THE
MARGARET ANN HUBBARD
MYSTERY OMNIBUS

THE MARGARET ANN HUBBARD MYSTERY OMNIBUS

MURDER TAKES THE VEIL

MURDER AT ST. DENNIS

SISTER SIMON'S MURDER CASE

COACHWHIP PUBLICATIONS

Greenville, Ohio

The Margaret Ann Hubbard Mystery Omnibus
© 2018 Coachwhip Publications

Margaret Ann Hubbard (1909-1992)
Murder Takes the Veil published 1950.
Murder at St. Dennis published 1952.
Sister Simon's Murder Case published 1959.
No claims made on public domain material.

CoachwhipBooks.com

ISBN 1-61646-452-6
ISBN-13 978-1-61646-452-3

CONTENTS

MURDER TAKES THE VEIL

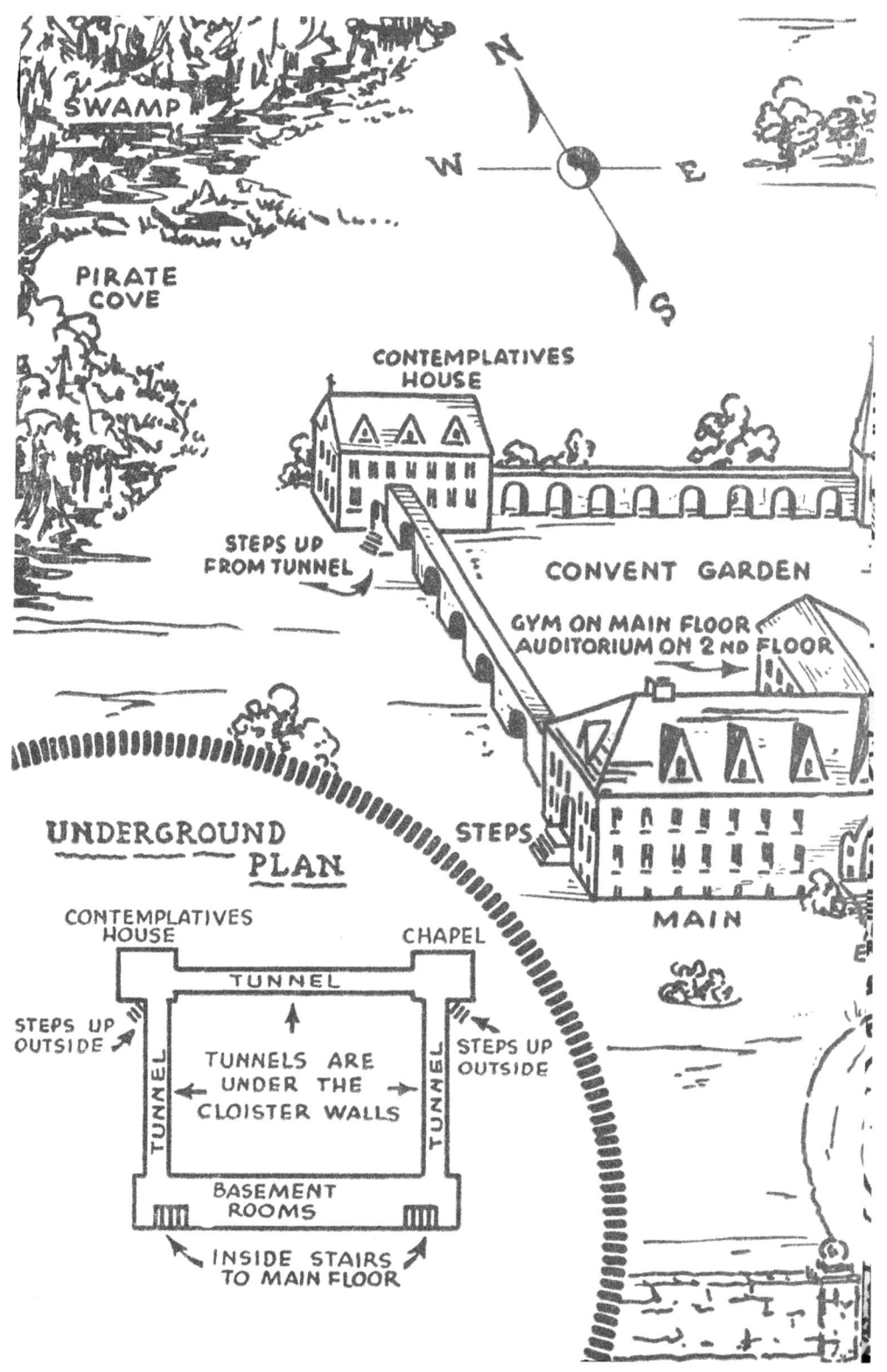

SWAMP

PIRATE
COVE

N
W E
S

CONTEMPLATIVES
HOUSE

STEPS UP
FROM TUNNEL

CONVENT GARDEN

GYM ON MAIN FLOOR
AUDITORIUM ON 2 ND FLOOR

STEPS

MAIN

UNDERGROUND
PLAN

CONTEMPLATIVES
HOUSE   CHAPEL

TUNNEL

STEPS UP
OUTSIDE

TUNNEL

TUNNELS ARE
UNDER THE
CLOISTER WALLS

TUNNEL

STEPS UP
OUTSIDE

BASEMENT
ROOMS

INSIDE STAIRS
TO MAIN FLOOR

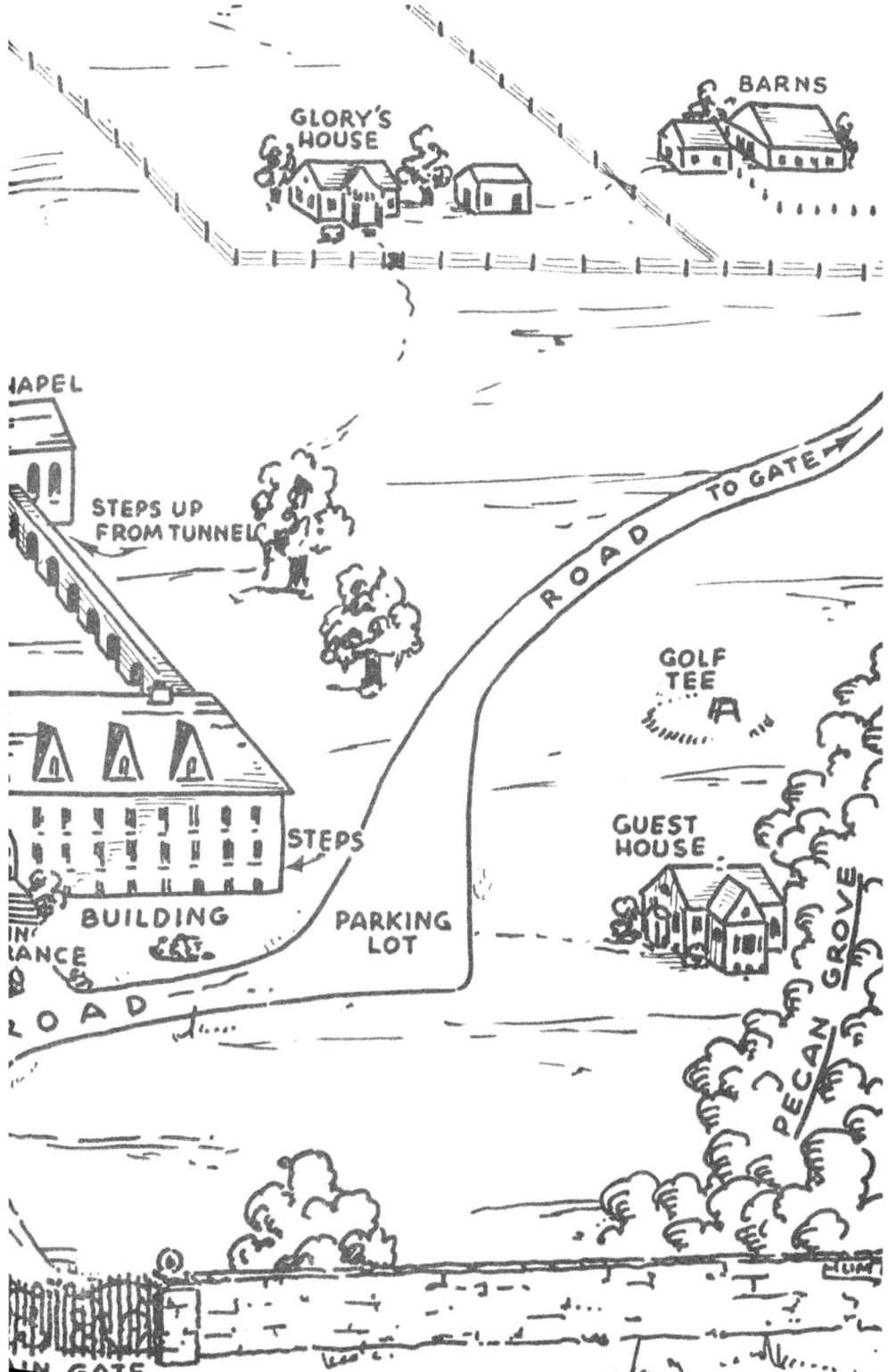

For Bessie, who said,
"Why don't you write one yourself?"

1

The door of Mother Theodore's parlor opened slowly. For the past twenty minutes Mother had been sitting absolutely still in her great, uncomfortable, carved chair, watching that door.

By neither nature nor training was Mother Theodore given to premonitions. Hunches, feelings in the bones, warnings by black crows, prophecies of death from the dank smell that often permeated the swamp—these were to be heeded only by the unknowing outside the convent walls. Mother knew better. It was excitement alone that had sent a strange tingle along her spine minutes ago when she had heard the whistle of the four-fifteen pulling into Marysville across the bayou; coincidence also that a crow had flapped, cawing, above the cypresses almost on the heels of the whistle; and nothing but imagination that scented the breeze with the odor of tombs as it moved through the open window.

But Mother's hand had gone out involuntarily to swing shut the casement.

And now the door was opening.

Mother Theodore rose, her eyes upon the dark wedge of hall twilight expanding inch by inch. It's not too late yet, she thought. I could refuse to see them. I could say I had changed my mind, that the College of St. Aurelien had prospered for nearly two centuries without lay instructors and it could go on—but that, of course, was the whole problem. Evidently it could not go on so well without some concession, for this year the enrollment was ten less than last; and so they were importing a writer, an artist, and an athletic instructor, all high in their fields. The very thought set Mother's brain to whirling in unorthodox panic, and she wiped her right palm surreptitiously against her habit. She must shake hands with dignity and enough welcome to fit the occasion, and trust that the gentlemen would not notice the unaccustomed clamminess of her hand. She had managed well yesterday, she believed, but there had been only one of the great Torvaldsen, the artist. Now there would be two to greet.

The door had now opened wide, and out of the corridor gloom Sister Osmond emerged, a large woman whom the amplitude of the habit made enormous. No one ever had been heard to remark that it was a pity Sister Osmond was so big, for her size was not only a fine attribute in a portress but a trait of personal dignity. Very erect, unhurried, she met all visitors at the door with her gracious smile and listened tranquilly to their requests. Those who were admitted felt that they had passed a test; but those who were turned away with the same gracious smile—usually masculine callers with designs upon the girls or the convent purse—never entertained the slightest rancor toward Sister Osmond. They simply had not measured up. That they might have gained entrance through several other unguarded ways never occurred to them.

Inside the door Sister stepped aside, inclined her head respectfully to Mother, slipped her hands up her sleeves, and turned a penetrating glance upon the two guests. The tall, dark young man stood gracefully at ease, the older looked across at Mother with an attentive smile. Unlike as the visitors were, they shared one reaction: neither was overawed by the decorum of the proceedings.

"Mother Theodore," said Sister Osmond. Then, having paused for Mother's permission, she indicated the guest who took precedence by age. "Mr. Crispin Archer."

The gentleman's head tilted in the conscious manner of people who have been often before crowds and consider without being aware of it the angle and effect of every mannerism. In Mr. Archer this learned poise appeared to be arrogance; and yet, as he advanced with a slow swinging gait, Mother Theodore realized also that it might be a compensation. For Crispin Archer was very oddly built. He was all wide—his head wide from ear to ear, his forehead broad under a broadly curving hairline, his eyes wide apart, his shoulders muscular as a boxer's, the hand he extended to Mother short and thick; still he was handsome. His hair, becomingly tousled, was of the tawny blond that photographs dark, and his eyes and complexion matched so perfectly that anyone seeing his picture would judge him to be swarthy brown. In the photographs which had accompanied the reviews of *Feathers of the Pen* and upon the back jacket of the book itself, Mr. Archer was pictured sitting down. He was not proud of his short legs, even though their shortness was only in comparison to his general width. Standing before Mother Theodore, he could meet her gaze levelly, and Mother was of more than medium height for a woman.

"Mr. Archer," she murmured, and at the same moment Mr. Archer murmured something polite.

His back was to the guardian Sister and his companion guest, still in the doorway; and suddenly Crispin Archer flashed toward Mother a most extraordinary smile. It slid around the strict impersonality of their meeting and became a recognition of the man for the woman, a bridge of humanness over the chasm beyond which all women retreat when they enter a convent and which few look back across. Mother Theodore gasped, but only mentally. Aloud she made no sound. In that instant Archer's eyes fell decorously, the smile retreated, he pressed her hand and stepped back, his manner all that one could ask, plus a nice touch of humility.

Mother turned her head slowly from him, and Sister Osmond took her cue.

"Mr. Franz Eric, Mother Theodore," the portress announced; and then, having completed her duty, she glided out into the wedge of twilight and closed Mother in with St. Aurelien's immediate future.

Franz Eric smiled also as he shook hands, but it was with the familiar deference of having said "yes'ster" and "no'ster" through eight years of grade school. He was young, half the age of Mr. Archer, dark and slim and olive skinned. Mother noted his dashing good looks. And the pixy way he had of catching his lower lip between his white teeth when he smiled. And the graceful nonchalance which had no doubt contributed to his fame as a fencing master in New Orleans. And the indolent charm which had made possible the evolution of Franz Eric from the grubby little larva which was Frank Ericson of the downtown Poydras Street Ericsons of New Orleans who had lived six to a room.

The list of his qualities added up to far more than the simple fact that Franz was just Frank with his face washed. To Mother Theodore, already shaken by Crispin Archer, he loomed as a promise of disaster—eighty-two separate disasters, according to the enrollment of St. Aurelien's. For Franz undeniably had magnetism. And in his lowly beginning perhaps lay the compulsion to raise himself high, to prove that the accidental poverty of his birth meant little.

Standing there, looking him over with every appearance of calmness, Mother was appalled at what she had done. The great Torvaldsen, nearing sixty and with a couple of grown daughters who no doubt had conditioned him through the years, would have been quite enough to modernize the curriculum. Admiring him respectfully, the eighty-two college girls would have continued about their business of submitting to education; but now, into their midst, Mother was about to inject two gentlemen of highly individual personality. That both had come well recommended was of small consequence where the basic urges were concerned. And that she had happened to fall upon two bachelors and a widower seemed indeed like a grim joke of Providence.

"Gentlemen, you will forgive me," Mother broke in upon her own confused reverie. "Please be seated. You had not too uncomfortable a journey, I trust? The connections were not bad?"

Gravely they seated themselves, the guests of necessity facing the light because Mother had lowered herself once again into the carved chair. But she did not relax. While Crispin Archer tactfully suppressed his opinion of the bayou country and Franz lied like a gentleman about the drudgery of the trip from New Orleans, Mother Theodore politely failed to listen. Firmness, she decided, that must be her course, a clear, straight statement of their position and hers. She could not back away from this situation, which after all was of her own inviting; there would be no sentimental yearning, even in the privacy of her own cell, for the dear old days when St. Aurelien's was a self-contained little world from whose portals Sister Osmond could fend off every enemy.

Mother Theodore turned to Mr. Archer. "I do not intend to dissemble before you gentlemen," she said bluntly, and then wondered if she should soften her manner. Archer's smile was one of surprise, and out of the corner of her eye she saw Franz come to attention. "You will be living inside the convent grounds, you see, and it would be quite intolerable for all of us—including yourselves—if we were to become too intimate objects of one another's concern. I hesitated long over taking this step. . . . We must compete, in a manner, with other colleges. In addition to religion, modern parents want also what they term 'advantages' for their daughters."

"And we are the advantages," Mr. Archer remarked.

Mother continued as if she had not heard the flippancy. "Sharing as you must in much of our routine, you will come to know a great deal about us, and it was that thought which made me uneasy. A writer must sketch from life, naturally, in the same spirit as a painter. Both can do it cruelly, or with human understanding. You have a reputation for keenness, Mr. Archer. I do not expect your months with us to be a hiatus in your creative life. I do, however, expect discretion. And I ask that you write nothing specific concerning St. Aurelien's."

Mother's eyes came to Franz Eric. "Our girls range in age from seventeen to twenty-one—the most impressionable time of their lives. Many of them have attended Sisters' schools always, through grade and high school; and it is going to be a thrilling innovation for them to sit at the feet of a masculine instructor. You may find a few of them troublesome, but you may limit your contacts to as little as you like outside of classes."

Franz coughed, and Crispin nodded gravely.

"Each of you will be given an office," Mother Theodore went on with her usual competence. "I understand you are a musician as well as a writer, Mr. Archer, so we have arranged a studio for you in the music department. For you, Mr. Eric, there is a small office in the gymnasium wing. The bookstore, where the girls buy their school supplies, is also in that wing," she added. And in the bookstore, as Mr. Eric would soon find out, old Sister Aloysius would be forever puttering about.

"Yes, Mother," Franz murmured with great docility.

"Since your time is entirely ours, Mr. Eric, we have already arranged your schedule. Mr. Archer's is not yet settled. The new book, you see, takes precedence over our own small needs."

And shrinks my salary, Crispin thought; but aloud he said, "You are considerate, Mother. However, I write like a maniac, at any hour of the day or night, or not at all. I'm not a consistent producer. Some of the reviewers, bless their black hearts, have expressed the notion that I'm not a creative writer at all but only a photographic recorder who happens to be a pretty slick craftsman. Which leads me to wonder, Mother, why I was honored by selection for St. Aurelien's."

Mother Theodore's eyes fell in the shadow of her coif. Here was the man who had been revealed in *Feathers of the Pen,* the detached observer who sat back looking at the world with a philosophic eye and setting down his record of it. The eye was now being applied to himself. Mother smiled at the toe of Mr. Archer's bronze-polished shoe.

"Fame is its own recommendation, sir."

"Ah, then who shall say it is worthless?"

Tolerantly amused at this thing called success, that was his pose; and so, thought Mother, upon that plane I shall meet him. "I doubt if one person can teach another to be a writer, Mr. Archer. Our personal gifts come from the hand of Providence. But you have already arrived in the literary world, and your knowledge of the practical side will constitute your main value to your students."

Mother's tone was very near to a reprimand, and Mr. Archer murmured something by way of apology. Franz Eric shifted in his chair. The nun regarded him with gratitude. Without her attention appearing to wander, her mind cast back over the excellent recommendations which had preceded Mr. Archer. In numbers and enthusiasm, his rooting section equaled that of the great Torvaldsen. Of the three, Franz had been the one to have merely adequate backing; yet that fact appealed strongly to Mother Theodore now. With two geniuses on her hands, how comforting it was to know that the third member was normal enough to furnish a balance.

Still, young Eric's eyes met hers with a strangely shrewd speculation as he asked with surprising seriousness: "If Mr. Archer's fame and experience constituted his recommendation, Mother, then exactly what prompted your selection of me?"

"We wished to give all our young ladies equal opportunity for something of added interest," Mother replied, hoping she did not sound as if she were mentally giving him a nice pat on the head. "Some will not take either to writing or painting, and for these we offer—ah—"

"Mr. Eric," Crispin suggested in that facile way he had of finishing a statement.

But Franz would not be led away from his question. With an eagerness approaching anxiety, he insisted, "And was that why you chose me, Mother—to temper the weight of culture?"

He was determined upon an answer, and like a flood tumbling into a spillway, Mother's premonitions rushed back. Where now was the balance of personalities that had soothed her a moment ago? And yet Franz had asked a perfectly legitimate question: why had she engaged him to complete her triumvirate of the famous when his fame was actually only a sort of harmless local notoriety?

Mother Theodore arose, and the two stood with her. Being upon her feet gave her confidence. "Carlyle once wrote that fame is no sure test of merit, but only a probability of such; it is an accident, not a property of man. If the accident has been slow in happening to you, Mr. Eric, it is no reflection whatever upon your merit. Your contribution to St. Aurelien's should be quite valuable in itself."

Franz was listening intently, as if he tried to clothe every word with far more than its meaning; and the thought struck Mother Theodore that this young gentleman was a good deal older than he admitted. Around his eyes were tiny lined proofs of it, proof again in the rather hard maturity of his mouth before the pixy smile took over.

Mr. Archer laughed.

"Forgive me, Mother, but your modernity amazes me. There is nothing archaic about you except your habit. The peasant dress of the Middle Ages, isn't it?"

Mother Theodore folded her hands under the brown scapular, which was the peasant apron of the Middle Ages, as Mr. Archer had assumed. There was no reason in the world why he should not know such a fact. The ancient dress was the historic mark of many an order, varying but slightly in color and in the design of the head-dress. Yet this common knowledge became, with Crispin Archer's statement, a personal revelation, as if he knew too much about her. Like what kind of toothpaste she used. And Mother Theodore knew how to deal with him.

"If you are with us long, sir," she said with faint emphasis on the if, "you will find that withdrawal from the world is one's best assurance of understanding it. Our convent walls are barriers, not obstacles."

Crispin bowed and Franz choked.

"You have a troublesome cough, Mr. Eric," Mother observed. "I'll see that you are served an eggnog with cream every morning. Very strengthening."

She walked to the door. Franz was ahead of her to open it.

"I hope your stay with us will be happy, gentlemen. Sister Osmond will show you to the guesthouse. Mr. Torvaldsen is already there. I think you will not find it crowded, even for the three of you."

"The great Torvaldsen!" Crispin exclaimed. "I've heard of him ever since I was a kid. Tell me, Mother, is he as great as his reputation?"

Mother met his glance coolly. "Torvaldsen has painted his masterpiece, one true picture, sir, and that assigns him a place with the immortals. One faultless contribution is enough for one man. But if he never had painted, he could still be a great *man,* Mr. Archer, and God makes too few of those. Good afternoon, sir. Mr. Eric."

Their exit was as ceremonious as their entrance, a fading into the gloom which had emitted them. When they were gone, Mother did not return to her chair. She went, instead, to the window and opened it wide.

Down on the green lawn under the magnolias and live oaks, groups of girls strolled or sat with their books open in their laps. Beyond the convent gates the road swung on to Marysville, a mile away, and between convent and village the bayous looped in currentless, brown stagnation, hidden by cypresses and tupelos. Back behind the convent the usual farm life was going on; within, it was the quietest hour of the day, the Sisters at prayers, the girls happily disposed according to necessity or temperament.

Why was I not satisfied with this as it was, Mother Theodore thought, and her automatic use of the past tense slapped at her sense of security. From the beginning, from that moment last July when she had held in her hand the letter from their famous poetess graduate and known she was about to pay them a visit, Mother had been uneasy. Marguerite Rontonga had always known too well what she wanted, and she had known immediately upon arrival what St. Aurelien's wanted. Opportunity. Never had opportunity knocked unheeded at Miss Rontonga's door. Writing under the name of Anacreon, the Greek lyric poet, she made for herself an exclusive niche that almost everyone envied. To her salons in New York had come Archer and Torvaldsen, along with a hundred others, and Marguerite had nipped them out and set their abilities before Mother. Then she talked to the patrons who already had contributed heavily to the support of the school, and each had telephoned Mother and come to tea. The result, in the light of the decreasing enrollment, was inevitable.

But it was my own decision, Mother reminded herself fairly. Not a single patron had done more than to suggest that she look into the fitness of the writer and the artist whom Miss Rontonga recommended, or allow a certain New Orleans connection to interview Mr. Eric. And so word had come to Mother, through the poetess, that all three would be willing. There had been no pressure whatever—except the Trend so much emphasized by Marguerite.

But perhaps nothing was changed after all. The new would very probably sift into the old; and soon the artist, the fencing master, and the writer would be no more a source of disturbance than any other of the very human frailties gathered together within St. Aurelien's.

Mother Theodore turned swiftly from the window. She was hungry in soul and body, and the sooner both hungers were satisfied the sooner would she return to her usual placid normality. Leaving the parlor, she hurried through the clean, dark halls and out the beautiful arched cloister walk to the chapel.

2

There were three cloister walks, one leading from either end of the long main building which formed the front of the square, the west walk terminating at the house occupied by the Contemplative Sisters of the order, the east walk ending at the chapel, the third joining the Contemplatives' house and the chapel. Within the square was a garden colorful with late-blooming flowers.

Crispin Archer, looking across the garden, saw the figure hastening to the chapel and smiled.

"It would seem that Mother is in need of spiritual sustenance," he murmured to Franz. "We must have proved a trial to her. Your cough, no doubt."

Franz grinned wickedly. Ahead of them Sister Osmond bustled, unconscious of the fact that the participants in this specially conducted tour were lagging and therefore missing most of her explanation of how the Sisters had come north from New Orleans in 1769 to escape the attentions of Count Alexander O'Reilly, the Spanish Butcher, and had remained to build the convent, much of it with their own hands.

"You may have noticed that our extracurricular activities are to be expressly limited," Franz replied in a low voice. "If we are to remain within this holy realm, we'll have to be, shall we say, circumspect."

"Let's do say it," said Archer.

Sister Osmond turned to meet the bland gaze of the two who had, from all appearances, been listening earnestly.

"Certainly no one could deny their pioneer spirit," Crispin said without allowing a second's pause. "Yes, I believe that's a sad lack in our own time, there is nothing left to explore. Those early trail breakers are to be envied, Sister."

Sister Osmond's manner became that of one whose dignity will not permit her to notice frivolity. "St. Aurelien's, as you see, is built in the form of a square," she stated as if those tons of stone must not be encouraged to jig around into any other pattern. Nodding toward the artistic tangle of angel trumpets, hibiscus, jasmine, and a crybaby tree, which wept tears of sap, she explained. "This is the convent garden. The Contemplative nuns of our order often work here. Their garb is like ours, and you will not know them from us except that they will not speak. You must not think them unfriendly. They have taken a vow of silence."

Crispin might well have said something flippant then; but in time to restrain himself he caught Sister Osmond's expression. She was looking across the garden to the Contemplatives' house, and in her eyes there was such longing that she was transformed. The older man was astounded, but Franz understood. Once he had very nearly gone down such a sun-arched walk and opened such a door himself. For Sister Osmond that silent life would have represented no sacrifice, the rigor of it no service because it would be what she loved. To meet the world at the convent door instead of withdrawing from it, to maintain her amiability while making explanations, apologies, and evasions all day long, there lay the sacrifice and the service. Even now, when she might be with the Sisters chanting Vespers in the chapel, she must lead around two intruders who said things behind her back.

Franz was moved by a sympathy that Crispin could never experience, and he said after an instant, "Don't stay with us, Sister. Show us where the guesthouse is and go to prayers. We'll find our way."

The Sister stirred with a wondering glance at Franz. So few ever understood, and to stumble upon this fellow-feeling in anyone so worldly as the young man before her was remarkable. She turned to lead the way out across the side lawn, her veil filling with the breeze so that she bore on like a seasoned windjammer bound on an important mission. Franz endeavored to keep up with her; but Crispin lolled along, enjoying his first real view of convent grounds. Coming up from the main gates, he had been able to see only the imposing pale stone front of the convent with the thickly matted foliage of the bayou forming the west boundary, and the groves and orchards on the east; but from this side lawn the farm buildings were in view back beyond the cloister, an efficient little village in themselves, and farther on were the pastures.

"The girls have done well, real well," Crispin muttered to himself.

The guesthouse, settled snugly at the end of the east lawn where the orchard began, was much to his liking. Picturesque without sacrificing comfort, he thought with approval. It was squat and gave the illusion of being small, but it was only an illusion. From the center of the roof rose a sturdy chimney, the outlet for several fireplaces, and over it two enormous pecans bent, dropping their nuts with gentle taps upon the shingles.

Sister Osmond advanced no further than the flagstone walk. "This house is yours for the school year, gentlemen," she announced with her usual urbanity. "Your meals will be served to you in a special dining room in the main building. Mr. Torvaldsen knows, he will show you the way." As with Mother Theodore, the mention of the artist alighted some inner fire, and Sister glowed for a moment before she came back to the matter at hand. "You are welcome to attend all our exercises in the chapel. Tomorrow we have an outdoor Mass in the cemetery—All Souls' Day, you know; and in the evening a procession to the village burying ground, both lovely traditional observances. Now if there is anything you wish?"

With their polite protests ringing in her ears, Sister Osmond departed. A gray squirrel leaped from the roof in beautiful flight and sped after her along the walk.

"Lovely traditional observances, all taking place among the dead," Crispin remarked. "Sounds like we hit the jackpot in gaiety this time. Well, this is our new home, my boy. Shall I carry you over the threshold?"

Franz did not answer. Over the bayou the sun was setting in a carnival display of color, and against it the cypresses and live oaks were black. A heron flew up, his legs trailing, and winged slowly away. On the convent roof the pigeons told their last gossip of the day, the cowbells jangled as the herd, which was the pride of St.

Aurelien's, neared the pasture gate. But Franz's eyes were on Sister Osmond's figure silhouetted on its passage through the arches of the cloister walk. He waited until she was gone before he entered the house.

Crispin was already standing in the middle of the spacious living room. If he had taken in the comfort of blazing fire, big chairs, radio, books, and the lack of clutter that appeals to a man, it had been at a glance; for his profound attention was centered upon the man asleep on the davenport. The sleeper lay flat on his back, his sock feet cocked up on a pile of cushions, his hands clasped across his stomach, and he was snoring in deep, rich tones. Even lying flat, his roundness was apparent. His cheeks were ruddy, the smile wrinkles deep around his eyes; there was a portly plumpness under the old-fashioned vest crossed by the heavy, gold watch chain. He was the typical uncle of the fairytales, the sort to rise up, eyes atwinkle, grizzled red-gray hair on end, and inform everyone that there was just time for a miracle before supper.

"So this is our Uncle Tor," Crispin said softly. "He looks more like a genial farmer than an exponent of the arts. I bet my typewriter the old guy's a fake."

Franz was intrigued. "How could he be? I mean, he came up from nothing, didn't he? I've heard his father was a fisherman, poor as a church mouse, lived in a houseboat on the bayous. You've got to have something on the ball to get started. Of course, after a good start, you can get away with murder."

Archer grinned. "Ain't it the truth?"

The sleeper gave a snort which startled even himself. His eyes flew open and came to rest upon the pair solemnly looking down on him. Immediately he sat up, ran his hands through his hair so that he looked like a Viking heading into adventure, and bounced to his feet.

"Gentlemen! You must excuse me, I'm an old man, I'm not yet rested from my journey. Mr. Archer? What a pleasure to meet you, sir! And young Mr. Eric—well, well!"

Torvaldsen's cheeks plumped into a smile that nearly closed his eyes. He shook hands, he brought out cigars, he showed off the good points of the guesthouse as if he were the official host; and yet in his manner there was nothing effusive, no false cordiality. He liked people, all types and kinds of people, and the result was a warmheartedness that overrode even Crispin Archer's cynicism.

Back in the living room, after a tour of the house, Archer bit the end off his cigar and grinned.

"I haven't smoked one of these in years, Torvaldsen."

The artist was down on the floor hunting for his shoes, and he sat back on his heels, chuckling delightedly. "I buy a box of that particular brand whenever I need to remind myself that I'm a success." When Franz turned in astonishment, he nodded. "Oh, yes, my boy, there are times without number when I wonder if Torvaldsen the artist might not have been a better blacksmith. That's when I buy the cigars my father used to provide for the grandfathers and all the uncles on Christmas, and the nostalgic aroma brings back the realization that I've risen from the poverty of those days. I haven't done badly, something has always come up. Like this." He indicated the whole situation of St. Aurelien's with a smile and a shrug.

"So you didn't come here with any high intentions of spreading art through an indifferent world?" Franz asked.

"I came because I needed the job," Torvaldsen said simply, and, having discovered his shoes, he sat where he was to put them on. "I know nothing of the ups and downs of your profession, Mr. Eric," he resumed. "Yours, Mr. Archer, I believe builds up a backlog for you, each new book adding to your income while the previous publications continue to sell? Yes. But in my work it's quite different. I paint a picture, I sell it, and there you are. In order to sell again, I must paint again. So I am never finished, you see. It is what keeps me young."

The statement had sounded in the beginning like a complaint, but ending as it did, it was confusing. In the days ahead the two young men would come to expect the unusual from Uncle Tor, but not yet.

"Then you wouldn't be an artist if you had it to do over again, Mr. Torvaldsen?" Franz asked.

The artist paused in the act of lacing one of his high-topped shoes. "I did not intend to imply that, Franz, I am what God and the devil made me."

"Exactly," said Crispin, almost as though he had been waiting for such a declaration.

Tor looked up without a trace of a smile. "If I were a blacksmith, I would still be an artist, just as a cypress board laid in a floor is still cypress. And won't you call me Tor? I was born to too long a name."

"I've seen your masterpiece, Tor," Franz said abruptly.

The old man laughed. "Which one?"

But Franz was serious. "The man walking alone along a woods road. You painted it in the north, I believe, because the woods are of brilliant autumn colors. I sat for an hour once, studying it; and I don't know why. The figure is quite unremarkable, walking away from you. There is even a blueness around him that nearly hides him. All the light is on the trees."

"I painted it in Normandy," Tor said. He finished tying his shoe-laces in a neat bow and clasped his arms around his knees. "Every man walks his road alone, Franz, often in the shadow although there is brilliant light above. That's why my picture fascinated you—you saw that man as yourself. I've seen people glance at it in the museum and pass on by, only to return with a somewhat puzzled air and study it as you say you did. It became so common a thing that the procurator finally put a bench at the proper distance from the picture, and now the viewers can puzzle in comfort."

Archer laughed and strolled into his bedroom to unpack. Some time later he looked up to see Franz in the doorway.

"Cris, he's not a fake."

"Uncle Tor?"

"Being an artist has little to do with it. Mother was right, it's the man that's great, not alone the artist. His simplicity, honesty, his genuineness, those are what make him what he is, not his pictures."

"Oh?" said Crispin. "I might argue several points there, my lad."

"Such as?"

"Such as his description of himself as an old man. He's not, you know—only well past middle age. But his manner says 'Be kind to me, I'm old, you must overlook any slight weaknesses or fancies I may have. And above all, protest that I'm not old, oh yes indeedy!'"

Franz scowled at the sport shirt Crispin held, pumpkin orange painted with moss-green ducks. "Are you going to wear that rig around here?"

"Certainly. But getting back to the fatherly attitude, I believe I'll adopt it myself. Unless I sublimate my natural gifts, I'm afraid I'll have a dull time in these holy precincts."

"Tor admits he came here because he needs the job," Franz pursued. "He was a lot more honest than we were."

"A rugged soul of vast integrity," said Crispin. "Could be. But I bet he seldom spoils the effect by combing his hair." Laying the yellow shirt in a drawer of the highboy, he shot a sly glance at the frowning young man in the doorway. "My reason for accepting Mother's bid is no secret, Franz. I like to be where I can work in peace and still be in close touch with people. These college kids are going to be people, some day, and the ladies under the veils are unexpectedly individual. I'm delighted with the whole setup. By the way, did you come because you can use the pesos, too?"

Franz grunted a monosyllable that could have been denial.

Then light-footed as the squirrel that had followed Sister Osmond, he was gone. A door shut hard down the hall.

In the living room the great Torvaldsen began to play the piano very badly.

3

Trillium was twenty, a convent-young, dreamy twenty and very happy. Not only was she happy because of the present moment, but because the future, as it met her and became the present, seemed to promise exactly what she wanted. Running down the stairs with her thin blue veil lifting around her face, Trillium paused on the landing to look over the eighty-two other veiled heads exactly like her own. Blue; but if the promise came true, she would be wearing the white veil of the novice when another All Souls' Day gathered the convent company in the big main corridor. No one, as yet, knew of her secret hope, although Mother Theodore might have guessed. As soon as her mother's letter arrived with the expected permission, she would go to Mother and ask to be admitted with the next class. The news, of course, would travel, and soon there would be about Trillium that aura of awe surrounding all the girls who had announced their intention of taking the veil . . . and the veil itself would be most becoming with her fresh complexion and dark eyes. . . .

"What're you mooning about, Trill?" Mary Elizabeth called, fluttering a hand to distinguish herself from the masses. "Come on or you won't get in line with Helen and me!"

Trillium sighed. There was nothing saintly about Mary Elizabeth except the way she looked, her blond hair and blue eyes accented by the veil. Helen, small and dark, was Trillium's twin in appearance and her second inseparable companion. What these two would say when they knew of her decision to enter the convent, Trillium could well imagine; for ever since their freshman year, the three had planned to be bridesmaid at one another's wedding.

Smiling mysteriously, Trillium descended; but her aloofness on the stairs had set her apart long enough to draw Sister Osmond's eye.

"The Bouncer's sending out distress signals. I guess it's you, Trill," Helen said. "Hurry up and we'll keep a place for you." Sister Osmond, looming large above the girls, held up a plain white envelope. Because the envelopes were always the same distinctive size, longer than an ordinary letter, Trillium knew even from a distance that her wait was over. Her mother had replied!

"You haven't time to read it now, dear, so you'll do an errand for me, won't you?" Sister Osmond suggested, handing her the letter along with a yellow envelope. "This telegram just came for Mr. Archer. Run over to the guesthouse with it, and then go straight along to Mass."

"Certainly, Sister," Trillium replied. She slipped her own letter into the pocket of her white dress. Mr. Archer's telegram felt important, folded and thick in its envelope. It must be very long and very expensive.

Sister Raymond passed her through the east door, and Trillium came out into the perfect morning. Behind her the processional line moved smoothly through the open door on its way around the buildings and up along the bayou to the cemetery. She would have to hurry if she didn't want to be late; but the arrival of her mother's letter filled her with a peculiar sadness and a faint stirring that she did not recognize as apprehension. Her throat was tight with the excess of emotion possible only to the very young. I must be alone, she thought, alone in this first moment, and started slowly across the lawn toward the guesthouse. She could not face her friends, the dear friends whom she soon must leave behind. Surely renunciation could claim a few minutes, particularly when she had Sister Osmond to give her an alibi. Picturing her own lovely movements, she felt that she floated across the lawn, a tear—a crystal tear—cool on her cheek. It was embarrassing that one eye always wept more easily than the other in these overemotional moments. Enjoying herself immensely, she stood still, her eyes closed.

If she had been gifted with second sight and a revelation of what lay in wait for her with the turning of the knob on the guesthouse door, Trillium would not have lingered in her romantic dream. She would have stood trembling, instead, with eyes strained wide for a final appreciation of the peaceful safety of St. Aurelien's; and she would have known then, also, that her supposed vocation was only affection for certain people and a place and a routine and a reluctance about leaving them all, an analysis that would have been gently made by Mother Theodore at the proper time.

But Trillium wandered, still in her dream, down the flagged path and up the two steps to the tiny stoop, and knocked at the guesthouse door.

There was no answer, no breath of sound from inside. From far over at the cemetery came the first chant of the Asperges, and Trillium knocked quickly again. When there still was no reply, she turned the handle of the door and entered.

She was in a small hall from which opened several doors, all standing ajar. The first she investigated was the living room. How masculine it smelled already—pipe smoke, leather, shoe polish, turpentine from Torvaldsen's paints. The room was cluttered with several packing boxes and their contents, piles of books, golf clubs, tennis rackets, a stack of canvases turned face to the wall, a beret and two caps on the davenport, the private possessions of all three tenants sprawled companionably together. It appeared to be a jumble that would remain as it was, granting the removal of the packing cases, and Trillium giggled.

"Why, they're all sloppy as can be!" she said aloud. She could imagine Rindy, the colored maid, rolling her eyes and muttering when she came in to clean. Rindy was used to convent neatness. How would she ever work her way through this? Even the mantel was loaded with a pile of books, ash trays, a can of tobacco, trinkets. . . .

Trillium's gaze tripped over an object and halted, fixed upon it. Her heart stopped for a matter of seconds, then gave a sudden flip and thumped until it shook her. The Sisters had set a statue of St. Joseph in the place of honor, centering the mantel. Now, beside him, his cat face smug and his paws embracing the world, was a six-inch silver image.

The girl remained still, staring at it as if the thing had eyes to see her. She could not think, her brain would not work. Only her heart was alive, choking her. How many minutes went by, she never knew, for time had ceased. The clock tapping somewhere in the room did not warn her to hurry. Nothing existed but that hideous little god upon the mantel.

She thought of his name, first. Billiken, the god of things as they ought to be. And then she remembered that there are many Billikens, just as there are many Buddhas, and certainly there would be in the world more than one made of plaster and painted to look like silver!

"Of course, this isn't the one!" Trillium exclaimed, even laughing a little. The paralyzing fear eased, she went softly over to the mantel, never wondering why she should be warned to silence in the empty house.

With her hand outstretched, she paused. What if this figure did have the mended break? It couldn't—but suppose it did? Wouldn't it be better not to know?

Before her dread could mount again and stop her, Trillium seized the small god, felt him cool in her palm, and turned him around. She had known it would be there, the little brown vein of glue, the plaster chipped white along its edge. Her mother had said the blemish would not spoil Billiken, no one would ever notice; but now it was a brand.

Trillium's hand left the figure, to clutch the edge of the mantel. Memory was a wild thing, running loose. She saw her father, huge in the cramped quarters of the houseboat, desperate, grim, shouting that he would not have that bounder giving presents to his wife; and her mother, small, dark-eyed like herself, emphasizing his roughness by her own withdrawal. He had looked upon her silence as a taunt, he had knocked the Billiken out of her hand and left with such tramping violence that the dishes rattled in the cupboard. Her mother had picked up the little figure, fitted in the broken part with glue. And that night Trillium had lain in bed, knowing her father had not come back, but hearing a whispered conversation in the next room between her mother and the stranger she never had seen. The next day the Billiken was gone. He had taken it—and brought it here?

Trillium touched the god with a shaking finger, turning him back to his former position. It was imperative that she leave no trace of her presence. She dared not think farther now. She had to get out of this place.

Stumbling over the litter, Trillium was at the door before she remembered the telegram. She had been going to lay it on the table, that was what brought her in. The table, like every available surface, was burdened. With a sweep of her arm she knocked a pile of books to the floor, then picked up one and propped the telegram against it.

Then she fled.

An onlooker would have concluded that Trillium ran so swiftly because she was late for Mass; a second glance would have set him wondering what punishment the Sisters inflicted on late-comers, for this girl was obviously in terror. It was a terror, however, that had nothing to do with tardiness. As she ran, a sickening realization came to Trillium: she did not know the present identity of Billiken's owner! She never had seen the man on that one night. His name, she knew, had been Jem. None in the swamp, never even heard his voice above the whispering of the three was named Jem—yet Billiken was here! Had he changed his name, or given the trinket to someone else—to Archer, Eric, or Torvaldsen?

Trillium forgot to slow down and catch her breath before actually coming into the cemetery, and so she was still panting from her exertions when she hesitated at the beginning of the long, open aisle. The scene was beautiful, familiar, and it called up inconsequential things: old Sister Etienne's conviction that it would rain, the stout optimism of the farm hand's wife, Glory Muckleroy; and Glory's faith had triumphed. The morning was ideal for the outdoor Mass, the sunlight infusing golden life into the magnificent stone crucifix with its Figure drooping above the altar. Flanking it were the tombs of the Sisters, dazzling white from recent cleaning, each banked with chrysanthemums which reflected a sunlight of their own. The girls in white with their blue veils, the Sisters in a protective cohort

of freshly pressed brown and black, the white-veiled novices unobtrusively at one side, the Muckleroys with all their children, every
employee and inhabitant of St. Aurelien's was in attendance.

And, ending the far curve of the crescent, the three new instructors, all down on one knee, Franz Eric with his head bent, the other
two observing the ceremony with solemn interest.

Trillium, still at the end of the aisle, knew she couldn't walk the
distance she must to reach Helen and Mary Elizabeth and the place
they had kept for her. She would be too conspicuous, he might be
attracted by the movement among all these quiet people, look over,
ask afterward who she was—and he would know her name. No one
was named Trillium. . . .

"It's all right, dear, go on," Sister Osmond whispered close to
her, and the girl realized she had been standing there much too
long.

She would have to go. She started up the aisle. What did it matter if he did find out who she was? That old incident was over—if
death could be termed an incident. Torvaldsen glanced toward her.
Then Archer.

Her eyes skidded away to the priest, to the blue veils, to Mary
Elizabeth's profile turned as far as permissible without looking back.
The scene grew misty, so near did she come to fainting, but she kept
moving with the peculiar sensation of the ground rolling toward her
while she herself stood still.

The congregation arose, and Trillium, sheltered, slipped in front
of Mary Elizabeth to her place. Helen passed over a missal. When
the girl took it, the thin pages fluttered, and Mary Elizabeth put
out a hand to steady her. It was not unheard of for girls to faint at
Mass, particularly when they had gone long without breakfast and
there were no chairs to sit on.

"I'm all right," Trillium whispered.

And, almost miraculously, she was. With commonplace sights
and sounds around her, Trillium regained enough self-confidence
to draw away from her apprehension and look at it clearly. In the
first place, there was no certainty whatever that the Billiken still
belonged to Jem; or that, because the little god sat on the mantel
of the guesthouse, Jem must be one of the three new instructors.

Someone might even have given the image to Mother Theodore, who had placed it where it was—but that was too farfetched an idea to entertain. Mother would not set Billiken up to rub shoulders with St. Joseph. She would go to Mother Theodore and tell her the whole terrible story, the tragic part Jem had played in her life, her suspicion that he was here on the campus; and Mother would listen earnestly and a few days later would call Trillium in and tell her it had all been explained. I need not bother my mother with it at all, the girl decided, and touched the letter in her pocket. For the moment she had forgotten the pleasure in store for her. Mother Theodore would be pleased to hear of another vocation, there were so few these days. . . .

By the time the Mass was over, Trillium had nearly recaptured her earlier expectancy. In the crowd breaking to straggle back into the building, she was able to lose Helen and Mary Elizabeth. They would insist that she go with them straight to the dining room for breakfast, and she couldn't. She had to read her letter. Alone, she ran across the lawn to the west door, up the stairs, along the corridors to her room in the east wing, and locked herself in. Throwing herself on the bed, she tore open the envelope.

She had been smiling in anticipation when she began to read, but at the first line the smile stiffened. Hastily she skimmed through it, dazed and fearful bewilderment growing in her eyes.

"Oh, no!" she breathed once. But there it was, in her mother's writing, not to be denied. A fit of trembling seized her, and she rolled over on the bed, the letter crackling under her. She didn't cry. When she could sit erect again, she picked up the crushed page and forced herself to read it through deliberately. As she read, the cold stillness inside her grew until it kept her even from trembling any more.

"My darling, I fear this letter will come as a shock to you, but there seems to be no way I can spare you. I must disappear again. The truth is, dear, that Jem is somewhere in the vicinity of New Orleans and has been trying to find me. It must be that he suspects I am coming close to the evidence I need to prove that he killed your father. I have known all these years that your father did not commit suicide, but there was no proof. Now we are in search of a witness who must have seen the whole thing happen. I cannot tell you more about it now, dear, but it will be a satisfaction for you to know that your father was blameless. I can't pretend I'm not in danger, because I am, but I'm taking every precaution. Jem is blaming me for what he did himself. All these years his fury has grown against me. I think now that he was keeping silent in order for me to build up a security he could destroy. No matter what happens, dear, say nothing. My life may depend upon this. Nothing could happen to you there, and it is a great comfort to me to know you're safe. And I know what he is doing. Above all, dear, don't mention this to Mother Theodore. And please don't worry. Henry will forward my letters to you as usual. . . ."

There was a little more, a few lines about the mother's happiness in giving a daughter to God. The daughter, however, lay curled upon her bed in a tight ball of fear, tears filling her head to bursting before they finally soaked into the pillow, the blue veil pathetically crumpled across her face. Against her closed lids she saw two figures: her mother, sad-eyed and remorseful, a hunted victim; and the silver Billiken smirking on the guesthouse mantel. No longer was she in doubt as to the identity of Billiken's owner. It was Jem, Jem who now bore a name her mother had not known when she read Trillium's account of the three whose arrival had then been imminent. Say nothing, no matter what happens—only what could happen in the security of St. Aurelien's? Nothing, except that her father's murderer had taken up residence on the campus.

Girls were wandering up to change into skirts and sweaters for the day. Someone knocked on Trillium's door, called, rattled the knob, and went away. Trillium lay still. She had an enormous welter to think through. Once she picked up the letter again, to reread a certain sentence. "Above all, don't mention this to Mother Theodore." But why? Mother was so good, so wise, so—The girl checked her rebellion swiftly. Always she had been an obedient daughter, not only because she loved her mother but because they two were alone in the world and their first loyalty was to one another. That was the way it had to be, else each would stand entirely alone. All that was necessary had been put into the letter. Reasons, of course, would be satisfying, but not required for her obedience.

So now I cannot go to Mother Theodore. Trillium made herself hammer home the thought. Very well, what then? Write to Uncle Henry? No, because the word would be passed along to her mother, and there was no point in adding to her worries yet. She might even come to St. Aurelien's, if she knew, and Jem would have his opportunity. . . .

A seizure of trembling shuddered through her, so that under her the bedspring made timorous little noises. I'll have to decide a course for myself and follow it, Trillium told herself firmly. Mother Theodore would approve of that. Even though I can't consult her, I can act as I think she would advise. The girl sat up, seeing herself in the dressing-table mirror, pink checked and eyes with the deep-washed look of recent tears. She had changed in seven years, grown from a little girl with a Dutch bob into a young lady with a fashionably long haircut and lipstick. He would never associate the child with this college senior. Unless he heard her name.

"I'll manage so he won't," she whispered, watching her lips in the mirror. "I'm really too dumb to take on anything extra, so Sister Onfroy will think I'm just being sensible when I ask to be dropped from the art class. I'll say I need all my time for my other studies. And if I don't take a class from any of them, he'll never hear my name. I'm not pretty enough or brilliant enough to draw attention, thank heaven. People don't talk about unremarkable other people when they are very remarkable people themselves. I'll just be one of the crowd—and he'll never know me. And the minute he gives himself away, so I'm sure of which one he is, I'll telephone to Uncle Henry and tell him to get out the bloodhounds!"

Trillium jumped off the bed and began to pull the hidden bobby pins out of her veil. Jem probably had no intention of harming her; but he might try to pump her, to find out where her mother had gone.

"Well, he'll see what a clam I can be!" she declared aloud. "I'll be so perfectly naturally uninterested that none of those three geniuses will ever notice me! I bet they're all too stuck up to see us, anyway!"

The jocular air of the girl in the mirror was pure bravado, but it helped. Trillium folded the veil, pulled off her dress, and got into a rose sweater and tweed skirt. She herself was in no predicament.

She could not ask Mother Theodore to receive her into the convent, not until she knew what this Billiken-Jem business involved; but after all, that meant only a postponement. A faint relief accompanied the thought, but Trillium was not yet ready to admit it was the dream that had intrigued her and that the reality was more than a little frightening. In the pit of her stomach there was a queer emptiness, as if her fear had made a vacuum.

"Golly, I'm hungry!" she exclaimed, and slammed open a drawer to hunt for her rose anklets. She had missed the late breakfast, and there would be no other refreshment until the middle of the afternoon when the juniors served their traditional tea in the parlors. Down in the kitchen the food committee would be at work cutting out sandwiches in the shape of stars and crescents. Fancy tidbits would not do for Trillium. She would get the kids to make her up a whopper, and she could take it out into the shade and have a private picnic.

She was fairly lighthearted when she opened her desk and slipped the letter in; then, frantically, she snatched it back. Hide it in her desk, when anyone coming in to borrow some paper might see a line or two and wonder—and run to Mother. . . .

All her fragile self-confidence gone, Trillium sank down on the little study chair. So this was how it would be! The one big decision to keep her secret would not suffice, there must be a constant watch for small slips, an endless sly planning to make all her actions seem normal when every minute she carried the most unnatural burden in the world—fear for the life of a beloved one.

I can't do it, she thought wildly, I can't! I'll run away, deep into the swamp until the mud sucks me down and I can crawl under the cypress knees! I'll know, there, if anyone follows, I'll hear the splash and plop in the mud!

But she couldn't run away, because then they would hunt for her, and her name would be shouted all over the campus. No, she must not show by word or action that she had anything on her mind. All she need do was watch and be careful. Through the entire school year, he might remain quietly following the schedule Mother had worked out for him and never suspect Trillium's identity.

And so long as he was here, he could not be endangering her mother!

"Oh, I can make a million pesky little plans if I have to!" she breathed. "It's worth anything! I can do it!"

Trillium seized the letter, about to tear it into bits. With the first split in the edge of the paper, she paused, staring at it. She could not destroy the letter, the only evidence in the world, outside of her mother's knowledge, that her father had not committed suicide. And it pointed out his murderer.

The memory of what she had almost done with the letter, placing it in her desk for anyone to see, was shattering, and she pricked herself several times as she fastened the envelope inside her slip with two large safety pins. The girls did not intentionally pry into anything. It was just that you might walk across the lawn and meet your green anklets and your charm bracelet and your sweater, each on a different person, and at the same time yourself be wearing things belonging to two other people; and all the articles would have been secured by simply going and taking them. No one minded.

"So you'll stay there, honey, until I know what to do with you," Trillium said, patting the letter in her bosom. Her appetite was gone, the emptiness giving her a clearheaded detachment quite removed from physical sensation or emotion. She knew, now, exactly what to do.

Since it was a holiday, many of the girls had gone into Marysville and would not return until time for the tea. Sister Onfroy was not in her office. Trillium found her out in the cloister walk, pacing slowly with her rosary in her hand.

Sister Onfroy was the registrar, and therefore accustomed to dealing with changes of mind. She listened to Trillium's apparently frank account of troubles with chemistry and history, the prodigious amount of time it took to do these subjects justice, and finally her invention of frequent headaches.

The headaches were a mistake.

"You need a lot more fresh air, child," said Sister Onfroy. "Something to take you outside, you see. None of you get outside enough. I couldn't sign you up for tennis, I'm sure there are already too many for the one court—but I'll put you into golf and fencing. Won't that be nice, dear?"

"Oh, Sister, I don't believe—" Trillium began.

"You don't look well, not at all well."

Trillium tucked her hand under the brown serge elbow. "I'm perfectly fine, Sister, only a headache once in a while, but not very often. I mean I'm really in wonderful health. I'd love the golf and fencing, but—"

"Then you shall have them," Sister Onfroy declared. "Mr. Eric is an exceptionally fine instructor. I've wondered why he consented to come here—oh, don't misunderstand, child, I feel that he will profit as well as ourselves—but still, Mother showed us those wonderful pictures of him taken at last year's Mardi Gras, I believe he was king of a parade, and—" The Sister wheeled, suddenly keen, to Trillium. "Why don't you want to take these instructions from him, dear?"

Trillium was startled. "Oh, but I do, Sister! It's sweet of you to put me in like this, at the last minute, and I just appreciate it heaps! I know I'll feel better, being out in the fresh air. And Sister, if you wouldn't mention to Mr. Eric that I signed up so late—well—"

Sister Onfroy patted her hand. "Of course I won't. He doesn't need to know he was an afterthought. Drop into my office in the morning and I'll have your schedule ready."

Trillium thanked her and escaped. I couldn't have done much worse if I'd thought it out for a million years, she ruminated bitterly. Out of the frying pan into the fire. Or was it? Wasn't Mr. Eric too young to be Jem? Helen, smitten already, had been conjecturing about his age in the shower room this morning and had started a discussion in which no two people agreed, the only unanimous sentiment being that he was the type, with his dark good looks and gracefulness, to look young until he was fifty. So he was old enough. . . .

That the fencing and golf entailed individual instruction had intrigued the girls this morning. To Trillium it was the most formidable detail. In the art class, Torvaldsen might have come to look over her shoulder, perhaps criticize her work, but his attention would be more upon the drawing than upon herself. Mr. Eric, on the other hand, would be concerned with her stance in golf, her grip of a sword—and she dared not drop the course now! Already she had drawn far too much notice from Sister Onfroy, who might pass the word on to Mother Theodore—and Mother would question her.

Trillium was so weary that her apprehension turned to rebellion against this circumstance which bound her like Prometheus to the rock. Reaching her own room again, she lay down, and in spite of her worries, fell asleep.

The supper bell woke her. She had a dull, pounding ache in the top of her head. *Because I fibbed about it,* she thought drowsily, *and this is my punishment.* As she lay there, half awake, the ache seemed to be the Billiken doing setting-up exercises inside her skull.

Fingernails rattled on her door and Mary Elizabeth poked her head in. "Trill, where have you been all day? We missed you at the tea. What's the matter?"

"Nothing." Trillium yawned. "I had a nap."

"Well, you look like you could stand a few morsels. Helen's just about ready. Meet us on the stairs, will you?"

The blond head was withdrawn. Trillium got up, put on too much lipstick, fixed her hair, and wondered how she could keep from being conspicuously ill. The ordeal of marching to the cemetery tonight, with *his* eyes upon her, would be too great an endurance test after all she had gone through during the day.

I'll not go, she decided abruptly, and opened her door. Sister Laurent, the prefect who supervised the girls on this floor, was just passing. At the sight of Trillium, she stopped short.

"My dear child, how ill you look! And on this night of all nights! I was a little worried about Kathy Thatcher. You know how she reacts to overexcitement, but I never thought of you—"

Sister Laurent bit her finger as she always did when perturbed. No tragedy could be more complete than to miss the All Souls' procession to the Marysville cemetery.

"I'm not at all ill, Sister," Trillium said quickly, but her brown eyes were wide with alarm and she glanced past the Sister into the deep shadows. "I'm tired, you know how you get a lot of tiredness piled up. I think I'll stay at home tonight and read."

Sister Laurent bit her finger so hard that she winced. Trillium, of all people, chattering about staying at home with a book when she hated reading and had been known to write book reports on movies she had seen. She hadn't even been considered for Mr. Archer's class in creative writing, and as for reading—

"Trillium, you seem to be afraid," Sister Laurent said quietly.

The Sister was young, her own school days not many years be-hind her, and she was used to keeping the girls' little secrets. But Trillium apparently had no intention of confiding in her. Such a spasm of terror passed over the young face that Sister Laurent in-voluntarily glanced around them.

"I don't understand, Trillium," she said in apology, "but, of course, you needn't go to the cemetery tonight if you're not up to it. I'll stay with you. I don't mind at all. My brother sent me a box of chocolates and we'll—"

Trillium smiled, but not before the shadow had flitted again over her face. "No, I'll go, Sister. I'll feel much better after supper. Thank you for offering to stay with me, but I'm going to be right there with the others!" And she hurried after Helen and Mary Eliz-abeth before the Sister could protest.

Stay at home with a Sister in attendance to emphasize her unusual behavior? Oh, no! There must be nothing out of the ordinary, Trilli-um warned herself. In the twilight, with the flickering light of can-dles as the only illumination, dressed exactly like the others in long white with a wreath of flowers, she would be one of the crowd again. It was unnerving to realize how nearly she had blundered once more. Her tension gave her a false gaiety, and through supper she laughed and talked with animation; but when supper was over she ran up a back stairs to her room and dressed quickly, even to the final touch of fastening the wreath in her hair. She looked lovely, but she didn't take the customary pleasure in it. Only one concern occupied her now: she had to get out of the building without seeing Sister Laurent, because Sister had not been satisfied with their conversation and she might decide it would be wise for Trillium to go quietly to bed.

How lucky, she thought as she let herself out into the hall, that she had no roommate, no one to question her. Through the closed door next to her own she heard the giggling of Helen and Mary Elizabeth; and across the hall where five girls roomed together there was a waterfall of laughter. Trillium walked slowly to the stairs lead-ing down to the main floor, then caught up her long white skirt and sped down. It didn't matter much where she went, for when the bell ordered the forming of the procession she would join it and everyone would be too excited to ask where she had been. Coming out at the west entrance, she half turned into the cloister walk; but over at the far end of the lawn the bayou lay in primeval elegance. Trillium stepped on to the green grass. "Primeval elegance" was her own term, and she had used it in a description of the bayou which had fascinated Sister Raymond into giving her the only A she ever had had on a theme.

Thinking of that proud achievement, Trillium raised her white skirt daintily above the grass and drifted along. This was not like the dream of the morning, when she had crossed the lawn to the guesthouse, but only the inevitable reaction of youth to the pleasure of the moment. Under it, pricking her, was the sharpness of what she knew. When she reached the soggy ground bordering the water, she turned to the right to stroll behind the Contemplatives' house. This was the least used part of the grounds. Farther over, directly behind the convent enclosure, were the farm buildings. No one came here except Hy Muckleroy cutting the grass.

It was startling, then, for Trillium to have the impression that she was being watched. She stopped dead still, one foot forward for another step. Her eyes darted over the lawn to the distant row of Glory Muckleroy's sunflowers rimming her garden, back to the solid wall. No one there, yet her scalp had needles dancing on it. Then to the swamp—and she saw the man standing precariously on a cypress knee, poised as if he mocked his own danger. He had watched her come clear across the lawn. And that, she thought, is how a spider sits watching a fly draw near its web.

Mr. Eric did not appear in the least spiderish. There was a sleepy air about him like that of an interrupted reverie, and Trillium caught herself wondering if his charming half smile had been directed at the cypresses before she came along. Not wishing to appear frightened, she clasped her hands before her and gave a small nod.

"Mr. Eric," she said softly.

"Good evening, Ma'amselle."

"I see you are not afraid of snakes, sir. The bayou is full of water moccasins."

His eyebrows went up, as if amused, but she was gratified to observe that he glanced somewhat apprehensively into the twilight under the trees. The fluted cypress trunks streaked high before the foliage began, and across the floor of the swamp were thick gray roots thrust up like knees above the water to allow the trees to breathe. That there was water at all was hard to see for it was hidden under a bulbous tangle of hyacinths. Mr. Eric, Trillium thought, must have leaped from the last bit of solid shore to his perch on the knee; but even as she thought it, he stepped lightly off on to the thickly woven plants and then to the dry land. The frail blossoms were barely crushed. Trillium stared wide eyed at Franz Eric.

With pleasure he returned her inspection. In short-sleeved white with the long skirt touching the grass, dark hair crowned with white flowers and a childlike mingling of alarm and admiration banishing whatever sophistication she might have had, Trillium was lovely.

"You might have gone through!" she exclaimed. "The hyacinths aren't solid enough to walk on!"

"I'll remember next time," said Franz. The child was entrancing. Something about her seemed familiar—his own young sister? He shook his head.

Trillium, fearing that the conversation might take a personal turn and he would ask her name, hurried into the first subject that crossed her mind.

"I'm glad you like Pirate Cove, Mr. Eric. It's named for a real pirate, Dominic You, one of the LaFitte gang from Grand Isle. There were no hyacinths in those days, of course. They were brought from Japan much later for an exposition and some of the planters set them out in the bayous and they ran wild. When Dominic and his men escaped up here in a skiff, the water was clear and it was a perfect spot to elude capture. The men were given coffee in the convent kitchen and Mother Adrian entertained Dominic in her own parlor."

"Really?" Franz encouraged her. "The same parlor where we were received, no doubt."

Trillium let her hand steal up to cover her heart, for it was pounding so that the tiny white buttons on her dress quivered. Mr. Eric's scrutiny had become something she could not read, and her chin went up. "The story is true, sir! Dominic You is a tradition with us! He was a very respectable pirate! He was the only one to go into business later in New Orleans and be buried in a tomb with his name on it. I've seen it myself!"

Franz bowed, hiding his smile. "Sorry, Ma'amselle! I don't doubt your veracity. I was merely picturing Mother—Adrian, was it?—serving her thick French coffee to the respectable pirate. If she resembled Mother Theodore, it would have been well worth seeing."

"Oh," said Trillium, rather flatly. She must go. The speculative light in Mr. Eric's eye was growing by the minute. . . .

The bell in the convent garden clanged. Never had its insistence been more welcome.

"Good-by, Mr. Eric," she said with the second note of the bell, and turned to run away across the lawn.

"But you haven't told me your name—"

"Sister Laurent will scold if I'm late for the procession! Good-by!"

Like Dominic You, Trillium fled. But where the pirate's pursuers had paddled swearing through the swamp, Trillium's supposed one did not pursue at all. When she looked back from the corner of the convent, she saw that he was still standing watching her.

Franz laughed aloud. He had hoped she would look back. The moment the white figure vanished, he was off around the back of the cloister toward the guesthouse.

The white ranks were a refuge. Trillium caught up her candle and chrysanthemums from the table where Sister Ignace was dealing them out, and, shielding the flame with her hand, took her place beside Helen.

"Where were you, Trill?" Mary Elizabeth, behind her, breathed down her neck.

"We can't talk now, we're starting."

The pitch pipe wheezed, the singers began, and the procession moved slowly down the road to the big gates.

In the village cemetery a half mile away the people heard the singing and saw the train of candle flames and became as quiet as one person. When the procession came in among the tombs, even the unbelievers were impressed. As it wound along the paths that were the streets of this miniature city, one girl after another turned aside to place her burning candle and her flowers before the tomb of a friend or relative. Passing the place where Torvaldsen, Franz

Eric, and Crispin Archer stood, many faces were shadowed, Trillium's among them because she had laid her memorial before the first neglected tomb she saw. Franz, watching for her, and Crispin, watching them all, did not see her; for as she passed them she looked quite naturally away toward a monument topped with angels spreading their wings. In the semidarkness she had many twins.

"It's unearthly!" Torvaldsen sighed. "No man could paint these young faces and do them justice."

Trillium heard him. She held her head turned away, very still. Don't be afraid, don't stumble, don't draw their attention; take one step, then another. . . .

Was that how Daniel forced himself to enter the lions' den?

4

Sister Aloysius, who did errands in addition to her duties in the bookstore, trudged by the students' dining room, paused, and returned to write a message on the blackboard beside the door.

"Trillium: a delivery for you in the office."

Not bothering to sign it, because all the girls knew her square block writing, she put down the chalk and tramped on. Her feet hurt and there were too many errands to be done.

Up in the auditorium, Sister Raymond sat watching the rehearsal of act one of "Mustardseed." The annual play, coming just before the Christmas holidays, was the cultural high point of winter. So far as audience approval was concerned, Sister Raymond had no doubt of the play's success. Let the doting relatives see their darlings walk across the stage without falling flat on their faces and the universal verdict would be that it was all just lovely. But Sister Raymond was a perfectionist. Not only for God, because she did His work, must everything be perfect, but to satisfy her own impeccable requirements.

"We'll get it, we'll get it right!" she kept assuring herself, fighting back the bugbear which for the past half hour had been nipping ever larger mouthfuls out of her belief in "Mustardseed." He was a silent bugbear, the great Torvaldsen, seated beside her with his chin in his hand, his attention so profound that it could almost be drawn in straight lines to the stage like the obvious art of the funny paper; but his silence was a threat. Like everyone else on the campus who had come in contact with him, Sister Raymond was finding his great simplicity not at all simple to meet. Almost, she reflected nervously, it was a monstrous characteristic because it impelled him to say exactly what he thought, kindly and sincerely, but nevertheless with the stubbornness of complete conviction. There was the matter of the studio, Sister remembered with a shudder. She had heard the story direct from Sister Osmond, whose graciousness had been ineffective for once. The artist had taken one look at the cozy, small room flooded with sunshine, nicely curtained, carpeted, furnished with easy chairs and a polished mahogany table—and was now installed, at his own insistence, in a barnlike storage room over the gymnasium in the wing jutting out into the convent garden: no curtains, cold north light, no rugs, an old pine-topped table, and a collection of wastebaskets.

Across one unbroken wall of that studio, Sister Raymond pondered, a huge canvas was hung, awaiting the artist's inspiration to become the backdrop for the last act of "Mustardseed." The other acts were being done against a sky drop with set pieces in the form of church spires, trees, and rocks. But the last act required something more, something to set off the climax of the play.

But if Torvaldsen didn't like the play he would say so, in his magnificently simple way, and the result might be no backdrop. Sister Raymond shot a glance at him around her coif. He was so intent now that he was whistling through his nose, but her movement broke in upon his concentration. She shivered, reminding herself that his verdict would probably be an excellent furthering of her humility.

"Beautiful!" he murmured.

"Oh!"

"Not the play, no."

"Oh."

"No, the play is rather bad. But the girls cannot be anything but beautiful. Not because they act well or speak well or sing nicely, for some of them are atrocious; no, but because of what they are. Youth is a beautiful thing in itself, you'll know that, Sister, when you're as old as I am. You see, they are not playing at acting Hope and Faith, they hold those wonders in their youth."

His eyes were upon the two girls who played the parts of Hope and Faith, Trillium Pierce and Helen Perry, coming hand in hand to downstage center in a challenge to their own destruction. They would not be destroyed, of course. Buffeted by all the wickedness the playwright could call up, they would persevere through two more acts and stand triumphant at the final curtain.

Sister Raymond, rebellious over Torvaldsen's frankness, listened to the stilted, poetic lines the girls were speaking and knew that he was right. The whole production, however, would be chalked up as another success in St. Aurelien's endless repertoire of successes because the audience would pay small heed to what their daughters said. That they spoke at all would be enough.

Sister Raymond turned to Torvaldsen with the idea of making some sort of apology for what she had been thinking; but the words never were spoken. The artist, his hair on end, was leaning forward, his gaze fastened on one of the girls so intently that the Sister was struck with a curious sense of violence. Startled, she traced his attention to the stage—to Trillium Pierce, young Hope, who stood lilting her lines.

Sister Raymond, rigid with surprised disapproval, made no movement; yet the man swung around to look straight into her eyes.

"I do not know the girl," he said softly, "I am unacquainted with all but the few who attend my classes."

Sister Raymond's mouth opened and closed, but she could not speak. To her relief, Torvaldsen again turned his eyes to the stage with the mien of any interested observer.

"Now for the backdrop, Sister, I believe an immensity of purple shadow. . . ."

He talked on in a low voice, Sister Raymond nodding at a few of the right times. The backdrop was now a matter of minor importance, pushed into obscurity by the burning question of whether or not she should report to Mother on Mr. Torvaldsen's upsetting behavior. Was this the raising of the viper's head which Mother had dreaded from the first moment? At his age—!

Sister Raymond realized that the stage manager had called "Last curtain!" several minutes ago, and she took advantage of the lull to leave her place.

"I'll dismiss them and be right back, Mr. Torvaldsen. I think your idea for the design is splendid." She hurried down the aisle.

"Now listen, girls, Sister Gaspard is ready for a costume fitting in the sewing room. . . ."

The Sister's mind went automatically along the well-known grooves, and behind them she came to a conclusion that had nothing to do with "Mustardseed." Since the Christmas season was always a rush, and hardly the time to bother Mother with vague assumptions, she would put Torvaldsen on probation, a sort of parole under her own surveillance. So long as he behaved she would say nothing; but let him make one misstep and every lift of an eyebrow would be promptly recounted to Mother.

Sister was so cheered by this resolution that when the girls filed out she went back to the discussion of the backdrop in a receptive frame of mind. And so gallantly did Mr. Torvaldsen behave that when they parted some time later, she had forgotten about the probation.

"Trillium, I saw your name on the blackboard," said Nerissa Brady as the cast left the stage.

Sister Laurent would have recognized the expression that tightened the girl's mouth. "Was it—what was it, Nerissa?"

"I didn't notice. Something about the office. You'd better go see."

"Oh, I will, right away."

But Trillium knew she couldn't. Her knees were shaking too badly, and she sank down on the stage steps. What could there be in the office to add to her burden of fear? Nothing, she told herself, nothing; and yet the gaunt emptiness remained with her as the manifestation of dread she had come to know so well during the days since All Souls'. They had been busy days, and that had helped; but there was always night when she lay wakeful, tired and yet afraid to sleep because of the horrible dreams. She rubbed her forehead wearily. In a moment she would get up and go along to the sewing room where Sister Gaspard awaited them, and afterward she could see what the message read. That would be time enough.

"Listen, Gaspard hasn't got the patience of Job! Come on!" said Helen Perry, dragging Trillium to her feet. "I'm just dead, but honestly dead! It takes so much out of one, doesn't it? I don't know whether I could go in for a career as an actress, but with a terrific impulse burning you, just actually burning you like a flame, it might be worse not to release it, don't you think, Trill?" Helen sighed reverently. Then her butterfly thought flitted to a new blossom, and she caught Trillium's arm, laughing, her eyes glowing. "Want to keep a secret with me? I've asked him to the play, and he's coming!"

"Who's coming, Nell?"

"Oh, honestly—Howard! Don't you remember that fascinating older man I danced with so much at the Freshman Mixer. Alison's brother?"

Trillium laughed. "An older man? Howard Cooper's only about twenty-four!"

"Twenty-five! And he's the most heavenly dancer! I happened to mention him in a letter to my mother, and she answered—by registered mail, imagine!—that I'm not to see him any more during the school year. But my goodness, all I've ever been out with him is to one movie in Marysville, and it was the early show, too! That certainly can't distract me too much! But I promised, of course, and I'm not breaking my promise now because everybody will be here at the play, and if he comes—well, I'll have to be careful, because I don't want my mother taking—steps."

"I get what you mean," said Trillium. The whole of last year had been enlivened by the parade of Helen's boy friends, most of them young football players who became red faced and speechless in the select confines of the visitors' parlor. Once, toward midyear, Helen had been caught almost in the act of eloping, and Mrs. Perry had indeed taken steps. No novice was more severely guarded now than the young Miss Perry.

"Howard is an older man," she repeated with a pertness that her mother would have called spunky. "I certainly have a right to lead my own life. And I'm absolutely not going to tell him not to come. That would be too childish. After all, Mother Theodore is always urging us to make decisions for ourselves. Why, my own mother was married and had me when she was my age! But honestly, they all seem to forget that they were young once! It's the most disgusting—good afternoon, Sister!"

They were at the door of the sewing room, now filled with girls in their slips and girls already in their costumes. Above the noise

Sister Gaspard gave out orders and advice and reprimands. At the calmest of times her voice was pitched to the stridency of a rescuer calling a ship in singlehanded out of the fog, a trait which, in conjunction with her general brawn, had moved an imaginative girl to nickname her the Virgin Most Powerful.

"All right, girls, all right!" boomed Sister Gaspard. "Helen and Trillium, you're Faith and Hope? All right, Ivy, where are their dresses?"

Ivy, a meek little sophomore who daily considered changing her major from Home Economics to something that would not involve Sister Gaspard, scuttled to the long rack where drifts of chiffon and tulle hung.

"Oh, aren't they the most divinely yummy things!" Helen exclaimed, pulling off her sweater. "And they're exactly alike. Which is mine, Ivy?"

"You're Faith, aren't you? This one, with the pink veil. Trillium's veil is blue."

"Isn't that sweet! Hope and Faith, wandering through the world in pink and blue, such innocent colors!"

"Sister sure let herself go this time," Mary Elizabeth said admiringly.

"She wasn't the only one," said Ivy. "What we've gone through! I've sewed until I feel like the Song of the Shirt. But she does twice as much herself. Every time I decide to get out of Home Ec, I get kind of a vision of the Most Powerful tearing around doing more than can be expected of mortal man, and I wind up with a rededication ceremony among my pots and pans. Doggone it," she added thoughtfully.

Trillium, diverted by the amazon accomplishments of Sister Gaspard, felt safe and secure. Safety in numbers was a cliché because it was true. In the crowded, busy college life lay her perfect refuge.

"All right, girls, all right!" Sister Gaspard intoned. "Quiet, please!" With one hand under her scapular like Napoleon in his historic pose, she waited until Ivy wanted to drop a pin and hear the crash. "All right! Now! Your costumes are finished, girls. The sewing classes have done a beautiful piece of work, right down to the final pressing. Since the dress rehearsal is tomorrow afternoon at four, I'm turning the costumes over to you now, and each of you will be responsible for her own. And notice I say responsible." Her head turned deliberately so that, in spite of the limited field of vision enforced by her coif, her inspection covered every young lady before her. "The dressing rooms are crowded, but there are racks provided where you may hang the costumes. There will be no excuse for damage to any. Senior girls will use the dressing room to the right of the stage, juniors and all others on the left. Any questions?"

"No'ster," the girls murmured.

"All right then, you may go. Oh, one more word. If—I say *if* there should be an accidental tear of any costume, bring it straight to me. That is all."

The room filled again with chatter, and under cover of it Ivy muttered, "All right, girls, all right! But *if* you rip something I positively dare you to dump it in my lap to mend!"

"Don't worry, we'd drown ourselves in the bayou first," Helen assured her. "Come on, Trill."

Hurrying to the backstage dressing room, then along the hall to the bulletin board, Trillium tried to keep down her apprehension. It could be a perfectly meaningless message. It could be.

But it wasn't.

She read it, then read it again. A delivery. And she knew what the delivery would be!

"I never thought of that!" she whispered.

"Huh? Trill, you look like you're going to faint!" Helen cried. "I'll get Sister—"

Trillium grabbed the tail of her sweater. "I'm fine, Nell, too many rehearsals, that's all. I'll go to the office later."

"But it's right on our way upstairs, why don't we stop now? I think something's wrong with you, Trill! Honestly, you look scared—"

"No!" Trillium said sharply, and forced a laugh, but it was not a success. "No, I'm not scared. I just know what the delivery is." She paused, took a long breathe to steady herself, and continued, "It's only my coat, sent out from the furrier's in Marysville. I stored it with him this summer."

"*Only* your coat, that heavenly thing! Listen, missus, we're picking it up this very minute! I'm dying to see it again!" And Helen pulled her along so that Trillium dared not hang back.

I've done the wrong thing again, the frightened girl thought, made a fuss over getting the coat and brought about the exact opposite of what I intended. Leave the coat where it was, that had been her impulse, take it up later when she would be alone and she could push it into the back of her closet without even opening the box. No one would ask about it. But now Helen would go around gushing over it, and if she told Helen to keep quiet, that would arouse suspicion, and there would be talk about Trillium's strange behavior . . . and the coat must not be seen on the campus. . . .

There was no time to think further. Already they were outside of the suite, which consisted of outer office, private office, and Mother's parlor. Helen threw back her shoulders.

"Head up, my child, radiate womanly vitality, be a credit to St. Aurelien's!"

The door of the inner office was closed, and from behind it came a voice in a masculine register. On one of the well-polished, uncomfortable chairs, Sister Laurent sat waiting.

"Good afternoon, Sister," said Helen.

Sister did not hear her. In the doorway behind Helen, Trillium stood, listening in evident terror, her eyes shadowed with it as they had been on the night of All Souls'.

"What is it, dear?" Sister exclaimed.

The girl remained staring at the closed door, and it was Helen who answered, "We came for her package, Sister. I see it here on the mail table. Maybe there's a letter for one of us, too, Trill."

Helen, oblivious to the undercurrent, riffled through the letters on the table. Sister Laurent was genuinely concerned about Trillium. What in the world could it be that was so intolerable, that could smudge circles under her eyes and drain her face of flesh and color?

"Helen, would you mind—" Sister began, thinking to give the other girl an errand which would leave Trillium alone with her.

But the door of Mother's office opened, and Mother's low voice came out with Mr. Archer. Mother herself stood in the doorway,

Mr. Archer bowing with his usual deep respect, Sister Laurent on her feet.

Since it was as natural for Helen to draw a man's attention as it was for her to breathe, she caught up the box, holding it against her, smiling from Mother to the gentleman whom she considered so romantic.

"Good afternoon, Mother. Good afternoon, Mr. Archer," she said in a tremulous voice.

Crispin bowed again, gravely. Helen's performance being what it was, it held Mother and Mr. Archer for divergent reasons; but Sister's eyes were on Trillium. No whiter than she had been, for that was impossible, she lingered in the outer doorway.

"I see you have your box, Trillium."

When Trillium did not reply on the moment, Helen said, "Yes, Mother, thank you."

Her nod dismissed the girls, but Trillium did not see it for her eyes were on the floor in unreasoning panic. Mr. Archer couldn't help hearing her name. He might repeat it in the guest house and Jem—whoever he was—would wonder if this could be Dulcie's daughter—

"Trill, wake up!" Helen whispered, nudging her companion into the hall with the box in her arms. She was in so exalted a state that she failed to notice Trillium's silence as they climbed the stairs. "Don't you think older men *have* something, Trill? Hilaria says I'm madly missing half my life when I don't take Mr. Archer's creative writing course, but getting to know him outside of class—I mean, that's a tribute to your personality, Trill! He *has* to be nice to those other girls, but us, after all—friendship is a selective thing, I mean!"

Trillium only nodded.

"Really, I don't think you're thrilled at all! Now let's open the box and see what this marvelous hunk of mink looks like."

"It won't be any different from last year, Nell."

But there was no shaking Helen. Thumping the box down on Trillium's bed, she cut the string and brought out the coat.

"Oh, Trill, would you—could you let me wear it the night of the play, I mean when I meet Howard? He'd be super-dazzled! It isn't every girl who has a fur coat, I mean they're a luxury in the South, and sometimes I think I'd be willing to live in the North if I could honestly have one!"

Trillium watched Helen in the coat, twisting and turning before the small dressing-table mirror. It was simplest now to let her think she could wear the coat, but no one, not even she herself, would appear in it. The soft fur rippled with Helen's posing, the sleeves fell away from her wrists luxuriously. This was a coat to dream about, timeless in fashion because the designer had had in mind a woman rather than a style. Exactly when her mother had come into possession of that coat, Trillium did not know, but it had been some time before her father died. In their terrible, hurried packing she had seen it jammed into a trunk; not again until Uncle Henry had shipped it to her, the summer before last, when she celebrated her eighteenth birthday. It would be a perfect thing to identify her if Jem should see it.

"Mink!" Helen breathed, stroking the silky sleeve.

Trillium felt a wave of physical illness break over her. She had been so careful about her name, yet today it had come out. This is what could happen, without warning, at any hour of any day, some unexpected thing to trip her up in spite of every precaution. . . .

She jumped up, snatching the coat from Helen. She couldn't think, now, of what to do; her mind was useless to her. But she would have to dispose of the coat before the night of the play. When Helen was gone, she hung it in the far end of her closet so that anyone opening the door would not see it. If only she could hang away her name—but how useless it was to worry! Mr. Archer's attention had been on Helen. In all probability he had not even heard the name.

Down in the office, Crispin Archer was answering Sister Laurent's polite inquiry.

"The novel is doing famously, Sister. Whether the reviewers will see its merits, I don't know. But I'm enjoying my first attempt at fiction. It's an experience."

"So you do not find your teaching duties too time-consuming?" Mother asked.

Crispin Archer made the expected protests, then said casually, "Trillium. Isn't that what you called the girl? An odd name. I'm always on the hunt for names with individuality, and they're fiendishly hard to find. I'll ask her permission to use Trillium for my heroine. I've been calling her Hetty Rose, and she's a slob. As Trillium, she'd scintillate."

Mother's mouth became firm. "You need ask no permission, Mr. Archer. Names are not copyrightable. A trillium is a rather common woods flower. You might come across it anywhere."

Archer's eyes danced, and it occurred to Sister Laurent that he was ribbing Mother. One of the tools of his trade would be knowing what was in the public domain and what was not.

"You relieve me of a pleasant chore, Mother," he said. "Good afternoon, Mother, Sister."

Although he really only nodded, he gave the impression of bowing from the waist, then swung to the door with his queer walk, and was gone.

"I wonder if I like that man," Mother said with unexpected frankness.

"Love thy neighbor," Sister Laurent laughed. She had come on an errand concerning her work, but the happenings of the past few minutes erased it from her mind. She turned to Mother with a puzzled frown. "Mother, what actually do we know about Trillium Pierce?"

"The name again?"

"No, Mother, the girl."

"Very little, I believe. It's surprising how little, now that I consider it. How strange that you should bring it to my attention. Come into the office, please."

They brought out Trillium's card from the files. Mother looked it over thoughtfully. "We seem to have scant information, Sister. Her father died when she was thirteen, I suppose from some illness, and about the same time the mother disappeared. Whether the mother died—or deserted her—I don't know. Her tuition has always been paid by an uncle in New Orleans, and he writes to her regularly. She spends her vacations there." Mother dropped the card back into the folder. "And that's all."

"Then she couldn't be having family trouble," said Sister Laurent. "She is coming along well in her studies, that is, well for her.

But I've had the impression that she's worried about something. Perhaps it's because I'm so fond of her. . . ."

Mother nodded. "It's the same with all of us, Sister. Trillium has a place of her own. Well, I'll wait a little longer and see if she comes to me. Quite often she does. But if she shouldn't, and her anxiety continues, I'll have a little talk with her."

"Thank you, Mother," said Sister Laurent.

Over in the guesthouse, Franz Eric was polishing golf clubs in the middle of the living room when Crispin Archer strolled in and flung himself into a chair. A week of existence under the same roof had weathered the three into "Uncle Tor" and "the boys," and the boys had already come into that easy stage of companionship where silence is as friendly as speech. Crispin lighted his pipe, squinting at Franz through the smoke.

After a long time he observed, "Some cute kids around here."

"So I've noticed."

"Know one they call Trillium?"

The club slipped in Franz's hand, knocking over the jar of polish, and he righted it before he replied, "Can't say that I do. I teach badminton to a Hilaria, tennis to a Nerissa, but I have not a single Trillium to call mine own."

"A little dark thing, enormous eyes—"

"Scads of 'em, but they're only sets of un-co-ordinated muscles to me yet, Cris. Tender little shoots, all fenced in by Mother's capable hands. Sometimes I wonder what that woman's past has been, to make her so suspicious of the male."

"Lurid, hey?"

"Maybe. Or frustrated. It could add up to the same thing." Franz blew on the metal club and rubbed hard. "Next time I'm going to get me a job in an old ladies' home where I can show my true colors and prowl to my heart's content."

"I'll be with you, laddie," said Crispin Archer.

Franz saw his own pixy grin reflected on the surface of the niblick in his hand. Tomorrow morning, if all went as scheduled, he would give her first golf lesson to Miss Trillium Pierce.

5

Sister Samuel was fascinated with Crispin Archer's playing. With her pretty, dreamy little face screened from him by her coif, she sat in his studio, in the main building, listening to his majestic rendition of the Finlandia. Through the great translation of the hopes of a people for freedom the music had been demanding, rolling in thunderous swells that shook the piano and Sister Samuel equally; but now the warriors were defeated, bringing home the dead, and he played softly, as if death were the inexplicable and even he dared not mock it. These were the only measures he treated with respect.

Never had Sister Samuel heard a musician play like that, snapping his fingers in the face of the composer, turning a pianissimo into a giant fortissimo and crashing chords into whispers. To one who always played carefully, reading the expression as minutely as the notes, it was an unforgettable experience. She was breathless when he finished and his hands fell to the bench beside him. She didn't know at what point in the music she had risen to her feet, yet there she stood, her back to the light, her face shadowed, dreading the moment when he would look over and expect her to say something.

But Crispin Archer was in a mood to play, not to talk, and Sister Samuel was the perfect listener. Without even wiping his forehead, which she saw was aglitter, he began a seldom-heard theme from Chopin. Sister Samuel would have played it with a light, gentle touch; but this interpretation was without reverence, as if the player enjoyed the spectacle of sadness which had led another to write such music. Oh, don't, don't, Sister Samuel wanted to cry out. But she didn't. With her lovely blue eyes on Crispin's stocky hands, she listened and said not a word.

Through a haze of music, the great Torvaldsen tramped down the stairs from his studio, a beret cockily over one ear and a sketch pad in his hand. He was a little late for his outdoor class, but Tor never had spoiled his students by being present to start them on a day's work. When he saw Mother Theodore in the hall, he paused, a smile wrinkling around his eyes. He had been at St. Aurelien's long enough now to have become an accepted adjunct, a serious artist absorbed in translating onto canvas all he could of the world's beauty in the time left to him. Everyone thought of him as old, unconsciously responsive to his lead. This morning, considering, he had decided to wait a few days longer before speaking to Mother; but this casual moment might do better. The corridor was quiet, with feminine voices chanting Latin behind a closed door at his left and Archer's music demanding to be heard on the upper floor. He's teasing someone, Torvaldsen chuckled to himself as he changed his course to come up with Mother Theodore. At his greeting, she halted, falling into the immediate repose so common to the Sisterhood and so seldom seen outside it. She was busy, as a superior always is, yet she gave the impression of having all the time in the world for Mr. Torvaldsen so long as he made good use of it. Chatting, they walked to the east door, and it was not until then that Mother was certain the artist had something on his mind. His red-brown eyes met hers and flashed away, returned and ran away again.

Mother Theodore was amused. She had one infallible ruse with which to bring people to the point. "Good-by for the moment, Mr. Torvaldsen," she said, and turned to continue on down the stairs.

"Oh, Mother, one second, please."

Gravely she came back and they stood looking out through the open door.

"Yes," said Torvaldsen, "yes, well. Mother, I don't believe there is any necessity for mentioning this, but from certain remarks of the boys—er—Archer and Eric—I appreciate the obstacles—" He broke off, chuckling. "I'm stammering like a schoolboy, Mother. The educational atmosphere, no doubt."

"I've had no occasion to produce my ruler yet, sir."

Torvaldsen's mirth died. "Ah—yes. Well. But to come to the matter: while I seem to have the health of Titian and may live, like him, for most of a century, still I feel that I should not put off until tomorrow what I can produce today. And the fact, Mother, is that I would be most proud to leave behind me here at St. Aurelien's a sample of my work, a sort of memorial to the Sisters and myself at once. Do I put it badly?"

"You put it very well, sir. If I may anticipate you, since you mentioned certain obstacles, I gather that you will need models for this project."

"Ah—in a nutshell, yes, Mother. Beautifully draped, of course, angels and children and suchlike."

Mother Theodore stood for a moment in silence, looking out across the quiet scene. A simple request, as simple as Torvaldsen himself. He had taken the harmless pose of being old, perhaps to emphasize his fatherliness; but genuine enough was his love for St. Aurelien's. Although there had been no discussion of his financial status, it was plain to Mother that he never would have accepted her offer if he had been able to do otherwise. Few artists elect of their own free will to teach. And he loves us all, Mother thought, and in his gratitude he would leave behind him here the most personal gift he can make!

Torvaldsen came nearer, and she could smell the turpentine and paint of his old smock. "There is a beautiful wall in the auditorium, Mother, an invitation for a mural. If it would be agreeable to you, that is where I would place my picture."

Mother nodded. "Years ago, when I was a novice, there was talk of a mural; but an artist pointed out that in this damp climate the paint would peel and the picture would have to be restored so often that in time there would be none of the original left."

"He must have planned to paint directly on the plaster, Mother. Now I would not do that! I would paint my picture on canvas. I don't say it would never need restoration, of course, all paint peels in this swamp region; but much less than the other way."

Torvaldsen talked on, Mother's enthusiasm taking fire from his. It was easy, he saw, to arouse her interest in anything which furthered the cultural and educational cause of St. Aurelien's. He spoke of line and color, even sketched a bit on the pad he held; and when finally he remembered his class and excused himself, the mural had become an accepted undertaking.

Mother Theodore turned to go down the stairs, then stopped as if someone had stuck her with a pin. She stepped back to the door. Torvaldsen was lumbering off toward the barnyard where his art class, having an outdoor lesson in sketching, moved slowly around after a cow. Mother, watching the ungainly progress of the artist, smiled a little wryly. The first resolution she had made, when at last it was decided to add art to the college schedule, was that the artist should not be allowed to use the girls as models. Personalities were to play no part. But Torvaldsen had skirted it neatly. He couldn't be expected to paint an ambitious mural without models. And certainly the huge barn he had selected as a studio was not conducive to intimate friendships. And he was anything but the type to inspire hero worship.

"I've been too thoroughly imbued with the protective instinct for our southern belles," Mother murmured aloud as she hurried down the stairs. "Most of them are hardy little weeds. But I'll be careful. Now if Sister Emery hasn't given up and left the linen room. . . ."

Torvaldsen, pondering the same phase of his art as Mother Theodore, was well pleased with himself. He could approach any of the girls now without having to give a reason, and therefore his approach to the special one would go unremarked. Very good, he chuckled, very good. He should do well at St. Aurelien's.

In the barnyard the students picked up their three-legged stools, followed the cow until she stopped to graze again, and all sat down.

"Land sakes, what they're learnin' I couldn't say," said Glory Muckleroy as she came out of the henhouse and met her husband, Hy, who was tinkering up the lawn mower. "Followin' that-there cow all around the pasture, they been, and I bet a skinned monkey there ain't one of 'em knows a soup bone from a rump roast."

"They ain't drawin' soup bones, honey," Hy remarked. "Now my idea of nothin' is that-there other young 'un whackin' away at the li'l ol' go'f ball. Ain't hit it yet, far as I can make out."

Trillium, at the practice tee between pecan grove and pasture, rested her driver on the ground while Franz Eric patiently repeated his instructions. She never would hit the ball, not with her hands shaking and her knees quivering as if the very earth itself quaked beneath her. With Crispin Archer's illogical music drifting over on the west wind, Franz Eric's hands touching hers as he explained the grip on the golf club and his tone very formal when he called her Miss Pierce, Torvaldsen swinging across the lawn toward them like a Viking setting out for the New World, Trillium suddenly felt surrounded.

"I'm sorry, I don't feel well, Mr. Eric," she said, and her pallor gave truth to her words. "Will you excuse me, please?"

She started toward the convent, encountered Torvaldsen, and streaked toward the barnyard. The artist quickened his step, realized he could not catch her without making a dash which would probably be both undignified and unsuccessful, and strolled on.

Franz laughed, slamming at the ball. "You're doing okay, Ericson," he said aloud. "She's gotta come back, some time." And he shouldered his clubs and meandered off to the tennis court without bothering to follow his ball.

Get away, get away, that was Trillium's nightmare urge; but it was almost like running in a dream when you never quite escape and yet never are caught. In her vegetable garden, Glory Muckleroy leaned on her hoe. It was late to be working in a garden, but Glory never could get enough of it. Slowing to a walk in order not to excite comment, Trillium waved to Glory and went on toward the cloister. The woman couldn't help her, Trillium thought, because she never had known real trouble, only the fussy trouble of raising five children on nothing, and now that she had come into good days the old times were the soil out of which the new were growing. No help there, no help from anyone.

Up in her room, Trillium shut the door and slid a chair against it under the knob. Crispin Archer had stopped playing in his studio. Someone was practicing scales on a violin. She threw herself flat on the bed. The only sound other than the violin was the short, heavy breathing of a runner, someone who had sped up stairs and through halls until her lungs were bursting. Herself.

Trillium jumped up and pushed at the chair again, making certain it was tight under the knob. The door had a lock, one that turned like a bolt on the inside and which could be opened with a key from the outside, an arrangement to assure a small degree of privacy but not planned for personal safety. Several people had keys: Mother Theodore, Sister Laurent, the refectory Sister, Rindy who did the cleaning. The chair, of course, was secure as any bolt. And no one could get in through the window. It was too high up.

Trillium lay down again and closed her eyes. This running away couldn't go on, particularly when she was not running to anything but only away. The thing to do was to think it out carefully, take her time, face her problem calmly; and she could do it now, with the autumn sunlight falling across her and the girls all up and about in the building.

There was the knowledge, first, that Mr. Archer had heard her name, Franz Eric had called her by it several times this morning, and Torvaldsen had been determined to meet her as she crossed the lawn. Each of the three knew her, the safe feeling of anonymity was gone.

"But they—he can't be sure!" she whispered.

Still, how many girls named Trillium Pierce would there be in the world?

And, to focus attention upon that strange name, there was the forthcoming publicity of "Mustardseed!" She could be ill, she thought frantically, she could even eat soap or something to make herself sick so she wouldn't have to stand up there before—him! But that was impossible as well as foolish; for Mother Theodore would call the doctor, and he would say that her illness was brought on by herself, and then they would all begin to ask why. And he would hear about it, and know for certain that she feared him. He might believe even that she knew him, could identify him whenever she found an opportunity, and she would no longer have even the slim safety that was hers now!

The spotlight of the play seemed infinitely preferable to such calamity. So there, at least, was one decision made. Under her clinging fingers the bedspread was crumpled into two damp little volcanoes. She must think about the letter, next. Through the week since All Souls' Day she had carried it pinned inside her blouse; but that was not secure enough. The paper might tear, the envelope fall and she would never know where it went. . . .

To destroy the letter would be the most final, just as she had always destroyed the others. But not this one. It held too much precious information. If she could hide it where no one would think of looking . . . and there was the coat . . . she had to get rid of the coat. . . .

For a quarter of an hour, Trillium lay still. When she sat up, the sunshine showed her to be paler than ever.

"I won't hesitate, I won't think any longer, because this is the only way out," she whispered. "Come on, kid, let's get it over."

She slid off the bed and opened the closet door. Digging back through the dresses, her hand met soft fur and she dragged it out. Quickly, as if the touch must not be allowed to soften her resolve, she threw the coat on the bed and snatched her nail scissors. The beautiful matched back lay there, brown and rich. Separating the fur, she plunged the little scissors deep into the skin and worked it until a flap was loosened. Then she caught the torn place and pulled. The skin was soft. When she stopped there was an arrow-shaped tear six inches long in the back of the coat.

"Well, that much is done!" she said aloud, but her voice broke. She couldn't see to find a face tissue, so she wiped her eyes on her sleeve. Then she hung the coat back where it had been in the closet and pulled the chair away from the door.

She had accomplished the first step. Now for the next.

The lunch bell rang while she was putting on fresh lipstick. She wasn't hungry. It would be hash, anyway. But she would have to go down. To miss lunch might invite questions, and there was only this afternoon in which to accomplish what she planned. Tomorrow, the day of the play, even the emergency she was about to bring on would not be enough to get her into Marysville.

Joining the other girls in the hall, girls atwitter over the approach of dress rehearsal, Trillium was as natural as any of them because none was quite herself. Voices were too high, laughter too shrill, tempers a little short. For Trillium there was also the exhilaration of awaiting her opportunity, the old thrill of playing cops and robbers. When the crowd broke up after lunch, she escaped to the dressing room and went straight to the rack where she had hung her costume.

There it was, misty white, the blue veil folded neatly over the inside of the hanger. Trillium hesitated then, more than she had over the coat. To destroy was horrible to her. Even as a child she had carefully leafed through the mail-order catalogue and felt regret when at last her mother said it was worn enough to be cut up for paper dolls. But there was no other way.

She had to get into town.

The costume drifted in her arms, light widths of chiffon artfully caught with a needle in exactly the right places to make it look free of all sewing. Sister Gaspard was an artist. Hastily selecting a breadth which was only a square of chiffon hung diagonally from the shoulder, Trillium caught the middle of it in her teeth and pulled. There was a rending tear, and the square hung with a bulging, ragged hole in the middle.

She had wept when she tore her coat, but seeing the ruin of her costume shook her with apprehension. What if she were mistaken, and the material had not been bought at Goldsmith's in Marysville? What if she couldn't replace it as she had planned?

"For heaven's sake!" she groaned. "I didn't think of that! But it has to be Goldsmith's! Dear Lord, let it be Goldsmith's"

It was late for such a prayer, like the time Helen set the Declaration of Independence in 1778 on a history exam and then prayed the Lord to make it that. Trillium pushed apart the other hanging costumes and thrust her own among them. Now she had to get into town, and fast!

Sister Raymond, luckily, was puttering around the stage, alone. There was nothing to be done, but she was too uneasy for meditation. She was wandering around with a potted fern, knowing she would put it back exactly where it had been, when Trillium burst out of the backstage shadows. Sister Raymond had turned on only one overhead spot, and outside its circle everything was hazy; but there was illumination enough to show the girl's white face and flying hair, and Sister's heart fell clear to her Cuban heels.

"Trillium, dear, now what?"

"Oh, Sister, I tore my costume! You know those wing pieces that sort of float out when we dance? Well, the left one, a big horrible hole!"

The fern was suddenly too heavy for Sister, and Trillium caught it before it fell.

"I'm just terribly sorry, Sister, but I couldn't help it!" Both statements were true. Trillium was terribly sorry; and she couldn't help it because this was the only errand she could invent which would surely take her into town.

"Sister, I still have some money from last month's allowance, and I'll go into town and get a length myself. There's no hem or anything and I can tack it in place and poor dear Sister Gaspard will never know the difference!"

"Oh, could you, Trillium? Did they buy it at Goldsmith's, do you think?"

"If they didn't, all is lost!" Trillium said truthfully. "If I could ask Hy Muckleroy to run me in—?"

"He's going for something else, if you hurry you'll catch him! You're sure you have the money?"

"Yes'ster!"

Trillium shoved the fern back into Sister Raymond's embrace and made off.

Sister Raymond, recovering from the shock, listened to Trillium's quick steps departing. "Oh, and take Helen with you, dear!" she called. She wasn't sure that Trillium heard, but it was Mother's policy never to allow the girls off the grounds alone. In the white glow of the spotlight she paused. Queer that Trillium, of all people, should have torn her costume. If it were Nerissa Brady, with her redheaded temperament, it would be perfectly understandable— but Trillium! She turned her back to the light, the shadows clown-black under her coif, and she stood that way a long time, holding the fern and patting its green-covered pot as if it might be lulled to sleep.

Trillium had heard the Sister's instruction, but she could easily pretend that she hadn't if anything came of it. She couldn't take Helen, not when the whole idea was to get the coat away from that determined young lady. In her room she yanked the furrier's box from under her bed. What she had to do took her less than a minute. She ran with the box cover bulging and string flying.

She was just in time to catch Hy Muckleroy. In the side yard by his house he was reviving the engine of the pickup truck, which was his care and joy, and only the lower blue-jeaned half of him was visible. Trillium climbed up into the high-rearing cab. Mother had been ready to junk the truck when Hy came to the farm, but his outraged protests had dissuaded her. Later Mother knew that Hy had the soul of a tinker and that a shiny new truck would never have had the appeal of this ailing vehicle. He overhauled it weekly, painted it a liverish red, and assured Mother every time he saw her that it was in fine condition.

"Well, Miss Trillium!" Hy greeted her, folding his long legs into the cab. "Comin' into town with me, eh? Welcome! Ever hear a nicer engine? Purrs like a baby, she does!"

Trillium giggled. There were other similes she could suggest, such as an earthquake in full swing. She liked Hy. He was tall and thin and had an air of always being delighted at finding himself in such pleasant surroundings no matter what they were. And to keep up with his position at St. Aurelien's, he had taken to shaving and changing his shirt almost every day.

"Quite a bundle you got there, Miss Trillium!" Hy shouted.

"I tore my costume!" Trillium shouted back. "Are you coming to the play tomorrow night?"

"Say, now, I'd admire to, but Glory's goin', and maybe she'll want me to stay with the kids."

"Oh, take them!" Trillium urged.

Hy hunched his shoulders. His cup of bliss would be running over whether he sat entranced over "Mustardseed" or hunkered on his back porch listening to the swamp settle for the night.

Marysville still had a baked appearance, the one street which was imposingly named St. Francis Boulevard was only a gasp away from summer indolence. But the furrier's shop was there, and Goldsmith's with a display of shovels and thread and kerosene cans and eighty square percale in the window.

When Hy stopped for her at the bank corner, having completed his errands, Trillium looked as if she had searched for the Holy

Grail and found it. Her large box was gone and in its place she carried a small flat paper sack with Goldsmith's name across it.

"Get what you wanted, Miss Trillium?" Hy inquired, throwing the truck into gear.

"Everything!" Trillium sighed.

It was true.

The first step accomplished, the rest would be easier. Tomorrow night the convent grounds would be crowded, the road a steady stream of autos winding out to the gates after the play, and almost any one of them would pick up a girl on foot. They wouldn't ask questions. She would be only another playgoer homeward bound. She would wear her brown wool and the dark red blanket coat, both inconspicuous in the dark, so when questions would be asked later the motorist who gave her the ride would be hard put to remember what she looked like and could only tell that he had given her a lift into Marysville. She had money enough, in spite of the expense of the chiffon. By the time anyone was actually worried, she would be in New Orleans. It was the only course to take, now that Jem knew her.

Ahead, casually crossing the parking lot, was Torvaldsen. At the moment Trillium caught sight of him, he observed the truck and stopped, obviously intending to waylay its passenger when she alighted at the east door.

Trillium grasped Hy's arm. "Listen, Hy, stop here! Right here! I'll run in the main entrance. Stop!"

She jerked his arm, and Hy, mystified but chalking her excitement up to the queer notions of women in general, stepped on the brake. Leaning across her, he pushed open the door and Trillium jumped out. When Hy chugged through the parking area and on to the barnyard, he waved at Torvaldsen who was lingering on the steps at the east entrance. Nose a little out of joint, Hy considered, but what was he after, an old stiff like him? He shrugged and began to whistle.

6

"I wish I could believe it!" Sister Raymond sighed. "I suppose I have morning-of-the-fatal-day jitters, but—" She spread her hands helplessly. This, at last, was the day of the "Mustardseed" presentation, and she had no more faith in it than—than Torvaldsen.

"But it's true, Sister!" cried Helen Perry, and Nerissa Brady added gaily, "It always happens, a bad dress rehearsal means a good performance. You'll see, Sister, honestly, we'll just act our hearts out tonight!"

"Well. . . ." Sister turned her head in order to see from end to end of the stage where they stood.

Trillium, in the narrow corridor leading from stage to dressing room, halted abruptly when she heard the next voice.

"I believe them, Sister," said Torvaldsen, and Trillium knew he was standing with a brush poised because he spoke musingly, as if his thoughts were only half on his words. "If they had given their best yesterday at the dress rehearsal they would be too assured to-night, they would see no necessity for trying harder. But knowing they didn't do well, they will be alert, they will use their minds as well as their voices. Perfection does not invite improvement, but imperfection puts one on guard. So!"

The Sister and the girls laughed, and Trillium heard Torvaldsen's voice again. "But I'm not joking! See, if my work had been perfect before, I'd never have thought of strengthening the shadows. But I lower the tone of the purple, and the white becomes more brilliant although I have not touched it. Marvelous!"

Light voices answered. Trillium glanced into the dressing room. No one was there. She went in and closed the door behind her. This would be the time to write her note, then she would have ample opportunity to deliver it. Seating herself at the built-in make-up shelf that ran the circumference of the room, she took a small envelope and paper from her cardigan pocket and wrote hastily.

"Dear Mother Theodore, Please forgive me for going away. There is nothing else I can do. I have money enough and I can take care of myself. I cannot explain because—"

She stopped, caution overcame her, and she sat chewing the end of her pencil. She should not have put in that last word since she dared not set down what ought to follow. The voices on the stage were growing louder, Trillium would not much longer be alone. Quickly she erased "because" and put a period after "explain." Then she added, "It is nothing that has happened at the convent. Please don't worry about me. With love, Trillium."

She had just written Mother's name on the envelope when the door flew open. A crowd of girls entered and began polishing the square mirrors, laying out make-up, and talking in a dozen assorted keys. Sister Raymond, Trillium saw, was quietly inspecting the costumes on the rack. All were in order. Even Sister Gaspard could not have told that one bore a new width of chiffon.

"You haven't anything laid out, Trill!" Helen exclaimed, pushing her own kit onto Trillium's section while she covered hers with a clean towel,

"I know, but I'm going to do it right now," Trillium said. She licked the flap of her little envelope and tucked it into one of the deep pockets of her sweater. Then she took off the sweater, hung it over the back of her chair, and began to sort her make-up.

"Oh, darn, I forgot my towels for tonight!" Helen complained.

"Use mine," Trillium offered.

"No, Sister says we each have to have our own. Sanitary, or something. Come on to the linen room with me. Why take your sweater? You don't need it."

Trillium hesitated hardly a fraction of a second. No one would touch the sweater. And she didn't need it. She had worn it to Mass this morning, but the early chill of the buildings was gone.

The auditorium and the adjoining dressing rooms were in the center wing, and at the leisurely pace Trillium and Helen set it was a long stroll to the linen room. Clear to the end of the west wing on the main floor, then down the stairs and into the tunnel which bore away toward the Contemplatives' house. A tunnel lay under each of the cloister walks, forming an underground square connecting the convent buildings as the walks did above ground.

"This place is a regular fort!" Helen whispered. "It makes me feel spooky. Where's the light, Trill?"

Finding the switch, Trillium said, "Well, wasn't it a fort in the early days? Indians and things? That's what I've always heard. Everybody used to pile down here when the Indians went on the warpath. Think how a Comanche would sound under this vaulted ceiling. Woo!" A long woo woo echoed her shrill cry.

"For goodness' sake, come on!" Helen demanded, and she dragged Trillium into one of the small rooms under the main building. Here the first Sisters had lived, but now the rooms were used for storage and laundry. Grabbing towels, Helen sped to the stairs.

Time was of no consequence today. Mother had dismissed all classes in order that the girls would be rested and fresh for the night's performance, and Trillium and Helen stepped out into the cool shade by the west door. They dallied so long that the crowd in the dressing room finished their undertakings and straggled away. Trillium's sweater fell on the floor. Someone picked it up by the tail and the note fell out, but the girl didn't notice. A hurrying foot kicked the small envelope far to one side. When the sweater hung again over the back of Trillium's chair, the note lay across the room. There was no reason, then, to connect the sweater with the note when another girl spied the envelope on the floor.

"Who lost this, kids?" she asked, waving it.

But no one claimed it, and she passed it to Sister Raymond. "Mother Theodore's name is on it," Sister said. "I'll leave it with her mail when I go by the office."

So the note went away in Sister Raymond's pocket.

When Trillium and Helen came back to the dressing room, everyone had left. From the high windows the light fell on all the neat make-up arrangements and upon Trillium's sweater, brilliant green.

She took it and with it swinging over her shoulder went with Helen to the dining room.

It was not until after lunch that Trillium felt again in the sweater pocket. The note was not there! She had made a mistake, felt in the wrong pocket. But the other was empty also. Frantically she searched again; but the sweater had only two pockets, and both were empty.

"Lose something, Trill?" asked Mary Elizabeth across the table.

"I—no, just my hanky."

"You look awfully worried for just a hanky."

Trillium was too panicky to dissemble now. She dipped under the table, but there was no small white envelope. Excusing herself, she left the other girls staring after her.

She was not acting naturally now, but she couldn't help it. I shouldn't have written the note so soon, she thought wildly, running along the old corridors; I should have waited, I needn't have written it at all! If someone had picked it up and read it, that person would wonder if Trillium had gone crazy—but St. Aurelien's personnel was too well mannered to tear open a note addressed to another.

"Of course no one has opened it!" Trillium panted, and forced herself to walk. But suppose the note was already in Mother Theodore's hands, suppose she sat in her office this very minute, reading the bungling excuse of a girl who intended to run away!

Without thinking of what she could say to Mother to undo the damage to her plan, Trillium ran until she reached the office door. The door of the inner office was open, showing a neat, empty interior, and on the mail table most of the letters from the morning post still lay. Hastily the girl scattered the pile sorted for Mother Theodore—bills, personal letters, advertisements—but no small white envelope without a postmark. The other letters on the table were for Torvaldsen, Archer, and Eric. The girls and Sisters had already taken theirs.

Relief made Trillium giddy, and she leaned against the table, stacking Mother's letters again neatly. Mother would not have picked up the least important looking of the lot and carried it away without taking the rest. So she had not read that scrawled little message! That was the inevitable, comforting conclusion.

Trillium's forehead was damp, but she laughed as she topped Mother's heap with a violent pink envelope bearing almost illegible writing in green ink. No wonder Nerissa Brady was flighty, with a mother like that. Trillium could think about something as inconsequential as Nerissa's mother's stationery because now her fright was over, and she would run down to the dressing room and find the envelope somewhere on the floor. That was where it would be, since no one had delivered it.

When she came into the dressing room, however, she saw immediately that she was wrong. The floor must have been swept during the lunch hour for she distinctly remembered a cloud of sawdust in one corner where something had been unpacked.

And Rindy would have done the sweeping, Rindy drooping through the halls with her curly white mop!

So certain was Trillium this time that when she found Rindy plodding along outside the visitors' parlor, she began without preamble.

"Give it to me, Rindy, please."

The African-brown face showed no surprise. "Give you-all what, Miss Tri'ium?"

"The note! You found it!" When the girl shook her head, Trillium cried out in a frenzy, "I know you did, don't lie! A plain envelope addressed to Mother Theodore! I lost it out of my sweater pocket!"

Rindy's head dropped and her lips bulged in a pout. "I didn' find no envelope! I ain't seen nothin' like that."

"But you swept the dressing room, didn't you?"

"That where you lose it? Yas'm, sawdust all over. But I didn' see no letter, no ma'am!"

Trillium tried to fight down her alarm. Of course Rindy had found the note! She was just waiting to be bribed, a business transaction, like her acceptance of Helen's red bandanna in exchange for services in mailing notes to Howard Cooper.

"Listen, Rindy," Trillium began confidentially, "listen, you've seen my new scarf, the aqua with the yellow roses? I'll give it to you if you'll tell me." When Rindy shook her head, Trillium wanted to slap her, but she dropped her voice coaxingly. "Then my anklets that match the scarf, I'll give you those, too, Rindy. You see, if I knew the note had been delivered to Mother already, I wouldn't mind a bit, I'd just ask her about it and she'd tell me. Did you meet her in the hall and give it to her?"

"I ain't seed yore note," Rindy insisted; and although her eyes remained on the mop she was shoving aimlessly, Trillium believed her. Rindy had been a last hope. Where shall I turn now? the girl's benumbed brain demanded. Her despair must have touched Rindy, for the maid added, "Must be somethin' powerful important, Miss Tri'ium. You-all looks like somebody's walkin' on yore grave,"

Trillium shuddered. Cover up, her caution warned her. "No, Rindy, it's not very important. But if you should find this little plain white envelope with Mother's name on it, you'll bring it straight to me, won't you?"

"I'll keep mah eyes poppin', honey!"

Trillium left her, and Rindy went on with her everlasting mop-pushing. The floors were of beautiful wide cypress boards, polished and waxed until they shone, and they were Rindy's pride. She pressed the soft mop tight against the wall to get every particle of dust, slipping it into the recess which accommodated the door to the visitors' parlor. The door was standing slightly ajar, and yet the pressure of the mop did not push it farther open. Must be something behind it, maybe the rug curled up, Rindy decided. The parlor was her concern only on Thursdays, and she went on by.

Sister Raymond, entering Mother's office, met Rindy outside the door and spoke to her. Sister had not until this moment thought of delivering the note she had picked up. She took it from her pocket and laid it with Mother's other letters, remarking to herself that Nerissa Brady's mother must be undergoing another period of concern for her only daughter. No one else used such raucous pink stationery and green ink.

The Sister hurried away, and Rindy went on with her work. She was at the far west end of the hall, going steadily on, when the door of the visitors' parlor opened and someone came quickly out and crossed to the office. Mother Theodore, coming in just before prayers, glanced at her letters, saw the pink envelope, and sighed. She did not know, of course, that there had been a white envelope on top of the pink. There was none then.

Trillium ran to her room, but there was nowhere she could go to escape from her terror. No use now regretting that she had written the message. It was done. And it was possible, more than probable, that the letter was mislaid, stuck off under a cupboard, kicked under a davenport, lying in a wastebasket. For a freakish instant she considered tearing through all the wastebaskets in the building, through the cloister, then over into the Contemplatives' house with a blizzard of paper flying behind her, and the Sisters would look up with that other-world peace and see her like a witch without a broomstick. . . .

Throwing herself on the bed, she fought off hysteria. There was no danger, really. Whoever Jem was, he could not be in the convent building where she had been this morning, in the dressing room— but Torvaldsen was on the stage, not fifty feet away—

Trillium jumped up, pulling the chair over to the door as she had done before and wedging it under the knob. I'll stay here, right here, she planned desperately, and then I'll go with Helen and Mary Liz down to supper and to the dressing room. During the performance I'll be either on stage or in the wings, always with a crowd. And afterward, when the autos would be sliding down to the gates, she could get away. It should be infinitely easier than what she had done yesterday to get rid of her coat. And once away she could breathe again, she would be safe. The only possible obstacle now was that someone still might find the note and give it to Mother. But there was nothing to be gained in speculating about that, and Trillium sat down to wait.

Below, in the cloister wing, old Sister Etienne had just put on her new habit and a clean coif. It was very early to be preparing for the evening's excitement, but she knew the Lord would not mind her expanding to its full this harmless little glow of pleasure. The Lord was very good to her. He had almost taken away her sight, but that was only so that she might look inward the better. She had no complaint. Her age and her partial blindness had actually brought her a deep contentment she had never known when she was young and busy.

And now she was ready, and she had nothing to do until Vespers. They were having Vespers early, an added little delight to upset the routine, but there was still plenty of time for a visit to Tom and Banty. Moving carefully, she left the cloister and went out along the walk. Getting a pan of sour milk from the dairy, Sister Etienne carried it into the barnyard. She never stumbled, carrying the milk. She knew the way too well. And she could see a little. She could see Tom fanning his tail and drooping his wings like a veteran gobbler, his royal head violet as he strutted before her; and Banty, the tiny chicken, jumping toward the pan of milk even before she set it down.

Tom always had been a pig about sour milk. Not only would he plunge his face into it, but he had to stand in the pan while Banty drank around him; and none of Sister Etienne's scoldings made any improvement in him. Squatted down beside them, stroking their firm backs, the old Sister was in a daze of happiness. She didn't notice that Tom, on his frequent trips out of the milk pan, planted his large feet on the skirt of her habit where it lay around her on the ground. In the fall sunshine the trio made a picture most pleasing to the two men strolling beside the bayou.

"Speaking of rural atmosphere, Cris, look," said Franz Eric. "Put the famous Archer sarcasm to work on that if you can."

"I don't know the meaning of the word," returned Crispin. "I'm in a mellow mood, I feel benevolent and kindly. Let's mosey over."

When Sister Etienne heard the strange footsteps and arose, they saw that the whole side of the habit was splashed with milk. Franz immediately understood. Neatness was a part of a Sister's godliness. He was so sorry for her that for a moment he couldn't speak, and Crispin made the first remark.

"I've seen you often here, Sister, but I hesitated to intrude. I'm Crispin Archer."

The Sister smiled. "Of course, sir, I know your voice, and I can still distinguish faces a little. It was such a pleasure for me to be in the assembly when you were all presented. And Mr. Eric is with you? Good afternoon, sir."

Franz murmured, "Good afternoon, Sister," as he used to do in school. Tom dropped his wings and gobbled, and they all laughed.

"Tom is not used to gentlemen," said Sister. "My little Banty raised him from the egg. She and I have spoiled him." She stooped, putting out her hand to the hen, and her eyes fell directly on the slopped folds of her skirt. Not trusting her sight, she felt of the wet white patches, her fingers swift. When she straightened, her cheeks were pink.

"I'm afraid there is no end to Tom's bad manners."

"You can sponge it out, Sister," Franz said quickly, so quickly that she knew he had noticed and been thinking out a solution. "Hang it in your drying yard, over there, and nobody will ever know the difference. You won't mind a little dampness, will you?" His eyes traveled over the cloister. Torvaldsen had come from somewhere and stood busy with a pencil and sketch pad at the far west end of the lawn.

Sister Etienne was quite flustered. How kind the gentlemen were, taking such an interest in an untidy old nun! She stammered an apology, excused herself, and departed with what haste she could. Tom's bad behavior was well worth while since it had resulted in such a nice little conversation.

Back in the cloister, she took off the habit, put on a plain black gown like a long-sleeved apron, and carried the habit into the Sisters' laundry. It didn't take long to sponge the soiled places, although she did a good deal more than necessary just to make sure. She couldn't sit through the play smelling of sour milk. When she hung it in the drying yard, which was screened by a vine-covered fence, she liked the idea of having a freshly aired habit. If the evening happened to be cool, she would take her shawl to wear when she stood outside listening to the conversation of the departing people; and then it seemed proper to air the shawl also, and she brought it out and hung it on the line with the habit.

Old Sister Etienne was very tired by that time. She would lie down, she planned, for a few minutes before Vespers. If the good habit wasn't dry, she could put on her old one, the one that had almost disintegrated before it was her turn for a new one. The moment her head touched the pillow the old Sister was sound asleep.

It was black dark in her room when Sister Etienne awoke. A minute went by before she realized she had slept through Vespers and supper. Horrified, she started up. The play would be beginning! In a rush she remembered the habit and shawl on the line, and everything fell into place. She went out into the lighted hall and threw open the door to the drying yard. At this distance the lines appeared to be empty. She stepped out, feeling her way in the darkness that was her own and the night's. Funny, she thought she had hung the habit on the first line, but that was empty. The second, also, and the third and fourth!

Sister Etienne couldn't believe her own discovery. The habit couldn't be gone! She slid her fingers along the lines for the third time before it occurred to her that someone must have brought it in out of the evening damp. Her name was in it. Whoever had taken the habit off the line had put it in her room.

The old Sister trotted back to her small chamber. Even her dim sight told her that the habit was not there, not in the closet, not on the bed. What had become of it? Had she not put it on the line? But she had! She could remember! Sitting on the side of her bed, she began to cry. She understood now. God was punishing her for taking too much pleasure in the play. The music was drifting down from the auditorium, the play was beginning. She could put on the ragged old habit and go. But it seemed like a defiance to do it. Perhaps if she missed the first act, that would be restitution enough. She hurried into the old habit, then went down on her knees and prayed earnestly for guidance.

7

"Trill, he's here!" Helen gushed in an exultant whisper.

"Who's here?" Trillium asked, dabbing on rouge. The dressing room was a babble of excited voices, nervous shrieks of laughter riding over Sister Raymond's earnest assurances that there was no reason to be nervous.

"*Who's* here? Honestly, Trill—*Howard!* I saw him just now! I sneaked around front and he's here!"

"Your folks are, too, aren't they?"

"Naturally. But I'm going to duck out and meet Howard right away after the performance, down by Pirate Cove. Mom won't know. She'll have to give me time to get dressed, and that'll be it!"

"Does Howard know you're doing that?"

"He'll be there," Helen said confidently. "He's like a pup after a bone where I'm concerned. Did you bring down your coat?"

"I forgot."

"Oh, Trill, you didn't! After you promised! Run up and get it now!"

Trillium pushed back her stool and arose as if she were going to obey. No one ever could argue with Helen and not feel that a spider web of nylon had been gently woven around them.

"Trillium, you're sure you're not nervous?" Sister Raymond quavered. "The audience wants to like you; remember, they're your friends. . . ."

With the others, Trillium listened to the pep talk Sister Raymond always gave before a performance. She was not nervous. She had come into a center of calm, knowing the maelstrom that whirled around her; but the make-believe of the play had nothing to do with it.

"Places!" called the stage manager. There was a final scurrying, and "Mustardseed" was under way.

The play was a beautiful fantasy that might well have drawn snickers from an audience who had lived through two world wars and come out of them to wonder what had become of faith and hope; but in the convent surroundings the message was right. By the end of the second act, businessman fathers tottered on the brink of realizing there was something more important than the dollar, and mothers became so misty-eyed they could barely follow the actors.

"And I told Sister the play was bad!" Torvaldsen murmured in the intermission, but low enough so that no parent heard him. With Franz and Crispin he sat well to the front near a side exit, the only seating arrangement Mr. Archer would tolerate since he expected to be afflicted with acute boredom. "But it isn't," Torvaldsen added in naïve astonishment. "With their interpretation, their youth, the convent setting, it's perfect."

Crispin shook his head. "You were right the first time, Tor. This is farce, pure and simple. What do these kids know about disillusionment? Wait until they're older and get slapped around a little, then they'll find out that the destruction of hope and faith isn't just a cute trick to act out in blue lights with soft music!"

"Faith and Hope won't be destroyed, Cris," Franz said, amused. "Going to put some of these kids in a novel, fit 'em all out with complexes?"

Crispin grunted rudely, and Franz laughed. "I wouldn't put it past you. But what's wrong with being cute? Gad, what a cure for a hang-over that young Trillium would be!"

"Which one's she?"

"Faith."

Crispin's program sailed to the floor. "Let it go. I never read 'em, anyway."

Torvaldsen, on the aisle, retrieved it and came up with his face very red. "I'll have to leave before the last act is over. I want to be in the parlor before the first visitors arrive to view my pictures."

"Lucky stiff," murmured Crispin.

The curtain opened.

The last act was, naturally, the culmination of the first and second. It left nothing to be desired. But Mr. Archer and Mr. Eric had not stayed until the end, either. When the curtain closed and the house lights came up, all three chairs were empty.

Glory Muckleroy, in the next row behind, looked over to Hy. It had all been too perfect. The baby, in Glory's arms, was sound asleep, but the others sat between her and Hy as if they could sit for the rest of the night.

"That's just the way things happen," said Glory. "You wonder and hope, and keep your faith growin' till you're fit to bust, and next thing you know it's all come out like in the play, the good gettin' the upper hand. You can't get away from it nohow."

Hy, who never could imitate his wife's ease of expression, only nodded.

Addie Pearl had a question. "Wasn't it funny, Ma, them men not stayin' for it all? Wouldn't you a-thought they'd want to see the end?"

"What men, honey?"

"That Mr. Eric and that Mr. Archer and the artist man. They was right ahead there."

"I didn't even miss 'em," said her mother.

Behind the blue velvet curtains the stage was dimly lighted and deserted, for everyone from the leading actors to the stage manager was eager to receive the congratulations of the audience now clotted in the halls.

All but Trillium. She had no one whose special pleasure it would be to praise her performance. But that was not what kept her on the stage. Slipping in behind the steps upon which Faith and Hope had posed for the final tableau, she sat down and rested her back against the network of braces. It was very quiet. If anyone came along, she would say she had a headache and was waiting until the dressing room would be a little less congested. But no one would come. The far-off noise made by a couple of hundred voices was soothing at this distance, and Trillium closed her eyes. She couldn't afford the time she was spending here—but she couldn't meet Helen again.

"Honestly, where is she?" she heard Helen's petulant demand. Half a dozen excitement-pitched answers came, none the right one. No one had seen Trillium. Helen would go in another minute, fuming, but without the coat because she would not delay long enough to run up to Trillium's room to get it herself.

"Oh, honestly!" Helen's exasperation carried plainly in to Trillium under the steps. That would probably be her last remark.

It was. It was the last remark Helen was ever to make within Trillium's hearing.

A cautious two minutes later, Trillium hurried into the dressing room and flung herself down at her make-up place as if she were rushing to a fascinating rendezvous and didn't have a minute to spare. Slapping cold cream on her face, she noted that Helen's things were exactly as she had left them at the beginning of the third act. So she had gone, as she promised, in her costume and make-up to meet Howard at Pirate Cove.

"You must have a heavy date on," said Lucille Thomas, who had portrayed Vanity in a pair of false eyelashes which she hated to give up.

"Oh, I have," Trillium replied, "but don't tell anybody!"

Lucille blinked the lashes, watching them dreamily in the mirror.

Trillium took off her costume carefully, loving it because it represented her last hour at St. Aurelien's. "Hope is a dream, but a waking dream wherein lies the beggar's wealth and the king's salvation." And the schoolgirl's refuge. Without the hope of escape, she would have died of fear tonight.

Swiftly she hung the costume on the rack and caught up her brown wool. She was nearly ready. The dressing room was empty except for herself and Lucille and the eyelashes, and Pansy Dodd pulling on her stockings wrong side out. Trillium's spirits rose. Everything was going to be beautifully simple. Buckle her gold belt, swish the comb through her hair, and then she could go. She knew hardly anyone in the crowd outside. No one would stop her now!

Her heart hammering under the brown wool, Trillium opened the door and closed it quickly behind her. As she had imagined, the small corridor immediately in front of the door was empty, but the wide hallway was jam-packed. She started through, elbowing politely, smiling her apologies for pushing. She was making excellent progress. An open space was ahead of her. She must not cross it too quickly. Trying to appear as if she were taking her time, Trillium stepped into the vacant spot. She was conspicuous, both because she was so pretty and because she stood apart from the crowd. Only a small mob ahead, she saw. Once through it, she would be away and free! She couldn't help quickening her steps.

But before she was across the open space, a hand was laid on her arm. Trillium stopped, dead still. And in that second she wondered how she could have been so certain that she would escape tonight.

Helen was mad at Trillium. Boiling mad. Promise to do a friendly turn and then welsh on it! Honestly! And it wasn't as if she'd hurt the coat, just wearing it for half an hour!

"Some people!" Helen raged.

She was glad she was in a temper because it made her feel quite brave, and she needed to be brave, standing here at the foot of the west stairs and facing the rounded void that was the tunnel.

"Honestly!" she said aloud.

The sound did nothing for her courage because of the echoes whispering back out of the dense blackness. She was silly to think she had to come this way. But if she ran across the lawn to Pirate Cove someone would be sure to see her, with her chiffon draperies fluttering white in the moonlight, and it would be reported to all the Powers That Be and she would be ordered in like any kindergartner and Howard would think her nothing but a child. In the dark sheath of Trillium's coat she could have crossed the lawn unnoticeably; and so it was Trillium's fault that Helen stood quaking, all by herself in the dim reflection of light from the upper hall, fumbling for the light switch. That there was a light switch she knew because Trillium had turned it on this morning, and she had seen far down the tunnel almost into the funny little room under the Contemplatives' house.

The button was under her hand, she pressed it, and the tunnel arch leaped into view as if it had just been built by some magic architect.

"There! What's so bad about that?"

Her voice, however, sounded flat and she took a long breath before she entered the tunnel.

It was like a very large sewer, well built to keep out swamp seepage, the floor of it worn dark from nearly two centuries of use. The girls were expressly forbidden to come here. Laughing to herself, her "mad" forgotten, Helen flitted along. Her only regret was that she would have so little time to spend with Howard.

The little octagonal room was just as she had seen it the day she and Nerissa Brady had sneaked over for a peek. One of the right-hand angles was another arch, the opening of the tunnel leading off to the chapel; and of course under the chapel there was another room exactly like this, with another passage turning back to the convent. In the twilight that filled the place there was a brooding quality, as if this might have been the scene of an Inquisition and held instruments of torture in its shadows.

"Glory be! Of all the creepy joints!" Helen shuddered. She must find the door to the outside. Trembling, she groped along the wall and her hand fell upon cold metal. She jerked away; but when she felt again she knew it was an old-fashioned wrought-iron latch. She lifted it, and the door swung open. Moonlight flooded the steps going up, and cold night air drifted around her.

"The luck of the Perrys!" she whispered through chattering teeth. She should have worn a wrap, but the costume was so lovely with the floating wings and the pink veil she couldn't consider covering it with anything less than Trillium's coat. Howard would just have to put his arms around her to keep her warm. Helen laughed and floated up the steps. Howard was no doubt already watching from the Cove, although she hadn't told him she would be here quite so early. But a devoted admirer would not wait until the last minute to arrive. She would be surprised to see him, naturally, and he would hear her lovely little cry and see her run across the grass with her chiffon wings drifting. She laughed again, glancing toward the black trees that hid the Cove.

And then, like Trillium back in the crowded hallway, she stood dead still.

Only a few feet away was an enormous Sister, motionless as Helen herself, her back to the moonlight so that she was all one towering shadow. From her position it almost seemed that she had come from the direction of the Cove, but that couldn't be. And why was she out so late, here in the solitude of the night?

Helen did not realize that her own elfin emergence, apparently from nowhere, was quite as startling to the other person. There was something horrible about the Sister as Helen stood watching her, so horrible that the girl could not think clearly. Was it because the figure was so tall and powerful looking, because it seemed to have no face, or was it because it stood so rigid that it had no pliant, human quality of life at all? Something about this strange creature hypnotized her so that she couldn't run or scream.

The wind flipped a corner of the Sister's garment, and Helen's eyes fell. Then she saw why the Sister was so terrifyingly unreal. Under the habit, which was far too short, there showed a pair of trouser legs and a large pair of man's shoes.

"You're not—not a Sister!" Helen gasped.

But her throat was constricted, the words a mere whisper.

The figure must have heard, for suddenly it began to move forward, a slow advance straight toward the fairylike girl. The head was muffled in a shawl, that was why it appeared to have no face, and the hands were invisible, thrust up the sleeves of the habit. But the feet were coming on, step by step, the distance lessening with a dreadful steadiness that was more frightening than any swift action.

Helen had no doubt whatever as to what the man was about to do. He was going to kill her.

"Why?" she breathed.

Still she couldn't move, she couldn't scream, she could only wait while those big feet carried him inexorably toward her.

It was when the arm came up for the blow that Helen's terror broke. She almost started for the steps; but the door might stick and she would be trapped. The man was looming over her. With every bit of strength in her slight body, she pushed under the arm and ran. Howard was at the bayou, he would save her, but the thought was not coherent. She ran toward the Cove because that was where she had been going. Her wings flying, she seemed hardly to touch the ground.

Ahead of her the cypresses were stark and unleafed, each with a black shadow laid like a plank upon a crazy pattern. "Howard! Howard!" she sobbed.

But she could not see him. She looked back over her shoulder. The big Sister was almost upon her. And now she knew that she couldn't save herself. She had to keep running, she had to run out on to the hyacinths. In the moonlight they looked like a solid floor.

Howard had known nothing of Helen's resolve to meet him so early. Howard was a nice young man who did all things methodically, and because his friendship with Helen was unpredictable, he found it fascinating. No whisper of Mrs. Perry's disapproval had come to his ears, for he had never met Mrs. Perry and Helen was resolved that he shouldn't. He hadn't minded, thus far. But as he worked his way in a leisurely manner out of the crowd, thinking of Helen's performance in more ways than one, he came to a decision. Helen was the girl for him. He would put it up squarely to her tonight, demand to meet her folks, and get their approval or else—well, or else he'd go on meeting her down by Pirate Cove, and he might as well admit it.

It would take her at least a quarter of an hour to dress, he decided, more nearly a half hour. He stood a while on the steps at the central entrance, smoking and wondering idly which of these smartly dressed, fortyish women might be Helen's mother. His own folks would be inside, pampering Alison. The kid deserved it. She'd said her lines so you could hear 'em, anyhow.

When Howard had finished his cigarette, he strolled around to the west door. Still plenty of time. The wide west lawn was deserted, the swamp a dark somberness beyond. He glanced over toward the Contemplatives' house. No movement around it, no light in a window, only the moonlight brushing the walls with pallor and shade. Gloomy spot, might as well wait here a while.

He had sat for twenty minutes watching the automobiles snake down toward the gate when he began to wonder if Helen might have reached the Cove without his knowledge. Helen loved romantic secrets. It would be like her to go by some sequestered circuit and surprise him. If she had done that, the surprise had certainly gone flat when he was not there.

He stepped on his cigarette and sprinted across to the Cove. From a distance, however, he could see that the place was deserted.

Helen had not come. He breathed a thankful sigh. Probably tied up with her folks, you never knew. He'd wait a while, and then if she didn't come he would go back to the auditorium and see if he could find her.

The cypresses stood black, and in the moonlight the hyacinths looked like a solid floor.

8

Trillium knew her face had gone white when the hand touched her, holding her still. She could see her own dread blossoming as astonishment in the eyes turned upon her from the crowd. Why, those people wondered, why did she cringe because Mother Theodore had laid a hand on her arm? But they don't know, Trillium thought in panic, they don't know that she is keeping me from running away to save my mother's life! For the girl had no doubt whatever that Mother had finally seen the note.

The reaction, then, was overpowering when Mother said quietly, "Did I startle you, dear? I'm sorry. I know you have no relatives here tonight, and these friends of mine have never seen the convent. Would you mind showing them around?"

Trillium could only nod.

Mother Theodore's hand pressed her arm. "No, I'll not ask you, dear. I can see that you don't feel well—"

"Oh, but I do!" Trillium cut in quickly. She must dissipate all that alarmed attention. "I'll be very happy to show your friends around, Mother."

"Well, just the library and the tunnel, don't bother with the chapel, then. It's too late for that."

Mother Theodore turned, smiling, to introduce a serenely middle-aged couple who loved Trillium on sight. But Mother watched them move away with the girl and wondered how long they would detain her. This very night, she decided definitely, she would have her talk with Trillium.

Mr. Penworthy was in the potato business in Nebraska, he told Trillium, buying, not raising; and his wife had been a schoolmate of Mother Theodore. The potatoes had necessitated the trip east, and Mrs. Penworthy's school memories had brought them to St. Aurelien's.

Trillium, answering politely, managed to look at her watch. Nearly eleven o'clock. The play had ended half an hour ago. People were lingering, there was still time. Show the tunnel, Mother had said. The west, leading to the Contemplatives' house, would do since they were only going to look into it. She led the way down the stairs past the west entrance. Someone had turned on the lights in the tunnel and left them. Answering the Penworthy's questions Trillium toyed with the idea of asking for a ride down to Marysville.

"Are you staying in a hotel here, Mrs. Penworthy?" she asked.

"A motor court, a quaint little place, but they do seem to have hot water. My dear, you couldn't imagine how nice it is to have . . ."

So that was out. Mother would telephone the Penworthys the first thing after the prefect discovered Trillium's empty room. She could hear Mr. Penworthy saying cheerily, "Oh, yes, gave her a ride down to town, fine little girl, showed us every cranny in that old rock pile of yours." That was how Mr. Penworthy would be.

Speedily, then, she delivered the pair back to Mother Theodore who still hovered in the hall, endlessly discussing other people's children.

"Thank you, dear," Mother said. "Run along to bed now. I may drop in for a minute a little later."

Again that strange fear blanched the girl's face, and she stammered, "Tonight? Oh, Mother . . ."

"Let's make it tomorrow morning," Mother suggested, genuinely concerned. "Come to my office whenever you're free. Good night, dear."

Trillium turned and almost ran through the hall. It was startling to realize how much she loved Mother Theodore, with her kind eyes and slow smile. Mother had strength; she never would go chasing off into the night to escape from anything. The 1 a.m. milk train would never be the solution for her.

But I'm not brave, Trillium admitted, or strong or sensible. I'm just plain scared. She paused at a window. A reassuring number of red taillights still slipped down toward the gates. She could make it if she hurried. Mother wouldn't be proud of her any more, nor of Helen, for Helen was drawing out her minutes with Howard into scandalous length. Trillium had seen Mrs. Perry talking brightly with a Sister while she watched the dressing room door for Helen and tried to keep Mr. Perry from saying something.

Trillium snatched her dark red coat from the closet, pushed her hat and gloves into the big pockets, opened the drawer of her dressing table for the last time and took out her purse. For the last time. She wanted to cry, overcome by memories of the three safe years she had spent in this room.

"Safe?" she whispered. That was funny enough to cry about. Brushing away her tears, she put out her hand to turn off the light. No, leave it on. Then Sister Laurent would think she was coming back. Shutting the door softly behind her, she hurried to the east stairs and down. No one saw her. In the parking space a car was just starting up. With her red coat flying, Trillium sped after it into the night.

A quarter of an hour later the east door opened again, and in that short time the scene had changed. Where the last bits of praise had fluttered around Sisters and girls, there followed a strangely apprehensive silence. In her office door Sister Osmond lingered, her gracious air very much askew. The prefects had herded the girls to their rooms, except for the few who still clung to their parents' company in the parlor, and the light, hushed voices made the only disturbance of the quiet. On the floor of the deserted hall a single cigarette stub was an impudent reminder that there had been company. Sheriff Thatcher still believed that there was nothing amiss; but his young daughter, Kathy, could have told him that the atmosphere was supercharged. Behind closed doors the question ran: what had Helen Perry done this time? Had she finally eloped? Giggling, excited quite as highly over the retribution awaiting her as they were over her flagrant absence, the girls whispered about Helen and the play and wondered when they had had so much fun.

At the moment the east door opened to admit a frightened girl in a red coat, Sheriff Thatcher was seated in Mother Theodore's office, his mind divided equally between two preoccupations: the fact that he dared not smoke in this holy place, and impatience with Mother's anxiety. Girls didn't leave their foolishness at the gates when they entered St. Aurelien's; in fact, the restrictions of convent life might well intensify a kid's natural yearning for the forbidden. Like his own longing for a cigar, the Sheriff pondered. Never in his life had he wanted a stogy so badly as now, when he couldn't have it. This young Helen was a highflier, boy crazy and rattlebrained into the bargain if half of what Kathy said was true. She was kicking up her heels and would be back in her own sweet time, a theory also held by Mrs. Perry who was expounding it with an eye to doing as little damage as possible to Helen's chances for remaining at St. Aurelien's.

The Sheriff pursed his lips under his neat gray mustache and nodded sagely, without giving much thought to it. Like Mrs. Penworthy, Jarvis Thatcher had been a schoolmate of Mother Theodore, and, since his motherless daughter was a sophomore at St. Aurelien's, he had attended the performance of "Mustardseed" and added his proud beaming to the universal glow. That was how he had come to be on hand when Helen's little escapade was discovered, and Mother had commandeered him in spite of his protests that the situation hardly merited a sheriff's services.

It was one of those times when a disinterested person would give anything to be somewhere else. Across from the Sheriff, Helen's expensively handsome parents sat, her mother being gay to cover the strain, her father striving for nonchalance and failing. Behind her desk Mother Theodore was too erect in her chair, stern, burning with righteous anger. St. Aurelien's was not a reformatory or a house of detention. When Helen returned, of her own free will since it appeared they would never find her, she would be expelled for conduct unbecoming a member of the college body.

Mother was about to deliver this pronouncement when a soft tap came at the door. All eyes but Mother's flared with instant hope; hers remained like granite.

"Come in!"

Sister Laurent poked her head around the door. "Mother, excuse me, Trillium Pierce insists on seeing you. She says she has something to tell about Helen."

Mrs. Perry gasped, her husband said a low word to her, and the tension broke in the room.

At Mother's nod the Sister disappeared and Trillium entered, pausing unhappily when she saw the strangers: the pretty, eager woman, the tall man in tweeds, the second man who stood rolling an unlighted cigar in his fingers, his gray eyes studying her. He was large boned and heavy, his face ruddy and pleasant with the expected guilelessness of a fat man; and yet his bulk was not excess weight because he was never designed for thinness. Without seeing him move, Trillium knew he would walk lightly, swiftly to wherever he was going; he would turn up where one least expected to see him—

Like here! What was he doing in Mother's office? She had met the Sheriff at another school affair. Was it something concerning her—or her mother—did he know why she had tried to get away? . . .

"Trillium, you have something to tell us about Helen?" Mother Theodore asked quietly.

Of course the Sheriff's presence had nothing to do with herself! Fear, in these days, needed neither stimulus nor reason.

"Yes, Mother," Trillium answered.

"Do you know where Helen has gone?"

"I think so, Mother."

The simple words had an amazing effect. The Perrys came to their feet, Mr. Perry quickly sorting through the emotions which crowded him and resuming the role of angry father. The Sheriff bit the end off his cigar.

And then, abruptly, Trillium was angry. Helen, with her silly behavior, had ruined more than the rules of St. Aurelien's. She deserves whatever punishment she gets, the girl decided wrathfully, she wrecked the only chance I may ever have to get away from here, she made me get rid of my coat; now I'll tell what I know and she can take the consequences for once!

"She went to Pirate Cove to meet Howard Cooper, Alison's brother," Trillium said, determined to crush any excuses Helen might try to make. "He came to the play tonight on her invitation. She told me she meant to meet him after the performance, and she did."

"Not Howard Cooper!" Mrs. Perry wailed. "Oh, she wouldn't! We had forbidden her to see him, or anyone! Helen's not a child to disobey—"

Her husband made an impatient gesture, and she subsided.

"Where is this Pirate Cove?" he demanded, implying that he himself would track it down personally if no one replied.

"It borders our grounds on the west, sir," said Mother Theodore. "The girls always regard it as a romantic spot."

"Then it's the place to look for Helen. Come on, Sheriff!"

"Oh, Henry, not you!" Mrs. Perry begged, and with reason, for her husband was plainly in a mood to turn Helen over his knee. "Let the Sheriff go with Trillium! Please! They'll bring her here."

"Have you anything more to tell us, Trillium?" Mother asked, cool as if she were gathering facts in an examination.

"No, not really, Mother. Helen said she was going, and I know she went because I heard her asking for me in the dressing room, but before I came she was gone."

That was the truth. Mr. Perry began what Helen would call the outraged parent routine, and Mother cut him short.

The Sheriff ushered Trillium out. At another time the girl might have found it amusing to see Mother handling a business tycoon as if he were a freshman; but now, hastening down the long hall and out along the west cloister walk, her fear for herself slid over her in fragments like the shadows cast by the moon through the old stone arches.

"I wouldn't be too much concerned over Helen, if I were you," the Sheriff said in the light tenor that somehow suited his size. "Some kids manage to wriggle out of things, you know. She'll be scolded, probably confined to the campus for the rest of the year; but she won't be permanently dented. This isn't her last secret date, by a long shot. Say, looky here!"

The Sheriff paused at the end of the cloister walk. Beside them was the door of the Contemplatives' house, and in the wall, sunken below stone steps, was the curious little door to the tunnel, all good solid masonry that in the moonlight took on ethereal beauty.

"Yeah, like old ramparts," the Sheriff said softly. "Kind of bulwarks thrown up against the evils of the world. Only in the moonlight, the world doesn't look so evil, does it?"

Trillium was uncertain, and as the Sheriff started out across the lawn she tucked her hand into his arm and kept close. The Cove was not far, not more than a good sprint away; but in the quiet night there was an unearthly quality about it. The bayou was not a river because it had no current; it was too thickly overgrown to be called a lake and yet it lacked the permanence of land. In the night, however, the hyacinths looked like a solid floor.

It took only a minute for them to see that the shore of Pirate Cove was bleak and deserted. A hoot owl gave a ghastly shriek, and Trillium shuddered.

"Helen!" the Sheriff called. "Helen, are you here?"

A flutter of wings was the only answer.

"She's gone!" Trillium whispered.

"Yeah, that's for sure. Say, what are you shaking about, little lady? You aren't scared, with me here, are you?"

"I—no, of course not, Mr. Thatcher. But I'd like to know what's become of Helen!"

"Well, I'd say that's easy, if Howard has a car. Wouldn't they have gone joy riding?"

Trillium laughed, and they walked quickly back through the shadowed cloister.

Seated in the outer office, listening to the ominous rumblings of Mr. Perry which greeted the Sheriff's news, Trillium had her first leisure to think. She was alone, the door of the inner office closed. Helen's senseless dilemma preoccupied her no longer. One single inescapable fact absorbed all her thinking powers: her own opportunity had gone by, there would be no further chance to get away tonight. What, then?

"Trillium," Mother said in the open doorway.

The girl jumped.

"Trillium, will you send Alison Cooper down, please? Even if she has gone to bed, have her dress and come down. And then go to bed yourself, dear, you look worn out."

Trillium hurried away. It was permissible to hurry, doing an errand for Mother.

Outside Alison's door she stopped. Alison had three roommates,
all chatterboxes, and with such news as Helen's brazen conduct
to make them feel virtuous, Trillium's knock was buried fourfold.
Opening the door, she peeked around it.

"Hey, kids! Message from Mother!" In the sudden silence, Trillium picked out Alison, the only one still dressed. "She wants to see
you, Miss Cooper."

"What about?"

"She didn't confide in me. But I imagine it's about Howard and
Helen."

"My goodness, I don't know a thing! A big brother never lets you
in on anything like that!"

"Tell it to Mother, Alison," Trillium suggested. "And I'd get down
there fast."

She shut herself out into the hall, thinking that Alison would
make more haste when there were no answers to be had. Immediately, however, the door flew open.

"Trillium! He's not with Helen!"

"How do you know?"

"Well, Howie was disgusted because he waited and waited, and
she didn't come, and he said she'd stood him up! He was sitting in
the car when I went out with Mother and Dad, and he was so mad
he wouldn't even speak to me!"

"Oh," said Trillium. It came out in a hoarse whisper. Helen beside the Cove, waiting, too early for Howard—and the black shadows around her—what had happened to her?

"Maybe she didn't think she'd better," Alison suggested.

Trillium gave her a push. "Go on, Al, Mother's in a tizzy already!"

Alison flew down the hall, wondering why she should be frightened.

Trillium went on into her own room, dropped her coat on the
bed, and snapped off the light to look out of the window. The scene
was peaceful as ever, the guesthouse showing yellow squares against
the blackness of the pecan grove. She wondered if Jem was really

there, probably discussing the play with his two companions, un-aware that his quarry had almost escaped. And so long as he doesn't know, I can try again, Trillium thought, and there will be no note to lose this time, nothing to give me away too soon. The flurry over Helen would claim all attention, and no one would notice if anoth-er girl acted a little off key. Why, it's my golden opportunity, and I didn't even know it, she reflected.

"Trill, you here?" Mary Elizabeth whispered from the door.

Trillium turned, feeling that she had just partaken of a reviving drink. "Sure, come on in. You were super in the play, Liz! I haven't had a chance to tell you—"

Mary Elizabeth squealed. "Oh, Trill, cover up that window! Hurry!"

"Well, honestly," Trillium said. Accustomed as she had become to Liz's imaginative scares, this one nevertheless impressed her with a different quality. Mary Elizabeth's blue eyes were almost black in spite of the glare from the two study lamps, the overhead light, and the dressing-table lady with the umbrella shade; and when she plumped down on the foot of the bed, her face was deathly pale and she clutched her old orchid housecoat around her as if for protection.

Trillium, being the handmaiden of fear herself these days, rec-ognized Mary Elizabeth's state too well. Quickly she shut the door and sat down on the bed, knee to knee with her frightened visitor.

"Liz, what's wrong?"

"I think I saw her, Trill!"

"You—what?"

"Saw Helen! Over by the Cove."

"Well, naturally, that's where she went to meet Howard."

"I know, Trill, but—" Mary Elizabeth's breath caught fearfully, "when I saw her, there was a Sister with her!"

"A Sister? Oh, now, Liz—"

"I did, I saw her plain as day! She was looming over Helen, only I thought the girl was you, Trill, you and Helen looked exactly alike in your costumes, you're so much alike anyway. . . ."

A black-spangled darkness broke over Trillium, cold moisture came out on her forehead and she lost the sense of Mary Elizabeth's explanation. In our costumes we looked exactly alike, that was why we were chosen for the parts, we were to portray the twin virtues of Faith and Hope; and with the moonlight to deceive further, Helen could easily be mistaken for me. Has something happened to her because she looks like me?

Mary Elizabeth had not seen a Sister, that was pure imagination; but she had seen someone . . . Jem? What would he be doing over beside the Cove?

"I wasn't going out with Neddie tonight, we were just making a date for Saturday," Mary Elizabeth rattled on, "and I still had my costume on and Neddie was—well, anyway, I saw this girl in white, and then this tall, muffled Sister standing at the far corner of the cloister, and I wondered who you were meeting, Trill. And then I turned to talk to Neddie for a while, and when I looked again the figure had grown to a giant, and its hands were extended like great claws and the face stood out like a death skull—"

"Liz, stop it!" Trillium choked, but she could not halt the unrolling of the monstrous tale.

In a soft, tense voice Mary Elizabeth continued to weave her spell. "When that horrible thing looked across at me, even at that distance I felt my soul shrink! Inside I was jelly! I know I'd have died if Neddie hadn't been there!"

"Did Neddie see her?" Trillium whispered.

"Are you kidding? With me there? No, he didn't, and I—oh, I didn't mention it. I know you stand in well with the Sisters, so I wasn't worried, even if you were getting caught." Suddenly Mary Elizabeth seemed to realize what she had been describing, and her eyes widened in horror and she clapped her hand over her mouth. "Trill! Where did she go? It wasn't you! It was Helen, and she's still gone! What did that terrible Sister do to her?"

"Why, maybe she's punishing Helen for—"

The door opened at the same moment that a tapping sounded upon the panel, and Sister Osmond stood in the aperture. "Mary Elizabeth? It's much too late for visiting."

The two girls stood up, from force of habit, and Mary Elizabeth said, "I was just leaving, Sister. We were talking about the lovely evening—you know—"

Sister Osmond smiled. She knew, indeed, that the subject was the missing girl and not "Mustardseed." "Of course, dear. Now run along to your own room."

"Sister, please, couldn't she sleep with me tonight?" Trillium begged.

Sister Osmond merely smiled again and turned off all the lights but one. "I think not. Helen will be back at any moment. It is much better that we keep to our regular routine. Good night, Trillium."

The Sister terminated her tour gracefully in the doorway, and all Trillium could manage was to whisper to Mary Elizabeth, "Don't say anything!" before the door closed behind the two. The girl stepped over swiftly and laid her ear against the crack. They were gone, the hall was settling to quiet. She turned the lock and pushed the chair with its back under the knob. Then she sat down at her dressing table, staring at her image in the mirror.

So the dread danger had not been imagined, Trillium admitted to herself, and knew then that there had always been a faint hope that she was wrong. The hope had been silly, baseless. The Billiken belonged to Jem, in no other way could it have reached the campus. After all, who would make another person a gift of a broken statue which had been of small value when it was whole? But what was Jem doing by the bayou? He had worn a cloak of some sort that made Mary Elizabeth see him as a nun, but that was not worth a second thought. Liz and the moonlight and the distance from the west entrance to the Cove all were responsible for the deception. Jem's reason for being there, that was what she must consider.

Even a long time later, Trillium had but one answer. Jem had come into possession of the note she had written to Mother Theodore. He knew she was trying to run away. Why he should think she would go up by the bayou was a problem, but no more of a problem than his own presence there. He must have said something to Helen to frighten her off, so that she instead of Trillium had run down the long road and hitched a ride in a car.

When she comes back, I'll have to talk to her, persuade her not to tell, Trillium decided. Exactly how she would manage to see Helen first, before the girl would be questioned by the Sheriff, she did not try to work out. She would stay awake, listening, waiting. Outside on the grounds, flashlights bounded in long arcs and men called, searching, their unbelief veering to dismay as the groups parted and met, parted and met, always with the same news. No trace. Through her open window Trillium heard them.

Helen was gone, and whatever had happened to Helen was meant for Trillium herself.

In some of the other wings, girls slept, but uneasily. At every window facing the front lawn, a watcher sat, her attention glued to the square of light laid on the grass from Mother's office. There were other squares as well from the long main corridor, but none with the fascination of that single one. It would go out, the girls knew, when Helen was found.

But the sun came up and pushed the shadows back into the bayou, and the watchers yawned and went for a shower to wake them up. Down in Mother's office, someone finally remembered to turn out the light. In the morning softness Mrs. Perry's face looked a little less ghastly; but when Sheriff Thatcher came in and made a bungling, compassionate attempt to tell her what they had found, she fainted.

He was able to tell her because Cris Archer and Franz Eric, having kept with the search party all night, had come back again to Pirate Cove. The place was still in twilight, but the twilight of early morning is revealing. And then they saw that it was only the moon that had given solidity to the hyacinths. The delicate bolls were crushed in a wide swath, and just under a gap in the trailing roots there floated a brown-soaked fragment of chiffon.

9

"I'll have to question her, Mother, you know that," the Sheriff insisted. "I have a feeling Trillium knows a little more than she volunteered last night when she popped in here from her walk. And young Cooper, too. He was too broken up when I got hold of him this morning, couldn't arrive at a coherent story at all. He kept insisting he hadn't seen anything of Helen or anyone else, but he must have seen something! That trampled place at the edge of the bayou tells its own tale. Either she struggled, or he stamped around afterward—oh, sorry, you don't need the details."

Mother Theodore closed her eyes as if to shut out some terrible sight, then crossed the room and looked down at the breakfast tray. "You didn't eat much, Jarvis."

"Will you get Trillium down here for me, Emmy?"

Mother seated herself in a small rocker and began to rock gently, her hands under her scapular. Sunshine flooded the visitors' parlor, brightening the rug, laying a high polish on the andirons and on the silver vase filled with chrysanthemums; but its touch upon the Sheriff's face was most unkind. A fat man does not easily look haggard; but Jarvis Thatcher, unshaven, red-eyed from lack of sleep, depressed by the torturing search and the scene with the Perrys, was haggard in the morning light. His neat blue suit and the shoes he had carefully cleaned before coming into the building still bore splashes of swamp mud; and when he leaned forward, rubbing his forehead wearily, Mother saw that his hands were scratched from swamp thorns. And yet, in spite of the fatigue that aged him, regardless of the mussed gray hair and his general air of being completely beaten down, Jarvis was more like the boy she had known than she had seen him in years.

Mother's rocking slowed and stopped. There was a long hiatus, of course, in the time she had known Jarvis, the years of her novitiate and his own early climb in politics and business, coming finally to the death of his wife and Kathy's entrance into St. Aurelien's. But the very young school days were nearer now than that, the days when she had sat in front of him and listened to his sniffling all winter because he never had a handkerchief, when he had passed over greasy pork sandwiches as presents to her and she had stuffed them down a gopher hole going home. At the basketball games he had smelled like a sheep in the high excitement of the rooting section; and the night of the Senior prom, when she told him she was going into the convent, he had cried and begged her to wait just a little while, she was so young, she knew nothing about life.

Curiously comforted, Mother began to rock again. Why she thought of such things just now she did not know, unless it was because Jarvis had called her Emmy, as he used to do. The parlor was quiet, it was wonderfully peaceful here, rocking, forgetting for the moment the awful hours just past, and not yet thinking of the other hours, perhaps quite as awful, to come.

Jarvis did not immediately repeat his request to see Trillium. Leaning forward, cracking his knuckles, he kept his eyes on the rug. After an interval, he spoke.

"I wouldn't have said a time like this would ever come for you, Emmy. Not with you choosing the sheltered life. It's something you don't expect, violent death in a convent."

Mother Theodore smiled, not at the mention of violent death, but because Jarvis, like countless others, regarded the cloister as a sheltered place. Sheltered, yes, from family cares and from the day to day struggle for a livelihood, now that the convent was well established; but sheltered from pride, jealousy, anger, small bickerings? Oh, no! Sheltered only to be closed in with them, to recognize and overcome them; but for all the graces showered upon their state in life, Sisters are nonetheless human.

"I'm glad I'm here, Emmy. I'll try to handle this thing as gently as possible. But I can't get around without slopping the puddle a little. I'll have to talk to the Sisters, see if they heard Helen say any-thing about—almost anything. And I'll have to question the girls. Helen didn't kill herself. There's a footprint, pretty shapeless in that soft muck, but it's a man's, and in a place where the searchers swear they didn't step—" He paused, and his eyes came to Mother's in sick appeal. "Emmy, they all know, don't they? The Sisters and the girls? I don't have to tell them?"

"Some of them saw the disturbance around the bayou," Mother said quietly. "We didn't try to keep it from them. But they think it was—accidental."

Mother Theodore sat a moment longer; but she took no comfort in it now. Postponing the answers to all that the Sheriff must find out would make it no better.

"I'm glad you're here, too, Jarvis," she said, and left the parlor.

A few moments later, Mother returned with Trillium.

The breakfast tray was gone, the Sheriff had combed his hair and, in spite of the whiskers, assumed a competence that was reas-suring. With a glance he requested Mother to remain; yet when she was seated again in her rocker and Trillium on the edge of a love seat, he kept riffling through his little notebook, wetting his thumb to turn a page, apparently at a loss as to how to begin. Or, thought Mother, he might be using this ruse to excite Trillium, to let her think over whatever it was she concealed. The girl was at her wits' end. Mother Theodore's compassion burned high, as her sudden resentment against Jarvis. He had no right to inflict such misery upon an already panic-stricken girl. She opened her lips to protest, but the Sheriff spoke before her.

"I'm sorry I've had to call you in, Trillium. The little Perry girl was one of your chums, I understand. But you see, that's the reason why I think you can do something for her now. I think it's possible that you'll be able to help me find out—eh—who killed her."

"Who—*killed* her? But I thought—" The girl's terror was in her eyes, in her hands clenched in her lap, in the stifled whisper that was all she could make of her voice. I thought it was an accident, that was what she had been about to say; but she didn't think it at all. From the first dreadful minute when Hilaria Thorns had burst into her room, screaming that they were pulling Helen out of the bayou, she had known it was not an accident. Jem had killed her, because he thought she was Trillium Pierce!

"Don't be nervous, dear," Mother said, and her pretense of naturalness was so good that neither the Sheriff nor Trillium even glanced at her.

The Sheriff, seeming to hesitate often, went over the story of Helen's last visit to the dressing room, leading Trillium on without haste; but that quiet manner was deceptive. Behind his apparent leisure he was thinking, putting together pieces of the puzzle, pieces fitting into the outer rim perhaps but nevertheless important; and in time, days from now, possibly weeks, he would have worked in to the center and the picture would be complete.

Mother Theodore, listening to the slow, somewhat aimless questioning, knew it was not aimless but driving straight to a point that had thus far remained invisible.

"So you suddenly decided you must talk to Mother last night," the Sheriff continued. "And when you came in, you went to the office to find her. That right?" The girl nodded. "Where had you been, Trillium?"

She answered, too pat for it to be anywhere near the truth. "I had gone for a little walk. I was too tired to sleep, and I had a headache. So when I went to my room and heard how noisy the girls were, I took my coat and went out."

"By which door?"

"The east. I didn't leave the grounds."

Trillium let her gaze meet the Sheriff's. She could do it because that small bit happened to be the truth.

"And you didn't see Helen while you were outside?"

"No, sir. She was out on the west lawn, I was on the east. There were cars still leaving. I just walked around a little and watched them."

"Well. Then I believe that's all, Trillium."

The girl sat still as a watched woods thing that knows its danger. If only she dared tell this kind, fatherly man—but her mother's letter had said plainly, don't tell, *no matter what happens!* Breaking that trust could not help Helen, she could not be brought back. Behind the warning was everything her mother feared—and if he killed Helen because he thought she was me, then he thinks I know him, that I can identify him—and I can't!

"Is there something more, Trillium?" the Sheriff asked.

She sprang up. "Oh, no, sir!" A second later, the door closed behind her.

Mother Theodore walked to the window. To distract him, the Sheriff wondered? But hardly that. Emmy was incapable of slyness.

"The assembly is waiting for us, Jarvis," she said.

"All right, Mother."

He stood up obediently, but Mother still remained with her back to him.

"They are very young, Jarvis, we shield them as much—"

"Too young to be in terror, Emmy, and one of them is. She just went out of here."

Mother whirled on him, and Jarvis knew that her mask of impatience was fright, rather, because she also had seen that Trillium was in terror. Educate them to stand on their own feet, to be self-reliant; but one learns by doing, and in the convent there was little to call up a show of independence. Let a situation require an important decision, and they would flounder, like Trillium, blinded by emotion, incapable of sensible thought. I'll help her, myself, today, Mother determined; but aloud she said,

"She is concealing something, I know, Jarvis, but it's nothing of value to you. She broke a rule or two last night, probably, and she doesn't want me to find out. Trillium is not given to untruths."

"Good, good," the Sheriff answered. "All right, we'll go along to the assembly. Oh, and Mother, wouldn't it be well to resume classes as usual today? There's something settling about routine, seems to me."

"And seems to me," Mother agreed. Routine was the backbone of life in the convent: a bell calling for prayers, a bell summoning Mother, a bell for dinner and supper and lights out. Always bells, and although sometimes to a tired Sister the compelling tones were the lash of the devil himself, she also could reflect that people climbed to heaven to the tune of bells.

The Sheriff, acutely conscious of his whiskered appearance, stood before the assembled staff and student body and depended upon his gentle-father attitude to reassure where words might fail. The case, he said, was not closed and would not be until it was solved. There was no explanation for what had happened. The building was open last night, strangers were everywhere, someone must have lurked in the grounds. But there was nothing more to happen now, deputies were investigating, it was over . . . mention it only as an accident in your letters home until more is known . . . the papers were being very discreet, very little publicity. . . .

Trillium, sitting carefully unclenching her hands whenever she could remember, kept her eyes on the back of Mary Elizabeth's neck and wondered what she should do. Not merely wondered, but ached with the emptiness of indecision. She would not be permitted to leave, she knew that now. Even though she might be able to elude the Sheriff's men, there was the one who would be watching, following. He had found and read her letter to Mother Theodore, and it had led him to act. He had killed in error, he would have to make another attempt. And flight would only make the attempt more necessary. Then he would be certain of what he suspects now . . . that I know him. . . . If only I did!

Many of the girls were crying, touched by Mother's tribute to Helen. Deliberately Trillium did not listen. Except for a strange quirk, Mother might have been saying these things about Trillium Pierce instead of Helen Perry. But I'll go crazy if I think about that, the girl cautioned herself desperately. I'll think about what to do— if I could only know—if I could talk with Uncle Henry—

"I can!" she breathed, and Hilaria Thorns, beside her, turned. Trillium, however, sat dry-eyed and oblivious to her surroundings. She could telephone to Uncle Henry. Not from the convent building, where Sister Osmond would have to note the call in order to make the charge to the proper person. Not from Marysville, for the Sheriff's men would allow no one to leave the grounds. There was one telephone on the campus unconnected with the switchboard . . . one she dared not use. . . .

The girls were rising, the group breaking up on the stage. As Trillium moved out into the aisle, Mary Elizabeth caught her by the arm.

"Trill, look!"

"Where?"

"Sister Etienne! She's like—like the one I saw—you know!"

Trillium stared at the old Sister who was humping slowly along, feeling for the backs of the seats to guide her, her shoulders swathed in a black shawl which was bunched to the top of her head in the back.

"Liz, don't be silly! Old Etienne isn't as tall as I am, and your spook was a giantess, remember?"

"She wasn't a spook, and I might have been mistaken about the size!"

"You could have been mistaken about the whole thing," Trillium said sensibly.

She reached the hall and in the crowd slipped away from Mary Elizabeth. She would have to watch a chance to use that one available telephone, and now, for no apparent reason, it seemed not so impossible.

Sister Etienne made her feeble way out of the auditorium. Sudden death did not impress her as it did some, she was too near to the gates herself. And she had another preoccupation, far more disturbing. She still had not found her missing habit. Under the shawl the neck of the old one, worn through to the white lining, was hidden, but it was a nuisance to be hugging something around her. Secretly, because she was ashamed to think she might have stuck the habit off somewhere and forgotten about it, or even not have put it out on the line at all, she hunted through the cloister. In the following days the Sisters would come upon her at odd times, going through the linen closets, burrowing in dresser drawers, and soon the word went around that poor old Etienne was really losing her grip. Everyone was kinder than ever, the younger Sisters remembered the times they had treated her slightingly and now made a point of keeping her company whenever they could snatch a moment; and so Etienne's searchings for the lost habit were to become even more secret and more of a worry to her because the Sisters' kindness left her so little time. They would indeed be miserable days for Sister Etienne.

Leaving the auditorium after the assembly, Franz Eric and Crispin Archer came out of the convent's east door and paused for a cigarette. Neither had a class the next hour, and they had fallen into the way of being together when no duties interfered. Since they had stood beside the bayou in the early morning and seen what lay under the trailing roots of the hyacinths, they had talked of nothing else; but now, looking out from the parking lot to the grand vista of lawn and pecan grove, they were silent.

"So," said Crispin at last, "having eulogized the dear departed and enshrined her silly little life among the immortals of the Old School, we now take up the traditional Hunt for the Golden Fleece. And what in the name of heaven that is, I'd admire to know. From the buzz following Mother's announcement in assembly, I'd say it's another of the lovely old traditions, no doubt also taking place in a cemetery. They all seem to have the same locale."

Franz was not in a mood for levity. Arms folded, mouth grim, he glared at the gentle countryside. It was impossible for him to appear unattractive. Certain young ladies would have maintained even that his glowering held more enchantment than most men's gallantry.

The Sheriff came out at the top of the steps and stood lighting a cigar. Whether Franz saw him was a question, but Crispin did, and quietly turned his back.

"The galling waste of it!" Franz muttered, and even before he continued, Archer knew he had gone back to the subject of Helen Perry. "Look at all that little kid had to live for! She hadn't done anything yet, she hadn't had time. What was she, nineteen, twenty? And now she's nothing but a heartache for her mother. Why did she have to live, if she had to die like that?"

Crispin blew out a cloud of smoke.

Behind the Sheriff, the door opened and young Kathy Thatcher danced out in the company of Torvaldsen. As if he were startled, Franz swung around.

"No, don't leave," Crispin said quickly, too low for anyone else to hear. "Thatcher questioned us this morning, most thoroughly. He's probably homeward bound for a shave if the kid ever lets him go."

Kathy, in a bright red dress, was a wonderful antidote for somberness.

"I didn't think we'd have it, anyway not on the traditional date!" she chattered to her father and Torvaldsen. "But the seniors are to have their class meeting and elect a chairman this very afternoon,

Mother says, and the chairman is always the most popular girl in school—"

"Then it will be you, pet," said the Sheriff.

"But I'm only a sophomore, Daddy!"

"And what is this Golden Fleece?" Torvaldsen asked, beaming on Kathy like the fairy-tale uncle.

"Oh, it's something different every year, and we hide it. I mean the seniors will hide it this year because they found it last year, and then all the rest of us hunt for it, and whatever class finds it can keep it for another year—"

"End of chapter," the Sheriff said firmly. "Run along now, honey, and I'll see you soon."

He kissed her, and Kathy ran inside. The Sheriff and Torvaldsen joined Franz and Crispin in the parking lot.

"The world is perfect, and only man is vile," said the artist, indicating the peaceful landscape. "My, my, trouble is very foreign to St. Aurelien's this morning."

"You weren't with us at the bayou," Franz said shortly.

"True, I was not. But Mother Theodore put it rather well, I thought, the young girl completing her journey with a little more swiftness than has been granted to us. Nice. It places the happy emphasis on reaching the goal, not upon the journey itself."

Crispin dropped his cigarette and stepped on it. "She'd lived through the only happy part of life, Tor, her childhood. I'd say she's better off. She'd have to hit the ball when she left here, probably marry some louse that would beat her every time he hiccupped. And in the immortal words of Mother Theodore, we all have to go sometime, so—" He ended with an expressive shrug.

Franz, glowering at the ground, said nothing. Torvaldsen took off his beret and stood tall and powerful, as if he offered another private tribute to the dead.

The Sheriff sighed. "Well, whatever the reason or lack of it, I have to find out why it happened. If I could be the Almighty for a few minutes and look into some of the silent partners in this business—yeah, I'd like to be the Lord and solve it quick."

"And what, for instance, would you like to know, Lord?" Archer asked with a quizzical smile.

"Where everybody was, for instance. If I knew that, I'd know everything."

The Sheriff's gaze slid carelessly over the three faces and came to rest on a far-off point in the pecan grove. Franz, he noted, registered exasperation with this thickheaded minion of the law; Torvaldsen was mildly hurt; Archer shrugged, found another cigarette, and gave it his amused attention.

"Well, we've accounted for our own whereabouts, Sheriff," Cris said. "As I explained this morning, I left the auditorium during the last act of the play. Gad, I can stand only so much sweetness and light, and I wanted to be at least normally alert to meet a battery of admirers. So I came out here for a smoke."

As if he were well satisfied, Mr. Thatcher nodded.

"Franz left with me," Archer added without even a glance at his impatient colleague.

"I did, but we didn't stay together. I went to my office in the gym wing," Franz muttered.

"Eric likes his public in small portions," Crispin explained. "Quality rather than quantity. The trek into that wing discouraged the fainthearted."

Franz growled something that was seldom heard at St. Aurelien's, and Torvaldsen said in the pause, "I need not repeat my—alibi, shall we call it, Sheriff?"

"Oh, alibis are not called for, yet," Jarvis said with quick friendliness. "No, indeed! You were showing your paintings until—how late—eleven?" When Torvaldsen spread his hands as if he turned time loose on its own, the Sheriff resumed, "See, you're all in the clear. Now there's another thing I'd like to know, and that is, where did Trillium Pierce go last night when she left the convent?"

"Trillium? Oh, the little dark one, Hope in the play?" Crispin grinned. "She looks guileless enough. Don't tell me she's holding out on you, Thatcher."

"I'm afraid so. She put on her coat, she says, and went out for a breath of air because she had a headache; but when she came back after that breath of air, she ran to the office, scared silly, and volunteered to tell us all she knew about Helen."

His listeners received the news equably, each intent upon some point in the really lovely view.

"She didn't leave the grounds," the Sheriff went on. "I think she was telling the truth there. But what she did in that time—" He let his eyes travel to the guesthouse and roam over it speculatively. It was a very short distance from the convent door to the guesthouse, short enough for a girl to run. . . . He began to whistle through his teeth, softly.

"I can tell you how she went, Sheriff, but not where," Torvaldsen remarked with every appearance of frankness. "I attached no importance to it at the time, which is why it happened to slip my mind when we talked this morning."

"I see. But this how business—"

"She went in a car, rather she came back in one. I was crossing the parking lot here when this car drove up and stopped, and the girl jumped out and ran into the building. I didn't speak to her, in fact she didn't see me at all. I thought nothing of it, beyond wondering whether she would be caught in her little escapade. Apparently she wasn't."

"Did you get a look at who was in the car?"

"No, the light was dim and I wasn't paying much attention. I was tired out with questions about the pictures on display. And of course at that time I didn't know that Helen was missing. There was no commotion about her then."

"Could you describe the car, Torvaldsen, anything about it you remember, the make, the color?"

"I recollect the color, a beautiful shade, sort of translucent blue. It was a wonderful car."

"Ah! You're pretty sure of that?"

"I don't forget colors, Mr. Thatcher."

"Well, say, that's really a help! Takes an artist to observe what the rest of us might pass up."

"Do you know who owns that car, Sheriff?" Archer asked idly.

"Oh, yes, only one like that in Marysville! Well, good day, gentlemen, see you later."

With his light step more nimble than ever, the Sheriff crossed to his car and climbed in. So Torvaldsen had been showing his pictures until eleven o'clock? But at a quarter before eleven, Trillium had come panic-stricken into Mother's office.

"His mama certainly had a bouncing boy, didn't she?" Crispin observed, watching the Sheriff's departure. "Funny to see a fat man so light on his feet. Like he's inflated."

Torvaldsen, appreciating the description, chuckled; but Franz made an irritable noise and strode off toward the golf tee.

Crispin's eyes followed him; but when he spoke, his remark did not concern Franz. "I'd be interested to know why you mentioned the girl's little adventure, Tor."

"We must be truthful, Cris. If we fail to be frank, and these incidents and our knowledge of them is found out afterward—well, we must remember our curious position here, strangers, we have nothing but our reputations to back up our innocence—"

"Good heavens, Tor, Thatcher doesn't suspect us!"

"Not of murder, I hope. But he was playing with the idea that Trillium had paid a short visit to the guesthouse. Not that I would blame her, in view of the provocation. I do look out for you boys, you see."

Cris grinned. "Very thoughtful. Thanks. Maybe I can do the same for you sometime."

Tor sighed. "I'm too old. But I appreciate the insinuation."

A bell rang inside, and the two men went their separate ways.

The same bell was a summons to Trillium to consider the history of civilization. Instead of pattering dutifully off to Sister Onfroy's classroom, she remained where she was, inside the east door, peeking out at the two men who stood talking at the edge of the parking lot. There had been three. When the bell parted the two, Trillium's vigil became a breathless, intense wariness. As the door opened under Archer's hand, she crept down the steps that led to the tunnels. It was very shadowy here. She heard Archer's steps go up, along the corridor, and fade. Whether he had a class she did not know, but at least he was in the building.

"Dear Lord, I almost wish You'd make Torvaldsen go along to the guesthouse!" Trillium whispered as she looked out again.

But Torvaldsen, striding mightily, was bound for his class of sketchers who today were doing pecan trees.

So now there was no reason why she should not go. Trillium let herself out into the warm sunshine, wondering how anyone could catch a glimpse of her and not know that fear was riding her like an old man of the sea. No one, apparently, saw her. As she had done a week ago, she walked across the lawn, the dream of that other morning never even entering her head. I look important, she thought, as if I had a message for one of the gentlemen. I'm the only one who thinks I'm out of place.

She stepped up on the stoop, as she had before, knocked, waited; and again as before, there was no answer. Turning the knob, Trillium went inside.

The small house was so silent that the clock tick sounded like a sledge hammer. She would not look for the Billiken—but she had to enter the living room to hunt for the telephone. And her eyes went straight to the mantel.

The strange little god of things as they ought to be was gone.

So he has packed it away, Trillium thought numbly, and Billiken's absence confirms what I knew. It belongs to Jem.

When the clock struck, she crossed the room and took up the telephone. She was not afraid now. She was acting wisely. The call would be charged to this number, but probably each of the tenants would have made calls to New Orleans and one more would never be remarked. The operator in Marysville answered, Trillium gave the number, heard a series of clicks, and then the familiar voice of her uncle's housekeeper.

"Mist' Alvard's residence. Long distance? Yas'm, go 'haid."

"May I speak to—to Mr. Alvard, please?" Trillium asked, pitching her voice low.

"No'm, he ain't home, not now. Mis' Alvard, she's here. You want to talk to her?"

"No!" Trillium said, too sharply, and she repeated. "No, thank you. When will Mr. Alvard be in?"

"Couldn't say, ma'am. He been gone since yestidday, won't be back for a long time. Gone on a business trip."

Trillium stood stiffly, the receiver pressed so tight that her ear felt brittle. So Uncle Henry was gone, on a business trip—to see her mother?

"You there, miss?" the voice asked. "You sounds like Miss Trilli-um."

"No, no, I—I'm a secretary, calling from Baton Rouge—"

"Baton Rouge? Didn' the operator say Marysville?"

"You're mistaken, I'm afraid. Good-by, and thank you very much."

She dropped the receiver before the anxious old woman could inquire again. Her heart was beating so loudly that she had to stand for a moment leaning against the wall, steadying herself. The house-keeper might be puzzled enough to report the call to Aunt Agnes, but her investigation would go no farther. Aunt Agnes was a club-woman with too many interests to waste much time on a college niece. When Uncle Henry returned, he might hear about the call, and come—

But for now, for the immediate dangerous now, there was noth-ing to do but wait.

A step sounded outside the front door. Trillium was instantly alert to her predicament. This was a phase she had not planned, that she might be caught in the guesthouse. She darted across to a wide arch leading into a hallway. It has to go somewhere, she thought, and turned into a small kitchen.

And the kitchen, naturally, had an outside door.

Someone had come into the living room, whistling, dropping something on the floor. In her haste to get away, Trillium lost her hold on the screen door, and the snap brought an instant response from the unseen man.

"Cris? Is that you?"

Franz Eric's voice! Trillium tiptoed to the edge of the porch. Behind her, she heard Franz moving, into the little hall, into the kitchen, then pausing before he pushed open the door and came out. His delight was evident. Trillium sidled toward the steps.

"Oh, don't go! I haven't a thing to do for the next hour."

"But I have, Mr. Eric. I'm very late for history right now!"

"History? We're making it ourselves." He folded his arms, look-ing down at her in a way that she found most disconcerting. Feeling her cheeks grow pink, Trillium tilted her chin high.

"I wanted to see someone—I mean, I have a message."

"Oh? For me?"

"Yes. I've sprained my wrist, rather badly, so I must give up fencing and golf for a long, long time!"

"That long? Surely it's not so bad as it might be. I notice it hasn't been bandaged."

"Well, I just did it!"

"Oh, how sad! On our front door, no doubt. Let me see it, I'm good at sprains."

He took her right hand, moving the fingers and feeling the tendons. Trillium knew he was laughing at her, knew he felt the trembling of her hand and most likely took it to be the shuddering of ecstasy at his touch. The conceit of him! And yet she did not pull away. Backed against the wall, her eyes on his handsome face, she saw a remarkable change come over him. The amusement faded, even the delight, and when he looked up it seemed to her that he understood her misery and shared it.

"Trillium, what's the matter?" he asked quietly. "Helen? That's over. And still you're afraid. Don't be." He took her other hand, laid in it the one he held, and stepped back. "We couldn't be friends, I don't suppose. Could we?"

Could they? Could she confide in him, Trillium wondered, tell him what she feared—

"Oh, no!" she gasped. "No!"

"I didn't think so," Franz sighed. Then his pixy smile flashed out. "But it would be more flattering if you weren't so sure!"

The smile lasted only for the second it took for Trillium to be gone around the corner of the house. He never had floundered before, and the knowledge that he could, even as others, kept him staring gloomily off into the pecans until the clock struck the next hour.

"Lord, what a waste!" he grumbled as he leaped off the porch. Ten little maidens would be awaiting him on the tennis court.

10

Jarvis Thatcher stopped at home in Marysville only long enough to make himself presentable before driving across town to an old white house on the outskirts. It was a genial place, its grounds rambling in a leisurely expanse from the street to the gardens at the back; beneath it, among the blocks which elevated the house above the dampness, a few chickens lay dusting themselves. As the Sheriff came up the path a brown hen stalked out from under the house, walked solemnly up the steps to the porch, eyed him, and hopped solemnly down. The performance was so prim that Jarvis laughed, and immediately a hammock stopped swinging on the porch.

"Jarvis Thatcher, of all people!" a woman exclaimed, struggling up out of the hammock.

She was younger than the Sheriff, sleek and well groomed even after an hour of laziness, her slightly gray hair cut close like a man's and her make-up so light it gave only vitality to her face.

"I've been trying to reach you, Jarvis. Come into the house, I was just thinking about a cup of coffee. You're working on the Perry case, of course?"

The Sheriff, following her into the house, answered her questions and wondered why it was that he never thought of dropping in on Erminie Wagner. She was the sort to enjoy a chat without expecting a proposal of marriage. She brought the Sheriff out to the kitchen and seated him in her upholstered breakfast nook while she made the coffee. He felt decidedly restful, Erminie's green linen slenderness was pleasant to look at. Listening more than he talked, Jarvis pondered matters that had nothing whatever to do with the tragedy at St. Aurelien's until Erminie sat down opposite him and poured the coffee.

"Now, Jarvis, you want to know about the girl I picked up. Did she tell you what she was afraid of?"

The Sheriff, pouring cream into his coffee, was surprised into slopping.

"Oh, I'm not clairvoyant, Jarve." Erminie smiled. "Anyone with an eye in their head could see that girl was scared. When I heard about Helen Perry, this morning, I wondered if—well, if they had been afraid of the same thing, possibly, and that I'd brought the other one back to more than she'd bargained for. It bothered me, Jarvis. The girl might have known what she was doing, running away."

The breakfast nook was not made for anyone of his bulk, but by shifting strategically the Sheriff was able to lean forward. "Suppose you tell me what happened, Erminie."

"Oh, I will! Not that I think this is so important, but it isn't up to me to judge. I went to the play alone, since I was unable to find anyone willing to face the talents of St. Aurelien's, and I wasn't in any hurry to leave. I talked to the Sisters, stopped to look at Torvaldsen's paintings—and by the way, Jarve, how did Mother Theodore ever snare a man of his genius?"

"Is he a genius?" the Sheriff twinkled.

"Certainly! And he's a personage, not merely an artist."

"And then you started home?"

"Yes, just as I was leaving the parking lot this girl ran out and started down the road, and I picked her up. I thought at first she was the one they had been asking about, Helen Perry. There was quite a bit of whispering about how she had scampered off on a date; and I didn't want to be an accessory to anything clandestine. When I told her, she denied it so vehemently I had to believe her. And then, I suppose to convince me, she said she knew where Helen was."

"Yes, Trillium even led me out to the Cove to look."

"And Helen—was she—then—"

"I'm afraid so, Erminie. She'd been in the water a long time when we found her, at least seven hours, the coroner said. Yeah, I'm afraid she was there when Trillium and I went out."

Erminie was not the woman to burst into tears, but she did take a moment to recover.

"I made the girl go back. She didn't want to, she almost jumped out of the car when I insisted; but I know Helen's mother, and I didn't see any point in prolonging her worry. Jarve, this hardly makes sense now, does it? It made so little difference that I brought Trillium back, it didn't help you to find Helen in time! But if she feared something herself—don't you understand what I did?" She paused, bewildered. "Only I don't see what there could be in a quiet place like St. Aurelien's to frighten a girl as she was frightened. When I went there, the most ungodly thing that happened was a bat in a dormitory. But Trillium is so afraid that she can't even tell what's the matter. The only answer she could find was to run away."

The Sheriff swilled the dregs of his coffee slowly around the cup. Trillium's strange conduct was his only lead. It could be something unconnected with the murder; but the two girls were friends and trouble was so foreign to St. Aurelien's that it was hardly possible for two unrelated forces to be at work, one resulting in a girl fleeing in terror and the other murdered. It couldn't happen.

"They're tied together in some way," Jarvis said, unaware that he spoke aloud. Erminie was one of those people with whom silence could be broken or kept. "I'll have to find that tie, and without Trillium's help. But where to begin —"

Erminie let him think for a minute. "Would it be something Trillium saw last night that made her panicky?"

The Sheriff's jaw dropped. "I hope not, Erminie."

"So do I. And it might not be. If you only knew when she began to be afraid—"

She left the words to trail through the Sheriff's mind, hoping he would pick them up. The same idea, Jarvis realized, had been in the back of his head all the time.

"That's something I can find out, Erminie. And if some new circumstance transpired at about the time that Trillium began to be afraid—"

Their glances met and slipped apart. The only new circumstance, they both remembered, was the advent of the three occupants of the guesthouse.

The Sheriff left soon after, going straight to the telegraph office. It would take time to unravel the past, but it could be done.

At four o'clock Mother Theodore, smiling rather wanly in answer to their excitement, shut the seniors into the auditorium for their class meeting and walked in deep meditation back to her office. Ever since Jarvis Thatcher left, Mother had been disturbed, not by any specific thing but intuitively, as any woman can be disturbed without reason. She was irritated with herself. The superior of an institution like St. Aurelien's had no business being bothered by intuition.

Perhaps it was because Mother was so annoyed with herself that she spoke sharply to Rindy, who was lingering in the corridor gloom outside the office. Rindy's back was turned to Mother, and to one approaching it seemed that Rindy was observing something she had no call to see for she was leaning forward, tense, her attention so completely upon whatever she saw inside that she heard nothing of Mother's advent. It was not until Mother Theodore was beside her that Rindy jumped, murmured something about givin' this-here li'l ol' door a good polishin', and flew to work.

"Good afternoon, Mr. Archer," said Mother Theodore.

Crispin Archer glanced casually at the letter he held and slipped it into his pocket.

"Good afternoon, Mother."

"Has the last mail come?"

"I believe so." He gave her his most captivating smile. "Would you have any idea of what might have become of Mercy Harding? We were to come to grips with misplaced modifiers this afternoon."

"Mercy is a senior, Mr. Archer. I'm afraid you'll have to excuse her today." Mother Theodore was not in the habit of making excuses for the girls. Normally she would have rung for Sister Osmond, who would locate the recalcitrant Miss Harding and forward her with all speed to her appointment. But Mother was in a mood to enjoy the sight of Mr. Archer being miffed. It was good for him to be forgotten by a lady, even a very young one. "The Hunt for the Golden Fleece is one of the high points of our year, sir, and only an act of God could keep a senior from this meeting today. They elect the chairman of the committee, you see, and no one would miss the voting. To be elected chairman is the greatest honor a senior can be given."

"How charming!" said Crispin, but the implication was the exact opposite. "Oh, well, we too once were young and gay. The Hunt has of course driven all else from their girlish minds."

"I trust so, Mr. Archer."

Mother nodded, coldly, she considered, and went on into her office and closed the door. I should have gone the whole way and been a Contemplative, she thought, and said a swift prayer for forgiveness for the uncharitable reflections she was entertaining toward Mr. Archer.

At that moment Trillium stood among her milling classmates, her thoughts in as dizzy a whirl as the scene. She had never for a minute expected to be chairman. Even when Mary Elizabeth, the inventive member of the class, suggested a baby muskrat to be the Fleece this year, she had made no objection. She would have nothing to do with the muskrat, it couldn't seem like a throwback to the past.

But in a landslide vote she had been elected chairman, and now she would have to creep through darkened halls with the muskrat in her arms, and if Jem should know. . . .

Trillium swayed, and a girl pushed a chair under her, and the joy mounted because of having elected a chairman who took the honor so to heart that she nearly fainted. And in the chair Trillium sat, smiling, drinking the water Hilaria brought—and all the time remembering that on the night the Fleece was hidden there was never a light showing and the halls were black as outer darkness itself. If only she dared tell Mother or the Sheriff how she had tried to get in touch with Uncle Henry, how Helen had been mistaken for her and it was no use to keep looking for a tramp who might be guilty of the murder—but her mother's letter had said, "No matter what happens, say nothing." But did that "what" include killing?

The girls were quieting down, waiting expectantly for her speech of acceptance, and Trillium made it. Thanking her classmates for the honor they had conferred upon her, she remembered under her conscious thoughts that this was the day for her weekly letter from her mother. It always came on the same day. Uncle Henry would have sent it on. She would go immediately after this meeting to get it.

Rindy, polishing, was still in the hall when Trillium sped to the office. Rindy was very happy. Good luck had come her way to-day. And how easily she might have missed it! If she had just been working even at the other end of the hall she would never have seen those three nice gentlemen come for their letters, or had them stop to speak to her. One asked if she would give his room in the guesthouse a special cleaning, another wanted something pressed, and the third—

Rindy giggled. "Oh, ain't he the one?" she muttered aloud. "And all the time he know like I know that Mother don't want him mixin' up widda young ladies!"

"Were you speaking to me, Rindy?" Trillium asked, pausing breathless at the office door.

"No'm, sho ain't," Rindy answered. She couldn't help giggling again. In her pocket was a five-dollar bill, dampened slightly from all the times she had felt of it with scrub-water hands. Easy money, the first that had ever come her way.

Trillium heard the laughter in the girl's voice, but she did not respond. The letter from New Orleans was not on the table.

"Rindy," she began. But what was the use in asking Rindy? She had nothing to do with the students' letters. "You look happy, Rindy, Santa Claus good to you already?"

"Yas'm, an' that's the truth!"

"Trillium, is that you?" Mother Theodore called from the inner office.

Trillium was startled. She had not noticed the door standing ajar. She stepped forward, pushing it open. Mother was seated at her desk, her pen in hand.

"I have a message for you from Mr. Torvaldsen. He asked me this morning for permission to have you pose for him. You may refuse if you wish."

The room spun around Trillium. Franz had tried the friendly approach, Torvaldsen wanted to get her up in that horrible, bare studio—

"Trillium, I think I must insist that you tell me what is troubling you."

The girl's face turned even whiter, and involuntarily Mother arose. With the desk between them, they confronted one another, and each knew that this was as far as the conference would go.

"I want to help you, dear," Mother urged, but the sealed, secret look in Trillium's eyes warned her that it was a vain attempt. "I know you are worried and I know that the very fact of telling someone would ease your mind. It need not be me. Wouldn't you like to talk with Father Michael?"

Trillium's gaze fell to her own hands gripping the edge of the desk. "I would like to, yes, Mother, but not just now. . . ."

Mother Theodore waited a moment, then seated herself again and took up her pen. "Torvaldsen is doing a mural for us," she said briskly, "several large portrait figures with a number of others grouped around them, possibly angels. He seems a little vague about it yet, but I understand these things grow from the original sketches." She smiled. "It's an honor, dear."

The girl managed to smile back. Two honors in one day, and both so deceptive, like the hyacinths blooming delicately with their roots hidden in slime.

"Has he asked some of the other girls to pose for him, Mother?"

"Yes, and they're both thrilled to be immortalized—Nerissa Brady and little Minna Marsh. I'm sure posing must be tiresome, but they don't seem to think of that."

I have to answer, Trillium thought; and it will have to be yes. Someone came into the outer office, and she said quickly, "I'll do it, of course. And thank you, Mother." She laid her hand on the knob, but instead of opening the door she pushed it shut. "Mother Theodore, I didn't mean to hurt you. It isn't you, it's just that I can't tell *any*one!"

The girl's misery was so touching that the sight of it blurred for Mother. "It's perfectly all right, dear," she said.

Trillium flung open the door and ran out, almost colliding with Sister Onfroy because her tears made it impossible for her to see where she was going.

Down in the guesthouse, Crispin Archer sat at the piano. For a half hour he had been playing the same theme with his own improvisations, each more weirdly minor than the last. Franz, sunk in a big chair with his head resting on one arm of it, his knees hung over the other, stared at the ceiling. Since the young ladies of St. Aurelien's had temporarily forsaken education, due to the Hunt for the Golden Fleece, there was nothing for either of them to do.

"Are you going to play that tune all night?" Franz grunted at last. "I'm seeing pink spiders on the ceiling."

"I'll quit when they turn purple."

Cris glanced at the picturesque black head in the chair, and a smile that was not quite amused played over his face. His square hands hit the keys with clumsy power, as if he had a greater strength than he dared use; but the harmony that resulted was a dance of capricious daintiness.

Suddenly Franz sat up, sniffing. Crispin continued to play. Without being deliberate enough to have a motive, Franz rose, stretched, and sauntered out into the little back hall from which opened the kitchen and bedrooms. Once out of sight, he became alert, sniffing again. The taint of smoke, here, was unmistakable. Noiseless on the carpet, he advanced to Torvaldsen's door. Perhaps the artist believed his door to be closed, because only a crack remained open; but through that crack Franz saw Torvaldsen, intent on what he was doing.

He was tearing up a letter and burning it, bit by bit, in an ash tray.

11

"You have a beautiful throat, my dear, exquisitely slender. And you carry your head well. You would think that all American women would stand proudly, they have everything in the world to inspire them; but no, they slouch and sag. In Europe, where sometimes a woman carries all her worldly goods in a basket on her head, that's where you see the beautiful postures."

Torvaldsen laid aside a brush and carefully selected a clean one. Trillium, seated on the dais, did not attempt a reply. The pulse beat hard in her throat. Perhaps he had noticed. He could require her to sit there under his minute observation, conscious of every heartbeat and change of expression; but she would neither make conversation nor pretend to enjoy it. He had asked her advice many times in the draping of the white material around her, explaining how she would be the main figure of the central group, the personification of the spiritual; and Trillium's acknowledgment had been small. Now, she thought, let him talk to himself if he finds the silence too oppressive. For her own, she had other preoccupations: the part she must play in the Hunt tonight, the dark halls and the stealthy journey to the hiding place with the object they had selected as the Golden Fleece. There could be no possible danger, she told herself for the hundredth time; the halls would be crowded, even though the crowd remained invisible in the darkness. And there was added safety in the secrecy surrounding the chairman's identity.

When the bell rang, Trillium shed her white draperies and, emerging in blouse and skirt, stepped down from the dais.

"Tomorrow, then, at the same time?" Torvaldsen asked as she left.

"Yes, sir," said Trillium and slipped past Nerissa Brady, who was entering.

Nerissa had no objection to posing. Dropping her books on a chair, she hurried over to look at the first sketch of Trillium resting on the easel. It was blocked in high lights and shadows, broadly done; but the eyes, gazing up at something far beyond the border of the picture, were so expressive of fear and sadness that even Nerissa was shocked. This was a Trillium she did not know, a stranger with familiar features. Torvaldsen was sitting back in the armchair against the wall, brooding over his work, the girl forgotten. And Uncle Tor, Nerissa saw, had upon him the same sadness as the painted face. Instead of questioning, as she would have liked to do, she stepped back quietly, afraid to interrupt the artist's reverie. It was not Nerissa's way to be still when she wanted to talk; but Tor's mood discouraged conversation. In the strong north light, surrounded by the bare studio setting, there was a starkness about him, a stripping away of all pretense, the genial uncle character gone. Nerissa was frightened. She was just deciding to move noiselessly to the door and leave him to his lonely musings when he spoke, deep in his throat as if it made no difference whether anyone heard but himself.

"I've had to bring myself to believe that everyone must be somewhat selfish in his determination to succeed, that too great generosity spreads the faculties too wide, that one's powers must be concentrated into more or less selfish service—but when I see her—" He paused, shaking his head.

"She looks afraid, there," Nerissa said barely above her breath.

"Yes. She is."

Nerissa's green eyes grew round. "Oh, please, don't paint me like that!"

To her embarrassment, he laughed.

"I won't have to, my dear! You aren't afraid of anything."

Nerissa smiled and went back to the portrait. "If I were going to be as scared as she is, I'd have refused to be chairman! I'd have said I was afraid of the dark and told them to elect someone else!"

Torvaldsen picked up a tube of paint and squeezed a long, white worm out on to his palette. "Is she afraid of the dark, Nerissa?"

"Well of course! What else is there? We hide the Fleece tonight, I mean, Trillium and whoever she chooses to go with her will hide it, and I'll bet a nickel it will be Mary Liz because she's Trill's best friend now that Helen—oh—"

The artist seemed to be far more interested in his paints than in Nerissa's chatter. He inspected the palette, grunted, and went into an explanation of her position in the group. When Crispin Archer wandered in a quarter of an hour later, Tor was engrossed in his sketching; but Nerissa saw that the visitor stopped in amazement when he caught his first glimpse of Trillium's portrait, and he was still studying it when the bell rang and the model had to take a reluctant departure.

"That's good, Tor," Crispin said. "Too bad it's only a sketch. But you made it on canvas, I see. Planning to do something with it?"

Nerissa's sketch was done on board, like all preliminary studies. Trust Archer to notice that the other was aimed at permanence. Torvaldsen laughed, gathering up his brushes.

"You resisted the temptation to make a siren out of the green-eyed redhead, I see," Crispin added. "You're well advised, Tor."

"I try. You'll have to excuse me a minute, Cris—have to wash these before the paint cakes. Be right back."

Torvaldsen, his hands bristling with brushes, departed; but when his footsteps had died away in the hall, he came quietly back and peered in through the crack of the door. Archer was sitting where he himself had been, arms folded, contemplating the dark, painted eyes of Trillium's portrait. When light steps began to climb the stairs, Tor hurried along to his destination, unsmiling, his expression remote and thoughtful as Nerissa had seen it.

He took his time with the brushes, and when he re-entered the studio, Archer was gone and little Minna Marsh, the blond of the mural trio, popped up from the edge of the chair where she had been seated.

"Mr. Torvaldsen, did you ever see a churn man? A real one?"

The artist dropped his brushes into their jar. What a very young question! "No, Minna, never have I seen a churn man. Why?"

"Because there's one down in the barnyard now! And everybody's out there! Just everybody!"

"Everybody but us, eh?"

"Yes, sir."

Torvaldsen sighed. The mood of a model was important to him, and for all Minna's heaven-blue eyes and golden curls, she could not assume an angelic expression while her thoughts twiddled around some sort of three-ring circus going on in the barnyard. "Ah, well, tomorrow then, Minna," he said.

"Yes, sir."

The girl was a streak of blue in the doorway; then a thumping of saddle shoes on the stairs, and Torvaldsen was alone.

He sat down in his armchair, but he could not stay where he had to look at Trillium's portrait. And the sun was bright, the day beautiful as Indian summer in the north. I shouldn't go to the barnyard, he thought, I should keep at work. But if everyone else was there, his absence might be noted more readily than his presence. Taking a sketch pad and pushing a pencil up under his beret, he tramped down the stairs.

It had been a case of love at first sight between Sister Etienne and the churn man's dog. With his master, who was small and quick and wizened like a monkey on a stick, the great creature paused to gaze across the barnyard to where the old Sister sat on an upturned bucket in the sun-warmed shelter of Glory's sunflowers. No one had challenged their walk up the long road from the gate, and the churn man was confident. He knew all about convents. If you could once get inside, get talking to one of the Sisters, the battle was half over.

"Muh pussonality, heh, heh," was how he would explain it.

But the dog broke the ice here. Lifting his huge paws precisely, he padded across to the old Sister, stepped neatly around the milk pan in which Tom was soaking his feet, and laid his enormous head gently in her lap. Banty cackled and Tom fanned his tail in majestic hatred. But Sister Etienne put her hand on the big, smooth head and looked down into the beautiful eyes and lost her heart completely.

"Name's Taffy. He's a Newfoundland, fine strain, maybe part St. Bernard, heh, heh," said the churn man, and his little eyes darted

around the farm buildings and over to the cloister. Everything solid, good financial state. Ought to be able to talk them into a churn.

The man began a sly sales line which was lost on Sister Etienne
because the dog's tongue had fluttered against her cheek and when
he lay down he was so big that his shoulder touched her knee; and
his head, which he placed immediately again in her lap, was so
heavy it was like holding a whole animal. Through the misery of the
past week, forsaken, worried, weary from the continual searching
for her lost habit, Sister Etienne had relinquished the thought of
ever regaining contentment, much less happiness. Then, suddenly,
across the barnyard, this marvelous trusting creature had come, and
Etienne's anxieties rolled away.

"Is he for sale, sir?" she asked. Foolish, of course. No one would
sell such a dog.

But surprisingly enough, the churn man replied, "Oh, sure, right
enough, ma'am. With the churn, that is."

"The churn?" Sister Etienne peered around and saw nothing but
a hazy little man before her.

"Nothin' to it. If I could give a demonstration it'd all be a open
book, yeah. Oh, how do, ma'am!"

This last was to Glory Muckleroy who had come out to lean on
her fence where the sunflowers had been pruned for exactly such a
purpose.

"My, is that a dog, Mister?" she asked. Without turning her head
she shouted, "Addie Pearl, bring the kids and come see!"

The Muckleroys—Munroe, Hattie Bell, Monessa, and Addie
Pearl with Palmer on her hip—responded with a slam of the kitch-
en door behind them.

"Havin' a bite of lunch, we was," Glory said by way of explanation for the presence of the entire brood.

She was drowned out by the shouts of the children crowding
around Taffy, who wagged his tail and accepted their homage with
dignity but continued to love old Etienne.

"Like I was sayin'," said the churn man, who knew an opportunity when he saw one, "I could give you a demonstration, easy. Got
my kit right down at the gate, didn't feel like I'd oughta drive in

till I'd spoke to somebody. I never was one to horn in where I ain't wanted."

"I can see you got real nice manners," said Glory.

The churn man winked at her. "How's about a demonstration, lady?"

"What of?"

"Heh, heh, muh churn!"

"Oh. Well, I guess we got one."

"Dasher kind?"

"Electric."

"No good," said the man with a fine wave of his hand. "Storm comes up, off goes the power, no churnin'. Now this-here dog churn—"

"Dog churn?" a chorus repeated.

"Right ho! You wait, just you wait here, ladies, that's all I ask. And prepare to be amazed!"

With another wink at Glory and a promising grin, the churn man patted Monessa on the head and departed with such speed that he had reached the barnyard gate before Glory found her tongue.

"I reckon the dog's the best part o' this outfit," she said. "I don't hold with strange men winkin'."

"Mercy me, did he wink?" Sister Etienne murmured. "I wonder if we shouldn't have had permission from Mother before we allowed him to demonstrate. . . ."

"Weren't much allowin' to it, seems if. But I was the one give in, Sister, you didn't have nothin' to do with it."

Whatever uneasiness the two might have felt was dispatched in the general wonder at the churn man's equipment. His old truck was painted yellow with "Churn With Burns" blaring across it in red.

"That's muh name, Burns," he said and winked again at Glory.

There seemed to be a great deal to the churn. When Mother Theodore discerned the unusual activity in the barnyard and decided to investigate, she came upon a scene of medieval proportions. In the center of a circle composed of the Muckleroys, Sister Etienne, all of the college girls, several of the farm hands and most of the faculty, the churn man's demonstration was taking place. Upon a large slanted treadmill the dog was walking, shut into a stall so that he never progressed forward but simply turned the table as he walked. The turning set in motion a great contrivance of machinery underneath, the machinery manipulated a long arm which ran out to a large barrel churn, and the barrel rolled on its axis, end over end. Far at the back stood a silent line of Contemplative Sisters, a little removed from them was fat Sister Emery from the kitchen in her stiff, white bonnet which she wore during working hours. At a good distance, for perspective, the artist stood, sketching.

And holding forth beside the churn with every eye upon him was the churn man himself, declaiming the merits of his equipage. That he had already been over his routine several times was no deterrent for such an orator. With so attentive an audience, he felt that he could go on for hours. The churn worked superbly, the great golden dog performed with endless patience, and the churn man wiped his forehead on the sleeve of his red shirt and brought out every adjective known to the language.

Unexpectedly, however, he ran down like a toy in need of winding.

"Oh-oh!" murmured Franz Eric.

"Yes, indeedy," said Cris, beside him.

For Mother Theodore, in all her vast respectability, had emerged in an opening beside the truck and into the churn man's line of vision. Mother was the personification of authority, quiet, inflexible authority, and the churn man's facility of expression suddenly ran dry. The dog raised his head and slowed his pace until the treadmill stopped, whereupon the churn halted its sprightly tumbling. The whole wide, entranced circle looked at Mother, and the only movement was the flutter of a Sister's veil and the flip of Mr. Archer's yellow tie in the wind.

Mother Theodore was not quite pleased. Everyone expected her to smash this pretty bauble of amusement with a word; and so, because she had both a contrary streak in her and a sense of humor, she smiled at the churn man.

"I seem to have missed the entertainment, sir. Will you not continue for my pleasure?"

Mother decided not to hear the universal gasp. The churn man bowed and, realizing he had gotten off easy, bowed again.

"Burns is the name, ma'am, Theophilus Burns, yes, ma'am! Now you see before you my invention. . . ."

He was off on another oration.

"His invention, my eye!" said Crispin Archer. "If I'm not mistaken, my grandmother had one of these contraptions. She wasn't sold on it. The dog always got sick, and she had a dickens of a time till she trained my grandfather to walk the mill. About all the old boy was good for."

Trillium, entranced as everyone, had gradually worked her way in to get a good view of the dog, and she had not noticed who were her neighbors in the crowd. Crispin Archer's voice startled her. But she didn't turn. She was learning not to respond to surprise. Franz Eric would be with him, the two were always together. Keeping her eyes ahead, she moved slowly away to the far side of the circle, then unobtrusively left it.

The churn man, always sensitive to goings and comings among his audience, saw Trillium's departure and, without interrupting so much as a comma of his discourse, scanned the crowd. There was a familiar face among them, and the churn man lifted his hand in friendly salute. Always best to recognize an acquaintance, even though, because of his extensive contacts with the public, he couldn't place this face immediately and give it a name. The one to whom he waved made no response, and the churn man thought absently that he must have been mistaken and went on with his harangue.

Glory Muckleroy heard Mr. Archer's remark about the grandfather. She liked Mr. Archer, with his comical way of putting things. Tossing her laughter over her shoulder to him, she wished she could think of a good answer. Talk back plenty to Hy, she could, put him in stitches; but Mr. Archer was the deep kind, like something in a dictionary that had a dozen different meanings you'd never think of.

"Glory!" came Mary Elizabeth's guarded whisper beside her. "Did Hy get it all right?"

"Sure thing, Miss Mary Elizabeth, it's right in my kitchen—"

"Sh!" the girl warned; but seeing no enemies within hearing, she continued audibly, "We have the cage all ready and we'll bring it over after dark. You be looking for us! But don't put on your porch light. It has to be secret, remember!"

"I'll watch out."

"Fine! 'By, now!

Mary Elizabeth moved away, and Glory, looking after her with a smile, saw that Mr. Archer was doing the same. "My, you're only young once, ain't you, Mr. Archer?" she said.

Mr. Archer patted Palmer on the back and received a display of two teeth in return. In the autumn breeze his tie stuck its tongue out, and in his eyes there was a distinct gleam of amusement.

The churn man finished going through his paces without much heart.

"The minute I set eyes on her I knowed she wasn't no easy mark," he said to Hy Muckleroy when he came back from an extremely short conclave with Mother Theodore. "Hardheaded, all them dames is, at the head of convents."

"They gotta be," said Hy. "Runnin' a shebang like this is big business. Somethin' like a flywheel you got under there, ain't it?"

The churn man dived half under the treadmill to point out the wonders of his invention, but before he quite disappeared he sent one more glare of rather disgusted admiration after Mother. "Well, I ain't sorry I done the settin' up, best crowd I've had in a coon's age. She offered me open house in the barn, too. Asked me to stay the night."

"A free night's lodgin' is money in the pocket," Hy observed. "Glory an' me, we'd be proud to have you eat with us. Now about this-here flywheel, seems to me like you'd oughta run another band. . . ."

The churn man followed Hy in under the machinery, since by that time the crowd had dwindled to two freshmen, Sister Etienne, the Muckleroy children, and Tom and Banty, all poor prospects.

At an ordinary time at St. Aurelien's, fame would not have been so fleeting for the churn man. Girls would have paid visits all through the evening to the yellow truck where they would have petted Taffy and listened to his master tell of stupendous adventures. The churn man expected it, he was entitled to hold court in the barnyard.

But twilight straggled in from the swamp, and the churn man stood on the Muckleroy's back porch with Hy, awaiting Glory's call to supper, and saw not a single candidate upon whom to exercise his powers of narration.

"Awful quiet," he said, "lock 'em up, do they, come the gloaming?"

"Not as a reg'lar thing," Hy grinned. "There'll be doin's inside them ol' walls tonight."

"Do tell," said Theophilus Burns.

Hy did. He knew, from other years when he had seen this strange night observed upon the campus, that the hiding of the Golden Fleece was like no other undertaking in the world.

There would be no appointed hour. At any minute from sunset to dawn, a girl might sneak out of a darkened room, slip to the hiding place with the trophy and back again to the darkened room, all unknown because on this night there would be no lights in the building. No prefect would challenge her, for every Sister except the portress in her little office would withdraw to the cloister and leave the way free for the hiding of the Fleece. But there would be spies, watching and waiting, freshman, sophomore, and junior spies in sneakers and blue jeans who would glide through the halls, following her. The seniors would thoughtfully provide decoys, of course, to lead them astray; but if by chance someone did follow the right one and guess where she hid the trophy, it would mean ignominious defeat for the defenders even before the Hunt opened, and unparalleled triumph for the Hunters. In any event, the Hunters had only thirty-six hours in which to find the Fleece.

Trillium, already in blue jeans, sweater, and gym shoes, sat on her bed and watched her door. In the two days since the letter from New Orleans had been due and had not come, she had haunted Mother's office. Uncle Henry was out of town on business. He could not forward the letter when he was not there—but his secretary could have done so. Never before had her mother's letter been late, always the distinctive, long envelope would be on the mail table with the other, unopened, inside it. Possibly moving to new quarters had delayed the writing. But as time passed and she kept tracing the weary circle around, it became less than ever possible for Trillium to believe that the letter had not arrived.

"It did come," she whispered through stiff lips, her eyes on the darkening hall outside her open door, "it did come, and he took it, and now he knows where my mother is, and he knows that I know he is threatening her. So I might be the only witness against him if he—found her. He can't leave me alone any longer. And all I'm sure of is that he is one of three . . . what would Mother Theodore have told me if I had dared confide in her? But I couldn't! No matter what happens!"

A soft shuffling approached her door, and she sprang up.

"You're ready?" Mary Elizabeth whispered. "Then come on!"

Trillium went softly out after her. When you don't know what else to do, do anything. There might not be safety in it, but at least you wouldn't go crazy with thinking.

Mother Theodore was in a like frame of mind. She could not remain quietly in her room or in the office or in the common room where the Sisters gathered in the evening. She walked through all the halls of the first floor, past the auditorium, over to the west stairs. All was hushed, waiting, the silence punctuated with giggles and once in a while the swift closing of a door. The moment darkness fell, the giggles and the expeditions from room to room would cease.

With no motive in mind, Mother descended the old stairs leading to the tunnels, thinking to find the passages black dark. Halfway along the corridor that ran under the building, the door of a room was open and light streamed out. For a long, hesitant minute, Mother stood on the stairs, apprehensive, wondering why she should not go forward and speak to whoever was in the storeroom. The general ghostliness of the ancient place, coupled with her dread of the night ahead, that was what held her on the stairs. It had nothing whatever to do with the presence of someone in the storeroom.

Ashamed of herself, Mother went resolutely toward that open door. Now she could hear the short scrape of a box being pushed along the stone floor, a rustle of paper. And then she saw into the room. In the brilliant light of the unshaded overhead bulb, a Sister was working with her back to the door, bent half into the large packing case she had pushed a moment earlier. Mother smiled. After all, who had she expected to find here in the basement depths?

And who was it? Even the Sisters themselves could not always be sure of another's identity from a back view.

"Sister?"

The packer almost toppled into the big box, and the hand she put out to steady herself was familiar.

"Oh, Sister Raymond!" Mother exclaimed. "Forgive me for startling you. What are you doing, so busy at this time of night?"

Sister Raymond laughed, catching her breath. "I'm putting away the 'Mustardseed' costumes. We just piled them all in here helter-skelter after the play, and I thought this would be a good time to sort them. I like to do it myself, then I know where everything is." She held up what had been a drift of white chiffon, now flattened and wrinkled from its sojourn under a dozen others. "It's still lovely, isn't it, Mother?"

But Mother Theodore stared at it in horror. When Sister Raymond heard a strangled sound and turned to see her superior's face, she was terrified.

"Mother, what's the matter?"

Mother's lips opened twice before her voice came. "The costume. I didn't know you kept Helen's!"

"Helen's?" The Sister's veil fluttered, so instantly did she turn to make certain of what she held. "Helen's? Oh, no, Mother, this is Trillium's!"

Sister Raymond shook out the delicate folds as if she must demonstrate beyond a doubt that they were neither stained nor torn, and Mother Theodore smiled, more than a little disgusted with herself.

"Of course, I might have known you wouldn't—I had forgotten how very much alike the two costumes were, Sister."

"Exactly alike, only for the color of the veils. Pink and blue. The girls looked like twins, I'll never forget it—never. . . ."

The Sister's hand lay gently upon the chiffon, lay until it went up to wipe away a tear that crept down under her glasses. Then she bent and dropped the costume into the box.

Mother Theodore slowly nodded. You could pack away the one remaining garment, but not the remembrance of its twin. "Sister, could you not leave this until another time?"

"If you wish me to, Mother."

"No. It was merely a suggestion. You may continue if you desire, Sister."

"Thank you, Mother."

The Superior looked back from the doorway. Trillium and Helen—what should she remember about them? Something tapped at her consciousness. Walking through the dark hall, wondering what the tantalizing thing could be, worrying a little about Sister Raymond down there alone with her quiet tears, Mother failed to awaken memory. She opened the big front door and came out on the main steps, then strolled on down to the drive where she loved to walk back and forth in the evening.

Tonight she had many thoughts to keep her company: Trillium's haunting of the office for the letter that had not been there; Trillium's fear—always Trillium. Mother's slow patrol halted abruptly.

The tantalizing thing had ceased to tantalize and had popped, full blown, into her mind!

The terrible realization held her still, her face turned to the west where the sun had already set, and she shivered under her warm cloak because her heart had stopped beating life through her body. She was certain of what she believed, sure she was right. Jarvis would have to know. At the thought of Jarvis, she felt warmth beat through her again. He was only as far away as her own office telephone!

She had reached the steps when she heard someone behind her, someone who walked with a steady, light tread, and swiftly. Mother wheeled, not realizing that her position on the step gave her the height of a giantess, that the twilight muffled her figure until she appeared to be a twin to Mary Elizabeth's phantom nun. She was amazed, then, at the strange expression upon the face of the young man who confronted her—stupefaction, incredulity?

"Good evening, Mother," said Franz Eric. "I didn't see you in the dark. I hope I didn't startle you."

"No."

He glanced around, and his eyes fell on the village lights twinkling a mile away. "I'm going into town to a movie. It's a perfect night for a walk."

"Yes," said Mother.

Franz hesitated, then smiled and saluted her. "Good night, Mother."

"Good night, Mr. Eric."

He strode away, a bareheaded, slight young man without a care for anything other than his own entertainment; but he could have cut across the lawn to the gates from the guesthouse without making this long circle up to the convent; and the last show, as Mother knew from various young ladies, started at eight. The clock in the tower had just struck a quarter past.

She stood watching until Franz was only a light speck well outside the gates. Over in the guest house a lamp glowed behind a window with an undrawn shade.

Mother Theodore went straight up the steps and into the main hall. The light from Sister Osmond's office was enough to show her the way. Without turning on any other, she hurried quietly to her own office. She had suddenly remembered that there was also a strange man in the barnyard tonight.

The strange man, however, was not at the moment in the barnyard but in the Muckleroy's kitchen watching the transfer of a young muskrat from a makeshift cage to a gaudy red one equipped with all the animal comforts of home. With Glory and the children kneeling around them, and advised by Hy and the churn man, Trillium and Mary Elizabeth coaxed while the little muskrat stared with beady eyes.

"Had quite a time gettin' him," Hy said importantly, impressing the churn man. "Don't know as anybody but me coulda done it. Them trappers is pretty persnickety about their mushqush, even just borrowin', like."

Glory looked up proudly at her husband; and Mary Elizabeth sighed, "He's just perfect, Hy! He's the most beautiful Golden Fleece we've ever had!"

The little muskrat crouched in the bedecked cage. He was young, half grown, and he was scared. With his pale belly fur clean and soft, his back shining dark with the guard hairs that make a coat so durable, his little round ears giving him the air of a defenseless baby, he stared into the circle of faces.

"I don't believe he appreciates all we've done for him," observed Mary Elizabeth. "Hy making the cage, Mercy Harding painting it with all these fuddy-duddies, and the crown sparkling like the king's jewels!" She touched the little pin which was tied to the cage with a ribbon.

"I reckon he'd rather have a nice mudhole," said Glory.

It was Trillium who remembered the urgency of the hour, the dark run to be made when Glory's door went shut behind them. Tonight there was no moon to hang like a witch's lantern over the swamp and make palisades of the convent walls and turn the hyacinths into a solid floor.

Mary Elizabeth was telling the Muckleroys how the Fleece would be hidden. The Hunters, of course, expected them to make a good many fake expeditions first and then, when the spies were occupied on false trails, to make a break to hide the treasure. And so, since that was what the Hunters looked to happen, the Committee planned to turn the tables on them.

"We'll hide the Fleece first and then lead them a merry chase afterward!" Mary Elizabeth confided. "Isn't that cute of us?"

"Liz, come on," Trillium broke in. "I'll take the little scamp, and you lead the way. Turn off the lights, Hy."

Glory let the two out into the night from the dark kitchen; when they left the porch, they were in a sea of blackness.

The swamp was as still as it ever is. A short distance away, on the road leading out from town, an engine chugged. Even the guesthouse was dark. Over between the chapel and the opaque mass of the convent the cloister walk arched blacker than the night.

"Come on," Trillium whispered. "We'll cut over to the cloister. No one can see us there."

Mary Elizabeth shuddered. Her imagination peopled the night with little dreads as they walked slowly across unseen grass, crept through a barely visible cloister walk, entered a building where familiar objects had assumed unfamiliar places in the pitch darkness. Trillium, holding the cage in both arms so it would not bump against some undiscernible object, trying to match her steps to Mary Elizabeth's, was grimly certain that every inch of their progress was being followed.

Once Trillium, on the stairs, halted, and Mary Elizabeth, instantly aware, stopped also. Neither of the girls breathed audibly. If there were a third presence anywhere on the stairs, it bided its time. And the time was not yet. When the girls moved on, the darkness stirred behind them.

12

"I don't hold with murder," said the churn man sententiously. The door was closed upon the dark night, and the children were disposed on the woodbox and in front of the kitchen range with Taffy. The pipe smoking of Hy and Theophilus Burns was infinitely peaceful. Glory was rocking the baby to sleep.

"I don't hold with murder, because it ain't never finished," the churn man further expounded. "Take a feller I once knew, when I was a mushqush trapper—"

"Oh, you trap mushqush in your time?" Hy inquired politely. At different points in the narrative Burns had mentioned many avocations and careers, all lawful, all extremely vague as to time.

But now he pinned himself down. "I did, some six-seven, maybe eight year ago. Down in the bayou country. Funny thing, I've always figgered nothin' woulda happened if that-there norther hadn't blowed up. Reg'lar stinkeroo, she was, ice an' sleet, an' cold!"

The churn man paused, reminiscing. After a moment Hy asked, "They freeze this feller to death, that how they done it?"

"Oh, no, no, the storm caught him in the swamp, see. One o' these dudes out on a huntin' trip. Got separated from his outfit and had to lay up at this-here trapper's houseboat. And the trapper had a good-looking missus." The churn man's eye met Hy's knowingly. "Seen her once myself." Settling in his chair, he drew on his pipe. "Well, sir, this hunter jigger didn't get enough of it in them two-three days of the storm. He kept comin' back. And pretty soon the husband tumbled to what was the attraction and raised right smart of a fuss. Well, like I said, the feller kept comin' back, and one night he come once too often. Bright moonlight, it was. The trapper met the guy out in the swamp, and pretty soon there was a shot and the dude skun out quick." The churn man looked at his pipe stem as if suddenly he hated the taste of it. "Peculiar, ain't it, how blood looks black in the moonlight."

There was a horrified silence, the children staring, Glory and Hy aghast. The only natural sound was Taffy licking his paws.

"Never did know what become o' the feller's wife and kid," the churn man added.

The kitchen was very still, the wood popping in the stove. Burns went on puffing at his pipe, so the sentences were curiously broken. "The murderer can't quit with them two alive, not and be safe. He wasn't never caught, never suspected. Suicide, they said. The story ain't never come out."

"How'd he get away, that night, I mean?" Hy asked.

"Easy, in the swamp. Why, a man could hide out in them back bayous for a elephant's lifetime. Bloodhounds can't track there—too much water. Take a feller don't know them back bayous, he'd be lost inside a day, but if you know 'em you can stay in or make your way out another direction, easy as you please. No, this guy got away at the time, but he ain't safe till he's fixed them two so they can't talk. Might be they ain't of a mind to talk, but he can't never be sure. That's why I said murder ain't never done up clean. There's always tag ends."

The Muckleroys listened, fascinated and horrified. To Glory, one terrible question stood out: why had the churn man chosen to tell this weird tale tonight? If only she dared ask him!

"Sounds like you might be a witness yourself, Mr. Burns," she ventured.

"Heard about it, that's all," he said shortly, forgetting his nice manners.

"Oh," said Glory.

The churn man arose hurriedly, turning only when he was half-way out of the door. "Oh, 'scuse me, I gotta see to somethin'. Thanks for the eats, an' all. Taffy!"

"Well, you come in and have breakfast with us, Mr. Burns," Glory reminded him.

"We'd be proud to have you," added Hy.

The big dog ambled to the door, and an instant later the churn man was gone, leaving behind him the rank smell of his pipe and a strange quivering sensation in everyone of the Muckleroys except Palmer, who was asleep.

"I didn't like him, Ma," whimpered Addie Pearl.

"Now don't you kids go gettin' worked up," Glory cautioned. "Hy, you look to the doors and the windows, too. And don't one of you mention a word o' this crazy yarn to anybody, you hear me? Land sakes, I'll be glad when this night's over with!"

Carrying Palmer into the bedroom, she looked out toward the convent. Not a light showed anywhere.

Trillium, crouched with the muskrat cage in the recess behind the prefect's desk in the dormitory hall, concentrated all her attention on her sense of hearing. This must be how it felt to be blind—inky darkness around you, nothing to compensate for the visual pictures of sight, no way to tell when someone came and stood near you! But there was a compensation in quickened listening, for with no eyes to offer diversion her ears were picking up sounds ordinarily unnoticeable. There was Mary Elizabeth at the entrance to this little hall recess, her blue jeans brushing once in a while against the wall. There were footsteps, once, so padded they were only a thinning of the close silence as they passed. And also, once, there was the rustle of a Sister's skirts, impossible to mistake for any other sound when a girl had listened for it through three years of little midnight snacks and visits. Straight by them and through the corridor, unhurried, deliberate, the slow sounds passed along and out of hearing.

"The old sneak!" Mary Elizabeth whispered. "She isn't supposed to be up here tonight!"

"Who was it?" Trillium breathed.

"The Bouncer! Who else?"

"Osmond wouldn't do that."

The muskrat began a scrabbling in the cage, his tiny claws scratching holes in the silence.

"Can't you keep him quiet, Trill?" Mary Elizabeth begged. "Rock him or something, maybe he'll think you're his mother."

Trillium rocked, and the little animal forgot his terror. Surely they had been in the alcove more than fifteen minutes! What if the juniors had somehow deduced that the striking of the clock was to be the signal and had stopped its old works? They could proceed without the signal, of course, because they were almost beside the hiding place right now. Around the corner into the hall, and there was the funny little door opening into the old chapel tower. Not far to go. Nothing to fear in the tower.

The secret of the hiding place had been well kept. This afternoon, when Trillium had come with Mary Elizabeth to do a little practicing in the tower, they had met Rindy in the hall outside.

But Rindy would never give them away.

In the clock tower, the old hammers struck four notes. "Excelsior! Onward and upward!" Mary Elizabeth whispered. "Come on, Trill!"

With Liz leading her by the front of her shirt, Trillium moved soundlessly into the hall, around the corner, past the broom closet, halted at the door leading to the tower. From other hiding places, decoys would be slipping out, carefully carrying empty shoe boxes to lead the spies astray; but there was no noise anywhere in the building.

Trillium quivered in every muscle as they stood, barely breathing, straining for any indication from the enemy. This was the most critical moment of the hiding process, when the door must be opened and the ascent made up the ancient steps. When Trillium had practiced it early in the day with her eyes shut, there had been the unconscious knowledge that she could open her eyes, and several times she had peeked. But there was no cheating in this utter blackness. Even with keeping her eyes so wide that the lids were stiff, she was a blind girl in a black world.

She knew when Mary Elizabeth opened the door because fresh air swam around her. Everything, then, must be just as they had left it in the middle of the afternoon, the small trap door propped wide at the top of the old tower stairs. For the first time since she had known she was chairman of the Fleece, Trillium was not afraid.

It might have been the stimulus of the night air from the tower, or Mary Elizabeth's competent guardianship, or the practical thought that the deed was so nearly completed. Whatever the reason, she was elated, lighthearted as a girl of twenty should be.

"Take it easy, Trill," Mary Elizabeth breathed in her ear, and Trillium realized that she had been fairly bounding around in the dark.

She laughed, but inside herself, and moved into the cramped space of the tower.

Mary Elizabeth would remain here, inside, the hall door closed, listening, while Trillium ascended to the bell chamber. Even the muskrat was behaving well now. Confidently, she put out her hand to steady herself against the wall, and with the other arm tight around the cage, began the perilous climb.

The Sisters, when the tower was planned, had not foreseen that it would be used for any purpose other than the accommodation of the clock works. The tower room itself was wide enough only to allow the pendulum to swing free, and over in a corner they had erected a steep flight of steps which had been hacked by an Indian out of a single cypress log. In the daytime, if the climber minded the business at hand, there was no danger of missing a step; but at night it was quite another matter to cling to the narrow log and lean hard against the wall to maintain balance. Another matter, also, to hold a muskrat cage suspended out over nothing so it wouldn't bump and make a noise.

Slowly, taking her time, Trillium crept up toward the opening above her head. The sky was shut away by the faces of the clock which walled the tower, but the west side, which had no face since the Sisters considered thriftily it would be wasted on the swamp, was fitted with louver boards. Feeling the cold air against her face, Trillium knew she was near the top, and pulled out her flashlight. In the little room the clock was busy; the bells were like plum puddings of different sizes set out to cool.

"I suppose you'll get scared when the clock strikes, honey, but try to bear up," Trillium whispered, laying down the cage. "You have plenty to eat, and this can't last forever!"

She would have liked to sit there a while with the muskrat for company and breathe the fresh night air and enjoy the odd certainty that her troubles were not any more insurmountable than the hiding of the Fleece; but Mary Liz waited below, the convent was crawling with spies, and back in her room she would be quite as well able to think as here.

"Good-by, Junior," she whispered. The jeweled crown on its ribbon sparkled no brighter than the muskrat's eyes.

Trillium snapped off her flash and edged backward on her knees to the yawning hatch. Working her way slowly, feeling for every inch of the steps, she reached the third and stood erect. Now she would have to pull the trap door into place after her. It was heavier than she expected, and she barely saved it from falling with a thud. She lay for a few moments against the old steps, smothering her breathing until the blood pounded in her head. I mustn't make any noise, she warned herself, no noise. And there was none, other than her own drumming heart.

Suddenly taut, she realized that there should be some slight movement down there below. Mary Elizabeth, safe in here with the door closed, could flash on her light, she could whisper some cautious word to know whether all was well with Trillium. But she didn't. No sound came from below.

She couldn't speak herself. Mary Elizabeth was the guard, the one to make the initial move. Had something happened down there in that very basement of the night? Could the door be open and Liz gone? Am I alone? Trillium's thought rushed on, for now all her foolish confidence was swallowed up in terror.

And then, in her intense listening, she caught a sound. Below her on the steps someone was creeping up, slowly, feeling the way as she herself had done with a hand on the rough old wall, breathing carefully, taking endless time.

And the hall door was open!

The tower smelled of dust and age and fresh air; but the outer hall held sweeping compound and the dinnertime roast beef, and there was no way for it to seep in except through the open door. And those homely odors were swirling into the tower!

Crouching on the steps, hearing faintly that creeping approach, Trillium sensed that this was not the hide-and-seek alarm of being caught with the Golden Fleece. In that moment she forgot the treasure hunt. Nothing was real but the open hall door and the appalling, slow advance below her on the stairs.

Trillium did not think out what she did next. Perhaps because she had used it a few minutes before, she jerked out her flashlight and pressed the button. The little tower room leaped into being, one segment of it very bright; and in that circle of light Mary Elizabeth crouched on the steps, her head on a level with Trillium's feet. She threw up an arm to shield her eyes, but she did not look up to where Trillium cowered. She looked back, to the open door of the hallway where the outer nimbus of light did not quite reach.

There, beyond that nimbus, shadowy but quite distinguishable, stood a giant Sister with her head muffled in black. Her habit was not quite long enough. Underneath it showed a pair of man's trouser legs ending in large, heavy boots.

"No!" Mary Elizabeth gasped, as if someone were choking her.

For an eternity the tableau held, the Sister simply standing with face hidden, hands hidden, an aura of evil emanating from her. Trillium wanted to swing the light up to that hidden face, over the whole muffled figure; but her arm wouldn't move. Her thumb fell away from the button; the flashlight snapped off.

Blackness again, but a blackness in which there were sounds: a series of bumps, a groan, the plop of a flashlight hitting the floor.

And in the underworld black of the hall there was the soft rustle of a Sister's skirts, exactly the sound that had gone so deliberately past the alcove so short a time before.

Mother Theodore, reading her breviary in her office, stiffened to attention. Within the close little room she heard nothing, but her nerves were tuned tonight to vibrate in the faintest breeze of trouble. For a moment she listened, straining. Suddenly she dropped the breviary and was around her desk and over to the door, out into the hall where the only light came from behind her and another patch down the hall where Sister Osmond was framed like a portrait of alarm.

For both the Sisters had heard the same sound, a high, piercing scream. Then silence, ominous, unnatural silence as if no one moved in the whole building.

Mother Theodore grasped the door behind her, helpless against this net of silence that was far more dreadful than any screaming. For she knew, without knowing, that the scream and the blank quiet had nothing to do with the Hunt for the Golden Fleece. Something had happened again.

And I don't know where Jarvis is, she thought dazedly, I couldn't find him earlier. In that moment the Superior of St. Aurelien's was as near to fainting as she ever had come in her life.

13

The convent building burned with light when the Sheriff swooped up the drive in his big car. A dark red convertible was already in the parking lot and the Sheriff, seeing it, sprinted for the main entrance. That sporty beauty belonged to young Dr. Chapman.

"And on the one night I'd get romantic-minded and take Erminie to the movies!" the Sheriff muttered. His thoughts fled ahead to Kathy, in her snug little room with Ivy Montgomery—or was it so snug? Was something even now happening to terrify her, to make her remember that other night?

The halls were as quiet as they had been a half hour earlier when the girls were divided into the Hunters and the Hunted, but with several differences: the Sisters were once again on duty in full numbers, each girl was in her proper room, and light was everywhere.

Nothing was known, actually, of what had happened. A scout had stumbled upon Trillium and Mary Elizabeth in the hall near their own rooms, and the scout, who was Alison Cooper, had taken rightful alarm when she heard stifled crying. In the glow of her flashlight Alison saw Mary Elizabeth drooping limply, supported by Trillium, who appeared to be half fainting herself, and both of them with their shirts smeared with blood.

"Turn it off!" Trillium begged, trying to shield her face from the light as Alison screamed.

"Mary Liz is murdered!" a girl whispered, and the word sped in a matter of seconds all through the black halls.

Alison, as Mother told her afterward, was the only one who kept her head. With her flashlight pointing the way for her, she flew straight to where Mother Theodore stood at her office door. And Mother called the doctor and the sheriff.

"Now what else, Emmy?" Jarvis asked quietly.

No reprimands, no blame for having allowed the Hunt to go on, not even the obvious suggestion that the whole enterprise should have been explained to him beforehand and his approval sought. Mother Theodore was grateful, so grateful that her throat tightened and she stood with her hands tightly clasped under her scapular, her eyes on the floor like anyone of her own charges called on the carpet.

"There is something more, Emmy," the Sheriff prodded, his voice still gentle. "Tell me." When she did look up, her distress was so intense that he added quickly, "Oh, it can't be that bad!"

"I saw Trillium's costume tonight, Jarvis. Sister Raymond was packing it away with the others." Quickly now the words tumbled out. "I thought it was Helen's! Trillium and Helen were both dressed exactly alike that night! It wasn't a tramp who killed Helen, it was someone who knew her, who thought she was Trillium, and I know I'm right, Jarvis, I couldn't be wrong because there is no other explanation for Trillium's fear!"

For a long minute the two were silent as if the room still echoed with the terrible truth.

"Yes, you're right, Emmy," the Sheriff said firmly. "Trillium is the bull's-eye; not Helen who looked like her nor Mary Elizabeth who got in the way. And here I've been trying to solve it from the wrong angle. I've dug into every friendship Helen ever made. I've questioned young Cooper till the poor guy's nearly nuts. I've rounded up more panhandlers than I thought we had in the whole state of Louisiana!" His voice dropped. "But tonight there were no panhandlers around. . . . Emmy, when did you first notice that Trillium was afraid of something?"

Mother Theodore could not face what she believed. Her mouth tight, she walked around her desk, seated herself, and folded her hands upon the blotter.

Jarvis leaned toward her upon the opposite side of the desk. Both knew the answer.

"She tried to run away on the night of the play, Emmy, we know that. Erminie Wagner insists that Trillium was deathly afraid when she made her come back. And what had happened shortly before that?" His voice dropped even lower. "The three geniuses had arrived upon the campus."

"She would tell me if—" Mother hesitated. Trillium had not told her, even with urging. She asked desperately, "Jarvis, why is she too much afraid to talk about it? What could be so dreadful that her life is in danger and still she can't ask for help?"

The Sheriff straightened and took a long breath. "I don't know. I've been investigating those three very interesting pasts, but so far there is no indication of anyone doing anything but minding his own business. Tor spent the summer painting in the French Quarter in New Orleans, Archer was up in the Evangeline country, Eric hanging his hat someplace in N. O. All perfectly natural—"

Mother Theodore glanced toward the door. "Here's the Doctor, now, Jarvis," she said.

The young Marysville doctor stood in the doorway. "Oh, hello, Sheriff! Well, I've looked them over, Mother, and they're both all right. Mary Elizabeth had a regular flood of a nosebleed and dripped over the two of them. Must have whacked her nose against that door she ran into. She has a broken rib, too, but it will mend. The other girl has nothing wrong with her that a couple of sleeping pills won't cure. I left something for them with the Sister up there."

"So they ran into a door, did they?" the Sheriff queried.

"That's what they said. The door must have had a punch like Joe Louis to do all that damage."

"Okay to go up and talk to them now, Doc?"

"Oh, sure, I told the Sister to hold the medicine till you'd seen the kids. I'll tell you, though, they aren't in a mood to talk."

"Oh, yes, they are!" the Sheriff declared.

But when he and Mother Theodore stood beside Mary Elizabeth's bed and saw her lying like another young corpse, her lashes dark on her white cheeks and her breathing imperceptible, the stern Sheriff melted into Kathy's father. On the other bed, which had been Helen's, Trillium was curled up, her eyes shadowed with more than weariness and her cheeks pink as if she had fever. She had changed her gory shirt for pajamas and a pink housecoat, and to Mother Theodore she looked fragile, certainly not the possessor of guilty knowledge.

Mother nodded to Sister Laurent who had been sitting with them, and the Sister went quietly out. The Sheriff sat down on the bed beside Trillium, but he glanced at Mary Elizabeth.

"She's awake," said Trillium. "She—I suppose she doesn't feel much like talking. But I'll tell you what happened, Sheriff."

"Fine! Just let me ask you first where you were when this tangle with the door took place?"

"In the clock tower!" Trillium whispered. "The Hunters haven't the slightest idea of where we hid the Fleece, because we were almost back here when Alison discovered us; so if you do have to go and look at it, please will you be terribly careful and not give away the hiding place? We'll lose the Hunt if they find it!"

The Sheriff seemed to be thinking this over. Mother knows I'm covering up, Trillium thought. She looks like the sphinx, sitting there on that straight study chair. But even she couldn't know the reason.

"What are you afraid of, Trillium?"

He asked the question so quietly that Trillium very nearly answered. That was how easily she might give herself away! Her eyes fell to his hand, fuzzy, blue veined, close to hers on the spread. If only she could grasp it, cling to it, and pour out the story—but no! No matter what happened. . . .

"The whole thing was scary, Sheriff, sneaking through the dark with nobody knew how many people after you. And we didn't want them to catch us, particularly this year when it's our last Hunt."

"All right, you didn't want to be discovered," Jarvis said patiently. Young girls were far too clever, leading one briskly up to a blank wall and then frisking blithely away. Trillium, he would have sworn on the Bible, was not afraid of the dark; and he was equally certain that she would never tell him. "Now, what did you do, where did you go, what did you hear?—you know, everything."

Trillium wanted nothing in the world less than to relive that awful time in the hall, the slow approach to the tower, the long ascent into the bell chamber; but it had to be done; and as she recounted it she became certain that the awful presence of the Sister had stalked their every step, pausing when they paused, so keenly foreseeing their movements that the ghostly progress was an echo of their own. Except for one time, when she and Liz had been in the alcove and heard the deliberate passing—

"What do you remember?" the Sheriff prompted.

Trillium felt the quiet gray gaze upon her. The man was almost reading her mind!

"Nothing—it's all so confused! I mean I was frightened, but who wouldn't be? I reached the bell chamber, and I set down the muskrat cage and started back down the steps, and—that's all, Sheriff."

"That's all? Didn't you hear any sound on the steps below you?"

"Why—Liz dropped the flashlight, and we couldn't see where we were going and we banged into the door, that is Liz did, and her nose began to bleed! That's all!"

Trillium waited, desperately hoping he would believe her. She had not mentioned Liz crawling up the stairs! If he could guess so much, might he not also guess that something stood in the doorway, cutting off their exit—

There was one escape, and Trillium took it. Lying back upon Helen's pillow, she sobbed, "I can't tell you anything more! Liz thought she heard a spy in the hall, and she started to crawl up the steps to warn me, and I turned on the flashlight and then-then she tumbled down the steps-and we—ran—"

The rest was a mumbled sobbing into the pillow. Sheriff Thatcher, recognizing the withdrawal tactics employed at times by his daughter, stood up shaking his head helplessly, his mouth grim. Mother Theodore was displeased. This was not like Trillium, this pillow-burrowing, crying, childish scene; yet Mother couldn't find it in her heart to reproach the girl.

"Mother?" Mary Elizabeth said suddenly, opening her eyes.

"Yes, dear. How do you feel?"

"I'm all right, Mother. And it's just the way Trillium said, I thought I heard somebody in the hall, and I started up the stairs to warn her, and then she turned on her light and I fell. I guess that's when I broke my rib."

"And then you ran into the door?" the Sheriff asked.

"Yes, sir."

"Had you left it open when you went into the tower?"

"No, sir—" Mary Elizabeth's eyes widened, and she choked back her reply. "I don't remember whether I had left it open or not."

"But it was open when you hit it?"

"Yes, sir."

"Who was in the hall?"

"I don't know, Mr. Thatcher," said Mary Elizabeth truthfully.

Together Mother Theodore and Jarvis Thatcher stood at the foot of the bed, disarmed by Trillium's nervous state and Mary Elizabeth's guilelessness. There was nothing to do but leave, and they left.

The moment the door closed, Trillium sat up.

"They're gone," Mary Elizabeth whispered after an interval.

"Yes, but Laurent will be back."

"I know." Mary Elizabeth pushed herself up on her elbow, gasped, and lay down. "Holy smoke, that hurt! Trill, you didn't mention—I mean, did you see what I saw in the door of the tower room?"

Trillium nodded.

"It wasn't Etienne, was it?"

"No."

"I knew it wasn't, I was just hoping. She was so bundled up and she—Trill, didn't she have man's trousers under her habit?" Mary Elizabeth paused, but she needed no reply to that. "I know she did, so it's the same one I saw by the bayou!"

"Hush, Liz!" Trillium bounded across the small space between the beds. "Oh, listen, Liz, please don't tell about it!"

"Well, I didn't, did I? I had promised to keep mum, and didn't I just get through keeping that promise?"

"I know, you were wonderful, Liz, and sometime I'll explain—"

"Jiggers!" Mary Elizabeth exclaimed.

Sister Laurent came competently in with two medicine glasses just as Trillium's bed spring stopped bouncing under the sudden return of its occupant.

At the foot of the stairs, the Sheriff and Mother Theodore paused.

"She's got to tell me, Mother," Jarvis insisted. The formality of the title meant that he was displeased. And I can't blame him, Mother admitted silently. I'm shielding that girl, perhaps foolishly, but I can't help it, I'm too fond of her—

"If it was anything less important than saving her own life, I'd give in, but I can't let this unholy killer go on with all the protection of secrecy! I'll leave her alone tonight, but tomorrow—"

"Tomorrow you may have a different lead, Jarvis," Mother interrupted calmly. "I don't question your responsibility in the matter, it's simply that I know what kind of girl Trillium is. I honestly believe you couldn't break her down. She has a great sense of honor and loyalty. If the danger was to herself alone, I think she'd tell you, in fact I think she'd have told me before now. And since she hasn't, my guess is that she is protecting someone very dear to her."

"And who would that be?"

"I don't know. An uncle seems to be her guardian."

The Sheriff sighed. For a long, wistful moment Mother waited.

"All right, Emmy," he said, "I'll see if I can come in by the back door. Heaven knows I don't want to torture that poor kid. But I'll tell you what I am going to do, I'm going to get a woman to nurse that young Mary Elizabeth, and I want Trillium to move in with her and stay there! Or maybe you'd better put both the girls in Trillium's room, that way they wouldn't think so much about Helen. Anyway, in she goes. The woman keeps an eye on the two of 'em, understand?"

Mother Theodore winced. Never had she felt unsafe in St. Aurelien's. "Sister Osmond will remain on duty—"

"Sister Osmond! I could march a whole deputation of men in here in broad daylight singing the Anvil Chorus and none of you would ever know it! Sister Osmond's fine for legal entrances, but anybody could get in at any time. No, I'm going to take a few precautions, Emmy, quite a few."

"Who will the woman be, Jarvis?"

"Glory Muckleroy."

"She won't want to leave her children."

"I'll talk her into it."

The Sheriff wheeled and started off along the hall to Sister Osmond's office. From her he would get the uncle's address, in a few minutes a call would be put through to New Orleans and the thorough fingers of the law would begin to root into Trillium's secret.

Mother Theodore walked slowly after the Sheriff, past her own office, past the closed doors leading to the cloister. When she came to the west stairs, she went down into the tunnel and through it to the chapel. The red sanctuary light was the only illumination in the beautiful, vaulted place. It was enough, for Mother did not need to see.

Jarvis Thatcher, having secured the information he needed from Sister Osmond and passed it on to a deputy in Marysville, strode up the stairs again and along to the clock tower. Nothing there, naturally, but a flashlight lying on the floor. Sometimes, he ruminated as he searched, he would like to take Mother by the veil and shake her, but that of course was a purely defensive reaction. Not so darn funny, either. If it hadn't been for the fact that he believed her to be right about Trillium's unshakable loyalty, he would never have agreed to a roundabout stalking of his problem.

When he left the tower, he did not pause again until he came out at the east door. The night air felt good on his face. Pausing for a long breath of it, the Sheriff glanced down to the guesthouse. It had been dark, he was fairly certain, when he drove up; but now, late as it was, a lamp glowed behind a window with an undrawn shade. Archer, Eric, and Torvaldsen. Like a firm of lawyers. A writer, an athlete, and an artist. But were they? Into the office at Marysville had come a good many telegrams, one leading to another, but all leaving gaps in the information he needed. At least one of the gentlemen, it appeared, had not been doing what his public assumed at a certain time in his past. One, and possibly another. But, of course, there would have to be proof.

Standing there, looking over at the lamp in the window, the Sheriff felt his forehead grow clammy in the cold night and his pulse begin to race unevenly, beating out a little Morse code of its own. The three had come to St. Aurelien's at the same time; and shortly after their arrival, one girl had begun to look as if doom stared back at her, and another had been frightened to her death. No proof for it, nothing even to indicate it except that soggy footprint.

Helen had been frightened to death; yet in her life there was no basis for fright like that, fright that could send her running out onto the hyacinths because even their treachery was better than what she ran from; and so the only conclusion could be that the thing she ran from was so terrifying she knew it would be her death, the threat in its appearance rather than its meaning. And who, or what, could it have been?

And what, the question followed naturally, what would be so horrible to Helen that she would run from it into the bayou, and that would also be terrible to Trillium, who had not seen it? Or had she seen it? Not on the night Helen died, because Erminie Wagner had given her an alibi. But tonight?

And why, above all, did Trillium conceal the reason for her fear?

"Glory be!" the Sheriff muttered aloud, dazed as if he had just received a blow in the midriff. But now he had it. Each time the killer had struck, he had come a little nearer to Trillium. Tonight he had almost reached her. The first time he had mistaken Helen for her, tonight Mary Elizabeth had been in the way. Even should he kill mistakenly again, it would make no difference. He would try again.

Jarvis wheeled to stare frantically back at the stone hulk behind him, at the dim-arched cloister walk, the hidden garden, the chapel spire pointing up to where the stars ought to be. Inside that old pile was Kathy, eighty-two Kathys, all infinitely precious. And their safety lay in his hands. What good would it do to install Glory Muckleroy as an unofficial guard? Anyone with the audacity to walk in among the Hunters, even in the inky darkness of the halls, would not be turned back by a single watcher—or by a dozen. And the killer had knowledge that apparently could be pried out of no one: he knew exactly where Trillium and Mary Elizabeth were to be at a given time.

The Sheriff crossed the lawn and his knock on the Muckleroys kitchen door was peremptory. He paid scant attention to Hy's apologies about how he had locked up extra tight tonight on account of the woman and kids being nervous over some wild tale that-there churn man had told. It took a good deal of persuasion to convince Glory that the children would survive the rest of the night without her.

"Listen, what are you afraid of, Glory?" Jarvis asked finally. "Did something scare you tonight? Somebody around the house outside, prowling?"

"Oh, nothin' like that, Sheriff! Just a notion, I guess, seein' all the goings-on over at the convent. Makes you feel spooky, it does. But if you need somebody to sit with that girl that was hurt, well, I guess Hy can make out alone."

The Sheriff, engrossed in his own mission, did not notice that Glory had given in almost too abruptly; and also he thought nothing of it when she called Hy into the pantry, ostensibly to tell him where to find the things for breakfast.

But what she whispered, out of the Sheriff's hearing, was a caution to Hy. "Don't you go spillin' no part o' what that-there churn man said! He saw a killin', mark my words, and maybe even now he's sorry he told us, and we don't want no part of him gettin' into trouble! He's a mean customer, with his winkin' and all. You keep a still tongue in your head, Hy Muckleroy, you hear me?"

"I hear you, Glory, honey." He kissed her. "There, now don't worry none about us. I reckon Addie Pearl an' me's about as good a team as you'd find in double harness."

So Glory accompanied the Sheriff over to the convent and up to Trillium's room where the two girls were now sound asleep. Between the beds Sister Laurent sat, a restful picture of a nun saying her beads.

"Glory," said the Sheriff, drawing her back into the hall and closing the door. "Glory, you're a sort of deputy, you understand? I'm putting you here to keep your eyes open and I want to hear about everything that happens, everything, no matter how unimportant it may seem to you. I have to try it this way, you see, because the girls won't talk to me. Oh, they tell me what floats on the surface, but down underneath there's deep water. That's why I wanted you. They'll talk to you, where they wouldn't either to a Sister or to me."

Glory's troubled blue eyes met the Sheriff's. "All right, Mr.

Thatcher, but I don't like it. Not that I'm scared, but I feel sort of dirty, spyin' on the girls."

Mother Theodore could have told them that all the spying in the world would do no good, but the Sheriff said, "It's the only way to help me, Glory. My daughter's here, too, you know."

A few minutes later, Glory was sitting on the cot the Sisters had provided for her in Trillium's room, and listening to the even breathing of the two she guarded. For Glory was not deluded by the Sheriff's neat explanation about finding out things. She was a guard, and she knew it.

The room was nice, crowded though it was with the extra bed for Mary Elizabeth and the cot for Glory. It had pretty furniture, and there were thin curtains and college banners and a bright rug. Exactly what Addie Pearl would admire to have. But Addie Pearl was safe, and all the nice things wouldn't half make up for it if she had to be scared all the time.

Glory got up and examined the door. It had a good lock, the kind that turns with a knob on the inside and opens with a key from the outside. She turned it, satisfied that she and her charges were secure. She didn't know, of course, that several people had keys— Mother Theodore, Sister Laurent, and Rindy.

Jarvis Thatcher, when he left Glory, paused in the dimly lighted hall and listened. Behind all the closed doors, girls were whispering, frightened; down in the cloister the Sisters, saying good night to one another, would go into their separate cells to keep the Silence until morning. It would be an attentive silence. And all of them, girls and Sisters, would think of the Sheriff as the bulwark between themselves and danger, a great perceptive brain boring straight into the maze, solving their ominous problem. Yet here he stood, his great perceptive brain staggering from one bewildering phase to the next, and his most definitive response was anger—at himself, at the ghostly presence which could apparently come and go at will, unknown and unseen. And the presence lived, undoubtedly, right here on the campus!

Inspired by wrath, the Sheriff tramped down the stairs and out into the night. The lamp still shone from the guesthouse window when he crossed the lawn and knocked at the door. It was opened immediately by Crispin Archer, his thumb marking his place in a book, his horn-rimmed glasses giving him the aspect of a benevolent professor, his hair tousled, and a purple tie loose under his collar.

"Too late for a visit, Mr. Archer?" the Sheriff asked.

"Not at this house. Come in, Sheriff. Eric just got back from disporting himself at the movies. Sit down and we'll wag the chins a spell."

The Sheriff, looking determinedly pleasant, followed his host into the living room. Already, before he was across the threshold, he had been handed Mr. Eric's alibi for the evening. By accident? Possibly.

"I rather expected to see Torvaldsen by the fire, or—oh, of course, he's in bed, eh?" Jarvis seated himself in a large chair.

"No, the old duffer's over at his studio. He'll be plodding along pretty soon, now. You're not here on business tonight, I hope, Sheriff?"

Eric was not in the room, but there were sounds coming from the back regions of the house. Jarvis' gesture made a molehill out of a mountain. "Oh, women's nervousness, Mr. Archer. The veil doesn't seem to make 'em any different, in some ways. The Lord may be watching over them with a special eye, but they still prefer the Sheriff in an emergency."

Archer smiled at this philosophy. "And this was an emergency?"

"Of a sort. Having some kind of Hunt up there tonight, and all the lights were turned off and a girl tangled with a door in the dark. Nothing to it. But Mother thought I'd better look into it, after the other unpleasantness."

"Naturally." Crispin seated himself opposite the Sheriff. "By the way, how are you coming on the—ah—other unpleasantness? Making progress, of course?"

"Certainly! But I'm just about convinced it was some tramp that wandered in. A place like this is honey to a fly." Jarvis nodded toward the book which lay face down on the arm of Archer's chair. "Reading anything good?"

Crispin's air of casual interest did not change. "Byron. He's almost too good to be good, sometimes."

The Sheriff laughed appreciatively, although all he could remember of the great bard was that he had had a game leg and had swum the Dardanelles.

Franz Eric, in pajamas and robe, his hair wet from a shower, appeared in the door.

"Hello, Sheriff. Cris, where did you put my shoeshine outfit when you got through with it this morning?"

"It's still on the back porch."

"Enjoy the movies tonight, did you, Mr. Eric?" Jarvis inquired.

Franz glowered. "Putrid."

"Oh? Well, of course I'm easily entertained, but I thought that motorcycle race was pretty good."

He waited for a reply, and Franz muttered, "Lousy!" before he disappeared. In a moment they heard him slamming around on the porch.

Crispin laughed. "That's life for you, Sheriff! Franz goes hunting entertainment and doesn't get it, and I stay home and it comes to me. Did you see that fellow—what's his name, Burns—goes around demonstrating a churn contraption?"

"Burns and Taffy," said the Sheriff. "Say, I haven't seen him in a month of Sundays. Here today, was he?"

"Put on a show in the barnyard. A fine dog he has."

"Yes, sir, Taffy's a fine dog."

"Burns came along tonight and sat here gabbing with me. You just missed him. Talk about a liar, that fellow's an eighteen-carat Ananias."

The Sheriff chuckled deeply. "That's about right, Mr. Archer. You sized up Theophilus. Is he an old acquaintance of yours?"

"Mine? Lordy, no, where would I meet him? No, he came asking for Tor, and I was alone so I had him come in. A great character."

"A character? That's Theophilus! Supposing you were to use him in one of your books, Mr. Archer, how'd you wind things up for him? Have him live to a ripe old age, a contented old reprobate running his face for a living?"

"Perhaps," said Crispin slowly, giving it every appearance of thought, "perhaps I would, Sheriff. But it would be just as logical to shoot him full of holes in about the tenth chapter."

"And then somebody like me would have to figure out who killed him, eh?" Jarvis arose. "Well, I'll be getting along, not as young as I used to be and I need to get my sleep. I'll step out and say good night to Mr. Eric."

The Sheriff stepped so quickly that he couldn't possibly have heard Mr. Archer's assurance that it wasn't necessary to be so polite. He came out on the back porch just as Mr. Eric slipped a very muddy boot out of sight. He couldn't, however, hide the basin of murky water in which he had been removing the worst of the slime; and the Sheriff glanced at it with a raised eyebrow.

"Some denizen ran me off the road tonight when I was walking back from the village," Franz explained grumpily. "I only got a bootful of mud, but I might have been knocked flat."

"Well, now, that's too bad," the Sheriff purred. "We try to watch out for reckless drivers, my men do, but we sure don't get 'em all. Drop in and see me when you're in town, Eric. I'll make you acquainted with some of the town lads. You must find it pretty quiet here, a young fellow like you."

"I do all right, thanks just the same," Franz rejoined. He picked up the basin of muddy water and tipped it into the darkness.

The Sheriff took himself off with a "Good night."

Doggedly he plodded back to the convent and came into the main corridor. When he had attended to his immediate errand, he would go over to the barnyard and have a chat with Burns. Mother Theodore's office was dark, Sister Osmond's a pale square in the light she always left on. At least they have confidence enough in me to retire to the cloister, he mused, and it's more than I have in myself. I wouldn't retire into a concrete dugout with any feeling of safety. Into the new gymnasium wing he went, then lightly up the stairs to Torvaldsen's studio. At the landing he drew back. Thus far he had not come stealthily, yet even on the bare old stairs the artist had not heard him.

In the barnlike room Tor sat before his easel, so abandoned to his study of something on the drawing board that he was disturbed by neither the sound nor the intuitive sensing of another person's presence. With two other images fresh in his mind, the Sheriff watched him. Tor was not working, merely sitting in the armchair which he had pulled forward to a spot before the heavy easel. A strong light under an opaque shadow threw a glare on the drawing board, and in the reflection the artist's face was a delineation in planes and shadows. Peaceful, that was the description that fitted. The round, plump face was a study in repose. The red-brown eyes were dark in the absence of light, thoughtfully serene, not fixed in a stare upon the drawing board but rather expressing a leisurely seriousness. The mouth was grave, relaxed, with a mobility that promised at any moment to cast aside the solemn mood. It was a face of great simplicity, given character by enjoyment of simple things, by the plain, uncomplicated sorrows which come to every man; no mark of bitterness or rebellion, but instead a deep contentment. And something else. Tor was thinking hard, so engrossed that he had not heard the Sheriff's approach.

His hair was pushed back in a wind-blown shag, and he wore a shirt printed in an oriental design, the collar open. He's a strong old gent, the Sheriff thought, noting the muscular neck. He could pick up a girl and throw her bodily into the bayou. So could Archer—so could Eric. But was the casual, easygoing, negligent Archer a murderer? Or Franz, who could be charming even in a temper?

Or this quiet, contented man who sat lost in thought over—what?

The Sheriff moved, and a board creaked under him. Immediately he stepped forward. Tor turned easily, almost as if he had been expecting a visitor. His smile was affable, guileless, not so expansive as to be irritating. Exactly right.

"I didn't hear you, Mr. Thatcher, come in! I was sitting here meditating. There is so much to work out, and I find little spare time during the day. Push that canvas on to the floor and sit down."

Jarvis unloaded the chair. If he sat where it was, he would be directly behind the easel and therefore unable to see what was pinned to the drawing board. Carelessly he swung the chair over near Tor, seated himself astraddle with his arms folded upon its back.

"Say, quite a place you've got here, Mr. Torvaldsen! You know, I've never seen an artist at work before. A little bit out of my line, but mighty interesting."

He laughed and let his eyes be drawn to the glare of the drawing board. Upon it a pencil sketch was pinned, a dog upon a treadmill and behind him a sea of faces, each face no more than a single line but so expressive that the scene had life. The picture had been hastily done; but up in the right-hand corner there was another sketch which had been lingered over, shaded and highlighted into a perfect portrait.

"Theophilus Burns!" the Sheriff exclaimed. "That's him to the life! How did you ever get him to pose for you?"

"He didn't know he was posing. I sketched him this afternoon while he was giving his demonstration. A wonderful bit of vanishing Americana."

"Old Theophilus!" Jarvis murmured. "It's hard to believe he won't turn around with that laugh of his and say something. Quite a fellow for the fast word, Burns is."

"The sketch is not that well done," Torvaldsen said rather shortly, and he took up the drawing board and disappeared swiftly into the shadows with it. His voice came back, however, genial as ever. "It's a habit with me to take notes, in a manner of speaking, on interesting faces. But this one is hardly worth keeping. Now here's something I think you may like, Sheriff. She posed for me this morning. A beautiful child."

Tor returned and set the study of Nerissa as a red-haired, green-eyed angel in the strong light. The mural was his pet subject, and a nod or two from the Sheriff sufficed to carry him along. But Jarvis' ponderings concerned the pencil sketch about which Tor had protested too much. Was it so insignificant, when it could hold a man spellbound as it had the artist? And what was the errand which had brought the churn man seeking Tor at the guesthouse?

Jarvis listened, managing an air of sober interest remarkable for one whose main appreciation of art was for lone wolves and leaping deer on calendars.

"I see," he nodded in reply to Tor's dissertation on symbolism. "There's a good deal more to a picture than the paint, sir! I'm afraid, though, that I'd have the wrong attitude toward my work, granted the talent in the first place; yes, I'm afraid I couldn't bear to part with a picture after I'd put in all this thought and planning on it. I'd just want to sit and look at it."

Tor shrugged. "Detachment has not been hard for me to learn, Mr. Thatcher. I never have felt that I painted with my lifeblood. While I am painting, the picture occupies my whole mind until I bring it to whatever perfection is possible for me. Then I sell it, the check is in my pocket—finis. I do not indulge in sentimentality."

"The best way, I'm sure," the Sheriff agreed. But Tor indulged in other sentimentalities. Calling himself an old man, for instance. "Well, I mustn't keep you too late, Mr. Torvaldsen. I'll be looking forward to another chat. Oh, by the way, about when did you come up here tonight? Sometime before dark?"

Tor picked up the portrait from the easel, answering absently, "I came up immediately after dinner, about seven o'clock. Why, Sheriff?"

"No reason to ask, really. One of the girls fell down some stairs and ran into a door. I wondered if the commotion had disturbed you."

The artist touched the hair of the portrait and rubbed the wet paint between his fingers. "So something else has happened." Although Jarvis waited, Tor only stood there, rubbing his fingers together, his plump cheeks sagging a little and the oriental figures on the shirt pathetically bright. "Who was it this time, Sheriff?"

"Mary Elizabeth Melville. Cracked a rib, the doctor says. Well, I'll be moving along. . . ."

"Sheriff."

Jarvis stopped in the door. Tor's face was pale now, and he made an obvious effort to speak naturally.

"Was anyone with her?"

"Yes, now you speak of it, there was another girl. Trillium Pierce."

"But she wasn't hurt?"

"No, seems like she wasn't. Well, good night, Mr. Torvaldsen, don't stay up too late! Oh, say, when Burns comes along, show him that picture you made of him and Taffy. He'd be proud!"

The artist's eyes came up to meet the Sheriff's. For only a second could Jarvis read that strange display of remorse—or was it pity?—before the mask fell, and Tor stood rubbing the wet paint between his fingers.

Clattering down the stairs, Jarvis halted on the floor below. The old place echoed like a well, any sound from above would be clearly heard; but there was none. The Sheriff went quietly on down and out to his car in the parking lot.

"Wake up, fella," he said to Pete Jenkins, snoring in the front seat. "Got a chore for you."

Pete was awake on the instant. "Okay, Chief, always on my toes."

"Yeah. Well, tiptoe in there and keep an eye on Torvaldsen. He'll be coming down from his studio any minute now. Escort him home, let him know you're on the job. I'll send somebody out to relieve you in a couple of hours."

Pete departed, and the Sheriff continued on toward his next goal.

But he saw before he reached the barnyard gate that his errand was to be fruitless. The churn man's truck was gone. And now Theophilus Burns, having disappeared, was more than ever intriguing. In three instances he had been mentioned tonight: Hy Muckleroy implied he had scared Glory and the kids with some wild tale; he had visited Archer, asking for Tor, and stayed to furnish Archer with an alibi; and he had been portrayed by Torvaldsen minutely, as if careful study had been made of that unattractive visage.

"Why?" the Sheriff spoke softly aloud. "And where is the connection, if any, between all these why's and the fact that Helen resembled Trillium? Well, we'll hunt up Burns and get a few answers."

Tom, asleep against the fence with Banty tucked under him as she had sheltered Tom himself when he was a chick, craned his neck and gobbled. Jarvis took a quiet departure. As he trudged back to his car, the chapel clock struck twelve.

14

Theophilus Burns was in a hurry. Crouched over the wheel of his ancient truck, he peered into the radius of light moving dimly ahead over the swamp road and heard with dread the commotion of his own passing. Muckleroy would probably have noted the exact hour and could hand the information to that businesslike Mother Whosis, and she would slip her hands up her sleeves and look wise and think—

The churn man cackled. What could she think, except that Mr. Burns had reconsidered his acceptance of her hospitality? She wouldn't know the extent of Mr. Burns's trepidation—had the fear of God knocked into him, so he had—so that even the curiosity to be aroused by his sudden departure seemed preferable to remaining longer on the grounds of St. Aurelien's. And the churn man, by nature and profession, was not one to court curiosity.

When the fine pastures fell behind and long scalp locks of moss began to show more frequently, dangling into the headlights from outstretched arms of live oaks, the churn man sat up straighter on the hard, springless seat. He was away, now. Any time he could stop and let Taffy out of the back and up where he loved to be, on the seat beside his master, his huge head resting where the breeze stroked him continually. Any time, Theophilus thought, but not quite yet. Put a little more distance between himself and what he had seen back there, maybe half the way to Bayou Fleurette. With every chug of the engine, his confidence grew. What had possessed him to tell that old secret to the Muckleroys he would never know, unless it was that redheaded woman with her pretty air of hanging on every word.

"Yeah, her doin's, all of it," the churn man muttered. "Me a born storyteller, and her eatin' it up. Yeah, that was it. Oh, well, no harm done, I've skun out on the double."

No harm, of course. Seven years was a long time, the fellow didn't recognize him, else why hadn't he returned the wave Theophilus sent him? Both of them had kept to themselves in that other era, never meeting more than to pass the time of day. The fellow hadn't been the kind you'd gas with.

By the time the swamp had thickened to mere patches of solid land among vine-clad, hidden waters, Theophilus was his old cocky self. He could look back on the day with his usual bravado and see it as a milestone upon his own particular road. It had been a diplomatic withdrawal only that carried him out the back way and along this trail so seldom traveled that it still held ruts from the spring downpours. He had planned, in the back of his head, to go to Bayou Fleurette, and he was simply taking the shortest route.

The churn man, as he would be the first to admit, was one to see an opportunity long before it walked right up and shook hands with him; and so when an inkling of an idea tapped at his mind, his foot grew lighter on the gas, the old truck coughed to a stop in the middle of the road, and he reached out automatically to shut off the switch. If he had not been so deep in thought, he might have noticed that another engine died with his, and not far back in the darkness. Theophilus also would have admitted that he had a one-track mind, and thus when he was blessed with a new idea, he deliberated with a consistency that balked description. It was long since he had had an idea with the possibilities of this one, and he found it almost overwhelming. There would be no end to its advantages, so far as he could see. It would warm him in the cold, comfort him in tribulation—in short, be a steady and abiding support in his old age. The fellow would have to trust him, since Theophilus had seven years of silence behind him to prove the stillness of his tongue; and so long as the fellow paid, the silence would continue. That wouldn't be difficult to put over.

The churn man opened the door of his truck and stepped out, whistling softly. He would have liked to work off his exultation in shouting and singing like a one-man revival meeting; but he didn't dare. Not that anyone would hear him. The swamp was as still as it ever is, whispering its own secrets.

In the morning, Theophilus decided, he would go back, he could afford the night to think through his beautiful plan. He put his hand to the catch which secured the back doors of the truck. He could hear Taffy moving clumsily inside. With his hand turning the catch, suddenly tense, the churn man stood listening. Those sounds were not all being made by Taffy inside the truck. Soft steps were coming along the road, businesslike steps as if the walker knew exactly where he was going and why.

Theophilus wheeled, flat against the truck. He had forgotten to turn off the lights, and in the pale red of the tail light he saw who it was.

He tried to speak, but the only sound was a feeble croak. All his slimy little ideas of blackmail whirled up madly into his mind. He wanted to shout, to beg, to implore, but he could not speak; the only sound he could manage was that feeble croak.

The gun spoke instead, and the churn man slipped to the ground like a broken toy.

15

Twisting her handkerchief into a rag, Glory Muckleroy sat on the edge of her chair in the visitors' parlor and kept her gaze on three well-draped marble maidens holding up a sort of birdbath in which grew tiny water plants. Glory was tired. The night had been an endless, waking dream in which she had lain staring at the doorknob in the fear that it would turn, then at the window in the hope that it soon would lighten with dawn. The girls had slept deeply, but such oblivion was not for Glory. Lying there, going over the evening, every word and gesture of the churn man became loaded with meaning. And when she came to that conclusion, she would slip away from it, only to return because of one inescapable fact: the man had been terrified when he left the kitchen, and since there was no other reason, then it must have been because he had told that horrible story. And if it had had no connection with the doings at St. Aurelien's, he need not have been afraid. She would tell the Sheriff, she decided, the first moment she could see him in the morning.

And now that she sat before him and knew he had called her in for information on that subject, the significance of it became appalling.

"All right, now, Glory," he said quietly, "neither of us had much sleep last night so we'll take it easy. I'll talk to Hy, but I'd like your story first. Was Burns there when the two girls came into your kitchen last night?"

"Oh, yes, sir, he'd been there maybe an hour by then. We'd had him to supper."

The Sheriff smiled, and Glory relaxed.

"Mr. Burns was real interested in the mushqush," she added. She could see the girls so plainly, Trillium white and scared, Mary Elizabeth thrilled over the possibilities of the evening, the two of them putting the little animal into the cage. Monessa had loved the sparkling crown and wanted to touch it. Everything had been so nice. Except, of course, for Miss Trillium.

"I didn't know it then, but I'd ought to of, because she was scared silly. Miss Trillium, I mean. You could see it plain as the nose on your face." She paused, then continued in an effort to be comforting, "I guess it's been Miss Trillium that was the most scared all the time, only nobody seemed to notice. This morning she's still dopey from that pill the doctor gave her, but every footstep that comes to the door, she starts up, listening. And she won't talk, Mr. Thatcher, not a word."

Jarvis took a turn across the room. Glory, himself, Mother Theodore, Sister Laurent, heaven knew how many more had looked at Trillium and yet not seen her.

He rubbed his eyes wearily. "Now about the Burns fellow, Glory. What did he talk about after the girls left? You said it was just business up till then."

"Yes, and the kids playin' with the dog, real cozy. At first when he started this rigmarole, I didn't take much stock in it because I thought he'd made up a good half of it; but before he got through—!" Glory shivered.

She went straight through the saga of murder as Theophilus Burns had told it, and when she ended, all the Sheriff's weariness had vanished. With its initial mystery, the churn man in his scarlet shirt spun the terrible little tale, slipped over to the door, spoke sharply to Taffy, disappeared into the night.

"And the last thing he said," Glory finished almost in a whisper, "he said he didn't hold with murder 'cause it's never done up clean, there's always tag ends. And then was when he got up sudden and left!"

Tag ends! Into the Sheriff's mind there sprang the old fairy tale of the boy who had gone walking in the forest and come upon an old oak which contained the pot of gold. The boy had tied his yellow scarf around the tree and run for help in claiming his treasure; but when he returned, the leprechauns had tied a yellow scarf around every tree in the forest. It might well be that Theophilus Burns was a mock clue, thus his only importance would be in furnishing Mr. Archer with an alibi. That the churn man, however, had scuttled away into the night because he no longer felt safe at St. Aurelien's was certain, because a gentleman of such roving instincts would not readily give up free board and lodging. Was it the murderer he had seen somewhere on the campus, the smooth-talking killer who had left a witness behind him in the swamp?

"By the way, Glory, you don't know at what hour Burns actually did leave the grounds, do you?"

"No, sir. The kids had the radio on, couldn't hear yourself think."

"Well, we'll find him. He can't have got far in that rickety old truck. I'll have a watch out for him clear to New Orluns. You go back to the girls, Glory. I want to talk to Hy, then I'll—"

"Mr. Thatcher!" Glory broke in. "Listen, Mr. Thatcher, somebody else has got to take over for me. I got to get back to my kids!"

The Sheriff looked at her sorrowfully. "I know, you hate this surveillance job, and so do I. But I have to get to the bottom of the trouble here, Glory, and I can't do it unless people help me. There's nothing we can do for Helen, except to find out why she died; but I honestly believe that we can save Trillium's life. No, I'm not exaggerating. I'd give a year of my own life to know what she's afraid of, but she's too frightened to tell us and so all we can do is to protect her as well as we can and try to find out in some other way. I think she may talk to you, Glory. And you know how grateful you'd be to anyone who looked out for Addie Pearl."

It was not fair, and Jarvis knew it, to appeal to Glory as a mother; but he had reached a point where he couldn't choose. Last night he had done a lot of thinking, and the result was something to make him wonder whether he ever would sleep again.

"I need time," he added, "and I don't dare take it unless I can be moderately certain that Trillium is safe."

Glory, her mouth trembling, stared at the Sheriff.

"I guess you can count on me, Sheriff. Poor little thing, with no mother! I'll be as good to her as I know how."

The Sheriff held out his hand to her. "Thank you, Glory."

But Trillium, lying in her bed with her eyes closed, listening to the soft rustle of papers as Sister Laurent sat correcting freshman English and filling Glory's post, was even then trying to think of a way to circumvent her protectors. In the drowsy intervals of waking, all the separate details of her problem kept jumping up like wild-eyed creatures on a merry-go-round, disappearing in the dizzy circling only to pop around again. There was the coat, but that was not an immediate worry; and with the coat she could pigeonhole her concern for her precious letter, the last she had received. Beside that thought a gargoyle leaped out: what had become of the letter which should have reached her several days ago? It hadn't come because Uncle Henry was out of town and hadn't been there to forward it; yet in the three years she had been at St. Aurelien's, nothing ever had happened to delay the letter before.

So he has it. I have to admit the possibility—it's perfectly logical that he has it. Trillium went back to the initial fact, that Jem had taken the letter, picked it up easily with his own from the mail table. There would be no return address other than Uncle Henry's, nothing to help him there. But so vindictive a person would not admit failure for long. He would try in some other way to find her mother—to strike at Trillium herself—and if I'm not in a position to warn my mother, she'll be in greater danger than ever!

So I'll go to Uncle Henry! The thought flashed in beautiful lightning across the darkness of her dread, and Trillium relaxed. In Uncle Henry's house, with the servants, she would be comparatively safe even though her uncle was not there. Eventually, possibly very soon, Jem would know she had gone and he would follow her, and his departure would leave St. Aurelien's in peace, and Mother Theodore would give up those long vigils in chapel and office. No trace of tragedy would remain, then, except the remembrance of Helen in their prayers.

"I'll do it," she whispered, and sighed to cover the sound. She would sleep for a little while, then plan what to do. It would have to be tonight. . . tonight. . . .

Down in the barnyard, the Sheriff was questioning Hy Muckleroy. Not with any conspicuous gain, he realized, for Hy's story was much the same as Glory's. Corroboration, nevertheless, was good, and there was no shadow of doubt that Theophilus Burns had left because he was scared. Hy, in the tool shed out behind the barn, enjoyed holding forth to the Sheriff, who was seated on a nail keg.

"Well, now for myself, bein' a family man, I don't see this life o' skitin' around; but to some, seems like it's the flavor in the stew."

"Did Burns say where he was bound for when he left here, Hy?"

"No, Sheriff, didn't even say he was leavin'.'"

"Do you know what time he went off in the truck?"

"Seems like I recollect hearin' a engine chuggin' around about, oh, long after Glory left."

"Long? How long?"

"I dunno, I'd been asleep a while. But it mightn't of been him. Lots o' times a tourist gets turned around and lands up in our barn-yard. Don't know this is a dead-end road."

"Glory thinks he went early, soon after he left the kitchen."

"Well, I ain't goin' to cross her."

The Sheriff gave it up. "I've had the highway patrol looking for him since midnight. If he'd taken one of the main roads, they should have found him long before this."

Hy sighted down the strip of tin he was hammering. "Should of, right enough. If 'twas me, I'd begin lookin' somewheres else about now."

"For instance?"

"For instance on our own private li'l ol' road to Bayou Fleurette. He's a great one for dawdlin'. Mebbe he's camped along there."

Hy, seeing the Sheriff's interest, gave a final bang and put aside his hammer. "That-there road ain't much used no more. In the early days the Bayou Fleuretters was mighty busy traipsin' over here. But we don't use it now, only sometimes for a short cut over to the high-way when we're goin' to New Iberia. Here, you step around the barn and I'll show you."

The Sheriff had got up, had gone to the tool shed door, and was looking hard at something outside. Hy went to his side.

Old Sister Etienne, bundled as always now, sat on the apple box with Tom and Banty slopping happily through their pan of sour milk; and beside her, sitting on his haunches with his beautiful head in her lap, was an enormous dog, the dog that Tor had sketched in the strange little picture about which he had been so secretive.

"Taffy!" Hy exclaimed. "Where'd he come from?"

The old Sister, hearing the voice, raised her head timidly.

The Sheriff squatted down beside her, patting the dog. "Say, now, you have a real friend here, Sister! Burns's partner, isn't he? How did he turn up?"

Sister Etienne, afraid to trust her memory, smiled and shook her head. It seemed to her that the churn man had been invited to stay overnight, but she was so often wrong. "He came to visit me," she said.

"The feller wouldn't of left the dog behind," Hy remarked. The Sheriff's frown silenced him. "He just came to you, did he, Sister? No truck around, or anything?"

"No, sir, I didn't hear one. I was sitting with Tom and Banty when he walked up to me. I think he must be hungry. Would it be all right to feed him?"

"Oh, certainly, Sister!"

Sister Etienne set off happily for the convent kitchen. Hy, bent on giving his conclusions before the Sheriff, closed one eye, fixed the other on a far cloud, and burst into speech.

"The way I figure it, Sheriff, there's fummy diddlin' goin' on. That Burns feller thinks the world an' all of his dog. An' still, he turns him loose an' the dog wanders back 'cause he'd took a shine to that old Sister. Looks like he's fixin' to stay, too."

"Not bad, Hy," said the Sheriff. "Now if you'll show me that road, or better still, come with me, we may find out why Taffy came back."

"You betcha, Sheriff. I'll open the pasture gate and you can drive right through."

The road was little more than a cow trail, overgrown until only two dusty furrows remained, and in the dust the fresh track of a car was plainly visible. Jarvis kept his own vehicle astride the ruts. A mile or so from the pasture gate, they rounded a bend and came upon the brilliantly painted truck. The residents of Bayou Fleurette would not have been able to pass this morning, for the flamboyant jitney stood in the middle of the road.

The Sheriff's car rolled to a stop.

"Well, there she is," Hy said unnecessarily.

"Right. Keep on the grass."

The truck, gaudily flaunting "Churn With Burns," was empty; but a few paces on, in a clump of brown weeds, the churn man lay on his back. All the bravado had gone out of him. The red shirt was stained now with an uneven shade, darker than its own dye. His eyes stared straight up into the sun, and in one loosely opened hand lay a curled leaf, dead as the churn man himself.

"Hey, I never thought—I was figurin' on him campin'—"

The disconnected sentences sounded like a gobble even to Hy's own ears. He pulled off his cap and stood clutching it, trying not to look at what was left of last night's arrogant storyteller and yet able to look nowhere else. A fly walked down the churn man's cheek, and the Sheriff pulled out a clean handkerchief and laid it quickly over the face. Kneeling there, he touched the hand that held the leaf. As he had expected, it was very cold.

So I'm too late again, the Sheriff admitted mournfully to himself. Nothing to do now but go back to Marysville, send more telegrams, try to fit the tag ends together. For it was quite apparent now that Theophilus Burns was a tag end, whether or not he had gone to the guesthouse asking for Torvaldsen and remaining to alibi Archer.

He got up, brushed the grass from his trousers, and walked around ahead of the truck. In the dusty ruts there was no trace of tire marks. If the assailant had been in a car, he had come up behind the churn man, not met him on the road. And if he had come up behind him, it meant he had started out from the convent grounds.

The Sheriff walked slowly back until he passed the quiet truck. Now there were tire marks in profusion, made by a new diamond-shaped tread. The churn man's truck was not equipped with new tires.

"Hy, where did you leave your pickup truck last night?"

'The pickup? Why, aside the tool shed, like always when it ain't rainin'. When it rains I run it into the barn."

"Is it beside the tool shed now?"

"Sure. You seen it yourself, Sheriff."

"You bought some new tires for it last summer, didn't you? Diamond tread?"

Hy swallowed hard at a trembling mass that rose in his throat. So that was why Thatcher had been examining the road!

"Sure, I bought 'em. But I—lordy, I didn't come out here—the feller winked at Glory, but I didn't—"

The Sheriff grinned. "Okay, Hy, I didn't think you'd resort to fire-arms. But somebody did, and it's ten to one he followed Burns out here in your truck. Could you tell if it had been moved in the night?"

"Well, come to think of it, Munroe druv it in last night. Mebbe he could tell, mebbe he couldn't. There's a kinda track all beat down from drivin' over it so much, but I dunno, if he'd left it about where Mun did, I guess you wouldn't know."

"How about the gas gauge?"

"Ain't got none."

"Well, you'll have to stay here, Hy, while I phone for my men. Don't mind, do you?"

Hy did mind. The Sheriff left him, a reluctant little human creature guarding another who needed no protection against ordinary disturbances. Turning his car carefully, Jarvis drove back to the convent.

Passing through the barnyard, the Sheriff hailed Mun, who was trundling a wheelbarrow of dirt toward the garden. Together they approached the truck which now stood in early morning shade beside the tool shed.

"Now, this is important, Mun," the Sheriff said. "Take a good look, go all around it before you answer: is that truck exactly as you left it last night?"

Munroe took off his cap, pushed back his cowlick, jammed the cap over his eyes, shoved his hands into his hip pockets, and, with a scowl that emphasized his deep absorption, sauntered around the truck. The verdict, Jarvis saw, would be weighed carefully. When at last Munroe was satisfied, he came back to stand, feet wide apart, beside the Sheriff.

He spat, first. "I tell you, Sheriff, I couldn't rightly say she's been moved from where I put 'er. I was pretty busy at the time, and I ran 'er up there—"

Suddenly Munroe's exaggerated seriousness dropped from him. He leaped to the running board and jerked the gear shift lever.

Jarvis bit back an exclamation. The kid would be spoiling possible fingerprints—only there would be none. This fellow was too clever to leave his trademark behind him.

"Hey, Sheriff, she's in gear! Looky, I don't never leave 'er that way!"

The Sheriff, jumping up beside him, felt the same rush of excitement that shivered through Munroe. "You're sure, Mun? You didn't accidentally leave it in gear?"

"Certain sure! That's one thing Pa's real pertickler about, he says some day I'll leave 'er in second and if she won't start and I have to crank 'er, she'll jump me and mebbe kill me. No, sir, I'd swear any way you like I didn't leave 'er that way!"

"Good! You've helped me, Mun." The Sheriff nodded toward the road he had just traveled. "See, somebody drove this truck up the bayou and shot Theophilus Burns." And the sound Hy had heard, Jarvis knew now, was the killer returning the truck to its parking place.

"You an' Pop found him?"

"Yeah, just now."

"Whillickers!" Mun's fascinated gaze went to the truck, then back to Mr. Thatcher's solemn face. "Listen, Sheriff, I betcha I know something about the guy that druv it!"

"You do? You mean when he left here?"

"No, nothin' like that. But I was readin' in a mechanics magazine, when you drive in hill country you learn to leave your car in gear when you park on a hill. if you park facin' downhill, you put it in reverse, leave 'er in second if you're goin' uphill. Kind of a extra brake. So," Munroe ended proudly, "this jigger musta learned to drive in hills, 'cause we ain't got none around here. He just left the truck this way outa habit."

The Sheriff gave a low whistle. This was the perfect explanation of one very small wisp, yet how did it help to know that the killer had learned to drive in hill country? Archer had been everywhere; Franz was a rover; in his beloved Normandy and Brittany Tor would have found numerous hills.

"Well, say, when you're old enough, I'll know where to find a mighty smart deputy!" Jarvis said confidentially. "I'd appreciate it if you wouldn't mention this to anybody, Mun. I couldn't say how important it may be, except that everything's important right now."

Munroe scowled, endeavoring to maintain a manly indifference. He did, until the Sheriff left him. Then he sat down on the running board of the truck and shook like an aspen in an autumn breeze.

16

Trillium, by late afternoon, knew as well as she could know what her plan must be. Once she had suggested to Glory that she dress and go down to the library to study, but Glory's horrified refusal had been so prompt that Trillium dared not ask again. Out in the halls the Hunters worked furiously against time, searching for the object bearing the crown, growing more fervid with every strike of the old clock. The bells rang, the chanting of the Sisters drifted over from the chapel at appointed hours, everything went on as usual; but underneath the homely, wholesome activity something else lay dormant, the relentless thing that would not be satisfied until murder had been done again.

When Sister Laurent came in to relieve Glory for an hour in the late afternoon, Trillium sat up, stretching, and asked, "Sister, can't I get up and dress? I'm so tired of lying here."

Sister Laurent, being young herself, knew how wearying a bed could become to young muscles, and she had not been over-cautioned by the Sheriff; so she agreed, and Trillium took her robe and went for a shower. The Sister, busily straightening up the room, failed to notice that Trillium had slipped a stub of pencil and a piece of paper into the pocket of her robe.

Glory, coming back, found Trillium neatly dressed in her brown wool, the gold belt buckled smartly, her hair freshly combed and her mouth bright with lipstick. Mary Elizabeth, in a pink bed jacket with a pink bow in her hair, languished upon her pillows and announced that she was hungry enough to eat a horse without cutting it up.

"Your patients are nearly well," Sister Laurent informed Glory. "You don't look very happy about it. Are you so sorry to lose them?"

"No, ma'am!" Glory murmured. A short half hour ago, when she had left, Trillium had been lying with her face to the wall, wide awake but pretending to be asleep. The change to the poised, quietly smiling young lady in the brown wool was too sudden not to be alarming.

"I'm going to pin the crown to our class banner tonight, Glory," she said.

"Oh, but Miss Trillium—"

Sister Laurent departed briskly, and Mary Elizabeth said with complacence, "The Hunters won't find the Fleece, don't you worry, Glory. That nice Mr. Thatcher didn't give us away. Trill is going to have her moment."

"But you aren't well enough, Miss Trillium! I mean, the Sheriff isn't going to think you're well enough—"

Mary Elizabeth laughed, then wailed as she hugged her sore rib; but Trillium gave a little secret smile and opened her chemistry book. Thus far, she had run into no obstacles. In the shower she had written the note for Mother Theodore, and this time there would be no chance for it to fall into the wrong hands because she would take it to the office herself, in the last moment before she left the building, and put it into the drawer of Mother's desk. Her coin purse and her flashlight were in the pocket of the red coat, a bandanna folded in with them. She could walk the mile in to Marysville without anyone being the wiser.

And, if the tiny clipping safe in her coin purse meant what it said, she would have a place to go when she reached Marysville. Planning ahead, that was what counted. Yesterday the clipping had been only a sort of hope, now it was a possibility, tonight it would be a reality. Feeling pathetically proud of her management, she sat pretending to study but thinking it all through again.

"Glory, will you get me a fresh drink of water, please?" Mary Elizabeth asked after a time.

Glory put down her crocheting and went obediently. When she was out of hearing, Mary Elizabeth asked, "Trill, are you going to the assembly?"

"Of course."

"But I don't think Glory will let you!"

Trillium laid down her book. "Liz, tonight means more to me than I can tell you. I—I have to go. You'll help me, won't you?"

"Well—sure, but—sure, if it's that important!"

Mary Elizabeth was deeply impressed, and Trillium went back to her studying with a guilty conscience.

Glory came back and sat down in the little rocker where she had spent so many hours; but now, busy as her hands were, the crocheting ceased to occupy her mind. She didn't like it, Miss Trillium up and dressed; for even though the girl seemed to be concerned with nothing outside of her schoolbooks, her air was that of a bird perched on a delicate twig while the cat crouched on the last limb that would hold his weight. If the bird had any sense he'd fly away, Glory followed the thought. . . .

The crochet hook jabbed her finger as Glory's hands stiffened. It was true. Miss Trillium's face, in the light of the study lamp, was quiet and determined, as if she had made a decision and was calm because of it. What if she had decided to run away?

Remembering all the Sheriff's warnings and her own promises, Glory was thrown into confusion. She had been ready to refuse permission for the girl to leave, but how to deal with this resoluteness she did not know. If only Hy were here to tell her what to do! If the Sheriff would happen along! She could telephone to either of them, but she would have to be gone some time to do it, and Miss Trillium would have her chance to run away.

But there was Mother Theodore, Glory remembered hopefully. If she could get word to Mother, then Mother could warn the Sheriff, and the responsibility would be his. Going back to her pineapple design, Glory felt eased. She would be the most ready to admit that she was not a diplomat. Still, having thought out this neat course for herself, she was equal to the game. She even knew now how she would proceed.

Glory was pleased when she saw Rindy's dark face looming over the tea cart. Rindy was trustable, and it was in the line of duty for her to carry messages. Having seen that the girls were settled with their supper trays, Glory followed Rindy into the hall.

"Rindy, please, will you tell Mother Theodore I'd like to see her, real soon?"

"Yas'm."

"I'm afraid she'll have to come up here. I can't leave."

"Yas'm, only she don' like it, comin' up all them stairs lessen you-all got a pretty nifty because."

If Glory had been less upset she might have wondered why Rindy should take it upon herself to judge the propriety of a request, but such was her state of mind that uncertainty came to her more readily than composure.

"Can't you just say that Miz Muckleroy's got to see her?"

"Yas'm," said Rindy, unconvinced.

"Tell her it's about Miss Trillium! That's all I know myself. Maybe it's just the convocation she's bound for, but there's something! Will you find Mother and tell her?"

"I'll take yo' message, ma'am, sho nuff."

Rindy pushed the tea cart against the wall to await the empty trays. Through the short conversation she had not met Glory's eyes, and as she glided noiselessly to the stairs and down, there was something so cunning about her that she might have been a spy slipping away with deadly information.

"Supper's getting cold, Glory," Mary Elizabeth called.

Glory went in and sat down with her tray. Mary Elizabeth, unaware that she was bridging an awkward moment, chattered on. Trillium ate her supper deliberately, answering sometimes, to all appearances merely a convent girl enduring a quiet hour; but she had not lain down or mussed herself up in any way. At the drop of a hat she could be out and gone.

Rindy, going down the back stairs to the kitchen, was more than pleased with the little incident. Clever, that's what she was. She hadn't promised to speak to Mother, she had promised to pass the word along, and that she would do. She laughed silently.

And there, below her, as if she were sent at the proper time, was Sister Etienne on her way to the Sisters' dining room. Rindy wiped her eyes and choked off her laughter. Old Etienne's timely appearance was a sign, and Rindy believed in signs. Without a second's hesitation she hurried down to intercept the old Sister.

Trillium guessed what had taken place between Rindy and Glory in the hall; but as the half hour became an hour and Mother did not come, she began to wonder. The convent, in this last desperate effort of the Hunt, was in an uproar. Thirty minutes more and the bell would ring out the seniors' victory; the underclassmen, dirty and brokenhearted, would make a rush for the auditorium where the crown would be pinned to the seniors' banner for another year. Through the day the fever had run high, and yet with the falling of dusk and the inevitable dwindling of hours into minutes, delirium was reached, sanity flew out the windows. If Mother Theodore did not receive Glory's message, or even forgot about it, that was hardly to be wondered at. Girls ran everywhere, burrowed into corners that already had been ransacked, even stood on the stairs and sobbed into their shirt sleeves.

"They've done it again!" the cry began, and soon the old halls were a wailing wall for the less valiant who could not take defeat.

In the auditorium the school band began to play, off key with excitement, but with full spirit. Up in the tower the clock struck, and the convent bell clanged the end of the Hunt.

"They didn't find it!" Hilaria shouted at the door, red faced, her hair on end. "Hear that, kids? We're the victors! Hurray for our side!"

"Oh, go away!" Mary Elizabeth snapped. "Don't tell us about your fun! Glory, you'll have to rub my back. Get the alcohol."

Trillium smiled at Hilaria, excusing the invalid. It was not natural, this peevishness, Glory thought, when the halls were alive with exultant seniors sounding like bees at swarming time. Mary Elizabeth should at least share as she could in the general gratification. If only Mother Theodore would come! But there was little hope now until after the convocation. Glory closed the door and went to the closet for the alcohol bottle. But Mary Elizabeth was in a tantrum.

"For Pete's sake, Glory, your hands are like ice! Go on and run some hot water on them!"

Glory was confounded. Her patient never had acted so badly before, turning her face to the wall, grumbling into her pillow.

"Don't mind her, Glory," Trillium said softly, "maybe she has a reason."

Glory cuddled the alcohol bottle. Her hands were always stiff with cold when she was nervous. The washroom was only down the hall, and if she were to leave the door open she could see Miss Trillium if she passed.

"I'll only be a minute!" she promised, and scurried away. Mary Elizabeth bounced upright. "Well, didn't I fix it for you, Trill? Scoot before she gets back!"

Trillium blew her a kiss and snatched her red coat from the closet. "Honestly, honey, I'll never forget this as long as I live!" she declared, and wondered how long that would be.

"Your good coat, Trill?" Mary Elizabeth asked. 'You'll get it filthy up in that old loft. Take your sweater."

"This night will never come again, Liz-baby! 'By, and thanks!"

She looked around the room, as if she were saying good-by to it forever, Mary Elizabeth would report later; and then she was gone.

A few minutes after, Glory returned to stand in the door, her face sickly white when she saw the empty chair by the desk, a thin figure in a faded dress and skimpy sweater which hung in peaks in front, seized with a fear that transferred itself to Mary Elizabeth.

"She's only gone to the convocation, Glory!" the girl protested. "She has to bring the Fleece from the hiding place to the auditorium stage! It's the crowning moment of the Hunt!"

But Glory seemed to be in a sort of stupor. "No," she said, "no, I've got to find Mother, right away quick." She stood mumbling, twisting her hands, unable to distinguish between the different urgencies that shook her—find Mother, find Miss Trillium, get word to the Sheriff. . . .

"*Glory!*" Mary Elizabeth wailed, but it was not enough to stop Glory. The girl was alone in the room, listening to footsteps hurrying away through the hall.

And now Mary Elizabeth was frightened. Trillium had taken her good coat. Why? Why did Glory go chasing after her as if it meant life or death? Mary Elizabeth did not get up to follow. She curled herself into a ball, hugging her sore rib, and lay watching the open door.

Sister Etienne, plodding along the cloister walk from a last visit to Tom and Banty, was bothered about something. Not about what was to happen this evening, for that was all quite clear. The Convent bell was ringing, and she was on her way to the auditorium for the Golden Fleece convocation. But back behind her knowledge of the present there lurked something else, something she ought to be doing, or that she should have done. Roast beef. Supper. Rindy. Rindy had given her a message for Mother—before supper!

"My old head is no good any more," she sighed. She couldn't even recall what Rindy had said. Only desirous. It was a curious word. If someone was desirous, and the message was for Mother, then it must be that one of the girls wished to see Mother in her office. That was right, she remembered now.

Sister Etienne plodded up the steps and in at the east entrance. Everyone passed her, but she didn't mind, she was used to that. She had to stop and rest on the first landing, and by the time she reached the main corridor all the girls were gone. All in the auditorium. Mother, of course, would be there, too. Mother, always kind, would forgive the late delivery of the message.

Shuffling along with her hand on the wall to guide her, Sister Etienne realized abruptly that she was in the wrong corridor. She had turned instead of continuing on straight ahead, and before her was the side stairs, seldom used, which led up to the second-floor dormitories. The second floor. That was where Trillium Pierce and Helen—no, Mary Elizabeth Melville lived, and Addie Pearl had told her that Glory was taking care of them.

That was the message! Trillium wanted to speak with Mother in her office!

Sister Etienne laughed softly. It was so wonderful to remember something. She turned to go back the way she had come; but now there was someone in the hall with her, someone who had come out of one of the little-used rooms on this corridor. The old Sister had not noticed, in her own perpetual twilight, that the hall where she stood was unlighted; but now she saw the figure ahead of her silhouetted against the strong reflection from the main hall. Mother Theodore, of all people! Mother, whom she wished to see before she would again forget the message.

"Mother, if you please—"

The figure halted as if startled.

"Excuse me, Mother, it's Sister Etienne. I have a message for you. Trillium Pierce would like to see you in your office. She's not very well, you know." Sister Etienne paused. When Mother made no answer, she took it as a reproach. "I'm very sorry, Mother, I should have remembered it sooner. If you'll excuse me, I'll not try to carry messages any more. My memory is too poor."

Sister Etienne was trembling by this time. Mother must be gravely displeased when she remained so silent and stiff against the light. The Sister, her eyes humbly on the floor, moved along past the tall figure. Mother's scapular seemed to be divided in a queer way, almost like trouser legs, and her feet appeared to be very large. Sister was not in a position to comment. Mother never had been so severe with her before. And without saying a word, too.

Sister Etienne was so troubled that she very nearly turned into the cloister instead of going on to the auditorium; but the evening would be lonely there and this upset with Mother brought back everything. The lost habit, which never had been found, sprang up before her with dreadful clarity. The doings of the girls would take her mind off it.

When she came into the auditorium, she sat down in a back seat beside another Sister.

"I was afraid you weren't coming, Sister," said Mother Theodore.

Sister Etienne gasped, then peered at the face beside her. It was Mother, there was no doubt of that. But how had she come here so quickly? And if they had met in the hall, why had Mother not seen that she was on her way to the auditorium?

"It was Sister Osmond!" the old Sister exclaimed.

"What was that, Sister?" Mother asked.

Sister Etienne smiled and nodded. She had encountered Sister Osmond in the hall, she was certain of that now. She recalled how big Sister Osmond was. And Sister hadn't spoken because she was miffed when she had not been recognized. So delighted was the old Sister with this explanation that she forgot entirely about the message, and turned to her enjoyment of the girls' performance.

Behind them, Glory Muckleroy slipped into the auditorium. All the Sisters were there, all counterparts of one another from the back. How on earth would she ever tell which was Mother? She couldn't walk right out into the aisle and look into their faces. Wait a minute, and Mother might turn around; but she didn't dare wait long—not long—

Trillium laughed to herself as she ran down the stairs, through the main hall and into the small corridor from which opened the dressing rooms and the stage entrance. It had been so easy to get away! The hurry and bustle reminded her of the night of "Mustardseed," when Helen had called as someone else was calling now.

"Trillium! Has anybody seen Trillium?"

Hilaria tumbled down the stage steps. "Oh, Trill, I didn't dare ask if you'd be here, after the way Liz snapped at me! Are you all right?"

"Fine! And don't be mad at Liz, she was doing it to help me get away. Listen, Hilaria, I want you to come with me for the Fleece!"

Hilaria made a delighted pretense of fainting, and Mercy Harding whispered down the steps, "Is that you, Trill? Okay, go get the Fleece! Everybody's rounded up!"

Silent, hand in hand, Hilaria and Trillium once again traversed the old halls, quiet now as if all noise had died in them and would never be resurrected. It was surprising to Trillium to feel so calm, almost detached from this girl in the brown wool dress who walked along with Hilaria. At the turn into the old passage out of which Sister Etienne had wandered so short a time before, they stopped, and Trillium swung on her coat.

"You go on, Hilaria. I'll stay here—"

"Not on your life! I'm not going up there alone!"

"Honey, don't be foolish! There could be spies still around, and if I'm on guard I can lead them astray."

"There won't be any spies, the Hunt's over!"

"Haven't you heard, Hilaria? We're leaving the hiding place to the juniors in our class will, a secret codicil, so we're still keeping guard."

"I haven't heard about any secret codicil, and I'm the class president," Hilaria retorted promptly. "What is this, dirty politics going on behind my back?"

"Please, don't make things difficult, honey chile!" Trillium begged. If her only chance was to go wrong now, when the open door was not fifty feet away around the turn of the hall.

"The juniors will probably think up their own hiding place any-way next year," said Hilaria. "Come on, let's get it over with before the ghosts walk."

"Hil, if I'd thought you'd be such a goose I wouldn't have chosen you, honestly! I'll go to the head of the stairs, but no farther, and from there I can keep an eye on the tower door and on this hall, too. And when you come back, if I'm gone—"

"Gone! For Pete's sake—"

"If a spy comes by, I'll have to lead her off, won't I? Now go on!"

"Well, I'm carrying a St. Christopher medal, so I may come back alive," Hilaria sighed; and then, thinking to get the frightening er-rand over quickly, she ran up the stairs.

Trillium waited only until her partner was out of sight. Her hand in her pocket told her that the coin purse was there, safe, the note for Mother with it. She tiptoed down the steps to keep her high heels from clicking and back along the corridor. Mother's office was dark, no trace of light showed through the frosted glass of the door; and yet, Trillium, her hand on the knob, halted, listening, her heart leaping in sudden warning. Run, run, her intuition cautioned, don't open the door, escape while you can!

Still, why should she stand there shuddering when all she must do now was to dart into Mother's office and leave the note on the desk? The note was not of extreme importance, asking only that Mother Theodore would not try to find her; but it was the first test of her courage to enter the dark room. She gave the knob a quick turn. The door opened as it should, noiselessly, swinging wide. Well, what did you expect, she thought, and stepped inside.

In a single second she knew she was not alone. Against the gray window a tall blur loomed, the exact silhouette of a nun. Before she could scream, the blur swelled until it blocked out the window, and powerful, purposeful hands caught her by the shoulders. Her choked exclamation was nothing more than a gurgle; and yet, in the blackness of the inner office, someone moved, striking a foot against the metal wastebasket. Then a heavy body struck her assail-ant; he staggered, lost his grip, and Trillium pulled free.

The door was still open behind her, and someone jostled her, escaping. She leaped backward, flew down the hall and out into the night. Who, she wondered in panic, who other than her attacker had been there in the black little room?

The enormous, quiet figure did not linger. A moment after Trillium's departure, it glided along the way she had taken; but when it came to the east door, it continued on down into the ancient passages below the convent. No one would follow into the tunnels.

When Hilaria passed the office, scanning the halls for Trillium, the door was closed and behind the frosted glass the darkness was unbroken. In the auditorium the band was putting all its lung capacity into the "Victory March." The entrance of Hilaria and the Fleece upon the stage touched off a celebration which could be compared only to a political convention when the favorite son has been nominated. The efforts of the band were noticeable only in distended cheeks. Juniors cheered for seniors, seniors cheered for themselves, and everyone else simply cheered in a colossal bedlam.

In the small corridor behind the stage, Mother Theodore, entering hastily, almost stepped upon a senior in blue jeans who was solemnly turning somersaults.

"Diana!"

"Yes, Mother?" The girl came up with flushed face.

"Ask Hilaria to step out here a moment, please."

Mother was provoked, but frightened far more than she was provoked. Glory had shilly-shallied so long that Trillium could be anywhere by now. Mother had overlooked the importance of being chairman of the Fleece committee, she had taken for granted Trillium's acquiescence in remaining away from the convocation. I should have spoken directly to her. . . .

"Hilaria, where is Trillium?"

Hilaria scrambled down the stage steps, and her face was blanched. "She's gone, Mother!"

Mother Theodore swayed against the wall. "But she was with you?"

"Oh, yes, she said she'd wait for me at the landing where she could watch for spies, but she didn't! When I came back she was gone! She'd have had time to lead a spy all over the campus and be back here by now! Mother, what will we do?"

Mother Theodore had read in books that brains sometimes went numb in terrifying circumstances, and always she had turned the page with superior pity, never giving a thought to the possibility that her own well-disciplined member could be capable of such inefficiency; but leaning there against the wall, seeing her own dread reflected in the young face before her, knowing that each separate event of the past days was not separate at all but only another fact of the terrible whole, her thinking powers were numbed. What will we do, Hilaria had asked her, as if there might be something they actually could do to turn the tide away from St. Aurelien's.

Although it seemed to Mother Theodore that she stood there, inarticulate, through a whirligig of time, it was only seconds before self-discipline, the watchword of the convent, provided an instinctive pattern.

"Go back and act in her place, Hilaria, and say nothing at all about Trillium. If the girls ask, say that I am having a talk with her. And no doubt by that time, I will be. Do the best you can, dear."

"Yes, Mother," Hilaria said obediently.

Mother left her, but if she had looked back she would have seen Hilaria's eyes dilated with fright and her hands pressed hard over her mouth. Because Hilaria knew now that all of Trillium's chatter about the secret codicil had been a deliberate ruse to give herself a reason for staying behind. And the minute Hilaria was gone, Trillium had run away!

Just up and went, that was how Glory had put it to Mother Theodore. Like the churn man. Theophilus Burns had up and gone, too. That was the first thought Mother had, an irrelevant one she was certain; yet it indicated that the numbness was lifting. Hurrying to her office, she had time to feel a definite impatience with Glory, even a slight apprehension when she cast ahead to what Jarvis would say.

She opened the door of the outer office quickly, snapped on the light, entered the inner room, and snapped on another light. There was no sign of any disturbance, except that a corner of the rug in the outer office was flipped back as if someone had tripped on it; but Mother had not looked that way.

Mr. Thatcher was at home when her call came. Hearing his clipped response, Mother realized that with his entry this time a new era would open for St. Aurelien's.

There could be no pretense that this was an accident, that Trillium had gone for a walk or strolled into town to the movies. Soon the campus looked like a northern meadow alight with fireflies as the Sheriff's men searched, sending the beams of their flashlights into every corner of the building and grounds. The girls knew, this time, what the hunt meant. Trillium had disappeared, perhaps as Helen had gone, and there was no attempt to mask the efforts to find her. With auto lights burning a hole in the darkness around the bayou, the hyacinths were torn away and the brown water dragged; and when they found nothing, Jarvis Thatcher did not know whether to be relieved or doubly apprehensive. It was possible that something even worse than drowning had happened to Trillium.

The Sheriff's knock upon the door of the guesthouse was peremptory. When Franz Eric answered it, Jarvis pushed past him into the living room and stood scrutinizing the homely scene as if he believed no part of what he saw. In pajamas and dressing gown, Tor sat dozing in a big armchair, his bare feet stretched out on a hassock toward the dying fire. On the davenport, with a multitude of papers laid out carefully on either side of him, Crispin Archer was arranged with a typewriter upon a card table before him. The davenport was low, the table uncomfortably high for typing; yet if one were to judge by the half sheets of paper covered with notes, he had been working in that position for hours.

Archer and Tor turned the same startled countenances to the Sheriff. Tor's feet hit the floor with a thump; Crispin half rose, bumped the card table, and fell back.

So much for you two, the Sheriff thought swiftly, you've shown me you're thunderstruck at my appearance here. As for Eric, he's the guileless schoolboy, caught off his guard a little more than the others but covering it up well. Wearing house slippers, too, fancy Mexican affairs. Strange how each was arrayed to scream out the information that he had been spending a peaceful evening at his own fireside.

The Sheriff stepped past Franz, who remained petrified in the doorway; but it was Franz who spoke first.

"Is she—" he began, and bit his lip.

"Is she what?" the Sheriff asked quietly. "And who, Eric? Who are you so anxious about?"

"Oh, come, Thatcher!" Crispin cut in. "Disaster is written all over you. What's up?"

"My dear sir, sit down," Tor urged. "Franz, get Mr. Thatcher a chair."

"Never mind. I understand from various sources that none of you attended the convocation tonight. During that time another girl disappeared. I must ask each of you to account for your movements from seven o'clock on. Who begins?"

Archer relaxed, at least in body, struck another key or two on the typewriter and pulled out the paper, glanced at what he had written and laid the sheet on one of the piles. Franz remained stiffly where he was, his dark eyes fixed upon Tor; but if the artist received any message, he did it so neatly that the Sheriff was unaware. Tor, feeling with his feet for his slippers, spoke as he would to a child, naturally taking the lead.

"I'll be first, Sheriff. But do sit down. You can't take notes very well standing up."

"I'll trust my memory. At seven o'clock—?"

Tor frowned, thinking deeply. "At seven, let me see. We had just finished dinner, a little late because we sat there talking. I believe it was Franz who asked if either of us was going to the convocation; but you, Cris, you said it was pretty juvenile for us."

The smile was so blatantly that of the good uncle fixing up everything that the Sheriff lost what patience he had.

"You didn't go to the auditorium. What did you do, you yourself?"

"Why, I went up to my studio."

"For an uninterrupted evening, of course?"

"Well, as it happened, no, I stayed about twenty minutes, not more. It was cold up there, dreary, and I began thinking of the warm sunny places I'd been until I worked up a dark-blue mood. I don't indulge myself often, Sheriff. But I managed to dispel any interest I had in my painting, and I came back here."

"That would be before seven-thirty, then?"

"I'm sure of it, although I didn't look at the time."

"And you have been in the house ever since?"

"Yes, Sheriff. I prepared for bed, but the boys came in and I joined them out here."

Exactly what an old codger like you ought to be doing on a cold night, a shade too characteristic, Jarvis reflected. Without a word, he let his inspection fall upon Archer, barricaded behind his table, a cigarette idly in his hand. Archer seemed rather amused, as if this were a staged interlude in which he pleasantly participated.

"I have a heck of an alibi, Sheriff. I did some work in the college library, about eight when I left. I didn't get lonesome, like Tor; it simply happened that I finished what I had to do and came home."

"And that's a heck of an alibi?" Jarvis snapped.

Archer pulled at his cigarette, grinning. "I'm afraid so. You see, I was alone the whole time."

"It's not funny, Cris," Tor reproved.

The Sheriff was becoming wrathful, a state of mind to benefit none of them; and Franz was not helping the situation. He crossed to the fireplace, his back to the room; but Tor, broadside to the others, noticed that his black eyes smoldered, although it was undoubtedly only the reflection of the flames.

"And you, Eric?" the Sheriff prompted.

"I looked in on the convocation, juvenile or not. The kids were having fun."

"Did you stay long?"

"No. One of the Sisters got her eye on me and I knew she'd bring me in and set me down with ceremony in a conspicuous place, so I skun out." He wheeled, defiance and arrogance in his bearing. "I went for a walk through the grounds, out by Pirate Cove, around through the barnyard, and over to the golf links. Alone. I came in about the time Cris did."

"What time?"

"Eight, a quarter to, a quarter after, I don't know."

"Not much concerned with time, are you, Eric?"

The young man shrugged.

Tor, perhaps with an idea of apologizing for these two, pulled himself out of his chair, a dignified figure in spite of rumpled hair and a split shoulder seam in his robe. "Have we helped you at all,

Sheriff? If there is anything else—no? Then let me say that I wish you godspeed in finding Trillium, both for her sake and ours."

The Sheriff's voice was as quiet as Tor's. "I didn't mention who was missing, Torvaldsen. How did you know?"

Instead of being thrown into confusion, the artist smiled. "Did I ever show you the portrait I am painting of her, Sheriff?"

A log fell in the fireplace, and across the room Jarvis' penetrating observation nailed Tor where he was, his profile to the firelight, the only lamp behind him. Another man would have squirmed, but not Torvaldsen. Head back, smiling so that his plump cheeks nearly closed his eyes, he met the Sheriff's stare as if it were a wind in the face.

The Sheriff's departure was as sudden as his entrance, a swift opening and closing of the door and footsteps dropping away into the night.

Cris whipped a piece of paper into his typewriter with a snarl of the roller. "What in the dickens made you say that, Tor?"

"Because it answered his question."

"I mean, how could you name Trillium?"

Tor seemed not to have heard. As if his thoughts had wandered to something of more importance, he sat down, pulled up the legs of his pajamas, and removed his garters.

"It felt like I'd forgotten something," he remarked. Then, with the green garters dangling from his hand, he puttered into his bedroom and closed the door.

Franz and Crispin studied the door for a long minute before Cris wriggled out from behind his table and approached the fire, stretching and yawning. They might have talked, but they didn't; and it was not because there was nothing to say.

"I wish we had the makin's of a drink," Franz said after a while.

"So do I," said Crispin. "I'm dismal and heartsick myself." Parting, they went to their rooms. Tor, they heard through the closed door, was yawning as if he relaxed for sleep.

"I'd be crazy right now if I didn't feel almost convinced she went off of her own accord," Sheriff Thatcher declared to Mother Theodore when, long after midnight, he sat again in her office. "I've alerted all the highway patrols, started inquiries in Marysville; but I had to drag the bayou just to satisfy myself. That story she handed Hilaria Thorns is what points to her going on her own, that and Mary Elizabeth's statement about the coat. She insists that Trillium is careful of her clothes, that she wouldn't take her good coat unless she intended to leave the building. If that young lady had had her flash of intelligence sooner, we might have done something. But Glory insists Trillium was building up to an escape all day." He glanced at Mother apologetically. "Glory did the best she could. She's a smart woman."

"Very," Mother said dryly.

"Oh, now, listen, Emmy—"

"Jarvis, what earthly excuse could she have for not sending word to me that she was worried about Trillium? She wasn't solely responsible, and she knew it!"

"She says she did send you a message."

"I didn't receive it."

"Well, she says she sent it by your maid, Rindy. Now I wonder, did Rindy forget?"

Mother Theodore caught her breath. Rindy, polishing the office door, brushing past the visitors' parlor, flicking impudence from her shifty eyes whenever she was corrected for something. Rindy had been different lately, independently different. That was the core of it! Rindy had been acting as if she didn't care about her job, as if the slightest hint might make her quit it.

"What is it, Emmy?"

"Rindy." Mother laid her hand on the telephone. "Would you like me to get her in here for you, Jarvis?"

When Rindy came in to stand before the Sheriff and Mother Theodore, her eyes downcast and her face the color of cold ashes, she could tell very little. Miss Glory had asked her to give Mother a message, but she was busy in the kitchen and she had forgotten.

"What kind of message?" the Sheriff demanded.

"She said to tell Mother she wanted to see her, but I thought it was just fussin', nothin' important."

"Was it up to you to decide, Rindy?"

The girl stood there, sullen. Not a very intelligent creature, but she worked hard. Without any reason in mind, Jarvis asked another question.

"Rindy, who cleans the guesthouse?"

Rindy's eyes met his, wide, terrified, and her arm came up as if to ward off a blow. But when the eyes fell, the defensive gesture ended in fumbling for a sweater button, and the unguarded reaction was under control.

"Who, Rindy?" Jarvis insisted, watching her closely.

Her tongue traveled around her lips before she answered. "Me, sir, Tuesdays an' Saturdays. They makes their own beds and I does the bathroom every day, but cleanin' only twice a week."

"What made your memory so brief where Mrs. Muckleroy's message was concerned? Was it because she didn't pay you that you forgot?"

Jarvis, seeing her mouth go shut stubbornly, knew he should not have lost his temper. But this girl was responsible, in a sense, for Trillium's disappearance, or worse. He should talk to her, try to worm out of her more information if possible; but he couldn't trust himself to do it now.

"All right, Rindy, you can go. And keep a silent tongue in your head, understand?"

Her eyes rolled until the whites showed, and the Sheriff groaned inwardly. Rindy was afraid of something, too. Of me, he decided, and waved her away.

When the door had closed behind Rindy, Jarvis snapped shut his notebook. "Well, all we're sure of is that Trillium's gone. And one more thing. I'm not kidding myself any more. I admit this killer has some means of getting around so that he's practically immune to detection. Otherwise he wouldn't have dared come in here last night, with kids swarming all over the place. Maybe he's the invisible man." He paused thoughtfully. "This sounds pretty farfetched, Emmy, but could there be a secret tunnel somewhere under the building, some entrance he can use unknown to us?"

Mother Theodore had thought of the same thing once, and she answered readily, "None, Jarvis. Last summer when the tunnels were being repaired I asked the workmen to look out for old forgotten passages. But there are only the three, from the west end of the convent building to the Contemplatives' house, then at a right angle over to the chapel, and turning again to come back to the east end of the building. They make a square, laid directly under the cloister walks."

"Well, it was just an idea." The Sheriff got up wearily. "If Trillium is alive, as I think she is, and turns up at her uncle's house in New Orluns, she won't find anybody home. Only the servants. But I'm trying to locate the uncle, and I've notified the agent at the railroad station in Marysville to keep her there if she shows up. And by the way, your three geniuses are alibiless for the hour between seven and eight, when our little lady was making her getaway. One gent was up in his studio, one alone in the library, one taking a solitary walk; and then they all toddled home and settled down cozy as bugs in a rug, and along comes the bungling old Sheriff and finds 'em there. And meanwhile, of course, Theophilus Burns was getting himself murdered on the road to Bayou Fleurette."

Jarvis walked to the door and opened it. In the harsh overhead light he looked old. "I'm glad we have capital punishment in this state, Emmy," he said softly, and went out and closed the door.

Mother Theodore heard him plod away almost like old Sister Etienne, as if he could see but dimly where he was going. All the lightness had gone out of his step.

17

By dawn, they had not found Trillium. Girls running to the showers stopped to look out of the hall windows, whispering an identical question which required no answer. Although the lawns were deserted and the Cove with its torn hyacinths resigned to the ghost of Dominic You, there was a grimness about that desertion as if the Hunt had merely shifted to other environs because there was no further need to search here. The Sheriff, so the news ran, was still on the premises, probably now eating breakfast from the bountiful tray which Hilaria had seen being carried into the visitors' parlor, gathering his strength for more determined efforts. The girls dressed quickly and hurried to the chapel for Mass, then down to the dining room, assuring one another that they couldn't eat a bite of breakfast. Mother Theodore, wan from her night-long vigil, was able to settle their apprehensions, convince them that the proper course was to continue with classes as usual; and when she left the dining room a line began to form immediately for the cafeteria breakfast trays.

Leaving the chatter in the dining room behind her, Mother Theodore walked slowly through the ancient ground-floor corridor, her mind blank except for the negative thought that she did not want to meet Jarvis Thatcher. All night she had remained in her office, explaining, listening, trying desperately to remember anything that might help in the search, talking frankly of Trillium's fear and bearing with fortitude the concealed exasperation of the Sheriff. She should not have taken it upon herself to conceal so vital a thing as a young girl's terror—yet, on the other hand, she had been uncertain that it was terror. For the past year, almost, Trillium had been slipping around the fact that she might have a vocation; and in the beginning Mother had believed her to be worried, as so many girls were, over taking the step that would cut her off forever from the world. It was a task requiring infinite tact and understanding to separate those with true vocations from the merely convent-struck, and the truest help lay in leaving a girl alone at such a time. So she had left Trillium alone, mistaking entirely the motive force behind her unrest, until the day she had tried to unveil the girl's secret. I should have insisted that she talk with Father Michael, Mother reflected sadly—but now it was too late.

Mother had come to the dark arch of the tunnel leading to the chapel, and she snapped on the lights. The passage offered an exit to the outdoors without the possibility of meeting Jarvis. The little bolted door in the chamber under the chapel would open into privacy for her.

Taking her time, Mother strolled along. History lived in this old place. The stones upon which she walked had been laid by Sisters' hands, an underground burrow in which the community had hidden from cannibal Indians and from the forces of the Spanish butcher with the Irish name. It was relaxing to dwell upon tribulations so old that time had solved them, and so when Mother saw the bundle pushed back upon the ledge she did not think much about it. The electric bulbs were dim and far apart, and the ledge burrowed in twilight between two fixtures. Mother Theodore was ten paces or more away when she paused, the thing she had seen tugging at her consciousness. She looked back. From this distance nothing was discernible. The old stones bulged and receded in heavy shadow. But something had been there, wedged into a break.

"Rindy!" she exclaimed aloud. "If that girl has been hiding dustcloths here. . . !"

Her ire and her curiosity both aroused, Mother Theodore bore back, her keen glance stripping the old walls of their secrets. She had not far to go. In the shadows between the lights, there was a recess in the solid stone, and out of it a brown lump of cloth protruded, exactly the color of a Sister's habit.

Mother halted so abruptly that one foot remained forward for another step. The old place was deathly still, now that her skirts had ceased their rustling; and in that incredible silence Mother stood, staring at the brown protrusion, remembering like a burst of a Fourth of July rocket something Jarvis Thatcher had said: he can come and go at will—in some unexplainable manner he is immune to detection. But why? How? Is he the invisible man?

And now Mother Theodore knew. He was the invisible man, invisible because he wore the garb of a Sister and could be seen and yet not seen because no one would remark him. He could go anywhere if he chose his moment carefully, at twilight, for instance. Mother recoiled in horror. She was jumping to a conclusion, of course, simply because Rindy had stuck a dust-cloth out of sight.

But she was shaking when she went slowly forward, trembling as she put up her hand to touch the bundle. It was large, from the solid feel of it, large enough to be an entire habit tightly rolled.

And there would be a name on it, inside the back of the neck.

That small fact seemed more terrifying than any other. Without having more than touched the cloth, she backed away. At the tunnel entrance she turned off the lights. Anyone who met her as she passed up the stairs saw nothing unusual in her deportment. It was only when the door of the visitors' parlor closed behind her that she gave in to her dread, and—the Sheriff had to put her into a chair and bring a glass of water before she could speak.

When she told him, Jarvis Thatcher sat for a long time staring at the dust motes dancing in the sunshine before the window. Mother had thought he would rush down to the tunnel and drag the bundle out to see for himself; but there he sat, evidently as reluctant as she to know more about this strange discovery.

"What do you do with your worn-out habits, Mother?" he asked finally.

"We burn them. They're blessed, you see."

"How many does each Sister have?"

"Two. An old one, and a good one which she saves for best."

"I take it no one has reported a habit missing?"

"No one, Jarvis."

"But there would be a name on this garment?"

"Yes."

He moved as if he were about to rise, but instead he drooped forward like an old man, his elbows on his knees. It was Mother Theodore who turned her eyes now to the dust motes.

Jarvis spoke painfully. "You see how it was, Emmy? Somehow or other he got hold of the habit, it doesn't matter how, and he saw that it would furnish him with the anonymity he had to have. He's clever, loves the dramatic, so the masquerade had a double appeal. In some way, too, he found out that Trillium was going to try to escape from the convent that night of the play, and so he had to move quickly. He already had the habit. He must have put it on somewhere back of the cloister and was just making his way around to where he expected to meet Trillium when she popped out before him."

"But it wasn't Trillium, it was Helen," Mother said dully.

"I know, but Trillium's twin in the moonlight. He must have been surprised to see her there, but our man's an opportunist, and he—acted."

The Sheriff stood up to leave. "I don't want to touch that habit. I'll go down and take a look at it, but I'm going to leave it where it is. Can you find out who it belongs to?"

Mother nodded.

Jarvis turned, his hand on the door knob. "I'd rather have had it any other way, Emmy. I guess you know that."

Mother kept her eyes on the sunshine. It was not nice to think that a Sister had missed a habit and not told. Whoever had kept the secret would have to face discovery now and explain why she had remained silent. Definitely, it was not nice.

Spurred by a small resentment and a very large curiosity, Mother left the parlor and went to begin a quiet questioning of all the Sisters.

Glory Muckleroy came out of the east entrance and cut across the lawn toward the farmyard and her own house. Absolutely, she was telling herself, she wouldn't take a skinned monkey and stay in that convent another night. Even with the door locked, she hadn't slept a wink. Miss Mary Elizabeth had tossed until midnight, when Glory finally decided to give her a sleeping pill, and now she lay like the dead, with Sister Laurent on guard. On guard, but it hadn't done much good to guard Miss Trillium, Glory reflected bitterly.

She would stay for the day, but when night came she would head for home, Sheriff or no Sheriff. Over the swamp the sky hung low, like a fleecy northern blanket. It would be raining by noon, or sooner.

In the portress' little office the telephone was ringing, a faint whirr cut abruptly when Sister Osmond answered. Within seconds the Sister popped out of her office and hurried along to the visitors' parlor, to knock discreetly. There being no answer, she opened the door and found the parlor empty.

"Oh, dear!" she sighed. It was troubling to receive a call such as she had just had and not be able to tell the Sheriff immediately. She went back to her office and pulled her chair into the doorway where she could see the Sheriff the instant he appeared. Or Mother Theodore. Mother would do as well.

But Mother Theodore was extremely busy that morning.

Classes were going on as usual in the college, as usual so far as routine was concerned. When Mother tapped at each classroom door and drew the Sister out into the hall, there was a stunned silence within instead of the expected buzz of whispering. Her question, always the same, brought always the same answer: the Sister had not lost a habit. But as her tour progressed, Mother gathered several bits of information. Three of the Sisters had received new habits this year, Sisters Raymond, Etienne, and Gaspard. Yet Sister Etienne, the other two remarked, had been seen only once wearing hers, and that was the Sunday before "Mustardseed." Often, in the past week, the other Sisters had come upon her searching through dresser drawers and closets. And she had been worried and jumpy and had given no explanation when they asked what she had lost.

Mother Theodore was far more unhappy than if the culprit had been either of the other Sisters. Coming to Sister Etienne's door, she knocked. No answer. She opened the door. The room was empty, but sniffling sounds came from the closet.

"Sister Etienne?"

The sounds continued. Mother quietly crossed the room and opened the closet door.

Inside, flanked by an old-fashioned long-sleeved nightgown and a heavy black cape, both on hangers, cowered Sister Etienne. Her eyes were tightly shut, and she was crying.

Mother took her gently by the arm and pulled her out. "Sister, you are not afraid of me. I know and I understand everything. You have lost your good new habit, haven't you?"

The old Sister shuddered through a long sob. "Yes, Mother! And when Sister Onfroy mentioned to me that you were asking about habits, I nearly died of shame!"

"Just tell me what happened, how you lost it, and I'll not ask you anything else."

"In the drying yard! I put it there because I'd sponged it out, and it had to dry. I wanted to look neat for the play! And they said I should sponge it, so I did!"

"Who were they, Sister?"

"I don't remember. It must have been Glory."

"And so you couldn't wear it to the play," Mother said, opening a small box on the dresser to bring out a clean handkerchief for Sister Etienne. If Jarvis was right in his reconstruction of that ghastly scene by the Cove, then the habit must have disappeared shortly before the performance began.

"Oh, I didn't mind, Mother, I still had my old one," Sister Etienne replied, smiling, her grief transient as a child's. "And it's quite wearable. I don't need another. I'm very happy with this one."

"And you're sure it was on the night of the play you lost the habit?"

"I couldn't forget that, Mother."

Of course she couldn't. No one could forget the initiation of such misery as Sister Etienne had been enduring.

"You'll have a new habit, Sister," Mother Theodore assured her. "I do not blame you in the least for what happened. The thief was very clever."

Sister Etienne cried again, but now it was with joy, and Mother left her. It had not occurred to Sister to ask whether it was because the habit had been found that Mother knew. She wiped her eyes, blew her nose, and felt her way out through the cloister for an hour with Taffy.

By noon, the telephone had rung again and sent Sister Osmond on another fruitless hunt for the Sheriff. By noon, also, Glory had encountered Rindy in the upper hall and dispatched her with a message to the Sheriff. But Jarvis Thatcher had gone into Marysville on another trail, and when he came back in the later afternoon he was busy.

Confronting Mother Theodore, he was no longer the old school chum who called her "Emmy" with an affectionate air of teasing. He stood with her desk between them, scowling down at the woman with the coif-shadowed face, and there was about him the brisk determination which had inspired the voters to elect him.

"I'm running into too many obstacles, Mother. I've put through a call to Alvard, the uncle, in New Orluns again, but there's only a couple of maids at home. First it was Alvard I couldn't get—out of town on business. Now the missus has gone to her folks in Tennessee and won't be back till after Christmas. And those stubborn maids insist they don't have her address, all they're sure of is Nashville. Poppycock!"

"Colored maids are cautious, Sheriff," Mother reminded him.

"Not that cautious! They're afraid of something, just like everybody else in this case! And I don't blame them, I'm afraid myself. Where is Glory Muckleroy?"

"She has gone home for an hour or so. Sister Laurent is relieving her."

The telephone rang. As Mother listened to Sister Osmond's voice, she closed her eyes.

"Very well, Sister, the Sheriff is here now. I'll tell him." She laid the telephone back in the cradle. "Sister Osmond is receiving mysterious calls, a man asking to speak with Trillium."

"Where's the call from?"

"Through the local exchange. It's not long distance."

The Sheriff grunted. "What about the habit, Mother?"

"I'm afraid it belonged to Sister Etienne. She's—not dependable—"

"Don't try to explain her to me, Emmy. I understand," Jarvis said, his brusque manner gone. "Trouble doesn't become either her or you—but about the habit. I left it where it is. Rats can always tell when something belonging to them has been moved, and they're likely to be frightened away. And I don't want our rat scared off. I want to catch him!"

"Of course, Jarvis," Mother murmured, but her impulse was to cry out that St. Aurelien's was never intended to be a rattrap.

"He has no moral character," the Sheriff continued. "He can't see anything wrong about killing to protect himself. And I think that's what he has done. The only bad feature, as far as he can see, is that he murdered the wrong one and it's put him to no end of trouble to try to catch up with the right one."

"So it's inevitable that he try again," said Mother.

"Unless he's already been successful."

Mother Theodore sat perfectly still, her eyes upon the Sheriff's hands clasped on the back of the chair. Her head ached unbearably. Still, pain was a comfort, in a way. If the life was to ebb out of her beloved convent, it was only fitting that she should feel the pain of its passing. The Sheriff said something about keeping her chin up, and left, but Mother did not move.

Sister Osmond, at her switchboard, was being very definite about the mysterious phone calls.

"Oh, yes, the same man both times, I'm positive, Sheriff. He asks for Trillium Pierce, and when I say she is indisposed, he cuts off the connection."

"Give me an outside line for a minute, Sister, and I'll set a snare for the elusive gentleman."

The telephone exchange in Marysville had a switchboard very nearly as old as the invention of the instrument. Above the usual line-up of plug connections there was a range of tiny trap doors. When a caller took down his receiver, the little lid fell open, revealing the number, while at the same time a buzzer gave a signal. It would be simple for the operator to keep a record of the calls for St. Aurelien's.

"Now, Sister, if this stranger calls again, you just ring Hattie back and she'll tell you where he called from," the Sheriff said. And leaving Sister Osmond in a flush of efficiency, he set off down the hall as if bound on urgent business.

At the east door he came to a stop and stood wondering where to turn next, pulling at his lower lip and catching glimpses of the parking lot through the rain swilling against the window. He had missed the onslaught of the rain, but already every concave surface was brimming. Hy's pickup truck slopped into sight and halted while someone got out on the far side. Bad day for a ride in that old jalopy, the Sheriff mused, no glass in the doors. With the storm slanting out of the east, whoever rode with Hy would certainly be soaked to the skin. The truck shuddered on, and a girl darted toward the entrance. The Sheriff swung the door open for her and let the wind drive it shut once she was inside.

For the girl who had sped in out of the rain was in the nature of a vision. During the past hours he had imagined her in so many states, including the sodden, that this sight of her seemed a fanciful continuation. She was dressed as they had described her. Her eyes were circled from lack of sleep; the small hand grasping the rail was dirty, as one might expect after a sojourn in the swamp. The Sheriff rubbed his forehead, shocked by this evidence of his fatigue. But when he looked again, the girl was still there. Not only was she still there, but she came close and swayed against him, and he steadied her with his arm.

A girl coming down the stairs saw her and screamed.

"None of that!" the Sheriff said sharply. "Trillium is perfectly well and safe, as you can see. You may tell the others, but no foolishness, understand?"

The girl stammered and fled.

With his arm about her gently as if she were Kathy, Jarvis led Trillium to Mother Theodore's office.

Mother received them as if she had been expecting such an event all day. She removed Trillium's wet coat, helped Jarvis put her into the armchair, and telephoned Sister Osmond to order hot coffee.

"Sister has a message for you, Mr. Thatcher," she said as she cradled the phone.

The Sheriff sat down. He had no intention of leaving Mother Theodore to extract the first information from Trillium. The girl lay back, her eyes closed, her hands limp, the right palm and nails pathetically black. Until the coffee came, Jarvis knew, it would be no use to try to question her. Mother would only seize upon the opportunity to banish him. But the girl will talk this time, he decided grimly, and occupied himself with framing questions until the coffee was handed in.

"I want you to drink this, dear," Mother said.

Trillium obeyed, and almost at once the color began to rise in her cheeks.

"Now you're beginning to come alive, Trillium," the Sheriff said. It was an unfortunate idiom. He went on rapidly, "We're entitled to an explanation of where you've been. You have caused us terrible anxiety. My men have been searching for you ever since last night. We dragged the bayou, we hunted everywhere we could think of. Mother Theodore was too worried to rest at all. The least you can do is explain where you went and why."

Trillium's lips quivered, her dark eyes were pleading. "I'm sorry, Sheriff, really I am! But I just—went away. I had to!"

"Why did you have to?"

"Because—I—" The girl began to tremble so that speech was impossible, and Mother Theodore drew a chair close and took her hands.

"Dear, the Sheriff has to find the solution to this quickly, there's very little time. Don't be afraid. Tell us where you went, what you did."

Trillium's head moved heavily against the back of her chair, her dirty little hands lay in Mother's, so pathetic that Jarvis could not bear to look at them. Swamp mud—evidently.

"Trillium," Mother said, "tell us what this is on your hands?"

"Silver polish."

The strange little answer hung between the Sheriff and Mother Theodore, bringing their attention together in bewilderment.

"It's what?" the Sheriff brought out at last.

Suddenly Trillium opened her eyes and sat up, clinging to Mother. "I didn't run away just to cause trouble, Mother. I had to go! Isn't it enough that I'm back now? I won't run away again, I promise!"

"No, Trillium, it isn't enough," the Sheriff said with all the sternness he could command. "There's too much behind it. You'll have to tell me now!"

"But I can't! I can't!" the girl sobbed.

"You can't, when two people have died because of you?"

"Two? Oh, no, not—" She bit back a name, in such terror that only the Sheriff's determination to help her drove him on.

"Not who, Trillium? Speak out! Who did you think might be the next victim?"

The girl was crying uncontrollably, and Mother said in a sick voice, "Jarvis, don't!"

Trillium heard them from a great distance, through darkness breaking in waves around her. She was not afraid any more. The darkness was thick and peaceful, she slipped down and down until it closed gently around her.

When she awoke she was in her own room, lying on her own bed, Mary Elizabeth's bed was gone, and she was alone with Sister Laurent hovering over her.

"Lie still, dear, don't talk."

Trillium's head moved against the pillow. Through her uneasy dreams some terrible question had drummed at her—"Sister!"

"Don't get so excited, child. What is it?"

"Sister, who else has been—been killed?"

"Why, that poor Mr. Burns. I should think it was a hunting accident. He was shot."

The girl's breath came in a long sigh. So it was not her mother, Jem had not slipped away from the campus and found her, defenseless, in whatever place she was hiding!

"Now go to sleep. I'll be right here," the Sister whispered.

Trillium smiled. It was easy to feel safe here with the rain walling the convent off into a world of its own. The grounds would soon be flooded, the guesthouse isolated so that even the purpose of a murderer would be thwarted. Not in days had Trillium felt so contentedly relaxed. Tomorrow's fear, of course, would rise with the new dawn; but tomorrow was too far away to be an immediate worry. How wonderful to be safe enough to sleep!

Jarvis Thatcher had deposited the unconscious Trillium upon her bed and hastened to other business.

"So she's found!" Sister Osmond exclaimed when he came into her office. "Thank the good Lord!"

She plugged in an outside line and waited while the Sheriff called his own office to end the search for Trillium; then she produced a paper upon which was written a telephone number, a name, and an address.

"What time did he call, Sister?"

"Twelve-fifteen, I noticed it exactly, Sheriff."

"And what did he ask?"

"He said may I speak to Trillium Pierce. And I said we couldn't call the girls to the telephone but if he would leave his number I'd give her the message. But he didn't seem to want to leave his number. The operator in Marysville had it for me, and I looked it up in the directory, and there it was: Abe Cohen, furrier."

"Give me that outside line again, Sister?"

His instructions were short. A deputy, Pete Jenkins, was to proceed at once to Mr. Cohen's establishment and ask some pertinent questions.

"He'll call back on that, Sister," said the Sheriff. "When he does, tell him to wait at the office until I get in touch with him."

He tramped away, and Sister Osmond settled into her chair with a sense of great accomplishment.

18

The Sheriff, turning up his collar, stepped out into the downpour. In his car, he remembered, were a pair of rubbers; but in two steps his feet were so thoroughly soaked that to put on rubbers then would be to shut water in instead of to keep it out.

The campus was a pool with large islands of sodden grass, the path to the barnyard a peninsula leading to the slightly higher ground around the buildings. The window of Glory's kitchen showed a light burning within, and the Sheriff headed for it.

Glory opened the door to him.

"I ain't goin' back!" she said instantly. "By night we'll have the Pacific Ocean between here and the convent, and I'm stayin' on my own side!"

The Sheriff, dripping a circle on the kitchen floor, saw that the family were celebrating Glory's return. Hy, with an apron tied around him, was earnestly wiping dishes for Addie Pearl. Baking supplies were set out on the table, and around this nucleus all the younger Muckleroys were ranged from the baby in his high chair to Mun who was stirring up batter in a blue bowl.

Jarvis fastened an eye accusingly upon the dishwiper. "Why didn't you come in with her, Muckleroy? You knew I'd want to talk to you. What was the idea?"

Glory gaped, the children rolled round eyes, and Hy stood in arrested motion, pressing the dish towel against the plate he held.

"Me? Come in with who, Sheriff?"

"With Trillium Pierce!" Jarvis snapped. "I saw the truck stop at the door."

"Miss Trillium? She's back?" Glory said in a sort of squeaky whisper.

"Certainly she's back! Didn't Hy bring her?"

Hy laid down the plate and folded his arms, the dish towel draped around them. "I didn't bring her, Thatcher, and I don't know what call you got to say I did. I come in from the barn when it commenced to rain, and I ain't been out since."

"How about the truck?"

"The truck went, sure 'nuff. But not me. I ain't got no information on that-there girl, and Glory ain't goin' back to sit with her no more. Now, you got any more questions?"

"Yes, who drove the truck if you didn't?"

"Torvaldsen."

"Thanks."

A whisk of rain swept into the kitchen, and the Sheriff was gone.

Glory sat down suddenly, her blue eyes upon her husband in adoration and misgiving, thrilled by his unexpected display of masculine fortitude yet slightly uneasy over this brush with the law. Not often did Hy assert himself. But there he stood, casually disregarding the admiration of his family, rubbing his chin with the dish towel. Later this incident would become known as the "Time Pa Put Thatcher in His Place," but as yet it was too freshly over to be labeled.

Already the short pilings of the guesthouse rose out of a lake. As the Sheriff stepped upon the small porch and knocked, it occurred to him that the rain might be going to accelerate matters in a very special way. If the house became flooded, as it well might here on low ground, there would be no solution other than to move the three occupants into the convent building for the duration of the storm. And if I have to do that, I'll stay with them myself, Mr. Thatcher vowed, and hunched his shoulders again. A dribble ran down his neck, his hat hung around his face, his shoes squished. And his trip to the guesthouse had been in vain for there was no answering movement inside. He stepped off the porch into the water before the door opened behind him.

"Sheriff, come in!" Torvaldsen cried. "I was changing my wet clothes, something you ought to be doing also from the look of you. But come in! You want to know about Trillium?"

"Exactly!"

"I was about to ring you up, Sheriff. I'm too old to go gallivanting around in the wet. The boys aren't in, and we'll have it all to ourselves. Make yourself comfortable by the fire. You won't mind if I do a little painting? It releases my thoughts, like a woman knitting."

A decoy, Jarvis thought wryly; but he skinned off his raincoat and hung it in the little vestibule. Tor's hospitality seemed genuine enough. The artist settled himself with his back to the north window. The small easel held a half-finished picture of a fishing boat on a bayou, the transparent shining surface of the water disclosing murky depths. Like Pirate Cove, when they had torn away the hyacinths, hunting Trillium.

"How did you know where to find her?" the Sheriff asked abruptly, standing before the fire.

The artist finished mixing a shade on his palette, applied it to the canvas, and studied it before he replied. "It was only by chance, Mr. Thatcher. I happened to be in the library one day, reading again the life of Da Vinci—it's wonderful how humble you feel after such an experience."

"Was Trillium there?"

"Yes, at the end of the table I was using. She was reading the local paper, but I didn't notice until she tore out the clipping. Isn't it strange how one notices nothing of another person's movements until they grow furtive about them? There I sat, reading with all my mind and heart, unconscious of the girl until she began to watch the librarian Sister, I forget her name. They all look alike, don't they?"

"Why was she watching the Sister?"

"Because no one is supposed to mar the papers. There's a sign about it, in very nice block lettering. Well, the Sister only sees what is straight ahead of her, on account of the coif, so it was very easy for the girl to nip out the clipping when the Sister's back was turned."

"And did you see what it was she tore out?"

"No. I didn't even think about it until this morning, when I went again to the library for a volume. Then I looked up the paper and found the cut space. It was simple to note what came above and below, and compare it with the paper we take here. Curiosity alone prompted me, Sheriff, I assure you." Tor laid down his brush and slipped his fingers into his vest pocket. "Here is what I cut from our own paper."

Jarvis carried the slip to the window. It was torn from the help wanted section, and it read: Wanted: maid, white, good wages. Mrs. O'Neill, first house beside the stone church, Marysville.

"So you took it into your own hands to investigate," the Sheriff said.

Tor smiled, his head on one side, the brush poised over the already perfect bayou water. "I brought her back, didn't I?"

"Why?"

"Because I'm sorry for her. And I thought she would be safer here."

Safer? When already there had been two attempts made upon her life? The Sheriff took out his wallet and stowed away the little clipping. It was not so important, now that Trillium had been found, but still unworthy to be tossed away.

The Sheriff's silent reception of his answer bothered Tor. He laid down the brush, and with a startling change to a businesslike manner faced the big man on the hearth.

"Mr. Thatcher, I discuss my work with no one, for obvious reasons. The subject of a painting is like the subject of a book, ideas are contagious and the most certain way to secure my own is to lock them in my own mind. But you are not satisfied, and so—"

He made a gesture that took in a wide space. The Sheriff tried to hide his surprise. Tor was wrong, he had been perfectly satisfied—until now. Now he was not.

"There is a good deal of competition for a mural design for a large hotel in the east," Tor resumed. "I am entering a subject, I hope unusual enough to catch the judges' fancy. And the central figure of my painting will be a young girl, not so beautiful as some, but with a marvelously expressive face—yes, Sheriff, Trillium Pierce. I had to use a ruse to get her to pose for me. She was reluctant, Mother Theodore's opposition had to be overcome, I felt compelled to keep my work secret—I even destroyed my correspondence on the subject. Oh, there were all kinds of obstacles. So when she disappeared and I knew where she could be found, I brought her back. A purely selfish motive, Sheriff. I want to win that competition."

Jarvis pursed his lips, nodding again. Tor was an upsetting old character, and no mistake. His explanation could be true. Crispin Archer, however, also admitted to spending some time in the library last night. Had he noted the clipped space in the paper and compared it with another? And had Tor brought Trillium back because he was afraid Archer would get to her first? Either could have the same reason for wanting her again at St. Aurelien's: for her own safety, or for his own convenience in disposing of her.

"What made you so certain Trillium had gone to this address, Torvaldsen?" the Sheriff asked.

"Wasn't it logical? The girl probably has no money. Domestic service would give her board and room, a little money eventually; and a strange kitchen would be the last place in the world a college girl would be hunted, until, of course, her absence was made public. But there had been no hue and cry, the woman would have no suspicion about hiring her. I think she was smart, very smart indeed."

"Then why didn't you get in touch with me when all this burst upon you?"

"I wanted to see her myself, to persuade her gently to return."

"And did you persuade her gently?"

"I used a little strategy. I told the woman I was her uncle, that she had run away from home—you know."

The Sheriff studied the guileless old face. Tor didn't in the least resemble a murderer, but neither had the white-haired gentleman who had fed two wives to the alligators not so long ago. There was no reason why the artist's entire story should not be gospel truth. Tor might have missed the significance of the paper clue immediately; yet here he had been sitting, quietly painting that bottomless bayou, while Trillium cowered in a strange kitchen, jumping at every knock of delivery boy and milkman, afraid for her life; and when the benevolent uncle had come and explained things to

Mrs. O'Neill, Trillium had been polishing the silver, and she had snatched her coat, with the polish still on her hands, and tried to get away—

"Where's Archer?" the Sheriff asked abruptly.

"Over at the college. He has classes all afternoon."

"And Eric?"

"I shouldn't wonder if he's still in the barn. We didn't realize it was raining so hard until we turned to come over—"

"Did Eric go with you to Marysville?"

"No. I let Trillium out at the east door and Franz happened to be there, so I picked him up. He insisted on letting me off here at the house, and taking the truck back to the barn. A nice boy, Franz. Must have had a good mother."

The Sheriff grunted and shrugged himself into his coat. Uncle Tor's brotherly love was a little more than he could stomach in view of recent incidents, and he plunged out into the rain with a sense of relief.

The deluge was now coming in solid sheets. At the pasture gate the cattle stood bawling, belly deep in water. If young Eric was still in the barn, the Sheriff thought without much sympathy, he would probably remain for the duration of the flood.

The convent was on a very slight rise, but even that would soon be inundated. There was no line of demarcation between bayou and lawn. Muskrats, taking refuge from the water, scurried around the old stone walls. As the Sheriff watched, a trapper trudged out of the swamp and began to scatter cut up carrots and turnips from the sack he carried on his back.

"Gotta keep 'em chewin'!" he called to Jarvis. "Them li'l ol' mushqush is muh bread an' butter!"

Inside, Sister Osmond was waiting with a call for the Sheriff.

At about the time the Sheriff was slogging across to the Muckleroy's, Pete Jenkins opened the door of Mr. Cohen's fur shop. A little bell tinkled above his head, and at the signal there was a response in the back room and Mr. Cohen stuck out a hand and then himself.

"Hello," said Pete, "you're the owner, eh?"

Mr. Cohen's soft brown eyes became wary, and he shrugged. "Owner, janitor, fur sewer, designer, what else?"

"I'm a deputy sheriff." Pete showed his badge. "I understand you've put in several calls to Miss Trillium Pierce at the College of St. Aurelien."

Mr. Cohen smiled uncertainly and pulled forward a chair. The shop was so small that there was barely room for two chairs, a table upon which lay several fur pelts, and the rack where a mink coat hung.

"I called her, sure," said the furrier. "You sit down, Mister? She asked me special to keep it for her, but it is mended, the season is short. I figure she should take the coat and wear it."

"What kind of a coat, Mr. Cohen?"

"Right there." He waved toward the rack.

Pete laid his hand on the fur and whistled. "Say, that's quite a piece of fluff, isn't it?"

"It's a very beautiful coat, Sheriff." Pete accepted the promotion with a nod, and Mr. Cohen continued, "I'll tell you about it, I don't want no trouble with the law. Two weeks ago she brought it in and showed me a big tear in the back. I don't say anything, but it looks to me like somebody deliberately tore the skins. She said keep it and she'd come back. Maybe I shouldn't called, I don't know. I got a daughter myself. She got little secrets I don't ask about. This girl I think got little secrets, too, maybe got her coat torn sometime she don't want to tell about."

The furrier stood impassive, his hands clasped over his blue denim apron, his spectacles pushed to his forehead.

"Is that a factory job, Mr. Cohen?"

"Ay, no, no-no-no!" Mr. Cohen caught the hem of the coat, fanning out the beautiful folds. "Special design, specially matched pelts! Made for beauty, no reinforcement because they want it soft and rippling! To me it looks like somebody designed it for one woman."

Pete was puzzled at the furrier's manner. "You mean somebody designed it for Trillium?"

"Yi, no! She is too young for mink! When this coat was made, she would be a little girl! No." He sighed, glancing sideways at Pete.

"Women like that want always mink, nothing else will do. It's a symbol, maybe, a laurel wreath—always it's mink."

"Well!" Pete exclaimed, looking at the coat in a new light. "Well! Could you give me any idea of what this victorious lady might look like?"

"Short, from the length, about a size fourteen."

"Fourteen? Seems to me my wife's been reminding me she's a sixteen. Christmas coming, you know. Fourteen would be smaller, eh?"

"Small, petite, very nice," said Mr. Cohen. "My wife is the fourteen in the height, but the girth, yi-yi, forty-four."

Pete reached for the telephone on the table and gave the number of St. Aurelien's. The Sheriff, said Sister Osmond, would call him back; but Pete was impatient.

"I'll take the coat and give you a receipt for it," he said to the furrier.

So Mr. Cohen, wondering how much trouble he had made for Trillium, trudged into his back room after a box. The memory of the girl had haunted him every time he entered his shop. Now it appeared that his part was finished and he was very much relieved.

"So Trillium is the owner of a mink coat," the Sheriff remarked thoughtfully. The beautiful garment was spread out on the table where the marble maidens usually held up their birdbath, the maidens having been transferred to the floor, and Mr. Thatcher and his deputy were discussing the furrier's tale. "And he thinks the tear was deliberately made, Pete?"

"That's what he said. But why?"

"Well, the furrier had just sent out the coat from storage, she couldn't very well cart it back to him without a reason."

"But why cart it back?"

"Somebody would recognize it."

Pete whistled, a favorite response when he wanted to register surprise. The coat, it seemed, might turn out to be the key to the whole business.

"I wonder why women wear fur coats in the south, Pete?" Jarvis asked, laying his hand on the silky back.

"Well, this one was a laurel wreath, according to Mr. Cohen's notion," Pete answered, and went into the explanation with elaborations of his own.

The result was swiftly forthcoming.

"Pete," the Sheriff snapped, "get along to Sister Osmond's office and have her put in a call to the New Orluns police department. I want to talk to them when she gets 'em."

"Settin' 'em on a trail, Chief?"

"The uncle. He can't have disappeared from the face of the earth! The sight of a uniform might open up those maids. Now scoot and get that call started."

"If the lines are down, it may take a week," Pete said dryly. "Remember our Lowsy-anna storms."

But he departed quickly. In the quiet room the Sheriff sat down to stare for a long time at the lovely, mysterious thing on the table. Had one of the three guests on the campus bought it? Which one? Anyone, if money alone was to be the clue. Each had earned for himself more than the price of the coat in the earlier years of his success. And none was too old or too young to have been the buyer.

19

By evening the bayou waters had met the waters covering the land, as if the Creator had reconsidered and was doing His great act in reverse. There was no longer any question of what must be done with the three gentlemen marooned in the guesthouse.

"I'll have to bring them here," the Sheriff told Mother Theodore. The lights were on in her office where they stood, but it seemed that there was no warmth in the brightness. The windows were flat, gray streams, the noise of the storm threatening as the voice of disaster itself.

"I don't want to do it, Emmy," he continued, "but we can't leave them there with water coming in over the floors, and that's about what will be happening by morning. I'll be here, and Pete, of course. We won't sleep, I promise you."

Mother Theodore regarded the grave face of her friend and read upon it what she dreaded: tonight might come the final attempt. He could not give up, whoever he was; one more murder upon his soul would be no deterrent to this final act which must be done.

Jarvis spoke quietly, and Mother felt his calmness flowing out to her. It steadied her, stiffened her resolution as a patient's is stiffened by confidence in his doctor. "If Sister Laurent will stay with Trillium, she'll be quite safe. For ourselves, Pete and me, we'll camp right in the corridor outside the doors of our guests. If anything should happen, Emmy—well, he can't get away. The flood will do that much for us. We'll catch him."

Mother Theodore smiled faintly. "Do whatever you think best, Jarvis."

"O.K., Emmy."

With a funny little salute, the Sheriff left her.

Pete was waiting for him in the hall, and while Jarvis gave his instructions for the transportation of the three from the guesthouse, Rindy worked her way out of the shadows with her everlasting dustcloth, noiseless on crepe-soled feet, so familiar a part of the convent picture that neither man noticed her. Her head down, crouched on her knees, she dug at a corner in the old molding.

"You get the skiff, then, Pete, and bring them over here," the Sheriff said. "Tor may give you a line about being an old man, unable to come out in the rain, but you tell him he'll drown if he stays there. I'll be in the parlor, call me when you come."

Pete ducked out into the rain, and the Sheriff went toward Sister Osmond's office. If either had looked back, he would have seen Rindy cowering against the wall, clutching the dustcloth to her, her eyes rolling in terror.

But the Sheriff was otherwise occupied, for Sister Osmond had a long-distance call for him. The voice coming over the wire was not the one he had hoped for. It told him, however, a tale which the churn man could have told if he had lived, a story of murder seven years old and of a murderer who never had been discovered.

"Yeah, the dead man's name was Pierce," the voice said. "I wasn't sheriff of this county then, like I am now; if it was in my time I reckon the verdict would have been different. Suicide, they said. I remember it well on account of the woman and the little girl. Pierce was a muskrat trapper, lived on a houseboat back in one of the bayous. Never did make sense to me that he up and shot himself for no reason at all. I'd sure of talked to that swell gent that was swingin' around just before Pierce died."

"Why wasn't he questioned?"

"No evidence. No witnesses. Nobody'd ever really seen him there. Nothing to identify him."

"Except—" The Sheriff's voice died. Now he knew. He didn't need the voice in his ear to confirm it.

"Sure, except for the wife and kid. They knew him. Say, is this connected with your case at St. Aurelien's? There hasn't been much about it in the papers, but I've heard talk."

"Well, I couldn't say. Listen, you can't tell me anything more about this fellow, what kind of a man he was—"

"You've got him there?"

"I've got three of him!"

"Oh?" The voice waited for an explanation, but when none came it continued, "He was pretty smooth with the ladies I guess. Brought Mrs. Pierce all kinds of fripperies."

"Was one of the fripperies a mink coat?"

"Say, yes, my wife said—"

The voice was suddenly blacked out. The Sheriff jiggled the instrument but only a small click came back.

"Line's down," he said.

"Oh, and you hadn't finished!" Sister Osmond exclaimed, fluttering about the switchboard as if she were personally responsible for its non-co-operation.

"I have all I need, Sister. Thanks for getting the call through."

"But now we can't get an answer from the New Orleans police, with the line down!"

Jarvis shook his head wearily and plodded away, muttering something about the sins of the fathers, and he moved as if he hurt in all his bones.

He passed Rindy again in the hall. Shrinking, she looked after him. The landing on the stairs leading down to the basement floor was dark, and she could creep down there and hide until the skiff came back with its unwelcome guests.

"I feels like a motherless child!" she moaned. She would have a long, dreary wait in the dark.

Up in her room, Trillium awoke, plunging into the immediate dread which had come to be her habit; but then she remembered. She was safe tonight. Between her and her nemesis rolled the floodwaters, black and dangerous in the dark. How wonderful it was to lie here safe and drowsy, and know that she could drift off to sleep again without awakening to danger. Yawning, she rolled over and curled herself up for sleep.

"Are you awake, Trillium?" Sister Laurent asked quietly.

"M-m-m, no."

"Dear, I want to run down to the cloister for just a moment. Shall I lock you in?"

"Lock me in."

"I'll be right back."

From far away Trillium heard the rustle of the Sister's departure, the turn of a key in the lock. The study lamp was on, the shade drawn, the rain washing the window, all extremely cozy; yet Trillium found herself wide awake, her eyes on the door just as she used to keep guard. It was being alone that brought back the old apprehension. She was safe, Sister Laurent would open the door in a minute. But her eyes remained upon the knob.

When it began slowly to turn, she thought she must be mistaken. And yet the smooth surface reflected changing light. Pressing a scream back, she watched. There was something so stealthy in the turning of that knob! It wasn't Sister Laurent who was doing it; she would know that the door was locked, she would insert her key and snap it over first, not try the knob, then slip in the key with only the tiniest click.

Urged by her terror to do something, Trillium jumped out of bed; but before she could act further Rindy slid in, pushing the door quickly shut behind her.

"Rindy, you scared me!" Trillium scolded. "What on earth do you mean by sneaking around like this?"

"Miss Tri'ium, you-all gotta come with me! I ain't got time to tell you, but you gotta come! Now!"

"Don't be foolish, Rindy! I'm safe here!"

"Safe?" The girl's dark eyes made an arc of fear. "Ma'am, you-all ain't safe noplace! Come on, Miss Tri'ium, grab some clothes and come!"

Trillium was almost beginning to believe in Rindy's panic. But the flood. . . .

"No'm," Rindy said in a ghastly whisper, "no'm, the flood ain't goin' to protect you-all tonight. He's here!"

A band tightened around Trillium's throat, a hammer pounded in her head. Here!

"Oh, no, Rindy!" she protested. "You're mistaken! He's in the guesthouse—"

"I seen 'em come. Sheriff's man brung 'em all over from there! What you want wear, Miss Tri'ium? You don' hurry, we goin' meet that Sister Laurent!"

That was the prod Trillium needed. She tore a dress out of her closet, gathered whatever else she could see, and thrust her bare feet into shoes.

"Take yo' coat!"

"It's still wet."

"Take it!"

Rindy was the leader, and Trillium obeyed. When Rindy reconnoitered and signaled to her to come, she followed out into the hall and down the back stairs to the old underground passages. She had given no thought to where Rindy might be taking her nor to the possibility that this strange girl might not be trustworthy. The unexpectedness of the new dread, coming upon her out of deep sleep, was numbing. Into the tunnel they went, the same tunnel where Mother Theodore had stood staring at a brown bulge upon a ledge. The habit was still there, but Trillium knew nothing about that. Unquestioning, she kept close on Rindy's heels as they entered the tunnel.

Sister Laurent, coming into the lighted room where the door stood open and the bed was unoccupied, realized instantly that it would do no good to look for Trillium in the washroom or to ask among the other girls along the hall. Down to Mother Theodore's office she hurried, but Mother was not there. The visitors' parlor, however, was filled with voices, deep masculine voices, and Sister Laurent looked in at the door. The Sheriff caught one glimpse of her face and joined her in the hall.

The Sister needed to mention no name. "She's gone, Sheriff! I left for a minute, but I locked her in! She was awake. She said she wasn't afraid to stay alone. And when I came back—she wasn't there!"

Jarvis Thatcher heard her as if he had known all evening that this would happen. It was a relentless progression: the flood, the rising of the waters around the guesthouse until it was impossible to leave the three men there, the transporting of them in the boat from the guesthouse to the convent. In the parlor behind him the Sheriff heard Mother's polite tones informing the three gentlemen of the arrangements for their comfort. Not three gentlemen, Jarvis corrected himself stupidly, two gentlemen and a murderer; and he didn't know which was which.

"Keep this quiet, will you, Sister?" What an effort it was to speak calmly. "You go back to her room and stay there, and if anyone asks for her, say she's asleep and can't be disturbed."

The Sister agreed without a word. Sheriff Thatcher, watching her go, was thankful for convent discipline. Another woman would have been in fits on his shoulder. He re-entered the parlor, hoping desperately that his expression would not sound a trumpet of alarm; but he might have had SOS written all over him without drawing attention because Uncle Tor was expounding upon the differences between equatorial floods and the type doing so thorough a job of deluging the bayou country.

Angrily the Sheriff surveyed the three: Archer debonair and amused, Franz impatient, Tor being the expansive entertainer; and not one of the three, so far as Jarvis had been able to see, had given more than a glance at Trillium's coat thrown carelessly over the back of a chair. Not carelessly, of course. Jarvis had displayed the coat in the hope that the one who knew its history would give himself away. A naïve idea, he knew now. So calculating and accomplished a killer would not be trapped by so simple a device as the sight of something brought up out of the past.

Mother Theodore was apologizing. "A double room and a single, I'm afraid that's the best I can offer, gentlemen. However, there is a connecting bath between the rooms, and I believe you will be quite comfortable."

"Splendid, dear Madam," Tor said. "I'll go in with one of the boys. Either one."

This drew protests from the boys, and they followed Mother out, squabbling amiably, Uncle Tor last and looking like a peddler with his night things rolled into a bundle.

"Pete," said the Sheriff, "there's trouble."

"She's not gone *again?*"

"She is."

Pete jumped off the chair arm where he had been perched. "Chief, the boat!"

For a silent instant the two stared at one another, then with a common impulse they were off, side by side, down the hall to the east door. In the wide rectangle of light thrown from the building, there was only black water spiked with rain. The boat was gone.

"Where can we find another skiff, Pete?"

"No place that I know of. Listen, Chief, I'll wade out around the walls, I might find something."

Rain slapped the floor as Pete went out, and Jarvis returned to the parlor. In a few minutes Mother Theodore would be back, and after all his assurances he would have to tell her that once again Trillium was in danger, that his precautions had been of no avail—

But when the footsteps sounded outside and the door opened, it was Pete who dashed in.

"Chief, I found the boat!"

"And Trillium?"

"No, but I don't think she's tried to leave the building! I waded along close to the east cloister walk, down toward the chapel, and there was the boat, pushed up good on that rise, you know, where the small stairs leads down to the tunnel door? There's another door just like it over under the Contemplatives' house, remember?"

"I remember," Jarvis said. That was the door out of which Helen had come on the night that now seemed years ago. Two weeks, from All Souls' Day to the fourteenth of December!

"The stair well is full of water," Pete said, "but there's this little knoll just outside of it, and that's where the boat is beached."

"Then she's got to be here, somewhere!"

"Sure, Chief, she couldn't wade off in all this flood. So, all we gotta do is find her! And when we do, by golly, I'll set with her on my lap for the rest of the night!"

Mother Theodore, accepting the new development with stifled horror, went quietly from room to room, assuring the girls that although the elements did appear to have got out of hand for the Almighty, the situation was entirely under control for St. Aurelien's. She went into all the shower rooms and the laundry, into Trillium's room where Sister Laurent sat waiting; even into the cloister. Pete had searched the more or less public corners where a manly presence was allowed. But both came back to Jarvis Thatcher with the same news.

"All right, she didn't leave and she isn't here!" the Sheriff summed it up. He sounded wrathful, but that was because there was a good deal of exasperation with himself mixed with his anxiety. "All right," he repeated. Like Sister Gaspard, Mother thought irrelevantly. "We'll have to assume that she didn't get away. So—" Knowing of no way to continue, he stopped.

"Rindy's room is also empty," Mother said quietly.

"Rindy?" Jarvis echoed. Through a long minute he sat transfixed, so obviously racing to the same conclusion Mother had reached that she could follow the process through his facial expression. Incredulity, wonder, then apprehension that had form to it now. "Rindy!" he whispered. Rindy had been deathly afraid when the Sheriff questioned her. Anyone, naturally, would be nervous over giving information to the law; but when he had asked her who had cleaned the guesthouse, Rindy had been struck dumb.

"Is that the colored girl?" Pete asked. "I wasn't looking for her, but I'm positive I didn't see her either."

"No," said Jarvis, "no, you wouldn't see her."

It seemed that there was no more to be said. Three small people, sitting in their separate chairs but sharing the same enormous thoughts; and with them, in the fourth chair with the mink coat, sat another presence, the twisted spirit of murder itself, old as Cain and new as the discovery they were bound to make tonight.

"And she had to get it away from here," the Sheriff mused, his eyes on the rich brown fur; and each of his listeners knew that "she" was Trillium, in tears over what she must do to her beautiful coat. "She didn't dare keep it here because she still was hoping to conceal her identity from—someone."

Jarvis pushed himself up out of his chair, stepped lightly across to lay his hand on the coat with a quick, searching touch. Neither asked what he expected to find. The soft folds rippled as they fell through his fingers, first the bottom of the coat, then the shoulders, every inch of the fronts and pockets, last the wide folds on the sleeves. With the left sleeve in his hand, he paused, feeling it over and over again. His excitement was not suppressed now. Digging into his pocket, he found his penknife and began hastily to cut the sewing that held the lining to the fur. Pete jumped to his side, Mother Theodore sat forward in her chair. She almost wanted to close her eyes, to keep from her knowledge a little longer the first opening of Trillium's secret. But this was foolish. And her eyes would not go shut. They remained upon the Sheriff's hands. They saw the lining open, the many-times-folded paper fall out. They saw the paper being smoothed flat.

And then Pete and Mother Theodore heard the Sheriff read what Trillium's mother had written to her two weeks ago, back in that other era when Pirate Cove was still a picnic spot for the girls on a Sunday afternoon. "No matter what happens, dear, say nothing. My life may depend upon this. Nothing could happen to you there . . . you are safe. . . . I know what he is doing. . . ." But all the time the mother had been hiding from Jem, he had been stalking the daughter in the peaceful confines of St. Aurelien's.

The Sheriff's thumb moved down to cover a short sentence, warning Pete not to read it aloud—"Above all, don't mention this to Mother Theodore." Emmy would take it as a reproach; but it was a tribute, actually, to her forthright attitude toward evil which would prompt her to call in the law and begin her own investigation. Mother would no more tolerate a stained character around her than she would a spot on one of her polished floors. But Trillium's mother knew better than anyone that there was no case against Jem, and could be none until the missing witness was found; and with the same stealth in which Jem had acted, she had gone about her task. She could not have Mother Theodore investigating, drawing attention to that part of the country in which she had hidden her daughter; but she could not know, either, the possible consequences of Trillium's obedience. And Trillium had concurred, blindly, loyally.

And all the time Jem had been here, going smugly about his business, catered to, flattered, given the run of the convent. And yet he had bungled the first try, because Helen looked like Trillium; and the second time Mary Elizabeth had been in the way . . . and there had been a crumpled figure in a red shirt, lying on a roadside with a dead leaf curled into a lifeless hand. The witness Trillium's mother never would find!

Jarvis raised his head slowly and looked across at Mother Theodore. The churn man staring up into the sun from the roadside had been no more inert than she. There was nothing to say to her. She would be blaming herself, naturally, for having brought the three to St. Aurelien's. He would tell her, another time, that the ways of Providence were past finding out. But Emmy knew that. And she knew that a girl's terror and loyalty could be unselfish when the object of both was the person dearest in the world to her.

The Sheriff folded the letter and pushed it deep into his pocket. His excited enthusiasm had vanished. Almost, Pete ruminated, the Chief seemed to be sorry he had found the letter.

The two men left the parlor and went quietly out into the old halls. Mother Theodore, her face shadowed, sat where they had left her.

"Don' nobody know 'bout this place," said Rindy, "nobody but me."

Trillium shivered, although the air was close. The old closet might have been a fruit cellar in the early days, for the shelves were still in place and furnished the only seats for Rindy and herself. A candle was stuck to the floor, its flame standing straight up as if something had frightened it. The walls were of stone, the door so cleverly concealed with thinly split stones that unless one knew where to look it could never be found; but from some hidden ventilator, air came in.

"It's a hideous little place!" Trillium whispered.

"No'm, mebbe it go save yo' life! It a savin' place long 'fore now. When the Injuns come, they gotta have a place to keep the Blessed Sacrament, them ol' Sisters did, and this-here was it."

"How did you get to know about it, Rindy?"

"I found it." Rindy's eyes were veiled. "Miss Tri'ium, you-all do what Rindy say now? You go away in the boat?"

"What boat?"

"You-all knows how to row, don' you?"

"Yes, but in the middle of a flood—"

"The flood's yo' deliverance, Miss Tri'ium! Oh, don' say no! I done played the Judas, but now I's gotta save you-all!"

There was no doubt about Rindy's sincerity, no reason to discount her fear. She sat on the old shelf opposite Trillium, her arms crossed, rocking herself disconsolately. She had betrayed Miss Trillium too often, and for money, exactly as Judas had done. She had seen the man take the letter from New Orleans—that was how it all had started, and he had given her money and had joked about it. He would take it to Miss Trillium, he said. It would give him an excuse to speak to her. He had fallen in love with her, and if Rindy would help him, he could often have little meetings with Miss Trillium in spite of Mother's rules. Rindy thought love was nearly as wonderful as the five-dollar bills she had received for telling him where Miss Trillium was going to be every single day. Luck had been on her side. She had happened along when the girls were practicing their ascent into the tower to hide the Fleece, and she had received ten dollars for that piece of information. It had been a little harder to make certain that Miss Trillium would be at the convocation, but Miz Muckleroy had been of the greatest help, although unknowingly.

And then Miss Trillium had gone into that dark office . . . and Rindy was there, in the inner office, because in the hall she had seen the terrifying big Sister with the trousers showing under the habit, and she had slipped into the first room she came to, taking refuge herself. Shuddering there in the blackness, Rindy's knowledge of the part she had played burst upon her like an explosion.

"I didn' know, Miss Trillium, so he'p me, I didn't Not till he'd got his hands on you," Rindy groaned. "I's been a Judas, but I's he'pin' you-all now, and mebbe he's goin' kill me for doin' it an' I don' care nohow."

"Then you—Rindy, you know who—"

But the girl clutched Trillium's knee across the small space. "No'm, don' ast me! You-all just nev' mind nothin'. You'll go, for Rindy?"

"I haven't any place to go!"

"Out to Miz Muckleroy's house!"

"What good would that do? The Muckleroys will have to come here if the water rises."

"No'm, they won't, they's got a upstairs to go to," Rindy whispered. "And once you-all's outen the way, I'll go to Mist' Thatcher and tell him all I knows! That kiln' man's slick. He'd know somehow where you-all is and he'd—"

Trillium shrank against the old wall, and Rindy's hand flew to shade the candle. Footsteps were coming through the tunnel, quiet, businesslike, steady. They died out of hearing toward the chapel, but Rindy remained still, as if the light of that small flame might fall through solid stone and give them away. In a few minutes the steps returned and went back into the hall that led to the east stairway.

"Not him," Rindy whispered. "They's huntin' you-all now. But the next one's gonna be him. And you-all ain't gonna be here, Miss Tri'ium! I can't have yore blood on mah soul!"

"Don't talk like that!" Trillium whispered harshly.

From then on, they sat in the dark, not speaking.

Pete had been gone a long time, the Sheriff mused uneasily as he sat in the darkness, waiting. He was in a room across the hall from the pair of doors behind which the guests had finally gone to bed, an hour having passed since the last light went out.

He didn't hear Pete until the deputy loomed in the door, his face a paler oval in the darkness. The thick cypress floors were not the kind to creak.

"It's gone," he whispered.

"You're sure you looked on the right ledge?"

"Sure, Chief. The habit's gone—nothing but an empty hole."

They crossed the hall noiselessly, Pete to one of the guest room doors, the Sheriff to the other. Simultaneously they opened the doors, felt for the switch inside, snapped on the lights. But their brisk enterprise died when, having coursed each through his assigned room, they met in the bathroom between.

Because both of the rooms were completely, undeniably empty.

"Couldn't I go now, Rindy?" Trillium whispered.

'Not till they quits huntin' you. We-all gotta have a li'l time."

Trillium stood up. "No, it's now, Rindy. I can't sit here like a trapped animal any longer. I'm going!"

Rindy knew determination when she met it. Cautiously lighting the candle, she helped Trillium into her wet coat. Then she extinguished the light, and the soft blackness wrapped them again.

Rindy pushed the old door. She had oiled the hinges, and it opened soundlessly. But instead of the darkness she expected, there was twilight in the tunnel. Trillium kept back an exclamation. The tunnel had been black when they came down, their way lighted by Rindy's flash. Whoever it was they had heard, he must have turned on the light. But not the tunnel lights, Trillium realized when her panic would allow her to think. This was a reflection from the main hall that ran under the convent building.

They stayed so long there, Trillium close behind Rindy, that they might have grown into their positions of tense watchfulness. There was no sound from the lighted passage. Was someone waiting there, watching, ready to pounce when the old wall opened? For that was how it would appear, Trillium knew. This old closet was perhaps a quarter of the way along the tunnel. Had he seen it already, the slight slant of the wall which made the open door? But that couldn't be. He could see far less than they, for he would be looking out of the light into the darkness.

"I'm going, Rindy," Trillium whispered barely above her breath.

Rindy opened the door enough to let her head out and took a long look toward the arch of the tunnel.

"Nobody there. Come on, Miss Trillium."

They slipped out. It wouldn't take long to reach the far end and the outside door under the chapel. If they could gain the end of the tunnel in safety, they would be free! Trillium started carefully along, keeping tight to the wall, hearing Rindy's cautious progress behind her.

And then, suddenly, she realized that Rindy had stopped moving, and somewhere back of them, toward the main hall, a curious swishing sound had begun. Trillium halted, frozen still. It was a sound she could not identify, sharpened though her mind was with the protective keenness that is nature's gift in danger. Horribly soft, evenly the swish, swish went on.

Regardless of whether she might be heard, Trillium ran for her life into the pitch blackness ahead. Helen had run like that, out on to the hyacinth floor of Pirate Cove.

Old Sister Etienne had been unable to sleep. The flood bothered her, the whine of the wind and the tremendous gurgle of rain in the drainpipes outside her window bothered her. She had always been afraid in flood time, and the only thing that comforted her was a tour through the building to reassure herself once again that the builders of St. Aurelien's knew the menace of creeping waters. And tonight, she thought contentedly, she would have a companion on her trip through the tunnels. She put on her heavy cloak over her long white nightgown and thrust her bare feet into slippers. She didn't need her coif, since she wouldn't be seen; so, with the long cloak brushing the floor and her small white nightcap tied neatly beneath her chin, she set out.

The night lamp was burning in the cloister corridor, plainly lighting the way for the old Sister. Grunting happily, she plodded to the kitchen and opened the door. She had had to take Sister Emery into her confidence concerning the overnight visitor since he had to be bedded before her stove; and Emery had been most co-operative. On her own initiative she had brought a clean old rug from the laundry and spread it for him; and so when Sister Etienne opened the door and called softly, the churn man's dog raised his head, thumped his tail, and came lovingly to her.

Equally content, Sister Etienne and Taffy started along the hall and down the stairs to the tunnels. It was very dark, but the Sister was used to darkness. Moving down, guiding herself by a hand on the rail, she pulled up hard against Taffy, who had stopped on the bottom step. Her surprise held her motionless for a moment, listening, but there was no sound from the black void. They had come down the east stairs, and straight ahead were the hall and the huddle of old rooms, the tunnel leading off to the chapel on her right. Taffy whined, bumping himself against her. She whispered something soothing and felt for the switch, and light leaped up in the hall. There was nothing out of the ordinary to be seen, she thought at first; but then she saw the water, a big black lake of it lying from the step to the tunnel entrance.

"Now where in the world—" she said aloud. But she knew the answer. Somewhere there was a break in the old stones, and a leak was coming in from the saturated world outside.

"We'll get us a broom, dearie, and then we'll open the drain," she said to Taffy. Sister Etienne had often scrubbed the halls in her novice days and she remembered the drain in the middle of the floor where she had so often swept the scrub water. It was a primitive old drain, with only a sort of sinkhole underneath, but it had saved her much labor.

With Taffy in attendance, Sister Etienne toiled up the stairs again to the kitchen to find a broom, leaving the lights on behind her. Once Taffy swung his big head and growled, but at Sister's touch he was quiet. In the darkness of a first-floor room the Sheriff sat, watching and waiting. It would still be a few minutes before he would go across the hall with Pete, snap on the lights, and find the two rooms empty. But if he had known then that the first of the silent departures was taking place, he would have followed the trespasser down to the bottom of the steps, seen him hesitate when he found the passage lighted, heard him splash across to the tunnel and disappear within it, crept after to sense rather than see him vanish in the chapel end of the tunnel.

Very soon, too, he would have seen Sister Etienne and Taffy return, the old Sister carrying a broom. The dog's ears were erect, his eyes wary, and when Sister Etienne sat down to take off her shoes he stood on the step beside her, straining forward, every muscle tense as if he were ready for a leap across and into the black tunnel. They were very quiet. The Sister slipped off her cloak, tied a dishtowel from the kitchen tight around her waist for an apron, rolled up her sleeves, and stepped carefully into the water.

She had to find the drain, first. Leaning over, her hand exploring for the ring in the drain cover, she was paying no attention to the unlighted hall behind her; but the fur on Taffy's neck rose. Something in the tunnel tantalized him, something on the stairs bothered him, and his great head turned uneasily from one direction to the other; but old Etienne, standing with the water cold around her shins, went on contentedly groping for the drain.

She was out of sight for anyone within the tunnel, and when she found the cover at last and pulled it aside, the only indication of her presence was the ensuing swish, swish of her broom as she pushed the water toward the drain. She was doing a good chore here, she knew, because in a little while the water would have risen and soaked the trunks stored in the passage. Mother Theodore would be pleased.

Thinking these thoughts, Sister Etienne was oblivious to the fact that she was almost surrounded by a cunningly quiet company. Someone crouched on the stairs, looking down on her. In the tunnel, Trillium and Rindy stood, transfixed with terror at the swish of her broom on the stones because they could not identify the sound. And there were others.

Abruptly, between strokes of her broom, Sister Etienne heard someone running in the tunnel. Her eyes flashed to the dark arch; but in that second, too many things happened for her to comprehend them all. The first thing she knew was that the lights went out, and with the sudden darkness someone screamed, a terrible, choked, agonizing shriek at the far end of the tunnel. Taffy landed with a bark beside her and rushed off into the tunnel, someone splashed past her, then another clatter on the stairs and the lights went on. As the Sheriff's hand left the switch he dashed across to the tunnel, and out of the tail of his eye he saw that Sister Etienne, clutching her broom, was seated on a trunk, her bare feet in the water, her nightgown splashed but her neat little bonnet still intact.

Later Jarvis might remember and laugh. "Lights! Where is the light switch for the tunnel, Sister?" But without waiting for a reply he ran on. He wouldn't dare touch a switch, anyway, standing in water.

Panting, with Pete neck and neck and then passing him, he pounded on into the gloom of the tunnel. Up ahead the dog was snarling, but the girl had stopped screaming.

"Pull on the door!" Trillium heard Rindy gasp, and she realized then that they were in the small room under the chapel, and that she had been thrown against the outside door by those murderous hands when the dog attacked her assailant. Her throat was aching and raw from the struggle she had made to breathe while she was being choked; but the air revived her. She could hear Rindy's frantic attempts to open the door. Clutching the old latch with both hands, she pulled with all her strength.

It was enough. The instant the door opened, water rushed in, drenching them from head to foot.

"The boat! Come on!" Rindy wheezed.

Scrambling up the steps behind Rindy, Trillium slipped over the little knoll and tumbled into the boat. The oars were there, Rindy caught them up, and without waiting to get them into the locks she pushed the boat out into the water.

In the room they had just left, men were shouting, Taffy barking; and Rindy moaned, "De dog! He ain't got him no mo'!"

She was right. Taffy was barking openmouthed. Even in the blackness of pouring rain, the water was a shade brighter, and when Trillium looked back she saw a black-draped figure struggle to the top of the steps and out into the water.

"He'p me, Miss Tri'ium!" Rindy panted, and shoved her an oar. "Don' drap it!"

Trillium was not used to rowing, but she pushed the oar into the water. Unevenly, because they were not pulling together, the boat started a crazy course out into deeper water. Behind it the black figure splashed, stumbled, always making more progress than the boat.

The Sheriff shouted from the knoll, Pete yelled as he plunged into the water, two more voices joined them. They'll never save us, Trillium thought, it isn't meant to be. There's no secrecy about this, but he doesn't care. It's vengeance now.

"Rindy, hurry!" she sobbed, glancing back over her shoulder.

He was coming steadily on, relentlessly, falling but always regaining his balance. Nothing could stop him. He would reach the boat, those hands would close around her throat again and he would fling her away from him into the water and she would die like Helen.

Now no one shouted, the only sounds were the rain splashing forever around them, the struggle of that black figure drawing closer, the frantic slop of the paddles pulling against each other. Water ran down Trillium's face like tears, but she was not crying. There was no time.

And then Rindy screamed. Trillium plunged against her, dropping her oar. The black giant was beside the boat, a hand coming out to grasp the side. The water was deep here, up to his shoulders, and as the hand shot out he stumbled. In the fraction of a second while he fought his way up, Rindy pulled away.

"He's going to upset the boat!" Pete shouted.

His voice told Trillium where he was, too far off to help them, and the Sheriff was behind him.

Through the splashing of the rain, then, another sound came, a puffing, wheezing breath, strong and steady, and a dark spot appeared.

"Taffy!" Rindy screeched. "Git him!"

Taffy, swimming easily, advanced as steadily as that other figure had come a minute before. The man shouted, and even though he needed his wind, Taffy growled. What happened then was a wild furor in darkness and rain. While the dog struggled against a fighter who was hampered by the long garment he wore, the Sheriff and Pete reached them.

"Get away, Rindy!" the Sheriff shouted.

There was no pursuer to follow them as the girl obeyed, weaving an eccentric course across the water to pull up at the east door of the convent.

The storm was so fierce that Mother Theodore had heard almost nothing of the commotion, and apparently neither girls nor Sisters had been awakened. Alone, with her face pressed against the glass, Mother waited at the door. When she saw the boat emerge out of the rain, carrying two bedraggled and hysterical girls, she realized that this was the culmination of all that had happened at St. Aurelien's; but how it had come about, she did not yet know.

20

Mother Theodore sat in her parlor, the front of her habit still damp from the wet clothes of the girls she had brought upstairs and turned over to Sister Laurent. Every light in the room was burning, not a shadow lurked anywhere except on Mother's face under the coif. Two weeks ago she had sat in the very chair she occupied now, watching for this same door to open; and she had heard the whistle of the train as it pulled into Marysville and insisted to herself that it boded nothing ill for St. Aurelien's. Strange, her apprehension that day, and quite unreasoning. Unreasoning also her dread of the coming moment when the door would open again. Scarcely an hour ago, the end of that terrible interval out in the dark and rain had come about, only a few minutes since the Sheriff had sat with her here and told her that all the trouble was over. The fellow had confessed everything, once they had him, Jarvis had said—stealing the habit from the drying yard, his mistaken identification of Helen as Trillium out by Pirate Cove, his belief that Trillium had known him and his resulting determination to eliminate her, his theft of Trillium's letter so that he knew also of her mother's whereabouts—even the churn man's murder. Everything, tied up neatly in the Sheriff's notebook.

"And he wants to see you," Jarvis had said. "I don't know why. There's no reason in the world why you should grant him the slightest consideration."

Mother had thought it over and then said quietly to her old friend, "I'll see him, Jarvis. What I begin, I like to finish. Perhaps he feels the same."

"Well, just as you please, Emmy," he had replied.

And now the door was slowly opening, just at it had opened on that other day, except that instead of Sister Osmond's politely formal presence there were Sheriff Thatcher and Pete moving grimly into the doorway behind the visitor.

He came into the room much as he had on the first occasion, his hands apparently clasped behind him. The handcuffs, therefore, were no more visible than if he did not wear them at all. And he smiled, nonchalant.

"It's good of you to receive me, Mother."

"Good morning, sir." Mother Theodore remained in her chair, her hands folded under her scapular. It was shocking, quite a little sickening, to see him so undaunted, boasting still the hint of swagger his public found so pleasing. Mother's eyes slipped down his arms. "I had thought to see you rather subdued, to say the least," she added.

"Already doing penance for my sins?" He shrugged. "Hardly. If your mistakes are written in the stars, what can you do about it?"

"Sir, do you call murder a mistake?"

"That depends upon the circumstances. Let's say I took a gamble, and lost. Fate had her tongue in her cheek."

Mother Theodore stiffened in her chair, and the Sheriff's scrutiny became sharper. There was nothing, however, to alarm the law. It was simply that Mother had come at last upon the reason for this man's unfathomable determination, his cool detachment that seemed to stem from a philosophizing turn of mind. And the reason was so unbelievable, considering the intelligence of the man, that Mother would have been less aroused if he had suddenly sprung up wearing horns and a tail.

"Surely you do not pretend to be a fatalist, sir?" she asked as sternly as she could. "You know there is no such entity as Fate! Divine Providence is quite another matter."

Whether the question itself delighted him, or whether it was rather juvenile glee over having kept his paganism secret, Mother could not tell. If he cared to gloat, he might do so with impunity. She had accepted him on what she considered good recommendations; to all intents and purposes she had approved him and his philosophy—oh, he had deceived her well! That he had deceived also the poetess and the friends who recommended him was of small comfort now. Upon Mother the final decision had rested; and her decision had very nearly wrecked the convent's future.

"Why quibble over a name, Mother?" he asked as if the question amused him. "Whether you call her Fate or something else, she is an inconsiderate mistress. That was why I asked to see you, to offer my personal apology. Not that it's up to me to apologize. But I respect you, Mother, and resent the fact that I had to institute this unpleasantness at St. Aurelien's."

Mother Theodore leaned back in her chair. She would not let him upset her with his cool, stupid arrogance. Calm to the point of frigidity herself, she let a long pause tighten between them before she spoke again.

"You surprise me, sir. I would expect a man of your brilliance to look for a better law to live by than the law that governs the inorganic world."

She had startled him, she saw; and she continued. "A lump of coal becomes coal because it must be subject to an unchangeable law. An object unsupported in the air falls to the ground because it cannot resist the law of gravity. That is fatalism, sir, the blind service of a higher power. These things must be what they are, act as they do. They have no choice. But man is free to choose the good or the evil. You, sir, have sought a mental refuge in a lower world to which you do not belong. You have brought yourself down from the place of the intellectual master to that of the vegetable servant!—You—you are like a lion seeking refuge in a bird cage!" Mother checked herself suddenly, and her voice fell to a low, soft tone, "I am sorry for you, sir, but it is too soon to despair. Even now, in the time left to you, all the evil of your life may be forgiven, the wickedness satisfied for. You may yet surrender to the love of a good God."

She never had liked him; yet now, when he stood before her still charming, handsome, wasted because of his strange beliefs, the pity she felt was a personal thing, acute and poignant.

The man's smile was gone. He even had the humility to address his next words to the carpet. "You must know, Mother, that you couldn't have prevented any of what has happened. It's all too old and rooted in too much that's past. A good woman like you might torture herself—later, I mean—because she didn't pray for me in time, or do so many of the things that she would consider might have saved me. I'll think of what you have said to me, Mother, and if I should feel any spark of repentance, you'll know. They're very good, I've heard, about delivering last messages."

He turned quickly, and the Sheriff and Pete stepped apart in the doorway; but as each took an arm, he looked back with a semblance of his old amused mockery. "Oh, Mother, will you give my thanks to Sister Etienne for the use of her habit? It was a very bad fit, but it served the purpose. Good-by, Mother."

"Good-by, Mr. Archer."

She said it steadily.

With a nod of farewell, he stepped into the gloom of the old hall, and the three were instantly gone, the sounds of their quick departure coming back to her. They could not take him away yet. The rain had stopped, but the road would still be flooded and treacherous in the dark. They would have to wait for daylight.

She slumped suddenly in her chair and laid her hand across her eyes.

"Down where we said, Chief?" Pete asked as they passed through the hall.

"Yeah."

The three disappeared down the stairs, now brightly lighted, where they had crept in darkness after a killer so short a time before.

A half hour later, when the pecans behind the guesthouse were beginning to blacken against the first gray dawn, Sheriff Thatcher looked into Mother Theodore's parlor. As he had feared, she was sitting exactly as they had left her when he and Pete took Archer away.

"All right, Emmy, come on," he said. When she only looked at him, silent, he added, "We're going down to the kitchen. Nothing like a cup of hot coffee to put the heart into you."

Mother smiled and glanced at the clock. "I'll watch you drink your coffee, Jarvis."

So it happened that the Sheriff and Mother Theodore came into a pleasant homeliness far removed from the tenor that had gone before. At the open oven Franz sat on a high kitchen stool, his wet clothes beginning to look dry. Tor, in his old dressing gown with the sleeves rolled up, was buttering bread and Sister Laurent pouring coffee. At a small table sat Trillium and Rindy.

Trillium sprang up, her dread almost as acute as in those hours they all assured her were over. "Sheriff! Where—where is he?"

Sheriff Thatcher answered directly. "Pete is guarding him. He won't get away. You'll not see him again, any of you. As soon as it's daylight, we'll take him to Marysville."

Trillium gave a queer little groan and sank back into her chair. In her old yellow dress, flat-heeled mules on her bare feet, she looked like a little girl; but the expression of lingering fear was one that no little girl should know.

"There's nothing to be afraid of now, dear," Mother Theodore said in as natural a voice as she could command.

The Sheriff smiled. Emmy, at least, was coming around.

"We'll get in touch with the New Orluns police as soon as the lines are repaired," he told Trillium. "But in the meantime, you know your mother is safe."

"My mother?"

"He tried to find out her whereabouts late in the summer, a cat-and-mouse idea of vengeance. It put her on her guard." The Sheriff smiled at Trillium. "Don't think about it any more. He never did reach her, he can't now."

The girl's eyes came to Mother Theodore, beside her. "Mother, you do understand how it was, don't you? If I could have told anyone, it would have been you! But I didn't know which one he was until tonight!"

"You had company there, Trillium," Franz said unexpectedly. "I should have suspected Cris since the night of 'Mustardseed,' when I mistakenly mentioned that you were Faith. You two kids looked so much alike, you and Helen, and I don't think Cris knew you even as well as I did. So when he saw a girl in a pink veil come out on the lawn he thought he had the right one. It was such a small incident, I forgot it until tonight."

Sister Laurent glanced at the lightening window. "Last night," she said. "The sun is coming up."

"Tor heard what I said, too," Franz added, his pixy grin flashing.

Torvaldsen nodded sadly. "I'm afraid I suspected both you and Cris also, son. Last night when I heard Cris go out of the single room, and you follow, well, I tagged along."

"So you all trooped out while Pete and I were keeping an eagle watch across the hall!" the Sheriff said wryly.

Tor's smile excused him. "It was pitch dark, Sheriff. And cypress floors do not creak."

"We'd have made it into the tunnel, only the lights were on," said Franz. "Sister Etienne turned them on just after Archer slipped through. She was sweeping," he finished, and his lips twitched.

"I should have known from the night of the churn man's murder," Tor said. "You see, Cris was not there when I came in. Franz was in the kitchen, and I took it for granted that Cris was with him. But I know now he wasn't."

"He wasn't!" Franz agreed savagely. "I can't stomach my own smugness! I let it pass without saying he wasn't with me in the kitchen because I couldn't think he—good Lord, he could have murdered a dozen more right under my nose without me smelling it out!"

"Recriminate me also, then, Franz," Tor invited. "I too clung to a comfortably unidentifiable tramp as our murderer."

"I was the—Judas!" Rindy whispered, but no one heard her.

"He says you spiked his plans several times, though," Sheriff Thatcher put in. "On the night of the Hunt, for instance. He made an attempt to get into the convent earlier, but you followed him, Franz. He wanted to get down into the tunnel, put on the habit, and come up out of the door under the chapel just as the girls passed on their way to Glory's for the muskrat. But when you tailed him, Eric, he had to wait till later and take a long chance in the tower. And he failed, where he probably wouldn't have failed outside."

"Do we have to talk about it any more?" Trillium whispered "I'm so grateful to all of you, I can't ever express it, but I—I can't bear to go over it—"

Mother Theodore's arm was around her, but Trillium shivered.

"He'd a killed us jes' for the killin'," Rindy said in a ghostly wheeze. "He'd a upset the boat, an' drowned us, an' all the time knowin' he couldn't get away, 'cause the debbil was ridin' that man!

The dark, it di'n' make no difference, nor the water, nor the law comin' up behind him, 'cause he had to kill, da's all."

Mother Theodore, surprisingly, nodded. "He had to kill, that was the answer. He didn't know how to stop. His intelligence could not guide him because of his fatalistic belief that all this was written in the stars, as he said, everything determined for him long before he lived . . . how pitiable. . . ."

"But ended, Mother," said Sister Laurent.

The Sheriff straightened, his eyes on the window as if the breaking light outside was a signal. He crossed the kitchen with that peculiar, poised step, all heads turning to follow him because everyone knew where he was going, and why. At the door, he paused, looking back at each in turn. When he came to Mother Theodore, he nodded faintly. Then he opened the door and was gone.

A few minutes later, the Sheriff and Pete started silently out of the underground room, between them an equally silent figure fastened to Pete by handcuffs. So intent were they upon making a noiseless departure that, until the dog growled, they failed to notice him with Sister Etienne in the high old arch of the tunnel. They halted, all of them taken aback except for the old Sister, who saw nothing out of the ordinary in such a meeting. She was becoming quite used to running across men in the tunnels.

Her sweet smile lighted her face. "Good morning, Mr. Thatcher, and—oh, it's Mr. Archer, isn't it?"

There was something so childlike and guileless about the little nun that the Sheriff instinctively stepped in front of Archer as if to shield her from evil.

Too low for the Sister to hear, Crispin said, "Don't worry, Sheriff," but Jarvis Thatcher remained where he was. Taffy sidled closer to Sister Etienne, wary, his big muscles tense.

"Will you excuse us, Sister?" the Sheriff asked quietly. "We are in something of a hurry."

"Oh, certainly! Perhaps another time—"

But Taffy was acting so badly now that she caught a handful of his neck fur to try to shake some sense into him.

As the men passed, the dog pushed her backward and growled deep in his throat.

"Why, Taffy!" Sister Etienne exclaimed.

The steps sounded swiftly, going up the stairs, then the east door closed on the landing. With the sound, the dog's head dropped and all the animosity left him.

The place now was very quiet. It almost seemed that the old remembered peace had returned to St. Aurelien's.

MURDER AT ST. DENNIS

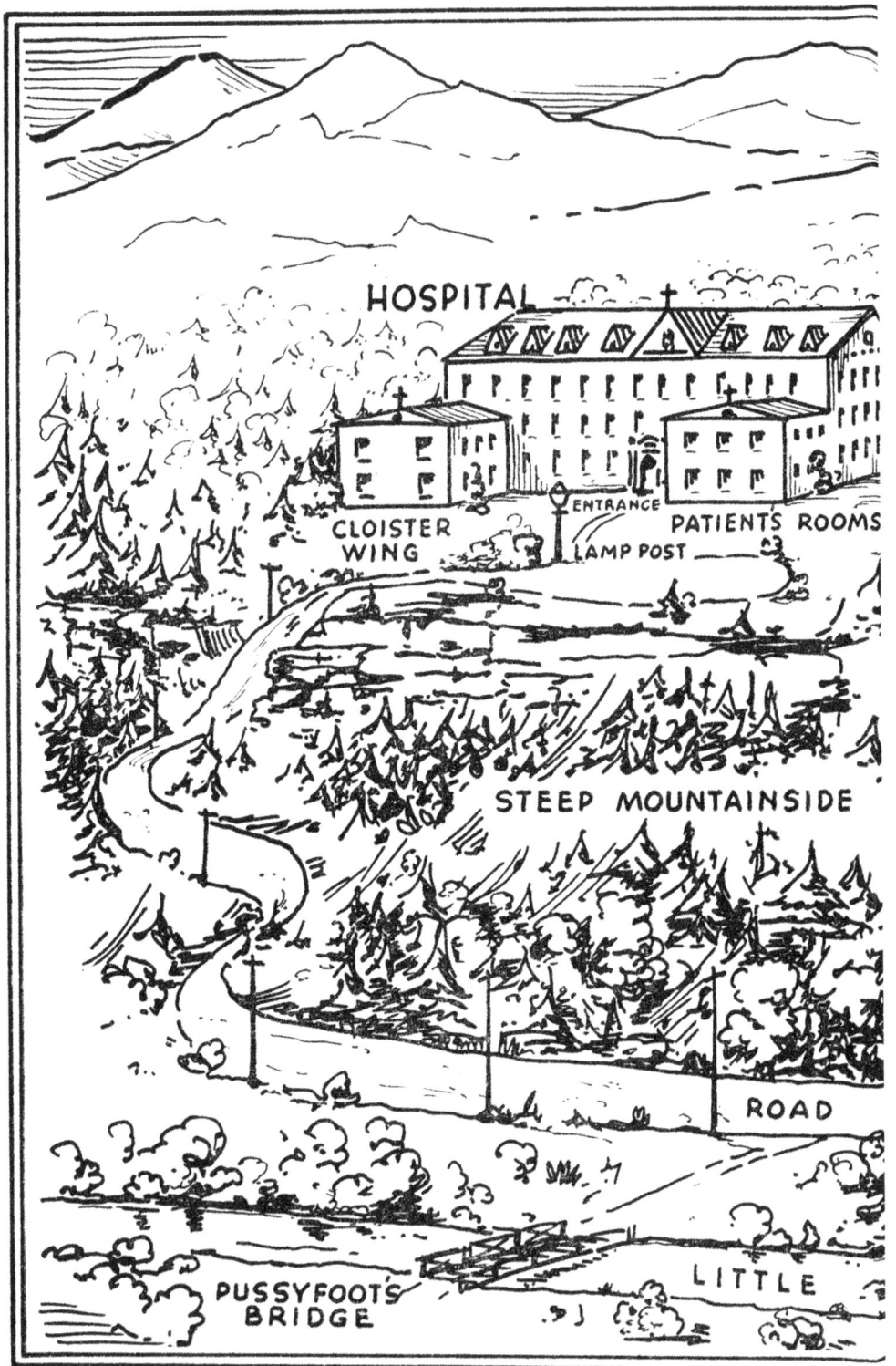

For Tuney and Paw

Thank you to Dr. O. Gordon Betts, Dr. L. L. Massa, and Dr. F. H. Dickson, who successively took care of Big Balsam for me; to Jackie Lambert, my advisor on medical technology; and to uncle Pat, who likes to see a man on the first page.

1

He knew as he watched her that she was frightened. And he knew almost to the second when her hesitation became more than natural diffidence in approaching a strange place. It was when she sat down on the suitcase. She had come up from the darkness of the long road and in under the driveway floodlight like a tall young phantom in a skimpy suit, her pale hair blowing and her cheeks pinched in the chill of the October evening. When she reached the clearing made in the night by the lamp, she stopped, and her big eyes fled over the rambling old hospital building. She did not see the doctor at the window of his lighted office, although the window almost flanked the entrance.

Formidable, that was how St. Dennis would appear to her. Three stories of solid brick before her, topped by outdated gables; the wings, a story lower, reaching out like squat fists to clutch the small lawn around the lamppost. The cloister wing, to her left, was dark at this early hour. The girl had hardly glanced at it. In the right wing the patients' rooms were bright behind lowered shades, but it was no sort of light that had drawn her attention. It was sound, the hollow, measured wheezing of the respirator that drifted out from the open window of the last room on the ground floor. To the lay person, that would be a fearful sound—the labor of a mechanical contrivance to drag a man back from the grave, the awful torture of the dying rather than the breathing in of new life. The doctor puffed out his lips, watching.

The girl listened for a long minute. Then she sprang up, looking back the way she had come, hesitant because she was remembering how she would have to walk alone, lugging the suitcase, down the long slope and through the Gulch with the mountains rising monstrously on either side; past the tributary gulch, where the ghost town rattled its bones; on in the dark to the village, where the miners' dogs would yap at her; and then to the highway to wait for the bus. The lonesome walk had most likely frightened her, coming in. She would not be looking for the solitude and isolation of another century just around the mountain from the busy young city. No one ever was. She heaved the suitcase up against her knee.

The doctor scowled. Johnny or Jock should be here to help her. Surely it was not too much to expect that either orderly be on duty at this hour, a little before seven. His impatience mounted while the girl drooped under the light, undecided. She would go away. He would never know what objective had brought her to the hospital. Furiously convincing himself of his unconcern, he strode out into the hall. Let her go back where she came from, wherever that might be.

Sister Magdalene, about to pull the shade at the window where the curtains seemed to bulge with the sighing of the respirator, glanced out idly, then with eagerness. So the girl had come! She smiled, her rosy cheeks plumped out over the tightly drawn wimple. The poor child was even thinner than she remembered, forlornly dressed with convent disregard for fashion, hollow chested, fatigue pulling at her like the suitcase.

The nun was about to call to her through the screen when the large entrance door opened. The girl knew no reason to be startled at the appearance of the hulking man in white who filled the doorway, who held out his hand for the suitcase, let her pass in ahead of him. It was no more than an ordinary courtesy, yet Sister Magdalene's gaze followed the closing door as if she had witnessed a miracle.

Slowly the Sister straightened at the window. She would not hurry. She would give King a little time. He would not know just yet that the girl was Marmion Pyus. The nurse was busy with her patient. Without speaking, the nun left the room.

Ignorant of having been the cause of a miracle, Marmion climbed the entrance stairs. The doctor ascended at a faster pace, giving her only a passing picture of a handsome, tousled head that was like a profile of anyone of the Caesars—Julius, perhaps, tramping the three infinite parts of Gaul. He had the build of a conqueror, the broad shoulders and deep chest, the fine height. Marmion, fresh out of a manless world, told herself it was thrilling to be thus initiated into the new—and stumbled on the stairs. The doctor did not glance around. She must focus her attention on her surroundings. That was easily done. She had often wondered what the old place would be like, the beloved old place, as Aunt Dorothy had termed it when they knew Marmion would be going back. Even now, no more than a dozen steps inside the building, she understood that description. It was a home, accommodating many guests, where someone had forgotten his rubbers at the door, where the cook had not shut the supper aroma into the kitchen but had allowed it to drift cosily up into the halls. A hungry girl could expect to be fed here, although the supper trays had been cleared away. The thought gave her energy to finish the ascent.

From small landings on either side of the stairs, archways opened into waiting rooms. In the one to the left, a woman with red hands and a safety pin in her coat sat anxiously peering out. The doctor paid no heed to her. He tramped through the wide doors into the main corridor, taking it for granted that Marmion would follow. Involuntarily the girl paused, listening for the respirator, but there was only a complexity of radio programs, a child crying, the clatter of dishwashing puttering up from the basement in the stair well across the hall. A nurse ran down from the second floor, glanced impersonally at Marmion, added a personal gleam for the doctor, and hurried on toward the quietly noisy wing where the iron lung sighed. As Aunt Dorothy had explained, they had done the best they could with the old place. The muslin curtains at the window on the stair landing were freshly laundered, a frame for blooming geraniums. The walls were pale yellow, reflecting all they could gather of light from the dim, high fixtures. But Marmion knew without inspecting it that the linoleum would be ridged from the warped boards underneath and cracked at the edges by soaking scrub water, that the woodwork would have broken away from the floor in long discouraging gaps. Not only time, but living had worn its mark. The stair rail was polished blond from sliding hands, the treads hollowed out by shoe soles.

The doctor gave an impatient cough. He had not turned into the hospital wing but in the other direction where a solid oak door with a white cross blocked the end of the hall, the entrance to the convent. He had opened a door only a few steps away and snapped on a light. Slowly Marmion walked toward him, her heels tapping indecisively on the linoleum. Her thoughts were of foolish things . . . cockroaches, which were most likely peeking at her out of the cracks; the tail of her blouse was stuck out; she was relieved to be at last within the shelter of St. Dennis. When Aunt Dorothy had taken her away, she had vowed never to return to the gulch. But time had changed her; she was different now. . . . And yet, this instant, Marmion felt herself to be more that child of twelve than a young lady of twenty-one going forth into life, as the bishop had said at commencement.

"This is Sister Magdalene's office," the man said gruffly. "She is the superior. I am Dr. Kingston. Sister will admit you."

Marmion entered the small office. There was age here, too, but useful age, dusted and polished. The old wooden filing cabinet gleamed dully, the solid desk was blond as the stair rail at the far side where elbows had rubbed for years. The swivel chair at the desk had a cushion tied to its back, the rose design faded to cabbage color. The girl stepped to the heavily worn spot on the carpet between desk and cabinet, and faced Dr. Kingston.

She had to clear her throat. It made her feel like a tight-voiced child about to speak a piece. "I am not a patient, sir.

That was a juvenile thing to say, as she said it. But her poise was returning. The doctor resembled nothing like a conqueror in the stronger light of the office. His hospital whites were limp, he assumed a clumsy pose with his hands in his hip pockets and chin sunk on his chest, too careless for a man who could hardly have touched forty. He watched while she seated herself, crossed her feet as she had been taught, folded her gloved hands. She was awkward, moving. Seated, her confidence grew. She could hold the silence as long as this big, rude young man who now, somehow, did not strike her as handsome at all. Clear around the office she let her eyes wander. They were violet eyes, her one real beauty. When she brought them back to the doctor, her interest was even less than she had lavished on the old desk and the filing cabinet. She felt well corseted with self-possession.

"Evidently you are unfamiliar with St. Dennis of the Hills."

The doctor's voice would have been worth a lot on radio. It failed to charm Marmion. Besides, why bother to tell him that she had been born three miles from here, up Hellbent Gulch?

"St. Dennis is a thirty-year-old institution of impeccable reputation—"

"Twenty-eight," the girl murmured.

He ignored the interruption. "Built in the days when Gopher Gulch boomed and there was no city. That it stands now in a ghost town is no reflection on Sister Magdalene's administration. She simply chose the wrong side of the mountain."

"How unfortunate. For her, that is."

Marmion had not given thought to the small remark, and she was astounded when the doctor flinched. Or perhaps he didn't. Perhaps he only turned his back to jerk down the window shade against the deepening night. She was glad. She had had enough of that particular darkness.

"We are not running a training school," he told her across the desk. "The people on our staff are of proven competence. They understand we do not maintain a refuge for frightened children."

Marmion gasped. So this man had spied upon her in the drive! And he had guessed her identity when she said she was not a patient. She had not imagined his dislike. Now she understood it—a natural aversion toward seeing his routine upset by the fumbling of a new-fledged graduate—but if he thought he could start her out on a cowed, excuse-me-for-living approach to her hospital career, he was wonderfully mistaken. It would take a great deal to intimidate the daughter of Little Job Pyus.

"Doctor, I may look like a refugee," she said with apparent mildness. "I imagine you might, too, if you had ridden three hundred miles on a bus without even a chance to comb your hair. But you may be interested to know that I'm a medical technologist. I was graduated cum laude from the toughest course offered by any college outside of medicine, I passed my board exams third on the list, and I was hired by Sister Magdalene as assistant to Sister Judith. Does that explain me?"

The doctor had the grace to shrug a half apology. Marmion rose and leaned across the desk. "I am very hard to impress with malice or contempt or ridicule. I was used to a homeful of it. I can be made miserable, but I won't be driven away."

"We need not indulge in personalities, Miss Pyus."

Marmion had grown very pale. These short spurts of bravery never lasted long enough to result in anything but confusion. Her mother had protested, infrequently, against Little Job's tyranny, and thus Marmion would lash out; but before any climax could be reached, she would be sick inside, and trembling, and in an hour her legs would be aching. She had promised herself, however, that once away from the convent where she had spent the past nine years, away from Aunt Dorothy who was Sister Alexis of Sister Magdalene's order, she would stand on her own two feet—no matter how her legs ached. Perhaps she had made a poor beginning, answering the defiance this doctor had invited. What would Aunt Dorothy say? But the nun's last bit of advice had in effect cut the old ties: you are an adult now, you will have the privilege of making your own mistakes.

And she had made a colossal one, Marmion realized, in her first five minutes at St. Dennis. The doctor's scrutiny told her so. His antagonism could toll the bell on her hopes. Her finger tips were pressed to numbness against the edge of the old desk.

"Doctor, I do have a reason for being here, outside of needing a job. Since I was twelve, the Sisters have given me a home and a free education. Reverend Mother assured me that I owe the Order nothing in money. But I feel that I do owe them success in my work. I'm going to try, very hard." The doctor, to her surprise, was listening with interest. She smiled faintly. "I was frightened out there in the drive when I heard the respirator because I wondered if . . . Who is in it, Doctor?"

"Mr. Cassidy."

Marmion's breath went out in a long sigh. "I knew it couldn't be anyone else!"

"Are you so familiar with the treatment for his particular illness?"

"Oh, no! It's just that everything about him has always been so big—his enormous fortune, his huge gold mine my mother told me reached clear to hell—and when I heard that giant breathing it sounded like a mammoth sort of dying, and I knew it must be Big Balsam. He is dying, isn't he?"

"How well do you know Cassidy?"

"I suppose I never knew him at all, really," Marmion said slowly. "I only know what he did to my father. And my mother. My father was his partner, in a way, but he never dared raise his voice around Big Balsam. He was hypnotized, Mother said. And then when he'd come home, he'd—" She paused, shaking her head as if she would dislodge the memory of the shouting pygmy that was Little Job. "My father might have been quite different, away from Big Balsam. He made the first gold strike here in Gopher Gulch, and Cassidy won it from him in a poker game. He never gave my father a cent of the profits. Big Balsam Cassidy haunted my home until my father was killed, although he never set foot in it. And now I wonder if I've escaped him."

"Then why stay?"

Marmion stared. She had gone back into the past as she had promised never to do, led by the doctor's interest; but that interest was deceitful. He used it to gather facts against her.

"Your work as a technologist would necessarily bring you into contact with Cassidy," the doctor continued. "He is a very sick man. Subacute bacterial endocarditis from an old rheumatic heart of childhood. Blood clot in the respiratory center of the brain, respiration too slow to keep him alive therefore the iron lung. A patient so ill requires constant tests. Sister Judith is not always available. You would be obliged to do your share."

"I understand that, Doctor."

"Feeling as you do about Cassidy, you would undoubtedly be happier somewhere else."

Marmion gripped her hands tightly together to stop their trembling. What stupidity to have been thrilled by this insufferable creature's attention!

"I would like to see Sister Magdalene, if I may."

The doctor shrugged. She was near to crying when he left.

Dr. Kingston was furious, lumbering up the stairs. Because he would not direct his fury toward himself, where it belonged, he had vented it upon a scared kid. In a minute, if he had guessed correctly where to find her, he would loose another blast at Sister Magdalene. But she deserved it, in a way. Build a better mousetrap, the philosopher said, and the world would beat a path to your door. Build a reputation for generous, unquestioning kindness, for feeding the hungry and clothing the naked and giving shelter to the homeless, and you would inherit all of the earth's confused and destitute who could pay or beg their way to your door. Many had come, a few had gone. This young stray down in the office was merely another. And judging from the size of the suitcase, she was here to stay.

The nursery, with its recessed door and side windows of glass, was opposite the stairs on the second floor. The doctor paused, looking in. Sister Magdalene was there, in the little rocker she loved, a pink bundle of a baby in her arms. Dr. Kingston pursed his lips into avoidance of a smile. Sister Magdalene had two escape hatches in times of mental stress: one into the laundry, the other into the nursery. Cassidy, of course, had driven her here. Even the veil could not shut out his violent presence. She was singing to the baby, rocking and patting. Her white habit emphasized her peasant ruddiness and the blue of her eyes behind the glasses. The patting hand was plump. Yet she must be old. The doctor did not realize how anxiously he studied the Sister for signs of senility, almost like a child wondering in the night if his mother would ever leave him. She had been a mother to him, this Mary Magdalene with the hearty chuckle. But she could retire to the mother house or die, and it would make no difference in his personal life. None.

He threw open the door abruptly. The Sister made a startled movement, and the baby complained. Laying the dark head against her cheek, she sang softly, "Little Totman's gone to town, to buy his love a wedding gown. Some say pink, some say blue, and that is all my song for you. . . ."

The doctor snorted. "There's another piece of debris in your office. Starved. Scared. No doubt incompetent. I'd kick her out. You won't."

"Thank you, King."

The door closed. The Sister rocked for another few minutes before laying little Totman back in his basket. She was tired. Sitting here, she had begun to believe she might be getting old; but that was only because the sight of Marmion had brought up thoughts of Little Job, and to remember Little Job was to think of Cassidy. Big Balsam, so King had said, had reached an age when recovery from a serious illness was problematical, seventy-four on the hospital records; and she was not so much younger. Not that she minded age for herself. But who would keep the life in old St. Dennis after she was gone? Around the mountain, in Balsam City, there were two newer hospitals, better equipped. It was sentiment that kept the old place going, people who had been born here, doctors like John Hamlin who had worked here since the early days.

"What a state of mind for a religious!" the nun said, tucking in the baby. She would not allow such foolishness to saturate her mind like dampening in a garment rolled up for ironing. With very nearly her usual briskness, she closed the nursery door behind her and started down the stairs.

Marmion heard the heavily starched rustle of white habit she had come to know so well in the college hospital, not at all like the Sunday ripple of black serge, and she turned to see Sister Magdalene on the threshold, her plump arms out in welcome, a twinkle in her eye, and a chuckle in her voice. You couldn't guess her age. All Sisters appear to be either very old or very young, the graying of their hair as secret as anything on earth. But she had walked the halls of the old building from the time they were only rafters; sat in this little office puzzling out her future while the carpenters were still hammering around her head; and St. Dennis of the Hills was far past its youth. It was easy to imagine her in her young days striding through the gulches with habit flapping in the wind much as Paul had gone striding through Galatia, facing down the bold, cold winters and torrid summers. If ever she proved to be a saint, she would be the rugged type who would act fast in answer to prayer. She held Marmion close, patting her as she had the baby, telling her how delighted they all were to have her with them.

"And you'll be glad you've come home, dear—back to the Gulch. You'll see now how little I could tell you of it on my few visits to the mother house. You have to be here to love it again."

And then the nun was asking questions about Marmion's trip, about Sister Alexis and how the new heating system was working out at the college. It was almost as if she did not want the girl to dwell on the strange reception she knew Marmion had received at St. Dennis.

"You'll get along well with Sister Judy, dear. Everyone does. She's our pet. You may find the hours long, at first, seven to seven; but there will be a while in the afternoon when you'll be free. And you'll have to arrange with Sister to take your turn on night call."

"We worked hard at school, Sister," Marmion replied. "I expect to work hard here—if I stay."

The nun maintained a lack of expression that would have been the envy of her early neighbor, Poker Alice. "You have met Dr. Kingston, Marmion."

"Yes, Sister."

"He is a brilliant man, professionally. Six years ago he came to us as our resident physician. He has nothing whatever to do with personnel."

"Nothing?"

"I'll show you to your room now, Marmion."

"Sister . . . he doesn't want me here. Why?"

The Sister turned to lead the way out of the office. Her voice lacked the chuckle as she answered. "We are all on edge, right now. Mr. Cassidy is a strain on everyone. He isn't the kind of person to keep either his living or his dying to himself. It's my fancy that he demands life from all of us, a sort of transfusion as we might give him blood. . . . But what talk is this for a nun!" She tucked Marmion's hand into hers. "We'll leave your suitcase; Johnny can take it up later. You'll have a room to yourself, but there's plenty of company. Nurses, the cook and her little boy, Blanche, Eloise—all of you on the third floor. You'll like it, dear."

Feeling mothered and protected, Marmion walked beside the Sister to the stairs. The protection was appreciated when the doctor came out of his office as if he had been waiting for them. He did not approach or speak. He planted himself to watch their ascent, and the girl became conscious of her every smallest movement, wondering if she would trip, seeing herself as the doctor saw her with hair stringing out of the page boy, and blouse collar lumped under her jacket. Although she was next to the railing, she did not look down.

So she feels safe with Magdalene, the doctor mused. She wouldn't turn and run now if she could.

He did not hear the nurse, beside him, until she spoke. "Will you sign this, please, Doctor?"

He glanced down at her clean cuff, at the pencil and pad she held for him. He scribbled his initials. She knew as well as he what treatment Cassidy required. But Lynn Baird was a faultless nurse, nothing ever taken for granted, almost primly precise. Her regard for him, however, was not prim. He knew that without glancing up. Of late he had taken to avoiding those brown eyes and therefore avoiding the derision that could have been amusing and was not. He was ashamed when he thrust the pencil at her with an involuntary twitch that struck her cuff.

"You're not having a chill, Dr. Kingston?"

He turned gruffly away. Her low voice followed him. "It's probably only the effect of this northern climate. Do you know the old superstition, Doctor? Shiver in the heat, and it means someone is walking on your grave."

He wheeled on the bottom step of the stairs; but Lynn was leaving him, walking like a duchess, quietly yet not with the innocuous silence of the other nurses. Lynn desired herself to be noticed. When she was gone the doctor continued on up the stairs, slowly, absently aware that he would have to invent an errand when he reached the second floor. Someone had walked on his grave.

And now there was Marmion.

The Sister was entering the well of the old-fashioned third-floor stairs when Marmion looked back. Dr. Kingston was at the chart desk, his head thrown back, but hardly like a conqueror. He was, the girl decided, just plain mad.

"Why?" she asked. "Sister, why does he act as if he'd like to wring my neck?"

Sister Magdalene chuckled. "He isn't angry with Marmion Pyus, child. It's with himself, and he's blaming the girl who enticed him into opening the door."

"You mean when I came into the hospital, Sister? But I didn't entice him! I didn't even know he was anywhere around! And anyway, isn't it just decently polite for a man to open a door for a woman?"

"Not for King, dear." The nun paused, looking up the narrow stairs as if she found them an aching prospect to climb. "Not for King. He hasn't opened that door in very nearly six years."

2

"We can do it if we work fast," said Eloise. Marmion had just returned to the third floor from her first visit to the laboratory, expecting to find her room empty. But Eloise, the X-ray technician, was spread out on her bed, and Blanche, in her blue kitchen uniform, sat lumped on the only chair. King would have classified Blanche as another of the homeless and friendless who had drifted into Sister Magdalene's comfortable arms to be instantly equipped with home and friends. Her eyes were fastened upon Eloise, who was obviously the only friend she wanted, and her full lips moved as she listened, repeating the racy observations she could never deliver properly even should she manage to remember them. Her heels were hooked on the rung of her chair in imitation of careless grace, and one finger twisted a lock of hair that was tinted as near as she could make it to Eloise's glorious auburn.

"We've been planning it for weeks," Eloise continued, giving a roll that spilled her hair wider over Marmion's pink blanket. She was a tomboy of a girl, apparently irresponsible, but, according to Sister Judith, one of the best X-ray technicians in the Hills. "The whole thing hinged on who got this room, of course. If it was a Spartan like Henny Penny Kennedy—"

"Or old Miss Hennessey," said Blanche. "Or Miss Baxter—"

"Or anyone but you, Marmie," Eloise broke in, "we'd have been stymied. You can't walk up to a gal like Baxter and tell her you're plotting to heave her bed out and turn her chamber into a parlor. Nursing is hard on the feet and hers have had half a century of wear, so she's got to rest 'em in solitude."

"And besides, she'd go straight to Polycarp," Blanche added.

"Polycarp? A Sister?" Marmion asked, perching on the foot of the bed. "If she's anything like my dear little Judy—"

"She isn't," said Eloise, but her green eyes danced. "Polycarp is all things to most people in this constricted little world of ours—I give you her own estimate, by the way. I couldn't guess how old she is. I know my Dad had her for a teacher in kindergarten, and she wasn't young then. That's how come I'm here. My loving parent thought I should be under the Polycarp influence on my first job, and I don't mind, it's near home. She's retired now, theoretically. Actually, she's busy as a little bee. And can she sting!"

"She's deaf, though," said Blanche.

"Her one good point."

"I liked it in the basement," the big girl went on thoughtfully. "I was closer to the kitchen."

Eloise shook a finger. "Tut, tut! You were also closer to Jock and the estimable Kingston, only a step across the hall. No, Polycarp has the system. She puts all the little boys in the basement and all the little girls in the attic, and then she patrols a beat in between."

"She's at recreation now," Blanche remarked.

Eloise sat up. "How about it, Marmie? We're going to have to hurry if we get through before she finds out what we're up to."

"Give it to me again, slow and easy," Marmion said. "We'd move my bed into your room, Eloise—"

"Right, and then we'd have a sitting room in here. These are the only rooms with a connecting door between. There are some chairs out there in the attic. And we'd have this closet for a kitchenette to make tea. Lovely?"

"Lovely. But how are we going to get the bed through the door?"

"Knock it down," said Blanche.

"She means knock down the bed," said Eloise. "She has talent that way."

Sister Magdalene left the chapel and entered the covered passage that led down the hillside to Methusaleh Hall, her oldest hospital building. It was a homely passage such as gold miners build in order to give them quick access to mill and smelter. For the hospital, this one and the second, going from Methusaleh to the main building, were ideal passageways. The chronic invalids who lived in the Hall were wheeled daily to prayers and Mass. There were only two wheel chairs tonight. Barney's was not one. The Sister let everyone go ahead of her. When she came into Methusaleh, she was alone. She went on to the last door on the corridor.

Barney knew when she came into the ward, for the other five men greeted her; and she knew he had been lying there looking at the ceiling because his eyelids twitched and his hand jerked when she laid hers upon it.

"You're not still thinking, Barney?"

He did open his eyes then. His white hair was in a kewpie curl on top of his head, but there was nothing comical about him. "And what else is there to be doing, Sister?"

"Barney, your hating him is not going to hurt Big Balsam Cassidy, but it's going to hurt your own soul."

"Is it my soul or not?" Suddenly he clutched her hand, pulling himself up on the pillow. "Sister, twenty wasted years I have behind me, all because Cassidy wouldn't make his mine safe for men to work in. And never a cent did I get for the accident! Do you think I don't lie here and curse him for putting a strain on your charity?"

"It's been no strain, Barney. You've always been so cheerful, such a fine example of spirituality, until now. But we must bear with this. Only the saints, remember, are given the privilege of asking, 'Why hast Thou forsaken me?'"

Barney shut his eyes tight. "I'm not asking, Sister. I know. The devil that's Cassidy has pushed God aside."

Sister Magdalene straightened with a sigh. She had been over this so often in the past few days. But as she turned away, Barney whispered, "I can't hate the dead, Sister. As soon as he's dead, I'll be cheerful again."

She spoke to the other men for a minute and said good night. The old passage to the hospital seemed long, looking into it. At the small windows, Sister Judy's geraniums bloomed. Sister Magdalene did not take her usual pleasure in them. The care of the great Cassidy had been a strain, but the sickening part was the unmistakable hatred the man gathered around him. He had earned it well, from Barney, from Philippa, who looked like a tired movie star and cooked like an angel—from Little Job's daughter, who had perhaps more reason than anyone in the world to hate him. And these were only the heart. Out from it eddied all the lessening currents: the nurses who must attend him, the thirty-odd patients who must bear his disturbing presence along with their own ills, finally the whole wide region where his name had been a byword for thirty-five years. That name would be forever stamped upon the country, for now there was Little Balsam Creek, cutting through Gopher Gulch, and Balsam Butte to rear its brown sides where none of the trees grew, and Balsam City around the mountain. Back in the early days the West had given him another name also, Hellbent Cassidy—no compliment intended—and he had taken it with a swagger and blazoned it over the hole in the ground he had just won from Little Job Pyus, the hole that proved to be a mint of gold.

And then, for a time, Big Balsam had subsided while a raw gang of insurgents brawled and shot their way to prominence. How well Sister Magdalene remembered! Before that summer was over, Cassidy's unnatural reticence became significant. An astounding number of heart attacks were killing the uproarious strikers of rich claims; and when it was noted that those claims all lay along the mineral belt centered by the Hellbent, and that the heart attacks were undoubtedly induced by cyanide in a drink of whiskey, many an adventurer sold out and hit for home. Nothing ever had been proved against Cassidy. People wanted to sell, the Hellbent was ready to buy. So the shafts went down and the stamp mills rose and the violent years became the foundation of industrial development. The prosperity of the Hellbent was the prosperity of the Hills. Those were the legendary days when Big Balsam, straddled at the head of Gopher Gulch, had roared down a mile of foaming sluice boxes. Now, down in the shafts and stopes the little gondola cars would go on being loaded with ore, the hoists would run with the same regularity, up in the mills the stamps would crush and the great vats fill and drain and fill again, all to produce the bricks of gold that look so disappointingly unprecious. But the mighty Cassidy had at last come face to face with the one adversary he could neither bully nor buy off nor knife in the back. Very soon, so it seemed, Barney would be able to pray again.

The Sister came slowly out of the passage and into the second-floor corridor of the hospital. To her left were the operating rooms, the delivery room, the laboratories where Eloise and Sister Judith and, after today, Little Job's daughter would be working together. Opposite the laboratory, the door was shut upon the stair well going up to the third floor. Strange sounds were issuing from up there, like a slipper heel pounding on iron. That was the moment Sister Polycarp emerged from the surgery, flashlight in hand, having proceeded thus far in her nightly pursuit of dripping faucets and left-on lights. Waste was an abhorrence to her. She had spent a life span urging students not to waste their time. She was still appalled at the flightiness of the young staff members who, she felt, should know better.

Sister Magdalene was beside the black space that entered the small, cut-up section of laboratories. She reached around inside the doorway, snapped on the light, gave the cubicle an inspection as if that were what she had come for.

Sister Polycarp watched with sharp black eyes. "I was in there, Sister. Everything is in order."

"Thank you, Sister. I can always depend on you." The Superior turned away, forgetting the light. It would please the old nun to snap it off.

A loud thump, then a dragging scrape floated down from the third floor. Sister Polly did not hear the racket. But having finished her round of the labs, she would climb to the crow's-nest, as the girls had named their domain.

Sister Magdalene hooked her arm companionably through the old Sister's, leading her toward the main stairs. "You must spare yourself tonight, dear. You're tired. Go now to the cloister."

She could not explain that she was thankful to have young spirits housed in St. Dennis, that whatever irreverence was going on upstairs was a blessing showered upon a desert-dry time. Marmion would be up there, forgetting with the facility of the young that she had ever been bitter and hating.

"I have not been to the basement," Sister Polycarp worried. "There is the leaky tap in the kitchen sink, the hot water. You have to use a towel on the handle or you'll hurt your thumb."

"I'll see to it, Sister."

"And close the window in the pharmacy."

"Of course, dear." Every night for six years, King had left the window up and Sister Polycarp had put it down. The feud over fresh air had become a ritual between them.

The Sisters had reached the main-floor corridor when a husky young man in white came leaping up the stairs from the basement, three steps at a time. His crew haircut stood straight and short as an angry cat's fur. He was whistling. Without losing a bar of the tune, he skirted the two, winked broadly at Sister Polycarp, and danced on up the stairs. Sister Magdalene tried not to smile. How many times had she reminded Johnny that he must not whistle in the halls, that he might as well learn early the deportment befitting a future doctor? And how many times, also, had she seen him wheedle and bemuse a refractory patient into behaving himself? Sister Polycarp, chuckling off toward the cloister wing, never accused Johnny of wasting time. School and his job as night orderly were enough even for her.

Sister Magdalene went on down, letting her weight fall ponderously from step to step. The stairs were not well lighted, the illumination from the upper hall reaching only to the landing. Below, a dim bulb dangled half around the turn, leaving the lower steps in shadow. That was why Jock, in the strong light cutting out from the dispensary, did not see the Sister. With no intention of eavesdropping, she paused. She was worried about Jock Turner. He had not been himself, lately. He performed his work as orderly with the old efficiency but with a new care to detail as if he knew there was danger of forgetfulness, and his grin often covered a most unusual inattention. Jock, slightly built, curly-headed, freckled and pug-nosed, was not the type to be taken seriously. The patients loved him and laughed at him. Some said he put on his comics in true clown fashion, to hide a broken heart; but the majority held that his sunny temperament was too shallow for any deep emotion, like a creek bubbling and dancing without concealing a single pebble in its course. The Sister, looking down on him, realized with remorse that Jock's change of spirit coincided with Cassidy's admission to the hospital. Overwork, that was it. He had been at the beck of the private nurses twelve hours a day, often answering calls when Johnny was on duty for the night, trundling oxygen tanks, helping to lift and turn the heavy patient. She would speak to him now, tell him he must keep his off-duty hours rigidly to himself. Before she could move, Lynn Baird appeared in the lighted doorway.

Lynn was beautiful, as perfect in appearance as a model. There was an air of indolence about her, in the faint drooping of the lids that made her brown eyes sleepy, in the impression that her skin had become tawny satin through lazy hours under a tropic sun. It was a charming indolence that seemed to lend thoroughness to her capabilities as a nurse; for Lynn was never in a hurry, always composed, bearing the strenuous days of caring for Cassidy with a tranquility that was the envy of little Dixie Bryan, who would be with him now, and Mrs. Hayes, who would toil up from the gulch at midnight. Lynn was not wearing her cap, and her dark hair was soft against the light. But Jock apparently took no pleasure in the picture. The Sister knew why. She had seen Lynn glance first over Jock's head, then down, as if she had expected to find him taller and remembered too late. Jock's face grew hot. Holding himself rigidly from limping, he retreated until his humped back was in the shadow. In his white uniform he was like a young boy dressed up for a Sunday school picnic; but when he limped around the corner to disappear, his dragging step sounded to the Sister as if he were running away.

Lynn, faintly smiling, went back to whatever she was doing in the pharmacy. Both she and Jock had been unaware of observation. Sister Magdalene, when she passed the door, did not glance in at Lynn. She was still indignant as she came into the kitchen.

The young woman peeling carrots jumped and the knife jabbed her finger. Sucking the finger, she slipped her feet into her high-heeled red slippers, her frown as deep as if it had been cut by the knife.

"I'm sorry, Sister! I didn't hear you coming. I'm all on edge today."

Sister Magdalene opened the table drawer and hunted for a bandage. "I'm the one to apologize, child. Let me see your finger."

Philippa drooped on the high stool. Her ears were pale today, standing out like frail china from her dark head. And her temper, too, was fragile. But even in this mood, Philippa was sweet.

"Sister, why can't I be like you? Why don't I say to myself, all right, this is the way things are, make the best of it? You do. Only of course being in the convent is different. Everything is smoothed out for you."

The Sister pressed adhesive around the finger. "If everything is smoothed out, it's because we do it for ourselves with God's help. Women don't assume new personalities when they take the veil. All their old faults are with them, a part of them like the color of their eyes. If their lives don't widen out toward God, then they become almost unbelievably narrow."

Philippa nodded. "I know what you mean, Sister. My life right now is narrowed down to despising that man upstairs. You don't know what it is! I was left with my tiny baby to rear and earn a living for, be mother and father and breadwinner all together—I was desperate two years ago, when you took me in! An unavoidable accident, they said, but carelessness is avoidable! My man died alone down in that black hole of the Hellbent because Cassidy didn't give a damn about the safety of his mine, but the great Balsam gets an iron lung and three nurses and—" She stopped, and her fist clenched until the bound finger grew purple. "I hope he dies. I hope he dies, and I hope it takes him a long time!"

In the kitchen rocker, two-year-old Chad watched his mother with serious eyes. When he slid off the chair and approached the table, reaching up to grope for carrot rounds from the neat row of ten, Sister Magdalene unobtrusively pushed a few within reach.

Philippa swooped to the floor to retrieve her knife. "Look, Sister, I blow off every once in a while, and then I feel better. I'm grateful as the dickens to you for taking me in. Where else could I go with Chad? I'm not a good mother, but at least I'm a substitute for an orphan's home. And as for that lousy Cassidy—Sister! Chad's eating up the Hail Marys!"

The little boy, sidling against Sister Magdalene, opened his mouth to let tiny lumps of carrot roll into his palm.

"Mommy doesn't want them back, honey," the Sister said, patting his ear. "She has plenty, and carrots are good for little boys."

Philippa laughed, her vicious mood spent. "Oh, sure, I can always start my rosary over. I like the Joyful Mysteries, anyway. They're something you can understand. Take the Visitation. I like to think about Mary walking all that way to Elizabeth's house, on that nice quiet road, just the same as me going to see my Aunt Susie up in Spearfish, only I'd go in a car and most likely have a flat in around Deadwood." She glanced up humbly. "I don't suppose it's sacrilegious, me counting prayers this way?

"Of course not, dear," Sister Magdalene said comfortably. "Mary was a housewife, too, you know."

The Sister was closing the cloister door finally and thankfully behind her when the last thump sounded in the crow's-nest.

"Now that's all, for sure," said Eloise. "We're right over Mrs. Totman's head, the poor dear. Even though she's used to pandemonium at home, we've given her enough of a workout for one night."

"Nine kids," said Blanche.

"Eleven. She just had two more." Eloise surveyed the room in high satisfaction. "As snug a little retreat as you could ask for. Your sacrifice is not in vain, Marmie."

Marmion sank down on the horsehair love seat. "If we had some silver polish we could shine up the brass on our center table. And it should have something set on it."

"We'll swipe a geranium," said Eloise. She stood in the middle of the cluttered room and nodded approvingly. "All I've ever dreamed of!"

"Until Sister Polycarp takes a hand."

"She won't. I'll quote my father. And the bishop certainly looks more at home in a sitting room." Eloise stepped around the table and reached up to polish the glass over the portrait with her handkerchief. Her finger moved gently down over the white-crowned, benevolent face. "Poor old laddie—he's another leftover now. We got 'em all up here."

"Uncle Josh, too," said Blanche.

Marmion giggled. "I don't get the connection."

"She's off on another tack," Eloise explained. "What about Uncle Josh, baby?"

Blanche pushed her home permanent up from her neck and rubbed thoughtfully. "On a record. For a gramophone. It's real old. I found it when we house-cleaned up here. It looks like a morning glory. Under an old quilt."

"Well, what are we waiting for!" exclaimed Eloise. "Come on!"

Marmion followed as far as the rubber matting outside the room. Only this main part of the building ran to three stories. In a long row across the front, where the windows would be utilized, small rooms had been finished leaving the remaining space beamed and dark, with the roof slanting down over a windowless gable. Marmion's room, which had become the sitting room, was the last in the long line, and next to it was the room into which they had cramped the two beds. Farther toward the stairs, the bathroom door stood open, showing light, and in the narrow stair well another bulb burned. The gloom was heavy back under the eaves where the Sisters' trunks were stored along with the nurses' luggage and the unused furniture and the mattress resting on a packing box like a huge jelly roll. In the deepest of the twilight, far back in a corner, Eloise and Blanche burrowed.

When Philippa and Chad climbed to the crow's-nest, the gramophone was installed on a footstool in the living room, its blue and yellow horn gaily swinging from a tripod, the cylindrical records neatly stacked on the floor.

"He's the one, that Uncle Josh," Blanche sighed as Philippa looked in. "It gobbles, kind of, but he's sure funny."

"You, kids!" Philippa, sagging in the doorway, pulled one foot out of a red slipper. "How long do you think this is going to last?"

Chad stood with his fat legs wide apart, a finger in his mouth, staring seriously at the portrait of the bishop. He removed his finger and a drip darkened his blue shirt front.

"Dat's my fodder," he said.

The girls collapsed into giggles.

"Out he goes!" cried Marmion. "Hide him under the quilt!"

But Philippa did not even smile. She looked down at her son as if what he said had frightened her to her very marrow. "He thinks the strangest things are his father! I have a container for string in the kitchen, it's shaped like a pig, and he says that's his father, too. The poor little tike, he doesn't know what a father is!"

"Oh, listen, Phil—" Eloise began.

Philippa was crying the hard tears she had not shed in the kitchen, and her voice rose. "That's what he's done to my baby, that damn Cassidy! I could kill him! If I only knew how, I'd—"

Eloise caught her firmly by the arm. "Take Chad to their room, Marmie, and put him in his crib. Or—never mind, I'll do it. You stay here."

"I'm all right!" Philippa sobbed.

But Eloise, with Chad cuddled in her strong arms, went out.

Marmion sat down beside Philippa in the chair with the leaky upholstery. For a little while, for the short time it had taken them to jam the beds into the other room and clamber sneezing after the dusty furniture in the attic, Marmion had forgotten the long past that had contained Big Balsam Cassidy. Listening to Philippa's crying, it seemed now that the interval of high school and college away with Aunt Dorothy had never happened at all, that this was her mother sobbing out the injustice of Big Balsam toward Little Job, and of Little Job to his wife and Marmion. She sat there, patting Philippa's shoulder, while memory rushed up like a bull before a storm, leaping all the fences she had built to hold it back.

3

Marmion had dreaded her first day in the new surroundings. But little Sister Judith, without any of the overassurances that would have added to her anxiety, started her off on the routine and left her to her work. She made no blunders. Steadily her confidence grew, her apprehension concerning the doctor's attitude faded. The first day passed smoothly, then the second and the third. Marmion had not been called upon to enter Big Balsam Cassidy's room. Passing through the halls, she heard the respirator, but the sound did not frighten her any more. Subconsciously, she had built up a belief that she would never be asked to attend Big Balsam because Sister Judy regarded him as her own particular care. But on the fourth morning, Marmion realized abruptly how false her relief had been.

It happened with as neat dispatch as even King could have planned. From seven o'clock, she and Sister Judith had worked together while the morning sun glittered over the beakers and tubes in the laboratory and finally took itself up out of sight. The tiny Sister, pushing one of her several wooden footstools from place to place, had amused Marmion at first. When she stepped off the stool, she was as small as a ten-year-old child; but her little hands were scarred from chemical burns and her little shoulders were rounded as if they never had quite straightened from the last load. Her face, however, showed a calm maturity. Even when the emergency call came from the operating room, she appeared to take her time assembling her tray, although the little hands moved quickly.

"I'll go, Marmion," she said. "Dr. Kingston is impatient, sometimes. Get me a gown and mask, please. And then you can pick up the first-floor wing."

"Yes, Sister."

"Dr. Hamlin wants a venous puncture on Mrs. Baker—tie it tighter, please."

The girl pulled the mask tapes into a knot on the back of the Sister's head. "Mrs. Baker and the little boy in seven. Is that all, Sister?"

"That's all, except Mr. Cassidy, of course. A prothrombin time. The doctor will want to order his dicoumarol, so you'd better do him first."

She hurried off, leaving Marmion with the strange sensation that she had been deserted. Nervously she prepared her tray. There was no reason why she should be nervous. Dr. Kingston was in surgery, safely out of her way. And seeing Cassidy immediately would end her foolishness over contact with the man who had been the evil genie of her life.

The mechanical sighing of the lung drifted out and around her as Marmion stood at last before the closed door. She tapped lightly. No answer. Her fingers opened, lying flat on the panel. Whether or not it was imagined, she felt a vibration like organ music in a small place—a place as small as the church a stone's throw from the Hellbent, where she had sat stunned and numb and heard someone whisper how lacking in feeling the great Cassidy must be, not even to attend the funeral of Little Job Pyus who had been his only friend. His absence had been of vague comfort to Marmion. Her mother would not have wanted him. Her mother was there, too, in the other casket.

She pushed on the door. It opened enough for her to pass in. The man's eyes caught her as she came, gray eyes with half their steel wasted away. His head was toward Marmion as he lay in the respirator, the eyes only a reflection in the mirror placed above him to give him a view of anyone entering; and yet the unexpected intensity of that gaze was unnerving. Because it seemed to be pleading. The all-powerful Cassidy, pleading?

The girl's blue eyes held fast to the eyes in the mirror. Clearly, the man was in agony, choking, his head rolling on the doll-size pillow, his mouth working around some exclamation he could not make. The nurse appeared to be paying no attention to him, although she stood close to the respirator, her back to the door. She had not noticed Marmion.

Big Balsam's forehead glistened as he made what appeared to be a last tremendous effort to speak. It was only an unintelligible, hissing whisper. Whether it was his inability to make himself heard that terrified him, the girl did not know; but suddenly he heaved his head back as if he would break away from the rubber cuff that sealed his neck into the lung. And then she saw the tracheotomy tube in his throat, inserted into the windpipe through a small incision. The tube was connected to an oxygen tank. Everything had been done to make his breathing easier, and yet the tube was what seemed to be choking him.

Marmion moved forward, and the nurse turned, startled. Anyone would have been startled.

"Sorry, Miss Baird," said Marmion, setting down her tray. "I did knock. I have to take a blood test."

"Wait a minute."

Lynn closed the open portholes, then with unhurried efficiency took out the small tube lining the larger one in the man's throat, cleaned it, and inserted it again.

Even so short a time ago as the moment she knocked on the door, Marmion had believed she could stand by and see Big Balsam's misery without being touched. But there is always something pitiable in the unconquered about to go down in defeat. And the sick man was so terribly alone. He was still handsome, with his iron-gray hair a shag on the pillow, his heavy black brows smooth. Those brows had never betrayed indecision. Their only trick had been a slight, disconcerting lift, a trick that had worked quite as well at the meetings of the Hellbent directors as it ever had at the bar of the Bloody Knuckle. They were the brows of a man who had never known opposition simply because he would not admit its existence. And now he was dying, alone. He had never had a friend, after Little Job.

The vibration of the respirator trembled through Marmion as it must through the man inside, inhale, exhale, so many long slow breaths to the minute. The thing was hypnotic, you couldn't be near it and not breathe that way yourself, deeply, deliberately, as if your life also depended . . .

"Don't do that," Lynn said. "You can't die with all of them. Don't let it get you." Her hand was on Big Balsam's forehead, stroking back the heavy hair. "You should know better."

Marmion was provoked. Surely the man must have heard! But his face remained expressionless, the eyes closed.

"Every respirator patient is extremely apprehensive," Lynn continued. "It's typical of them. They're always afraid something will happen, especially that the power will go off. Everything here is electric, you see. This one is particularly anxious. He has never had to be dependent. Big, Big Balsam." Her hand paused, cupped under his chin. When he did not move, she smiled faintly. "He takes spells of fighting the lung. They all do. Then he remembers that if he wants to live, he'll have to cooperate, and he settles down. In the long run, of course, it won't make much difference."

Quickly Marmion took a syringe from her tray. "I've never had to do this for a patient in a respirator. I know I'll have to work fast so I won't have the porthole open too long."

"I'll help you," said Lynn. "We'll open two holes. I can hold his arm for you."

The rubber panel blubbered around the man's quiet face, the warm air breezed out against Marmion as the pressure rose and fell. The figure under the white blanket looked strong and vigorous, merely at rest. You could imagine that the lung vibrated with the energy of the man rather than from any mechanical stimulus, and that at any minute he might open his eyes, kick himself free, and go bellowing off about his business.

"Take your time," Lynn said quietly, and Marmion knew she had remarked the trembling of the needle.

Dr. Kingston could not have chosen a more critical moment to enter. When he saw the two busy at the lung, he paused at the door, evidently interested in this first glimpse of the new technologist at work. But he doesn't belong here, Marmion thought while she forced her hand to remain steady—he's up in surgery yelling bloody murder over an emergency!

"You're doing fine," Lynn whispered without moving her lips.

And so Marmion finished without incident while the doctor strolled to the table to read the chart. Apparently he was pleased with what he saw.

"You're getting better, Mr. Cassidy," he said.

Marmion took up her tray and withdrew to the far side of the room to write her slip. Big Balsam was blinking in the strong light, trying to speak. It was a wicked thing for the doctor to have said, when there was no hope. But King was beside the respirator, looking down eagerly at his patient.

"Your pulse is stronger, fever down. You're definitely better."

Cassidy's head moved on the pillow. "Damn rubber collar!" he whispered plainly.

The doctor laughed. "You'll be rid of it in a few more days, I promise you. You could breathe right now without the lung. Want to try it for a minute?"

Big Balsam nodded.

"Good! I'll be right here. If you can't breathe, don't be afraid. Now take it easy. Ready?"

Lynn clicked a switch. Silence rushed in like air into a vacuum.

Marmion held her own breath; and then she heard the soft hiss of oxygen through the tube, a short pause, then the hiss again. Big Balsam was breathing. That small sound was the proof that he would not die as Lynn had predicted. The nurse stood with her hand on the switch, Dr. Kingston leaned close to the porthole; and the steady, quiet hissing went on.

"Enough?" the doctor asked.

But it was characteristic of the great Cassidy that he shook his head even though sweat ran into the pillow, typical that he should force himself to do a little more than he was able.

"Turn it on," said King.

Once again the wheezing of the respirator filled the room, and the nurse uncapped her pen to set down the indisputable evidence that she was wrong, that Big Balsam would some day return to the busy thunder of his mills. His gaze was upon Lynn, triumphant, the brows tipped to a derisive slant, and Marmion knew then that he had heard his nurse's remark. He gagged a little, as if laughter caught in his throat.

Dr. Kingston, leaving, turned. "How often do you aspirate that tube, nurse?"

"Every ten or twelve minutes, Doctor."

"I'd do it right away."

She glanced at her watch and went on writing. The doctor's vexation called for slamming a door; but when he went out, the door whispered shut.

Lynn arose the instant the doctor was gone and went to carry out his order. The patient lay with his eyes closed, his mouth eased to the mild expression one often sees on the faces of those who have died quietly. Marmion picked up her tray and left the room.

The doctor stood with Eloise before the open door leading to the small porch. Although he obviously had been speaking to the other girl, Marmion had the feeling that he had been waiting for herself.

"Miss Pyus."

"Yes, Doctor?" What sort of reprimand would he deliver? She had taken the test properly. . . .

"Miss Pyus, you must stop living in the past. Your father is dead, all of the past is dead, don't let it walk on your grave. You should not have come here, but now that you're here, exercise a little common sense. Cassidy is not dying. Give him a few more weeks of convalescence and with a bit of luck he'll be back to his old tricks, pitching his own brand of bravado high and wide. For how long, no one knows. That doesn't concern me—what he does after he leaves here. You don't concern me either. I'm interested only in my patient's recovery."

"Yes, Doctor," the girl murmured. If he were not concerned for her peace of mind, why should he care that she had come to St. Dennis?

Whether he might have added anything, she never knew, for the doctor's signal was struck on the gong in the main corridor. Never had she heard so lovely a sound nor seen so pleasant a sight as the big white back, departing.

Eloise relieved her of the tray. "I'd better take this before you drop it. Evidently you don't find these little encounters stimulating.

Some day we'll have round two, King and I. Subject: agoraphobia.
The Greeks named it. Fear of the market place. Ever hear of it?
Well, the good doctor must have."

"I'm afraid I don't get it, Ellie. You mean—"

"Don't keep saying you're afraid! You're not. You're only bewildered by some of the antics of dear Magdalene's private zoo. We're
just amusing ourselves, hon. With me, a good argument is the soul's
signal for rallying."

At the corner, Marmion looked back. From this distance the
echo of the lung was like a whisper from eternity. It did nothing
whatever to rally her soul.

"I'll keep a stiff upper lip, Ellie. I'm all right now. Give me the
tray."

She reached the stairs and saw the white head coming up from
the basement, a head with a clean pink line parting the hair. Although the old man paused, looking up after her, she did not stop.

He leaned on the newel post, getting his breath. The bent elbow
made the hole in his sweater sleeve very conspicuous. Even had he
known, he would not have minded. In thirty years, old St. Dennis
had seen him through all stages of new sweaters and old. When the
girl disappeared up the stairs, he pushed his glasses to his forehead
and rubbed the twin footprints they had left on the bridge of his
nose. With all things temporarily appearing to be at the bottom of
a tub of water, he did not see Sister Magdalene until she spoke.

"Good morning, Hal," she said. The old preacher was beginning
definitely to show his age. The corollary, unavoidable, was that she
also was growing old. She had come to the Hills in the same spring-
time that brought Mr. Wilkins and Big Balsam Cassidy. In years,
she was the middle of the trio; and now one was making a heavy
business of recovery from an illness that would take his strength,
and the youngest was old.

Mr. Wilkins nodded upward in the direction Marmion had gone.
"Little Job's daughter? I knew her mother. I've wondered, at times,
why a just Providence saw fit to put both parents into the white
racer when it smashed into the cliff."

"Our finite minds understand so little of the infinite," the Sister
replied. Someone had said that to her, long ago. Perhaps it was Hal

Wilkins himself, for she saw recognition in his half-smile, and she knew they were both being swayed by the same thought.

"Father Anthony, too, Maggie." The old preacher bowed his head and the white fringe of hair sprang out of his collar. "So young, that brother of yours, when he was killed. A rain-sleek trail, they said, and the horse losing its footing in the dark, plunging down the cliff. . . ."

"Not now, Hal."

He drew a long breath, and put on his glasses. The lenses were smeared from too many polishings with his thumb, but they enabled him to see again. He made an apologetic gesture.

"I'm sorry, Maggie. I say it clumsily. The thought is that we must so often make blind acceptance serve in place of reason. I believe even Cassidy has done that. They say he lost so much of his bluster in the last nine years, since Little Job died. Death came as near as it dared to the great Cassidy, taking Little Job. He seems to have bowed before it."

The conversation was disturbing to the nun. Mr. Wilkins seldom was anything but a mild, kindly, dear old man scuffing through the hospital, trailing invisible daisy chains of faith and good will, easing the day for every patient who cared to hear a Bible verse or play a game of checkers or merely wake for a second or two when his smile came around the door. Today there seemed to be an edge to his mildness. He had no reason to fear the behemoth of the Hills, no personal hatred; and yet the gentle soul was touched by both of those ungentle emotions as the beach is wet from the sea and yet is no part of it.

"We all came in the same year, you and Cassidy and I," he said. "I preached the gospel in the gold camps from Deadwood to Custer, and my words are as dead now as the fish Peter netted in the Sea of Galilee. You added the ministry of healing the sick to your living of the word of God, and your good deeds will be remembered after you. But Cassidy lived entirely without God, and he has made history."

The Sister could bring up only one small, troubled comment. "Hal, would you change places with Big Balsam Cassidy now?"

"Would you?"

They smiled at one another, and as if some soreness were healed between them, they turned to walk side by side to the entrance stairs. Long ago each had given up trying to influence the other's religious views. After all, as Mr. Wilkins had observed years ago, why waste time heading into defeat? Sympathetic friendship was a different matter.

Mr. Wilkins settled his old elastic-sided shoes one after the other down the hollows he and so many others had worn on the treads of the entrance stairs. The shoes stepped very precisely, as if they had come this way a thousand times before and the man in them needed no longer guide them. It was just as well. His mind was on where he had been, not where he was going. He was thinking how Cassidy's presence seemed to contaminate this precious place, and that he should chide himself, a man of the cloth, for harboring so un-Christian a thought. But he was too weary—that is, a little weary at the moment. Part way down the stairs he stopped to rest. This was the step where he always paused coming up. Never, until today, going down.

"Ah, well," he sighed.

He came out into Indian summer, golden sun, aspens and poppies quaking with golden leaves, heat radiating from dry-baked earth. In a day, even in a few hours, all the golden warmth could sizzle out under the first snow. Autumn ended that way, in South Dakota. But it was next to paradise while it lasted.

Pussyfoot Rayburn, down in the gulch where Little Balsam Creek slogged through its bed of black slime, saw Mr. Wilkins small as an ant walking on its hind legs down the long road from the hospital terrace. Against the brawny height of Balsam Mountain, St. Dennis was a dollhouse. Pussyfoot sat on the tumble-down bridge, the sun hot on his back, his shoes beside him and his bare feet swinging. Little enough time left to go barefooted. He hated shoes, never would wear them in summer if it weren't for Sister Judy coaxing him to uphold his dignity as engineer—only he knew he was a janitor—for St. Dennis.

Disregarding the Reverend, he squinted upstream, letting his tongue move around his lips as though he tasted something sweet. Up there, three miles to the north in the mountain-folded gulches, the Hellbent shafts stuck against the sky like grain elevators in the wheat country, slim above the low buildings cluttering the mountainside. You couldn't see the shafts from here; but that was where Little Balsam, splashing in harnessed pools through the Hellbent's stamp mills, turned black and picked up the cyanide. It would have been a dandy trout stream, without the cyanide.

A gravel truck rumbled between Pussyfoot and the nearing Mr. Wilkins, smoothly enough on the black top, kicking up a cloud of dust when it dropped off on to the old stage road that now led to the gravel pit. Pussyfoot waited for the dust to settle. Then he spat in Little Balsam's face.

"Some folks is stinkers," he observed. "And then, some ain't."

"Judge not, lest ye be judged," said Mr. Wilkins, but without conviction since he had just come through a small session of judging, himself.

"Phooey," said Pussyfoot. "You know who hated Cassidy uncommon bad? His best friend, only friend he had. Little Job Pyus." He squinted at the water. "She's got reason to hate him, too. Good reason."

"She?"

"Little Job's daughter."

Mr. Wilkins stepped off the road to let another gravel truck go by. He never liked this walk through the gulch. Like an old horse going home to the hay in his manger, he used to say, all that sustained him was the sanctuary ahead in Charity Chapel. He walked quickly, for him. But he could not walk away from his unwanted companions, Big Balsam Cassidy and Little Job Pyus. Until the flashy racer had crashed into the cliff, the two names had been synonymous with the Hellbent. Why there should have been any importance attached to the name of Pyus, no one seemed exactly to know. Little Job was a bluffer, a trampler, a loud and tawdry talker when he lorded it in a saloon alone. It was only in Big Balsam's company that he became small as a two o'clock shadow. Whatever his function in regard to the Hellbent, it had died with him. He had never been replaced. Little Job's daughter had gone away. And now she was back. . . .

4

Marmion well knew there was no sound other than trifles in the little sitting room—the tap of Eloise's knitting needles, the tiny blowing of Lynn's cigarette smoke toward the ceiling, the chirp of the sparrow on the flat roof outside the window. The respirator's wheezing could not possibly reach up here. And yet Marmion heard it in the way one catches an offensive odor long after coming into pure air. This was her rest period, from three to five. She had come upstairs with the idea of playing Uncle Josh and proving he had taken a hog and not a dog to the county fair, as Blanche insisted.

But Eloise was already there, in her slip, barefooted, her feet stuck out before her to hold her ball of yarn. In a few minutes Lynn had wandered in, off duty at three but looking as fresh as if she had just spent the past eight hours in sleep rather than in the exacting business of caring for Big Balsam Cassidy. She wore a scarlet satin robe, too stunning for a women's dormitory. In the front of it, a safety pin had pulled a hole. She lay back in the chair with the leaky arm and blew a smoke ring.

"He's a showman right to the core," Lynn said.

"The estimable Kingston, of course." Eloise nodded. "What's he staging now?"

"He stopped the lung. My stout Cassidy loved it. He's another miracle man."

"Well, it demonstrated that Big Balsam is recovering," Marmion declared, but as Lynn shook her head, she added, "Didn't it?"

"No. If Cassidy had been paralyzed, then I'd say yes. But he never was. His respiration is slowed to the point where he couldn't breathe in enough oxygen to keep him alive, but he could always manage a few breaths. Shutting off the lung was mostly a stunt."

"Then why do it?"

"A therapeutic measure. Persuade him he's better and he will be."

Eloise thoughtfully rolled the yarn between her feet. "I'd bet on King knowing what he's doing, though. And he's a marvelous surgeon. I don't deny he's excruciating to work with, temperamental as the dickens. Magdalene is the only one he can't browbeat. Still, I guess I'd rather work with him than with some old slugger that didn't know a scalpel from a buttonhook." The yarn rolled away. Swooping after it, she added, "I'd certainly love to despise Guy Murray Kingston, M.D."

"Join the sisterhood," said Lynn.

"He can't stand the sight of me," Eloise went on. "He's as introverted as a bear with a sore paw. D'you know what I've figured out? That I remind him of some dame that done him wrong, so every glimpse he gets of me, he wants to throw up."

"You're sure it isn't his liver?"

Marmion lifted a strand of blond hair from her shoulder and studied it. "We're not."

"Not what?" Eloise asked.

"Alike. But he hates me, too. Maybe he detests all women. What's the word for it?"

"Misogyny," said Lynn.

"Plus agoraphobia," Marmion observed. "Our good doctor has quite a cross to bear."

Eloise jerked the knitting. "Dram!—I told Sister Judy nobody could learn to knit without using profanity, so we compromised on dram. It's a reasonable facsimile."

"When are you kids going to get some ash trays?" Lynn asked, looking around lazily.

"When somebody gives them to us," said Eloise.

Lynn arose, stretching, the scarlet gown shining against her long limbs. These two were like a pair of conspirators, circling between Marmion and King, on guard for the man they professed to loathe. Well, you won't get away with concealing information, Marmion vowed.

"Agoraphobia, fear of the market place," she remarked. "The opposite of claustrophobia, fear of being closed in. Is King so morbidly afraid of open spaces that he never sets foot outside? Is that why Sister Magdalene was so astounded when he stepped out to take my suitcase?"

Lynn was in the doorway, her brown eyes wide as Eloise's.

"You're kidding!" Eloise exclaimed. "King actually went outside? I don't believe it!"

"He did. But what I'd like to know is, where did he get this unnatural fear? Was it because something awful happened to him in a wide-open space of some kind, and he can't forget it?"

Eloise shrugged. Lynn dropped her smoldering cigarette on the floor and stepped on it.

"A wide-open space, or a closed-in one. It would have to be either, wouldn't it?"

The gay figure went on out, and the two girls sat in silence, listening to Lynn's footsteps padding away.

"Our lovely Baird isn't immune to King, either," Eloise remarked.

Marmion sat down in the chair Lynn had vacated. "She gets his goat, though. This morning he told her to aspirate Cassidy's trachea tube right away, but she didn't do it until after King was gone. He was mad."

"An attention-getting device. If you can't make him notice you because he likes you, get him mad enough to notice you anyway."

"But if she hates him . . ."

"She doesn't. She's just like all the rest of us. She's more than a little bit in love with him."

"I'm not!" Marmion declared heatedly.

The argument was still going on when Blanche wandered in and asked was it hog or dog.

"I haven't had time to find out," said Marmion. "We're just getting down to a definition of love. I say it's Nature's clever way of fooling us into carrying on the race."

Blanche regarded her with sorrow. "You've never been in love."

"Have you?"

"Usually. There's different kinds. Take Johnny. . . . I think how nice it would be to have him up here, maybe listening to the gramophone, and him and me laughing and kidding—"

"Where is Polycarp about this time?" Eloise inquired.

"And there'll be more like Johnny. But then there's the other kind. It takes your breath away, like you went outside on a thirty below morning and it hurt to breathe."

"And someone has made you feel that way, Blanche?" Marmion asked.

The big girl cupped her hands around her elbows and rocked gently. "Sure. The doctor."

The knitting fell to Eloise's lap. Blanche ducked her head, hiding her little embarrassed smile, but she continued. "Course, he don't even know I'm alive. I wouldn't ever get to marry a man like him. The most I'll ever have is a fella on wages and a runty house with everything shoved under the bed when I get company. But I like work, so I guess I'll make out. I gotta go now. I'm carrying trays."

They listened to her steps going away as Lynn's had done.

"Ellie."

"Do you suppose you'll ever look at a man and feel like it hurt to breathe on a cold morning?"

"I wish I knew," said Eloise.

The storm was already rising in the west when Marmion recollected her duty and hastened down to the laboratory. Sister Judy was not there to note her tardiness. Marmion was just finishing her work when a nurse came in with a tray of bottles.

"I had to bring my own, so I picked up Hennesseys, too," she said.

She was not pretty, and yet the most common description of her was that pretty little Miss Bryan. Her brown hair curled out from under her cap like a baby's under a bonnet. But her forehead showed the cramp of pain and her eyes were squinted against the light.

"Headache, Dixie?" Marmion asked.

"A brute. What time is it—six thirty? Glory be, it's a long time till eleven!"

"Can't you get somebody to pinch hit for you?"

"I suppose Mrs. Hayes would come early, if her helpmate isn't plastered. He usually is. What a life, listening to that bum all day and Cassidy all night!"

"If there's anything I can do, Dixie . . ."

"Well, as a matter of fact, there is. Look in on Mrs. Totman. She wants some little errand done, I don't know what, and she won't ask the floor nurse because they're having a battle. I'll have to run now. Hennessey is staying with Cassidy while I'm up here. You can't leave these patients alone at all . . . thanks, Marmie, and don't forget. . . ."

Marmion worked on, completing tests that could just as well be done tomorrow. She did not want to be idle, with a storm coming up. Thunder was her terror, a senseless terror because the lightning never bothered her. The boom and crash of the thunder would be right over her head in the crow's-nest. But eventually everything was finished, the sink scrubbed and every bottle washed. She would bring her reports to the nurses and at the same time do the errand for Mrs. Totman. As she turned out the light, the creeping, growling bear of a storm touched his forepaw to the gulch and began to spit snow.

It was nearly nine on the clock above the chart desk. The floor nurse was not in sight. Marmion set an ink bottle on top of her small sheaf of slips and went on into Mrs. Totman's room. The patient was sitting up in bed reading a newspaper, her pink flannel sleeves rolled up from arms that would have been a handy size for a wrestler.

"Oh, it's you, dearie! Come in. You're not going to prick me at this hour of the night, are you? That's good. I was up today. But I says to Doc, don't push me, I says, the only vacations I get are when the stork comes. You seen the twins?"

"Tomorrow I will."

"You got to prick 'em?"

"Oh, yes, every day."

"Well, try not to gash 'em too deep. Look, dearie, would you do me a favor? I won't ask that frizzled-up Miss Bacon."

"That's what I came for, Mrs. Totman. Miss Bryan—"

"She's a sweet one, that! You open the middle drawer of the dresser. See a long white box?"

"This one? It could be a dozen long-stemmed roses."

"No, it's Sister Peter's corset. I guess the bones in the old one were stickin' her something awful. This one's got steel ribs, regular girders, awful heavy, but she won't mind. My oldest girl, Mellie, was going around to town today so I had her get it. Sister said to take it good and big so if she ain't spared to wear it out, Sister Magdalene can take over and be comfortable. I couldn't look forward to a thing like that, myself. Seems like when I buy a new girdle I kinda take a new lease on life."

Marmion pretended to be smoothing the paper on the box, a box too sturdy for roses. "I'll deliver it, safe and sound."

"Fine. If you could catch Sister Peter before they go into the Great Silence for the night . . . oh, and tell her Mellie'll be glad to change 'em if they ain't big enough."

The girl looked back at the kind, florid face framed by the sparse little braids. "I'll tell her," she said. Although the thunder crashed just then, she barely noticed it.

Marmion went slowly down the stairs. It would not be easy to reach a Sister once the good oak door of the cloister had closed behind her, a door that no lay person ever opened except a repairman thoroughly chaperoned. Down at the bottom of the entrance stairs, the black doors still showed tiny splashes of rain and snow. The wind threw itself about, a pine cone snapped against a pane, one of the old panels rattled as if someone leaned shivering against it. Any minute now the crawling giant would fling himself into the gulch. The thunder was almost continuous, the lightning flared white on the hillside.

With the box under her arm, Marmion glanced up and down the hall. Far off to the right the cloister door was closed on shadows. To the left were King's office, the diet kitchen, a ward or two, the wing where Big Balsam Cassidy was returning to life as boisterously as he had gone about dying. The storm violence outside lent the place coziness. Nothing in the quiet setting to warn of murder, nothing to tell the girl that this was the chosen hour, that her own safety was to depend upon her turning back up the stairs and forgetting the lab reports in her hand and Mrs. Totman's box under her arm. She hesitated, but only for a second. Then she walked down the dim hall to lay her slips on the chart desk.

It was the vague thought that the night supervisor, Sister Ursula, might be in the wing that kept Marmion lingering—that and the fact of the storm being shut away somewhat by the flanking rooms. Waiting, she leaned against the wall. Once long ago, on this very spot, a miner's wife had tried to kill herself because her man had been blown to bits up in the Killjoy. The ghosts still lived. When the door at her elbow opened, Marmion was startled. She had heard no voices inside, but now Dr. Hamlin came out—he had been the first doctor to hang out his shingle in the Gulch, but he would not remember Little Job's daughter—and King with his stethoscope around his neck; then Miss Hennessey who was always at logger-heads with everyone but her patients. She was wheeling a stretcher on which a young boy lay, wrapped to the chin.

The small procession passed Marmion without notice. When she was asked, later, how long she remained there, she never could tell. She heard the creaky old elevator ascend to the second floor. If the clock struck, the small tinny sound was consumed by the storm. No one else entered or left the hall, she swore to that, no one until Lynn Baird came out of Big Balsam's room. She stood in the wedge of light for a second, looking back at her patient. Then she closed the door. And saw Marmion.

She approached swiftly. "Do you know where Hennessey is?"

"She just took a patient on a stretcher—"

"Oh, the broken leg. I've got to have Cassidy's medicine. I suppose Dixie didn't think of it, with that horrible headache."

"You took her place? That's sweet of you, Lynn."

"Not particularly. I have nothing to do evenings. Listen, if you'd stay with Cassidy, I'll run down to the pharmacy myself. King must have put out the medicine, and Dixie forgot. I don't like to leave the patient alone—he's too restless. But I've just cleaned his tracheotomy and I'm sure he'll be all right for a few minutes."

Something within Marmion recoiled, as if she smelled food that had once made her very ill. But she couldn't refuse.

"Of course I'll stay. Only hurry, won't you?"

Clasping the corset box, Marmion went reluctantly to the end of the wing. She opened the door, and the suction of the lung seemed to draw her into the room. Big Balsam lay as he had before, his head protruding from the clown's ruff of cotton, but this time his eyes were closed and a faint blood color had crept deep into the flesh of his cheeks. Had the therapeutic measure, as Lynn termed it, been responsible for all this?

"You are better, really better!" Marmion said.

She was close to him, but Big Balsam did not hear. She did not hear herself very clearly. The thunder smashed at the old building, shaking the very hillside on which it stood. She never knew how many minutes she remained there, beside him, before the gagging began, only a few small bubblings at first but terrifying to Marmion because she was alone and because she remembered his misery of this morning and because his head began to jerk away from the confining collar.

"Help me!" He mouthed the words noiselessly.

"Don't struggle like that!" she begged. "And don't be afraid! I'll get Sister Ursula. Or Miss Hennessey. You're all right!"

He nodded faintly. She started toward the door. But only a step. Before she could take another, the storm lashed viciously against the windows. The whole of Balsam Mountain quaked.

And the lights went out. Sudden, complete night fell upon the room, and under the stunning blow of it, Marmion stood motionless. She did not think, for that first minute, to fear the crashing thunder or to wish that the illumination of the lightning might enter the room through the drawn shades. She did not think at all—until she missed the sound of the lung.

She moved then, quickly, and came up hard against the cool side of the respirator. The feel of it was the impact of terror. The thing had stopped! Inside it, gagging and choking, Big Balsam lay helpless in the dark. Her panic scattered any coherent reasoning Marmion might have done. Disconnected bits fled through her mind. Cassidy could breathe without the lung, he had done it this morning; but the doctor had been there, the patient was not frightened. There must be a way to work the lung by hand, if only she knew how, if she could find the mechanism in the pitch dark.

Marmion's hand slid down to the man's face. "You're all right, Mr. Cassidy, I'll help you, don't be afraid!"

She didn't know whether he tried to answer. His efforts to breathe were surely not so vigorous as they had been.

"Help!" she screamed. "Help! Come quick, somebody!"

She left the lung, to feel along the wall, find the closet door and be fooled by it until the clothes brushed her face, then fumble on again, screaming and sobbing, in her panic not knowing the outside door when she came to it, on past it until she stumbled against the dresser. That was when the door opened across the room behind her. She would not have known about it except that a flashlight beam struck across to her and was instantly shut off.

"Lynn?" she sobbed. "Is it you, Lynn? Help him! Hurry!"

The light did not come on again. Beyond the window shades, the lightning flashed but its brilliance was shut out of the room. Whoever had entered was invisible in the darkness, the sound of any movement imperceptible in the uproar of the storm.

"Who is it?" Marmion begged. "Turn on your flash! I'll help you. . . ."

She stopped; for suddenly, so late, a warning sense told her that she would not be answered. Someone had come in, of that she was certain. A stealthy presence, uncannily hushed, moved somewhere near the lung. And then, in a moment of comparative quiet, she became aware that the man's struggle for breath had ceased. At the same time, there was a new sound, a steady, small hissing. She didn't know when the bubbling breath had stopped and the hissing began. Her fright had become a physical state, freezing her screams into a faint mewling, sucking darkness into her brain. The hissing was a snake, rising green-eyed and swaying beside her, a monster she could not fight off . . . and she fell into a gaping, quiet cavity of night that had nothing to do with the storm. . . .

It was Dr. Kingston who tripped over the unconscious girl, knelt to feel her pulse briefly, roared at Johnny to never mind her and get light wherever he could. There were a half-dozen flashlights by then: Lynn's turned on the pressure gauge of the lung, Dixie's on the floor while she pushed and pulled the hand lever of the bellows and tried to keep in time with Lynn's counting. Johnny held a trembling light for the doctor and Sister Ursula. Marmion, coming slowly back to consciousness, heard the respirator and thought it was her own breathing. Her bed was too hard. She moved, her elbow struck the wall. And then she remembered.

The doctor turned suddenly and looked straight down at Marmion. "Are you all right?"

She nodded.

"Then get out of here."

She was still sick and weak, and his curtness made her want to cry. She pushed herself to a sitting position, and the effort riled up the darkness into which she had fallen. The doctor, she saw through a giddy haze, was paying no attention to her. Dixie, doggedly working the hand lever, was a strange sight in pajamas and fluffy housecoat. They were an other-world company, all of them, casting great shadows, silent, their hands and faces pale and inhuman. Sister Magdalene alone stood back, perhaps because too many hands would hinder; but her gaze was fixed on the man in the lung. Marmion could not see him. She didn't want to see him. She got up slowly and dragged herself out of the room.

Someone had lighted a kerosene lamp on the chart desk, and through the flood around it, dazzling in comparison to darkness, Marmion made her way. In the soft gray mist of the stairs, she sat down. Her head was splitting, she could not think. But she knew she had behaved very badly, screaming and fainting, acting generally like a schoolgirl, as King would have expected. How good it would be now to remember that she had kept her wits, taken a few seconds to orient herself in the darkness, and then gone competently to find a nurse. And she might have controlled her terror, at the last, if that person hadn't come in. . . .

Groaning, Marmion dropped her head into her hands.

"What's the matter, baby?" Eloise asked, sitting down beside her because the stairs were narrow and she must leave room for all the hurrying nurses.

"My head!"

"Run into a door in the dark?"

"Not exactly. I was with Cassidy just now, when the power went off. And of course the lung stopped. It was pretty ghastly." She felt the other girl's thigh tighten against her own.

"Marmie, he didn't—he—they got it going again—in time?"

Marmion stiffened against the railing, and a bit of carving dented her shoulder. "In time? What do you mean?"

Eloise's cold grip was upon her wrist. Into the pool of light at the chart desk, three people emerged from the dark wing: Sister Ursula,

Sister Magdalene, and the doctor. As King seated himself and took down a chart, Lynn joined them; then Dixie, folding the blue robe about her. The doctor began to write. All the eyes followed his pen, shocked and unbelieving. Even for those who have seen the transition, it is hard to accept the fact that the burly living have suddenly become the dead.

"Oh, no!" Marmion breathed.

But King's pen went on writing, setting down the record that meant the end of the embattled, formative period of the Hellbent and the Hills. Because Big Balsam Cassidy was only a name, now. He had died while Marmion stood helpless beside him. Everything they had done since had been done for a dead man.

Huddled together on the stairs, the two girls did not see the small figure come quietly up from the dark end of the hall and go in silence up the stairs behind them. When they were asked whether anyone had passed, both were positive that no one had.

5

The storm winds were so spent that they were barely able to whistle around the rimrock when Jock and the doctor, by the light of a kerosene lamp, turned off the oxygen tank and opened the respirator. The coroner made his examination of the earthly remains of the great Cassidy, the sheriff thankfully accepted his colleague's opinion that a freak of nature had been the cause of accidental death; and then they had checked, for certainty, with the power company.

"Yeah, line's down somewhere." The night foreman's assurance had come over the wire. "Lucky the phones aren't knocked out too, eh? No, the lights are all out on that side of the mountain, Sheriff. Somebody else just called me from down in the Gulch. We can't do a thing about it till daylight, but I'll get the boys out just as soon as it's bright enough to see. We've got a small airplane now. Flies right over the line. We can locate the breaks fast that way. . . . Huh? O.K., we'll speed it up."

The sheriff was more relieved than he would have cared to admit. Range battles over grazing rights, hotheaded shootings with plenty of witnesses—those had been his career. He was tall and gaunt, with hooked nose and tight mouth, and he had been sheriff for more years than most people remembered—too old, they said, to have run for office again; but he had gone in, as usual, on a landslide vote. In the hospital waiting room he sat writing carefully at a table where a kerosene lamp burned. Like the others, Marmion watched the movement of the pencil up to the sheriff's tongue, down to the notebook to write blacker for a few words before fading into gray. He was putting down all the facts they had told him so precisely,

301

adding them up into the sum total of the historic period his own life had spanned.

The sheriff did not look up until King and Jock appeared in the open arch of the waiting room. The entrance stairs were a dark well behind the two white figures. All the silent people turned to look with the sheriff, although there would be nothing new to hear. Sister Magdalene and Sister Ursula were deliberately composed, Lynn interested as she would be in a critical operation, Dixie still frowning away her headache, and Marmion benumbed.

"Done, boys?" the sheriff asked.

King nodded. Everyone moved, relaxing. This was the conclusion of all the horror they had endured.

But Marmion leaned forward, her face stark, her eyes nearly black in the lamplight. "I'm to blame, Sheriff. I lost my head completely. If I'd only been calm, run to get someone instead of groping around like that in the dark. . . ."

Before the sheriff could protest, Lynn replied with the first agitation she had shown. "I know how you feel, Marmion! But if it's anyone's fault, it's mine. I shouldn't have left you with him, I should have waited until Hennessey came back . . . and then I'd have been there when the power went off."

The sheriff turned over his notes. "Just why did you leave, Miss Baird?"

Lynn's hesitation was slight, but Marmion caught it. She won't involve Dixie, the girl thought. She's too fair to put the blame on someone else.

"I had to have Mr. Cassidy's medicine," Lynn replied. "I didn't think I'd be gone over two minutes. The pharmacy is just at the foot of the stairs, in the basement."

"How did you get the medicine, other times?"

Jock answered from the archway beside King. "I brought it up, Sheriff. I knew Cassidy's nurses couldn't leave him."

"Then how did you happen to slip up tonight?"

Sister Magdalene was like a mother coming to the defense of her children. "Miss Bryan had a terrible headache, Sheriff. She must be excused for any oversight. And Jock was not on duty after seven.

Also, we had an emergency, a little boy with a broken leg. And then the storm was making the patients. . . ."

The words trailed away as a scream cut down through the darkness, a high, piercing scream, persisting until the quiet was cut to shreds. At first it seemed only to come out of the night, from neither place nor direction. When it gathered identity, it became a woman screaming somewhere on the second floor near the laboratories.

The sheriff shot to his feet, rocking the lamp dangerously. Then he was out of the room, sprinting after the doctor, Jock hippety-hopping in their wake, all running up the stairs toward the screaming that had now become a terrified sobbing. There were other sounds in a moment, tumbling down out of the dark, patients awakening to that grotesque weeping and beginning a frightened wailing of their own.

Sister Magdalene gave orders hurriedly. "Miss Baird and Dixie, see if Miss Hennessey needs help down here. If she doesn't, come to the second floor and help Miss Baxter."

The Sisters were gone, Lynn and Dixie with them, all running to duty that came ahead of their own fears. And Marmion was left alone with hers. Suddenly she was on her feet and running like the others up the stairs. She stumbled on a step and skinned her knee, but nothing stopped her, not the dark lying everywhere between fitful pools of lamp and candlelight, not the fact that every step carried her nearer to the spot where someone still sobbed and moaned. They were over at the stair well of the crow's-nest, a group of excited people, and the object of their excitement apparently lay at the foot of the stairs.

Marmion caught hold of Dixie, who was running past. "What happened? Who is screaming?"

"Eloise. Poor kid, she found her."

"Found who?"

"Sister Judy!"

Dr. Kingston was coming toward them, carrying a small nun who lay limp against him, one arm dangling like a child's. She was in her good black habit and a fresh white coif. But the coif was not so fresh as it had been. Now there was blood on it. Miss Baxter slipped past King to light the way down the stairs, and the stain on the white glowed bright red. The stair rail was etched in black for a minute, then they were gone. Eloise's crying died away.

"Dixie, where did—" Marmion began. But Dixie also had vanished. Down the stairs there was the rustle of a habit, another reflection of light growing from below. The girl peeked over the balustrade. Sister Polycarp, of course, in pursuit of trouble. The nearest door stood open a couple of inches. Marmion pushed it wider, felt it strike an obstacle, pushed harder, and slipped inside.

Someone was there, breathing beside her, not in bed as a patient should be but close in the very black room! A fuzzy thing brushed her elbow.

"Mrs. Totman?"

A relieved sigh came out of the pitch dark. "And who else, in my own room? What on earth is going on here? Who knocked out Sister Judy?"

"Knocked her out? Oh, for goodness' sake, I never thought of that!"

"Well, somebody did, heaven knows, prowlin' around in the dead of night! And her goin' up them stairs like she belonged up there! What was she doing out of the cloister?"

Marmion swayed and caught herself against the door. This was the first of the dizzying dread she would know in the next few days, the foreboding she should have felt in time to turn away from the wing that was so soon to be dashed into darkness.

"Mrs. Totman, tell me what you mean!"

"Nothing. But there's some kind of funny business goin' on here tonight, and that's no lie. I'm gonna get back in bed, honey. If Baxter saw me up like this she'd have Doc send me home tomorrow. Oh, by the way, you found Sister Peter all right?"

"Sister—oh, the corset. It's safe," Marmion fibbed. What had she done with the box? She had been clasping it when she went into Big Balsam's room because she remembered how it had struck against the door jamb. And then what? She must have dropped it when the lights went out. Unless someone had kicked it out of the way, Sister Peter's corset would still be lying, wrapped like a sheaf of roses, beside the respirator.

And she would have to retrieve the package, Marmion insisted to herself as she helped Mrs. Totman to feel her way under the covers. Nothing in the world was more horrible than the thought of entering that fearfully empty room again. But whoever picked up the box would open it, naturally, and then there would have to be an explanation, and dear old Sister Peter would be embarrassed to tears at a public display of her underpinning.

Mrs. Totman was rambling comfortably on. "Mellie wants Rollo and Roscoe, but their dad says it's gotta be something manly. I'm sure glad the others come one at a time, so's we could name 'em— you leaving, dearie? Well, maybe it's better. You sure need your rest."

Marmion let herself out into the dark hall. Sister Polycarp was not in sight. She could run down now to the quiet room, ask Miss Hennessey to come with her to find the box. . . . But she didn't. She took a candle from the box on the chart desk, lighted it, and fled up the stairs to the crow's-nest. Sister Peter's discomfiture was of small account compared to her own terrors. She was only halfway up when the candle went black out.

6

The diminishing storm still whipped around the building, sifting in at every window, and it was the down draft from the upper floor that had blown out the candle. But Marmion was not being reasonable. Scraping her shins wickedly, she groped up in the dark, saw a dimness at the far end of the rank of rooms, and ran stumbling toward it. When she came into the little sitting room, she saw what an impression running footsteps in the night could make on frightened people. Eloise in her white uniform, Blanche in a housecoat with her hair in pin curls, Philippa on the edge of the big chair and Chad asleep in her arms—the three gave the illusion of being huddled together, their pale faces turned to the door. Blanche had picked up one of the gramophone records and was holding it like a missile in her hand.

Philippa gave a long sigh. The storm wind rattled the sash as if someone tapped to gain their attention. Blanche laid down the record.

"Ellie, you're all right?" Marmion asked.

Eloise, her face tear-stained, was not nonchalant any more. She was like a child frightened sick, chastened but petulant. "Of course I'm all right!"

"But you—you screamed so—"

"Wouldn't you if you fell over somebody in the dark?"

"I know I would, Ellie!"

"She'd been taking the X rays of the boy's leg," Philippa said as if this were a story she had learned. "When the power went off, there was no use staying down there. A nurse was with the boy. So after a while, when they were sure the current wouldn't come on again, she started up here."

"You were with me, Ellie, on the stairs," Marmion said without knowing why.

"I went back to the lab, after that. But they'd taken the boy downstairs, so there was nothing for me to do. And I started up here—and I tripped over her."

Marmion slipped an arm around Ellie. And then, because no one spoke, they heard the running on the stairs, then along the rubber matting. Blanche leaned toward the candle, her lips pursed to blow it out. Before she could blow, the steps reached the doorway. It was Dixie who had been running in flopping mules, taking a chance on a turned ankle.

"If there hadn't been a light, I'd never have come!" she panted. "There's been too much going on up here tonight."

That was what Mrs. Totman had said. But instead of Marmion, it was Philippa who asked the question.

"Like what?"

"Like Sister Judy coming up here and finding the master switch disconnected. And somebody jumped her in the dark!"

The small group tightened, one moving a fraction nearer to another. When Chad whimpered, his mother tucked the blanket closer around him.

"Dixie, what do you know about the master switch?" Eloise asked hoarsely. "Don't hold back! *Tell* us!"

"Baxter told me. She was with Sister Judy when the sheriff questioned her. . . . I'm cold," she observed irrelevantly. The little room was warm and stuffy. Blanche pushed forward a footstool and she sat down, shivering. "I don't know why Judy thought of the switch, but she did. She got up and dressed, and took her flashlight and came to look—and the switch handle, it fits tight into the connection, but it was dangling loose against the wall. It's right—out—there. . . ."

The girls drew even closer together. Not fifteen feet away, in the attic darkness beside the dim old gable window, was the master switch that controlled the entire intake of electric current for the hospital. Pull that switch and you plunged the whole building into darkness. Someone had done it tonight.

"If—if someone pulled the switch . . ." Eloise's stiff lips could not finish.

"Yes," said Dixie, "if someone pulled it, then it was because that someone knew the respirator would stop without current, and Cassidy couldn't live. But whoever did it would be two floors away, safe because everyone would run away to Cassidy, to help. . . ."

Neither could Dixie finish. She could have put it all into one short word: murder. But the word was too terrifying to utter, too secret and menacing.

"The switch isn't near the stairs!" Marmion whispered. "How could Sister Judy?—"

"She was attacked over here. Right here. And she lay in the dark for a long time. And then she says she fell down the stairs because she was running too fast."

Dixie's whisper overlaid, for a moment, the sound of the steps coming up the stairs, heavily. Blanche leaned swiftly forward and blew out the candle.

"I want to talk to that girl again. Pyus. How do I get to the third floor?"

The sheriff was not merely asking for information, he was demanding. The doctor, seated in his old-fashioned office chair, his feet resting on a desk drawer, was a good deal like a Buddha with a candle burning before his shrine.

"Have you thought of walking boldly up?" he suggested.

"Come with me."

The doctor and the sheriff reached the foot of the crow's-nest stairs just as a large puddle of flashlight beam flowed past the sitting-room door. In the puddle, a man's feet walked in high-heeled riding boots. He went straight to the master switch. Marmion, on Blanche's lap, breathed hardly more than Big Balsam. The man was tinkering at the switch, making soft breathing noises quite audible to the tense group in the little room.

And then Sister Polycarp's voice came sharply from just outside the door. "Sir, what are you doing here? We have rules!"

The man dropped something that clattered.

"Gentlemen do not come up here unescorted, sir!" The Sister's flashlight snapped on, showing her bristling and outraged.

"I'm sorry, ma'am, but somebody's already been up here."

"A likely excuse!" Sister Polycarp declared, a remark that covered everything she could not hear.

"He wiped his fingerprints off'n the switch handle, too," the stranger drawled, unperturbed. "A right thorough gent. Hey, that you, Sheriff?"

"It's me. No fingerprints, Joe? You're sure?"

Sister Polycarp wheeled to face the newcomers. Her flash cut across the sitting room, paused, then swooped in to rest upon one girl after another. "In the dark? Have you no candle?"

"Light it quick!" Eloise whispered.

Marmion struck a match. The flaring up of the candle was like the brightness of the sun upon the morning glory horn, the bishop's portrait, the brass center table, and the chair with the leaky arm. Behind the Sister, in the door, were the sheriff and King.

"Ah!" said the sheriff.

He was so close to her good ear that Sister Polycarp could not mistake his satisfaction. She crossed to the love seat, set herself firmly down, slipped her hands up her sleeves, and fastened her gaze upon the two men. Now, she said wordlessly, badger these young ladies if you dare!

"Here, Sheriff," Dixie invited. "I'll sit on the floor."

The tall old man folded himself onto the chair. King, impassive in what might have been an amusing situation, lounged in the doorway.

"I'm not going to bother you long," the sheriff remarked. He was a tired old friend, come in for a chat, no notebook, no sharpness in his voice or manner. "It just occurred to me that maybe some one of you might have thought over something or other, maybe seen it in a different light. It makes a difference, our accident being—murder."

He dropped the new name deliberately, yet he watched the flickering of the candle rather than the flicker of possible fear upon a face.

"This has been an awful disappointing evening for somebody," he resumed. "We'd pegged it an accident. I'd called the power company, and they'd said the line had blown down. Our disappointed friend couldn't have known the line would blow down, of course, the way it did. He was counting on us thinking it was a tree limb fell across the line and grounded the current till the wind threw the limb off again. Happens all the time. There was a great line-up of coincidences in his favor, you see: the storm, Miss Baird having to go for medicine, then the actual shutting off of the current. He'd gone back to put the switch on again when he ran into Sister Judith. Rough luck. Real disheartening, when everything else had gone off so well."

The sheriff picked a bit of lint off his trouser knee and rolled it under his thumb. "But the real disappointment is that if he hadn't done a thing, nature would have attended to the job for him. The only hitch might have been he'd have had to knock out Miss Baird. She'd have known how to run the respirator by hand." He tossed away the lint and for the first time looked directly around the voice-less company. "The electric clock in the surgery stopped at nine twenty-eight. The fellow at the power office—I called him back—he says he's positive it was a little later when somebody phoned from the gulch and said the current had just gone off. I'll find out for sure tomorrow. All these things make a difference, Cassidy's death being murder."

Marmion's hands clenched hard in her lap. She was on the floor now beside Dixie, in the sheriff's shadow. He was not paying much attention to her.

"As far as we can find out, nobody left the hospital tonight after the lights went out. All the visitors had gone before nine, on account of the storm. So, if nobody left, then our disappointed one is still with us."

He glanced down carelessly at Marmion. She knew when his glance clung and hardened. She knew when all the other eyes alight-ed upon her in alarming accord.

The admission was forced from her. "He came back—while I was there."

Eloise gasped. If the others recoiled, Marmion didn't know. She was again in the dark beside the respirator, sensing those quiet movements somewhere across the room, and again the waves of blackness rolled toward her.

"Miss Pyus!" the sheriff said firmly. "Who was it? Tell me!"

Marmion shook her head. The sheriff took it for refusal to answer, but she was only trying to remain above the black ocean.

"It was dark," he reminded her. "Didn't he have a flashlight?"

"Yes."

"Then you saw him."

"No. The light was on for only a second, just on and off. And my back was turned. By the time I whirled around, the light was gone."

He doesn't believe me, she thought dully. I've piled on too much. I should have said my back was turned and let it go at that.

But surprisingly, he accepted her answer. "All right. Then what?"

"I don't know. I mean—he worked in the dark—"

"Worked? What doing?"

"I've told you I don't know! The storm was too wild for me to hear. Really, I just had the impression he was there and doing something."

"Where? In what part of the room?"

Marmion dared not say again that she didn't know. She made a limp gesture. "Over there." That was when the nightmare of the snake began, the hissing, weaving thing.

"At Cassidy's head or feet?"

"Head, I suppose. I was at the foot of the respirator."

"So if he'd been trying to work the lung by hand, he'd have been right beside you. And he wasn't?"

"Oh, no, I'm sure of that."

Marmion's gaze was on the floor.

Someone white-shod had come into the doorway beside King several minutes ago, to stand listening. Now, to Marmion's relief, the sheriff addressed the newcomer.

"Was this mysterious intruder there when you came, Miss Baird?"

"I didn't see him. I was turned around a little, in the dark. I'm not too familiar with St. Dennis, Sheriff. I had never worked here, you know, until I took this case."

"But you'd got the medicine from the pharmacy—"

"No, I didn't go that far. I was just at the foot of the stairs when the lights went out. So of course my first thought was for my patient, and I hurried as fast as I could back up to the wing."

"Who came next, after you?"

"I'm not sure, I think it was Sister Ursula. And Jock. They came almost together. Everybody thought of Cassidy."

King's flashlight, hanging in his hand, made a quick arc and fell back.

"And you, Doctor?" the sheriff prompted.

"I was down in my room. I'd finished my rounds."

"But you thought of Cassidy?"

"Naturally."

"Who was with him when you got there?"

"Miss Baird. Sister Ursula. Jock. Johnny. Miss Bryan, I guess."

"Miss Bryan." The sheriff looked down at Dixie in the fluffy robe, her bare feet tucked under her. "What have you to tell me, Miss Bryan?"

Dixie shrugged faintly. "Only what you know, Sheriff. But I'm wondering why Marmion can't help you a little more. I shouldn't think it would be too hard to tell whether the mysterious person was a man or a woman."

No, no, Marmion wanted to scream, don't make it any harder for me! Nice, dear little Dixie, don't be so undear!

"By the rustle of a uniform, for instance," the nurse was going on. "A nurse's skirts aren't like the swish of an orderly's fresh trouser legs. And she uses bath powder, usually—"

"It wasn't either!" Blanche burst out.

Everyone jumped. The sheriff turned to her with interest. "Wasn't who?"

"Johnny! He's our only clean orderly at night!"

Eloise smiled. "She means Jock works all day. His whites wouldn't be in shape to swish by evening."

"But I couldn't hear anything!" Marmion insisted. "The storm—"

"If he'd come in from outside, you could have smelled wet clothes," Dixie prodded.

"I didn't! I didn't! Why do you keep saying I know when I don't! Cassidy was murdered, somebody hated him that much. I did, I hated him! But I wouldn't protect his murderer!"

Sister Polycarp was instantly on her feet. But it was King who knelt beside the hysterical girl, jerked her erect, and slapped her face smartly. Marmion gasped, her fingers going to her stinging cheek. But she was quiet. The only noise was Blanche's frightened whimpering.

The sheriff spoke earnestly. "Miss Pyus, the person who came into that room had an excellent reason for keeping mum. If he wasn't guilty in some way, he'd have identified himself to me long ago. I think he'd pulled the switch or knew who had. Later he attacked Sister Judith. He's already killed once; the punishment wouldn't be any worse for two murders. Don't you see you're asking for trouble?"

"I'm not!" Marmion sobbed in a hoarse whisper. "I don't know anything! I didn't see—I didn't hear. . . ." There was something, if only he would allow her to think!

She dared not cry aloud, not with King's big hand opening again. Sister Polycarp intervened.

"She has talked enough for tonight, Sheriff. Where are your beds, Miss Campion?

"In there, Sister," Eloise quavered. "Mine has the Teddy bear."

Chad had awakened and was crying lustily into his mother's shoulder. Blanche, on the floor, hiccupped without tears, watching King warily. Someone knocked an Uncle Josh record off the table and it rolled out of sight.

"I'll just get out of here quietly," the sheriff suggested.

Sister Polycarp, in the bedroom door, turned. "Not without escort, sir! Miss Baird, see that Miss Pyus gets to bed. Come, sir. And walk slowly!"

She marched out of the room and down the rubber-matting trail, closing doors firmly ahead of the sheriff. She seemed to forget that she was leaving another gentleman, unchaperoned, behind her. But the doctor was not in a mood to linger. Almost on the sheriff's heels, he was down the stairs.

Because he remembered his notebook lying on the table by the lamp, the officer returned to the waiting room. Even his pencil still lay where he had dropped it when he heard Eloise scream. But he halted in surprise on the threshold. Sister Magdalene was there, waiting with the patience that goes beyond mere lack of restlessness and becomes a virtue in itself. She stirred when he came in, watched while he picked up the notebook and dropped it into his pocket,

then seated himself away from the light. She was thinking of how
he had come once before, in the middle of the night and in a storm
as vicious as this one—many times, of course, to investigate other
accidents but only the once like that. They had been younger then,
both of them. If sorrow was sharper, physical strength had at least
been better able to endure shock.

"Thirty years, isn't it, Sister?"

She nodded. Sympathy rather oddly softened the man's weathered face. She was comforted to know he remembered also. "Twenty-
nine last April. It was spring, a spring rain."

"A spring rain, a freak of nature," the sheriff mused. "The horse
slipped on the slick mountain trail—I've had it happen to me. But
Father Anthony fell harder than I ever did." He raised his head and
looked across at her thoughtfully. "Those were tough years for the
priests, Sister. I remember one over in Popple Run about that time,
used to carry a gun when he went out on sick calls at night. A kid
jumped him once, just for a joke, and came mighty near to getting
shot."

"I begged Anthony to carry a gun, too. His life meant so much to
me, my only brother. . . ." The Sister paused, and when she resumed
her tone was quick. "Anthony's death was an accident, a plunge in
the dark from Horsethief Trail. That ravine was treacherous, everyone said. And he went everywhere on sick calls!"

"Sure. Cardinelle's house was no different from any other. Only
her ladies wore silk, and rode through the town in fancy carriages."

Sister Magdalene settled back into her chair. She spoke so seldom of Father Anthony. The sheriff mistook her sudden quietness.

"Holy smoke, Sister, you're ready to fall over! You get along to
the cloister! And don't sit down and start thinking again, either. You
go to bed!"

The nun smiled. Murmuring that she was all right, but letting
him persuade her, she said good night and walked slowly to the
cloister. How many years had it been since a man had told her what
to do—and she had done it? Self-sufficiency with dependence on
God, that was what maintained you as head of any convent group;
but no matter how well you had mastered the technique of being
self-sufficient, let a man give an order and the eternal woman in you

obeyed. Even with nuns who had learned the lesson to the point of complacence, Sister Magdalene pondered, the natural impulse to submit would often give them a struggle. For herself, meekness was welcome, at the moment. She closed the cloister door behind her. All was peace and quiet. Yet in that peaceful quiet, she would find she could not sleep.

Marmion had stubbornly refused to take the sedative Lynn said the doctor had left for her.

"Later," the girl insisted, "Ellie will be getting ready for bed for a while, and she'll keep me awake. The minute she's ready to hop in, I'll take it."

"Well, make it soon or you'll be asleep half the morning," Lynn remarked, and went away.

When she was gone, Marmion sat bolt upright in bed. Eloise had not taken off even her uniform. She sat on the foot of her own cot and stared into the candle flame on the dresser, and when Marmion spoke, she jumped.

"Ellie, I'm going down there to get it! I just can't let somebody else find it!"

"Find what?"

"Sister Peter's corset."

"Sister Pete's—*what?* Honey, you're delirious!"

Marmion did not want to get the giggles and perhaps go into hysterics again. But the story was funny, as she told it to Eloise. Mrs. Totman's kindness and her own cherishing of the treasure and the old Sister's certain embarrassment if the box were found by—heaven forbid!—a man!

"Look, I'll go," Eloise said. "I'll get the dram thing and be done with it. Here's your pill. Down the hatch. That's the girl. Afraid? Why should I be?"

"But it's so far down there! And dark. Ellie, let me come—"

"Not on your life, baby! I'm going to do this little errand without fanfare. You'd pass out on me before I'd be to the second floor. No, you lie down now and let that pill get busy. I'll be back instanter."

"We'll wait till morning," Marmion objected, but she lay down. She was too relieved to argue. And soon, too sleepy. With her last conscious thought she wondered why Eloise should have practically grabbed at the chance to venture again into the heavy blackness that had already thrust terror upon her. She did not know exactly when Eloise went. She didn't know that someone came softly into the sitting room, hesitated, listened to her own regular breathing, and then went away. The quiet feet made noiseless descent where Eloise had gone a few minutes before.

Downstairs, the girl entered the horribly vacant room where Big Balsam Cassidy had died. Like Marmion, she neither saw nor heard anyone behind her. The storm was calmer, but the sound was only a faint rustle and there was no light to see. No one could identify a rustle of the night itself.

Nothing else touched her until the dawn broke and the rosy light made a flame of her hair where it spilled across the floor.

7

Eloise stirred when the sun touched her. Then she sat up. She was in the room with the empty respirator. Her head throbbed. Gingerly she felt of the painful spot and found a swelling that shot daggers through her brain. Reeling, she sat there. She had come for a box. There was no box on the floor or on the dresser. If she could get to her feet without splitting her head wide open, she would look in the dresser drawers and in the closet. But the torturing hunt yielded nothing. Sick, she dragged herself to the door, down the hall, up the stairs, on up to the crow's-nest. No one was astir. She had been too miserable to try to avoid being seen, yet nobody saw her. When she fell into bed, Marmion, soundly asleep, did not move.

Down in the bare and chilly basement room where Big Balsam lay, there was no bright sunlight, nothing but grimy shadows in the corners and white twilight around the sheeted stretcher. The stretcher was very narrow, even narrower than the lung had been. They had laid pillows over him, bringing him down here, smoothing the sheet over the pillows so that an aroused patient glancing out would think only that Jock was wheeling a load of bedding. The pillows were gone now. The sheet, wilted in the dampness of the room, clung far too revealingly, as if the man's features and powerful limbs were carved in marble like the ancient figures reclining on the stone caskets of abbeys. Big Balsam's feet were not crossed. He had not been a crusader. Nothing moved in the small place, not even a breath of air, until the doorknob turned stealthily. It was a long minute more before the door swung in, so slowly, so silently that it was more like a parting of the gloom back there along the shadowy wall. The corner of the sheet moved as it might move with a slight easing of the stiff position on the stretcher.

Pussyfoot, who had let only his head into the room, jerked back. It was all he could do to keep from slamming the door. Clutching the knob, he stood panting, listening, shaking, his tongue salty from the spot he had bitten. He didn't want to go in there. He didn't want to at all. He hadn't wanted to go into that other room, either. But it had been good for him in the long run. The faint draft through the door was damp and smelled like a grave newly dug in wet clay, a natural enough phenomenon since he himself had mopped the room early in the afternoon and left the customary puddles on the cement floor. What was there to be scared of in a place where he had slapped down spiders and slopped around suds only a few hours earlier? It wouldn't be like that other room, somebody poking in. . . .

With a gathering of courage, Pussyfoot pushed the door wide enough to let himself in. He wouldn't shut it after him. Should someone discover him, there was no explanation necessary. Anyone could keep company with the dead, even one who had been quite unwelcome in life. Reluctantly, a step at a time, feeling every grain of cool wet cement under his bare soles, Pussyfoot stole forward. He wished the pillows were still between Big Balsam and the sheet. He wished he had never come in here. But more than anything, he wanted to look once more at Big Balsam.

He shifted the box under his arm, the box that looked as if it might contain a dozen long-stemmed roses. Then, furtively, he took hold of the smooth, wide hem of the sheet and lifted it back. For the better part of the past two hours he had thought over what he would say, contemptuous, biting, uncautious things that had ding-ed at him for years and never dared come out. He would say them now, probably in a whisper, but with venom.

And then the sheet was down to Cassidy's chin, and Pussyfoot's hand on it was still. He studied the face cleared now of all human emotion. The ruthless lines were gone about the mouth, around the eyes were none of the crow's feet that had screwed them into boring intensity, in the solid jaw the muscles were relaxed to the roundness of youth. This was the face of the man he could have been, not the man he ever was. Pussyfoot's hand crawled up to his own bristling hair, the reverent gesture of taking off his hat. But he had not worn a hat into the presence of the dead. Remembering, he let his palm rest on his whiskers, his little finger between his teeth. Then, finally, he laid the sheet gently back in place and the end brushed the wet cement floor.

"Rest in peace, stinker," he said softly.

The door moved as if a breeze shoved it an inch more open, but there was no breeze. When Pussyfoot left to pad back to his lair off the furnace room, he saw no one at all in the dark old corridor. He wanted to get to his desk right away, open the locked drawer, and go through his papers. Not that he would have far to go. The one he wanted would be first, on top. He dropped the long box on his cot and went to his desk. When the paper was in his hand, his haste seemed to be satisfied. Like a man in a great quandary, he put the yellowed envelope into his right hip pocket, took it out and put it into his left hip pocket, then into the breast pocket of his shirt with the flap buttoned down. The buttonhole, however, was old and stretched.

"There just ain't no safe place!" he muttered, and hunted through the litter on his dresser for a safety pin. "Man can't never find nothin'. By golly, tomorrow I'm gonna buy me a safety pin, whole dang package of safety pins!"

But he didn't. He had no opportunity.

The dawn had lost its rosiness and the white-faced cattle on the hills were getting up to begin their first nuzzling in the sticky snow that had followed the October thunderstorm when Mr. Wilkins was aroused by an insistent knocking on his door. Pulling on trousers and sweater over his nightshirt, he went to admit the sheriff. A few minutes later they walked across the road to the small mined chapel. The little place had been scorched by fire, then partly torn down, leaving one room still intact. What had been an inner partition, gay with flowered paper, had become the outer wall, and the heater that once had warmed both rooms stood with its rump jutting out like a kibitzer fascinated with what was going on inside. At this hour, every inch of the roof and piled lumber was decorated with wet, melting snow. The sheriff was not interested in nature's cosmetics. He followed Mr. Wilkins onto the porch of this odd remnant, bending to clear the sign which read "Charity Chapel" in red that had run a little. He saw the old preacher push open the door that was never locked, and they stepped together into morning twilight.

"You see, there it is," Mr. Wilkins said, "just as I laid it down. I even remember the passage I was reading: 'Look not mournfully into the past, it comes not back again; wisely improve the present, it is thine.'"

The book, as he said, was lying face down on a small table that in other days would have been called a center table. Beside the table was a wooden rocker padded with a thin cushion of no color. Kitchen chairs of many designs were set in neat rows, a bench or two against the wall. The place smelled of barrenness, of dim old dust sifted into the wallpaper and around the pictures hung almost touching one another, small black-framed pictures of people in clothes of forgotten decades, stiffly sitting to have their portraits made.

On the table, touching the book, was an electric lamp. Mr. Wilkins, his white hair mussed and eyes still swollen from sleep, reached out to turn on the lamp. There was only a fruitless click.

"I was sitting here, reading, you see, when the current went off. But my flashlight was in my pocket—I use one crossing the road at night, on account of the ruts. So I turned it on to see the time." He smiled faintly. "One might wonder why time could be so important to me—"

"And your watch said—?"

"Nine thirty-seven, exactly."

"Your watch was right?"

"Always, Sheriff. I check it every day with the noon whistle at the brick kiln. I haven't had to set it in nearly a year."

Although Mr. Wilkins had just done the same thing, the sheriff reached out and clicked the lamp button. "Nine minutes for murder," he mused.

"Nine minutes that could have been golden."

"Yeh. If he'd been able to get the switch connected again without discovery, nobody would ever have asked whether the lights went off in the gulch and the hospital at precisely the same minute. But Sister Judy had to trip him up."

"I didn't mean quite that." Mr. Wilkins picked up the book, closed it, ran his finger along the back. "It will be hard for her."

"Sister Judy? I wouldn't say so. She'll just get a day's rest that she needs anyway."

"I referred to Sister Magdalene." The preacher's eyes were on his finger as it rubbed the book. "I must remember not to lay a book open, face down. It cracks the binding." Rather abruptly, he turned and stepped out onto the porch.

Across the road a cow bawled. Houses, set in no sort of order, sidled against the base of the cliff, which in its turn was the base of Balsam Mountain. The vertical crag also was the rimrock holding back the terrace upon which the hospital stood. Early visionaries had seen beautiful residences nestling upon that mountain. Their only error was in mistaking the side of the mountain upon which the nestling would be done. On the far slope Balsam City had been built. In Gopher Gulch, none but a lumberman's ax had ever been set to the pines.

'We all came together," Mr. Wilkins said reminiscently. "Sister Magdalene, and Mr. Cassidy, and I. And, of course, Cardinelle."

"Of course?"

"From Big Balsam's viewpoint. But in her own right, also, she was noteworthy. You remember her."

The sheriff had forgotten how Cassidy's name had been linked with Cardinelle's—not that it mattered now. For an instant, standing in the bright sunshine, feeling the natural lift of the clean, tangy air, he wondered whether, after all, it was so imperative that he stir the decay of the past, find what had come out of that rottenness to kill the man. That the thing stemmed from the past he was certain. Who would be moved to unpremeditated murder by the sight of a man struggling for life in a respirator? No, it had been planned, brooded over. Look not into the past, it comes not back again—something like that, Mr. Wilkins had read in his book. But when the past lashed out in murder, when the law was your business . . .

"The most beautiful woman I ever saw."

"Cardinelle?" The sheriff caught up a phrase of the old man's recollection.

"Yes. She had magnificent red hair. I think it was from the hair that she took her name, cardinal red. None of those women ever used their right names. Remember her place, Sheriff, up Horsethief Trail?"

The sheriff brought up the detail that lingered in his wife's hearsay memory of Cardinelle. Yellow taffeta curtains. The curtains had hung to the floor, the envy of every woman who wore calico and hung scrim over her windows. But the envy had died when Cardinelle's blood stained the hem of one curtain a thick and ugly brown.

"There was another facet to the Cardinelle story," the sheriff remarked. "Father Anthony. Sister Magdalene's brother."

"Anthony Dumont?"

"He brought the last Sacraments of his Church to a girl dying in Cardinelle's house. But when he reached the house, there was no dying girl, and no one would admit to having called him. Strange, that on his return from a bogus call, his horse should slip and they would tumble together down that vertical madness. . . ."

The sheriff, remembering how he had been obliged to go to Sister Magdalene and tell her of the accident, did not at once comprehend the meaning of a small orange point that flashed suddenly on in a house across the road.

"By jolly, they've fixed the power line! The boys sure didn't waste any time! You keep in mind what you've told me this morning, Reverend. There'll be an inquest and you'll be called on to testify." Mr. Wilkins appeared to be slightly puzzled, and the sheriff added, as he started toward his car, "The lamp going out, you know. Looking at your watch."

"Oh, to be sure," the preacher assented.

The sheriff, maneuvering the car into a turn, speculated briefly upon the capacity of death to nibble away whatever secure foundation a being had managed to build under himself. Mr. Wilkins seemed to have no safety but his faith, this morning. Sister Magdalene, last night, had been the same. Even the sheriff's faith, a practical one based upon the eventual triumph of the law, was quailing before the fact that Big Balsam Cassidy had always been his own law and the mystery of his death might never yield to another. He drove as slowly as his conscience would allow him around the mountain and up to the hospital.

Gus Omley had climbed the long hill an hour after dawn and taken Big Balsam away; but no hearse could hold the thing that seemed to have wings, that hung in every corner, crouched just outside of every door, flitted behind everyone who walked alone through a deserted passage. Marmion, working in the laboratory, desperately trying to keep her mind away from what Eloise had told her this morning, tried to dwell on the story of Sister Judy's adventure that was going the rounds. It was a fantastic story. Sister had gone to the crow's-nest for some reason as yet unexplained and straight to the master switch. She had had an instant to see that the switch was loose. Then he had come up behind her, unheard. He could see her plainly because she was standing against the aura of her flashlight. He caught her veil and wound it firmly around her face, then laid her carefully down on the floor. She had heard the click of the switch being thrown back in place. Then he was gone. The storm had covered his departure. But the little Sister had been too terrified to move. When she did go, finally, she ran. And tumbled down the stairs. And now she was confined most unwillingly to bed in one of the regular hospital rooms.

And Eloise had been struck down last night . . . because someone thought it was Marmion who had come back to get her box? But why? Who knew she had had the box? Marmion's hand trembled on the adjusting screw of the microscope and the black pepper of corpuscles grew hazy in the slide. Don't tell, Eloise had urged while she reeled into her clothes this morning, and Marmion had agreed. Eloise could not identify her assailant any more than Marmion had, or Sister Judy, and the admission of her prowling would only bring a reprimand from the sheriff and most likely from Sister Polycarp. So Eloise had combed her hair gingerly, keeping away from the sore tenderness on the back of her head, and put on a faint touch of rouge, and tucked a scarlet handkerchief into her white pocket to pick up the color in her cheeks. And Marmion, wondering where Sister Peter's corset had gone, worked very slowly in the laboratory trying to avoid mistakes. You are asking for trouble, the sheriff had said. But how could you identify a figment of the night? Suddenly Marmion turned away from the microscope, took up her tray, and left the laboratory.

Down in Sister Judith's room, King was leaning on the foot of the bed. The small nun was dainty in her modest white gown and nightcap. The only mark of her accident was the adhesive patch on her forehead.

"But there are only the two of us in the laboratory, Doctor," she pleaded. "There's far too much work for Marmion alone and she's inexperienced. . . ."

"You may get up and dress, Sister, and go to my office. The sheriff wants to talk to you again. But after that, you're coming back to bed."

Sister Judy closed her eyes and leaned back against her pillows. King stepped around to the bedside and took her wrist in his fingers. The pulse was rapid.

"Would you rather not talk to the sheriff today?"

"I'd rather get it over, Doctor."

The doctor was puzzled. Puzzled, he believed, not worried. Affection for a person is a requirement for proper worry.

"All right, then, signal for the nurse when you're ready. And lie down if there's any waiting. I don't want you up any longer than necessary."

"Yes, Doctor."

He went out, closing the door quietly. The convent was a humility mill, he told himself, grinding down every individual trait until all that was left was a pious, one-track zeal. At intervals, the track swung around to him, and he would find on his desk various books and pamphlets, which he dropped into his wastebasket without reading—all but the ones he knew belonged to Sister Judy. Those he unobtrusively returned to the laboratory. He never tried to explain why he should boil with rebellion over ties that did not bind him and rules that did not govern his own life.

When Sister Magdalene entered the room King had just left, Sister Judy was combing her hair. It was gray hair, wiry and curly and very short. She stood to the side of the dresser so she did not see herself in the mirror. A Sister must guard against vanity. But she saw Sister Magdalene, who had come with a clean coif. Sister Judy bound the headband tight around her forehead and pinned it. Then the soft folds of white went around her neck and up under her chin, to be pinned on top of her head. The veil was laid on last and pinned, the same veil that had been so smothering a blindfold last night.

She turned then to the Superior, her eyes submissively on the floor. Together, the two walked to the waiting room the sheriff was again using as an office.

The sheriff was weary. He seated the nuns with their backs considerately to the light and sat down to listen to a story he believed he already knew backward. But you never could tell. There might be something he had missed last night. He listened absently, rubbing his lean, stubbled chin, his gaze going on out the window. An automobile zoomed up the long hill and scraped to a stop. Reporters, most likely. Cassidy's death in a normal manner would have made news, but his murder would he a sensation. And it would have to be solved by a tired old man who had started out in life as a cowpoke.

"And then he took off his shoes, sir," said Sister Judy.

The sheriff clamped his jaw shut and bit his tongue. Blinking back tears of pain, he stammered, "He—what, Sister? He—"

"He took off his shoes, sir."

"How could you tell?"

"He was very close to me, as I lay on the floor. And you know the little tapping that the tin tips of shoelaces make against leather? That's what I heard. And when he left, the steps were very soft. Thumps, you know."

"Wasn't the storm making enough rumpus to cover footsteps?"

"You'd think so, sir."

Sister Judy attacked by an assailant who took off his shoes, Cassidy The Great now lying on one of Gus Omley's slabs, the Pyus girl stubbornly unable to identify the almost certain killer—and running up the entrance stairs were three reporters who would ask deft questions and perhaps uncover the bewilderment of the investigator. Helpless, that was the only adjective the sheriff could apply to himself at the moment.

"Reporters. I'll see 'em, Sister Magdalene. They don't need to bother you."

But Marmion Pyus, leaving the first floor, was meeting the three gentlemen head-on in the hall. They had just come up the entrance stairs. One was very tall and thin and blond, one was short and ruddy, the third mildly nothing but middle aged.

The ruddy one spoke. "Good morning, Miss. I'm Williams, of the *Atlas Syndicate*. Quite a racy incident here last night, eh? Oh, this is Jensen, *World Press*." He indicated the middle-aged man. The tall thin youth evidently did not rate an introduction. "We'd like a human interest angle, you—excuse me, but haven't we met somewhere?"

"I shouldn't wonder," said Marmion. "I run across all sorts of queer things under the microscope."

Mr. Williams had the grace to smile. "Well, all right. But how about a few impressions? Front page—"

He stopped as if his tongue stuck to the roof of his mouth. Marmion knew why. She had heard the rustle of a habit behind her. She stepped slightly aside, amused at the young man's discomfiture. Sister Magdalene, her hands up her sleeves, was the very personification of dignity.

"You are newspaper reporters, gentlemen?"

The middle-aged man made the gentle reply one would expect from him. "We have been sent by our respective editors to cover a story, Sister. Mr. Cassidy's passing is of national interest."

"I understand, sir," the Sister answered with corresponding mildness; but when she turned to the one who had spoken first, her severity would have been approved even by Sister Polycarp. "I realize that you are performing your duty in coming here. Perhaps you will appreciate that I am performing mine when I ask you to sit quietly in the waiting room until the sheriff can see you. I will not permit any of the staff or patients to be questioned. I do not wish any pictures to be taken. I forbid you to go anywhere in the hospital. Do I make myself clear?"

The ruddy Williams grew ruddier. Mild Mr. Jensen bowed. The young man gulped down something that choked him.

"The waiting room is immediately behind you, gentlemen," the Sister added. And without staying to see whether they entered, or whether Marmion spoke further to them, she turned and walked away. Her departure was a more effective guarantee of obedience than if she had slapped their wrists.

The girl went on up the stairs. At the landing, she looked down. The tall, nameless young man was watching her with transparent appeal, and not all of the appeal was for a story. A warm, pleasant sensation tingled through her, quite the opposite of feeling your lungs scorched with cold on a winter day. . . .

What an odd thing to remember!

8

The shadows were long in the gulches when the sheriff drove up the hospital road with Coffer Daniels. Daniels was not the one to trip breezily around the country attending to his law practice. He never had been known to visit any client, except one. And that one was now being embalmed. The sheriff, however, had been curt; and when Daniels finally had been convinced that if he wanted to be included in the proceedings he would have to go where those proceedings would take place, he went.

Sister Magdalene's worn, muslin-curtained office was not a sumptuous setting. Mr. Daniels sat with his blue trouser legs pulled up to preserve the crease, his candy-striped silk shirt and stiff collar giving him the air of an outdated sport, and offered unctuous remarks about the heat. The sheriff's forehead was beaded. Mr. Daniels' was not. Sister Magdalene, on the far side of her veined old desk, waited patiently for the lawyer to come to the point.

The sheriff was not so patient. "Suppose you get out the will, Daniels."

The Sister became mildly attentive. Whose will? She glanced at the sheriff and saw that he was more excited than in the days when he had ridden a bucking bronco at a rodeo and been pitched into the stands.

Coffer Daniels opened his brief case and took out the one document it contained, typed sheets clipped to a backing of pale blue. "Because of the peculiar circumstances of Mr. Cassidy's death, the sheriff ordered the will to be opened immediately."

"A question of motive." The sheriff hooked an elbow over the back of his chair. "That is, I hoped to find a motive. As it is—go on, Daniels."

The lawyer cleared his throat blandly. "This is a testimonial, one might say, to the truth that the greatest of virtues is charity. And—at times, I might add—the most surprising." His eyes sped over the typed lines he had found so obnoxiously hard to believe an hour or so ago. "To put it briefly, Sister, this is the last will and testament of Michael James Cassidy. In it, he makes disposition of his very considerable worldly goods. And you, Sister Magdalene—" he paused, enjoying this moment which was all he would get out of the amazing document. "You, Sister, are almost the sole inheritor."

The Sister's reaction was disappointing, because there was none— no delighted exclamations, no joyful disbelief. Nothing. Because it was thirty-four hours since she had slept, and because there was no precedent for Mr. Cassidy's benevolence, she sat in a daze and stared at the lawyer and wondered what, exactly, he had said.

Mr. Daniels seemed to understand. "You are practically the sole inheritor. The other bequests are of small importance."

When he paused, the nun said, "It was kind of Mr. Cassidy to leave a legacy to St. Dennis of the Hills. I cannot own property, personally. The hospital is greatly in need of funds. Reverend Mother will be most grateful." She knew it was inadequate thanks. Except for the mention of Reverend Mother, she had often thanked a farmer in the same tone for a load of rutabagas or a side of beef.

The lawyer's smile was ingratiating. In that moment he was nearer to liking Sister Magdalene than in all the years he had never been called upon to do business with her. He hated brilliant women. This one, he saw now, had a reputation for brilliance she did not deserve.

"You have inherited a large fortune, Madam, very large. Its administration will be a responsibility, but one Mr. Cassidy—and I myself, if I may say so—are happy to put in your hands." He pursed his lips. Until it was found in the safe at the mine office, he had known nothing of this will. Cassidy had not called upon his trusted friend Daniels to draw it up for him. "Allow me to read: 'In consideration of my long-felt desire to render assistance to the hospital known as St. Dennis of the Hills, I hereby give, devise, and bequeath to this organization all the rest, residue, and remainder of my estate of which I may die possessed or to which I may at the time of my death be in any way entitled, the estate to be administered under the personal direction of Sister Mary Magdalene Dumont. Because of my admiration for her outstanding ability as a businesswoman, her sincerity and her goodness, and because I know that under her hand my fortune will be expended wisely and for the benefit of the people of the Hills, I leave this legacy. I ask that she, in her Christian charity, pray for me. . . .'"

Pray for me. Out of the well-turned phrases, Sister Magdalene caught the familiar entreaty. Big Balsam had seldom taken the name of his Maker except in profanity. Now he was putting forth the handmaiden to speak for him. She could understand that. Prayer is so practical, so precise and simple. But the money—that was different.

"He had no reason to leave the hospital any gift, however small," she said. Money, so provokingly necessary and of such exaggerated importance when there was little, could not come so easily.

"But it is not small, Madam!" Mr. Daniels protested. "You are almost the sole heir to nearly a million dollars—even after taxes!"

Faintness stole over Sister Magdalene, and far distant she heard her own voice. Mr. Cassidy owed St. Dennis nothing . . . it was extremely kind of him . . . and under the spoken thoughts, others ran: two of the pioneer quartet were gone, Big Balsam and Cardinelle, and two more whose lives had touched them, Father Anthony and Little Job. Anthony's connection had been so short, hardly more than a determination to fight the great Cassidy, and it had died with him. Only one tie had bound together that small divergent group, the fact that they had come west at one time. Now there were only Mr. Wilkins, peacefully amounting to nothing so far as the world could see; and herself.

"Little Job's daughter, Marmion Pyus? Did he leave her a bequest, perhaps?" the Sister asked.

Mr. Daniels pretended to search the pages, a superfluous pretense because every disgusting word was burned into his brain.

"No, no, it seems Miss Pyus is not mentioned. Well!" He flipped the document back into the brief case and arose. "May I be the first to congratulate you on your good fortune? And also, may I offer my personal interest as well as my professional services? I shall save you every unnecessary concern, dear Sister, of that you may be certain! Yes. Well! I'll enter the will for probate as soon as possible. Let us not postpone the enjoyment of our blessings, eh, Sister?"

He could have been reciting "The Village Blacksmith," so far as Sister Magdalene comprehended. Words fell upon her ears, a hand clasped hers, she walked with the two men to the office door. She would have to be alone, soon.

They left her; but in a moment the sheriff, having shed Daniels, was back.

"Sister, I don't quite know how to congratulate you. I had some nice remarks all roped, but I can't get my tongue around 'em!" He grinned. "This business has sure throwed Daniels!"

The Sister nodded. "We don't understand his charity, which only proves how little we understood the man."

"Well, we all want money, for one reason or another, so we figure the fellow that has it, he's got the world by the tail. Up on a pedestal."

"And a pedestal is very small to sit on. There's no room for anyone else."

"Now that's what I mean, Sister! Cassidy never had a home, even if he had the biggest house this side of Denver! This gulch, right here, was as near to being home to him as any place. I expect that's why he did it."

"Why he did what, Sheriff?"

"Put the clause in his will that Daniels didn't read you. It said he's to be buried in the old cemetery here in the Gulch. And his funeral's to take place from Charity Chapel."

A few minutes later, Sister Magdalene climbed the path to the hospital chapel. The day was cloudy and still. The backfiring of the sheriff's car, going down the steep road, shot holes in the quiet. At the chapel door she paused. The hospital cut off her view of the Gulch, but the broad old hillside was there opposite, faintly dented by the prospect holes that had named Gopher Gulch. At its base a small section of Little Balsam Creek shambled along, black between black meadows of overflow mud, all refuse from the Hellbent mills where the gold was taken from the slime, the gold that was to be hers now. . . .

She remained a long time in the chapel, having spoken to no one of the great good fortune that had come to St. Dennis. And yet, before she was far into her thanksgiving, the news had traveled.

The boiler room was a vantage point for Pussyfoot Rayburn. Not only was it directly around the corner from the pharmacy, where almost every nurse could be seen at some time of the day, but its shoulder-high windows looked out upon the front drive. When the sheriff's car pulled up to disgorge the sheriff and Coffer Daniels, Pussyfoot had hastily disposed of his repairs on a thermostat, caught up his hedge clippers, and was trimming the bridal wreath under the office window about the time Mr. Daniels opened the brief case. He heard everything. Only once did the clippers pause entirely. That was when Big Balsam's plea for prayers fell from Daniels' dry lips. Him, of all people, asking her for prayers! His arm made a long, wiping motion across his mouth. When the clippers snipped again, they cut the bridal wreath to the quick.

A bit of news, to Pussyfoot, was of only half value until he could recount it. Sometimes you had to pick your hearer with discrimination in order to get the most out of your big-man moment. But not so with the tidings he carried now. Anyone would marvel. Dropping the clippers barely inside the boiler room, he started for the stairs, and met Jock Turner coming out of the pharmacy.

"Hey, Turner, hold up a minute!"

Jock stopped. In his hand a bottle of medicine glowed jewel pink.

"Sheriff just left, Turner. That trick lawyer from the Hellbent, he was here, too."

"What for? Do they know who killed Cassidy?"

"Set quite a spell. I just happened to be attending to my own business outside the window—"

Jock lurched forward on his bad leg, and somehow the bottle of medicine slipped to the cement floor. He didn't even glance down at the pink splash on his white shoe.

"Answer me!"

"Listen, they ain't found who done the guy in! But they know who profits by it!"

"Who?"

"A million dollars, too!"

"*Who?*"

"Sister Magdalene."

"Ah. . . ." It was a long sigh. Jock went down on one knee, poking at the broken glass in the brown, odorous puddle. The place seemed dark. Pussyfoot snapped on another light, and the particles on the floor glittered.

He didn't know why he wanted to be good to Jock, just then; but he did. He elbowed the orderly aside. "You lemme get 'em, you might cut yourself. Ain't good goin' around sick folks with cut hands."

Pussyfoot, taking his time, gathered the glass. Once, leaning far over, his shirt pocket gaped and a yellowed envelope fell to the floor. Before Jock could touch it, Pussyfoot snatched it away. With his hands dripping medicine, one filled with glass, he couldn't open the pocket flap. He stuck the Paper between his teeth.

"C'mon, Jock, I'll get a mop."

Jock followed him through the furnace room and into the lair at the back. The old man went to the dresser and dropped the Paper on top of the accumulated junk.

"Puss, was there . . . look, you heard everything, you said?"

"Sure did, certain sure."

"Was there anybody else mentioned in the will as a beneficiary?"

"No."

"You're sure?"

"Ain't I told ya? You seddown a minute, and I'll wash my hands and be right back. I got a snort hid under the bed. You look like you could use a nip, eh?"

He waited until Jock shoved a pile of papers to the floor and sat down on the one chair. The fellow didn't look so good, kind of green. But Pussyfoot would not be so certain of that until afterward. And he would believe, afterward, that if he had washed his hands and returned straightway—but the washbowl was beside the door to the hall, and when Pussyfoot heard heavy steps coming down the stairs he had to go look. And when he saw Dr. Kingston, he forgot Jock.

"Hey, Doc, you hear? About the will?"

"Whose will?"

Pussyfoot snickered. "Cassidy's. Him and Magdalene musta been friends on the side. He left all his money to her!"

The doctor's reaction was disappointing. He didn't respond like a man of the world. He gave Pussyfoot a glare of deep disgust and tramped on into the pharmacy.

The old man, not to be defeated, followed to lean on the half door. "You're surprised, I betcha, Doc. I was close to that there shyster lawyer as I am to you, and I heard—"

"Eavesdropping outside the window? Or did you manage to crawl under the rug, this time, where you'd meet some more of your own kind?"

"O.K., but didn't I tell you the news?"

King gave an aggravating grunt. "I don't credit gossip."

"This ain't gossip! Didn't I hear 'em lickin' his dirty hand like he was the high smackdab up in heaven? Why, that yellow claim-jumper, he wasn't nothin' but a bullyin', murderin' sneak! And scared? Listen, who am I? Nobody! But he'd—"

Pussyfoot's jaw dropped, his tongue flashed out as if he would gather back the words he had just uttered. Trying to impress King, he had gone too far. And Jock, he saw, had come around the corner, white as a dead man.

"Go on, Rayburn," the doctor suggested. "He'd what?"

Pussyfoot cringed, side-stepping to the turn of the hall where he looked back with imitation jauntiness. "No skin off'n my nose if he wants to bury his money in Gopher Gulch! Buryin' himself here, too, what ya think of that? Rest in peace!"

Jock limped slowly into the pharmacy. He and King shared a silence that somehow impressed them both as irresolute. They could have called to Pussyfoot to come back, or gone after him into the furnace room, or even expressed their doubts of the old man's news. But they folded their arms on the workbench, and between them lay an invisible thing neither would touch.

"It's true, I guess," King said finally.

"I guess so."

"Hearty rejoicing. Congratulations."

"Hip, hip, hooray." Jock's tone was as dull as King's. "Sorry I smashed Finnegan's medicine."

"Doesn't matter. I'll put up another bottle."

Finnegan was late in getting his medicine, but only Finnegan attached any importance to that. Within a quarter of an hour, the news of Cassidy's generosity had swept through the hospital, and the wondrous delight of it occupied every tongue and mind. "Why?" everyone asked. "Why did he do it? Because he had no family, no one near or dear?"

Asking, they glanced at Marmion, if she happened to be within view. After all, she was nearest to the lonely man, daughter of his only friend. But no one asked her directly. She kept away from those curious glances whenever she could, working quickly in the laboratory to finish her work and Sister Judith's. This evening she would seek out Sister Magdalene to congratulate her on her good fortune; and after the congratulations she would tell the Superior every fear and misgiving she had had, how terrified she had been there in the dark with that unknown person, and Big Balsam dying; how horribly certain she was that Eloise had been attacked by mistake because she came on Marmion's errand. But why? Over and over every detail she went, until she could think of none clearly. Then she would glance at the clock and remind herself that she must not look forward to all the hours of the night ahead but rather back to the night and day she had lived through, an infinitely longer time. Between supper and prayers, that was the most leisurely interval for Sister Magdalene. . . . That's when I'll try to catch her, Marmion decided.

She was in the sitting room in the crow's-nest, killing time by pretending to write a letter to Aunt Dorothy, when Lynn strolled in and dropped into the chair with the leaky arm.

"I think it's the least we can do for her," she remarked.

"Do what for who?" Marmion asked idly.

"Carve our Magdalene on Mount Rushmore, the fifth Great Stone Face. She belongs up there with the Great Emancipator and the Poor Man's Champion and the Father of Our Country. The indomitable spirit of the West, that's our gal. She'd translate into stone with her personality intact. We should start a movement to immortalize her, Pyus. And let her pay for it, of course."

Sister Magdalene in stone coif and veil, her glasses suggested in granite shadows like Teddy Roosevelt's, her mouth firm as Washington's, perhaps the quizzical peace of Jefferson about the eyes—who but Lynn would think of a thing so readily imaginable? Marmion smiled, drawing umbrellas across Aunt Dorothy's letter.

"Are you staying on to do general duty, Lynn?"

"Heavens, no. I'm specialing for that motorcycle accident case, Jimmie Anderson. Nights." She took a package of cigarettes out of the pocket of the scarlet robe. "Why I stay in this bottom of God's pocket, I'll never know. I got Cassidy's case because the registry called the kid I was rooming with, and she was scared stiff. So when I offered . . . oh, well!" Lynn flicked open her cigarette lighter. "I'm disappointed that we're not going to see our petticoat dictator perform at the inquest tomorrow."

"The inquest? I hadn't heard about it. Oh, Lynn, will I be—"

"Nobody will. They'll draw a jury, have them view the body, then adjourn. The sheriff wants to have more evidence lined up before he asks for a verdict."

"More? But what more is there? He thinks I know who came into Cassidy's room, but I don't!" Marmion's breath caught on a frightened sob. "Honestly, I don't!"

"Then I wouldn't protest so violently." Lynn gave her a cool inspection. "You're stuck with a story, aren't you? Either you imagined the entry of someone, which is certainly understandable; or you had some indication of who the person was and you're afraid to tell."

Marmion rose slowly. The writing tablet fell, the pencil after it. "I don't care a great deal whether you believe me or not. Sister Judy didn't recognize her assailant, and her story rings true enough. And—" She paused. Neither she nor Eloise had told about the incident of the corset box. "I really don't care," she added. Then she went out and down the stairs.

The clock struck in the hall below. Seven. Too late now to find Sister Magdalene in her office. The Sisters would be assembling for prayers. She felt not in the least foolhardy, walking through the elevated passage to Methusaleh. There were lights, Sister Judy's geraniums flared pink on the narrow window sills. She reached Methusaleh, went on into the second passage to the chapel. Coming into the chapel balcony, she left the light behind her. The organ showed its white teeth in the twilight. Down the few steps to the body of the chapel the real darkness began, reddened at the altar by the sanctuary light and the vigil lights the Sisters had set burning. But the nuns were not there, now. Marmion did not know that prayers had been advanced to seven-thirty in order that Father might come and give Benediction on this great occasion. She looked around the small, empty place, smelled the faint incense and varnish and candle wax, and realized that her head was aching. There were two pews beside the organ, and she knelt in one. Closing her eyes, she thought of nothing but the intense quiet.

Perhaps that was why she heard the sound in the passageway. She turned her head, leaning her cheek on her folded hands. There was no repetition of the sound. That was when the quiet became frightening. She heard a rustle, or footstep, some disturbance of the walled-in silence. And yet no one came out of the passage! It was a full minute before Marmion admitted to herself that the sound had been the almost inaudible retreat of someone who had no intention of entering the chapel. Her own presence would not deter anyone coming to say night prayers. But if the unseen lingered there with the purpose of doing bodily harm, then he would behave exactly as he was doing! He would wait, just out of sight, near enough so that her first step into the passage would bring her upon him, and there would be no time to scream. . . .

Trembling, Marmion turned back to face the altar, what anyone deep in prayer would do after slight distraction. If he were watching, he would know she had heard him, but not that she attached any significance to the sound. Deliberately, she yawned. Don't alarm him, don't precipitate an attack. The chapel was a dead end, she was cornered, he could afford to wait. Even a killer would hesitate to desecrate a chapel.

And then her eyes, raised to Mary's altar, took in a fringe of the high, dark panels of the door. An outside door! If she could manage to reach it—if it was unlocked, she could escape! But she must not hurry. When finally she stood up, she walked without haste down the steps. He would think, she hoped, that she was about to start around the Stations. Perhaps that minute of his indecision would be enough—if the door was not locked!

She came to the door and laid her hand quickly on the latch. And pressed. In the same moment she heard running feet start across the balcony.

Sister Magdalene met Mr. Wilkins in the main corridor. He was breathless because he had taken the hill too fast. By the time he reached the top of the stairs, he was puffing. He spoke with many hesitations as if he were lost in thought, the hesitations giving him time to get his breath. Sister Magdalene, he felt confident, did not notice. She showed her age tonight, dazed still from the impact of good fortune.

"I didn't think he'd come back from the dead to jeer at me and my poor chapel," he said. "The sheriff explained nothing, except that the funeral was Mr. Cassidy's wish. A telephone conversation is so terse, without body or soul. But your great news, Maggie, it rang true even over the wire."

Sister Magdalene smiled. She had just climbed the basement stairs and she was short of breath, but she believed she disguised it too well for Mr. Wilkins to notice. He was looking every day of his years, tonight.

Together, the two old friends walked to the sun porch, each thoughtful of the other's decrepitude. The sun-porch windows were gay with Sister Judy's African violets. Beyond the building the lawn made a short sweep to the rimrock, then the cliff fell away to the gulch where the ghost town was hidden. From the windows there was only a long vista of pleated hills, invisible now in the night.

"From almost anyone's point of view, I haven't been a success, Maggie," the old man said, deeply troubled. "In the beginning, I believed as you did that the city would be built on this side of the mountain. It was logical. The stage road followed this canyon; it seemed probable that the railroad would do the same. . . . Oh, well, my small chapel was to be only a sort of semicolon between my open-air preaching on the hillside and the fine new church the people would surely desire. In a place where God walks as He does here, they would want to give Him shelter. I suppose it's been my fault. If I had pushed them into building a church here before the new cornerstones were laid in Balsam City, they would have stayed with me. The debt would have obligated them, if nothing else. . . ."

"You don't mean that, Hal. You're only borrowing gall and wormwood. You've never brewed bitterness for yourself."

Mr. Wilkins gave a sigh that gently tipped a violet. "Forgive me, Maggie. In my Father's house are many mansions. Perhaps Charity Chapel qualifies as the woodshed." The Sister chuckled, and he turned to look straight at her for the first time. His plump cheeks were still pale, but his eyes had regained their old tranquility. "I feel better, having told you this. I slap out because I don't like Cassidy's post-mortem joke. When my little chapel was partly burned last winter, there was no money either to tear it down or to rebuild it, although my faithful miners made much ado about it. By next summer, I believe, we'll be at work. But in the meantime, I preach and we pray with the same spirituality. I don't care for Cassidy's joke."

Sister Magdalene let him finish, even allowed a short pause. "I saw it as you do, at first, Hal," she said slowly. "A dramatic effect in keeping with the grand charity of leaving his money to the hospital. But since we don't understand his charity, how can we understand his desire for a simple funeral? It could be sincere. This softness, this loneliness, might have been at the root of all his bluster. Perhaps there was something in his life we know nothing about, some hurt that made him cover up any human longing that might have led him toward people. He could have been ashamed to reach out. Now, of course, no one will ever know why, so he can allow himself what he really longed for in life—a gesture of friendship."

"He couldn't buy it, Maggie."

"He didn't try. He left you nothing in his will. You'll be given a generous stipend, of course, for the funeral, but nothing more."

The old man sighed again. "How you have relieved me! I couldn't disregard the wish of the dead, but now I have no desire to. Yes, you have given me reassurance."

But he didn't turn to go. There was something else heavy on his mind. He was frowning, his hat nervously slapping his knee, his eyes again on the pleated hills.

"Mrs. Burkish is having a bad attack of arthritis," he said at last.

The Sister could have chuckled aloud. She let her coif hide a smile. "Bring it to us, Hal."

The hat stopped slapping. "I wouldn't dream of asking you, Maggie—but I have only the one good shirt, you see, and I can't ask Mrs. Burkish to do it up, and there isn't time to send it to a laundry in town. The sheriff called me so late, and the funeral is to be the day after tomorrow. I thought I might wear it again. It's plenty clean for a small wedding or a christening, but for this—"

"If we were to have the funeral in our chapel, we would wash and clean the vestments," Sister Magdalene said, relieving him of his explanation. "The good shirt is your vestment. Could you bring it up in the morning?"

They shook hands, smiling.

Mr. Wilkins nodded. "My prayers have been answered. I don't mean the shirt. I've prayed very hard for some great opportunity to come to you. I didn't dream of Cassidy. Who would?"

As the preacher and his old friend were shaking hands, Marmion was yanking frantically at the chapel door—and Pussyfoot was making the discovery that his envelope was gone.

He couldn't believe it. He had laid the Paper on the dresser, right here, on top of everything else, there was no possibility of its being lost. His heart was thumping as hard as Marmion's when he began to scrabble through the newspapers, cards, string, old envelopes, the accumulated trash he was always salvaging from the wastebaskets. Pussyfoot had the soul of a scavenger. That was why he had picked up the long box when he scuffed against it in the dark room. He had hidden it away because it had a right smart dent in it. But the box didn't matter now. It was the Paper he must find. It couldn't be gone!

He started through his pockets, even though he knew he hadn't absently stuck it back in. He had held it in his teeth, bringing it in here—

That was when he remembered. Jock had been with him. He had offered Jock a snort. Then he had gone out to wash the medicine off his hands, and he had heard King—and Jock had come out of the furnace room looking like the ghost of a ghost.

And the envelope was gone!

Standing in the middle of the room like a scarecrow with limp pockets all turned out, Pussyfoot gaped at nothing. Turner, the stinkin' thief, he had taken the Paper! And he'd know what it meant, too. Get him a smart lawyer, like Coffer Daniels, and he might even take a crack at breaking Cassidy's will. And then all kinds of evidence would be aired. . . .

Righteously indignant, Pussyfoot strode down the hall to Jock's room. He knocked on the closed door, waited half a second, and opened it. The room was empty. He didn't know why he snapped on the light. All he saw was the closet, the door open, the hangers empty. On the bed lay a suitcase, fully packed, ready for the lid to be closed. Pussyfoot backed out of the room, forgetting to turn off the light. He would listen for the fellow, with his own door open he would hear that scuffling step. There was nothing to worry about.

But all his guarantees to himself could not keep Pussyfoot from going half crazy with terror. He cowered on his bed, listening, waiting. The only sound he caught was the patter of footsteps, running by.

A few minutes earlier, Sister Judith had laid down her prayer book as her door opened. And then she dropped the book and snatched the sheet up to her chin. Although she was a hospital patient, she could not have such a visitor as this.

"You can't come in here, Jock! Go away instantly!"

Jock's little smile was pleading. "Sister, please, just let me—"

"I cannot have a layman in my room!"

"I know. I'll go." But instead of leaving, he came and leaned on the footrail. His hair was sleeked down, still wet from the shower, his cheeks were powdery with talcum.

"You're dressed up, Jock." And then the little nun asked a question that seemed irrelevant. "Why did you take off your shoes?"

The young man's mouth twisted for a second into a grimace that would never be a smile. "I thought you'd recognize my step."

"I didn't, Jock."

"Bless you! I tried not to choke you, but I didn't have the time to be extra gentle." His voice strengthened and steadied. "Sister, I didn't kill Cassidy. I had nothing to do with it. Do you believe me?"

"Of course."

"All I've done is . . . No, I won't burden you. I just wanted you to know that my leaving now has no bearing on anything that happened. And I wanted to say God bless you. . . ."

Sister Judith was not readily moved to tears; but Jock had the very clean look of all the polished little boys who trooped to the hospital every summer with such desolate bravery to have their tonsils out, and she was always tortured with sympathy for them. She snuggled the sheet up higher and heard Jock go. About the time Marmion ran along the drive, Sister Judith reached for the cord which would turn on the signal light for the nurse. But all she did was to wind and rewind it around her finger.

Marmion met Jock at the front door, but she didn't stop. Her feet barely touched the stairs, hardly tapped the silence of the old halls. Anywhere, now, was refuge after that cornered interlude in the chapel, the eternal minute it took to open the door, the never ending run through the black night over unseen ground from the chapel to the basement entrance. But down there was the room where Big Balsam had lain like a fallen crusader, the empty kitchen and the black furnace room and the shadowed pharmacy, and even in her fright Marmion could not force herself through that door. So she ran around to the front, then up all the stairs to the crow's-nest. Over under the rafters, the rolled mattress eased itself a little out of its coil as she flew by. The bedroom was unoccupied. Marmion stumbled in, slammed the door and locked it, drove Eloise's bed a little harder against the second door into the hall. And then she collapsed on the floor. Whom did she fear? Not Lynn, or Dixie, or King. Nor old Miss Hennessey, or Miss Baxter soaking her corns in the bathroom, or Philippa, or Jock. Still, there had been no stranger, to the sheriff's knowledge, in the hospital on the night Big Balsam died, and yet the danger persisted from that time. The attic darkness had covered the stealthy movement of someone's hand on the master switch, and the same darkness had hidden her assailant from

Sister Judy and from Eloise . . . and tonight, the quiet had rustled just out of sight in the chapel passage. She had not been followed down the hillside. Had she, possibly, imagined the whole thing?

Marmion got up, pulled off her uniform and kicked off her shoes, sat down on the end of her bed and tucked her feet under her, covering them with the hem of her slip. The room was chilly. But that was not why the girl sat shivering. It was because she was fitting the garments of a murderer on to all the people she knew in the hospital and finding they fitted everyone except the Sisters.

When Eloise came, she had to plead with Marmion to open the door.

Mr. Wilkins walked slowly down the hill from the hospital. He had seen Barney and been delighted to find him cheery.

"If I could just know nobody'd suffer for the good deed," Barney had said, referring to Cassidy's murder.

Mr. Wilkins could not admit to having the same opinion. He was feeling most placid tonight. The item of the shirt was off his mind. He did not usually come down the long road in the dark. Today, however, so much had happened, excitement enough for a lifetime crowded into a few hours, and he knew he would not sleep. The night was restful. All the commotion of the day backed off, leaving him a lone person trudging down a hill in the starlight. Step cautiously, feel the heel tendon press against the back of the old gaiter, first one foot and then the other; wonder if black shoe polish would do enough for the scuffed toes; be thankful again over the shirt; glow with simple pride over the coming, great day. . . .

He heard the footsteps behind him and stopped.

"Hello! Nice evening! Bound for the gulch?"

The steps halted abruptly. Silence.

Mr. Wilkins was troubled. He had spoken out of an innocent desire for companionship. Surely no one would object so strenuously to him as to remain hidden in the dark, rather fearfully hidden, because the fellow could not be far away. Neither of them had been guided by a flashlight. Mr. Wilkins had not expected to be out so late as to need one. But the other fellow, if he had a light, was not betraying his position by it.

Curious. Unless, by chance, this was a stranger returning from a visit to the hospital, hurrying down the hill to the bus stop, and startled half out of his wits by a voice coming out of the night.

"I'm the preacher from Charity Chapel," said Mr. Wilkins. "We might as well walk together."

No reply. The night birds circled with hoarse cries.

The old man did not flee down the road, but he did not quite take his time. Behind him the quiet one might have moved. He never knew. He was at his own door when a leftover returned to his mind, something he had put aside at an odd time to ponder at leisure. He tried to remember, standing on his porch looking up at the velveteen sky. The solid, arching wall of hills made the sky a little lighter. Contrast. . . . The leftover was almost within reach.

The hours crossed the barrier of midnight and became a new day. In the hospital everyone slept, except the night nurses. And Pussyfoot. Rising once in a while to walk the cramps out of his legs, he never went farther than the furnace room door, for he knew Jock had not returned. The hills were walling pink sky when he slipped down the hall to look for sure. He came back running on tiptoe.

They began asking around about Jock even earlier than Pussyfoot had anticipated. A nurse called down to remind him of surgery; Sister Peter telephoned from Methusaleh. But no one pair of hands, it seemed, could take the place of Jock's.

"Where is he?" everyone demanded on this busy morning.

It was Dr. Kingston, out of patience, who finally tapped on the closed door and, receiving no reply, nearly jerked off the knob and went in. The light was on. He was there only a minute. Then he went out and shut the door.

9

They stood beside Jock's empty bed, the sheriff and King. The bed was smoothly made. Nothing lay on it but the suitcase, packed and waiting for a hand to close it. They looked at the dresser where not one single thing littered the clean scarf, and at the two white chairs and the row of empty coat hangers in the closet. The sheriff walked to the closet and poked his head in. He brushed the hangers, and they made a thin, wiry jingling.

"The bed hasn't been slept in."

The doctor shook his head. "Yesterday was the day for clean linen. The pillow slip isn't wrinkled."

The sheriff had seen the unwrinkled slip. He came back to the suitcase. It was cheap, flimsy even in its prime. He poked a rolled pair of socks. This was the sparse accumulation of either a very poor man or one who cared nothing for belongings. Or of one who had purposely rid himself of everything that could connect him with the past. There was a small radio with its cord looped around it, underwear and shirts gray from hospital washing, hand-kerchiefs a better color than the shirts. All of it might have belonged to anyone.

"I don't get it. He planned to light out, because he packed up. But he's already lit without the suitcase. Why didn't he come back?" The sheriff answered his own question with another. "Because he couldn't?"

The doctor's jaw clamped hard, raising the tendons in his temples. He had called the sheriff immediately after discovering the emptiness of Jock's room, and that, it seemed, was to be the total of his contribution. Fists in his hip pockets, he stood in his favorite pose, puffing out his ups as he scrutinized the suitcase.

The sheriff closed down the lid much as one would let the cover of a casket fall over the face of a beloved one. "Well, I'll organize a search. . . ."

"He might be dead drunk somewhere."

"How's that?"

The doctor shrugged. "He's gone on a binge quite a few times in the two years he's been here."

"And he didn't get fired for it?"

"Orderlies are hard to find."

"Go on, Doc.

"Most men drink to escape from something. With Jock, it's his physical disability. Remember when he was a champion rodeo rider?"

"Gad, yes! I'd forgotten! Throwed, wasn't he?"

"He got off with a broken back and a crushed leg. Thrown against the fence and then kicked. Carelessness, it sounded like to me. Either too cocky or else he didn't give a damn. He spent a while in another hospital, then they brought him here. I thought I could tinker him up."

"Looks like you got him on his feet again."

King lifted his shoulder. "If you could call it that. Jock's a rider. He's never been thankful for a bad leg."

"Isn't he pretty lucky to have a job at all?"

"He's not an irrepressible optimist."

The sheriff whistled thoughtfully. "Had a dress-up suit, didn't he?" At King's nod, he went on, "It's not in the suitcase, so he must be wearing it. Did he dress up mostly when he went on these bats?"

"No, he knew he'd ruin his clothes."

"Well, we'll pick him up, wherever he is. I'll telephone my office and tell Brandt to alert the police in all the Hills towns. We ought to have him by evening, easy enough."

But long before evening, the sheriff knew that King would have called him an irrepressible optimist. Even before the reports began filtering into his office—Jock Turner not seen by any of his cronies in the familiar haunts—he began to doubt the doctor's diagnosis.

He had gone to the sun porch to use the telephone and found Sister Magdalene in conversation with Mr. Wilkins. Jock's absence was already a subject much discussed, and now to the sheriff's lean information there was added Mr. Wilkins' account of the stranger behind him on the road and out of that a time set for the young man's departure—that is, if the preacher had not been mistaken about the footsteps, if the unseen follower was Jock. Seven thirty, or thereabouts. Jock had no car. Seven forty-five was the next bus for town, eight if he wanted one going in the opposite direction.

"So he could have been catching a bus," the sheriff pondered. "Well, I'll get the boys started."

"Terry Turner," Mr. Wilkins remarked to himself.

The paper sack in the Sister's arms gave out a suddenly crushed crackle.

"Terry Turner," he repeated. "The history of this region has always fascinated me, Sheriff. In a place where there is little to look forward to in the future, the past can be alluring. It has been my life interest."

"What about Terry?" the sheriff suggested.

Sister Magdalene turned to lean on the arm of her chair. The morning was fresh over the mountains, Sister Judy's violets like soft new suede; but the past lured her back, as it must be luring Mr. Wilkins, to a night when the hills were slippery with rain. . . .

"Is it old Terry you mean," the sheriff continued, "the one that had some kind of trouble with Cassidy in the early days? Over a mine, wasn't it?"

The identification fitted almost every homestaker in the region. Nearly all had had trouble with Cassidy over mines. But Mr. Wilkins nodded.

"Terry was Jock's father. He had a claim over here on Little Balsam Creek, just outside the gulch. But he couldn't work it. It turned out to be a dry claim."

"A dry claim on a creek?"

"Odd, wasn't it? Little Balsam rose on Cassidy's land, and so naturally he could keep control of the water. He offered to buy the claim, but Terry wouldn't sell. That was when Cassidy found that he'd have to divert the water to a new channel in order to work his own claim at top capacity."

The sheriff remembered the picturesque term men had used then in referring to Big Balsam. It was a good one, not to be recollected in genteel company.

"And this diversion business," he said, "I suppose it only held long enough for Cassidy to—eh—acquire Turner's claim?"

"Terry didn't sell."

The sheriff's fingers drummed the table. He could have sworn the preacher was not speaking at random; and yet where was the connection between Jock's ownership of a forgotten gold mine and his disappearance?

"If Terry didn't sell out, maybe Jock did."

"Not to my knowledge, Sheriff."

"Why didn't he develop the mine, then?"

"It takes a fortune to make a fortune in the gold business today. A lot is low grade ore, and he'd have to build a stamp mill and cyanide plant to make the mining pay. Where would he get the money?"

"Then say he didn't build a plant—couldn't he get some other outfit to do the milling after he got the ore out of the ground?"

"He could. In Denver. But look at the distance, look at what it would cost for shipping. If there was any way to recover gold without investing a mint of money, you'd see the gulch gophered again with mines. No, the easy pickings are gone. You can't go out with a gold pan any more and wash yourself a year's wages in a day. The gold is here, but aside from the Hellbent, nobody has the money to get it out."

Mr. Wilkins excused himself then. As he hurried away down the hall, passing open doors, the light fell on him, first one side and then the other. Sister Magdalene, watching him go, was obviously thinking of something else.

"Sister Judith is back to work this morning, Sheriff."

"Good!" The sheriff paused in the act of lifting the telephone.

"It seems that she saw Jock last night."

"She did? Where?"

The nun's mouth tightened. "She will tell you. You will find her in the laboratory.

She arose with the paper-sack package and went off through the patches of light and shadow. The sheriff's attention was on the veiled figure that appeared to drift away from him. There, now, where she paused at the newel post, she looked exactly as she had on that rainy night twenty-nine years ago, in the little old hospital near the Hellbent. Never in his life had he been so sorry for any human being . . . and then he gave a low whistle. Father Anthony! That was the night Father Anthony was killed! And the young priest had been a very close friend of Terry Turner. . . .

"Hello. Sheriff's office," the voice in the receiver repeated.

Quickly the sheriff gave the orders that would start the search for Jock. "And look, Brandt," he added, "send somebody to the courthouse to look up the record on old Terry Turner's mining claim. The name of it? I don't know, maybe he never got around to naming it. It's located some place near this gulch, could be in it, even. You find out."

"O.K., Boss. That all? Then listen here. I checked on the bank accounts. Several banks got 'em, Kingston's and the hospital account at the Balsam Butte National, Hennessey at the—"

"Skip the extra details."

"Well, they're all about what you'd expect. Only one. Caspar Rayburn."

"Cas—"

"Pussyfoot. Boss, he's got an account would knock your hat off. Close to sixty thousand dollars!" The silence was so long that Brandt jiggled the hook. "You still there?"

"I'm here. You're sure about this, Brandt? There could be another Rayburn, it wouldn't have to be—"

"It is. I didn't believe it either, but the bank manager's positive. Their depositors wear shoes as a rule. Pussyfoot don't. He comes in regular on the tenth of each month and makes the deposit. Always in cash, too. And the same amount every time, a hundred and fifty bucks."

"Maybe it's his wages."

"You kiddin'? Your Mary Magdalene pays him thirty-one smackers a month. He deposits her check."

"How long ago did he open that account, Brandt?"

"Uh—let's see—twenty-nine years ago last May."

"Ah!"

"What you mean, ah?"

"When did he make the last deposit?"

"The tenth of September. . . . That tell you something, Boss?"

"Yeah, I just reckon it does!"

The sheriff dropped the receiver back in place. The next step was obvious. He would get Pussyfoot by the scruff of his hairy old neck and choke out of him the story of how and why he came to blackmail Big Balsam Cassidy. For there could be no doubt as to the source of the old renegade's bank account. Cassidy had been admitted to St. Dennis on October fifth, making him unavailable to Pussyfoot on the tenth. That was why the last payment had been made in September.

"So now we're getting places," the sheriff muttered.

He clattered down the stairs to the furnace room. Pussyfoot was not there. Nor was he to be found anywhere in the hospital or grounds. So the sheriff made a second call to Brandt, directing that a man come to the gulch with the single purpose of finding Pussyfoot. The old fellow could not be far away, not so far as Jock, who continued to be missing from Deadwood to Hot Springs.

Marmion, on a high stool with her back to the sheriff and her eye tight to a microscope, gave half of her attention to the slide and half to Sister Judith. They had not had much time to talk this morning, and the small nun's story of Jock's visit was a revelation to Marmion as well as to the sheriff.

"I almost wondered, at the time, if it could have been Jock in the attic," the Sister said, her eyes on the spoon which stirred a bubbling saucepan of germ culture. "He was so careful and so gentle. I've seen him handle patients that way."

"He didn't explain what he was doing in the attic?"

"No, sir."

"Protecting someone," the sheriff said mildly.

Marmion's hand trembled as she took up her pencil.

"Protecting someone," he repeated. "He knew the switch was off or he wouldn't have gone up there. And if he hadn't pulled it himself, then he knew who did. Now who was important enough to Jock for him to take a chance like that?"

Marmion swung sharply to face him. "Me, for instance, Sheriff? I'd only been here four days, but these things happen fast!" She hated to be so savagely angry. Almost in spite of herself, the bitter words poured out. "He came into Big Balsam's room and I recognized him, is that it? Because he had neglected to take off his shoes? Well, let me tell you this, Sheriff—it wasn't Jock who chased me out of the chapel last night! He couldn't have been there and with Sister Judy at the same time! And besides, I met him at the front door when I ran in."

"You were chased out of the chapel, Miss Pyus?" the sheriff demanded, and even Marmion could see his consternation.

"Yes, I was. But I'm surprised you believe me. I thought I'd have to take the veil and hang a rosary at my belt before you'd—"

"Marmion!" Sister Judith snapped. The culture slopped out of the pan and a vile odor filled the laboratory. With a corner of her apron for a holder, the nun lifted the pan off the heat. And she, like Marmion, was shaking.

The sheriff glanced at his watch as if he noticed nothing unusual in this little byplay. "Well, we're hunting two men now, old Rayburn too. I'm putting men here from now on, a twenty-four-hour guard. If you feel an urge to stroll through a dark hall again, Miss Pyus, ask one of my men to go with you. It would be safer."

"And more exciting!" Marmion said shortly. She was ashamed of herself, almost.

The sheriff departed. Sister Judith replaced her pan and went on stirring. Marmion tried again to concentrate on Mr. Walker's peculiar germs, but she couldn't keep at it. Unwillingly, she turned to the little nun.

"Sister Judy, I'm sorry! But that man aggravates me! He seemed to believe I met Jock at the door, all right, but he probably thinks we were going to elope. And he's struck with the idea that I hated Cassidy. I did, but not enough to kill him! I mean, I'm not the kind to do much about what I don't like . . . not murder!"

"He was a foundling," Sister Judith said softly, so softly that Marmion wondered if she had heard correctly. Although her face was shadowed by the veil, the girl had seen her lips move around the strange word, and still it was unbelievable.

"A foundling? Mr. Cassidy? I never heard that, Sister!"

"If you had known, you couldn't have hated him. He had no home but an orphanage, and he ran away from that. So he had to be successful in a worldly way in order to overcome what he felt was the handicap of his birth. He used to tell me I was rich because I had the most precious treasure in the world, a name. If you didn't get it as a free gift, he said, you couldn't ever buy it."

"He told you this himself, Sister?"

"Yes, dear." She brushed her cheek, leaving a bright smear. "He was very lonely, the loneliest man in the world, I used to think. King is the same. They aren't hard, men like that. They've been badly hurt, and the hard surface is scar tissue. I made up a story about Mr. Cassidy. I was only fourteen, then. I pretended he had been in love with a beautiful girl who spurned him because she wanted wealth and social position, and that experience destroyed his faith in people. He had to have something, then, to take its place, so he set out to make the world envy him. Envy isn't much, but it was all he had."

"Sister, but you—how did you—"

"I worked at the Hellbent as a cleaner in the offices. I was too young, but Mr. Cassidy knew my father had no money to give me and I had to earn what I needed to enter the convent. Reverend Mother would not have required the fee, I suppose, but I wanted to come like the others. I didn't mind working, especially when I came to know Mr. Cassidy. He used to come early, sometimes, and listen to the stamp mills starting up for the day, and I'd be finishing the night's cleaning. That was when he would talk. He never knew who his parents were, and the names people gave him, like Big Balsam and Hellbent, used to amuse him in a fierce sort of way. He said they were quite as authentic as the name he had chosen for himself."

Marmion listened in the awed wonder she had felt when she first saw Mount Rushmore, when she walked into the college chapel for the first time—when she had come face to face with any incarnation of the sublime. Sister Judy, stirring the pan of soup, had touched the clouds. She must have loved the lonely man who had talked to her while the stamp mills were starting up in the morning. And with those talks, perhaps fifteen years back, the change might have begun in him, his realization of loneliness, his initial desire for friendship, possibly his first wondering as to the eventual disposition of his great wealth. Was it because he remembered the little scrub girl, saving her skimpy wages, that he left his fortune to the institution which housed her?

"He knew I wanted to earn my own money, that it was important to me," the Sister added, "and so he never overpaid me. It took me two years to save what I needed. He understood so well. . . ."

She turned her back, going about her work.

Marmion swallowed hard before she could speak. "Sister, I didn't know—my father was his best friend, but—how can I hate his memory now?"

"That's why I told you, dear."

Late in the afternoon, Marmion was alone in the laboratory. Her head ached dully, her lungs seemed to be filled with milkweed fluff. Sister Judy had not mentioned Big Balsam Cassidy again, but the story had hung between the two as they worked and they had never reached such accord. Because she was still thinking of Sister Judith, Marmion did not realize at once that someone had come in and was standing behind her. For a frozen instant she could not turn. Safety—call one of my men, the sheriff had said, but how could she call now, when the visitor stood between her and the door?

It took a mighty effort to look around slowly, casually. But when she beheld him, a tall, thin young man, blond, peering wistfully around his large nose, her apprehensions melted away. No murderous character would have such pathetic, bony wrists, or an Adam's apple jumping above his open collar, or eyebrows jumping with the Adam's apple, or his head ducked in a question he could not quite utter. And on top of all that, Marmion knew him. At least, she had seen him before.

Trying not to allow her smile to become too friendly, Marmion slid off her stool and approached him with her hand out. The young man hastily shifted his notebook and shook hands.

"Your slip, please!" Marmion said severely.

He blushed with a painfulness that could not be less than genuine. His sleeves were too short, the shoulders of his jacket skimpy like her own old suit. She struck down a sympathetic feeling.

"If you've come for a blood test, you must have a slip from your doctor. Or—you're not a donor?" Here was one that could almost he counted upon to faint in spite of brandy and cool cloths. Perhaps she should call the kitchen for black coffee.

The young man smiled, and the effect was that of the double rainbow over Balsam Butte, unexpected, twice as beautiful as most rainbows. "Miss, I'm a reporter. Scully, of the *Daily Bulletin.*"

"You were here this morning! That's when I saw you."

"Yes, ma'am. I shook off the other fellows. I know I shouldn't be up here, but this is my first chance at a real story! I only got it through a fluke, and it's up to me to make good on it. Couldn't you please . . ." A pleading gesture went with the entreaty.

Marmion kept her glance away from the bony wrist. "Up to you, not to me, Mr. Scully. Now if you'll excuse me, I have my work to do."

The Adam's apple gave another leap. She knew he would persist, perhaps in the end even draw out of her the sweet, pathetic tale of Sister Judy and the great Cassidy which was uppermost in her mind. In self-protection, she picked up a needle.

"I might as well take a blood sample as long as you're here, Mr. Scully. We use so many donors, and you could be something we're short on."

"Ma'am, I never disclose a source of news, so you'd be perfectly—"

"Even if we never call you, it's a good idea for people to know their own blood type in case of emergency. Take me, for instance." She pinched up her finger until it grew rosy. "There's gold in them there veins. Rh negative."

"You were with Cassidy when he died, weren't you, ma'am? The sheriff said the nurse wasn't—"

"The left hand, please," said Marmion. "Calluses from typing? I'll have to prick deep. It may be sore for a while."

She turned away, considerately taking a minute to find a new card. She believed she had scared him out. Before she was through fumbling, the young man was gone. Protection, you owed that to yourself above all, and if you talked thoughtlessly to a reporter . . . and Sister Magdalene had forbidden her staff to see reporters. But there had been something about him. . . . Marmion went quickly to the window and threw it wide open. Sam Scully was legging it down the hill. With a sigh, she went back to her work.

The laundry was an escape world for Sister Magdalene. The moist, soapy smell brought her back to childhood when her mother had soused away in suds to the elbows and there was the froggy sound of clothes rubbed on the washboard and there would be soup and pudding for dinner on washday. Problems then had been elemental, such as concerned a whole roof over their heads and money for tomorrow's meat. Nothing like quiet, stalking evil that struck out of the dark and left death and injury behind it.

Old Sister Margaret was running the small washing machine in which she laundered the nurses' uniforms. The big mangle and the drier and the large washer were not in operation. When she saw the Superior, the old nun shut off the machine and came with all her wrinkles smiling, wiping her hands on her apron.

"Are the women gone so early, Sister Margaret?"

"No, Sista. It is their half day off. You have something for me to wash?"

Sister Magdalene opened the paper sack she had carried from one task to another for several hours. "I had thought I would do it myself, Sister, not to add to your work. But since you're using the small machine, and it's white . . ." She tucked the empty sack under her arm and shook out the garment. "Mr. Wilkins' best shirt. He was in deep trouble about it because it must be laundered before Mr. Cassidy's funeral tomorrow. I offered to do it up for him."

"Yes, Sista," the old nun murmured, the habit of a lifetime. But she did not touch the shirt. "You will excuse me, Sista?"

Sister Magdalene nodded, surprised.

"Then you will remember, please, that we are forbidden to take part in Protestant religious ceremonies?"

The Superior folded the shirt against her front and stroked out the wrinkles. She had not been so diverted since the night of the storm.

"I believe we may do this with a clear conscience, Sister," she said after a pause. "It is a corporal work of mercy to bury the dead. We are assisting, in a small way. And we are doing a sort of round-about honor to our benefactor."

"Yes, Sista."

"Is this load ready to come out?"

"No, Sista, it just went in."

"Then we'll put the shirt in also."

She could see that Sister Margaret turned on the current reluctantly. In a moment, the shirt disappeared under the suds. They stood watching, one on either side of the machine, a warm, soapy haze rising between them.

"Are you planning yet for your new laundry, Sister Margaret?"

Surprisingly, the nun began to cry, the tears running down her cheeks as if the question had burst a dam. With each hand cupping an elbow, she rocked back and forth. "I know I'm selfish, Sista, I should not regret our great good fortune. It is what we have prayed for and done without all our years together. If God had not wanted us to have it, He would not have sent it. But I am ungenerous, Sista, I think of myself, I do not want to leave this room where I have spent my life! Always I have dreamed of the day when I would come here with my last strength and make an offering of all the work of my hands. Each day I offer, but I wanted to make the last here—and I could never do it in a white, new laundry!"

The old Sister's sobs were little childish hiccups. Sister Magdalene was stricken. She should have remembered that Sister Margaret and Sister Peter, also, had been with her from the beginning, young in her own young years, hopeful and disappointed and afraid with her. It had been wicked to forget them. She put her arms around the frail old Sister. In health, Big Balsam Cassidy had never set foot in St. Dennis. Now, from the grave, he was reaching back into every smallest corner.

The two nuns stood long together, while in the washing machine Mr. Wilkins' shirt worked itself into a gay entanglement with the nurses' uniforms.

10

The sheriff did not know he was about to solve the secret of Jock's absence when he stopped his car in front of Charity Chapel—not why, yet, nor even exactly when Jock had gone, but where. He slammed the car door behind him and glanced at Mr. Wilkins' house on one side of the road, the chapel on the other. The chapel door stood open. He strode to it. The old preacher was going to disclose why he had seen fit to bring up the subject of Terry Turner's mine at the time he did. Brandt had uncovered the legal information in the courthouse. Now Mr. Wilkins would be given the opportunity to add what would not be recorded, every detail of the trouble between Turner and Cassidy, Father Anthony's connection—none of it any great feat for a historian who found the past so alluring.

The sheriff stamped into the chapel to find Mr. Wilkins, as he expected, seated in his rocker with a finger marking a passage in his Bible. With him, however, were two boys of high school age, bright youths with clean hair showing they had mothers who cared, and very ripped and dirty overalls indicating that they had been up to some sort of rugged boy-business. Evidently Mr. Wilkins had been listening to an incredible tale, for his customary mild absent-mindedness had been startled out of him. He barely caught the Bible before it fell.

"Sheriff, thank heaven you're here! I was about to call you. Marty and Charlie, they've found Jock!"

"They have! Where? Did he come back with you fellows?"

The boys looked scared. Mr. Wilkins slowly laid the Bible on the table and polished his glasses, each lens separately, with his thumb.

"He didn't come back, Sheriff. He couldn't. Jock is dead."

A fly, one of the season's last, buzzed into the room, a veritable bomber in the intense quiet.

"He's—*dead?*"

The taller of the boys nodded. "He was shot. But there's no gun.

The sheriff let go his breath suddenly. "You kids didn't move him!"

"Gosh, no! But you can see, the way he's lying. Right beside the water."

"Balsam Creek? Here in the gulch?"

The tall lad gulped. "Uh—no—"

"Turner owned the Mary Ellen mine," said Mr. Wilkins. "Cassidy owned the Killjoy, right next to it. They found Jock in the Killjoy shaft."

The sheriff found he had to sit down for a minute. Cassidy again! Big Balsam had asked for murder. But Jock, sunny tempered, inoffensive, in spirit no older than the boys who had found him, how could he inspire the unlawful taking of a human life with malice aforethought?

"All right, kids, let's have it. How'd you happen to find him? And who are you, by the way?"

"I'm Marty Spree," said the taller boy. "My dad's the butcher. He's Charlie Morlund. They've got the filling station—"

"I know. About the mine?"

Marty hitched his Sam Brown belt, and the sheriff noticed then that Charlie wore its twin and that each belt was hung with flashlights, knives, pencils, pads of paper, rope, and a compass.

"We're the Gopher Gulch Mine Mapping and Exploring Team," said Marty. "We been working in the old mines all summer, making maps. This afternoon we got to the Killjoy."

"You're sure it's the Killjoy?"

Charlie grinned. "We know them mines, Sheriff. We're gonna be mining engineers—"

"Jock," said the sheriff. "How do we get to him?"

"We'll take you there. Down the main shaft. You go down a ladder. He's right beside a great big black puddle of water."

So Jock had packed his suitcase last night, intending to run away from the thing that menaced him; but first he had gone to Sister Judy to make his peace with her, and then he had taken himself off to the Killjoy to die in the dark. Why?

"Okay, kids, we'll go as soon as I call my office and get some men started out here," the sheriff said. . . . Never mind the why, just now. Go to Jock, look at him, try not to remember what a swell little guy he'd been because sentiment would make you so howling mad. . . .

They bumped off over the ruts of Main Street leaving Mr. Wilkins sadly behind, then out to the highway and swiftly across it to the dirt road that once had led to the gold mill. The mill was a ruin of odd wheels and sections of wall towering nowhere, set in its own desert of shining black slag plateaus.

"There's an old logging road goes around the back of the mountain, if you wanta take the long way," said Marty. "Or we can shinny straight up from here."

The sheriff stopped the car and squinted up the hillside. "That the entrance, that kind of brushy place?"

"Looks like an overgrown hole," said Charlie.

"Let's climb."

The slag was slippery as ice, allowing few toe holds on the bulging sides of the plateaus; but once they reached the top, behind the mill, the grassy slope offered scrub pines to catch and old stumps for steppingstones. As they climbed, the boys set forth an amazing knowledge of the old mines.

"See, the way they mined then was to tunnel in, horizontally, at the top," said Charlie. "There was another tunnel away down there at the base of the mountain, but that's caved in now. The upper one had a vertical shaft running down a good ways, and the men would go in through the upper tunnel till they came to the shaft, then down a ladder with dynamite strapped to their backs, and they'd set off the dynamite so's it would blast out a kind of room right above the lower tunnel. The room was a stope."

"And then they'd make a hole about eighteen inches across, in the floor of the stope," Marty took it up, "and they'd push the ore down through the hole into the little mule cars in the tunnel below; and the mules 'ud haul it out to the mill."

"This stope," said Charlie, "it had pillars of rock, maybe thirty feet through, so's the whole thing wouldn't cave in. You'll see, Sheriff. It's just like a room. Kind of a ragged room."

"And water's seeped in," added Marty. "Looky, here's some of the ore."

They were at the mouth of the Killjoy. A few rotting sacks of ore lay there, and a pile of short, stout timbers like the ones which had been used to brace the entrance. The tunnel gaped black dark beyond the welcome mat of sunshine.

"Here, Sheriff, you'll need a flashlight," said Marty. "You can have this, it's extra. Come on."

Their first sensation, aside from the dark, was the chill. Dank and clammy, it met them ten feet in. Underfoot the smashed rock was jagged, the low ceiling and walls treacherously hung with thin slabs ready to fall crashing into the passage. It had been like this when the miners tramped through here with dynamite on their backs, dragging picks and shovels, and there had been amazingly few accidents.

The darkness intensified. Marty's legs were like long shears cutting into the black void. Suddenly he stopped.

"Now we go down," Charlie whispered, behind the sheriff.

There was no reason to whisper, nothing could be disturbed here—nothing living. A hole gaped in the floor and up out of it stuck the rusty prongs of a steel ladder. The hands of dead men had clung to those prongs, men who had gone down into the old stope and set their dynamite, scrambled up to wait and earnestly count the blasts from below because their lives depended upon counting right. If ten charges had been set and nine went off, there would be one remaining to splatter a man into eternity.

The sheriff backed around and felt with his foot for the first rung of the ladder. Foolhardy, these boys, poking into the innards of the earth. But lucky, for him. Who could ever conceive of a man going deliberately down into this old mine for any sane reason?

The chamber was, as Charlie had said, a large room, with an immense black pillar in the middle. Toward the side was the hole through which the gold ore had been shoved to the cars below, broken with age far wider than it had ever been in the old days. The ceiling was high and cavernous, the walls echoing.

"Over here," Charlie said, and the walls threw back the "here."

His flashlight cut to the jagged pillar, then around it, onto the pool of water black as ink. The three moved toward the pool reluctantly. A drop fell from above with a musical clink. Water was to be expected in an old mine—but not what lay at the edge of it: a pair of man's shoes, and there were feet in the shoes, and above them were tweed trouser legs, no longer natty, soaked from the black pond.

The sheriff had known what he would find, and yet the beam of his flash wavered and fell away. The curly head was too boyish, lying on the black old floor. But there was nothing juvenile about the bullet hole in the temple. Except for the counterevidence of that wound, Jock might have been lying there asleep.

The activity of the next hour was such as the old mine had not known since the early boom days of Gopher Gulch. Thirty years ago, when the rungs were new and shining, men had been carried up that ladder in the stope; but none had been carried as they carried Jock. For the miners there had been hope, and the rescuers worked fast. But they could be slow with Jock, slow to come out, slow to lay him on the grass. There was nothing they could do for him, except to find out how he had come to die. The sheriff spread his clean blue handkerchief over Jock's face.

Marty and Charlie stood aside, following at a distance when the men, walking with uneven step on the rocky slope and over the black plateaus, went down with the stretcher. It was Marty who had stumbled upon the gun, tossed away behind the foot of the ladder in the stope. He had not touched it. A deputy had picked it up, wrapping it carefully to preserve fingerprints. That was when they first named, for certain, the ugly thing that had happened to Jock.

Murder.

The word swept through the hospital. Sister Magdalene told King, and then Dixie, because there would be no way of keeping back such news; and no one knew what tongue carried it next. The atmosphere tightened as if an unseen force compressed the very air.

You breathed it, choking; you made a dozen trips to the drinking fountain and still were thirsty; when you came around a corner, a whispered conversation would be abruptly cut and only resumed when the whisperers saw who you were. Tension everywhere, suspicion and fear and bewilderment.

For Marmion, there was more. The others were bewildered, but she was in a waking coma. They were afraid, and Marmion feared for her life. You are asking for trouble, the sheriff had said. Had he cautioned Jock, also? But Jock had put on the natty tweed suit, just as she might dress in the suit that was the best she had, and started out as she might to try to solve some phase of the awful puzzle. When she saw him, he had not looked like a man going to his death. But had she looked like a girl who had just escaped a murderer? Could you tell, after all, by appearances?

She sat alone in the laboratory while the daylight crept out of the gulch. She would have been startled, perhaps to screaming, if she had glanced up to see anyone else standing in the doorway; but not when it was the blond young man with the jumping Adam's apple. His hair was still wind-blown in the same way, he clutched his notebook as he had before; and because he had been in the laboratory only a short few hours earlier, because he had Jock's gentleness, Marmion saw him as a friend.

"He was alive, last night. I saw him," she said, jabbing dots on a piece of paper. The young man's head cocked. "He was always hurrying somewhere, doing a kindness for somebody. That's how I see him, limping off step after step the way you'd say a rosary, and the number of steps getting less with every hour. And then last night, when he went—even then, the rosary was running out. He had only a few steps left." She dropped the pencil and her lovely blue eyes stared as if she actually beheld the limping figure. "I might have been the last to see him alive! If I'd said something to him, maybe asked him what was the matter, it might have made a difference!"

The young man came into the room, laid his notebook on the desk, then pushed the notebook farther, and sat where it had rested. That was the way Jock would be with a patient who was afraid of being hurt. Her hand was on the desk near him. He didn't touch her.

He was not being timid, only considerate. How, Marmion thought, how could I ever have seen him as gawky and homely?

"I wasn't—I'm not afraid," she faltered.

"Of course not. You're a very brave little girl."

And Marmion began to sob against the back of her chair. She would have pulled away if he had put his arm around her; but he didn't, and she sobbed on and wished he would.

Sister Magdalene kept a tight rein on the crying thing inside her. It had been difficult in Methusaleh with Sister Peter, trying to rearrange the schedule so there would be someone strong to lift Barney into bed and turn Benny without hurting him. Endeavoring to fill his place, the two nuns realized fully that Jock was gone. Sister Peter could not talk about him. He had not taken on the dignity of the dead, yet. He was still a quick grin, a joke, a pair of feet hurrying despite the dragging one, absent for a little while. . . .

So Sister Magdalene had hurried away from Methusaleh, and now she was in her office, answering the telephone. King had followed her in and stood planted in the middle of the floor, defiantly untidy, his pallor more pronounced than usual.

The nun laid the instrument back in the cradle. "The sheriff is coming. He'll be here in a few minutes. He sounded very much excited," she added as if it didn't matter.

King puffed out his lips. "Murder is exciting. For a time. Like a game of run sheep run. The sheep are frightened now, but a week after it's over you'll hear somebody make the asinine remark that it seems like a year since All That. And then before you know it, it will be a year, and everybody will have forgotten how they drank of terror till they had nonalcoholic d.t.'s. And Gopher Gulch will be famous because the great Cassidy favored us the same way Wild Bill Hickok favored Deadwood—he got himself murdered here."

Sister Magdalene, if she had not been so wearied by her own troubles, might have reminded King that he spoke as if he were one of the frightened sheep himself. But she was not in a state of mind to analyze her own emotions, much less his. This little room had been her office ever since its early stages of damp plaster and nail-littered floor. Here she had prayed and planned, known every degree of expectancy and trust and resignation. But never rebellion. Never the feeling that she was knocking at a locked door to which the key would never be found. Once, years ago, when Anthony had been killed, she had gone through a similar darkness of soul. Now there was the magnificent gift of the legacy to lighten the darkness, but all the money in the world could not alleviate the dismal pain of murder. . . .

She did not want King to talk, so she reached for the *Daily Bulletin* and opened it. The first page glowed with Cassidy's murder. She turned to the sports page. There was a knock on the door.

"Let him in, please, King, but don't leave," she said.

The sheriff entered swiftly, dropped his hat on the back of a chair, nodded to the doctor. "They're doing a post on Jock. He died early last night, probably around nine or a little later. Sister, I'll have to talk to everybody again, find out exactly where they were. Rayburn hasn't showed up yet, either."

The newspaper lay flat, the Sister's eyes were on a picture of basketball players who seemed to have too many legs for the number of boys; but she saw also the sheriff's hand resting just above the legs, and the hand held an envelope, letter size. The envelope bore a two-cent stamp. And there was writing. She knew that writing, bold and square. My heart stood still, she had heard people say. Now she knew the meaning of that trite expression. Her own inner stillness did not contain even a heartbeat. She heard the sheriff's alarmed, "Hey, Doc!" and King's calm, "Get it over, she's all right." To reassure them, she nodded, but her only sensation was the feel of the veil slipping along her shoulders. She had loved that feel since she was a novice.

The sheriff's finger tapped the envelope. "We found this in Jock's pocket. It's stamped, you see, not postmarked, therefore never mailed.

"Anthony's," Sister Magdalene said.

"Yes. It's signed Anthony Dumont. I don't know where it's been all these years, but I've got an idea. Jock didn't have it, that's for sure."

"You mean he took it from somebody who killed him to get it back?" King asked.

"No. It was in Jock's pocket, within easy reach. Whoever killed him either didn't know or didn't care about the letter."

King's eyelids were swollen. Perhaps that was why they seemed to fall nearly shut. "Then why the murder?"

"Because Jock knew who pulled the switch the night Cassidy died. He was protecting that person, either because he wanted to or because he had to. That's what brought him to the attic, to get the switch back before anybody'd find out." The sheriff paused, and the letter tapped the desk. "And then, in some way, he got hold of this letter, I don't know exactly how, but I know who from. Rayburn. I can't tell what connection it made with something Jock already knew, but it must have proved enough to make him want to get away. So he packed his suitcase. And that was what finally spurred our unknown to silence him for good."

"Old Rayburn?" the doctor asked.

"No, not Rayburn. Jock went to the Killjoy to see . . . well, you'll understand when I read the letter. Our man is unlucky on coincidences that seem lucky, at first, like Jock going voluntarily to the mine, the perfect hiding place for a body; and then the boys coming along and finding him."

The nun heard the words without meaning. Anthony was here. His pen just raised from the letter, he was about to speak across a span of thirty years. The sheriff was opening the envelope, taking out a sheet, and unfolding it. The paper was yellowed with age, the ink the greenish shade of ancient black.

"Sister, I'll have to read this to you. I want you to help me. If there wasn't a good reason, believe me . . ."

Sister Magdalene roused herself from her memories. "I understand, Sheriff. Go on."

"The date is twenty-nine years ago last April. And it's addressed to somebody named Jim. See, the writing on the envelope is all worn off, it's been handled so much. But he says 'dear Jim,' in the letter." He skipped the first part. He could spare her the vivid picture they gave of a young man alive. This was undoubtedly the last letter ever written by Anthony Dumont. Slowly he began to read. "I've already had one close call. A rock big enough to bury a man and horse fell across the road one day just after I had passed. Many rockslides occur in this country but seldom do they kill anyone. I would have been the exception. I want you to come out here as soon as you can and confirm what the local engineers tell me. If it's true, then I have at last found evidence that can be proved against Cassidy. That is, I'll prove it unless he has me murdered, first. The whole thing lies in a mine they call the Killjoy. There is even a blaze to mark the boundary. I can't tell you any more on paper. Wire me when you'll be here."

The sheriff laid down the letter. The clock ticked. A woman's voice came casually from the hall.

"The Killjoy," Sister Magdalene said, hearing her own words from far away as if she stood back with Anthony and a double sat across the desk from the sheriff. "The Killjoy was where they found Jock. Was that why he went there, to see what Anthony meant?"

She saw the sheriff glance at King, wondering if he should answer. The doctor was watching her with the critical attention he gave a very ill patient.

"Was that why, Sheriff?" she repeated.

"We'll never know for sure, Sister. He still owned the Killjoy, it would have been the natural thing to do. He knew the whole history of the trouble, from his father." He stroked the paper. "Do you remember any friend of Father Anthony's named Jim?"

"This evidence that Anthony had," the nun persisted, "it lay in the Killjoy. And he would prove something unless Cassidy had him murdered first. Isn't that right? But Anthony did die even before he could mail his letter."

"Sister," the sheriff said unwillingly, "I thought about it quite a while before I made up my mind to tell you this. There's hardly a chance that we could clear up the circumstances of Father Anthony's death at this late date. For one thing, the witnesses would be either scattered to the four corners of the earth or else across the Gulch in the cemetery. And if we did find 'em, they wouldn't admit they'd been where they were, at Cardinelle's place. But this business of the mine is different. It's the background of Jock's murder. And that's why I want to locate this Jim, if I can. Father Anthony might have told him more in an earlier letter. Do you have any notion of who he could be, Sister?"

"Jim. Jim Cartwright, I wonder? Anthony and I went to school with him. He was a brilliant student. He used to say he wanted to be an engineer. He might have gone into mining."

"And where was this, Sister?"

"In Denver. He could be anywhere now."

"Well, we'll start with Denver. Now about old Terry Turner. Father Anthony was a pretty good friend of his, wasn't he?"

"Yes. Terry was young, then. He had been so hopeful, when he made the rich strike . . . and then his wife died, Mary Ellen, and left him alone with the little boy. . . ." Sister Magdalene could not go on. They had found the little boy, today, beside the black pool in the Killjoy.

The doctor was forcing her to bend over until her head was between her knees, saying something to the sheriff about driving a woman to faint. And all she thought of was that she must have taken on more weight than she realized because it was very difficult to bend so far.

She was relieved when at last they left her alone.

The two men appeared to be companionable, walking together down the hall. They paused at the stairs.

"So he killed Anthony," said King. "Cassidy did."

"There's no doubt of it. Then thirty years later he gets an attack of conscience and pays for the life he took. A good price, too. A million bucks."

"You call that conscience, Sheriff?"

"Why not?"

"It could be spite."

The sheriff grunted. He clattered down the stairs and was outside before he realized what King meant.

Marmion cried for as long as it took the sheriff to read Father Anthony's letter down in the office. She heard the young man get up and take a turn around the room, and she would have stopped then if she hadn't been quite certain he would return to his perch on the desk beside her. And he did. So she cried for another minute. Then she raised her head.

"You're sweet, Mr.—"

"Sam. Sam Scully. *Daily Bulletin.*"

"I wish you weren't a reporter."

"I won't be, long. I'm doing very badly on this Cassidy business." He held out a tangled wad of one-inch gauze. "This is all I could find for you. Our office is much handier. We have a roller towel."

Marmion was surprised to hear herself laughing. She took the gauze and mopped her face. "You're getting nicer all the time, Mr. Scully. But how can you come up here any time you please without being caught?" The question confused him, and she added quickly. "Never mind. It doesn't matter. But I can't tell you anything. Sister Magdalene would do nip-ups if we talked to reporters. And now that Jock is . . ."

Sam's honest brow crinkled with earnestness. "I wish you didn't have to be unhappy about it, Marmion."

Unhappy, only, when she dared not walk through a dark hall? The adjective was so inadequate and so like this young man that she giggled again. "How did you know my name?"

"The first article I ever sold was a feature on the Hellbent. I sort of played up Little Job Pyus. I felt sorry for the little guy." He smiled, squeaking his finger on the varnished desk. "I saw you get off the bus, too, the day you came. You had a suitcase. I was in my jalopy. I wanted to offer you a ride, but it was getting dark and I didn't think you'd go with me."

"I suppose I wouldn't have," Marmion replied. Sam knew her so well. Had he seen that she was dead tired but filled with expectation that night? The delight of being on her own, her confidence in her own abilities, the lovely and imagined marvels of life at St. Dennis—all had helped her up the long hill despite her fatigue. And then at the top of the road she had met the sound of the lung. Nothing had been right since.

"What a long way I had come—Sam. A girl on her first job travels so far, even though it's only half a block from home instead of three hundred miles—you know, leaving school behind her and everything. I didn't realize it, then."

"Sure. The journey of five thousand miles begins with a single step."

"Or a single misstep, Sam?"

Whether he would have answered, she never knew, for someone was hurrying in through the passage, through the twilight, and Marmion sprang up.

"Sam, you shouldn't be here! Pretend you're a donor. I'll be making out a slip for you—oh, Miss Baird, it's only you."

"Should I be complimented?" Lynn asked. "Get me another pint for Jimmie, will you, Pyus? He has a terrific thirst for blood. Oh, sorry, I didn't see—"

"Sam Scully," said Marmion.

"*Daily Bulletin*," Sam added. "I was just leaving."

"The *Bulletin* has done a fine coverage on the Cassidy story," Lynn observed.

Marmion sighed with relief. Anyone but Lynn, coming upon an outlawed visitor, would probably have tattled. Anyone but Lynn, or Eloise. Neither of them was enslaved by edicts. Sam, after a startled moment or two of eyebrow-jumping, was enthralled by Lynn's sleek, diverting talk. She would be beautiful, too, to Sam, looking out at him from the inside of sophistication, bedazzling him as a girl hauling a suitcase off a bus could never do. A bottle of saline solution slipped out of Marmion's hand, cracking hard against the sink.

"Darn!" she muttered.

Good saline solution down the drain because she resented another woman's God-given glamour! Lynn was at the window, gazing casually down on the drive, the young man giving the impression that he was frisking around her begging for attention although he remained beside Marmion's desk.

"You were on duty when he died, weren't you?" Sam inquired. "Wasn't there something about the regular nurse having a headache—"

"Your facts are not quite accurate, Mr. Scully. Miss Pyus happened to be with Mr. Cassidy."

"I was with him and he choked to death," Marmion snapped. "Your tray, Miss Baird." She came forward with it, a bottle of clear liquid and another of crimson, a coil of tubing beside them.

But Sam was not ready to give up. "He choked? I thought he just didn't get enough oxygen—I mean—"

Lynn took the tray, checked it completely, and her amused little smile grazed Sam. "Conjecture is a dangerous field, Mr. Scully. Only an experienced writer should attempt it, and then not unless he has the boldness to back up his guessing. It takes considerable backbone."

Sam, confounded and confused, gaped at the empty doorway where Lynn had been. Marmion began to pick the broken glass out of the sink. Sam was not worth a bottle of saline. Stubbornly she remained with her back to him while he shuffled, cleared his throat, and finally left.

Even before his steps had stopped echoing forlornly in the hall, she was mulling over what Sam had said. I thought he just didn't get enough oxygen . . . but Big Balsam had choked, gagging horribly. Marmion knew. She would never forget the terrible sounds of his dying. There was something frightening about what Sam had said. Like Mr. Wilkins when he stood under the stars, she could not quite catch up the memory and hold it. But something was there . . . the snake? Was it something to do with the hissing?

She walked to the window where Lynn had stood looking down. The sheriff and Mr. Wilkins were talking together under the lamppost, the light flooding them as it had herself when she hesitated out there on that first night. If she had turned and run away, as she had wanted to do, she would be safe now.

"So tell me," the sheriff said. "I remember, but tell me."

Mr. Wilkins was mildly amazed. "About the mine? Terry Turner would not sell to the Hellbent—"

"Not the mine," the sheriff prodded patiently.

The old preacher sighed. He could well be forgiven a reluctance to look back, although the mists always rose for him at this hour. He had just come from a visit to Barney, who had spoken of ghostly miners climbing the mountainsides to the Killjoy and the Mary Ellen, the White Hope and the Jingo and the Benison, miners long dead but climbing again every twilight with candles in their hats. Mr. Wilkins had very nearly seen them, too. He fixed his far gaze on the artificially lighted faces of Mount Rushmore.

"She was the most beautiful woman I ever saw."

"Cardinelle?"

"Cardinelle. She was like her name, scarlet to the heart, young only in years when she came out to this country. You don't need me to describe her gambling house, up Horsethief Trail?"

The sheriff shook his head, and Mr. Wilkins resumed. "It was in a good location, near enough to the mines, far enough from town. The law couldn't touch her."

"The law was busy with shooting scraps and a few other little items," said the sheriff, "items such as trial by jury for a lawbreaker before a mob could string him up on the Hurdy Gurdy Tree."

"No criticism intended, Sheriff. And Cardinelle ran an orderly house. Then, of course, she was Cassidy's friend."

"So?"

"Father Anthony was summoned there to attend a dying girl. The messenger—an Indian rider—urged him to great haste. And yet, when the priest arrived, no one would admit to having called him. There was no dying girl. It was a treacherous night, the rain was greasing the trail. What wonder that a man and horse fell to their death that night?"

"I know all that," the sheriff reminded him.

"Well, then the raid on Cardinelle's place, a couple of weeks later. By a sheriff's posse, supposedly—"

"It wasn't. I was the sheriff."

Mr. Wilkins gently lifted his shoulders. "I said supposedly. None of the deputies, so called, could be identified afterward, and they made no arrests. There was shooting. They said it was a stray shot that killed Cardinelle. She was the only casualty."

The sheriff drew a long breath, relieved that the thing had at last come out. "Yeah!" There was reverence in the little word. "Yeah, she sure was a humdinger, lying there. A shot corpse has it all over every other kind, for looks. They're waxy, sort of. And she was a looker, anyhow. Wearing something pink, and this big red pool around her, and that hair. . . . She was under a window, and the curtain was all that got messed up." He paused, embarrassed. "I remember well because I was just getting shaken down into office when that deal broke loose. Maybe if I'd been older, had more experience, I'd have been able to make some headway. . . ."

Mr. Wilkins shook his head. "I don't think so, Sheriff. It was all too cleverly planned. A fake raid, men dashing in out of the night and gone again, and one victim left behind, dead. It could have been an accidental shooting, some of the boys staging high jinks and getting in deeper than they expected. Or it might have been on purpose, somebody that lost too much at gambling and wanted revenge."

"Or it could have been because Father Anthony had gone over the cliff two weeks before."

"But that also was accidental, Sheriff."

The sheriff began to whistle softly, enclosed in a speculation that shut out Mr. Wilkins and his murmured good night. The dowdy figure disappeared in the darkness. The sheriff turned back to the hospital entrance just as the door flew open and a young fellow, vaguely familiar, halted for a second of eyebrow-jumping and then dashed past and away. The sheriff continued on in.

Mr. Wilkins, plodding down the grade, heard the steps behind him and he stopped instantly. This would not be a repetition of last night's performance, when the silent stalker had turned him to jelly.

"Who's there?" he demanded with authority. "Come forward, please!"

To his immense relief, the gravel crunched again, and because Mr. Wilkins was downhill he saw the young man against the sky. Contrast, dark and light—the teasing memory nagged again, but he had no time to pursue it.

"Tell me who you are, sir!" he ordered.

"Scully, Sam Scully of the *Daily Bulletin*."

The baritone voice was of fine quality, and Mr. Wilkins coupled it with a splendid physique and handsome face. And it sounded trustworthy.

"Well," he said mildly. "Well! Will you walk with me to the Gulch?"

"I sure will, sir, and thanks. I left my jalopy down below, for security reasons.

"Security?"

"My own. I thought they'd throw me out on my ear."

The old preacher made an absent reply. Memory was riding him and holding a tight rein because the sheriff also had wondered why the fake raid had taken place but a short time after Father Anthony's death. Wondering over facts thirty years cold could produce nothing. And yet when Mr. Wilkins began to talk to Sam, he spoke of Cardinelle and the yellow taffeta curtains that had been the envy of every woman in the Hills.

"Where's he been, Merve?" the sheriff demanded, clattering down the stairs behind the deputy. "In here, the furnace room? What's he been doing all day?"

"I guess Pussyfoot figures he's a law unto himself. Right through here, Boss. Ain't this an awful old barracks?"

Pussyfoot was cringing on his bed. But at least he had managed to get the long, slim box out of here. He'd have to be careful, though, maybe explain a little. . . .

"I been tendin' to my own business! And I'm hungry, that's why this feller found me in the kitchen!—I ain't done nothin', Sheriff! You think for a minute Sister Magdalene 'ud have me here if I was . . ."

"A blackmailer?"

"You ain't got no call to say that! She hired me outa the goodness of her heart, like Jock and all them women—"

"Then where did you get the money you deposited every month in the Balsam Butte National Bank?" The sheriff opened his wallet and showed the letter. "This is the answer, isn't it?"

Pussyfoot's recognition of his Paper was awkward to see. No man should cringe as he was doing, doubled forward, his head wagging from side to side.

"Why didn't Cassidy kill you?" the sheriff persisted. "He killed other men for less. Or did you know how far you could bleed him without him trying to get out from under?"

Pussyfoot went on rocking. The sheriff winked at Merve. "All right, put the cuffs on him. He killed Cassidy for some reason connected with this blackmail scheme, then Jock. We've got plenty on him without him saying a word."

At that, the old fellow bounced off the bed. "I didn't do murder, Sheriff! I was collectin' on a commodity, like, but I didn't kill him! Lordy, he was worth more to me alive than dead!" Anxiously, he watched for the sheriff's reaction.

So long as they didn't ask why he went to Cassidy's room that early morning after the guy had died, it wouldn't be so bad. The truth would sound weak, that he had wanted to see where and how the stinker had given up the ghost. He had been as surprised as the girl, not to be alone in the room. He had to get away unseen, he couldn't afford to be connected with murder. So he had biffed her with the corset box, harder than he intended. But they'd never believe such a story. . . .

"How did you get hold of the letter in the first place?" the sheriff demanded.

"Father Anthony gimme it to mail. I was his helper, sort of. He was gettin' Turner to start a lawsuit, and this-here Jim Cartwright—he's a minin' engineer—he was comin' out here. I just didn't happen to of mailed the letter 'fore we started up Horsethief Trail."

"You were along on that ride?"

"Sure. I didn't like the looks of him goin' to Cardinelle's place, alone, only for that Injun." Pussyfoot paused. "I ain't one for pokin' in. I stayed outside."

"So you saw Cassidy come out and loosen the horse's shoe?"

"I didn't! I swear I didn't see nothin'!"

"And then you had the letter to back it up—'I'll fight him unless he has me murdered first'—something like that? A valuable commodity, Rayburn."

"The letter was all I had!" Pussyfoot whispered. His hand went up to his cheek, his teeth caught the little finger and bit until the blood started.

The sheriff stared at him for a long time. "You contemptible wretch," he said quietly. "You've lived off his sister all the time you were using his dead name to pile you up a fortune in a bank. You're scum, rotten scum! I could—"

"Take it easy, Boss," the deputy cautioned.

"Yeah. O.K., you can manage him alone, Merve."

"I ain't admitted nothin'!" Pussyfoot whined.

"You're doing fine," Merve assured him. "Come on." The handcuffs clicked loudly in the little room.

Marmion was nervous, waiting, and very tired. They had taken Pussyfoot away. She knew that. The news had run through the hospital before the deputy's care reached the Gulch. So the dirty old man had done it! everyone had exclaimed with a lightening of the heart. The reason for his misdeeds was of no concern. The murders were solved!

And then, just when those off duty were climbing wearily up or down to their rooms, the sheriff had begun summoning each member, separately, to what they had named the grill room. He was asking the questions one would look for if the mystery remained: Where were you at the hour Jock died? When did you see him last? Was anyone missing from duty?

"All that!" Blanche told Marmion in a shocked whisper. She had just emerged from the room, giving way to Dr. Kingston, who had gone in glowering. "Why did they want Pussyfoot if he isn't the one?"

Marmion shook her head dumbly. Fear had, for a few moments, flown away, a dizzying deliverance she had not had time to enjoy before the thing was back. What would he ask her now, this grim old man who never seemed to believe a word she told him?

"Gas," said Blanche, "on my stomach. Honest, you don't know! If I'd a belched, I'd a blown the sheriff out the window."

"Sh!" Marmion whispered.

Sister Magdalene came slowly along the hall. She did not notice the girls. She was wearing her black habit, her hands tucked up under the wide cuffs that would be let down to cover those hands when the habit became her shroud. She would not feel colder then, nor more alone, and the coldness and the desolation were in her drawn face and her tired shoulders.

"Sister!" Marmion exclaimed softly. "Sister, what has happened?"

At that instant, the door of the grill room opened and Dr. Kingston lumbered out. The Sister paused. The big man's rumpled appearance indicated an ugly mood.

"You've heard, King?"

"Yes. It's going to make a difference—or is it?"

"Evidently Mr. Cassidy thought it a fair exchange. Anthony's life for a new hospital."

"I'm no judge of fairness, Sister. Right and wrong, to me, are matters of personal preference. I wouldn't know what to think of restitution that was ground out of a man by his conscience."

"I have already made my decision."

The doctor shrugged. "Was there any to make? Money is power and prestige, and it's only human to want both. Not for yourself, naturally, since you're bound by a vow of poverty. And you would see a distinction between expending the million on a house and fine clothes, and on a cause that's your very life. If you spend the money for God, you have the power and still you gain the reputation for great unselfishness and holiness. St. Magdalene of Gopher Gulch! Congratulations!"

The Sister paled a little more. "I have not made the decision you suggest, Doctor. I am not taking Mr. Cassidy's money."

The silence in the hall was overpowering. It was Marmion, after a long minute, who broke it, stepping out from the shadow to face King squarely, her head high.

"You're a wicked, cruel man, Dr. Kingston," she said barely above a whisper, and the words lashed the more because of the low tone. "You don't know what decency is. When you see something good you have to cut it down. Can't you even respect Sister Magdalene?"

King's big hands opened as if he would settle them around the girl's slim throat. Then, deliberately, he clasped his fists behind him.

"The sheriff is waiting for you, Miss Pyus. Don't waste his time."

As if on cue, the sheriff opened the door. Her fury at King helped Marmion through the next quarter hour. She answered the sheriff's questions with a confidence she had not shown before, a confidence based on inattention until nearly the end.

He had been asking about Jock: how well Marmion knew him, whether he had appeared to be worried; and she hardly realized that he had switched to King.

"And you've never known him to leave the hospital?"

"The doctor? No, never. But then I've only been here . . ." Suddenly she realized where the question might have led. "Sheriff, you couldn't think Dr. Kingston would—didn't you arrest Pussyfoot for Jock's murder?"

"No."

"But King never leaves the hospital!"

"I'm not saying he did. But if you have a phobia about keeping inside, doesn't it make an airtight alibi for the time you might want to sneak out?"

Marmion was stunned. The sheriff was not merely an old man now. He was ageless in a menacing way, as if he knew all and simply waited for these blundering humans to arrange their own downfall.

"Miss Pyus, we have reached a point where we can't be polite any more. What do you know about Dr. Kingston?"

"Why—nothing!"

"He seems to be attracted to you."

"Then he takes a strange way of showing it." But in spite of herself, Marmion felt her cheeks flushing. "You're mistaken, Sheriff. The doctor dislikes all women. Me in particular."

"Isn't it possible that a man can try to hate a woman because he likes her too much?"

When Marmion only shook her head, the sheriff insisted, "He's never talked to you about himself?"

"Hardly!"

The officer hitched impatiently in his chair. "It's unbelievable that a man could step into his position of trust without disclosing something about his past! Sister Magdalene advertised in a medical journal for a resident doctor, Kingston applied, she looked up his scholastic record because he wasn't long out of medical school, found he had been in the navy, and, by thunder, the job was his!"

"He's done some wonderful work here," Marmion said, shaken, wondering why she should defend him.

"It's the same with the nurses," the sheriff went on as if this were a personal grievance. "Sister hired them through the registry or because they asked for a job or because she knew their mothers, and what do we wind up with? Murder!" He jumped to his feet and began to stride about the small room. The deputy, writing at the bed, shifted his chair out of the way. "Miss Pyus, people murder

other people for a good many reasons—revenge, jealousy, to gain
something the other fellow's got, like his money or his wife. But
there's the innocent bystander that saw too much, sometimes he
gets murdered too."

The girl also arose. "Why can't I make you believe—?"

"Oh, I believe you, all right. But I think you know something
you don't know is of any importance. That can be just as dangerous
as the conscious kind. More so. You can't tell when the thing will
pop full bloom into your head."

The door opened, slamming against Marmion.

"Oh, sorry," said the deputy who put his head in. "Long distance, Sheriff. Denver."

The sheriff hurried out. The secretary-deputy went on catching
up on his notes with the notebook spread wide on the bed. His forehead was girlishly white where his hat always covered it.

"He said you could go, Miss."

"I know. But is there anything else you want to ask?"

"Me? I guess not, Miss. The boss asks the questions."

He would tell the sheriff later that he'd bet his boots the girl
had something on the end of her tongue right then. Ask me questions, Marmion was silently begging, dig out this treacherous thing
I know and don't know. But the deputy did not respond. She let
herself out into the hall just as the gong was sending forth an emergency call for the laboratory.

The sheriff was in Sister Magdalene's office, listening eagerly to
the voice on the telephone.

"This is Jim Cartwright, in Denver, Sheriff. Your office got in
touch with me. Something I can do for you?"

"I expect you've heard about the death of Big Balsam Cassidy?"

"I read about it. The papers are full of it here."

"You knew Cassidy in the early days, Mr. Cartwright?"

"I knew of him. Every mining man did."

"You had a mutual acquaintance, Father Anthony Dumont."

The line was silent for a second, then the voice came dryly. "It's
a good thing you said acquaintance, Sheriff. Cassidy sure didn't call
him a friend."

"But you did?"

"Absolutely! Anthony Dumont and his sister Hettie and I, we were all schoolmates, public high school. Hettie went into the convent."

The sheriff grinned. Hettie's present whereabouts must be unknown to Mr. Cartwright. "I have a letter here, addressed to you. Father Anthony wrote it."

"Good lord! How could that be?"

"It's turned up in the middle of this murder investigation. I'll read it to you." He laid the letter under the desk lamp and read, and the crumbling old paper dropped another flake or two under his handling. "That's it," he ended. "Evidence he could prove against Cassidy, he says, down in the old Killjoy. A blaze at the boundary. Would you have any idea of what this boundary business could mean?"

"That mine lies right next to the one owned by a fellow named Turner, doesn't it?"

"Right. The Mary Ellen."

"Well, you could get an engineer there to confirm this for you, Sheriff, but I'd give you ten to one I'm right. The Hellbent outfit was undermining Turner's property. Turner wouldn't sell out to them, so they just proceeded to follow the lead right along underground into what rightfully belonged to Turner. It was most likely a pretty deep drift. From the outside you might hear the blasting, but you couldn't tell where it was coming from. And the Hellbent wouldn't let anybody go down into their workings. But Anthony must have got hold of an engineer who determined the boundaries, because he hinted it in a letter. You haven't run across anything like a mark?"

"There's a slop of white paint on the pillar just about where we found Jock. The old man's son."

"Then that's it! The blaze!"

"I'll be jiggered," the sheriff muttered.

"Anthony had a good basis for a lawsuit," Jim Cartwright continued. "One suit wouldn't faze the Hellbent, but it would establish a bad precedent. Others might get the same idea. Too bad Anthony had that accident before Turner started proceedings. I guess the whole thing just petered out when he died, eh?"

"It was meant to, yeah."

After he had hung up the receiver, the sheriff sat for a long time, thinking. He had the motive to back up Pussyfoot's tale. Cassidy was defending his right to poach on another man's property, a justifiable ground for murder, to him. And Cardinelle had either not been a party to the plot which brought Father Anthony to her establishment, or else she had known and later been appalled by the outcome. Even a Cardinelle could well be revolted at the murder of a priest. And so in her turn she had become a menace to Cassidy, and was removed. The whole thing had been sloppily planned, but the plan had sufficed. Only Pussyfoot remained, of those who knew. It would take a renegade's egotism to allow a man a night's sleep, in Pussyfoot's position. Cassidy must have known his blackmailer well enough to realize that money was all he wanted, not even a large sum in the great man's estimation. Possibly he did not care to risk another killing so soon. Whatever the reason, Pussyfoot was allowed to live and collect. Somewhere there had to be a connection between the old story and the new. Somewhere.

"By golly, it's gotta be that way!" the sheriff muttered.

He was almost too tired to think.

11

Marmion read the flaring headline in Mrs. Totman's room the next morning.

"Go see!" Eloise had urged. "Her husband brought her the morning paper, and she's the only one that has it on this floor. She's holding court like a grand duchess. Go on, Marmie!"

The headline was spread across Mrs. Totman's feet—Sam's headline. To Marmion, it was what her speech instructor in college had called an emotional blow in the midriff.

"Where is Cardinelle's daughter?" the banner demanded, and in decreasing size, "Cassidy linked to unsolved mystery of murder in mine. Chain of events begun generation ago may lead to solution."

Then in twelve-point print, the type used for a child's easy reading, Sam's scoop began to explain itself. "Who," he demanded, "is Cardinelle's daughter? Where is the baby who was left motherless twenty-nine years ago when the flaming-haired beauty of the gambling casino was shot down by an unidentified gunman? Who was accountable for the accident that took the life of Father Anthony Dumont, popular young missionary, a few weeks before the murder of Cardinelle? The answer to these questions may contain clues that will point the way to a solution of the recent killings in Gopher Gulch."

As if someone who knew all had stood looking over his shoulder, Sam continued with his story: the discovery of the ancient letter in Jock's pocket, a short but colorful history of Cardinelle and Father Anthony's contrasted goodness, dwindling back into the hackneyed facts of the murder of Cassidy whom he designated as a far-famed business tycoon. Marmion skipped the last paragraphs to return to the beginning. Cardinelle had been married to a dimly known character named Smith who had disappeared either through adventure or misadventure several months before her death. He had no importance, apparently, except as the father of the mysterious daughter. There was no hint that he had raised a gun against his glamorous spouse. And who, Sam asked again, is Cardinelle's daughter? Is, not was. Sam took it for granted that she had grown to womanhood.

"Thirty, or thirty-one," Marmion said aloud.

"How's that, dearie?" Mrs. Totman interrupted a monologue of her own.

"That's how old she'd be. Cardinelle's daughter."

"Oh. Well, like I was sayin', I shoulda got to know her. I was real sorry I didn't, afterward. I said to Totman, I felt like some of it was my fault, not because I did but because I didn't."

"Who are you talking about, Mrs. Totman?"

The woman regarded Marmion with affectionate reproach. "You ain't been listening, honey. I was talkin' about his wife." She pushed the sleeves of the pink nightie up her brawny forearms and nodded sagely. "Jock Turner's wife."

Mr. Wilkins had been worried about the funeral. It would seem like presumption on his part, he feared, to invite the great of the region to pay their last respects to Big Balsam Cassidy in the confines of his little chapel. But when he saw the assemblage, silent and expectant, and how it overflowed to the porch and into the street, up to the dead end against the cliff and down to what used to be the post office, he knew his doubts to be rooted in personal vanity. The chapel, although better than a stable, had not been chosen by the mighty Cassidy as a setting for a final gesture of sham humility. The building was only incidental. He had come back to the Gulch where as a prospector he had possibly known the only happiness of his life, when the dream was all ahead but well within the power of realization; and this was the last return of a friendless and lonely man.

The old preacher stepped out on the porch as the organ music ended. He had not planned to speak from here. But if he were to remain inside, near the fine bronze casket and the organ drayed in for the occasion, it would seem like a private service for the benefit of the Hellbent dignitaries and other important people gathered inside. They could hear him perfectly well on the porch. Clasping his Bible with a finger marking the place, he let a moment pass while his eyes strayed over the crowd. If Cassidy wanted friends, he had them, today, jammed into the sun of Main Street. Sam's lurid story had only spiced with romance the charity of this man who had stooped so low that he had risen high. Not that one of them would condone murder. But so long ago—and nothing had been proved. . . . A good many were weeping, he saw, shedding the almost involuntary tears always called forth by organ music at a funeral. They wept, not for Cassidy who lay in the satin-soft coffin, but for all the dead they had buried before, and for themselves who would die, and for the frail living who could hardly be expected to last out the winter and yet would most likely surprise everyone by attending the funerals of some of the weepers. Mr. Wilkins understood so well. One never attends another's funeral, solely. He sits also at his own.

He opened the Bible, finding his place. He would have been shocked to know that some of the tears were inspired by emotion over himself, a dear old man in a shirt ironed to a fine gloss, his white hair professionally trimmed but not too short, his suit brushed to a good blackness, his hand trembling a little over the page—a childlike, guileless soul. The sheriff was not one of the emotional ones.

The officer stood alone at the edge of the crowd. He had spent the morning insistently digging facts out of Mr. Wilkins' copious memory. The old man, he felt, had had a motive in giving that young whippersnapper reporter such a yarn. But listening to the rich voice reading the psalm as it should be read—"out of the depths I have cried unto Thee, O Lord . . . there is forgiveness with Thee . . . my soul waiteth for the Lord more than they that watch for the morning"—listening, the sheriff wondered. It could have happened exactly as Mr. Wilkins declared: Sam had caught him in a reminiscent mood, he had rambled on and chanced upon the fact of the baby daughter, something long forgotten. It was no secret that Cardinelle had had a daughter, perhaps a year old at the time the mother was killed. No one had ever seen her. As those women almost universally did, Cardinelle had sent the baby away. Possibly, if the girl were alive, she was still ignorant of her parentage. That was the one thing Cardinelle's kind could do for their children—protect them from their own way of life.

The prayer began. The sheriff bowed his head. An instant earlier, he had noticed a familiar profile ahead of him. A woman. One of the nurses from the hospital? Funny he couldn't place her, then. But they all looked quite unlike themselves in street clothes, even Marmion Pyus. She was there, clutching her purse as if it helped her to keep her balance.

The sheriff was near enough to Mr. Wilkins' house to hear when the telephone began its irreverent racket. No telling how long the ringing would go on, with no one to answer. People were turning their heads in annoyance. Quietly the officer made his way to the house and entered.

"You're disturbing the proceedings, Brandt," he said into the old-fashioned wall telephone. "What's up?"

Brandt's lazy drawl answered. "I'm sure sorry, Boss. But you got two calls here that look pretty important—one, anyway."

"Who's it from?"

"That pretty kitty at the Hellbent, Bolivar Mannering."

"Cassidy's secretary?"

"Right-oh. He called around noon but I didn't know where to find you. He's at the funeral now—I bet he's chief mourner—but he'll be back at the Hellbent right away after. He sounded like something outsize was biting him."

"What about the other call?"

"Oh, that's some girl, Marmion Pyus. She called this morning, too, and again about noon. Said if you got up to the hospital to be sure and see a patient, Mrs. Totman. That's all."

"Well, that one can wait," the sheriff said, and hung up the receiver.

Mr. Wilkins' blunder might not prove to be such a bad break after all, he pondered. Up to this point, no one had volunteered information of any kind. But out comes Sam's story and suddenly there are two calls. Both from people who had done as little as possible to co-operate before. What prompted them? Fear? Most likely. An ounce of funk weighed more than pounds of persuasion.

He had abundant time to go to the hospital, see Mrs. Who'sit, and still be at the Hellbent ahead of Mr. Mannering, the sheriff decided. As he stepped out of the house, the crowd began to sing, led by the expensive quartet which had expected to perform alone. But Mr. Wilkins was not presiding at a performance. He was initiating Big Balsam Cassidy into the brotherhood he had never known, alive.

"What a beautiful hymn," said Sister Ursula as the tremendous voice poured up over the rimrock. "Safe in the arms of Jesus. Somehow, I never imagined Mr. Cassidy needing safety."

"He was mortal," Sister Judy said gently.

They stood well back from the rimrock out of view of the crowd below, all the Sisters together, and the singing of the invisible hundreds swelled up and around them as if it came from inside the hills themselves. Mr. Cassidy would have been impressed by it, Sister Judy thought. Perhaps he would even have seen something of the kingdom and the power and the glory if he had heard the magnificent praying of those voices a few minutes ago. The tears ran down her cheeks.

Sister Margaret, beside her, was wondering if she had been correct in assuming that Mr. Wilkins would like starch in his shirt collar; and then she had a twinge of conscience over letting her mind wander from a religious ceremony, and that twinge was followed by another over even this long-distance participation in a Protestant service. But Sister Magdalene had given permission to all the community to pay this final tribute to their benefactor. Theoretically, they could have attended the funeral, but Reverend Mother would never have allowed it, to say nothing of the Bishop. So they stood out of sight on the crown of the rimrock and said silent Hail Marys during the part of the services they could not hear.

Their Superior did not speak during any of the forty-five minutes of the ceremony.

"Twins, this time, Sheriff," Mrs. Totman beamed, shaking the sheriff's hand stoutly. "My husband's calling them Doc and Spike, but we haven't decided on names, yet. You a family man, Sheriff?"

"One grown daughter." The tired officer eased himself into the rocker. "I understand you wanted to see me, Mrs. Totman."

"Me? Land, no! Where'd you get that notion?"

"There was a call to my office from Marmion Pyus. She said for me to—"

"So that's it!" Mrs. Totman stiffened against her pillows with a gleam in her eye. "I knew there was some skullduggery about that corset!"

The sheriff blinked. "A corset?"

"Oh, not just any corset. This was Sister Peter's. And I give it to that girl, trustin' her like I would my own, and I says will you see that Sister gets it, and she says yes. But I know perfectly well she never did give it to Sister because she ain't mentioned it, Sister Pete ain't, and she would if she'd got it because Sisters are that polite, even to each other, let alone—"

"Mrs. Totman, I don't believe—"

Mrs. Totman's gaze was unseeing upon the footrail of her bed, and her ears were hearing nothing but Marmion's treachery. "I'll be glad to, she says, and off she goes. And what she coulda done with it, I dunno. It 'ud make two for her. She's a slim thing, but just you wait till she's had a few kids—"

"Mrs. Totman," the sheriff interrupted firmly. "I'll be glad to question Miss Pyus about this—eh—garment. But there must have been something else. She'd hardly call me on to her own trail. Think hard, please."

"Then it musta been Jock. I was tellin' her about him. But land, I didn't think it was that important!" She pushed herself more erect and her plump face glowed. "My, that poor young fellow came to an awful end, didn't he? Down in that mine and all! What in the world ever possessed him, Sheriff? And his suitcase right beside him, too, they said, and they said he looked real surprised. My, you just never know, do you?"

Rumor had indeed added picturesque touches to the story of Jock's death. The sheriff took out his notebook. He didn't intend to write much in it, but Mrs. Totman was one of those overworked, taken-for-granted beings who would love to have her words recorded in a notebook.

"How well were you acquainted with Jock, Mrs. Totman?"

"Oh, not much. I don't suppose I can tell you anything you don't already know. They lived near us for a while, twelve miles bein' near in our neck o' the woods. Alkali Flats."

"They?"

Mrs. Totman's nod humped her hair against the pillow. "I don't get off the ranch very often. Doc and Spike's number ten and eleven. Course I only had eight then, but they're like steps on the stairs, one right after the other. The girl wasn't much for visiting, either, kind of hoity-toity. But all us neighbors kind of blamed ourselves afterward. Seemed like the lonesomeness might of drove her to it."

The sheriff's hand opened loosely. "The girl? You mean Jock was married?

Mrs. Totman looked at him with reproach. "Look, you dropped your notebook, Sheriff." She waited until he had retrieved it before she continued. "Sure he was married. He had this ranch, near us, like I said, and they lived there, oh, six, seven months, maybe. I could figure it to the last week if you give me time. By Mary's hives. Mary was the baby then, always breakin' out with something. And around the time I took her to the doctor—"

"The approximate time will do," the sheriff told her. "How long ago was this, Mrs. Totman—approximately?"

"He changed her formula . . . well, like I say, Mary was the baby when they come, and she's four now. Three years, a little longer, I guess. I had one in between."

"You don't happen to know the girl's maiden name?"

"Not her maiden name. But I know I've heard her first name, something short. Maybe it'll come to me. I guess I better tell it to you my own way, and some o' these things I've forgot might pop into my head."

"A good idea," the sheriff murmured, making the notebook very prominent.

"Well, I've always thought I understood better'n some how that girl felt. She'd come from a city, like me, and she must of thought

ranches were awful romantic places, the lady ridin' out like a duchess and the cowboys circlin' the herd in full moonlight and singin'
while a coyote howled in the coulee. Well, the coyote was all that
turned out like she expected, if she was like me. And I know how
Jock's place looked. The ranch house was a little unpainted one
rarin' up in a ravine with one cottonwood for shade, and the corrals
were just plain ol' pole fences, and the one cowboy on the place
couldn't carry a tune. There just ain't no West like in the movies.
She used to play her fiddle, some. She was a musician, I know that.
But the fiddle wouldn't sound like it used to, with nothing to go
with it but a little dogie bawlin' down the draw. Jock was a rodeo
rider then, getting up into the money, national champeen bulldog-
ger or something. He was everlastingly off to some rodeo. At first
she'd go with him, but that wasn't any life for a nice girl that'd done
all she'd done. So she got so's she'd just stay home."

"Just what had she done, Mrs. Totman?"

"Oh, I dunno, maybe not so much. But all that fiddling was sure
nice. And she had lots of clothes. She must of had some use for 'em
in the first place or she wouldn't a got 'em."

Mrs. Totman's eyes were on the undertaker's calendar which offered helpful services in time of need. It was evident that she had
given much thought to the disillusioned young wife in her unpainted house down in the ravine with the one cottonwood.

"Now this part I don't really know, Sheriff, only that the house
burned down and nobody seen her after. Nobody, that is, but the
railroad ticket agent in Rapid. They traced her that far. But I guess
she didn't go where she'd bought her ticket for. Anyway, they never
found her. See, Jock was gone, we knew that much, and from the
looks of things somebody figured out she'd maybe dumped a lot of
kerosene in the kitchen stove to make it burn faster, and it explod-
ed. I expect her fiddle was burned up, too. Poor thing, I've often
wondered what she did after she left here."

"And Jock sold the ranch?"

"Yes, a few months after. He got throwed in a rodeo pretty soon,
and he was in a hospital over in Cheyenne for a while, then they
brought him here. Couldn't even walk till Doc Kingston fixed him
up. My, there's a grand doctor, only he—" She glanced toward the

door and lowered her voice. "Sheriff, is it the bounden truth that he likes his nip? I ain't ever smelled nothin' on him!

"And Jock sold the ranch," the sheriff repeated.

"That's right. I guess he'd seen too much trouble there."

"And you never saw the girl?"

"Never, more's the pity. She was real good lookin', I guess. She'd brought all her evening dresses with her. My, I sure wisht Ida seen em!"

"But you did know her name."

"Well, if I could think of it. Something short."

"Ann?"

"They don't come much shorter'n that, do they, Sheriff? No, seems like it had a little more to it."

"And you're sure you don't know where she came from?"

"No, I never did hear. I guess all I know for sure is she had a short name and her house burned down and she played the fiddle, and her and me, we both seen too many Western movies before we got married."

"Oh, well, we all make mistakes," the sheriff said, closing his notebook.

Mrs. Totman laughed heartily. "Land, I didn't make no mistake! I wouldn't live any place else! It ain't like in the movies, but, my, I wouldn't wanta be married to a man that went around singin' all the time. He wouldn't ever get nothing done!"

The sheriff grinned for the first time in days. "Maybe you got something there. Now I don't want to be hard on you, Mrs. Totman, but if you feel up to doing a little ruminating on that name, I'd sure appreciate it."

"It ain't goin' to hurt me one bit, Sheriff. I'm sorta siftin' through names, anyhow, for Spike and Doc. How would you favor Leonard and Leopold? We could cut 'em to Lennie and Lee. We're great for nicknames. When I named Mary, I said there's one they can't nickname, but the kids call her Mare."

"Fine," said the sheriff absently. "I'll get in touch with the sheriff of your county."

"You can, but it won't do much good, there wasn't nothin' to the investigation. Jock didn't want to push it, seemed like."

"The sheriff might remember the case—"

"He don't," Mrs. Totman interrupted. "He got shot. See, there was this rancher, Plumbag Ollibar, he'd put up a gate to keep this neighbor's cattle from trespassin'. But the other fellow—land, I'd oughta know his name as well as my own—"

"Well, thanks, you've sure helped me, Mrs. Totman," the sheriff said quickly. "If you remember the girl's name, you might ask the nurse to call me. I won't tire you out any longer, now. So long!"

"My, I ain't tired. And say, don't forget about the corset, will you, Sheriff? Sister Pete wouldn't mind, you bein' a family man—"

"You bet. Thanks again."

The sheriff made his escape. The funeral procession was winding out of the Gulch to the highway, where they would travel a few hundred feet and then turn back onto the opposite hillside where the cemetery was scarred by an open grave. The sheriff, at the tail of the serpentine line, fumed at the delay. When finally he reached town and his own office, he had to hasten his instructions to Brandt, starting the search for Jock's wife. He did not wish to keep the magnificent Mr. Mannering waiting.

The day was very still. Dr. Kingston, at the open window of his office, heard the wheels rolling over clay and gravel on the other wall of the Gulch, slowly, no hurry about getting there. He could see the grave, a small dry spot on the hillside. The black beetles climbed toward it, wound around below it, subsided into quiet. All the tiny people would move now to the open hole. He slapped his thigh impatiently and was about to turn away when he saw the girl again, much as he had seen her on the night she came, climbing, tired from the long road. She had been to the funeral and it had torn her to shreds. He waited until she opened the door below, until her slow feet carried her up the entrance stairs.

Marmion paused when the doctor loomed in the hall before her. He was intimidating because of his sheer physical size, but the girl was not afraid. She stopped because he would not let her pass. She was holding her hat, her hair was damp where it touched her forehead. King scowled viciously at her.

"You shouldn't have gone to the funeral. It was totally unnecessary."

"I had permission to go."

"I was not speaking of permission."

There was a chain of little white plastic daisies around her neck. Cheap. Her hair curled over one of them.

The doctor jammed his hands into his pockets. "Miss Pyus, you are not the type to integrate well into our hospital staff. Don't you know that by now?"

Marmion looked up into his glowering, handsome face. So this was the man who was so attracted to her, according to the sheriff's way of thinking; who, in Sister Judy's judgment, had been badly hurt, scarred like Big Balsam Cassidy, and all the fighting was simply a defense mechanism. Exciting! We're all a little bit in love with him, Eloise had said; and to Blanche he was a scintillating breath on a cold morning. And now he stood here stoutly hating the young convent graduate, who had never had a date other than a few proms arranged by the Sisters, hating her because—he liked her too much?

With the poise instinctive to every woman who knows she is admired, Marmion smiled. Afraid of him? Never again!

"If I may pass, Doctor . . ." she murmured, and still with that little secret smile she stepped around him and went on up the stairs. From the landing she saw King standing where she had left him, astonished, bewildered—but respectful? On his face there was the first hint of frank amusement she had ever seen.

Blanche, alone in the kitchen, wished she had disregarded her stomach and gone to the funeral. Even Philippa had gone, leaving Chad down in the Gulch with Mrs. Hayes, who had been Cassidy's night nurse. Nothing could be worse than being here by herself, listening to the quiet. Blanche had slight imagination, and yet the kitchen—in fact, the whole of the old ground floor—seemed to brood, hiding something, holding back. There was nothing to do. Philippa had planned supper so they could get the trays ready in a jiffy. Scrub, maybe? Blanche loved to scrub. The floor was already clean. The old stove, ready to roar like a blast furnace when the gas was turned on, was cool and polished. The refrigerator had been defrosted this morning, Chad's toys put away, everything in order. But she could always chase cockroaches in the cupboard under the sink.

Slowly Blanche went down on her knees and opened the cupboard doors. The cold water pipe had been sweating and the seldom used pans they kept here were wet again. She pulled out the roaster, tipped it so the stagnant puddle raced to the other end. She was not much interested in the problem of sweating pipes. She didn't even bat at the cockroach waving its feelers from under the muffin tins. She was back to her fearful wonderings: who was Marmie afraid of; why had Ellie never mentioned the sore place on the back of her head, a thing Blanche knew about only because she had heard her groaning about it to Marmion in the bathroom. And why had Phil suddenly gone into a fit of the screaming jeebies this morning, when Blanche, hungry for a little cheer, had tuned in a music program on the radio? Such nice music, too, violins like silk threads over deep velvet.

She caught a glimpse of the cockroach and clattered the muffin tins down on top of it. At least it was something to do. Do? Why not do something about her own unhappy situation? Her stomach would never be better while she stayed here. So why stay? The sheriff wouldn't like it if she were to leave, but on the other hand, if he didn't know she was going, he couldn't stop her. . . . She could pack up and be out of here before the others were back from the funeral. . . . The Sisters wouldn't know, they were still out on the rimrock. And the few nurses left on duty, Miss Bacon and a couple downstairs, were too busy to oversee an escaping. . . .

Blanche's brain had been too preoccupied to pay any attention to what her eyes were seeing. Now, suddenly, the realization broke through that there was a box in the cupboard with the pans, a long thin box that had no business being in under the pipes because it would soon be soaked. Without thinking, Blanche pulled it out. And then she began to wonder what was in it. Something Philippa had stuck away? There was no paper wrapping. All she had to do was to lift the lid. A new pink corset lay neatly rolled inside.

Puzzled, but not so puzzled as she would have been without worries of her own, Blanche pushed the cover back on the box. The side was dented so that the cover didn't quite fit. The thing would be ruined if she were to leave it here. On top of the cupboard then? No, someone had put it down with the pans so it wouldn't be seen, a nice modest gesture.

"Gosh, I gotta be goin'!" she said aloud with a glance at the clock. So she carried the corset box with her when she climbed to the crow's-nest.

Get the suitcase first, she decided, dump everything in, never mind how; then hurry down to the kitchen again and hide the suitcase under the sink. It would be all right—she could set the roaster to catch the drips. Then tonight, after dark, she would catch a bus into town.

Although the sun shone outside, the attic space was shadowed. The luggage, pushed helter-skelter back near the jelly-roll mattress, was all dimly alike. She made foot space by nudging aside an overnight case. Then she leaned far over and pulled out the suitcase with the tweed finish. There was another like it, but farther away. Perhaps because she jerked so impatiently, the lid fell open. She caught it with her knee. A long white envelope slid along the blue lining. Her suitcase didn't have blue lining. In another minute she might have reflected that the envelope was not her property since the suitcase was not; but it was an intriguing envelope, with a fat paper folded inside. There was no address. That made it even more interesting. The flap was unsealed. No reason in the world why she shouldn't take a peek. She took out the paper and unfolded it. It was very pretty. Fat, dimpled cupids wreathed the page, beautiful little boys as pink as the roses that entwined them. There was printing, and writing, too. She would need time to read all this. Quickly she closed the suitcase and slipped it back in the exact spot where she had found it.

She was looking for a stepping place when she heard the first tread on the stairs. For an instant she stood there, her heart hammering in alarm. She had blundered into something, just the way Marmie and Ellie had, and now she would go around in danger of her life! What to do? The envelope was too large to go into her pocket, and there wasn't time to reach any door without being seen.

The corset box was her salvation. Stooping quickly, Blanche

picked it up, raised the lid, and thrust the paper and envelope in-side. Then, because her own room was near the stairs and she would meet the steadily climbing one face to face if she went in that di-rection, she scuttled as noiselessly as she could back to the sitting room with the box under her arm. Lucky the climber was so slow! Where would she hide the box? The closet, which had become the pantry, was the only possibility. She pushed the box onto the high shelf just as the steps came along even with the bathroom. There wasn't time to push the box clear back out of sight.

She was in the chair with the leaky arm when Marmion, tired but apparently satisfied about something, slumped in and threw her hat and purse in the direction of the bedroom.

"I'm beat out, Blanche! What a day! At that, though, I have more pep than Lynn and Dixie. I left them down in the gulch hoping they'd get a ride. Where have you been?"

"Me? No place. Why?"

"I just thought you seemed out of breath. What time is it—quarter to four? I'm going to make a cup of tea before I go back to the lab."

"I'll make it for you," Blanche offered instantly.

"Thanks, but I'd rather have something to do. I want to get the funeral out of my head."

"I'll get you a tea bag and you can take it down to the lab and make the tea there."

"The lab isn't appetizing." Marmion turned in the bedroom door. "Is there some reason why I can't have my tea here?"

"Gosh, no!" Blanche replied hastily. "No, I just thought—you go right ahead, Marmie. I gotta be going, anyway."

Marmion, alone, forgot the big girl's behavior. She changed into her uniform. Then she went to the bathroom to get hot water. They couldn't have boiling water for their tea, but the water from the tap was always steaming. She came back with a full cup. Groping to the high shelf, she shoved aside a white box that had pushed the tea almost out of reach. The box was a nuisance. She barely managed to finger the tea into her grasp.

She was sitting in the leaky chair, squeezing the tea bag with her spoon, when the strange familiarity of the white box began to impress her. She had seen that box before. And it had not been on the closet shelf. Cookies? They had a cookie jar, empty.

Setting her cup on the table, Marmion went purposefully to the closet and took down the box. And then she stood there gaping at it. It was the shape to hold a dozen long-stemmed roses!

"Sister Peter's corset!" she whispered. She raised the lid. The corset was there, the lacing neatly uppermost; and on top of it lay a paper and an envelope. Blanche's paper? But why in the corset box? And where had the box been all these days?

The nurses were coming up the stairs now, talking and laughing. Any one of them might come in. Marmion replaced the box on the shelf, but without the folded paper. She glanced at it, saw inane cupids and bulbous roses. She didn't dare try to read it now.

When Marmion went down to the lab, her large purse was under her arm. And in the purse was the envelope and the paper with the cupids.

In the plush office adjoining the other, which had belonged to the great man of the Hellbent, the sheriff was ruminating. The man nearest to Cassidy in life sat across the mahogany desk, a sad young man with white hands folded on the very clean plate glass before him. He wore Oxford gray with white shirt and black tie, and the impression was that of a sensitive undertaker about to close the casket in the presence of the bereaved. Last summer there had been a rumor afloat that this same Mr. Bolivar Mannering had dug himself a swimming pool in his back yard, then stood in the hole when he opened the dam to let the creek rush in, and nearly drowned himself. The sheriff found the rumor believable, all except the digging. He couldn't imagine a shovel in those dainty hands.

"Your message sounded urgent, Mannering. Have you unearthed a new angle? Or is it something you recollected since our first interview?"

The young man let pained brown eyes fall to a point on the desk. "It's—neither, really, Sheriff. I didn't think this incident would be of the slightest significance, and it does reflect upon me because— well, I overstepped the bounds of good taste, a thing I've never—"

The sheriff let his annoyance speak. "You understand you may have withheld evidence? There's a penalty for that, you know, Mannering!"

"I realize what I've done, Sheriff. But honestly, it didn't come to me with any force until this morning when I read that—that yellow story in the *Daily Bulletin!*"

"All right. Begin at the beginning."

"My duties sometimes take me out of the office, even when Mr. Cassidy is—was here. I'm not excusing myself, Sheriff, this is simply the truth. I inform the switchboard operator when I'm leaving, and she holds all calls and visitors, except the staff."

"So you were out and somebody got in."

"Yes. I'd been down to the mills to get the time slips, and when I came back in, this woman was with Mr. Cassidy. When I heard raised voices—well, it was a degrading thing to do, but I—"

"You listened. What day was this, Mannering?"

"A few days before Mr. Cassidy was taken ill."

"Go on."

"I had reached this desk when I heard the voices, and I looked up and saw that the door there was ajar, and I went over to close it. But when I heard what they were saying—"

"Yeah?" The sheriff forgot his irritations over too discreet secretaries and overly bright reporters. "What were they up to?"

"The woman—she was young, I knew that from her voice—she was giving Mr. Cassidy a tongue lashing, calling him a devil incarnate and a terrorist. It seemed to me that she was delivering a rehearsed speech, not memorized but excellently thought through. She never paused for a word."

"And Cassidy?"

"He didn't say a thing."

"What did she want?"

"I don't know. Perhaps she had made her demands before I came in. But I thought her attitude was one of utter hatred, that if he had offered her anything she would have thrown it back at him. Really, she gave me crawlies down my spine!"

"And you thought this was of no importance!" the sheriff sighed. "You're sure you don't know what she wanted?"

"Honestly, I don't. I missed a lot of what she said because I was in such a quandary myself. I couldn't decide whether to close the door and hope Mr. Cassidy wouldn't notice, or leave it open and go out myself—which is what I did, after a minute. When I came back, she was gone."

The sheriff sat deep in thought for a moment. Now he had something to root out, a woman's identity, name her, and give her a past and a present. Her future, too, would come under his jurisdiction if she had connived to kill Cassidy. She had disclosed a motive, cold and calculating hatred. Cardinelle's daughter would hate him that way.

"Did this affect Cassidy at all?" the sheriff asked. "Make him moody, for instance?"

"Oh, definitely!" Mr. Mannering replied. "Yes, you'd think a wand was waved over him. He lost his appetite, for one thing, because he didn't go out for lunch, just sat in there with the door closed. I wanted to get him coffee, but he wouldn't have even that. I don't believe he ate a thing those days. And of course he began to look thinner. If it hadn't been Mr. Cassidy, I'd have thought he was frightened and—well, perhaps remorseful. Then that last afternoon, I heard him fall. I ran in, and when I saw him lying there I thought he was dead."

"Can you give me the exact date the woman was here?"

The secretary turned to a calendar. "Yes, October second. That would be the date for picking up the time slips for that two-week period."

"Good. Would you know her voice if you heard it again?"

"I doubt it. I was very much confused."

"Well, if you think of anything else, call me even if it's the middle of the night, eh, Mannering?"

The sheriff grabbed his hat. He had given up any idea of reprisal against Mr. Mannering for withholding evidence. He was at the door when the young man spoke again.

"There's one more thing, Sheriff."

"Something she said, quite horrible because she said it so softly and clearly. I could imagine her screaming it and it wouldn't sound half so terrifying. But in that low voice, you'd have to believe her."

The secretary's voice fell to a hoarse whisper. "Sheriff, she called him a murderer!"

When Marmion reached the laboratory, she saw the reason for the doctor's amusement. He had lined up a full evening's work for her. Exasperated, she flipped through the slips. Nothing unnecessary. But he had marked them all for tonight!

"Dram him!" she muttered, flinging her purse into a cupboard. "All right, Kingston, M.D., you'll get them tonight, and from me personally!"

Sister Judith had left the laboratory, no doubt before King sent up the slips. He would never have dared do it if the nun was on duty. And Marmion would not call her. Straight through the supper hour she worked, and her hair grew damper on her forehead and her uniform clung to her shoulders. It was nine o'clock when she was finished. She stacked the reports neatly and went down to the doctor's office.

To her surprise, he was there, seated in his swivel chair, the lower desk drawer pulled out for a footrest, a medical journal tossed open in front of him.

Marmion slapped down the sheaf of slips. "My reports, Doctor."

"How efficient you are, Miss Pyus."

"Thank you. Will that be all for tonight, Doctor?"

"I believe so. If anything comes up, I can always call you."

"Oh, don't hesitate! Sister Judith is on call tonight."

"Thank you. Good night, Miss Pyus."

He whirled the chair until his back was toward her. But instead of looking over the reports she had worked so hard to provide, he picked up the magazine and began to turn its pages.

Marmion was not surprised. Striding angrily back up to the lab, she told herself that this was what she had expected of King. She would not leave voluntarily, so he would persecute her. She was not at all thrilled by him now. Through the dark little labyrinth that spewed off to the X-ray room she went without thinking of being afraid; and when she took her purse out of the cupboard where she had kept it all evening, it was with never a thought that someone might be lurking out of sight but within hearing. She was going to peruse the mysterious paper right here and now, without being disturbed. Upstairs there would be Eloise, at least, possibly Blanche and Lynn and Dixie to come in upon her and ask what she had. Opening the purse, she mused that she could return the thing to Blanche, or put it back in the corset box for her to find; but all the time, she was taking out the paper. A week ago she would never have considered reading anything belonging to another person. Now, quickly, although her hands shook, she smoothed the sheet out on her desk.

The page was printed, with names handwritten in the spaces provided. She read it, then read it again. On the tenth day of September, four years ago, Eleanor Ann Roberts had been united in marriage to Joseph Terence Turner.

Jock was Joseph Terence, Sam's article had thus named him. And he had been married, just as Mrs. Totman had said. The wife would be the logical owner of a marriage certificate. But how could Jock's wife, a stranger, have hidden it in the hospital where only an insider such as Blanche could find it?

She didn't for a moment consider that Blanche might be Eleanor Ann. But the elusive Eleanor was not a stranger; she knew her way around the hospital. Therefore she must have taken another name. She did not want to be identified as Jock's wife. Why not? Because she had killed him?

"Oh, no!" Marmion whispered, so faintly that anyone listening in the outer passage would hardly have heard. There was only silence out there, anyway.

When the sound finally came from the darkened rectangle beyond the door, it was tiny as a mouse's frisking. Marmion did not hear it. She was putting the paper into the envelope.

And then Eloise spoke. "What's that, Marmie?"

Marmion jumped and gave a choked exclamation. "What—oh, Ellie, you scared the daylights out of me—" She stopped, horrified. What had she just said? Oh, Ellie . . . and Ellie could be short for Eleanor Ann . . . but it wasn't! This was Eloise, her friend, her confidante, Ellie who had gone down to Big Balsam's room to get the corset box, who had insisted on going . . . and she was too young to be Eleanor Ann. . . ."

"Marmie, what in creation is the matter with you? So help me, you look as if you'd seen a ghost."

The tall girl was in pajamas and robe, her feet in soft slippers. Anyone could walk unheard, like that.

Marmion fumbled at her purse, closing it clumsily. "You just startled me, Ellie. You know how we all are."

"What are you hiding in your purse?"

"Hiding? Nothing."

"Yes, you are, baby. Tell Mama." Eloise came softly over to the desk.

Marmion laughed shakily. After all, why not let Ellie see the certificate, watch her and try to detect any recognition? It would be a quick test. And she would know, then, whether Eloise was friend or enemy. She opened the purse.

"Can you keep a secret, Flue? This is a whopper. Look!"

She unfolded the paper quickly and thrust it at the girl. And Ellie's reaction was the same as her own, bewilderment first, then comprehension, then awareness of danger. When finally she looked up, her eyes were dark with fear.

"Marmie, this isn't good!" she whispered. "How did you get hold of it?"

"It was in Sister Peter's corset box, on our closet shelf." Marmion, reassured by Ellie's apprehension, felt her own doubts fade. "There's nothing to get us into trouble, really. I'm going to telephone the sheriff right away."

"Of course." Eloise folded the paper and tucked it into Marmion's purse. But she was listening, oddly, as if half her attention remained in the dark little hall she had just traversed. "Come on, Marmie, upstairs. You can phone from there."

"But this is more private—"

"No!" Ellie's green eyes slid away from the door to Marmion, and her face was whiter than if she had fainted. "Oh, Marmie, come on!"

There was nothing else she could do. She had to obey Ellie's insistence. And Eleanor Ann, perhaps, had never been nicknamed at all. Talk about jumping to conclusions!

"I'm with you, Ellie. You go ahead and turn on the lights, then I'll turn off this one. Everything's under control."

Queer, for her to be encouraging Eloise. They ran together all the way to their sitting room.

Mrs. Totman lay on her back staring into the comfortable dimness made by the night light down in the base of her floor lamp. She had been thinking, ever since the sheriff's visit, mulling over names. She had not come upon a pair that would do for the twins, but her efforts had not been entirely wasted. Out of memory, at last, had come the name of Jock's wife. A simple one, but tricky to remember. Several times she had picked up the string of her signal light to call the nurse and ask her to telephone the sheriff, since she had promised; but Baxter-with-the-corns was on duty and probably not in a frame of mind to deliver messages. Tomorrow, too, the sheriff would be here and there would be the great satisfaction of telling him herself. She wouldn't forget the name, either, once she had remembered it. She turned over and settled for sleep. She wouldn't forget. The name was Ellie.

12

Indian summer abandoned the Hills for good in the night. Morning came dismally, under a gray sky and over ragged veils of fog trailing the valleys. In the hospital corridors the lights burned without dispelling the gloom. But the day was beginning.

Dr. Kingston, coming up from the basement floor, stepped back to avoid meeting the procession of two: Sister Magdalene with her lighted candle and her tinkling silver bell, the young priest in white vestments bringing Communion to the patients. King nearly always managed to escape the halls at such a time. This morning, particularly, he was disgusted with his blundering up the stairs; but his mind had been on Marmion and the invention of a casual errand that might take him to the laboratory. Once there, he would consider what to do about an apology for his boorishness of last night.

He was further incensed at Marmion, then, for the distraction that brought him face to face with Sister Magdalene. He had not seen her since the night before last, when he had heaped such bitter censure upon her.

They passed on by, the priest's robes rustling softly. He was very young, recently ordained, still looking starved from his seminary days, a mere assistant at the cathedral in Balsam City. No wonder Magdalene had not consulted him about the moral problem involved in Cassidy's legacy; no wonder she had Johnny drive her into the city to consult the Bishop last night . . . as if she remained in doubt! King's lips made a derisive plop, but the derision was difficult to maintain. When he continued on up the stairs, his head was not high like a conqueror's. And he did not go to the lab.

Sister Magdalene tried not to be disconcerted by the sight of the doctor. She had been worried, naturally, by his outburst and more than ever by his avoidance of her yesterday. She had mentioned it to the Bishop, last night. Had she been lax, she asked, in bringing an unknown to the staff, into the inner life of the hospital, with so little investigation as she had made? The Bishop had kindly set forth all the arguments she had already thought out in self-defense: a hospital such as St. Dennis was lucky indeed to have a resident physician and surgeon; his brilliant record in the past six years proved she had judged him rightly as a doctor. And as a man, he had behaved himself. His past actually did not matter. And then they had gone on to the urgent problem of Cassidy's money.

It was still a problem. She must decide for herself, the Bishop had said. There was no moral reason why she should not accept the gift. Cassidy had based his fortune on wrongdoing in the early days, but there was no possible manner in which she could make restitution now. Except as the great man had indicated. A fine hospital would benefit all the people of the Hills.

Ringing her little bell, the Sister walked slowly on. And even for her, preoccupied as she was, the Healer walked again among the sick, comforting and restoring.

An inch at a time, without a betraying creak of the springs, Marmion pushed herself cautiously out of bed, listening, halting at every tiny slide of the sheets. Eloise's breathing was a steady, comfortable sound, one you'd wish might go on through the gray day this promised to be. There was barely light enough for Marmion to grope for her clothes. The luminous face of her watch set the hour as a little after six. Plenty of time, before anyone stirred, to run downstairs to the telephone. Ellie had been so very firm about not calling the sheriff last night. You're too tired, Marmie, she had insisted. Call that old buckaroo and he'll be out here half the night. . . . What would you gain? Nothing but lost sleep. . . . The thing will keep till morning.

So together Eloise and Marmion had left the laboratory, hustling through the black little passage, and in the hall they had met Dixie coming up with a request slip. Again Eloise had taken the lead, determined that Dixie would summon Sister Judy who was supposed to be on night call, and she had piloted Marmion up to the crow's-nest. Always Eloise. A wonderful friend.

Marmion carried her uniform out to the sitting room so the starchy slipping on of it would not arouse Ellie. She would have to make one more trip into the bedroom. She had left the marriage certificate under her pillow. The sheriff might want to read it, word for word. The floor complained when she stepped in between the beds, but Ellie was too deeply asleep to be disturbed. In a few minutes the alarm would go off, and she would awake groaning and sighing as if she climbed up from the bottomless pit.

No one, so far as Marmion knew, had seen her when she tiptoed along the rubber matting and over to the stairs, the long envelope poking up out of her pocket and the corset box under her arm. She would go to Sister Magdalene's office. Only the office telephone was on a private line. All the others were on one extension and anyone could listen in. At this hour she would have to rout the sheriff out of bed, but he wouldn't mind when he heard what she had to tell him. And then she would deliver the corset—at last—to Sister Peter.

Sister Magdalene's little bell tinkled off in the wing where Big Balsam had died, but Marmion met no one. The small office was gray and deserted as she came into it. She would not turn on the light. Someone might recall an errand, seeing a lighted office. So she walked in, into the quiet and the faint chill that always seems to hang in deserted places. And then she did something she never could explain. She pulled open the top drawer of the filing cabinet and dropped the envelope in among the folders. Even she could not have put her hand instantly upon it, after that.

Marmion smiled as she perched on the edge of the desk and took up the telephone.

The sheriff had gone extremely early to his office. His wife was thankful to see the last of him. He had not slept, he would not eat. He had talked until midnight about the secrecy surrounding Jock's marriage. It had taken place in a county at the other end of the state, which was why the fact had not been unearthed earlier. And after the tragedy of her house burning down, the young wife had completely disappeared. And as if this was not enough, there was the alarming possibility that Cardinelle's daughter had returned. Someone, within Mannering's hearing, had called Cassidy a murderer.

"Not that quite a handful of other people couldn't say the same," the sheriff had surmised at three minutes to twelve. "But let me find those two women and I'll be satisfied."

"I'd imagine the grandmother would want Cardinelle's baby to have all the nice things she could give her," his wife said pensively. "I know I would, to try to make up for what she couldn't ever have."

"Sure thing," the sheriff replied with the indifference of a man who often pursues unrelated subjects with mind and tongue.

"Like music," the wife continued. She appeared to be half asleep, stretched out in her chair with her feet on a hassock, one of the last batch of kittens curled in her lap. Sitting upright, she would have no lap. "Music is nice, for a girl. I've never seen anything prettier than a girl playing the violin."

The sheriff suddenly began to listen. "How does this go again, Lucy?"

But her answer seemed to be off on another tangent. "Would Jock's wife have a motive for murdering Cassidy?"

"She could have. He'd done Jock out of a lot of money."

"He'd done Jock's father out of the money, wasn't that it? Jock ought to be used to the idea by this time, even though his wife . . ." She paused, absently stroking the kitten's pencil of a tail. "Cardinelle's daughter would have a swell motive. Even a jury would sympathize with her while they set her in the Chair. And Jock's wife played the violin," she added. "I bet she had a good fiddle, too."

"And you think maybe Cardinelle's daughter played the fiddle?"

Lucy nodded sagely. "Granny would have seen to it that she had music."

"Lordy Lord!" the sheriff sighed. His fatigue couldn't keep him in his chair. He sprang up and began to pace the floor. He made several turns before he stopped before his wife. "So you think the daughter and Jock's wife . . ."

"I think they're the same one." She straightened, the kitten rolled over, and she caught it in her cupped palm. Then she got up and carried it out to its mother in the kitchen.

So the sheriff sat at his desk in the very early gray morning, wondering and fitting together pieces of the puzzle. Although the two women were one, he still had to find her. Nobody at the Hellbent had seen anyone who might have been Mr. Mannering's mysterious lady. That was understandable, if aggravating. There had been many outsiders from Balsam City coming to the Hellbent offices around that time, collectors for the Community Fund, the Red Cross, ticket sellers for all the fall festival suppers of the various churches. If the young woman was also Jock's wife, then that would put her at the hospital because it would explain Jock's protection of her . . . but no one at the hospital, other than the orderly, was named Turner. . . .

The sheriff sat motionless, seeing the snow come down like drifting tissue paper, the initial touch of a winter that would leave cattle starving in the ravines. His wife had done this sort of deducing on other cases. Early in his career he had endeavored to find out how she did it. He had given up.

When the telephone rang, he jumped, glancing at the clock. A few minutes after six. He had been sitting here for over an hour.

"Hello," he said into the phone. It was too early to be official.

"Honey, is that you?"

"Sure is, Lucy."

"Listen, I've just had a call from the Pyus girl—Marmion, is it? I think she's in trouble!"

"She called the house?"

"Well, of course, it's so early. She asked for you. And then, when I said you were at the office, she said something about yes, doctor, she'd attend to it right away. So I said for her to never mind trying to call you, I'd do it and send you straight up there."

"Good work, Lucy. I'm on my way."

"All right. But listen, honey, have you had your breakfast? All this on an empty stomach—"

"I'm fine, lovey. Good-by!"

The sheriff was on his feet as he dropped the telephone back in the cradle. Opening the door, he nearly scuffed aside the telegram which lay on the floor below the mail slot. It hadn't been there when he came in—or had it? He tore it open, grunted his satisfaction as he read.

Guy Murray Kingston, according to the navy, had spent two years in prison. Charges: jumping ship and insubordination. He had been released six years ago. Whereabouts unknown.

But not unknown to the sheriff. The doctor had come straight from his prison cell to his own voluntary confinement in the old hospital of St. Dennis of the Hills.

Marmion sat for a long time on the edge of the desk in Sister Magdalene's office. No one entered. The sheriff's wife, blessedly, had realized the emergency indicated by her mumbled foolishness and made it unnecessary for her to say a great deal. The sheriff would come as fast as he could cover the three miles around the mountain from Balsam City. But would that be in time? Would the white shoulder, just glimpsed outside the door, materialize into someone who would dart swiftly in, slam the heavy oak barrier shut, and then go leisurely about the task of murder?

She sat there so long that when she finally slid to her feet, pins and needles jabbed up through her soles. I'll meet it, she decided. Whatever is waiting there, I'll meet it. It was almost an anticlimax to come to the door, look out into vacancy, hear the first clatter of trays being prepared in the kitchen, the first radio blatting the news. Leaning against the door jamb, Marmion began to laugh. That would never do. Someone would see her, ask her what was the matter. And she must get away from the office, where the marriage certificate lay safely in the file.

Once again, Sister Peter's corset was performing a function. Its delivery was taking Marmion through the old passage to Methusaleh Hall where, even at this early hour, Sister would be trudging around like a pigeon with sore feet, her head bobbing at every step, her convex glasses almost disguising the beautiful kindness of her eyes. At the end of the passage, Marmion paused. She was not called here often, because these were chronic cases, but she recognized the usual morning hubbub: the old refugee from the prairie dugout demanding alcohol to drink, not rub; Barney cracking an Irish joke; fat old Mr. Larson reading the morning paper aloud. The Country Club, Johnny called it.

Sister Peter, carrying a washbasin, came out of a ward and stopped when she saw Marmion. Her day would not end until nine, or later, this evening, and yet she was beginning it with placid expectation.

"Sister, this is for you," Marmion said, offering the box. "Mrs. Totman gave it to me nearly a week ago. I'm sorry I didn't get it to you sooner."

The Sister's homely face flushed with pleasure. "So she remembered! Thank you, dear. Did she happen to tell you to mention the size?"

Marmion searched her memory hurriedly. "Plenty big, she said."

"Exactly right."

Running back through the passage and up to the crow's-nest, the girl mused almost enviously upon Sister Peter's tranquility. Did it come to you when you took the veil, or was it something you made for yourself? But tranquility was too ethereal, too unattainable to ponder long. Ellie, she thought more practically, would be gone by this time. She didn't distrust Ellie. It would be easier, however, not meeting her. The third floor was noisy now, a girl laughing, someone running a shower, another singing the "Prisoner's Song"—a normal awakening to a new day.

If Marmion had paused in the sitting room, she would have noticed that the bishop was hanging crooked on the wall. It was Eloise's tumbled bed that caught her eye. Not only was the bed tumbled, but the bottom sheet was ripped off and hung torn over the footrail. Dazedly, Marmion reached the door and saw the full turmoil of the room. The dresser drawers had been pulled out and dumped, clothes thrown out of the closet, her own bed with even the mattress crooked. She didn't have to ask herself why. Or who. She knew. Eleanor Ann had come hunting her marriage certificate.

Only Eloise, she thought after a blank interval, only Ellie had known she had the certificate. But Ellie had seen her put it under her pillow. She wouldn't tear the room apart like this. Relief flooded Marmion's tired brain. Now she could admit that she had been foolishly wrong about her roommate, especially last night when

Ellie wouldn't allow the call to the sheriff. What a wonderful thing to know there was someone to trust!

With the relief, Marmion could think again. Quickly she closed the open door to the hall. No one must see the mess in here until the sheriff had come. She remembered Philippa standing in that doorway—how many nights ago, surely more than six—and young Chad taking his finger from his mouth to remark concerning the bishop, "Dat's my fodder." Poor Phil had cried. Chad was always adopting inanimate things as fathers, she said, because he didn't know what a father was. Cassidy had done that to her baby. She would kill him, she screamed, if she knew how.

The house phone rang down the hall.

"Pyus! It's for you!" someone shouted. "A man. Felicitations!" It would be the sheriff, Marmion knew. He would ask her to come downstairs. And she would tell him everything.

Sister Magdalene knew she was sadly neglecting her duty that day. In an uneasy round she had gone from one patient's room to another, up to the laboratory where Marmion jumped at every footstep and Sister Judy worked in silence, into the X-ray room to help Eloise shift a heavy patient, to the nursery where the babies slept like Christmas dolls, anywhere but to her office and the pile of mail lying on her desk and King tramping in from time to time to see if she was there. She did not wish to meet him. Her unpreventable interview with the sheriff had been enough. Marmion Pyus, he said, had at last told him a straight story, given him the marriage certificate, been as helpful as she had been hindering before. But now he was uncomfortably certain that Eleanor Ann, under cover of some other name, was here. The girls who had been in the crow's-nest during the ransacking of Marmion's room seemed to have formed a conspiracy of false clues and denials. No one had heard or seen anything that someone else couldn't explain away. There had been people all over the place. The ransacker had evidently chosen a foolhardy but foolproof time for her search.

"Well, I'll have to get her from another direction, then, but I'll get her!" the sheriff swore to Sister Magdalene. "I'm going to put more men out here, that's for sure. And if you hear or see or even smell anything out of the ordinary, call me, will you?" With that, he had gone away.

One could almost gain an illusion of peace, looking out on the gently falling snow. The ponderosa pines were becoming heavy with it, their branches drooping until the wet load slid off and the branch snapped up again, dark among its white neighbors. Sister Magdalene watched the lovely process from the sunporch. In a minute she would go and find something to do. . . .

But it was too late. She recognized the step coming in behind her. How she wished she had gone straight to the cloister.

"May I see you a moment, Sister?"

"Of course, King."

"You've been busy today."

Because there was a bit of ridicule in that, she didn't answer. When the silence became cumbersome, the doctor broke it.

"It's not easy to talk to a person who won't look at you, Sister."

She turned around. King's hair was tousled, his linen rumpled, but there was something different about him. His shoulders were straight, that was one change. And he was not glowering.

"The sheriff told you, I see." The words were what one would expect from King, but not the manner. He was ill at ease—humble, if he understood humility.

"The sheriff told me what, King?"

"About my prison record. Do I lose my job?" Without waiting for her answer, he swung impatiently to the window. "I didn't want you to know, naturally. A man is never proud of being a jailbird. You ought to understand my crime, you've put up with more of it than the navy could stomach: insubordination. They gave me two years. I'll not tell you the reason. I wouldn't tell the sheriff, either, even though I know he can dig it out for himself. And I'll not ask your pardon for anything I've been or done. An old priest told me once that your God provides irritations for saints in order to develop their perseverance—I remember he said he had already pushed his bishop far along toward sainthood—and I've done the same for you. So I've not been wasted. Even a negative blessing has its place."

Sister Magdalene smiled faintly. "I've often said you were our salvation, King, but I didn't mean—"

"Don't obligate me further with praise! You don't owe it to me. But I have a debt to pay." He wheeled, facing her belligerently. "Whether you build your hospital is up to you. I'd do it, in your place, but then I have the scruples of a skunk. If I have a streak of decency, too, would it surprise you? Probably not. You can always find the good in the worst of us, can't you? Well . . . you'll see. . . ."

Sister Magdalene had no pious homily to deliver. Tonight she was as bleak of spirit as old Barney ever had been. Twenty-nine years ago Anthony had died, and because she could not see her way to going on without him, she had been ready to return to the mother house. Not that she would have found it impossible to bear the personal loss. But Anthony was her only entry, it seemed, into the places where money abounded. Without his help, she could not hope to build beyond the log cabin that was her hospital up near the Hellbent, the small and pathetic attempt to care for the miners and their families. She had finally persuaded Sister Peter and Sister Margaret, and they had even packed their belongings and were ready to leave when Little Job Pyus came with his gift—this beautiful tract on Balsam Mountain. The city would grow here, he predicted; the hospital would stand in the middle of the new boom. But more to the Sister than the deed to the land was Little Job's sympathetic understanding. When he left, she had gone back to her room and unpacked. The other Sisters had rejoiced with tears of thankfulness. But the gift had not been given in charity; it was only a means to keep her here, too busy to wonder what actually had happened to Anthony. . . .

There was a small sound behind her, and the Sister turned. Mr. Wilkins stood in the doorway, his hat in his hand, the new haircut giving him a briskness quite out of keeping with the sag of his shoulders under the old overcoat. The coat was embossed with melted snow beginning to fall in small drops around him.

Sister Magdalene was touched by the appearance of her old friend. He had always been unassuming, but now there was a timid buoyancy about him as if somewhere he had found hopefulness and enthusiasm he had never chanced upon before.

She smiled. "The walking must be very bad, Hal. Should you have come out?"

"It's slippery, yes. There will be accidents tonight."

He hesitated, and the Sister was afraid she had not sounded cordial. "Do take off your wet overcoat. You're not in a hurry, surely?"

The old man was pleased at that. Carefully, not to soil the floor, he slid out of the coat, folded the wet side in, and laid it over a chair. "I suppose I have no right to risk broken bones that my parish would have to pay for mending. But I love to be out. Except for the snow, I imagine this old gulch resembles the country around Jerusalem."

"The Valley of Hinnom, perhaps?"

His eyes twinkled. "Ah, yes, the valley that was the model of hell for the rabbis' sermons. You know, Maggie, that valley was nothing more than the city dump. They kept fires burning in it to do away with the refuse. No doubt from the hillside the smoke and flames did look like hell."

Sister Magdalene chuckled. She had seated herself in a rocker, and now she began a gentle rocking, her arms folded as if she held a baby. "You're good at banishing ghosts, Hal."

"I've come to banish another, I hope." He sat down with his back to the window, and the snow seemed to fall around him as he went on. "Big Balsam Cassidy's ghost, Maggie."

She stopped rocking. "His ghost is laid, for me."

"If I could be sure of that, I'd say nothing. But—" he leaned forward with kindly determination, "one look at you and I know it can't be true. If you had reached a decision you felt was binding, whether it was to take the money or not, you would be at peace. And you aren't. You believe you have turned down the legacy, of course. Actually, you haven't. I would guess that your bishop, being a very wise man, counseled you to follow your own inclination in regard to the money, and so you are considering again." He paused in embarrassment rather than uncertainty. "I am not so wise as your bishop, you see, and I have come to offer advice—to urge you to accept Cassidy's fortune. I've prayed for such an opportunity for you. I want my prayers to be answered."

Sister Magdalene smiled, about to thank him and assure him that she had quite irrevocably made up her mind; but Mr. Wilkins' gesture stopped her.

"Let me say it out, please. I've never thought it was by an odd run of luck that we all came west at the same time—you and Cassidy and I—and in the past few days I've been more convinced of it than ever. Our lives were meant to be lived out together. One can believe in a divine plan without being a fatalist. You saw the practical vision of service. Cassidy made the money so you might carry out the dream before you die. What my part was meant to be, I don't know, Maggie. I do know that my regard for you has kept me in Gopher Gulch all these years."

The nun wondered, for a moment, whether she had heard correctly. Mr. Wilkins had lost a shade or two of his usual healthy color and his eyes were fixed on the wet circlet where he had stood with his overcoat dripping. But elderly ministers did not sit in sun parlors speaking of lifetime affection for nuns. She had mistaken his meaning.

Mr. Wilkins continued. "Until yesterday I would have said that my dowdy little round in Gopher Gulch amounted to zero in the general scheme of things. In fact, I did say as much to you. But then I conducted Cassidy's funeral, and I realized suddenly the loneliness of everyone's passage, and that there is so much loneliness because we don't know how to go about finding real friendship. Cassidy didn't. He didn't know how to make a generous gesture, beyond buying a few tickets for bazaars. He was the Lord's instrument, like Judas—I've always been sorry for Judas—he had to be the one to strike Father Anthony out of your life because you were to be enabled to build uncommon spiritual strength. And now the Lord is using the same instrument to endow you with temporal means." The old man's hands were lying upon his knees and he turned them suddenly palm up. "I have not said this well, Maggie. The excitement of these days has tired me. I'll have to leave the rest to your understanding."

He rose, shrugged on the overcoat, and stood before her with his hat in his hand. "I've brought tears," he said gently. "I'm sorry. Whatever I have said that needs forgiving, I know you'll forgive. Good night, Maggie."

He left her. He had never felt so tired in his life. He would go straight home, and to bed, and he would sleep until his brain was perfectly clear again; and then he would think over what he had said to the Sister that he should not have said. After that, perhaps, he would go back and ask her pardon properly. Although why, indeed, should he degrade by apology the affection that had been the splendid experience of his life?

The old man stopped because he had run almost headlong into King. He did not know that the doctor had been watching him from the time he left the sun porch.

"You're out on a bad day, Mr. Wilkins."

"God never makes a bad day, Doctor. He knows we can attend to that ourselves."

"It's coffee time in the kitchen. I'm on my way down. Come along and have a cup."

Mr. Wilkins needed no persuasion. He was a little surprised that the doctor, usually brusque, should seek his company.

It was, as King had said, coffee time in the kitchen. Quite a group had assembled. Mr. Wilkins knew every one of them by sight. He answered the chorus of greetings with a bow and smile, which always sufficed when he could not remember names. How pretty the women were in their white uniforms, so clean, the cook in her blue. . . . Contrast. . . . The strange, teasing uneasiness that had been with him under the stars was back again, only now it rushed over him like a dry river of dust, choking out all sight and sound and even the pleasant aroma of the coffee. He swayed and would have fallen, except for King's hand instantly under his elbow.

"Here, sir, sit down! Get him some coffee, Blanche."

They were agog around him, putting him into Philippa's rocker, pushing Chad and his fire trucks aside to make room, exclaiming in sympathy like a bunch of high school kids instead of people who were trained to be unemotional about illness. Mr. Wilkins was disconcerted by all the attention. It had one good feature, however. The young woman would never guess that his sudden realization of her identity was what had set him reeling. He would not look at her now. And he would decide, in a minute, what to do.

"Put some sugar in—did you put some sugar in, Blanche?" the doctor was asking. "Never mind whether he likes it, it's going to give him quick energy."

Mr. Wilkins raised his head with a faint smile. "I'm only a little tired, really. I'm not ill. The excitement of yesterday, perhaps, and then the long walk. . . ." And he realized vaguely that the "young woman" herself seemed to be watching him with great concern.

"We have to begin taking things easy, at our age, sir," said Johnny, who should have been at school.

"Now drink this," King said, putting the cup into Mr. Wilkins' hand.

The old man drank it without complaint, although he never took sugar in his coffee. It really was a poor brew, too bitter under the sweetness. But it made him feel stronger at once.

"There's nothing like coffee for a harmless stimulant," the doctor said. "Don't let anyone ever talk you into giving it up, Mr. Wilkins."

They had stopped fluttering around him. Several of them left. Little Job's daughter was one. Mr. Wilkins was still shaken, but he knew now what he would do. He would get back down to the chapel as quickly as the snow would let him, and he would take one more look at the picture, just to make certain. Then he would call the sheriff.

When Mr. Wilkins started down the road, the gravel was greased with snow. He had to walk slowly, digging his heels in. He saw a stout branch hanging from an aspen, pulled it loose, stripped it of twigs and went on down the hill using it as a staff. The staff was a great aid. The falling snow was dizzying, and coupled with the slippery descent it gave him an unbalanced sensation. As if he would tumble into sleep right there in the snow.

The going was easier once he reached the gulch. He paused and, taking off his hat, raised his face to the sky. The snowflakes were tiny cool pats on his eyelids, fairy puppy dogs licking his cheeks. A fanciful thought for an old man. Leaning heavily on his stick, he opened his eyes. The snow fell from slate gray, coating everything but Little Balsam Creek, which still ran dead black through the white. Contrast. He had no excuse for not having remembered earlier that red hair photographs dark. He should have known the young woman immediately. But many people during the summers asked him about the Gulch and the mines, and she had seemed no different from any other, coming along on that lazy Sunday afternoon. She had known about Cardinelle, he recollected now. He might have told her the old story of the fake raid and the yellow taffeta curtain stained brown. It was almost a legend, he would have attached no importance to the telling. He drooped over the stick while the little fairy pats of snow went down his neck and turned soggy inside his collar. There was no reason to hurry. If he had collected his wits two days ago, Jock would still be alive—a week ago, and Cassidy would not have had to die.

His shoulders became so blanketed that when Mr. Wilkins finally moved, a soft crust slid away as it did from the branches of the ponderosas. Midway between his house and the chapel, he stopped. The sign, Charity Chapel, was almost obliterated by the wet casing of snow. Even the ruins did not appear ruinous.

"A beautiful world," he sighed. "I have loved, O Lord, the beauty of Thine house, and the place where Thy glory dwelleth." He liked remembering that. Gopher Gulch had always been the place where the glory dwelt.

Mr. Wilkins could fight off sleep no longer. He dragged himself to the chapel, leaving a small trough behind each foot in the snow. Juicy Parker's white dog bounded up to him, barking a greeting. He was too sleepy to speak. As soon as he had looked at the picture, he would go straight to his house and to bed. He pushed open the door. The organ was still there. They would take it away tomorrow. The stick fell from his hand. The little room was cold.

13

"I ain't telling," Blanche insisted doggedly. It was evening, and she was humped on a high stool beside Marmion in the laboratory where she had been for the past half hour, ever since Sister Judy left for her rest period before going on night call. "I ain't telling nobody where I found that paper, whatever it was. I told you I didn't say nothing to the sheriff. I'm not—"

"I know, not getting yourself into trouble," Marmion said with an exasperated sigh. "Look, Blanche, I only asked you once and you said you wouldn't tell me, so I believe you. Now will you please be quiet so I can get this job of matching done? I don't want to be here all night!"

"Blood is blood, ain't it?"

"Huh!" said Marmion.

The telephone rang. She went to answer it.

"Hi!" Sam greeted her, and her heart turned a flip-flop. "How's stuff?"

"Not bad. Congratulations on your story, Sam."

"Thanks. It kept me away from the hospital today. I dassen't set foot in the sheriff's beat. I wanted to, though."

"You did, Sam?" Marmion glowed.

"Sure did. I wanted to ask you what you meant by Cassidy choking to death. Why wasn't it more like smothering? Why would he gag? That's worried me."

"What a pity!" she snapped. So Sam couldn't come to the hospital because he was afraid of the sheriff! And if he had braved the perils, it would have been merely to get another story. "I'm afraid

423

you'll have to get your information from someone else," she added coldly. "Good-by, Sam!"

"Oh, now, listen, I didn't mean—"

She broke the connection with her finger, leaving the receiver against her ear. After a few seconds she listened again. Sam was protesting in very satisfactory anguish. And then, in a tiny pause, she heard the unmistakable sound of a receiver going down. Not Sam's. He was still talking. Someone was listening on another extension in the hospital.

"Gee, you're mean to him," Blanche remarked.

Softly Marmion dropped the receiver onto the hook. Why should she feel a blast of raw cold in the overheated little room? The dark gray window was tight shut, two stories above ground, safe from prying fingers.

"Come on and get this stuff done, if you're not going to talk to him," Blanche urged. "I want to get upstairs."

"Why don't you go ahead?"

"I'm scared. Look, you got two Johnsons here. Is that poor guy ever going to have a bill!"

"It isn't the same family. I wish you'd go, Blanche, honestly!"

But Blanche remained. She was not, she insisted, getting herself into trouble. Marmion, concerned with her own frightened thoughts, worked quickly. She had said nothing to Sam that could be of any consequence. How could it matter, then, that someone had overheard the pointless conversation?

Even in the security of the crow's-nest, Marmion could not relax. Eloise had not come up, although it was nearly eight. Throwing herself on the bed, she tried to face her apprehensions and reason them away. The sheriff had been here today. He had listened to her story, seen the ransacked room, talked with Eloise as he had with everyone else, and apparently seen nothing alarming in the similarity of names. So why be concerned? Think about Sam, instead, perfidious Sam. A little determination had scared him away on that first day when she had pretended she thought him to be a blood donor—blood? Marmion closed her eyes tight. She had just set out a bottle before coming upstairs, Rh negative for Lynn's Jimmie. But was it negative she had left ready for Lynn, or, in the confusion of listening to Blanche's chatter, had she inadvertently taken Rh positive? For a minute she lay there, thinking. Only one way to be sure. Go down to the lab and look.

Wearily Marmion sat up, swinging her feet around to find her shoes. Lynn might notice the mistake, if there had been one, but she might not. It wasn't good to take a chance. And the trip to the lab would be very quick.

She was not even afraid when she started past the rooms. Ellie was up here, she could hear her talking to Philippa. Silly to feel relieved. The laboratory was opposite the stairs to the crow's-nest. Marmion switched on the lights in the small passage, hurried through it with only a glance at the dark X-ray lab. Her own workroom looked cozy tonight, the white walls gleaming, Sister Judy's little footstools neatly shoved out of the way. She glanced at the bottle, saw she actually had made a mistake. In a minute she would find the right one. She sat down at the desk and laid her hand on the telephone. Really, it would be only decent to call Sam, let him know she wasn't always a witch with a temper. On the other hand, a short period of squirming never did a young man any harm. Tomorrow she would telephone him. That would be time enough.

Marmion didn't realize she had sat thinking of Sam for ten minutes. She was faintly smiling when she arose, went to the refrigerator, found a bottle with the correct type for Jimmie, and took it out for labeling. And then, backing against the door to close it, she caught a glimpse of the passage. It was dark! She had left the light on when she came in! Had Sister Polycarp flicked off the switch? But Sister would have seen the bright lab, then, and come to investigate. . . .

The red flagon was cold in her hand, but Marmion was aware of no sensation but terror. She was not alone! No one was in the room, to be sure, but out in the black little passage there was the gentle unrest of breathing. Sister Polycarp would not stand out there, just beyond the barrier of the wall. Panic beat in Marmion's throat. She would scream—someone would hear her!

But before she could make a sound, the lights went out in the laboratory. Not even a hand had been visible because the switch was on the wall in the passage, convenient for a person entering

at night and lighting the way before him. But not convenient for
the one who stood half fainting against the cool door of the refrigerator, remembering how like the lung that smooth enamel felt
and clutching an ice cold bottle in chilled palms. She could hear
someone moving now, around the wall, slowly, breathing softly. The
window was gradually becoming a gray rectangle, masked by snow.
And against the grayness, something moved.

Marmion screamed. But even in her own ears, the scream
amounted to nothing. Miss Bacon, at the chart desk down the hall,
did not hear her. The blot grew, padding out all but tiny slivers of
the window. Then even the slivers were gone, and Marmion felt the
warmth of a human body and heard a long intake of breath, as if the
intruder gathered strength for a blow.

"No, no!" the girl choked.

In panic, to get away from that warm, breathing thing, she
plunged aside. She tripped over one of Sister Judy's footstools. And
she fell and lay still.

The sheriff, heading into Gopher Gulch at a speed that would not
have been reckless on a dry road, held his car to the highway with
absent-minded skill. Where Pussyfoot's favorite bridge spanned the
black creek, he turned sharply up toward the ghost town clasped
between the hills. He was too preoccupied to see, as Mr. Wilkins
had, the clean beauty of wet snow on the false-fronted saloon, kind
beauty that made the saloon and the Gulch mysterious rather than
vacant. The car slewed on the turn, the rear swung across the road
like something dangling on a string and with a jarring thump came
to rest against a snowy hummock in the ditch.

"So I'm stuck," the sheriff muttered as he let the clutch out and
in, trying to rock a wheel hold. He gave it up after a minute and
climbed out. Not too bad a break that the hummock was there.
Without it, he'd have careened clear back to the highway. Flipping
up his collar, he started up the road. A few lighted windows glowed
orange, but not the right ones. He had expected darkness in Charity
Chapel, but Mr. Wilkins' house should be alight. The hour was early,
seven thirty or so. Yet if it had been midnight, the sheriff would

have come straight along and routed the old man out of bed. When you had been smitten by a burst of perception, when all you needed to tie up your case was identification of the suspect, then regardless of the hour you would seek out the one who could establish that identity. Murderers and their hunters don't wait for morning.

He tramped up to the small house and pommeled on the door. "It's the sheriff, sir! I'd like to see you for a minute."

There was no reply, no shuffling of an old man arising from bed. The gulch was so still that the large wet flakes could be heard landing. The officer knocked again, then tried the knob. The door swung open, and he turned his flash inside. Even before he saw that there was no one at home, he felt the chill, as if the fire had gone out long ago. Strange. The preacher was no great hand for being out in a snowfall. Why should he be away tonight, when of all times he must be tired to death?

A white dog barked and wagged out from between the houses as the sheriff stood undecided in the road again. No tracks led away. The small dents the dog made, the man's own large plowing were all that broke the snow. The chapel was dark. Where to turn next, that was the question. What would be the use of storming into St. Dennis and declaring his case to be solved when he still could not identify the evildoer? Through the afternoon, the feelers he had sent out for information had been paying off, one by one, building his case to a climax. And now it appeared that the climax had fizzled to a cold ash. All he had accomplished by driving so impetuously to Gopher Gulch was to get his car stuck in the snow and keep company with a roaming dog.

The dog had been leaping in circles around his new friend, throwing the snow high as he burrowed through it. His last circuit had taken him close to the chapel. Suddenly he stiffened his legs, sliding deep into a drift. The hair rose down his back, his neck stretched, and slowly, one stalking step after another, he crept to the chapel porch. His low growl was a warning and a summons. The door was open a crack. The dog did not like what was inside. The sheriff caught him in the beam of his flashlight, but the animal was not distracted. One paw raised, his nose only a foot away from the dark crack, he crouched there and growled deep in his throat.

The light fell from the man's loosened fingers, and the next thing he knew he was on his knees in the snow, hunting. He had to have the flash. No sense in shaking like this. The old preacher had simply come out of the chapel and neglected to close the door tightly, and the wind had blown it open. He got up, brushed some of the snow off his clothes, turned on the light, and strode to the porch.

"All right, Buster," he said, "one side with you!"

The dog backed a slow step. A wave of snow had curled in through the crack, a small dune out of which an aspen stick protruded. The dune did not reach Mr. Wilkins' feet. The old man sat in his chair with the dingy cushions. He must have sat down in daylight for he had not turned on the lamp beside him, and he had been looking at something, a picture lying under the hand in his lap. He was wearing his overcoat and overshoes, his head lay against the chair back and his eyes were closed. He was ready for a journey, but he had already gone.

The sheriff touched him only once. At the touch, fury skimmed away the dread that had come with him across the road. How dared she do this thing! His wrath was as cold as Mr. Wilkins' flesh. Harmless, mild old man—but not harmless to the one he could have identified as Cardinelle's daughter. And this last act would not protect her. Somewhere in the world there would have to exist someone else who could do what the preacher had been denied. And I'll find him, the sheriff promised solemnly, if I have to walk after him barefooted to the ends of the earth. I'll find him.

He turned the light away from Mr. Wilkins' peaceful face, and the beam fell upon the picture. Eagerly, he bent down to look. The picture was one of the type sometimes taken as a news shot for a feature story. It was a group of people around a gambling table, four men and one woman. The woman was nearest to the camera, and her charm had not faded with the dulling of the old print. She was beautiful, not young, not smiling, her eyes narrowed in supercilious amusement. Her red hair had photographed dark. The picture of the mother was more like the daughter than the two could be in real life.

The sheriff did not straighten for a long moment. Then he gently disengaged the picture. Mr. Wilkins had framed it. For some reason, he had prized it.

"You've done it, Mr. Wilkins. She didn't stop you. Bully for you."

A small doubt struck him. The old man's heart might have been unable to stand the strain of the walk through the snow, after the cumulative excitement of Cassidy's death. But when there had been two murders, and Mr. Wilkins had been about to point the finger at the one who was Cardinelle's daughter. . . .

He turned away quickly. The dog's eyes shone like iridescent grapes. The man kicked out the snow and closed the door. The dog trotted at his heels as he crossed the road to Mr. Wilkins' forsaken house.

Dr. Hamlin, riding up the Gulch on horseback, saw the car in the ditch where the sheriff had left it, but he did not stop. Guiding his horse as best he could, he held the blanket-wrapped child with arms that were numb. He would be in no shape to operate tonight. But King would do it, if necessary. And they might be safe in waiting until morning. A blood test would tell the tale. He urged his horse onto the long slope where the snow lay unbroken. The child stirred and whimpered.

"We're doing fine, Beth, we're almost there," the doctor said. "Sister Magdalene will put you in a soft bed and you can go right to sleep."

"It hurts, Doctor!"

"I know it does, honey. Hang on, now."

Beth had been a great little soldier. For nearly two hours he had ridden with her, down from a cabin that was inaccessible by car. Why these fellows with families wanted to live off in the wilds, he'd never know; but there were too many of them to wonder about any more. Even their wives, having babies in the dead of winter, would stay at home until the doctor was frantic about them. And when there was a case of appendicitis, like Beth's . . .

Johnny met him at the hospital door.

"All right, you take her," the doctor said, "I'm about whipped. Her father met me at the road with a horse, and when I came back out, the snow was so slippery I figured I'd make better time if I stayed on Dobbin. He's out there on the drive. You take care of him when you get a chance, eh, Johnny?"

"Sure thing, Doctor," said Johnny.

But there was a good deal to do, and Johnny forgot about the horse. So the tired beast, tied Western fashion with the reins hanging to the ground, stood on three legs while the snow melted over his wet sides, and the fourth foot, bent under to rest, was soon lost under a small, driven mound.

Marmion came back to consciousness in a dream. Her bed was floating away with her, the pillow moved under her head. And then she realized that someone was carrying her, that the pillow was a shoulder, and finally that the shoulder belonged to Dr. Kingston. But why was he carrying her downstairs instead of up to the crow's-nest? She was not alarmed until he reached the main floor and, instead of turning toward the patients' rooms where he would be taking her if she were hurt, he continued on down.

Fully awake, she began to struggle. But the powerful arms held her easily. Down here were the boiler room, the dark and vacant little room where Big Balsam Cassidy, at the end of his crusade, had lain awaiting Gus Omley, the undertaker; the deserted kitchen, the other closed door behind which Jock's packed suitcase still remained.

"Please! Let me go!" Marmion begged.

The doctor was at the bottom of the stairs, the black open door of the pharmacy immediately beside them.

"No!" she cried.

"Be quiet."

He carried her inside. Holding her with one arm, he threw shut the lower half of the door, found the hook and pushed it into the hasp, swung the top half tight shut and hooked it. Only then did he turn on the light and release the girl.

The change in him was shocking. Marmion had seen him contemptuous, defiant, sullen; but now it seemed that the darkness of this weird night had crept into his very soul. He looked at her, but she wondered if he saw her. She would know in a moment. Without taking her eyes off him, she backed a step to the door, let her fingers slip along to the lower hook. She could never open both halves. The lower would be enough. If she could open it quickly and duck out—

"Leave it alone."

Marmion snatched her hand away from the hook. And then, surprisingly, as though he trusted her to obey him, the doctor turned his back on her and sat down at the work counter under the window.

"Come here, Marmion."

She moved, felt her clothes sticky against her, and glanced down. The whole front of her uniform was bright red. "I'm hurt!"

"No. You had a bottle of blood in your hand when you fainted. It broke." King got up, opened a drawer, took out a clean gown, and tossed it to her. He perched on the stool again, his back to her. She slipped out of her uniform and into the long gown.

"Marmion," the doctor said slowly, "Marmion, do you know what prison is? Walls. Walls of stone. Walls of estrangement from the world. There are no gates in them."

Heavily he turned on the stool. She had rolled up the long sleeves, folded her arms over a voluminous pleat in the gown. The neck of it showed one thin young collarbone shadowed by soft hair. She didn't feel like a madonna. She looked at King with misery in her blue eyes, and fear, and bewilderment.

"Walls," he repeated. "You get to want them, you know, for their shelter. You're safe in them, until you're turned out." In the pause there was no sound whatever of life anywhere in the old walls. "If I had it to do now, I'd kill her."

Marmion stared at him. The stickiness was coming through from her other clothes into the clean gown. But that was a strange thing to be thinking while a man was speaking to her regretfully of a murder he had not committed.

"Her name was Angel. Angel! She had the blackest heart the devil ever contrived. Come to the beach with me, she said. On the white sand under the palm trees we'll forget that the blue ocean is the highway of war, forget that you are ashore without leave, our importance to each other far exceeds any surgeon's duty to his shipmates. The captain had a smaller idea of my importance. He sailed without me. You know what the navy calls that? Jumping ship. They don't like it." The doctor shook his head slowly. "She wasn't like you. You're sweet, you pity me right now, even though you're afraid of me."

"I'm not afr—"

"Angel lived up to her name for twenty-four hours. But then she had to leave me. I found out afterward that she had a date with someone else on the white sand under the palm trees. When I sobered up—they said it was a week later—she was gone, and I was in jail. If I'd killed her, I'd have saved a long parade of other poor devils the same misery. She didn't want us, or our money, nothing but our sanity. Lord, I should have destroyed her. She's malignant. . . ."

His lips finished the sentence noiselessly. He had been speaking almost as a bystander who had seen all this nightmare happen and not been touched by it himself; but he was as gray of face as Lazarus when the winding sheets fell away from him in the tomb.

"I didn't see her again until four years ago. She came here, pretending to be a patient. She had me in a good position for blackmail, but she didn't demand it. She didn't have to. By then she knew that Jock had a gold mine." King laughed without pleasure, shortly. "When she turned up a month ago, I should have killed her—"

The telephone rang sharply. He looked at it until it rang again with an insistence that warned of emergency. Muttering under his breath, the doctor went to answer. Marmion was benumbed by fear that suspended time. He might have stood a minute or an hour with his back to her, talking. His excitement told her that some new incident must have taken place. If she were to scream now the person at the other end of the wire would hear. He would come or send someone to her rescue. Her throat was constricted and dry, too parched for even a whisper . . . and then she heard it again, the soft hissing of the snake in the nightmare when she had stood half fainting in the room where Big Balsam Cassidy was choking to death. She was not dreaming now! She spun around in the direction of the sound, and at the same moment the radiator clanked. Of course, the steam was coming on! The man substituting for Pussyfoot in the boiler room was sending up heat to combat the early chill. So that was what she had heard in Cassidy's room, the memory that had tormented her for the past four days! Weak with relief, Marmion leaned against the workbench, watching the radiator as if she expected it to give some indication of agreement. The heat would feel good . . . but there had been no need for heat on the night Big

Balsam died. The day had been warm. It was not the radiator that had given off the hissing sound, the hissing she had not heard until after the door had opened and the unknown person had come into the room.

The doctor, she saw, had come back and was standing before her in silence. She didn't realize that it was the silence of shock. She clutched the bench behind her for support.

"What *was* it?" she whispered.

"The sheriff. The old preacher is dead. God in heaven, what can I do?"

Marmion shook her head dumbly. "The sound. The hissing. I heard it in the dark, that night." King was staring at her, and she stumbled on. "After the person came in. I'm sure I didn't hear it before. It started up, and I fainted. . . . Doctor, what could it have been!"

The doctor's eyes were upon hers, hypnotic as the snake's in the dream. For an eternal minute he held her that way, incapable of movement or thought. Then he gave a long sigh.

"So you did know!"

"But I didn't! I don't yet!"

"The oxygen tank," he said wearily. "It was turned off in order to make Cassidy's death certain when the lung quit. But it had to be on again, everything normal, before help came. . . ."

His voice fell to a hoarse whisper. Marmion watched him drop to the stool where he had sat before, flip a piece of paper into the typewriter he used for writing prescription labels, and then begin to peck at the keys with two fingers. He was not excited. He appeared, rather, to be on the edge of despair.

"Doctor. . . ."

King frowned. "I'm sure, now. I'll have to do this. It's the only way. Don't talk to me, Marmion."

The girl remained very still. She could see what he was writing, even read it. . . . *I confess that on the night of October twentieth I caused the death of Michael James Cassidy.* . . . The type blurred. There was more, but she need not read it. Jock's name would be on the page, later—and then her own? The doctor knew now what she had known from the beginning, and her testimony would be damning. She had never thought of King as the murderer. All her fears had been of Ellie, her best friend or of an unidentified Eleanor Ann. Never King. Barely breathing, she held herself tightly erect. She would have to try—at least try!—to get away. When the faint tapping came at the door, the man did not turn. Oh, don't hear it, King, don't, Marmion pleaded silently. Let me back away from you, step by step. Don't tap too loudly, whoever you are. Don't draw his attention! Stealthily, her eyes never leaving the hulking white figure, she crossed the room. Now she was in the shadow; she could open the lower door, if only the hook didn't stick. It scraped lightly, coming out of the hasp. The doctor did not hear.

He finished the page and ripped the paper out of the typewriter. "That's it. Now she can sign it Angel, or Eleanor, or . . ."

Abruptly he turned. He was alone in the pharmacy. The lower half of the door stood open.

"Oh, Ellie, I didn't know it was you!" Marmion whispered in the hall. "How did you know I was here? Where—"

"Marmie, there's no time! I saw King carry you down here, and he looked lethal! And then I saw her upstairs with a splash of blood on her uniform—" Eloise made herself pause for a steadying breath. Her red hair was dull in the shadowed passage, her profile cameo-white as she lifted her head, listening. There were footsteps, above. Swiftly, her strong fingers in a bruising hold, she pushed Marmion around the bend in the old corridor. The kitchen was black dark. She dragged Marmion in, shut the door behind them. It was like being in a vault that smelled of cooked onions and soup.

"Ellie, who—"

"Don't ask questions! You've got to get upstairs. There's a deputy in the front entrance. Marmie, you'll have to get out of here quick! The door is bolted, but you can open it. Then run around outside to the front!"

"But you, Ellie—"

"I'll stay here and distract her for a minute. I know she's following me—run! *It's your life!*"

Marmion was too panic-stricken to argue. With her hands out before her in the dark, she crossed the kitchen, found the door knob and the bolt, opened the door, and stumbled up the area steps. The snow was instantly cold on her feet, tiny chills of it dotting her face and arms. But she was out, she was free! And then, down in the darkness of the kitchen, she heard the footsteps, lacking caution, running, now out on the steps.

"Ellie?" she called.

Even as she spoke, she knew it was not Eloise. This was the one who had come into Cassidy's room, been able to work so quietly and efficiently in the dark because the apparatus was familiar . . . the one who had listened and waited for Marmion to recognize the remembered sound of the oxygen hissing out of the tank. Sam had blundered upon it: I thought he just didn't get enough oxygen, Sam had said. But still she had not redeemed the memory.

The instant of hesitation had been too long. The steps were muffled now in snow. Marmion caught a glimpse of a white figure. Then she ran on into the storm.

She couldn't see where she was going, sliding and slipping, by some miracle keeping her feet. Run around to the front door, Ellie had said—the sheriff's man is there. But how could she find direction in the blinding moving night? She veered to the left, felt the ground slanting and nearly fell. The pursuer was gaining on her. The flight was a nightmare in which Marmion ran in a treadmill, the same snow falling before her and the same wet, stony hillside under her feet. If only that silent one would cry out, scream, or gasp, or make any human sound! But all she heard was her own painful struggle for breath. The wall of the hospital was close beside her now—turn again to the left. She hesitated for a split second—and fingers curled into claws raked down her back!

Marmion gave a terrified scream and her feet skidded from under her. She fell, a wrist twisting painfully. Pain did not matter. In another moment those raking fingers would be at her throat. She screamed again. And miraculously, there was an answer, a man's shout from out on the drive. She did not recognize the voice. Help called to her somewhere within reach. Frantically she fought away from her attacker, a fight that was easier because a man had shouted. The white figure was up as soon as Marmion, but not running, simply standing there in indecision.

New voices were shouting now. Someone thundered around the building from the direction Marmion had come, and the indecisive figure whirled. That was the first time there was a sound. The girl did not recognize any voice she ever had heard, a hoarse, terrible gasping. The instant was very short. Running, desperately fast, the white wraith fled in the only direction unguarded, around to the front of the hospital.

Dr. Hamlin's horse, drooping away from the storm, gave a sudden startled snort. The sheriff was near enough to see something like an enormous white bat spring to the animal's back. Rearing and plunging, he tried to dislodge that clinging thing. When he could not, he started on a dead run in the only direction that did not blind him, heading away from the wind.

"Good Lord, the rimrock!" the sheriff shouted.

The doctor lumbered out from the protecting wall of the hospital, almost under the striking hoofs.

"Don't try to stop him!" the sheriff yelled. "He'll kill you!"

The horse pitched violently, narrowly missing the crouching man, and bolted into the curtain of snow.

They knew later that the beast, plunging pell-mell to the edge of the rimrock, set his legs stiffly, for there were long skid marks in the slush. They heard a scream, the terrified scream of a horse stampeding to its death. Then there was the awful, thudding fall down the broad face of the cliff. And nothing more. The flakes were already covering the skid marks when the men ran up. The white rider had gone over the cliff, still clinging to the horse's back.

Marmion sat in the snow, crying hysterically, palms flat over her ears. "I can't hear it, I can't, I can't," she kept sobbing long after there was only silence over by the rimrock. It had seemed to her that it was Eloise she had seen in that ghastly glimpse as she fell, Ellie whose hair would look dark, plastered wet to her head.

She didn't question his fortuitous arrival when Sam dropped down beside her, pulled off his coat, and wrapped her in it, then picked her up as easily as King when he found her on the lab floor.

"There, now, baby, you're all right. It's all over!"

"Oh, Sam!" Marmion groaned. "Who was it?"

"That doesn't matter, does it?" said Sam.

Over on the crown of the rimrock, the sheriff and the doctor stood looking down into moving white.

"We can't go this way," the sheriff said. "Doc, you'll have to come with me, around the long road. You'd better go in and get a coat."

They both knew there was no need to hurry. There was no sound from below. In King's pocket, the confession was a wadded paper. She had not signed it by any of the names she could have used: Angel or Eleanor Ann . . . or Lynn. She had not signed it at all.

14

The doctor, standing close to the wall of old St. Dennis, looked out into endless space. With dawn the snow had stopped, and the sun was reflected everywhere in white that appeared to throw off sparks. There was no mark on top of the rimrock where a horse had skidded to his death last night. If the doctor were to tramp through the snow to the rock and look down, he would see no mark either of the place where Angel had lain, a sleeping beauty, her lovely face unmarred. But he was not quite ready to walk out and away from the sheltering wall of the hospital. Angel was dead. It would take a little while for his resentment to die, like the sensation of the patient who had complained to him that she missed the weight of the tumor he had removed, or the old man who still felt the pain of an amputated leg. But the load of his hatred was gone. If ever he had loved Angel, it had been only for those few hours under the palm trees . . . not as Jock had loved her, protecting her, knowing she was following him to the mine but willing to trust her even then. Perhaps he had told her of Father Anthony's letter. And, afterward, he had been going to take himself away with his dangerous knowledge of what Lynn had done the night of the storm.

I wasn't quite such a fool, the doctor thought. I only let her make me into psychopath. Marmion had already begun his resurrection. Last night, when she screamed, he had run out into the storm as if it were the natural thing to do. That was the sweetness of Marmion. She was so real and timid and determined—but why think of her when he would so soon be leaving St. Dennis.

Quietly the door opened behind him and Sister Magdalene came out. She was in her white habit. The doctor had intended to avoid her this morning. She knew it.

"I'm out," he said gruffly.

"So I see."

"What I mean is not apparent to the naked eye. I'm out of prison, outside the walls because the jailer is dead . . . if you can understand that."

"Of course I do, King."

He glanced down at her with a shamed grin. "Sister, why am I always so damned hateful to you?"

"Because you want to get even with me."

The Sister chuckled. "You do, you know, King. You can't bear to have anyone think well of you. Because I see the good in you, as you reminded me the other day, you're bound to be bad."

He smiled unwillingly. "We won't discuss it. Whatever the reason, I've been enough to try the patience of a saint. Not that it matters too much now. I'm leaving." He paused, and because the Sister did not appear to be either surprised or impressed, he continued belligerently: "I apologize for what I said to you about Cassidy's money. I've never been as sure of heaven as I was of hell, but I do have the perception to see that there's a difference in the powers of money. Cassidy made it his god. You would make it serve your God." King paused again, ruffling the snow with his white shoe. "I wish, somehow, that you were taking it."

"I am, King."

After a long interval, during which both she and the doctor looked at the radiant snow without seeing it, she resumed.

"I couldn't turn down the money now, not when there has had to be so much clearing of the way to make it available to us—from Anthony's time down to last night. Only yesterday afternoon Mr. Wilkins spoke of it. He said he couldn't see what his role was to be in the general pattern that had involved himself and Mr. Cassidy and me. But now I know. He was the defining link between the old pattern and the new. There will be the new hospital, you see, built with Cassidy's fortune, and those of us who care will realize that the memorial is not to the great man of the Hellbent but rather to the lonely man Mr. Wilkins saw, the man who fought away from friendship because he did not know how to ask for it. No, the past is all ended, King, even for me." Sister Magdalene smiled. "May I shake hands with my new chief of staff?"

The doctor stared at the plump hand. Finally he took it.

"I'll repay you with all my working days!" he said hoarsely.

Melodramatic, the Sister thought as she opened the door to go back in to her work. But he would become a fixture in Gopher Gulch as Mr. Wilkins had been, as Sister Magdalene herself would still be; and he would be surly at times, brilliant, exacting, hard to work with, an outstanding doctor, and, in time, a more or less normal man. Climbing the stairs to the second floor, pulling herself up by the railing, she thought of Hal Wilkins: how many times his hand had slid over the smooth old wood, how faithfully he had helped to wear the hollows in the stair treads. . . . The sheriff had told her what he knew of Lynn's past, that she was Cardinelle's daughter and Jock's wife. Jock had made himself vulnerable by loving her. Cassidy had earned the wages of sin, but Hal—Hal had done nothing but remember too much. . . .

Marmion, in the laboratory, looked up to see Sister Magdalene standing in the doorway, and she slid hastily to her feet. Sister Judy, on her little footstool at the microscope, turned to nod. The floor was washed clean again, the sun slanted in through the snow-trimmed window. But the girl, turning around the desk chair for Sister Magdalene, reflected that no amount of cleaning and sunshine could span the unnatural gap of the past five days. Nothing would ever be quite the same again.

"Dixie is on the Anderson case now," the Superior said with what might have been irrelevance; but Marmion nodded. Jimmie would be cared for, efficiently and perhaps more sympathetically, by a pair of hands other than Lynn's; but in the room would be the pillows and tumblers and medicine bottles that she had touched. The patients still would look up and feel a small flare of disappointment when it was not Jock who entered. Mr. Wilkins was not yet missed, but even by noon he would be. Cassidy, the great, was the only one of the four who would leave no regret behind him. Still, Sister Judy bent over her microscope with the utmost concentration as if she found it difficult to keep her attention on the beautifully colored slides.

Marmion could find no reply other than an inane, "Yes, Sister." The needlessness of Mr. Wilkins' death, that was what made the Sister desolate, the girl thought. For the others there was a reason, however twisted, but not for him—padding up the stairs, sighing when he thought himself unobserved, shabby, wistfully anxious to share with his old friend the faith that had been his wealth.

Sister Magdalene picked up the glass paperweight on the desk, turned it upside down, and set it back to watch the snow fall around a tiny pair of children. "She was a strange girl, Lynn was. Like Big Balsam Cassidy. They both lived to exact satisfaction for a wrong done to themselves. His blame was never specifically against the parents who had left him nameless and homeless, it was always turned upon his immediate world, and he had to become greater and richer and more influential to prove that what other people had—a name—was of no consequence to him. He could rise and gain by his own powers. Lynn, of course, had a precise grievance against her mother's murderer, which she extended to many men. I've wondered . . ."

Suddenly, out in the hall, there was a swift patter of light feet, a child's high, delighted laughter, and Chad came running into the laboratory, his eyes wide with the excitement of the chase. For an instant he hesitated. Then, seeing Sister Magdalene, he shouted and ran to her, burying his face in her lap. His bib was smeared with breakfast cereal, one fat hand sticky with it. But the Sister smiled and cuddled his head between her hands.

"Now you're safe, Chaddie! She can't get you."

Blanche, thudding in from the passage, stopped short when she saw Sister Magdalene. "Oh, my gosh! Chad, you're a bad, bad boy! But it isn't Phil's fault, honest, Sister, she tries like mad to keep track of him, but just lately he's started running away to get us to chase him—" She finally paused for breath. "And the doctor and the sheriff's on their way up here. I passed 'em on the landing.

Sister Magdalene lifted Chad into her lap. "Get me a hand towel, will you, Marmion? And wet one corner of it, please. You can take him in a minute, Blanche."

Marmion, wetting the towel at the sink, wondered how much of Blanche's panting was a nervous twitter. They were in the passage now, the doctor and the sheriff. And suddenly Marmion shared Blanche's excitement. She had not seen King since last night, when she had been so desperately afraid of him down in the pharmacy. Would he be different this morning, with the chapter of Angel definitely closed? She gave him only a glance as he loomed in the door with the sheriff, but that was enough—his hair combed, his white linen fresh. The sheriff, unshaven, slouching with fatigue, was an unflattered contrast to King; but he had the composure of one who has triumphed and can go home to relax.

"The sheriff has news for you, Sister," King said. "I'm sorry it has to be—what it is."

Apprehension stilled every voice and motion—Sister Judy stepping off her footstool, Blanche with a hand pressed to her lips, Marmion near enough to Sister Magdalene to hear the soft sigh that was almost like life leaving a person.

The sheriff regarded the Superior with sympathetic understanding. "I wanted to tell you. About Mr. Wilkins. It didn't hurt him—I mean, he just dropped off to sleep, you'd know how it would be—"

Sister Magdalene went on wiping Chad's fingers. The officer glanced uneasily at King. When the doctor nodded, he cleared his throat and continued, groping for the right words. "It was an overdose of sleeping medicine. Barbiturate. The coroner found enough in his stomach . . ."

"She said it was saccharine!" Blanche whimpered in the tense silence. "I didn't know! The doctor said to put some more sugar in the coffee, and I started to, but Miss Baird whispered that too much sugar wouldn't be good for him and she took these little pills out of her pocket and crushed them up real quick and told me to stir—" Blanche's voice rose hysterically. "How would I know? I liked Miss Baird! I thought she was beautiful!"

"Honey, don't!" Eloise put her arm around the weeping girl.

The sheriff seemed relieved at the distraction. "I can't understand it, a good-looking, intelligent girl like that. Why, my wife says we heard her play in that dance orchestra she traveled with. Four years ago, when they were up at the Silver Flute. I didn't remember. But Lucy says they were great. That musta been when she got mixed up with Jock."

Sister Magdalene appeared not to have heard the sheriff. When Chad complained, "Hurt!" and pulled his hand away, settling back against her shoulder, she held him tight.

"I thought she was beautiful, too," Marmion said slowly. "So assured, and poised, and glamorous. But still, she nearly killed me. When Ellie went down to Mr. Cassidy's room that night to get— what I'd forgotten, and she thought it was me—"

"That was Pussyfoot in the room, not Baird," said the sheriff. "He's come clean. Says he wanted to see the respirator, the thing that had finished off the man he despised."

"But in the chapel," Marmion insisted, "she would have killed me, then, Sheriff. I told you but you wouldn't believe me."

"Oh, I believed you, all right. But I thought then, and I do now, that she was only trying to scare you away. She couldn't have you here, with what you knew about the oxygen tank being turned off. She was about the only one that could have done that, you see. You could practically have identified her any time you recollected that noise. So when you wouldn't scare, she had to try to shut you up, permanent."

"I did remember, last night, when the radiator began to hiss—" Marmion hesitated. The doctor was answering the telephone, telling the sheriff there was no urgency about the call to Charity Chapel because it was already too late. Lynn, entangled finally by her own desperation, had performed her last unnecessary misdeed. "I'm sorry!" Marmion said.

To her surprise, Sister Magdalene stirred and looked up at her with a faint smile. "We're all sorry, dear. But I've brought to mind one of Mr. Wilkins' quotations: 'Look not mournfully into the past, it comes not back again; wisely improve the present, it is thine.' And our present is composed of people who need our attention." She gave the baby a gentle slap on his fat leg. "Hop down, Chaddie, Sister has to get back to work."

They all moved then, speaking, even smiling, buoyantly thankful for this common-sense return to normal. Marmion found herself beside King. He was observing her uncritically for the first time. Attracted to her, the sheriff had declared. To keep herself from blushing, she thought quickly of something else—Angel. Judging from the discussions this morning, King had not disclosed the episode of Angel. Why should he? It would serve no useful purpose. Angel was a separate identity. In the course of the sheriff's investigation, the doctor had learned of Lynn's second role, as Jock's wife. Of the third, that of Cardinelle's daughter, he would have had no knowledge unless she had told him. And it was hardly a subject to be discussed under the palm trees. Jock was the only one who had possessed the dangerous knowledge of Lynn's parentage. Today they were clearing away the snow and digging a grave for him not far from Cassidy's on the far side of the gulch.

Marmion absently rolled a pipette between her fingers. "She might have confessed, King . . . or would she?"

"I was going to try to make her sign the confession I'd written. Whether she'd have done it—" The doctor shrugged. "You said you were sorry about the old preacher. So am I. But not about Angel. Even I am not vindictive enough to wish that she had been tried and sentenced to die. And she lived as she was meant to live. Who can do more?"

"We can accept God's guidance," Sister Judy said unexpectedly. "And we are capable of acting with the right intention. The choice of intention is an almost terrible responsibility. An embryo lives as it must, under the divine law governing its kind. A man—or a woman—doesn't live blindly. Therefore we must not interpret their actions blindly. It seems to us that they built, Mr. Cassidy and Lynn, without the Lord because we judge by what we see of the building. But what they intended, what they hoped to come by . . . how can we know?"

The little question fell into a silence broken only by the sound of Chad sucking his finger.

"Yeah," said the sheriff finally. "Yeah. Well, I'm going along home and get some sleep."

"Come on, Chad," Blanche urged. "Listen now, no monkey business. Mommy wants us!"

The little boy went with surprising docility. In a few moments only Sister Judy and Marmion were left in the laboratory. And then only the small Sister remained because Marmion followed the others to the hallway. But she did not go further with them. Leaning against the door, she watched King and Sister Magdalene walking away from her, the light from open rooms falling upon them. They were not talking, their silence was more companionable than any amount of speech.

Marmion smiled. She was not afraid . . . not afraid of a dark passage or of the future or of anything in the world.

SISTER SIMON'S
MURDER CASE

To the man in my life who, though he seldom has time to read my books, is nevertheless my most devoted fan and press agent, my ever loving husband, Joe.

1

The slim little woman sat on the green bench in front of the curio shop, her eyes shifting with the crowd that passed inches beyond her knees. Too bad she could not enjoy herself in this vacation mecca. But she tried at least to relax, every time she thought of it. At these times she would straighten her small shoulders, remember how her hair always straggled in the heat—for the August mugginess still hung over into the evening—and feel for wisps to tuck under. Then her hand would go a little higher to touch the three pink roses on the hat. The roses looked nice. She had snipped new edges on them and pressed the veil over wax paper. The cotton dress was too wide in the neck, but fastened up with the brooch, it was all right. Appearance was unimportant anyway. She had come here with a purpose. In a minute or two she would get up from the bench, go down the long cement stairs that led from Main Street to the little park on the water front. . . .

She couldn't help it, her chin trembled. Fingering her chin, she felt the tiny white whisker that persisted in growing in the mole. She should have thought to pull it out. But it was no wonder, really, that small things slipped her mind.

The Indian on the other end of the short bench began to scratch, thoroughly. Under the bench his dog cuffed an ear, tapping the little lady's ankle. She moved her foot, then raised her small suitcase from the pavement and stood it between herself and the Indian. He went on scratching.

The little woman drew a long breath and set her gaze deliberately upon the crowd. All were vacationers, all in pursuit of amusement.

That was why she felt so apart from them. But she liked the general bedlam—snatches of conversation, jukeboxes blasting from open shops, the solid zoom of traffic uphill from the river and the hooting of downbound cars for the right of way on the narrow turn to the bridge, the whistles of boats seemingly distant but actually right down behind the buildings, the roar of skates from the roller rink. And the evening had a frivolous smell of popcorn and arid summer and engine exhaust that called up pictures of travel and fun. A bus prowled past, nosing between automobiles. Its breath was different, heavy with burned kerosene. At every stop this afternoon the little woman had caught that oily stench and it had made her sick. The same nausea rolled over her now. Only, to be fair, she couldn't put all the blame on the bus. She always felt sick to her stomach when she was worried. And tonight she was not only worried, she was in actual physical dread.

Her hand flew again to her hat, a reflex so abrupt that her elbow knocked the suitcase against the Indian. He turned, mildly curious.

"Excuse me—so careless of me!" she murmured.

Jumping up, snatching the suitcase, she dived into the crowd. No more dallying. Get it over. Using the suitcase as a rudder, she pushed between a teen-age couple who were strolling arm in arm, shoved aside a middle-aged man who bristled, "Well, pardon me for living!" and ran hard into a small boy. The boy squealed in the manner of children who are much too tired and use any excuse to raise a commotion. His mother, a fat, moist woman, jerked him out of the way. With all this justification he opened his mouth and bawled.

"Oh, I'm really sorry!" the little woman apologized. What was the matter with her, barging into people, endangering children? She never acted that way!

"I'm so sorry," she said again. "Could I buy him an ice-cream cone?"

"He's fulla ice cream, that's whatsa matter with him," the mother replied. "Anyway, I got popcorn. Dannie, cut it out!"

The little woman started at the name, then covered the movement with a gesture toward her hat. But the mother hadn't noticed.

"We're gonna take the boat ride. I wanta see them educational sights. I put in all year chasin' kids, now I'm gonna enjoy myself if it kills me. Dannie!"

Yanking her screaming son after her, she charged off into the crowd. Her bag of popcorn broke open, dropping a trail of white kernels as if she were a fairy-tale character bound to mark her way back.

The small woman stepped to the curb where she could stand for a minute to catch her breath. She had felt so anonymous, coming here on this secret little mission—so secret she hadn't even made up her mind yet whether to see Diane this time—and it had been shocking, in a way, to hear her own name blurted out of the crowd. Not that the name had been addressed to her. But now she had a sense of urgency she hadn't had before. If someone were to come along who really knew her, there would be at best a delay while she smiled and explained how she had just happened to drop into town. And if the person also knew Diane—one of the student nurses from St. Matthew's, for instance—that would be even worse. How could she say, don't mention this meeting to my niece because if my suspicion is right then I wouldn't dare go near her. . . .

The suitcase skidded down rattling against the lamppost. Dannie opened the old black purse, took out a clean handkerchief and pushed up her hat. The hat left her forehead with a sticky little break. It would be pressing a red rim below her hairline. Carefully she wiped her brow. A few people were doing that, mostly men. They would think she was hot, if they thought at all. The cold clamminess of fear was as foreign here as the winter snows.

She put away the handkerchief. She was in front of the great building owned by the boat company, a cavernous affair architecturally somewhere between a mausoleum and a railroad station. If people were not hurrying in they were hurrying out. Between this edifice and the roller rink there was a gap of a quarter of a block where the sidewalk became a gallery topping the retaining wall. A crowd hung on the railing, looking down on another throng in the miniature park below. There would be an excursion boat loading at the dock for the moonlight trip up the river. With the departure of the boat most of the crowd would straggle away. Quickly, Dannie picked up the suitcase.

At the very corner of the boat company's building the long stairs began, plodding in low, wide steps down into the paper-strewn, smudgy park. Halfway down Dannie stopped. The statues were still there, close in by the wall, mummies of mud and shadow; but she couldn't take time to look at them now. Over on the riverbank, under the glare of the raw electric bulbs stringing together the docks and the ticket booth, there were clots of people. The big white excursion boat was in a frenzy of light and fluttering banners. The whole place was bright, almost fearfully so because the brilliance washing over all the faces touched her own.

Dannie leaned hard against the railing, her neck stretched tense as if every inch nearer might help, and her eyes cut into the crowd, slipping over the women, not even seeing the children, clinging for a second or two to every man. It was difficult to follow them, shifting as they did—almost like viewing the designs in a kaleidoscope and thinking surely you had seen that bit before. Down the ticket line face by face, across the scattered groups and the moving couples her gaze paced along, discarding everyone. She couldn't be quite positive about the people on the boat. With the distance, even though the deck was wide open to the sky, it was hard to tell exactly. But as the last few straggled past the ticket taker her confidence flared into open bloom. He was not here! She had been mistaken in believing she had seen him before. If she hadn't gone scuttling off like a scared rabbit, she would have sorted away those imagined similarities, known that this was the last place in the world he would ever be. And she would have saved herself three weeks of utter misery.

Almost weak with relief, Dannie turned slowly away from the bright lights. No reason now why she should not get a better look at the mud figures. They had intrigued her on that previous visit, but the first throbs of apprehension were driving through her then and she had thought of little else. Deliberately she crossed to the small, roped-off area and set down the suitcase. How nice that no one had destroyed the statues, for they were oddly beautiful even though they were only made of mud. Not perfect, any of them, but all so right, exactly what you might expect to find by a river. There was a drowned woman still clutching her baby, and a bearded riverman who had thrown himself down to sleep—you could actually see the difference between the sleeping and the dead—and a camp cook squatted beside his fire. A dog lay curled around her two small puppies. There had been more than the two in the beginning. That was why the mother was so protective toward these. The sculptor, whoever he was, possessed real talent to be able to express such delicate shadings through the ugly medium of mud. And he had revealed something of himself in his work. Tenderness, for instance, in the guarding pose of the dog's head, in the curve of the woman's arm about her child. But there was impatience, too. A face, nicely started, was caved in by a big footprint. Several mounds showed the first forming of hands or heads. Why had he not broken down these attempts and used them over instead of digging up new earth? The digging must be laborious. He had few tools, merely a spade, a bucket of water, several small instruments that looked like nut picks.

Dannie's little imaginings stumbled and fell apart. As one knows instinctively at times, she knew that someone was watching her. Nothing to be alarmed about, of course. She did have a few acquaintances in the Narrows. Casually she turned to the stairs, glancing over the crowd. Her glance did not go far. Like her thoughts a moment ago, it stumbled and stood still.

It was not he, she told herself numbly, it couldn't be. This was a stranger. The face was different. But not the eyes. Only one pair of eyes in the world could induce the beat of fear that leaped thumping against her ribs. They had not always looked at her that way. She had seen them laughing, impudent, pleading once in a while; but now they nailed her to the ground, cold and bleak, daring her to remember. I don't remember, she wanted to cry out, I don't know you, all I want is to get away and forget I ever saw you . . . let me go. . . .

She managed, somehow, to bend and pick up the suitcase. Yet how could she run? A woman chasing up the stairs, banging people with her suitcase, would stick out like a sore thumb in this leisurely crowd. Remember how conspicuous she had made herself up on Main Street! But she could leave, quietly, taking her time, and even if he should follow her—the thumping nearly overcame her—if he should follow her, what, after all, could he do? Nothing, if she remained with people. And she could sit on the green bench for the entire night if necessary.

With all the bravery she could muster, Dannie raised her head. And then she knew that fear was not only a lonely emptiness in the middle of the night. In that moment it became for her a cold gray thing against the heat and color of the carnival—a pair of eyes forbidding her to move or think or even breathe. And they blocked her only escape, the long stairs up to Main Street.

Down on the dock where the big white *Triton* was taking on her eight o'clock load of passengers a girl leaned back against the railing, one red sandal hooked into the bars behind her, her dark eyes eagerly upon the crowd. She never grew tired of watching people. In one way, vacationers were like the patients in the hospital, a tribe in themselves, cut off from the groove in which they spent their daily lives, and it was interesting to try to discern the marks of the groove. She was always doing that at St. Matt's, picking out the lawyers and shoe clerks and teachers, and then during the chitchat of nursing care she could find out if she was right. There was no way of finding out, here. Not that it mattered. She could always move on to a new face. That woman, for instance.

The woman had come into view at the top of the long stairs, a tiny person, not very well dressed, eye-catching because she carried a suitcase which in spite of its small size appeared to be quite a burden for her. Why hadn't she checked it at her hotel? the girl wondered idly. It would just be in her way on the boat ride. But perhaps she was not planning on taking the excursion for she came slowly, finally stopping to study the crowd. Even at that distance something about her was familiar. The girl unhooked her sandal from the rail and spoke to the blue-uniformed young man who was taking tickets at the gangplank.

"I'm going over there a minute, Ted."

"We're ready to pull out. Don't go far, Liz."

"I'll be right back."

The little woman had come on down the stairs to stand looking at the mud figures, so intent that she was entirely unaware of being an object of interest herself. Lizette approached the bed of drooping cannas. From here she could see the woman's face plainly. Somewhere they had met, herself and this little stranger, possibly at the hospital. Her cotton dress fitted her badly, and all you could say about her hat was that she had done the best she could with it. Her stockings were cheap but gartered up nice and tight so they only wrinkled slightly around the ankles. There was no permanent in her limp, soft hair, and she was alarmingly pale.

But she was beautiful. The goodness in her face shone forth like another light, surrounding her with the spiritual cleanness of a saint. There was fragility about her, too, a delicateness that called out for protection in this every-man-for-himself sort of world. You wanted to take her hand and pat her on the shoulder and assure her that things were going to be all right, if they weren't already. And things were not all right. The woman was worried, and worry had taken away her appetite, and lack of food had made her pale. Tiny lines of distress showed around her eyes and her lips had a tired sag. Lizette's mother feelings boiled up. Ted was always laughing at her for feeding stray cats and giving dimes to bums. But this woman was worthy of at least a kind word. Something about the mud figures, that would be a good opener, and then haven't-we-met-before. Somewhere, Lizette knew, she had seen that high-crowned hat with the three pink roses. There couldn't be another like it.

Lizette had stepped forward and was about to speak when a sudden, startling change came over the small stranger. She had been standing with the quietness of keen attention as she studied the statues; but now, as if she had received a physical blow, she stiffened. Her face became a death mask. For half of a frozen minute she did not move. Then, seemingly impelled by some force she could not resist, she turned toward the long stairs and again stood still.

In bewildered wonder Lizette scanned the crowd for some person or thing to account for this amazing change. But so far as she could see there was nothing fearful anywhere. Several people appeared to be watching the little woman, a natural consequence in view of her behavior; but none with lethal interest. Over on the stairs, a step or so up, was a garish figure in black Turkish trousers, white satin shirt, and orange turban—the mind reader who held forth in the purple tent up by the roller rink. Jinny was always going to him. A ludicrous creature, really. A little nearer, a paunchy tourist had planted himself, hat on the back of his head and jaw swinging around a half-eaten cigar. Very much diverted by the woman, Lizette thought fleetingly, but certainly not contemplating bodily harm. The neatness of his short beard was a contradiction to his general air of carelessness. The sculptor of the mud figures had appeared also, probably from a lair under the steps for he looked as if he had been heavily asleep a minute ago. He was a handsome animal of a man, tall and broadly built, his black shirt open far down over a powerful chest, graying hair tumbled back from a broad forehead, his whole bearing that of a vagrant. Lazily his gaze slid from the woman and came to rest on Lizette. In haste she looked away. Don't have anything to do with the carnival drifters, Ted was always telling her, keep clear of them. There was amusement in his smile, even derision, but nothing sinister. The only real animosity came from a frowsy, redheaded woman who glowered frankly and blocked the path to the stairs with the wide, solid stance of a man; but since she was glowering at everyone it was hard to tell how much of her ill will was directed at the little stranger. Which of these people, Lizette mused, which is the alarming one? Or was it someone she hadn't noticed. . . ?

Down at the dock the *Triton* gave a warning toot. If Lizette were to help the woman at all, it would have to be immediately. She stepped forward and laid her hand on the shoulder of the cotton dress.

"I'm sure we've met somewhere," she said. "At St. Matt's? I'm a student nurse."

The woman spun to face her. For a fraction of a second Lizette was certain she saw recognition in the really beautiful blue eyes. But a hand went to the trembling mouth, cutting off a very audible gasp; and then with the suitcase batting her knees at every step, the little woman darted around the glowering redhead and rushed up the stairs.

Lizette could only stare after her in complete astonishment. Surely she herself was not a frightening sight, yet the woman was scrambling up the stairs as if her life depended on it. Sidestepping away from the mind reader, she stumbled on to the top and disappeared in the crowd.

"Friend of yours?"

Lizette jumped. The artist had come closer and was regarding her with a very charming and very personal smile, most appreciative of her young slenderness and her summer tan and her dark hair blowing in the wind. She could feel the catalogue being made. Raising her chin high, she looked him up and down.

"I don't believe it's any concern of yours," she said. He cocked his head as if he might be a little hard of hearing; but she wouldn't repeat her statement, and then turning she walked slowly past the canna bed.

The *Triton's* whistle jerked an insistent summons, but Lizette would not hurry. That mud-pie character was not going to think she was running away from him. She arrived on the dock just as Ted began to lift the gangplank.

"Holy smoke, Liz, will you straggle aboard!" he urged. "You know how Jerry is! What kept you?"

"I'm sorry, Ted, honestly I am," she said. Jerry, the *Triton's* pilot, was old and a stickler for promptness because he wanted to get home to bed. The guides were not supposed to take their girlfriends free on the boat rides, but all of them did it. Jerry only put up with her presence, Lizette knew, because she never bothered him. "I won't be late again," she promised.

"Maybe there won't be any again. He's mad."

Meekly, Lizette slipped past to stand beside the rail. Ted slammed the gangplank into place and shouted to the pilot, and the boat eased away from the landing. She fully expected Ted to stride off forward, then, and take his place on the high stool where he perched for his discourse to the passengers. Instead he stopped beside her, looking straight ahead, his profile solidly masterful as Caesar on a Roman coin.

"What did he say to you?"

"Who?"

"Don't hedge. That whole carnival outfit is a bunch of tramps! Why did you go over there, anyway?"

"The woman. I thought I knew her."

"Was he asking you for a date?"

"Ted, really! You haven't any right to . . ."

"Haven't I? Whose frat pin are you wearing?"

Lizette slipped her hand under his elbow. There was no response.

"Jinny thinks he's wonderful," she said, putting a smile into her voice.

"Tell Jinny to keep away from him! He's no good!"

"All right, Jasper."

"What woman?"

"Just someone I noticed in the crowd."

"Why bother about her?"

"Because she interested me! Don't you ever wonder about people?"

"Sure. When I'm helping lay 'em out at Waddy's. You ought to see 'em sometime."

Lizette jerked her hand away.

"We gotta guide this trip or ain't we?" Jerry's voice came over the mike.

"Be seein' you," Ted muttered, and dived off into the twilight under the awning.

It wasn't what he had said about Waddy's, Lizette pondered furiously, it was the implication. He had become very insistent lately that she go with him to the mortuary. At a nice, quiet time, he said, when there was no one around. He hadn't exactly fancied his job as night man at first, either, he always explained; but it was good experience for a future doctor, and it fitted nicely into the night hours after he had finished on the boat. And a nurse who was expecting to be a doctor's wife would have to get over her aversion to seeing the dead because dying, he always ended up, was as natural as being born. A trip to Waddy's would be the first step in the getting-over process.

"Well, I'm not going," Lizette said aloud, and folded her arms firmly on the rail. "Ever," she added.

Wearing his fraternity pin didn't mean she had to knuckle under to Ted. She was going to keep the pin. And she wasn't going to Waddy's. And she was going to talk to whoever she pleased down on the water front, man or woman.

The lights of the town seemed to be receding while the boat stood still. Back there, somewhere, probably up on Main Street, the woman would be plodding along with her lonely little fears. Surely,

Lizette worried, there was something she could have done to help. Maybe tomorrow . . .

"Good evening, ladies and gentlemen," Ted began through the mike. "You are about to see the Narrows by moonlight, an unforgettable sight. We are now entering the Jaws of the Narrows. . . ."

The jaws of rock, standing out against the moonlight, looked savage. How long had they guarded the river? Against their age the span of a human life was a mere second—but still important to eternity. Tomorrow, Lizette promised herself, she would haunt the water front until she found the little woman again and she would make her understand her desire to help. And she wouldn't tease Ted any more. He was too wonderful a guy. But she wasn't going to Waddy's.

Dropping her cheek on her folded arms, she watched the path of moonlight spinning out behind the boat on the water. Life, she felt, was a very nice proposition.

2

Reaching the top of the stairs, Dannie struck off blindly into the crowd. It didn't matter where she went. There was an awful giddiness swirling up somewhere out of the middle of her into her head so she felt as if she were staggering heavily yet floating at the same time. Something tapped at her brain like fate knocking at the door—but that would be the three pink roses bouncing on the hat. She must sew them down tighter. Diane would have a needle . . .

She stopped dead still. She could not go to Diane. She could not go because the worst had happened. She had met him. Face to face. And she had known him. And he had known her.

And then she had been confronted by the girl. That incident was a tag end, really, when you considered the terrible significance of the first. Yet you never knew into what importance a small beginning might grow. Lizette hadn't remembered her, quite, but she would. And what would be more natural than to ask Diane, at breakfast perhaps, if she had had a nice visit with Aunt Dannie. And Diane would be puzzled and hurt, and Lizette would recall how Aunt Dannie had been scared to death and gone scuttling away into the night, and there would be questions—why had her aunt been so frightened, why hadn't she come to Diane, where was she now . . . ?

"Oh, dear!" Dannie whispered. Her hand went up to the hat and the old black purse whacked to the pavement. Retrieving it, she was bumped by a man who said, "Excuse me" and three teen-agers who did not. She couldn't stand here in the street. Gripping the suitcase, she hastened up the long hill.

Movement was good for it gave her the illusion that she was doing something. But she couldn't rush hither and yon all night. Her heart was pounding, her breath short, and worst of all she was leaving the crowd behind. She stopped, gazing up the hill. A block or so ahead, above the softly rounded trees, sharp old-fashioned turrets stuck up against the sky. They were familiar turrets, in a way. She passed that place on the bus every time she came to town . . . Henry Waddy's mortuary . . . Henry! Why hadn't she thought of him before? Henry was used to counseling people in trouble, he would be calm and fatherly. Whether he would realize the significance of her discovery, that was something else. She would deal with Henry's possible doubt when the time came.

Nearly running, Dannie started ahead. Her arm was sore from lugging the suitcase. If only she could check it somewhere! She paused, glancing back down the hill. She had just passed a laundromat. They would have shelf room, they were used to bundles. Edging to the door, she looked inside. A man sat on a high stool with a newspaper spread out on the counter before him. On benches at the back of the long narrow room a dozen or so women flipped through magazines while their laundry did itself in the white machines ranged around the walls.

Dannie opened the door. The man laid down the paper. He had very clean hands.

"Hi," he said. "You come at the right time. I got a couple machines empty."

"Oh, I don't want to wash anything!" She hoisted the suitcase to the counter and tapped its shabby paper side. "Could I leave this with you? For an hour or so?"

The man rubbed the back of his neck. He was almost bald but on top of his head was a tiny patch of hair which he had parted in the middle. It gave him a dapper air.

"Well, I guess I can oblige. If you're comin' right back, that is. We don't make a practice of checkin' parcels."

"Oh, I am! And I'll pay you for your trouble, of course."

"No trouble. But I close at eleven."

The clock on the wall showed only a little after nine.

"I'll be here long before eleven," Dannie promised.

He pushed forward a tag and a pencil. "Name, please, lady."

"I'll be here," she repeated, nodding brightly, and hurried out into the street.

She was a little surprised at herself. There was no reason why she should not have given her name. Perhaps caution was being born of fear. She even peered back over her shoulder as she started up the hill under the dark maples. Henry's place, luckily, was only a few minutes away.

Dannie always knew that Henry Waddy had done well for himself. Except for the sign, *Funeral Home*, his establishment might easily be mistaken for another of the old but comfortably spacious residences of the neighborhood. Venetian blinds slit the view of lighted rooms within. There were geraniums in the window boxes with vinca vines trailing their green and white leaves. Hydrangea and bridal wreath and honeysuckle bulked against the white walls. A green rubber runner led from the street up to Henry's door where a rubber mat said Welcome.

Standing on the mat, Dannie pressed the doorbell. Soft chimes sounded inside. Perhaps Henry himself would open the door. He might not know her just on the instant. But it would take him no time at all to remember.

The door opened. Dannie's flicker of expectation died; for it was not Henry who stood on the threshold. This man was younger, tall and thin and stoop-shouldered. Never had she seen so bald a head. Down around his collar where it did nothing for his appearance he had a fringe of hair, but over the skull there was none. The light above him skated across a dome as shiny as the doorknob. He inclined his head and the light slid back.

"Good evening, Madam."

"Good evening. Is—I'd like to see Mr. Waddy, please."

"Mr. Waddy is not in. Perhaps I could help you?"

Dannie's heart sank.

"I make arrangements in Mr. Waddy's absence," the man added. "Of course, later you may talk with him. He always sees personally to all of our services."

"Oh, I—I'm not a customer!" Dannie said quickly. "No, Mr. Waddy is a friend—a friend of the family. I'm sure he'd see me!"

"Indeed, yes." His manner became slightly less formal. "I didn't quite understand. But Mr. Waddy really is not in. He left only a few minutes ago on a call. He doesn't go out any more, as a rule, but these people asked specially for him, and in such a case he never refuses. Mr. Waddy is very considerate toward the bereaved."

"I'd expect so," Dannie said. Henry would be like that, considerate toward everyone. Toward her, too. "Could I come in and wait? I wouldn't care how long!"

The man had nice eyes and they lingered on her in sympathy. "I'm sorry, madam, but I'm afraid it wouldn't do a bit of good. The place is far out, an hour each way—they can't drive fast, you know. It will be close to midnight when they get back and I'm sure Mr. Waddy won't return here. He'll have the driver drop him off at home. By that time Ted—our night man—will be here to help with the unloading."

"I see."

Dannie turned back down to the green matting. She had never felt more desolate in all her life. Behind her there was the soft twang of a spring as if the man had opened the screen door wider, and his voice was quick with concern.

"Couldn't you stop by in the morning? Mr. Waddy is always here around nine."

Morning was a night away, and fear nipped at her heels like a hound out of the dark. She murmured yes, she'd stop by in the morning, but the man must not have heard.

"Mr. Waddy will be asking who called, Madam. What name shall I say?"

Dannie increased her pace, pretending not to hear his question. She reached the end of the green rubber and turned once again toward the distant bright lights of Main Street.

She walked very fast, going downhill. There was one other possible source of help: Vince. He would *have* to come to her rescue. Not that she doubted his willingness. Quite the contrary. The difficult part would be to keep him from flying into instant action, calling the police, chasing down to the water front, embroiling everyone in wild confusion. Well, what if she couldn't restrain him? What difference would it make? At least the awful weight would be off her shoulders.

The jukeboxes were still making a gay affair of the evening when Dannie came again into the midway but she scarcely heard them. Just beyond the laundromat she crossed through the traffic, hurried on until she came to the bank corner, paused briefly, then sped off into the dark. If she remembered the location of Vince's house correctly, she wouldn't have far to go. Half a block later she saw that she had not forgotten, except that she was on the opposite side of the avenue. There could be no mistaking the place, bare of trees on a tree-lined street, a tall unlovely hulk making no pretense of being a home. Vince Barron never had cared about comfort. You'd never guess, looking at the house, that he had made a million in the lumber business. He must still have his offices crammed on to the lower floor, for the windows were dark. Upstairs, where he had always lived, one broad uncurtained window was lighted.

Eagerly Dannie came out to the curb, ready to cross. But then she stopped. A man had appeared in the window, a tall rangy man with a handful of papers which he began to flip one by one onto some surface below the sill. Twice as she watched he made quick dips out of sight, most likely to snatch at a paper that had gone sailing. Impatient, stormy Vince. Was he the one to trust with a secret which required calm deliberation?

"I don't know!" she whispered. "I don't know!"

But of course she did know, and the knowledge kept her from crossing the avenue and climbing those dark steps. She couldn't send Vince rushing around with a hotheaded charge of murder, not unless she was very sure. And was she that sure?

Slowly Dannie turned once again toward Main Street. She was so tired now that she could scarcely drag one foot after the other. Better go to the hotel. But she had so little money. And if she were to remain in town—rather, since she must remain in town long enough to clear up this matter, then she dared not be extravagant. There was the practical certainty, too, that Lizette would mention something to Diane about having seen her aunt, and the only way to keep Diane from feeling hurt would be to go out to the hospital. It would conserve the small funds in the old black purse. And when you came right down to it, where was the danger—yet? She hadn't given herself away—at least, she hadn't spoken to him. He knew her, but how could he be sure that she knew him? And why exactly should he fear her? When she hadn't gone to the police twenty years ago, why should she go now?

A bus came just as she reached the bank corner and she sprinted to catch it. It had carried her on to the river bridge before she remembered the suitcase. She jumped up and staggered to the front of the bus. "I—I forgot something. How soon would I get a bus going back?" she asked the driver.

"That'll be me, lady." He looked at his watch. "Ten twenty-six now. It'd be about eleven. I go clear to the Heights before I turn around. Want me to stop?"

Dannie peered out into the black night. The laundromat would close at eleven. And besides, she shouldn't walk in on Diane any later than this.

"How's about it, lady?"

"No, I'll go on to St. Matthew's Hospital. Thank you."

Tomorrow morning, on her way to Henry's, she would stop and pick up the suitcase.

The corner where the bus stopped was well lighted. The hospital, too, was checked with lighted windows and there was a mellow flood around the entrance. But between, for half a block, lay nothing but darkness. Dannie would have to walk through it. Or run. For a panicky moment after she alighted she thought of shouting after the bus, making that friendly young man take her with him to the end of the line and back. But what good would that do? The hour would be later on the return. Go ahead, now! And walk, don't run. There was nothing to be afraid of. After all, the only difference between night and day was that you could see things in the daytime. At night you couldn't see . . .

But you could hear.

There were steps behind her. Long steps. Keeping the rhythm of her own. But catching up to her because of that long stride. Only a man would pace along like that.

Only a man. And the sheltering trees made a black tunnel ending a lifetime away at the hospital entrance.

3

Lizette, rocking the baby, hummed softly to him. In the shadowy room seven other babies slept in their cribs. This was her favorite time in the routine of pediatrics. The uproar caused by the departure of parents was long past and all but the most restless children were settled for the night. Life in general was a very satisfactory proposition. Ted had been nice to her on the boat ride after he had worked off his ire over the sculptor, and they had made a date to go up the river to their favorite picnic spot and cook breakfast. Morning dates were different. And practical. Ted was always being practical. That was why he couldn't understand her phobia about going to Waddy's.

The baby grunted, pushing the bottle away.

"Full up, Butch?" Lizette whispered. "O.K., we'll cuddle. But don't breathe a word of it to Sister Simon."

She laid the baby against her shoulder and patted him softly. A student nurse appeared in the doorway.

"Liz?"

"All right, Jinny, tell Simon I'll be there."

"She didn't send me. I had to tell you, I got my time off!"

"For the whole Festival?"

"Ya, the whole three days! Sister Pete didn't say a thing. I've got to make up the time, of course. That's what I'm doing now, I should of been off at eleven. But I don't care! I don't care about nothin' as long as I can be queen!"

"Hey, don't wake up the kids," Lizette cautioned, but she did it gently. In Jinny's drab life there had been one beautiful, cherished honor. Up in the woods last summer in her home town of Marshlands, population six hundred twenty-nine, she had been elected Blueberry Queen. Next week, courtesy of Sister Peter, she would return to Marshlands for a brief reign before passing her crown on to the new queen.

Jinny doubled down on a chair and hooked her elbow awkwardly over the back. It was easy to imagine Jinny at the age of eighty with the same tired droop and the same bowed shoulders, for the hard work she had been obliged to do throughout her childhood had made an old woman of her. And she was never really neat. Even in the immaculate pink uniform and white apron, with her long blond hair netted, she managed to have a tousled air. That she remained in nursing school at all was a tribute to the ability of her classmates to cover up her mistakes. Other classes knitted for the lepers or adopted babies in the Far East as their projects. This one looked out for Jinny.

"Liz, you don't think it's funny, do you?"

"What's funny?" Lizette asked, absently because she was running over the possible blunders Jinny might have made since coming on duty at seven. Probably none. Anybody could tuck the kids in for the night. "What do I think is funny, Jin?"

"Me being queen."

"Of course not!"

"The others do. They think I'm too dumb to catch on, and mostly I am, so how can I help being calm as a cucumber? But I dunno. . . ." Jinny twisted around into another awkward attitude and a forlorn note crept into her voice. "It makes me feel like the fun I had being queen, it wasn't really fun at all and

maybe people were laughing at me. But you never laugh, Liz. You're just wonderful to me."

"I'm always wonderful to my roommates," Lizette said. Jinny's outbursts of devotion were sometimes burdensome. "Listen, go rinse this bottle if you want something to do."

"Is that Randy?"

"Mm-hm."

"I don't see why you fed him when I just got through."

"You just—oh, Jin, you didn't!"

"Isn't he a ten o'clock feeder?"

Count ten, Lizette told herself, take it easy. Evidently Jinny had not looked at the feeding board; and having fed the baby, she hadn't charted it. Two large blunders right there.

"Liz, if Simon finds out she'll have me campused! I won't get to the Blueberry Festival! I'll even get kicked clear out of school!"

"If you're kicked out you'll have plenty of time to be queen!" Lizette snapped. "And you might give a thought to Randy. After all, he's in here for regulation of his formula!"

Jinny by now was crying into her apron, muttering her contrition. The baby seemed happy. Could it be possible Jinny's mistake had uncovered the answer to his finicky appetite, feed him in two courses instead of one?

"Are you going to tell Sister Simon?"

"Why shouldn't I?" Lizette retorted, but at Jinny's wail she added quickly, "All right, I won't. I'll chart it all as one feeding. But for Pete's sake pay attention to what you're doing! And stop bawling! If Simon sees you like that she'll want answers you'll never think up!"

"Do the charting quick, Liz!"

'Well—I'll see."

Lizette, hurrying down the hall to the nurses' station, reflected that someone, sometime, should permit retribution to catch up with Jinny. Why not now? Of late she had been more careless than ever. It might do her good to be given a thorough scare on the eve of her great day, since no amount of lecturing seemed to impress her. And the baby, too, might benefit if it were known how he had enjoyed his supper.

But when Lizette saw Sister Simon bent wearily over the desk, her pretty, young face drawn with fatigue, the determination left her. The Sister was peckishly strict, often a peevish disciplinarian because she was very little older than the students herself. Yet she would give in to the parents when she should have been firm. Overworked, of course, but that seemed to be the normal state for the nuns in the hospital. She shouldn't even be here, close to midnight. The end of a sixteen-hour day, Lizette decided, was no time to present anyone with an incident which called for extreme forbearance. She reached for Randy's chart. Just this once—but never any more—she would cover up for Jinny.

The telephone rang. Still writing, the nun lifted the receiver, said "No!" with severity, and hung up. Lizette turned the pages of the chart slowly. Why should she think the call had been for her? Ted would know better than to ring the floor. And her family was three hundred miles away. In case of emergency Sister Simon would let her take a call. It couldn't have been anything of importance, most likely not even for her. Yet the stiffness of the nun's back gave her the uneasy impression of resistance. The little office was so quiet that the electric clock, shifting its minute hand, made quite a small disturbance.

Sister Simon frowned hard at the work schedule before her. She was not going to pass the message on to Lizette. She was too busy. People should not call at this hour. She moved her head from side to side, trying to relax. Since she had become a supervisor she was always tired. If only she could have a short vacation! But in the convent there were few vacations. If you had your shoes on you carried your full load.

And the load, today, had been heavy. Johnny Phelps's mother, for one thing, demanding a certain crib for her son. And getting it. Sister Paul would never have yielded. But Sister Paul was older, she knew how to handle people. Upsets were always happening on pedes. No use pretending she didn't feel the burden of her youth and inexperience; but it was Mother's wish that Sisters be supervisors wherever possible, and since there were not enough nuns ever to go around and Sister Simon had passed her registry with a nearly perfect mark and she loved children, it was inevitable that she be made supervisor of pediatrics.

The neat writing began to swim. She lifted her face to the open window. Lizette had finished her charting and gone. The warm summer night sent in its sounds—the disharmony of the midway across the river, faint and toylike; the whistles of the boats, an automobile humming by; and under it all the vast quiet that was the night itself. Life was like that, a medley of annoyances but with certainty underneath. Never in the least confused as to her religious vocation, she had allowed the human irritations of supervising to beat her down. To keep peace she had given in to Mrs. Phelps. When an aide had telephoned, late, that she would be absent from duty there was no reprimand although these absences always coincided with some escapade of her worthless husband. One thing after another kept cropping up to break down discipline. Like Evvie's call a few minutes ago. Evvie knew the rules perfectly well. They were posted right above the switchboard.

Thrusting her pen into the red ink, Sister Simon reached for a slip of paper and with a force that spread the pen point she printed in large letters, "ATTENTION." The telephone rang. She took it up, listened, and a flush of annoyance warmed her cheeks.

"Why do I have to tell you this again, Everine? Visiting hours are over at nine. And you know perfectly well that the students do not receive visitors on duty."

I shouldn't be explaining, Sister Simon thought. She cut into Evvie's apologetic pleading.

"Certainly you can tell the woman that! Why not?"

She dropped the receiver into place. Evvie would not have given Sister Paul any argument. With herself, from now on, it would be the same. A rule was a rule and every single one would be kept. She took up the pen again, carefully recrossing the t's. A dear little person, Evvie had said, and something about Diane being out on a date and so the woman was asking for Lizette.

"Ambulance just pulled in," Mrs. Popnesky announced, trudging into the chart room. "Wanta bet we get it?"

"I'd probably lose."

"That kind of a night, huh?"

Sister Simon nodded and crumpled up the paper, for she had absently drawn a villainous face in the letter O. The wad hadn't hit the wastebasket before the phone rang again. Poppy reached for it.

"We better turn down the bed in 32," she said before she answered. "I'm gonna win the bet."

Sister Simon felt herself smiling. Poppy had that effect on people. Her hair was usually stringing out and her cap had been seen to wear a dash of chocolate for a week, her slip hung down and her uniform hiked up in the back; but for dependability and cheer she had no equal.

"I toldya," she said. "Kid hit by a car. I better get movin'."

Sister Simon dropped the red pen. It would be a good deal later that she would remember her irritation at Evvie's infringement of the rules—remember and wonder whether she herself had actually measured out for someone the difference between life and death.

Everine leaned out of her cubicle as far as the harness on her head would permit. She dared not leave the switchboard because the ambulance was screaming up the alley, but she did look anxiously after the little woman. There was something so very pathetic in the way she had asked so diffidently for Diane, then for Lizette, accepting the discouragement as if she really deserved nothing less.

"It's right there," Evvie urged. The woman glanced back. Her cotton dress was crumpled, but the three roses stood up stoutly against the crown of the hat. Evvie's finger poked the air. "There! To your right. The light switch is right inside the door."

"I'll find it. Thank you, dear."

She did go into the waiting room, but no light came on. The room would not be completely dark, of course, for the archway was wide open. Sit down and wait, Evvie had said, Lizette will be down in a little while. A white lie, but what could you do? What a time for Simon to stiffen her backbone! Which was more important, anyway, the darn rules or this little scared woman?

The switchboard buzzed and Evvie sat down to answer. Emergency wanted things. It was several minutes before she could peek around her corner again. Still there was no light in the waiting room. Honestly!—the poor soul didn't have to sit in the dark! Troubles looked bad enough with a lamp on. Evvie lifted the headset carefully off the curls she had made blond for the summer. She could scoot to the waiting room, turn on a light, give the little woman a reassuring word which she probably wouldn't believe, in view of everything, and be back inside a minute.

But with the headset in her hand, she paused. Up and over the archway which separated the hall from the lobby a Christmas ivy grew. Even in summer when the front door opened there was enough draft between the door and the freight elevator shaft to swing the delicate tendrils. They were swinging now. Evvie ran her hand around inside her belt to tuck in her blouse, lifted her bosom, and pulled in her stomach. She was "Information" at night and she had picked up some nice acquaintances here, particularly young men with mothers in the hospital.

A minute went by. No one appeared. Well, then the little woman must have gone out when the ivy swayed. There was another doorway, unseen from here, from the waiting room into the lobby. O.K., so she was gone. But the ivy began to swing again, gently. Now somebody would have to appear. Two people couldn't go out one after the other when there was only one to go in the first place.

Yet the hall remained empty. The switchboard buzzed. Mechanically Evvie capped the headset in place. Another buzzer joined the first.

"Oh, murder!" Evvie muttered, and flung herself into her chair. First chance she had, she was going to walk down the hall and look in the waiting room. If the woman was gone, fine, she'd forget about her.

But there was a flurry of calls and Evvie hadn't a minute to herself. When she heard footsteps beating hurriedly through the hall, she leaned out of her corner.

"Jinny? Hey, you're on pedes, aren't you?"

Jinny, almost by, kept stepping away backward.

"Yes. It's a little girl. I'm going to the blood bank."

"Listen, tell Liz to give me a ring right away, will you?"

"Maybe she won't even live."

"Jin, will you tell Liz? It's real important!"

"Tell her what?"

But already Jinny was running away.

Honestly! Evvie told herself bitterly, you'd think the fates were dead against the little woman. It would never do to ring pedes again and ask for Liz. She would have to count on waylaying Jinny on her return.

Jinny, however, must have taken the elevator over by emergency because the only human being to appear within the next ten minutes was a timid man who asked if it wasn't much too late for him to go up to see his wife.

Lizette glanced at her watch as she ran down the stairs. Nearly half past twelve. Call Evvie about something, Jinny had said, it's real important. Sister Simon was still on the floor so she didn't want to use the station telephone. The simplest thing was to run down to the switchboard.

"What does he want in the dead of night?" Lizette demanded almost before she was around the comer.

Evvie looked up from the confession magazine rolled open on her lap. "What he?"

"Ted. Didn't you tell Jinny . . ."

"Oh, not him. This woman. But she's gone now. I guess she didn't think it was any use her waiting."

"What woman, Evvie?"

"I dunno. She didn't seem to know you very well, just your first name."

"But if she asked for me . . ." Not the little woman from the park! With an odd sensation that reminded her of dread, Lizette pictured the small figure hurrying up the stairs to Main Street. "Didn't she tell you what she wanted, Ev?"

"No. She was scared about something, though. I sure wish Diane had hit on some other night to take a one o'clock pass."

"Diane? Was it her aunt?"

"I guess so. Know her?"

"So that's who she was!"

"Come again?"

"Remember that tea the student nurses gave for their parents about three weeks ago? Diane brought her Aunt Dannie. She was better dressed that time, but she had the same hat. I knew I'd seen it before! Why didn't I think of it!"

"Did she go upstairs, after I went and told her. . . ."

"No, no, I saw her this afternoon. Tell me what she said to you, Ev."

"Not much. When I said Diane was out on a date, she asked for you. She sure needed somebody, I could see that. So how could I say Simon wouldn't co-operate, for gosh sake! Honest, that nun thinks being a supervisor is saying no all the time."

"What did she do then?"

"Slammed up the receiver."

"No—the woman!"

"Oh. Well, I said sit in the waiting room a while and Liz will be down. I was going to get you, too, if it was the last thing I ever did under this holy roof. And I bet it woulda been. I guess maybe she went in there for a minute, but then she left."

"Did you go look?"

"I didn't hafta. The ivy started swinging, you know how it does when the door opens."

Lizette started down the hall toward the waiting room.

"She's gone, Liz," Evvie said.

But the girl hurried on. The waiting room was empty. She turned into the lobby which was illuminated only by the patch of light striking in from the hall. The outer door was closed. Opening it wide she stepped on the doorstop, pushed open the screen, and was outside.

The old lamp above the door was bleary, its globe dark with the moths that had fluttered themselves to death inside. The moonlight was almost brighter than the lamp. Leaning on the balustrade, Lizette looked down past the stone steps to the street. The little woman would have had to plunge into the darkness under the oaks, fly along with their leafy prattle surrounding her like enemy whispers. Evvie should have told her about the short cut through the basement, for the nurses' home was almost certain to be her destination.

Lizette ran down the stairs to the pavement to look in either direction. Silly, of course. Aunt Dannie would never dally here. By now she would be safe in Diane's room, probably sound asleep.

Lizette took a long breath of the sweet air. The nicotiana Sister Joe had planted in close to the building was perfuming the whole night. Against the dark wall the pale flowers were plainly visible. A few sprigs in a glass of water would do a lot for the nurses' station. The girl started up the rather steep terrace. And stopped.

Something had been tossed into the shadow of the wall. Something black. She had stopped because the thing was against her foot. She pushed it with her toe. It was light, moving easily. Slowly she bent to touch it—a black straw hat.

After a moment she straightened with the hat in her hand. It was an old-fashioned hat, high in the crown. Across the front were three roses. In the moonlight the roses were gray.

4

Lightly, Lizette touched the roses. The little woman must have lost her hat when she ran down the stairs. That was the logical explanation. But suddenly the girl wanted no more of the darkness. Clutching the hat she whirled, even took a long stride back down the terrace.

And that was when her gaze fell full upon the plum tree.

It was a peculiar tree, less than waist high even in maturity, the branches spread like an umbrella and bowed to the ground with green fruit. Small boys of the neighborhood, playing cowboy and Indian, often used it as a wigwam. Its shelter now was no part of a game. From under the wide fan of a limb a small foot protruded, a foot that she could see even in the poor light had on a worn black shoe. The stocking above the shoe would be wrinkled around the ankle.

Lizette stared at the foot. It was almost as if she expected to see it there and so she had no reaction at all. After a minute she moved slowly across the grass, bent, and touched the ankle. There was a spot right in front of the bone where you could feel for a pulse. If there was one. Her fingers explored. Then, still with that sensation of numbness she rose, walked to the steps and up, through the door, and into the lobby.

She knew exactly what to do in caring for the dead. Call the intern, get the clothing list, put the belongings together with the body on the stretcher, and cover it with a sheet—only you did all that when the body lay decently in bed, not sprawled with a twisted foot under a plum tree. . . .

Someone was holding her by the shoulders, pressing her so hard against the archway that the ivy cracked behind her spine.

"Liz, what in the dickens hit you?"

Her vision cleared. It was Merle, the curly-headed night orderly, who was doing his best to ruin the ivy.

"You look like you've seen a ghost, kid. What's up?"

The numbness broke and she sagged weakly down on the edge of the jardiniere. Merle looked from her to the hat, then caught it up on one finger and twirled it.

"Hey, quite a chapeau."

"Stop that!" Lizette clapped her hand over her mouth to keep back the scream. Merle, with the hat at a tipsy angle, stretched his neck in surprise. He looked very funny, like a cartoon she had seen of a rooster swallowing a string.

"Listen, Merle," she said quietly, "there's a woman out on the lawn. Dead. You'd better go quick before—before somebody . . ."

Before somebody what? Nothing could hurt the little woman any more.

Evvie was there by now, backed against the wall, trembling, her eyes wide as if the stiff lashes propped them open.

"Liz, our little lady? She isn't really—*dead?*"

"Yes." Lizette stood up, not even swaying. "Death is a natural thing, perfectly natural. Go on, Evvie, call the intern. And Father Paul."

The words didn't come out very well. But Merle went. Evvie, too, for in a moment the speaker high on the wall gave the small scratch of the switch being turned on and Evvie's voice came softly but urgently, "Dr. Barney. Father Paul." Now all would be done that could be done for the little woman.

Carefully Lizette walked to the freight elevator, opened the grating, pushed it shut behind her, and pressed her thumb on the third-floor button. She felt competent, no faintness, no confusion. The second floor slid down from above and slipped away below. She stopped at exactly the right instant and pulled open the grating.

And then, unaccountably, panic seized her. There was no reason for it by that time. The floor kitchen was black dark but quite familiar, the wide door to pediatrics a dimly lighted oblong. Lizette ran toward it, heard the buzzer in the elevator snappishly remind her that she had not closed the door, and stumbled as she turned back. The slam she gave the door was enough to shake the whole shaft. She didn't care. She couldn't hold back the storm inside her any longer.

By the time she reached the station she was crying in long sobs that sickened her and made a great deal of noise. Poppy, sitting pigeon-toed on a high stool, nearly fell headlong getting off. Sister Simon, at the desk, looked up. The pen fell from her grasp and made a big red blot on the white paper.

"It's your fault, Sister! All your fault!" Lizette sobbed, and she would have gone on except that her face was being pressed against Poppy's shoulder and Poppy's arms were very tight around her.

"Let's not wake every kid in the county," Poppy soothed, but there was alarm in her voice. "What you been up to, anyhow?"

"Ask Sister! She knows!"

Lizette heard the scrape of the Sister's chair being pushed back, then the rush of water at the sink. Shoving Poppy away, she confronted the nun.

"You couldn't let me go, could you, Sister, not even speak to her on the phone, and I was sitting there, *right there,* when Evvie called! You wouldn't even tell me she was here!"

The water overflowed the glass, running down into the Sister's sleeve. She shut off the faucet and held out the glass to Lizette. The girl dumped it and slammed it upside down on the drain-board.

"Your rules are so important, aren't they? No visitors during duty, no leaving the floor except on necessary errands! Oh, we have the most law-abiding floor in the whole. . . ."

"Lizette!"

Lizette whirled to Poppy. "Since when is a rule more important than a woman's life?"

"What woman?"

"Aunt Dannie." She turned to the nun. "How are you going to tell Diane?"

"Tell her—what?" That was the first thing the Sister had said.

"That Aunt Dannie is dead. Somebody killed her."

"Somebody killed her? How?" Poppy gasped.

Lizette's tumbling thoughts stopped short. Why had she said Aunt Dannie was killed?

"I don't know. But you don't toss away your hat—your hat that you've fixed all up the best you can—and then crawl off under the plum tree and die! Not if you're scared to death of the dark in the first place!"

"Is that what . . . what she . . ."

"Yes, and if Sister had let me go, she might be alive right now!"

"All right, ducky," Poppy said in the tone she used for the children. "Let's not split our seams."

"You'd better get some seconal for her," Lizette heard the nun say, and her voice was strangled as if the coif had suddenly become too tight.

"Maybe she hasn't reported it, Sister. When you find a body you're supposed to—"

"I did, I told Evvie," Lizette managed to choke out, "but not Diane. She's out on a date!"

"Oh, lordy!" Poppy breathed. "Sister, we can't put this kid to sleep. The police will want to ask questions."

"They can question her tomorrow, nothing will be changed by morning."

You're so right, Lizette wanted to say, but what was the use? She had said a lot of things to the nun. Too many. But Sisters were human. If they made human mistakes, why shouldn't they bear the consequences?

Obediently the girl swallowed the capsule Poppy offered her. It was disgraceful, really, to go to pieces like this. How dependable would she be as a nurse if she became hysterical every time a patient died? But this was not just a patient, it was a poor creature she might have helped except for Sister Simon's stubborn regard for rules.

"Come on now, dearie," Poppy said. "Off to bed with you."

"You'll be alone on the floor, Poppy."

"In a manner of speaking, yes. But Jinny is here, remember."

Lizette knew Sister Simon watched them leave, and it seemed to her that she was still watching as they proceeded down in the elevator, through the basement, across the alley, and into the nurses' home. By that time the seconal was beginning to take effect. She was not going to dream of Sister Simon. Nor of Aunt Dannie, either. Dying was as natural as being born—Ted said so—only there was nothing natural about the foot sticking out from under the plum tree. . . .

The last thing she felt was her head falling against the pillow and someone lifting her feet up onto the bed.

Poppy remained with Lizette until she was certain the girl was asleep. The kid had had a terrific shock and somehow she had tied it all up with Sister Simon. A pretty unstable reaction, but then it wasn't every day you'd run into murder. . . .

"Murder?" Poppy quavered aloud.

Why had she put it that way when she'd have to scoot back across the dark alley alone! She peered out of the window. The moon had set. The hospital grounds were as black as the inside of Jonah's whale. She would run, fast, and nobody would have a chance to grab her. Lizette was breathing deeply, sound asleep. Go on now, before she lost her nerve.

Poppy slipped through the hall and in fear and trembling let herself out into the alley. She looked up and down. Once your eyes were used to the darkness it wasn't so bad. She could see the ladders stacked where the window washers had left them, the garbage cans over by the basement door. The whole bulk of the hospital stood between her and the front lawn. From the third-floor windows, of course, she could see perfectly well but it wouldn't be the intimate view she would have from the ground. Go around the building and there she'd be, screened by the lilacs, in a dandy position to see for herself what was going on around the plum tree.

It was even better than Poppy had expected. She could look out unseen right onto the terrace. There were men, half a dozen of them, and they were flashing lights all over. A photographer's bulb whitened the little tree for a split second, enough for Poppy to determine that no one now lay on the grass. They must have carried the woman into the hospital morgue. They kept their voices disgustingly low. All she could make out with any degree of certainty was that they were searching for a weapon and not finding one.

Quietly Poppy backed out of the lilacs and groped again toward the alley. If they were hunting a weapon then Liz was right, the woman had been killed. Murdered. And she was Diane's aunt. Poppy dredged up all the memories she had of the student nurses' relatives. They were sparse, mere greetings at Christmas parties. She should circulate more, then when something interesting like this came up she'd know. . . .

A loud, resounding clang echoed through the alley. Poppy shrank against the old bricks. She thought she screamed. In a single wild second she saw herself flat on the pavement in a pool of blood with a monster leering over her.

And then a cat yowled. The garbage cans, of course. She had surprised the scavenger at its nightly prowling. But she sprang for the door, yanked it open, and shot inside. That was the worst of murder, it wasn't inflicted upon the victim alone but upon every mortal and thing around it. Every small sound became the possible warning of danger. The cops hadn't found the weapon. Maybe the guy was stalking around in the dark, making ready to use it again. . . .

"Lordy, lordy, don't let him be in the elevator!" Poppy prayed frantically.

He was not. The grating stood open upon a lighted cage.

But next to the elevator was a small door, lower than most, with a pane of glass so thickly frosted that even when the room was lighted no one would see in. Behind the window was a glow of light. Only members of the staff were permitted in the morgue. But anyone else could go in if they felt like it, simply by opening the door.

Tiptoeing, Poppy approached the door. She touched the knob. In the same instant a man's shadow fell, black and giant, against the frosted glass. Poppy had not been awed by the morgue since her student days when she had stepped into the disinfected little place with such misgivings that she usually forgot to duck her head, and whacked it against the low lintel. The sight of the man's shadow hit her with the old impact of the lintel. She turned and ran.

Slamming the elevator door, Poppy flattened her thumb on the button. Everywhere, in the dark rooms and corners and especially down below in the shaft where the dark mounted into a skyscraper as the elevator rose, there the murderer lingered. And every small creak of the cables was the same bugaboo that had cried with the cat.

"Lord, just let me make the third floor," Poppy prayed, "and I'll camp there the rest of my life!"

She put her hand to her tousled hair. Somewhere down in the dark she had lost her cap. The lilac branches had streaked the whole side of her uniform. She would indeed be a lovely sight for Sister Simon, the immaculate. But she had one point decidedly in her favor. She was alive.

5

Ted paused on the ramp that took the place of steps leading from the hall door down to the floor. He had been here several times but the room still intrigued him. Aside from the entrance and the extreme bareness, you wouldn't remark anything unusual about it. Knowing it was a morgue was what made the difference. A long table cluttered with beakers, not very clean, ended in a sink. In one corner of the room was a large partitioning which could have been a closet. Mr. Waddy, jogging down the ramp, nodded toward it.

"She'll be in the cooler, of course. Well. Close the door, Ted. Tightly."

The young man tried the already closed door. His shadow fell like a black giant on the frosted glass. Then, carefully, he let his stretcher roll before him down to the floor. Care was the watchword when the old gentleman was present. Mr. Waddy had just returned from a lengthy jaunt into the country when the call from the hospital came in. Ted had been surprised when Mr. Waddy, listening in at home, said he would accompany him. The mechanic who slept at the mortuary would have done as well. But the news of murder had apparently banished any fatigue Mr. Waddy might have felt at the end of his eighteen-hour day. Briskly he nodded to Ted and trotted over to the bulletin board.

"Always take a look here first, son. Sometimes they post a note for you. Although the body, of course, will be tagged."

"Yes, sir," said Ted. He knew these things. But it was Mr. Waddy's way to educate a new man.

Amused, Ted watched the old gentleman push his good gray hat to the rim of his gray curls, tip back his head, and bring the bulletin board into range of his bifocals. Even in high curiosity, he would never cut corners. He had found a note and was perusing it thoroughly. A stranger guessing his business would never have taken him for a funeral director. He was, rather, a child's dream of a grandfather, lively of eye and limb, short enough for his ear to be on easy level for whispered secrets, plump enough to have a cuddly lap when he sat in a rocking chair. His favorite Sunday pastime, so the boys said, was to take his wife and the grandchildren on long walks to gather wild flowers in the country. In his young days he had preached in small country churches where they could not afford a minister. A popular toastmaster for local banquets, he had served also as chairman of the school board and had passed out high school diplomas on every graduation night for twenty years. It was all extremely good for business. People, bereaved, naturally thought of Mr. Waddy. And he was never a disappointment.

Ted, lounging on the ramp, began to whistle absently. Mr. Waddy turned in reproach.

"My boy, we are in the presence of the dead."

"Oh. Sorry."

"If I teach you nothing more, do remember in your future practice of medicine that a dead body is not a thing, it is still the God-made image of Himself and during its years of life it housed a soul. Therefore it commands reverence. Right? Well."

Ted had been advised ahead of time about these little lectures and he had expected to find them very funny. They were not. He was even embarrassed enough to try to bring up some sort of apology. But the old gentleman would never permit any molehill of thoughtlessness to be made into a mountain. A correction, once over, was a closed incident.

He stepped across to the cooler.

"Allow me, sir."

Ted strode across the room, threw the heavy handle and swung back the door. The temperature, somewhere around forty degrees, felt like Antarctica after the heat. He took hold of the cart to shunt it out.

"Read the tag, son, read the tag," Mr. Waddy advised.

"O.K., sir. But there's only the one." Ted squinted briefly at the cramped writing. "Diana something. If you'll step back, sir, I'll get her out where there's more light."

It took him a minute to push out the cart and secure the door. When he turned Mr. Waddy, with the tag in his hand, had folded the sheet down as far as the little woman's shoulders and he was staring at her with a most amazed expression. The apples had faded entirely from his cheeks. The room was so quiet that a car, swooping through the alley with its horn blasting, sounded like a devil abroad from the underworld.

"Sir, do you—you don't know her?" Ted asked. "I mean, people that are murdered, you don't usually know them."

The white bosom of Mr. Waddy's shirt lifted and he laid a gentle hand on the sheet.

"Yes, I know—knew her. Dannie Grear."

For the first time Ted really looked at the woman. Where her dress showed above the sheet there was a drying dark red stain. Mr. Waddy examined it briefly.

"Stabbed. The hand that struck her down was a violent one. But she died without violence inside her. It's how I'd expect her to go."

He gave the arm another light pat, a gesture of comfort to himself, perhaps, since the little woman could not feel it. "But she shouldn't have had to go like this," he added. Then he laid the sheet back in place.

He was too old, Mr. Waddy often said, for the heavy lifting a mortician must do; yet now, although Ted was at his elbow, he wrapped the sheet tightly about the body and lifted it without aid to his own cart. Then he turned the cart so it would ascend headfirst. There was never any willy-nilly either-end-first with Mr. Waddy.

"We're ready, Ted. If you'll get the door . . ."

With one hand on the door, the other holding the head of the cart, the young man hesitated. "I'm sorry, sir. I mean, seeing her like this, if she was a friend, it's quite a blow."

Mr. Waddy nodded. "Quite a blow. Yes. Now let's be on our way, son."

They had good footing on the rubber matting which, Mr. Waddy said, had been his suggestion years ago, and the cart moved readily. Ted reached behind him to open the door. Swinging out, the door bumped someone who had been standing very close to it in the hall.

Sister Simon left the floor as soon as Poppy returned. Not that she felt like going to rest; but Poppy, with her usual tactlessness, would begin asking questions and the Sister had no answers. She stood a minute before she entered the freight elevator, hesitated again before she pushed the down button. She knew she was acting with unusual deliberation; but if she were to proceed with the haste that had become habit, then she might catch up with some of the things that were waiting for her to think about. Two floors slid up past the elevator. She hadn't intended, exactly, to go to the basement; yet, reaching it, she pushed back the grating and stepped out.

The place smelled of soap and food from laundry and kitchen, leftover workaday smells that made the total quiet more noticeable. Slowly the nun ascended the short stairs to the alley door and looked out. A few paces away across the pavement was the entrance to the nurses' home. Half a minute and she could be with Lizette. But what could she say? That nothing is more important than a rule?

"Her duty was on the floor, to me and to the patients!" the Sister whispered vehemently, and her fist struck the door. "I was doing my duty when I refused to let anything interfere! The woman had no business being where she was at such an hour with such a request. I couldn't foresee what would happen! I have to keep order."

Something moved out in the alley. A cat. She turned quickly away. Next to the elevator was the small door to the morgue. Light showed behind the frosted glass. They wouldn't be doing the autopsy on the woman yet, for the pathologist lived miles away. But someone was there. She could go in and look at the body herself. Then she might know whether a few seconds snatched in spite of a rule might have meant the difference between life and death. It would all depend on how the woman had died.

She laid her hand on the knob. From inside someone turned the knob and the door bumped her as it swung open. She was looking right into the face of a strange young man.

He was as startled as she. At the far end of the stretcher stood Mr. Waddy. In spite of her preoccupation the thought struck her forcibly that Mr. Waddy was getting on in years. Never had she seen him appear so tired. His face was almost as gray as the hat he held nipped against the stretcher.

He nodded politely. "Good evening, Sister Simon," he said, and gave her a kind little smile.

She forgot that the little smile was probably as professional a piece of garb as the striped trousers he wore at funerals. His kindness touched off a terrific urge to cry. Like the time she had cut her finger as a youngster and borne up bravely until her mother said, "Oh, you poor darling!" and the flood had come. To dam it back now, she said very stiffly,

"Good evening, Mr. Waddy."

He waited a moment, then said apologetically, "If we might proceed into the hall, Sister—the cart is a bit difficult to hold on the slant."

"Of course," the nun murmured and moved quickly out of the way. The young man was very competent. In a minute the cart was in the hall, the light off in the morgue and the door closed. Now they would be leaving, up the steep stone flight to the alley, and her only opportunity would be gone.

"Mr. Waddy?"

"A moment, Ted. Yes, Sister?"

"Mr. Waddy, was she—you don't know what happened to her, how she died?"

He shook his head gently. Then he took off his glasses and rubbed hard at the marks on his nose. Putting the glasses on again, he inspected the front of the Sister's apron.

"That is for the coroner to say, of course, Sister. But she appears to have been stabbed."

"Oh. Oh, thank you." Death by stabbing could be very swift. "Thank you," the nun said again.

"Yes. Well. Suppose we trade places, Ted. This end of the cart will have to be lifted very high to keep it horizontal. If you'll excuse us, Sister."

Mr. Waddy gave a small bow and set his good gray hat on his curls. He couldn't very well put all his strength into the job of carrying and be hanging on to his hat at the same time.

The young man threw open the door to the stairs. The areaway was enclosed at the top and bottom, and the air of it even in summer was tomblike. No one had considered lighting it. The economical twilight of the hall and the glimmer from the alley above were supposedly enough for a stairs not commonly used. It was startling, then, to meet a pair of eyes gleaming green in the darkness at the top.

"A cat," Mr. Waddy said quietly. "I must have neglected to pull the door shut when we came in. See, it's gone now."

Walking carefully backward, he started up the steps.

The nun did not wait to watch that cautious exit. She did not even turn back to the elevator. She threaded the old labyrinth of halls, hurried up the stairs to the emergency entrance and out into the night. It was very dark. The alley was well populated with cats, she reminded herself. Every moving shadow need not be the murderer.

It was only a short run across the avenue to the convent. The old Octagon House was a landmark built in the heyday of the lumber barons and it had been cut up into rooms oddly shaped because of its eight sides, a make-do convent with inconvenient plumbing and almost no closets. But to Sister Simon it was the most blessed shelter in the world tonight. Up the steps she fled, not pausing until she was inside the screened porch where the lumberman used to stand waving tipsy good-byes to his guests at about this hour of the morning. Nothing had chased her nor even frightened her. On into the house she went, through the central lobby where the circular staircase wound clear up into the cupola, and paused before a solid door marked with a white cross. Behind this door, in the cloister, she had always found peace. The small cares of daily existence had peered through at her, sometimes even made grotesque faces, but she had always been able to push them back across the threshold. The door must close upon her burdens tonight. She could not bear them longer.

Dipping her finger in the holy-water container, she made the sign of the cross. Then she went inside and shut the door.

6

Mr. Waddy had not gone home. The early morning sunlight, falling through the Venetian blinds of his office, laid neat slats across the tapestried wall and across Mr. Waddy himself on the davenport. When a slat touched his face he opened his eyes, blinked, and crooked an arm up to shut away the light. It was a little hard for him to tell whether he had been asleep. He did not feel either drowsy or rested. And what he remembered of the night was certainly not a dream.

Shading his eyes with his hand, he looked across the room to the clock on the desk. Six o'clock. It wasn't too early to make the phone call. Vince was an early riser. Mr. Waddy sat up and reached for his high-laced shoes. Not for years had he spent a night at the mortuary. Mrs. Waddy had been somewhat difficult to convince that there was a real need for him to remain here, but in the lethargy of two o'clock in the morning she had been unable to produce much argument. He hadn't known himself exactly why he felt he should stay. Only seeing Dannie again . . . and like that. . . .

He tied the shoelace into a bowknot, pulling at the loops until they were precisely the same size. Then, dangling the other shoe, he looked up and around the room. He had chosen every detail so carefully. The wallpaper was like woven grass, softly green and tan, the tapestry of ladies and prancing white horses was a museum piece. The carpet was a lovely continuation of shaded green, and against it the cherry-colored chairs and the mahogany desk were richly set off. A far cry, all of it, from the bare room in the back of the furniture store where he had started his undertaking business.

The preparation table then had been a storm door laid on saw-horses, the caskets nothing more than grim black boxes. And he had so little in the way of supplies to make a dead person look present-able, especially one who had died in a fire. . . .

Mist swam between Mr. Waddy and the cherry-colored chairs. Fumbling with his other shoe, he pulled out the laces and had to wipe his eyes with the back of his hand before he could see to thread them in again. He was feeling seedy after sleeping in his clothes. He'd get his face washed, then he'd brighten up.

When Mr. Waddy came out of the lavatory off the office, his hair was combed and his glasses polished. There was even an imitation of his customary briskness in the way he slipped on his coat and snapped shut the Venetian blinds to keep out the heat. His hand was on the telephone when a light knock came at the door.

"Come in," Mr. Waddy said.

A tall, very bald man let himself in and closed the door behind him.

"You're early, Snodgrass."

"Yes, sir. I saw the morning paper. The minute I read about it, I knew it was she!" The man came across to the desk with a lithe step. He leaned so close that Mr. Waddy could catch the scent of shaving lotion on his smooth cheeks. "She was here, sir! Last night. She asked for you."

The old gentleman laid his hand on his watch chain. He felt as if he were going down very fast in an elevator.

"Why wasn't I summoned, Snodgrass?"

"You had just left for the country."

Mr. Waddy's eyes fell to the desk, to the picture of the grandchil-dren under the plate glass. Almost any evening of the whole year he would have been available.

"Tell me about her, John."

"That was all, Mr. Waddy. When I said you weren't here she seemed terribly disappointed. She wanted to wait. But I knew you'd stop off at home, just as you did, sir, and I told her that. Didn't I do right?"

"What else could you have done?"

SISTER SIMON'S MURDER CASE

"But she was so frightened, Mr. Waddy, scared to death! She wouldn't even tell me her name!" The man's voice rose. "I feel now as if I—my goodness—I should have put her on a slab if I had to, just to keep her here!"

Mr. Waddy cleared his throat. Snodgrass' finger tips, pressed on the desk, showed nails freshly bitten to the quick.

The role of comforter had never been difficult for Henry Waddy; but now, perhaps because he needed comfort himself, he could find none to pass on. He took Snodgrass by the arm. The arm was tense. All Mr. Waddy could do was to pat it. His voice was gone. Snodgrass had been with him a long time—but not long enough to have known Dannie.

"Go down and make us some coffee, John," Mr. Waddy said when he could speak. Snodgrass' coffee was like seepage from a swamp but it would be a distraction. "Go on. I'll be down as soon as I water the cactus."

The man left. Picking up the telephone, Mr. Waddy dialed.

"Vince? Henry. Could you come over?"

"Yes. Dannie, isn't it?"

"How did you know?"

"Radio."

The line went dead. That was Vince, no waste of words. Mr. Waddy went into the lavatory, ran a cup half full of water, and spilled it on the cactus as he did every morning. Then, setting the door ajar behind him, he went out of the office.

The hall was still shadowy. Up a couple of steps was the general office, down a few was another door opening off a small landing. Mr. Waddy glanced toward neither. Close to the railing side, he proceeded down the stairs.

More than once in the past Mr. Waddy had come into the airiness of the entrance hall and felt a definite lifting of spirits. On the bottom step he paused, hoping for the lift to come. Trying to help it along, he reviewed how well he had done with transforming the old house. The wide archway made only a gesture of separating the hall from the drawing-room chapel, giving spaciousness to both. Mr. Waddy never had cared about pews. Folding chairs sufficed for funerals and between times, as at present, they could disappear, restoring the pleasant living-room atmosphere. The only feature not commonly found in living rooms was a large recess in the wall opposite the archway. Now the recess held a coffee table upon which stood a pink cyclamen in full bloom. The soft pinks and grays were repeated in the upholstered chairs, davenports, drapes, and carpet, a gently cheering combination. . . .

Abruptly Mr. Waddy's head turned toward the narrow hall leading off the lobby. The workrooms were back there. Some too discreet sound had caught his attention.

"Snodgrass? Is that you?"

But not even Snodgrass' version of coffee could be ready yet. And Ted wouldn't be up. Once, long ago, the boys had left the rear door unlocked and a tramp had wandered in. Mr. Waddy started to investigate. The small corridor was so dark that he was well in before he recognized his visitor.

"Oh," he said. "Vince. Well. I didn't think you could get here so soon."

It almost seemed, from his position, that Vince had just come out of the preparation room. Mr. Waddy knew better than to inquire.

"I hope I didn't phone you too early."

"No."

Vince always talked that way, as if he hated people. And mostly he did. Henry Waddy was about his only friend. The fellow belonged in the woods, really. Tall and gaunt as a Norway pine, he looked like a lumberjack in the plaid shirt and heavy boots he always wore. You'd never take him for a millionaire. Although there was no big timber left in these days, nothing but pulpwood, still he kept to the woods.

Perhaps, Mr. Waddy decided, it would be best to disregard the possibility that Vince had already been in the preparation room.

"I want you to see her, Vince," he said. "If you'll step aside—yes. Thank you."

Together they entered the room, white and clean as a surgery. The one window had a beveled pane with a rim of blue stained glass, and the sun laid a blue rectangle on the gray terrazzo floor.

Mr. Waddy opened his cooler and wheeled out a white-sheeted stretcher, pushing and pulling until he had it exactly right. Slowly he lifted the hem of the sheet, folded it back and down until the small face was uncovered. Part of the blue line of light lay around the face like a frame.

Vince drew an audible breath. Considerately, Mr. Waddy did not look at him. But he did note that Vince's horny hands made lumps in his pockets like knots on an oak tree.

"I hadn't seen her for years," Mr. Waddy said. "She came here last night, asking for me. I was out. Would you have any idea what she wanted, Vince?"

"No."

"You hadn't talked with her lately?"

"No."

Mr. Waddy's glance flicked his friend. The bony jaw was dark and unshaven, the muscles tight.

"She reminds me of Elizabeth," Mr. Waddy said.

"Elizabeth McArthur's dead twenty years."

In a near room a radio blasted on and was immediately quieted to a drumbeat. Mr. Waddy cocked his head in the listening attitude that had become a mannerism.

"Yes. Well. Twenty years is nearly a generation, isn't it?"

"If you mean the girl, Diane, she's grown up."

"I was thinking of Elizabeth."

Vince finally looked at him, and Mr. Waddy continued. "She was the first one I used the wax on. She wasn't too badly burned, considering she was in the house when it went. But I couldn't have let anyone see her without the wax. One of the nuns—can you think of her name, Vince, a strapping big woman—she said I'd made her natural as life."

He paused, but Vince made no reply. "We still use the wax in the same way, only now we rebuild features mostly after auto accidents. It's very soft, to prevent cracking, and people are sometimes curious, they want to touch a face, and fingers leave dents. So we drape the veil of net from the lid of the casket out over—"

Vince wheeled. Before he could reach the door, the old gentleman's quiet voice stopped him.

"You understand my code of ethics, Vince. I never volunteer information. If the police want to get something out of me they have to obtain a court order to do it. Not that I wish to place obstacles in their way but I feel very strongly . . ."

"You've told me before, Henry."

"I feel very strongly that a funeral director must never be connected with anything in the least sensational. It would be bad, very bad for my name to be linked with this case in any way." Again Mr. Waddy paused. "There may be no reason, of course, to dig into the past."

"Can't we wait and see?"

"Certainly."

There was a ragged look about Vince that Mr. Waddy couldn't bear. "I'll see that she has a nice funeral. I can't exclude the thrill seekers, I'm afraid, for the manner of her death invites them, but I'll make sure that there is no disrespect. . . .

No point in continuing. Vince had charged out into the hall as if the whole place were crammed with underbrush to be trampled down. Mr. Waddy cocked his head, listening. You couldn't exactly say that Vince slammed the door, but you did know unmistakably that he had gone out.

Mr. Waddy drew a deep breath. He must not keep Dannie out here in the warmth too long. The sun had moved, laying the blue frame a little closer about her face. Women always fascinated him from the time they attained the use of reason at the approximate age of three until they were carried in through his back door. You'd almost swear that some of them, during their last seconds of life, had stood before the pearly gates and seen inside. The men, judging from their expressions, might have gone anywhere. The women made you believe in heaven.

"Yes. Well," Mr. Waddy said aloud.

With a delicate sort of tenderness the old gentleman laid the sheet back in place. If the call hadn't come to take him away last night, if he had been able to talk with Dannie—but why go over it in vain regretting? Vince was the one to think of now.

7

Lizette sat in the second chair in the third row and stared at the blackboard. This was the room in which the nurses' aides had their classes, and someone with a flair for slogans had written on the board, "Carefulness, Cleanliness, Courtesy." The word "Courtesy" sat neatly on Chief Wakeley's shoulder as he stood at the desk, talking. Seated at the desk was a young policeman who wrote earnestly in a notebook and never seemed to get caught up because his pencil always went on writing through the pauses. Not that there had been many pauses. The questions had come rapidly. Everyone was assembled who could conceivably know the slightest detail about the little woman's visit to the hospital and her subsequent death—even Diane, who hadn't had to come. Right up to the door of the room Lizette had heard Mother Richard explaining to her that she need not be questioned with the others, the Chief had said so. But Diane insisted on hearing everything for herself. And now she sat in the chair ahead of Lizette with Mother Richard beside her. Over at the end of the row, nearest the door, was another nun, Sister Simon. Lizette had glanced at her but once. She had very raw feelings concerning Sister Simon.

Since eight o'clock—it was nine now—the Chief had been digging away at the scant information the hospital staff could give him. He had the look about him of a very determined woodpecker, probably because he combed his black hair back in a shining crest. His shoulders were even wider than Ted's and he had a way of pushing his chin forward as if he were literally uprooting facts. It could be, Lizette reflected, that his collar was too tight; but the gesture gave him an air of stern tenacity. And stubbornness. You probably couldn't change his mind about anything. For instance, about the picture he was building up of Dannie Grear. Like any tourist, he said, she came to town and went sight-seeing down on the water front.

"She arrived by bus, we know that," he said, although he had gone over all this before. He turned to Lizette. "Judging from the time you saw her, Miss Carter, she must have gone straight down to the river. Apparently she was under your observation the entire time she was there. You say she spoke to no one, not even to you. Isn't that the normal conduct of a person among strangers?"

"Yes, sir. But she was afraid," Lizette said. She had said it before. She could be stubborn, too, particularly when she was telling the truth.

"Did you see anyone or anything to frighten you?"

"No, sir."

"According to her niece, Miss Grear had no enemies."

"Of course she hadn't!" Diane broke in. "She was a wonderful person! Everybody loved her. Think of what she did for me, raising me after my mother died in the fire! Why, she was the dearest, sweetest . . ."

The girl's voice broke, and Lizette leaned forward to lay a hand on her shoulder. "Diane, I know! I only meant that somebody . . ."

"Mr. Peters said she was the best clerk he ever had, too. And she was with him twenty years! She brought all kinds of customers to the store!"

Mother Richard whispered something, and Diane subsided.

"We've pretty well established the kind of person she was," Wakeley said. "Let's return to the facts. She did have a suitcase when you saw her on the water front, Miss Carter? You're sure of that?"

"Yes, sir, the paper kind that looks like tweed. They're not very expensive."

"And a purse?"

"Yes."

"Now Miss Barlow." He faced Evvie. "You saw that she had the purse when she came in here to the desk?"

"Sure, I told you about it. Black. But she didn't have the suitcase. I'd of noticed."

"She could have left it in the waiting room, couldn't she, without you knowing?"

"Well—I guess so."

"But when you found her, Miss Carter, you didn't see the purse or the suitcase anywhere around?"

"I didn't look," Lizette said shortly.

Mother Richard's veil made a small motion of annoyance. She expected her people to co-operate fully with the police. She had made a few remarks on the subject, precisely and formally, before Wakeley came in.

"She was scared, all right," Evvie said suddenly. "I could tell."

"How could you tell?"

Good for you, Evvie, now don't back down, Lizette urged silently. But Evvie, confronted by a situation which called for brainwork, was at a loss.

"Well, I just knew. Like I know I'm scared now!"

There was a rustle of laughter and people shifting in their chairs. Wakeley even smiled, a rugged, he-man smile that put women and their intuition in their proper place. Lizette fixed her gaze upon Mrs. Van Courtland, the life-size dummy whom the nurses' aides had tucked up primly in her hospital bed. It would be very handy to be like Mrs. Van Courtland, no feelings about anything.

"You are probably right, Miss Barlow," the Chief said. "She was scared because she knew she had been followed out here. Somebody, seeing her down on the water front, decided she had some money. So he followed her, hung around outside while she was in here, and when she came out again he struck. The purse and the suitcase are both missing." His chin prodded forward again. "But we'll find them, and we'll find who killed her. It may take time but we'll do it. That's all for now, ladies and gentlemen, and thank you for your patience. If you remember anything more, no matter how small, call my office."

Everyone stood up, talking with conscious ease, and began to move out of the room. Lizette walked to the back windows. She was not going to face Sister Simon. The room grew silent, the voices became a disappearing drone in the hall. She turned, and discovered that she was alone with Sister Simon.

The nun looked as if she had not slept at all. She was beside a chair, holding on to the back as if she actually needed the support.

"I've taken you off duty for tonight, Lizette," she said. "Virginia needs to get in some extra hours."

"Thank you, Sister. But I'd rather work."

A faint flush rose in the Sister's cheeks. Lizette added coldly, "You need not upset your schedule, Sister. Rules are so important."

"My duty last night was to my patients, not to a strange woman who had no claim on us. You should understand that, Lizette."

"Oh, I do! But isn't it a little rough on people who need help and can find nobody in the world with time to help them?"

The nun bit her lip but even then it trembled. Lizette looked away. She was going to cherish the resentment she felt against everyone who refused to see into Dannie Grear's tragedy, and everyone included Sister Simon.

"She asked for Diane, Evvie said," Lizette went on, addressing a chart showing the complete digestive system. "When Diane wasn't in, then she thought of me. Not because she knew me well—we'd only met once at a tea—but because she had to have someone to be with *then!* Not an hour and a half later, when Diane would be home, but right that minute! She didn't want to be alone because she was *afraid for her life!*"

To her dismay, Lizette felt a tear start down her cheek. Slapping it away, she cut through a row of chairs to the door.

"But don't let it bother you, Sister," she said in the doorway. "You did the right thing."

Then she ran because she knew she was going to cry and cry and cry.

Sister Simon stood for a long minute hanging on to the chair back. She *had* done the right thing. Lizette was heartbroken now over her memory of the woman's suffering. In her replies to the police officer's questions, her remorse had been evident. She was scourging herself because she had not helped the woman when she met her on the water front, and anyone who touched upon the incident would be scourged also. The girl's resentment was understandable. And perhaps there *might* have been a way out. . . .

Sister Simon left the room, walked down the two flights of stairs to the emergency entrance and out into the alley. Mother Richard could still be with Diane; but also she could be in the spot she always said was her choice, next to the chapel, for meditation. Crossing the avenue and skirting around the old Octagon House, Sister Simon went quickly out through the vacant lots toward the bluff.

She could see from a distance that Mother Richard was on her knees in the vegetable garden. No other nun wore the same kind of striped apron. She had pinned back her sleeves and her veil and she was breaking over onion tops. A few rows away Sister Joe was working. The old nun was so deaf that her presence would not hinder a private conversation.

Sister Simon halted between the rows. The pungent odor of the crushed greens and the perfume drawn out of the clover by the hot sun was as homely a mingling as one could imagine. Impossible to relate onion juice and murder.

Mother Richard sat back on her heels. She was not wearing gloves and the pulp stained her hands. She rested them, palm up, on her knees. Her age was right to make her the mother of the younger nuns. The smile failed to put the customary twinkle in her eyes.

"Have you come to help pull the radishes, Sister? They're going to seed."

Sister Simon tried to return the smile. The attempt was a sorry affair. Better to gaze out over the river. The bluff where she stood was a lofty lookout, affording a panoramic view of the far bank. Over there, a few miles back from the shore line, the glacier of an ancient age had crept to a halt and its melting torrents had cut chasms down through rock layers so deep that a person exploring them on a summer day would shiver in the moist twilight, and so narrow that he would have to turn sideways to pass through. Small creeks now trickled down the beds worn by those mad, whirling streams. A man could hide there for weeks, undiscovered—a murderer. Her father had been killed by a murderer he and another policeman were trying to apprehend, and she had promised herself then and there that she would become a detective and avenge all murders. At thirteen, there had been nothing impossible about that. Her father had taught her to shoot "from the hip," that is, without using the sights. She could hit a moving target at fifty feet with a pistol—a skill you seldom needed in the convent. She still could do it, as she had proved at the last nurses' picnic. . . .

"What is troubling you, Sister?" Mother Richard asked, getting to her feet. She was short and portly, a comfortable housewife of the Middle Ages in the ancient dress. Behind her, in spirit, were ranged all the thousands of women who had worn the habit and kept the rule, losing the world to gain heaven.

Sister Simon bent and pulled off a sprig of radish blossom.

"Mother—duty has nothing to do with sentiment, has it? Duty is assigned, a law requiring administration on the one hand and obedience on the other. Because I'm a supervisor, I'm an administrator. But I still have the obligation of being obedient to the law myself. I must not set it aside for personal considerations. Am I right, Mother?"

"Of course."

"Then . . ." The radish flower slid down against her apron. "Then why am I in such a state of confusion?"

"All this has something to do with last night, Sister?"

"Yes, Mother. The woman—Dannie Grear—had Everine call up to the floor for Lizette. I told the police officer about it. He thought nothing of it, as evidence."

"I remember. You had an emergency at about the same time."

"A few minutes later. But not just then. Mother, I could have let Lizette go down!"

Mother Richard stepped over the onions. Taking the Sister's left hand, she spread her own pudgy, freckled left hand beside it. Each wore a plain silver band.

"We both wear the ring, Sister," she said, pushing her thumb up against her own. "See how tight mine has become? I doubt if I could get it off now. It's made a groove for itself right in my flesh. Forty years deep. Yours is still loose, you see." She patted the hand. "We wear the ring because we chose it, Sister. Nobody made us do so; we entered the convent of our own free will. While I was a novice I had long talks with Sister Joseph, she was Mother Superior then—the same kind of talks you had with me. You understood before you took your vows that the life of the convent is all according to rule, right down to the smallest detail. A bell rings and we obey, our superior speaks and we obey without question. We agree to live by the rule, that's our way of life." Mother patted the hand again and released it. "Don't worry about your doubts, Sister, just dismiss them. By the time your fingers are as fat as mine you'll have no doubts any more."

Sister Simon smiled faintly. "That will be a happy day, Mother."

"You did the right thing last night, Sister. The woman's death is tragic but it had nothing to do with you. Forget about it as best you can."

"Yes, Mother. Thank you."

Pondering the simplicity of Mother Richard's wisdom, the nun started back along the path. Sister Joseph was ahead of her, trudging with a pail of beets. She caught up to the old Sister and stepped out to pass her.

Sister Joe nodded a greeting. Her wrinkled face was browned to the hue of an Indian in sharp contrast to the white coif.

"There seems to be excitement in the air this morning, Sister," she boomed. Her tone was loud because she could barely hear herself.

Sister Simon beckoned for the pad of paper and the pencil the old nun always carried in her pocket.

"A woman died last night. At the hospital," she wrote. Then for no obvious reason, she added the name, "Dannie Grear."

Sister Joe read and reread the message. "Some doctor's carelessness?" she asked finally.

In haste, Sister Simon wrote, "Murder," and handed back the pencil. It was pathetic, she thought as she hurried on, that Sister Joe must depend on someone's whim to hear the news. She must pay more attention herself and she would remind the others.

But she didn't think long about the old nun. She had been gone too long from the floor and her work was waiting. She knew now what to say to Lizette, and she would say it at the first opportunity. She could make Lizette understand.

In the hospital corridors Lizette had managed to elude everyone who might ask questions; but when she sped across the alley and yanked open the door to the nurses' home, she was afraid her luck was ended. The very air was vibrant with the hum of voices. Even the kids who had come off night duty must be chattering away. And there would be only one subject. The murder. How would she ever get past all those open doors to the telephone? Someone did call out, but Lizette pretended not to hear as she ran by.

Mr. Waddy answered her telephone call. He said that Ted had gone out.

"He isn't there? Where did he go?" Lizette asked childishly.

That, she knew, was silly. Mr. Waddy would have no idea of what his boys did in their free time. He told her so, kindly.

"Thank you," Lizette said, ". . . No, no message."

What message could she leave—that the bottom had fallen out of the morning, that she had become such a clinging vine as to feel all uprooted when she couldn't find Ted?

"Here, kitty, here's your breakfast, come kitty-kitty-kitty!" a girl called over by the alley door.

Antonia was putting out scraps for Liz's dependents, as they called the cats. The kids would all be good. But thoughtless. They would want a million details.

"Hi. I thought I saw you flit by my door. Without so much as a good morning, either."

Lizette looked up wearily. Sybil, as usual, was barefooted. But her red hair was brushed into coppery highlights and her silver-flowered housecoat was the kind most of the girls would only sigh over in a store window.

"I shouldn't even tell you what I'm supposed to tell you," she remarked, draping herself against the wall. Sybil always moved as if a gallery of eligible males were watching. "But I'm a superior-type maiden. I won't even make you suffer." Her green eyes came languidly to Lizette. "Boy, do you look shot!"

"What are you supposed to tell me?"

"Your boyfriend's waiting for you in the mush room."

"Not Ted?"

"None other than. I was going to hold back until you'd given me a firsthand account of finding the corpse, because I knew you'd dash off—sure, there you go."

"Well, get me some clothes, then. I'll dress in the shower room and give you a blow-by-blow description."

"Goody. What do you want to put on?"

"Shorts. The white ones. And borrow a blouse from Jinny."

"Our little Jinny, what would we do without her."

"And tell Ted I'll be right there."

"I'll tell him that in the course of human events you'll show up. You owe me a decent minute, dearie."

Sybil drifted away and Lizette ran for the shower room.

Ten minutes later she entered the violet parlor. Ted, relaxing on his spine in a lavender chair, removed his gaze from the painting of a white madonna with purple pansies which took up the space above the violet love seat.

"Hello, hon. I was just sitting here wondering who decorated this cheery little spot, anyway."

"For goodness' sake, does it matter? Ted, Dannie Grear was mur . . ."

"Any guy with dishonorable intentions would sure feel he was getting the cold shoulder." Ted pulled himself out of the chair. "Old Waddy never uses purple—too chilly."

"Ted, aren't you even interested in . . ."

"I'm interested in you, punkin. And I want you to stay in low gear. I'm going to take you on a picnic."

"Are you really? Up the Gorge?"

"Absolutely." He kissed her on the forehead. "See, out of deference to the saintly nun who put her all into this room, I won't even kiss you here. But out in the primitive wilds—aha!"

He picked up the large paper sack from the floor beside his chair. Lizette laughed shakily. Ted always did that to her, made her feel cared for and carefree. It was perfectly possible that he wouldn't let her mention the murder at all.

Eddie was skulking, not walking, up the narrow sidewalk that threaded the Witches' Gorge. Knees slightly bent, putting your heel down first and rolling, sort of, on to your toe, that was how you skulked. Eddie knew because he had seen Indians doing it on television. He was not an Indian this morning, though, he was a sheriff's scout. A band of outlaws had held up the stagecoach right out in the oak grove behind the barn and he had seen the whole thing while he was gathering eggs in the henhouse. He had sneaked off as soon as he could make it, trailing the gang cross-country to the Gorge. It wasn't far from home, exactly, but you could make it seem farther if you took it easy and doubled back quite a bit. His mother never wanted him to come over here—letting the kid run wild, she called it—but his dad couldn't see anything wrong with it, provided he got his chores done first. Mom wouldn't fuss today. She was too busy making little sandwiches for her bridge club this afternoon, and she'd want him out of the way anyhow. Eddie hated the bridge club. The ladies all acted as if they were going to pat him on the head, and somebody would always ask how old he was. Next time he wasn't going to say eight, he'd say about forty-seven and maybe they'd quit. . . .

He stopped, stock still. High up on the rock wall there was a scrambling sound, too small for a bandit but enough to let Eddie bring the gun up in position against his shoulder. Sighting along the barrel, he looked smack into the face of an astonished chipmunk. The chipmunks didn't often come down here, too dark and damp.

"Bang!" he said.

The chipmunk flicked its tail. Eddie swung the muzzle up, sighting for more game. The Gorge was deep as a house, the sky a narrow blue ribbon running along up there with ferns and things hanging over from the forest floor. The walls were of cross-bedded rock, smooth sometimes, then again stacked up like a giant's dinner plates with moss in patches as if the giant's wife hadn't scraped the plates very clean. Down here where the sidewalk was, nothing lived, not even snakes. But from about half past two in the afternoon until dark there would be tourists tramping through here led by a guide in a blue uniform. That was why the boat company had built the sidewalk, so the people could walk along and not get their feet wet. Eddie dropped to his stomach and peered over the edge of the planks. The creek was still there, all right. But little, like somebody farther up was maybe just dumping out their canteen. It sure sounded like a tall story that about a billion trillion years ago the creek was a great big river tearing through the rocks, running down from the glacier when it melted. He wouldn't believe all that, only his dad had told it. The water had whirled so hard it had scooped regular little round rooms out under the dinner plates. Some of the rooms were plenty big so a bandit could get in there and hide if he wanted to. A dandy place to cache the loot from the stagecoach, too.

Eddie laid the gun carefully on the sidewalk. His hands were all rusty from it, but that didn't matter. He'd wash them good in the chickens' drinking trough when he got home. It was possible that his mother wouldn't take the gun away from him even if she discovered it, but there was no sense taking chances. The skulking had sure been more fun since he'd found the shootin' iron in the river. That was another reason for not letting Mom know about the gun. She'd said not to go near the river.

Sliding between the boards of the guard rail, Eddie hooked his bare toes into the cracked rock that was the threshold of the room. The rock was awfully cold. Even a stagecoach robber would have to be pretty desperate to hide in here very long. He peered back into the dimness. Maybe there weren't any snakes in the Gorge, but it sure looked like there ought to be. Or lizards. Something tiny moved, away in the back.

Eddie scuttled out so fast, backward, that he slipped under the sidewalk, caught at the planks, ran a long sliver into his thumb, got himself mostly soaked in the creek, and finally swung in under the guard rail. Grabbing the gun, he streaked up the Gorge. Wet like this, he was cold. In his den the sun would be hot and he'd be dry in no time.

He was breathing hard when he reached the Witches' Glen at the head of the Gorge. It was big as a living room, overgrown with scrubby trees and ferns, and partly roofed by the cross-bedded rock. He could sun himself here, but the den would be even better. Jumping to a rounded rock, then to the next, he used the left foot first. He always did it that way because the left foot never got to be first and it deserved some turns, too. Part way up the side Eddie paused, looked around for enemies, and then slipped between the vertical layers of a rock wall.

The chamber he entered was open to the sky but sunken to the depth of a room below the forest floor. The rock ledges were padded with moss and vines, and tall trees threw shade from the plateau. Eddie had always known—about two weeks—that someone else used the den, too, because the ashes of the campfire in the middle of the rock floor were sometimes different. But he never had met the other user. Now he did. A girl, down on her knees beside the fire, was frying bacon in a black old pan, and she had a pot of coffee bubbling so hard it made little spittings out through the spout. She was alone now, but she probably wouldn't be for long because two paper plates were set side by side on a ledge, and there were two forks.

She didn't seem a bit surprised to see a visitor. She was pretty, like his teacher last year. Sitting back on her heels, she smiled. She was even prettier then.

"Hi," she said. "Had your breakfast?"

Eddie scowled. He liked the girl already, but none of the strong men in the TV westerns got friendly right off the bat.

"Where's he?" he asked. She did look surprised, then, so he pointed the gun at the paper plates. "Him. You got two."

"Say, that's pretty sharp of you. He's up there getting more wood."

She waved the fork toward the plateau, then began to nip the bacon out of the pan and drop it on a paper napkin.

"Have a bite with us? I'll put in an extra egg."

"Oh. . . . I dunno."

"As long as we use your hide-out, we'd better be buddies."

"O.K." Eddie watched the eggs bubble up in white blisters, "How'd you know this was my hide-out?"

"Well, once I left the frying pan right side up in the pantry over there, and when I came to get it next time, it was the way it ought to be, bottom up. Nobody but a real woodsman would have bothered about that."

Eddie scowled hard at the rocky recess she called the pantry. He remembered very well how he had taken everything out and examined it. Putting the frying pan back as she said was pure accident.

"I figured you'd forgot," he muttered. "You gotta be careful with frying pans."

"Sure, they rust," she said as if Eddie knew all about it; so he nodded as if he did.

There was quite a crackling now up on the plateau and a tall young man appeared.

"Timber-r-r!" he called, and dropped down his armful of wood before he came skidding after it. "Hi, fella," he grinned at Eddie.

"This is Ted," the girl said. "I'm Lizette. He's a guide for the boat company."

"I seen you yesterday comin' up the draw," Eddie told the young man. "I seen you lots of times, two maybe."

"I bring settlers in regular."

"You never even knew I was there, did you?"

"No, siree, you're a pretty smooth scout, good as Jim Bowie."

"You and Jim Bowie could dig into the buffalo steak if we had another plate," Lizette said. "And a cup. I'll give him a little coffee."

"She makes the finest coffee this side of the Pecos, Jim," Ted declared, winking. "Pure smoke and ashes." He reached into the pantry right from where he sat, his arms were that long.

Eddie couldn't get over it, the way they fell into playing the game without any questions. The girl portioned out the eggs and bacon and a piece of bread and handed a plate to him. It smelled wonderful, just as you'd imagine when you'd see the campfires leaping on TV.

Eddie laid aside his gun to take the plate.

"Dandy shootin' iron you got there," Ted remarked. "Put up much gold for it?"

"Didn't cost me nothin'. I hooked it in the river, fishin'."

"Whadda ya know! Hand it over a minute."

Eating with one hand, Ted examined the gun, even sighted along the rusty old barrel. He wouldn't have to be told that the working parts didn't work.

"I bet it's great for antelope, eh, Jim?"

"I ain't brought down much with it yet, just a few chipmunks."

"How do you suppose it got into the river, Ted?" Lizette asked.

"Hard to tell. Somebody was deer hunting and lost it, maybe. Could have been crossing the river and his boat upset." He ran his thumb over the wooden stock. "He cut his initials here. W something."

"W L," Eddie said. "I washed it off good in the chickens' trough. You could see it plain when it was wet."

"Too bad it isn't W E," said Lizette. "Then it would be Wyatt Earp."

Ted seemed to consider this seriously. He even put down his bread so he could study the lettering better. Eddie held his breath.

"It is W E, dogged if it ain't!" Ted exclaimed. "Funny I didn't notice it!"

Eddie scrambled over on his knees until he was hard against Ted's shoulder. "Where? Where's the E?"

"Right there, bright as day, only you can't make out the arms of the E because the waves wore them down till you'd swear it's an L. Looky here, I'll get out my knife. . . ."

"Your Bowie knife," Lizette corrected.

"Sure thing. And I'll carve that E out real fine."

"But eat your pemmican first," Lizette reminded him. "You have to keep up your strength, you and Jim."

"Absolutely. To the feed bag, Jim!"

"And don't gobble. I'm going to have a nap here in the shade so you'll have time to carve the whole alphabet if you're a mind to."

"Women," Ted said, and winked broadly.

Eddie crawled back to his plate. He was so excited he felt like the balloons down at the river park, light and dancing. He hadn't had such a great time all summer.

Sister Joseph was sorely perplexed. She didn't have the slightest idea of what to do about the letter. She sat in her rocker and leaned forward with her elbows on her knees, the letter in her hand, her brooding gaze on the contents of the box on the floor before her. It was an apple box she had covered, lid and all, with calico years before and it still was a good box. It contained her treasures: a scrapbook, a chipped statue of the Blessed Mother, old rosaries, papers, a piece of crocheting, and a deck of cards. With the lid down, and under her bed, the box was as safe a place as one could wish for. No one ever touched another's possessions in the cloister. But put the letter in there and every time she came to the box she would see it. No, definitely this letter must go into the book. Her old face took on a softening of relief. Laying the lid in place, she pushed the box back under the bed. She saw that the Japanese glass chimes on her bookcase swayed and touched as she tramped across to the closet. It would be nice to hear the chimes. But at least she could see well. And the crown of her head still touched the six-foot-one mark made on the kitchen door by the novices so long ago.

Pushing back the curtain which shut away her closet, Sister Joe reached easily to the top shelf. Two books? Hadn't she always had but one up here? *Muskox, Bison, Sheep, and Goats,* by Caspar Whitney and Others. That was the old stand-by, the best book she had ever had for forgetting. She frowned at the other, bound in brisk new red: *Uranium Prospecting in Northern Minnesota.*

"Of course," she said. She knew she spoke aloud because she felt the vibration in her throat. She did remember now about the uranium book. She had picked it up in a room the nurses' aides were cleaning and the aides had said, every last one of them, that she should keep it. A book you never read is an excellent place to tuck away a letter you'd like to forget about. Mr. Whitney's volume had been entrusted with enough secrets through the years so that they were likely to fall out, which was disastrous to forgetting. She really needed this second book.

She flipped through the new pages. She had put nothing at all in it yet. A perfect hiding place for Damian's letter. Sister Joe laid the envelope between the pages and closed the book tightly. But then she hesitated. Was it right just to forget what Damian had said? Not said, exactly, but certainly hinted. I'm going to talk it all over with you, that was what she had put in the letter. But she hadn't said when the talk would be.

It would be never, now. Sister Simon had said that Damian was dead. And since death had ended the long tragedy, surely it was best to forget about the letter. Stretching up, Sister Joe pushed the book far back on the shelf. Then she looked at her clock. At ten, she would go to the kitchen to slip the skins off the beets for Sister Mary Clement. She had fifteen minutes. Seating herself again in the rocker, she pulled out the apple box and carefully extracted the scrapbook. Niagara Falls, on the cover, was faded until it looked like a wheatfield after a hailstorm. She laid open the book across her knees, turning the pages cautiously. They were broken around the edges and tiny bits fell in chaff down her scapular. Photographs, name's day cards, and little notes of spiritual bouquets she turned past, page after page.

"Ah," she said aloud.

The page under her hand was pasted full of newspaper clippings on which the glue showed through in brown patches. But the print was readable. "Hunter Accidentally Shot in Cabin, Brother Missing." With what impact that headline had hit the convent on the morning it came out!

Propping the book against the bed, she turned the page. On the back she had pasted something of less importance. In fact, she couldn't remember now why she had saved it at all. "Third Hunter Lost in Woods." She read the first line. "The sheriff's office reported this morning that Willis Lawrence of Beechwood Falls failed to rejoin his party. . . ."

Her attention wandered. A man named Willis Lawrence could have nothing to do with Damian. Turning back to the first page, she began to read. Someone else had slipped the skins off the beets before she remembered her duty down in the kitchen.

8

Late in the afternoon Lizette lay on as much of her bed as Evvie had left to her and did her best to think about nothing. She and Ted had prolonged their picnic until nearly one o'clock, coming back barely in time for him to change into his uniform and make it to the dock for his first boat trip. The pleasant relaxation of the morning still lingered with her. Because of Sybil's foresight, the "Do Not Disturb!" sign on the door was having its effect. On the other bed, Jinny sat crosslegged in her slip, little piles of papers all around her. Sybil, the volunteer guard, was curled up on Jinny's pillows.

"I'm going to poison that lousy ivy," Evvie said. "Hey, you don't care if I use your nail polish, do you, Liz?"

Lizette grunted. She had been smelling the strong banana odor for quite some time.

"What ivy?" she asked.

"You're not supposed to talk to her, Ev," Sybil said. "She's asleep."

"She'd sleep better if you kids got out," Jinny remarked. "I'd be real still. I'm studying."

"What ivy?" Lizette asked again.

"The one over the lobby arch. In the hospital. The way it swings, it gives me the willies."

"Just when the door is open, though," Jinny put in. "That's all it swings."

"Well, sure. But look at last night, the stupid thing swinging away and nobody coming in."

"Couldn't they of gone in the waiting room? You wouldn't see."

"The woman was in the waiting room—oh, glory, it could of been the murd . . ."

The word was cut off as if a hand had been clapped over Evvie's mouth. Sybil's hand, because Jinny took up the idea in a frightened whisper.

"D'you suppose he dragged her outside and plunged a knife in her . . . ?"

"*Jinny!*" Sybil cautioned.

Lizette sat up. Jinny was looking as if she herself had just confronted the murderer face to face, and Evvie had spilled the nail polish in her lap.

"Now look what you made me do!" Evvie squealed, and Sybil snapped, "It was your own fault! Don't move or it'll go all over the bed."

"Like blood," Jinny whispered.

"Jin, I'll choke you yet!" Sybil warned.

But Evvie cut in excitedly. "I don't see why we shouldn't talk! My brother-in-law says Liz is going to be next."

"What does your brother-in-law know about it?"

"Plenty! Gordie says maybe the guy was right down there on the water front when Liz talked to the woman, because that's when she said the woman got so scared, and the cop didn't believe you, Liz, but Gordie does. He says you've sure got good reason to worry!"

"I haven't been worrying."

"Then you better! Because Gordie says you're the only one could really identify him. You looked maybe right *at* him and he knows it!"

"But *I* don't know it. I mean, I have no idea what scared the woman. . . ."

"Sure, but even the cop says it was somebody killed her, who followed her up from the water front and robbed her!"

"Robbery wasn't the motive! How could she be afraid ahead of time of somebody that was going to hold her up?"

"You see?" Evvie declared triumphantly. She leaped up and a sticky puddle of polish streamed to the floor. "See, you talk just like Gordie. He says you better look out. . . ."

"Ev, will you shut *up!*" Sybil commanded. "Get your skirt off, it's ruined anyway, and wipe up this mess."

"Well, it's fair to warn her, and I wouldn't be in her shoes for a million dollars," Evvie muttered, but she stepped out of her skirt and went down on her knees, mopping.

Surprised at herself for trembling, Lizette lay down again. Her own possible danger was something she had not considered. She hadn't seen the person who frightened Dannie Grear, she had told the police so; it would most likely even be in the paper tonight! But the criminal couldn't be sure. The only certain means of preventing identification by her would be to . . .

"The darn stain isn't coming out at all!" Evvie wailed, rubbing at the floor. "What'll I do?"

"Use some polish remover," Sybil retorted in a tone short of patience. "Not Lizette's, either. And get a move on. I've got to wash my hair."

"Well, go ahead. And you don't have to bite my head off! I guess I'm just as good a friend of Liz's as you are, heaps better if I—"

"We're all friends," Lizette broke in, "so let's act like it. Going out on a heavy date, Sybil?"

"The only thing heavy about it is the character I'm going with."

"Chuck?"

"Roger. I can't stand him."

"Then why go?" Jinny asked.

"I wouldn't if somebody else . . . Jin! How about you?"

"Me?"

"You *must* hate the guy," Evvie remarked, getting up with the skirt wadded in her hand.

"Shut the door as you leave," Sybil suggested.

"Oh, cut it out, kids," Lizette sighed. "Leave us have peace and quiet."

Everine's large dark eyes, so effective with the ash-blond hair, filled with tears. "Liz, you're so good! I just hope nothing—nothing—I mean . . ."

"Farewell, friend," Sybil said, and she marched over and kicked the door shut on the very tail of Evvie's slip.

"Friends are *nice!*" Jinny burst out unexpectedly. "And Evvie has real good common sense. I haven't; Mother Richard says so. I haven't got any judgment at all, except bad. And Evvie's scared, right to the marrow of her bones! That's what friends are for!"

"To scare the liver out of you?" Sybil asked.

"To do things for you. When you're in trouble or in need or something, then your friends help you out. I'd do anything for Liz!"

"How about for me?"

"But that's different! I've never been out with a boy in my life!"

"You handled the queen business last year without breaking a leg, didn't you? So you can muddle through this. And look what's in it for you, a meal that didn't come out of a wash boiler, scintillating conversation with a razor brain."

"I wouldn't know what to talk about."

"Worms," said Sybil, seating herself again on the bed. "He's a biologist. Or dead cats. He's taking anatomy, too."

"Now you're laughing at me! I'm not so dumb I can't tell when you're . . ."

"Jinny, dear," Lizette said, doing her best to remember that patience is a virtue, "honey, why don't you go out with Roger and have a good time? Don't be so tense. You're a sweet child and you have a lot more on the ball than you think. Roger will love you."

"If I could be like you, all poised and everything, I'd go in a minute."

"Forget about poise and you'll have it."

"I haven't got a thing to wear!"

"How about my orchid nylon?" Sybil asked. "You'd look like the Czaress of Timbuktu, with your blond hair."

"You haven't even worn it yet yourself! What if I tear it?"

"Dearie, this is a dinner party, not a wrestling match."

The door burst open and Antonia bounced in.

"Phone for you, Liz."

"Who is it?"

"Your one and only."

"I thought he was on the high seas," Lizette said, but she reached for her housecoat. "Thanks, Tony. Bye bye, kiddies, see you much, much later."

"Aren't you coming back?" Jinny asked.

"She means we won't be here when she gets back," Sybil explained. "O.K., just for that, we'll borrow her shampoo. You can dress in my room, too. Grab the unmentionables and we won't have to bother Miss Exclusive again."

Sybil certainly meant business, Lizette thought as she went down the hall. Sybil never lent her clothes. And never shampooed any hair but her own. She probably had another date up her sleeve for tonight.

"Hi, Ted," Lizette said into the telephone. "What's new?"

"Nothing much. Did I wake you up?"

"In this monkey house? Hardly."

"Going on duty tonight?"

"Of course. At eleven. Why?"

"You'll sleep through the dinner hour?"

"I was planning on it."

"Then I won't come over between trips. I'd like to go back and see what's up with poor old Waddy, anyway. Looks to me like he's in a bad state."

"Sick?"

"Practically. Wanders around like a chicken with its head cut off. He knew Dannie Grear, I told you that."

"I remember."

"I've been wondering if the old guy didn't maybe want to marry her sometime. Before Mrs. Waddy, that is."

"She'd have been too young. He has grown-up sons."

"Yeah, you're right. But he's sure taking it hard. Liz . . ."

"What?"

"Wouldn't you come over and see her? He's done a swell job on her. . . ."

"No. N O."

"Well, have a good sleep."

"I will. Ted . . . I . . . The kids were saying . . . I mean, Evvie thinks . . ."

"Thinks what?"

"Nothing."

'What is it, Liz?"

"Nothing, honestly. Will I see you tomorrow morning?"

"I'll be on the doorstep with the morning paper. Jerry's tooting for me. 'Bye, honey."

Lizette put down the telephone slowly. Ted was not an alarmist—he would never agree with Gordie. And she could hardly be in danger for the next few hours. Let the future take care of itself. She picked up a scrap of chalk and wrote on the blackboard, "No calls. Carter."

When she reached her room the girls were gone. A great deal of chatter issued from Sybil's room down the hall. Lizette shut herself in, pulled down the shade and flopped onto the bed. Almost before she kicked off her slippers, she was sound asleep.

"There's no help for it, Snodgrass," said Mr. Waddy.

Still, he came once again to the door of the small room and looked out across the lobby into the drawing-room chapel.

"No," he said finally, turning back, "no, it's much too public. We couldn't protect her out there. Here we can."

"I feel that this is rather cozy, sir," Snodgrass said, and he tilted his head to one side, a mannerism he had picked up from Mr. Waddy. They had pulled the heavy drapes shut and turned on the ceiling light, and the glare skidded across his bald head. He moved a candelabrum two inches farther away from the head of the casket. Then he stepped carefully around the kneeler to move the candelabrum at the foot two inches. He had to step carefully, for there was very little room.

"A nice layout, sir," Snodgrass said.

Mr. Waddy knew it was a nice layout, the nicest he could devise. The casket was lined with the palest of shell pink, and they had found a dress of the same shade. It had been worth the trouble. Dannie looked like an angel asleep. And she would have complete privacy here. This little room, tucked in behind the stair well, was entirely removed from the usual range of visitors. Vince would be pleased.

"Snodgrass, will you make a call for me?" Mr. Waddy asked.

But Snodgrass had disappeared. Vaguely Mr. Waddy recollected that the telephone had rung. When Snodgrass, a moment later, called him to answer, he turned out the lights and closed the door upon Dannie. He would give Vince a ring himself.

Mr. Waddy had rather been expecting Chief Wakeley to get in touch with him and he was not surprised when the officer's terse greeting came over the wire. What was a little surprising was the question he rattled into Mr. Waddy's ear.

"Mr. Waddy, who is paying for Dannie Grear's funeral?"

The old gentleman closed his eyes and drew a long breath. Wakeley was smart.

"Mr. Waddy?"

"Yes. Yes, Chief. I'm sorry."

"I asked you . . ."

"I know what you asked me. I cannot give you an answer."

"Why not?"

"Because, sir, I must not divulge private information. A mortician must maintain the same code as a lawyer or a doctor. The dead have no dignity except what the living preserve for them. Perhaps the police hold to the same belief?"

There was a short pause.

"I'm going to have this information, Mr. Waddy. You'll have to give it to me if I get a court order."

"I realize that, sir."

"Then I'll get it!"

Without the formality of a good-by, the line went dead.

Slowly Mr. Waddy replaced the receiver. Judge Deever would have to issue the order and he was out at his summer cabin. The order couldn't come through until tomorrow. No need to be concerned about it. Take care of the other matter first. He put his finger into a hole ready to dial a number when the gong for the front door stroked the quiet.

"I'll get it, Snodgrass," Mr. Waddy called.

But before he could do so the door opened, admitted a man, and closed. Mr. Waddy was disturbed. The sign over the bell outside advised the visitor to ring and enter but this one hadn't waited even a second. And he was not a particularly soothing individual.

He was a big fellow. The sleeves of his black shirt were wrinkled, as if they had only recently been rolled down. The shirt was buttoned to the collar but he wore no tie. He had, in fact, the remains of mud on his blue jeans.

"Yes, sir?" Mr. Waddy inquired, putting a frown in his voice.

The fellow looked him up and down. "You're Henry Waddy?"

"I am."

"I'd like to see Dannie Grear."

Mr. Waddy returned the scrutiny in silence. His was not the only undertaking establishment in town. It was the oldest. And the best, naturally. But that was no reason why this unruly looking stranger should assume that Dannie should be here.

"I want to see if I can identify her," the man added.

"That will not be necessary, sir. The police are already satisfied as to her identity."

Mr. Waddy took a step forward, definitely suggesting that the unkempt boots should remove themselves from his good gray carpeting.

But the fellow didn't budge.

"The identification is for my own satisfaction, not for the police."

Mr. Waddy merely folded his arms. The fellow would have to do better than that.

The strong, darkly bearded chin lowered a trifle; the eyes, gray and cold, remained upon Mr. Waddy. If he had combed his hair he had done a poor job. But artistically poor. Something about him—the set of his head, that wild hair—something tugged at Mr. Waddy's memory.

The eyes narrowed. "I'm a tramp," the man said, and there was the viciousness in it of old tempers. "A carnival tramp. I make figures out of mud down on the water front."

"So that's where I've seen you," Mr. Waddy said. "Not this summer, though."

"This summer."

The old gentleman shook his head. "No. I haven't taken the time to visit the carnival this season."

"I've never been on the water front before this summer."

Mr. Waddy's plump shoulders lifted. It did seem much longer ago. Surely he couldn't have forgotten a recent visit to the river because Mrs. Waddy would have objected strongly and he never went anywhere like that without her.

"Pico, Pico della Mara," the fellow added. "But you wouldn't know my name. Nobody does. I'm 'hey, you,' down there."

"No," said Mr. Waddy, "no, that name is not familiar at all. But—about Miss Grear?"

"She stopped to admire my work. That is, I believe it was her. The cops were around this morning asking questions. I'd like to be sure."

"Didn't they describe her to you?"

"Listen!" the fellow began roughly, and immediately amended his tone. "Listen, do you have any idea the number of people stop during a day? Even if I model one of those dinky mud heads of them, I couldn't tell you what they looked like a minute later. All I know is they pay me a buck. Think the cop can understand that? No, he gets sore because I can't say right, right, right, she's the one. Burned me up! I'll drop by and see her, I told him, that's the only way I'll be sure. And he says O.K."

Mr. Waddy could reasonably hesitate no longer. He couldn't quite restrain another glance at the dirty boots. But he led the way around the stairs to the small room, opened the door, and snapped on the light. The fellow, he hoped, would be content to glance in over his shoulder.

But he wasn't. Pushing past Mr. Waddy, he went over close to the casket. The candles were not lighted but even without their softness Dannie was a wax angel. The man took a long time to look at her.

"It's her," he said. "Dannie—what was her name?"

"Grear," Mr. Waddy said softly. "Dannie Grear."

His hand was on the light switch. He was not going to permit this carnival tramp to remain any longer than necessary within the clean confines of his establishment.

9

Jinny was alone. Posed on the end of Sybil's bed, she could see herself in the mirror. The orchid dress was thin as a cloud and embroidered in white, and her hair fell in shining blond waves to her shoulders. Sybil had given her a skillful make-up of lavender eye shadow, a touch of rouge for the china shepherdess effect, but no powder.

"Roger will eat you up," Sybil said as she departed on a date of her own. "He'll be back for more, I promise you. And don't try to talk much, just open your eyes wide. The mascara will do the rest."

Now that Sybil was gone, Jinny was so frightened her stomach felt like an empty bubble under the tight-fitting bodice; but she practiced opening her eyes wide. It all seemed a little silly. She'd give anything if she didn't have to go.

"Carter!" someone called out in the hall. "Hey, Liz, telephone!"

Jinny bounded off the bed and over to the door.

"Tony, don't call her! She's asleep!"

"I know it. I see her note on the board. But this guy really wants her."

"Is it Ted?"

"No, some other fellow." Antonia, wrapped in a large towel, grabbed a corner as it slipped. "You talk to him, will you, Jin? I'm dripping all over. Wow, do you look scrumptious!"

"I feel awful," Jinny said. "I wish you'd hurry up and get some clothes on. The monitor isn't supposed to run around like that. And you're supposed to put Roger in the mush room when he comes."

"Sybil told me. I'll be there in a fresh paint job."

"Then hurry up!"

"O.K., O.K. But you answer that creature before he blows a fuse."

Tony pattered away. Jinny took up the telephone.

"Hello," she said. "This is . . ."

"Lizette? Listen carefully. I'll only explain this once."

The voice was not Ted's. It was low and gruff, fearfully commanding.

"Lizette, can you hear me?"

"Yes," she quavered. "Yes, but . . ."

"All right. Now get this straight. Go to the laundromat, the Snow White. Do you know where that is?"

"Yes." The time was past for telling him she was not Lizette.

"The woman, Dannie Grear, left her suitcase there. I want it. You go to the Snow White and get it, then bring it down to the water front. Be sure you come down the stairs with a crowd, not alone. You don't want to be noticed. Put the suitcase back under the stairs. Then leave. Got it straight?"

"I think so."

"Don't tell anybody where you're going and don't bring anybody with you." There was a second's pause. "If you double-cross me on this, you'll wish you hadn't. And you'll never live to identify me, remember that. The only way we'll get along is for you to play ball. Understand?"

"Yes."

The little word was only a whisper, but he must have heard it for the line went dead. Jinny let the receiver fall in place. She was oddly numb. Not frightened, just numb. Slowly she walked back to Sybil's room, her high heels tapping. In the room she closed the door, sat down on the end of the bed, and folded her hands. A beautiful girl in an orchid dress looked back at her from the mirror.

The girl had just talked to Dannie Grear's murderer.

She stared into the mirror while cold paralysis held her body and brain. One small thought broke through: Gordie was right. The murderer did believe that Lizette could identify him. So that put Lizette in the same peril Dannie Grear had faced. And Dannie was dead.

The clock ticked busily through empty minutes. Time might be precious, for the man sounded as if he expected his order to be carried out instantly. Not that Jinny needed time to decide what to do. From almost the first minute, she knew. Liz was her best friend, her defender and her rescuer times without number. Liz would be in very real danger if she were to take the suitcase down under the stairs, because the man might go back on his promise to play ball. After all, he had killed once, and to kill again would not make him any worse off than he was already.

"I can't! I simply can't!" Jinny whispered.

But this was a chance to do something for Lizette. The one-sided friendship would be well balanced, even tipped to Jinny's side, for nothing in the world was so important as saving a life. And that was what she would be doing for Liz. She herself would be in no danger. She didn't know the man.

She jumped up and started to unzip the dress. But why take it off? She wouldn't be gone forever and upon her return she would be ready to go out with Roger. He would have to wait a little but he was used to waiting for Sybil. And she could ask Tony to explain. . . .

She couldn't. Don't tell anyone where you're going, the man had said. Glancing out of the window, she saw that the sidewalk was empty of everything except a few dragonflies darning a pattern over the petunias. A quarter to seven. Roger would come around seven. Being conditioned to Sybil, he would wait until half past without getting the fidgets, and by that time Jinny would be back. She snatched the pretty beaded purse Sybil had lent her. In it were fifty cents on lend-lease from Evvie, a lipstick, comb, handkerchief, and her rosary, all the temporal and spiritual insurance she would need for the evening.

Tiptoeing out into the hall as if she must sneak past a dozen spies, Jinny headed for the alley entrance. Voices came from rooms, but there was no one to see her go. Perhaps no one would see her come back, either, and the secret of this great thing she was doing for Lizette would be her own until she would choose to tell it.

Right at the doorway, she met Sister Simon coming in.

Sister Simon took a second glance before she recognized the girl in the orchid dress.

"Jinny, how lovely you look! That color is heavenly on you."

She paused then. Was she not saying the right thing? In the girl's eyes there was an expression of fear. She glanced at her watch. The time could have nothing to do with it. All the girls off duty were free in the evening.

"Thank you, Sister," Jinny was murmuring. "I . . . it isn't mine . . . I'm going . . . good-by, 'Ster!"

"Have a good time, dear. Is Lizette in her room?"

"Yes, 'Ster. But she's asleep."

The nun, on the steps, watched the blond hair flying as Jinny ran away down the alley toward the street. Some little mission she didn't want discovered, no doubt something so harmless you'd wonder why she had bothered to cover it up. Smiling to herself, Sister Simon walked down the alley past the emergency entrance and on across to the convent. She would have preferred to have her talk with Lizette, but since it had to be postponed she was relieved. Tomorrow, perhaps, would be even better. She might not be so tired. There was still work that could be done, of course, paperwork up on pedes. But where did duty end and martyrdom begin? She couldn't remember exactly when she had gone to recreation. Tonight, in the close family company of the nuns, she would forget the cares that nagged her, and finally she would be able to sleep.

She was thinking about her crocheting as she climbed the steps to the lumberman's porch. In the chest in the recreation room, it seemed she had left it there. She couldn't remember exactly what she was making, either a doily or a chair cover, pineapple design, for her niece Betty. It didn't really matter. Betty was not likely to use it anyway in her modernistic living room. . . .

"Simon?"

Old Sister Joe was getting up out of a rocker, leaving it to whack against another, coming forward with a step that shook the porch. She must have been waiting for me, Sister Simon thought, she wants to know more about the murder. The old nun took her by the arm.

"Sister, will you come with me to the mortuary? I must see her."

"See who, Sister?"

"Dannie Grear."

"I can tell you about her. We wouldn't have to . . ."

The wrinkled face came closer, and the voice took on anxiety.

"I have permission, Sister. Mother is so very kind. She says we may use the car. It's not only that you can drive, Sister, but this morning you told me—I'm sure you told me about Dannie. I couldn't forget that, could I, dear?"

"Oh, no, no, I told you," Sister Simon replied quickly. She wanted nothing less than to go to Henry Waddy's and look at a dead woman, but she added, making the gesture that would explain her words, "I'll have to change into my black habit, Sister."

The old nun nodded. "I didn't do anything for her when she asked me to, dear. You see, I thought, when we could talk—well, we never can, now. But I'd like to pay my respects to her. You understand, Sister?"

"Oh, of course," Sister Simon answered, unpinning a sleeve.

"She was Damian when she was with us," Sister Joe remarked. The pin bit into the young nun's thumb. "I knew she wouldn't stay. Even without the fire, she wouldn't have stayed. Now run along, dear. Mother won't like it if we're out too late."

With her thumb in her mouth, Sister Simon hurried into the cloister.

The Snow White was a bedlam of thunderously churning machines when Jinny entered and sidled up to the counter. In the steamy rear a dozen women shouted companionably at one another as they stepped around piles of laundry. The girl attendant looked as if she had just been lifted out of a hot tub, clothes and all. She pushed a pad and pencil toward Jinny.

"Write it."

"What?"

"Name. I can't hear nothin' above them machines. Saves a lot of time if you write your name."

Jinny's heart gave a fearful leap. The man hadn't mentioned a name. If she were to say Dannie Grear, and the girl had read the papers—and who hadn't!—she would most likely call the police.

The girl swiped her face with the back of her wrist and leaned over the counter. "That's sure a pretty dress. But it won't wash. I don't buy nothin' won't wash. Only I'd sure like somethin' like that."

"Thank you," Jinny said. "I'm after a suitcase."

"A what?"

"Suitcase. I'm calling for it. The woman can't come."

The girl swiped her face with the other wrist. "They don't generally put their stuff in suitcases. Must be somethin' the boss took in."

"Please look!" Jinny begged. "I promised I'd get it!"

The girl drooped down under the counter, reappearing almost immediately with a small tweed paper suitcase.

"This it? Only one we got."

"Oh, that's it!" Jinny exclaimed. This was the one Liz had described, tweedy and poor. "Thank you so much!"

"Wait a minute. Let's see how much I collect."

"Collect?"

"We ain't in business for fun, ma'am."

Jinny knew a moment of panic, then. She had fifty cents.

What if the charge should be more? Was the whole success of this mission—Lizette's very life—to hang on a few cents she didn't have?

The girl found a slip of paper stuck to the side of the suitcase, read it, and shrugged.

"No charge. He must of felt softhearted, for some reason. Well, there you go."

She pushed the suitcase across the counter. Jinny grabbed the small handle.

"I just don't know how to thank you!"

"Don't bother. I ain't used to it." The girl smiled. "You been in here before with another student nurse. Real cute."

"That's Lizette. Good-by, and thanks again."

"Goin' out on a date, huh? Have fun."

"Oh, I will!"

Out on the sidewalk Jinny wondered briefly how the girl knew they were nurses, started to run, then slowed to a walk. People would look at her, dashing by. She must be inconspicuous, stay with this crowd, and perhaps when they reached the boat company's big building enough of them would go down the stairs to make a cover for her. She had obeyed orders to the letter, thus far. And it hadn't been so difficult. She felt strong and courageous when, at the top of the stairs, she looked down on the river park.

Mr. Waddy knew he should go home. Twice since six o'clock Mrs. Waddy had called, urging him to end his long day. He would have done so gladly if it weren't for his conviction that he would only carry his restlessness home with him, and he couldn't face a new frontier of sympathy. The boys had borne with his anxieties all day, kindly and for the most part wordlessly. But they had shown their concern. Ted, for instance, had rushed back on his supper break, stood on one leg for a moment before Mr. Waddy, and then dashed to the kitchenette to start the percolator. Snodgrass had been brewing coffee all afternoon and Mr. Waddy had meekly drunk so much that by the time Ted came in with his tray he had worked up quite a case of sour stomach. But he couldn't turn the boy down.

Susan, whose mind was normally on something entirely extracurricular, even forgot to repair her lipstick. Mr. Waddy hadn't been so fortunate in keeping secretaries—they were all either too thrilled or too awed by the surroundings—but Susan Chapin had been here quite a while now. She was a good girl. Each time Mr. Waddy entered the office today her fingers would trip over the statements she was typing, and her large eyes would fasten on him, brimming with concern. At five o'clock, however, Susan departed. Snodgrass disappeared, and the place became so quiet that the old gentleman, who had been longing for solitude, found he could not bear his own company.

It was around seven fifteen when he wandered through the hall past the preparation room and the kitchenette and out into the garage. Young Lombard was there, shining up the hearse although his hours of duty were over long ago. He waved to Mr. Waddy with an alert air of fellow feeling. They wanted to help, all of them. The old gentleman's vision clouded a little. He'd certainly explain as soon as possible.

"Very nice, Gene," he said. "Don't forget the steering wheel. We must have it all perfect for tomorrow."

For tomorrow. For Dannie. He had been saying things like that all day. Really, he must be quite a trial to have around.

Very quietly, so as not to arouse Snodgrass with another cup of coffee, Mr. Waddy re-entered the passageway, went safely past the kitchenette, and reached the front lobby. Two nuns, one extremely tall and broad and old, the other young and pretty, stood just inside the front door. They were all in black, even their hands, and their white coifs made shadows around their faces.

"Yes. Good evening, Sisters," Mr. Waddy said. He had the queer feeling that this had happened before, long ago. . . .

"I am Sister Mary Joseph," the tall one said very loudly. Deaf, of course. "This is Sister Mary Simon. We have come to pay our respects to Damian."

"Dannie Grear," the younger nun added.

It was fitting that nuns should come to pray for Dannie, so fitting that Mr. Waddy didn't waste a wonder on the new name. Not exactly new, either. Like the appearance of the tall Sister, it rang a faint bell.

He opened the door of the small room, snapped on a shaded lamp, and stood aside. They went straight to the casket and knelt. Mr. Waddy folded his hands. Dannie looked so young. Perhaps all the soft pink helped the illusion. But it was the way he had laid her out, too, giving that tiny tilt to the head that no one had ever discovered and yet it made all the difference between funereal stiffness and the impression of natural sleep.

The tall nun, Sister Joseph, rose from her knees. She had been crying. Mr. Waddy liked her for it.

"Poor Damian. I'd know her anywhere," she said. "She had a beautiful life, you can tell that. She made no mistake, leaving us."

The memory snapped to the surface of Mr. Waddy's muddled mind. "Of course! You were the Mother Superior then! I remember!" He held out his hand.

Sister Joe smiled, a miracle of wrinkled pleasure, and took his hand in both of hers. "You've done a beautiful job, Mr. Waddy. Why, she looks as young as the day she entered the convent!"

Mr. Waddy smiled tremulously.

"She seemed to be so uncertain while she was with us," the old nun went on, and her eyes returned to Dannie. The younger one still knelt. "She didn't belong in the convent. I knew it, but she had to find out for herself. Girls come in for all kinds of reasons besides the right one, and they always find out. She had been disappointed in love."

"I know," Mr. Waddy said.

"You remember Elizabeth? I never thought she was quite fair with Damian. She didn't like Steve, you know, she thought he was a ne'er-do-well—and of course he was. So she told Damian that Steve was about to marry someone else. You never heard whether he actually did, I suppose?"

Sister Joseph was looking at him, and Mr. Waddy shook his head. His hands, clasped behind him, were wet with perspiration.

"Well, it might not have worked out, anyway. So much tragedy, all related somehow to Steve. You have to wonder, sometimes, why the Lord permits these things to happen."

"Not Steve," Mr. Waddy said. "Steve wasn't good."

Sister Joseph went right on, not having heard him. "I've often thought how providential it was that Elizabeth brought the baby to the convent that day. If she hadn't, the child would surely have been burned up with her. You know Diane? A beautiful girl. I gave Damian permission to keep her for the day. As it happened, she kept her for twenty-one years."

"A wonderful sacrifice," the old gentleman murmured. The Sister must have read his lips, for she replied.

"Not a sacrifice in the ordinary sense, Mr. Waddy. There was nothing Damian wanted when she couldn't have Steve. That was why she entered the convent, and it was why she left. The baby took Steve's place in her heart." Sister Joe paused. "I've been looking over my old scrapbook, you see, and it's all back with me so clearly. The hunting accident, that was the beginning. Perhaps nothing would have happened if they hadn't gone hunting that time."

"Perhaps not," Mr. Waddy whispered.

Sister Simon crossed herself and rose from her knees.

"Yes, we must go," Sister Joseph said in her customary boom. "Thank you for your kindness, sir."

"Not at all." Mr. Waddy, bowing, stood aside. "Could one of the boys give you a ride home?"

The old nun's eyes twinkled. "In the hearse, sir? Thank you, no, I'll be in it soon enough. We have our own car."

Mr. Waddy murmured politely and went through his usual hand-shaking. But when he had closed the outer door behind the nuns, he sat down on the first chair he could reach. Once, on a country hike, he had been caught in a hailstorm and the effect of being pelted with ice was like this. He had crawled into a thicket, and the tangle of branches had somewhat broken the battering downfall. There was no thicket here.

Voices sounded from the direction of the kitchenette, something about coffee. Mr. Waddy got to his feet and went as quickly as he could manage up the stairs to his office. It was cool and dusky there, tranquil as a woodsy dell. Buzzing the house phone he told Snodgrass, in the kitchen, that he and young Lombard might leave now. No, indeed, there was nothing more for them to do. He himself would be here until Ted Benedict returned at eleven. Then he sat down at his desk, snapped on a light, and opened his Bible.

"How long, ye simple ones, will ye love simplicity, and the scorners delight in their scorning, and fools hate knowledge?" Wise old Solomon! Wearily Mr. Waddy rubbed his hand over his eyes. How long? Only until tomorrow morning, ten o'clock, even nine. Judge Deever was an early riser, and Wakeley wouldn't dally about getting the court order.

Pulling the telephone toward him, Mr. Waddy fingered the dial. He dialed one number, then broke the connection. Outside on the avenue Lombard's jalopy started up with a loud series of reports. Loyalty was a touching thing. Although sometimes misplaced. Again Mr. Waddy picked up the phone and began to dial. Vince Barron, having about as rancid a nature as any human being ever possessed, might not understand or appreciate loyalty; but he had always leaned on it, taken it as his right from his friend Henry.

The Bible had flipped shut. Mr. Waddy's eyes rested on the worn black cover. In his ear the bell ringing in a far-off room made an insistent summons.

Like a diver out of ocean depths, Lizette struggled out of sleep. The ceiling light was on full in her eyes and someone was shaking her awake.

"Cut it out," she mumbled, "Le' me alone." And she tried to roll over to bury her face in the pillow.

But the shaking went on.

"Liz, wake up! You've got to tell me where she is!"

"Where who is?"

"Jinny."

"She's out on a date. Turn off that dam light!"

"Liz, she didn't go out with Roger! Come on, wake up!"

Determined palms slapped her cheeks. Fighting them off, Lizette came awake. Tony was crouched on the side of the bed, her round face anxious.

"We can't find her anywhere, Liz. She's skun out."

"Maybe she didn't like the looks of Roger."

"She didn't even take a peek at him. I felt sorry for the poor guy, stood up by two girls in one night. He sat in the mush room nearly an hour, waiting."

"And Jinny didn't show up?"

"No. And she looked absolutely ambrosial. She was all ready when she came out to . . ."

Tony broke off as if someone had knocked her breathless.

"Came out to what, Tony?"

"To answer the phone. Oh, Liz, that couldn't have anything to do with her disappearance, could it?"

Chill fingers ran down Lizette's spine. "Maybe you'd better tell me the beginning, the middle, and the end. What phone call?"

"It was for you. I answered first."

"Who was it?"

"I don't know. A man. Come to think about it, I didn't like the sound of him one bit!"

"Now don't imagine things, Tony," Lizette said sternly. "Why didn't you call me?"

"Because you'd left a note on the board, no calls. I let out one yell and Jinny came running and said she'd take it. And—that's all."

That was all. A call from a strange man who didn't sound nice. And this afternoon there had been Evvie's talk about her brother-in-law's opinions, and a heated discussion about friendship—I'd do anything for Liz, Jinny had said—and tonight she was gone.

"You're thinking something, Liz," Tony accused. "You're scared!"

"What is there to be scared of?" Lizette asked, but she jumped out of bed and began to gather clothes. "What time is it?"

"Almost ten thirty."

"She goes on duty at eleven. I bet she's in Sybil's room right now, getting dressed. She doesn't want to disturb me."

"She isn't there."

"Maybe she left a note for me out on the board."

"No. I looked."

"Try over on the desk."

Tony bounced across the room. "I don't see anything. Boy, what a mess!"

She paused, frowning. "Liz, I just thought of something! If she took off the orchid dress, wouldn't that mean . . . well, she didn't intend to come back?"

Lizette, rummaging in a drawer for a clean slip, sat back on her heels. "Possibly. But where would she go?"

Tony gave a large shrug. "Sybil isn't in yet, either. I'll scan her closet."

"Grab me a cap from somebody, too, will you? Mine has spinach on it."

Tony bounded away. Lizette began to put the buttons in a fresh uniform. But her fingers trembled so badly she made slow headway, and a peculiar emptiness began to stir at the pit of her stomach. Would it bode ill or good if the orchid dress was in the closet?

"Not there," Tony reported, coming in to toss a cap on the bed. "That's one of mine."

"Then she'll be back. She'd never risk a demerit for being late, much less a whole flock of them for absence."

"Not with the queen business coming up," Tony agreed. "Why didn't we think of that before?"

The assurance, however, had worn thin by the time Lizette reached the nurses' station on pediatrics. There had been no telephone call from Jinny frantically begging that Liz cover up for her until she could arrive, no note found hidden under a pillow or under the dresser scarf or pinned to the stuffed rooster. Lizette tried to work up a defensive impatience over Jinny's nonappearance. Anything was better than the fear that swelled and grew with every minute.

Poppy, going over the charts with the relief nurse, merely glanced up as Lizette came in.

"You're on the small end tonight, Carter. I'll let Johnson take the big kids."

Lizette nodded and said something. She and the aide could do all right since most of the young patients were asleep. Jinny could appear with an armful of diapers and the only reprimand would be for not reporting to the station when she came on duty. With any luck, it wouldn't occur to Poppy to inquire when she actually had come.

But a half hour went by and Lizette finally met Poppy head on in the utility room. Poppy came straight to the point.

"Where's Johnson?"

"Jinny?"

"Virginia. Your dear friend and roommate. I'm sure I'd of noticed if she was here. Something would of gone wrong. Is she sick?"

"No. Anyway, I don't think so."

"Just having herself a night off? Looky, this idea of putting in extra hours was hers, not mine, and I'm depending on her. I told the aide with the drinkin' husband not to come tonight."

"I'm sorry, Poppy. But Jinny'll get here."

"Well, if I have to dig her up she's gonna get a demerit."

Poppy filled a hot-water bottle and tipped it expertly to expel the air. Lizette, watching the water rise in the neck, made a sudden decision.

"She's gone, Poppy."

"Come again?"

"She got all dressed up for a date and then she disappeared."

"Got scared of the guy? Well, if that's it we won't be too hard on her. I sure remember my first glimpse of the character I married." Poppy slapped the bottle. "But with Jinny that Gooseberry Festival's so all-fired important. . . ."

"Blueberry."

"I could keep her from even seeing a blueberry, for this performance."

"It would break her heart, Poppy!"

"I know it. Well, let's make us a quick novena of nine minutes, see if St. Anthony can put a bug in her ear. I can't give her much longer."

"Midnight?"

"O.K., midnight."

"Poppy, you're a friend in need!"

"It's my Irish grandmother."

But midnight came and passed, and no one but an orderly came through the swinging door to pediatrics. Poppy, meeting Lizette at the station desk, glanced up at the clock.

"Time's run out, Liz. Five after."

"What will we do?"

"Call the nurses' home. I don't think she's there, but try. It'll be less official, coming from you."

Lizette made the call. Neither of them was surprised when a sleepy girl said no, Jinny hadn't come back. Poppy picked up a pencil and tapped on the desk absently.

"I could wring her neck sometimes," she said slowly, "but you've gotta admit she's the soul of faithfulness. Something big, fat, and important has sure come up, bigger'n the gooseberries. The question is—what?"

"Poppy, she took a telephone call for me. From a man."

"Swiped a date on you, you mean?"

"Not like that. Tony said he didn't sound a bit nice. But Jinny talked to him, and that's the last anybody saw of her."

Poppy leaned forward, her knees spread, and a button skipped off her uniform and across the floor.

"Liz, we might as well face it. Last night a woman was killed here, tonight a girl's missing. Maybe they have nothing to do with each other, but . . ." She spread her hands eloquently. "If Jinny's—well, in trouble, then the demerit won't count. And if she isn't, she deserves one. I'll give Simon a jingle."

Lizette stretched after the button and her face was hidden from Poppy. "Does it have to be—I mean, why not the police?"

"Oh, ducky, Sister would never forgive the slight to her authority if I called the cops on my own!"

"You'll wake the whole convent."

"So what?"

Poppy reached for the phone. Down the hall a child cried.

Lizette jumped up. "There's that little Phelps demon. I better get him quick. Poppy, make it as light as you can, won't you?"

But Lizette knew, just as Poppy did, that the facts couldn't be lightened. For how could you minimize the fact that a girl who was the soul of faithfulness, who wouldn't risk her cherished reign as Blueberry Queen for anything in the world—that girl had thrown faithfulness and caution to the winds and was unaccountably missing?

10

Sister Simon sat with the old scrapbook open on her lap. She was not looking at it. Her hand lay on the pasted clippings, her eyes were unseeing upon the pillow where her tired head should have been resting for the past two hours. Her shoes stood side by side at the foot of the bed, but she still wore her black habit. Her mind was filled with what she had just read. "It's all here, dear," Sister Joe had said. And no doubt it was, if you knew what to make of it. Two tragedies, both accidental, had touched Dannie Grear, changing the course of her life completely; and twenty years later Dannie herself was murdered. In every life the present is somehow the harvest of the past. How often her policeman father used to say that! Was it possible that here, on these brown old pages, the planting of the deadly seed was recorded?

I don't really want to know, Sister Simon thought; yet her eyes again sought the headline, "Hunter Accidentally Shot Near Beechwood Falls, Brother Missing," and underneath it the smaller line, "James McArthur, Fourth Fatality of Season." Somebody named Willis Lawrence had also disappeared on the same night Jim McArthur was shot. The reporter ended with a remark about the awful toll of lives during the deer hunting season. So impersonal in print, so hurtfully personal to Elizabeth and Diane. And Dannie?

Out in the hall the telephone rang. The nun was instantly on her feet. In the daytime the ring would be a routine interruption, but at night it was the sharp rap of emergency. Sister Simon made such good time that she cut off the third ring. It was Poppy. Virginia hadn't come on duty. No one had seen her since sometime around six thirty.

"Then she didn't come back?" the nun asked needlessly.

"Back from where, Sister?"

"I met her at the door at a quarter to seven. She didn't say where she was going."

"Well, all we know is she took a telephone call intended for Lizette, and then she disappeared. I think you better call the police, Sister. She's sure not staying off of her own accord, not with that blueberry business coming up."

"I'll call Wakeley."

It was all Sister Simon could say because the pounding of her heart was suffocating. She stood for a long minute staring at the newel post, trying to get her breath. So she hadn't been mistaken about the fear in Jinny's eyes. The girl had been on her way to do something that frightened her to death. . . . To death? Would there be another headline tomorrow or the next day, "Body of Missing Girl Found. . . ?"

Her trembling hands dropped the phone book, and she at last fumbled out Wakeley's number. He answered in a voice thick with sleep.

"If she's out on a date, wouldn't that explain it? Kids lose track of time."

"Not Virginia. And she was afraid! I saw her go!"

There was a short pause. When Wakeley's voice came again it had snapped to attention.

"All right, Sister. I'll get out a bulletin and then I'll be over to the hospital. Give me a rundown on what she looks like, what she was wearing, anything that would help us spot her."

The description, the nun knew, was the merest outside of Jinny. What had happened on the inside to make her disappear? Was it something concerning the call she had taken for Lizette? Was she still running, her lovely orchid dress billowing out? Fleeing away from something . . . or toward some person or thing only she knew about? All the policemen and highway patrolmen and sheriff's deputies within two hundred miles, Wakeley was saying, would be alerted, they'd find her, don't worry.

"Thank you," the Sister said, and hurried back to her cell to put on her shoes. She was out in the hall again when she stopped, turned back, and took the old scrapbook from the bed where she had dropped it. Then, with it under her arm, she went noiselessly out of the convent and over to the hospital. Come to the visitors' waiting room on the first floor, she had told Wakeley. The room was dark and empty. Going on to the switchboard, she instructed Evvie to call pediatrics and ask Poppy to come down.

"O.K., Sister," Evvie said, but she didn't reach for the plug. Her brown eyes were wide and frightened, and her midnight sandwich lay in the wax paper with one bite out of it. "Sister, couldn't we maybe lock that front door at night? It's awful public, I mean, any-body can come in. I mean . . ."

"There's nothing to be afraid of, Evvie," the Sister said sternly. "Dannie Grear's death had no connection with us."

"Well . . . but where's Jinny?"

"She'll be back. Now don't worry."

"The cop's comin' though, ain't he?"

Sister Simon pressed her lips together, decided not to call Evvie down for listening in on her telephone conversation, and answered briefly, "Yes, he's coming."

"That darn ivy is what bothers me, that's what it is!" Evvie went on. "We were talking about it this afternoon and I was telling the kids how it swung . . . Sister! There it goes again!"

The delicate tendrils were swaying above the arch but there was no sound of anyone entering, an eerie performance indeed if one were alone, and watching.

"Don't be so silly, Evvie! It's Chief Wakeley, naturally."

The Sister said it firmly enough. But she was not totally without doubt herself until she came right to the door of the waiting room and saw the Chief switching on a light. The good solid size of him was most heartening. Even in the self-containment of the convent, she thought as she seated herself on the brink of a settee, there was a certain dependence on the strength of a man.

Wakeley was alert and fresh, his black hair smoothly shining and every button properly buttoned.

"Now about this girl," he began, and stopped when Lizette appeared in the archway. "Oh, Miss Carter."

"Poppy sent me, Sister," said Lizette. "I know more about this than she does."

"Of course, dear. Sit here."

She patted the settee; but Lizette dropped into the nearest chair. The Sister clasped her hands on the scrapbook in her lap. If the tight, quick way in which the girl began answering Wakeley's questions was any indication, she was very near the breaking point. How sinful was my neglect, Sister Simon thought as she listened. I should have had a talk with her today. This tension is my fault. Yet, with the development of the story, another reason for the tension became evident: the girls, Evvie in particular, had been very certain that Lizette herself was in danger.

"Because the man—whoever killed Dannie Grear—might think I saw him on the water front and I could identify him. But I can't! I didn't see anyone suspicious!" Lizette's voice shook to a whisper. Her hands were so tightly clenched that the knuckles were white. "And Jinny said she would do anything for me, and then this call came and I know it's what sent her out, wherever she's gone. And he's done something to her, that's why she hasn't come back! She *cant!*"

Wakeley took out his pencil. "Did anyone else know about the call?"

"The girl who answered the phone. Tony Burke. She'd just got out of the shower so she called Jinny. I was asleep."

He wrote the name on a folded paper.

"You can't just write things!" Lizette cried. "Don't you understand, he'll kill her if you don't find her right away!"

"We're looking for her already, Miss Carter. But it might help if we knew why she went off."

"I've told you why! She's protecting me!"

"Possibly so. Well, we'll know when we find her."

Wakeley shoved the folded paper into his pocket and made a movement to rise.

"Officer," Sister Simon said, for it was now or never. "Officer, have you looked into Dannie's past at all?"

"Of course, Sister."

"And what did you learn?"

"She had a very routine life, clerked in a store in Beechwood Falls for eighteen years, some friends, nothing out of the ordinary."

"But farther back than that?"

"She grew up here in the Narrows, went to school, the usual thing."

"Do you know about the accident—two accidents, really, that placed Diane in her care?"

"The girl herself mentioned them."

"It's more important than a mention." Sister Simon tapped the picture of Niagara Falls on the cover of the scrapbook. "Sister Joseph—she was Mother then—kept clippings from the local papers. There's something here, I'm sure of it!"

"You may be right, Sister. There's always a high road and a low road to the solution of every case. I could dig into the past and probably in the course of time come up with something, but it would be a long process. In the first place I'd have to hunt up everybody connected with Dannie Grear—how long ago was it, twenty years? And they're scattered to the winds, maybe even dead. That's the long road. The short cut is to find out who followed Dannie up here from the water front. Somebody saw him, somewhere. The suitcase and purse are somewhere, too. So . . ." Wakeley spread his hands, palms up, "find the suitcase or the purse, or a witness who can give us a clue or two, and there we are."

"Or find out where Jinny went," Lizette added. "That would be the shortest cut of all!"

"It's a possibility, Miss Carter, nothing more." The Chief made another movement to rise.

"Please!"

Sister Simon was faintly surprised at the urgency of her own exclamation, a surprise she saw reflected in Wakeley's pause.

"Yes, Sister?"

She felt her cheeks growing warm. Why should she hesitate to put her theory before him? Hadn't she heard tales of the detection of crime from her father in place of bedtime stories ever since she could remember? He might knock her idea into a cocked hat, but . . .

"Will you listen just a minute, please?" she begged. "It's all in my head, so I can tell you quickly. Jim McArthur was Diane's father, the one who was killed in the hunting accident. And the same night, Jim's younger brother, Steve vanished. Steve had been with the hunting party."

"If you have all the clippings, Sister, you know what happened to him. Seven or eight years later, some geologist out on a scouting expedition found his skeleton in a ravine. So if there was any suspicion attached to Steve, that's where it ended."

"But the other tragedy—Diane's mother Elizabeth burned to death. And only three weeks later!"

"In a fire that swept in from the woods. Half the countryside was aflame that fall, one of the worst years in history for forest fires. No, Sister." Wakeley got to his feet this time. "No, it was just one of those things. The only connection with Dannie Grear was that the double tragedy landed the baby in her lap."

"Dannie was in the convent at the time. She left to care for Diane."

"Too bad."

He said it casually. The emotional conflict involved in such a decision was beyond his ken. If he had a thought at all it would probably be that with Dannie's departure Mother would have been short of help to scrub the floors. A rush of explanation flooded to Sister Simon's tongue—but what good would it do to try to explain to a nonbeliever at one o'clock in the morning?

The Chief said good night and took himself off. Over in the corner Lizette got up, ready to fly away.

"Lizette."

"Yes, 'Ster."

The nun rose and walked across the room to face the girl. Lizette remained looking down the hall as if something of great importance had caught her attention, but there was no heart, really, to her stiffness. She's ashamed, the Sister thought, ashamed and obstinate and terribly hurt. Her eyes were red from crying. Jinny was her friend.

"Lizette, I was reading St. Augustine tonight. About duty. He says, 'In doing what we ought we deserve no praise, because it is our duty.' And the reverse is also true. In doing what we ought we deserve no blame. Think about it, dear."

Lizette pressed her lips tight together. But she was not being stubborn now, she was trying hard not to break down. The nun went on evenly, addressing the urn out of which the ivy grew.

"I believe the Chief is wrong. It seems to me the real short cut is through this." She tapped the scrapbook which she held in her folded arms. "If we could find out why, then surely we would know who. There must be a link somewhere."

As she spoke, something teased her memory, perhaps a name she had skipped over in her reading. Frowning in concentration, she sat down and opened the book. She scanned the first of the clippings which was the bare report of the shooting accident. Nothing there. But at the end of the second article the names of the other hunters were given. Her finger stopped under the last.

"For goodness' sake!"

"What is it, Sister?"

"Henry Waddy! He was one of the hunters!"

"Henry Waddy?" The girl dropped down beside the nun. "Sister, he must have been a good friend of Dannie's! Ted told me the poor old guy was absolutely knocked out when he saw her on the stretcher. Do you think . . . Sister, what do you think?"

I'm thinking how blessed it is that the barrier between us has fallen, the nun might have said. But she shook her head.

"I'm not thinking anything yet, Lizette. But couldn't it be that he's our link?"

"Oh, but he wouldn't kill her!"

"He might know who did."

"He couldn't be mixed up in murder! He's so gentle and so cute. . . ."

"And so worried. We were at the mortuary tonight, Sister Joseph and I. And Mr. Waddy was . . . not frightened. . . . Heartsick, that's the right word. Sick right to the heart."

"And you think it was about Dannie?"

"I have no way of knowing. I'd soon find out if I could talk to him. Only how could I?"

"I can talk to him, Sister."

"Of course you can."

Sister Simon responded almost automatically. But you don't send young girls chasing after possible clues to murder. You call up the policeman—the policeman who already has said he will not delve into the past?

"We're talking foolishness, dear," the nun said, closing the book. "This is definitely no business of ours."

"We've made it our business because we both feel guilty about not helping Dannie."

Before the Sister could gather her nice assortment of facts concerning duty, Lizette hurried on.

"Whether we admit it or not, it's true, and the only way we'll get to feel better is to *do* something. And it would be so easy, Sister!" The girl laid her hand on the Sister's arm. "My boyfriend, Ted Benedict, is Waddy's night man, and I can stop by and ask for him. He'll find a casual way to talk to Mr. Waddy. There'd be nothing to it, Sister!"

"Well . . . but when can you go?"

"As soon as I'm off duty. Ted said he'd be over at seven. He'll go back with me."

"Make it a little earlier, then, and catch him before he leaves. I'll come and help Poppy for that last half hour."

"Oh, thank you, Sister! Now tell me what to ask Mr. Waddy."

"All about the accidents, both of them. Who went on the hunting trip, exactly how Jim McArthur was shot, everything he knows about the fire. And about Steve."

"I don't see where Steve comes in," Lizette said. "Anyway, not after they found his bones."

Not after they found his bones. The little phrase hung in her mind as Sister Simon went back to the convent. Steve was dead. The geologist couldn't have run across his bones unless he was dead. Steve belonged to the past. In the present there was a more immediate concern: knowing that Mother Richard would never allow even the slightest participation in a murder investigation, was she begging the question of obedience by sending Lizette to talk with Henry Waddy? St. Augustine, it seemed, had the answer. She had read it this evening. "Let the superior be obeyed like a mother, with all due honor, so that you offend not God through offending her." But how could Mother be offended through a short friendly conversation she would never hear about? For that was all it would amount to. Kind, benign Mr. Waddy would assure Lizette that the stories were exactly as stated in the clippings, two regrettable accidents, and Chief Wakeley would go straight along his high road to the solution of the mystery. Lizette herself would know the satisfaction of having done something for Dannie Grear. And Sister Simon would share the satisfaction.

Sighing deeply, she closed the cloister door behind her. In four hours the rising bell would ring. The only thought she would carry to bed with her was the reassuring one that the chip had fallen from Lizette's shoulder.

11

The morning, at twenty minutes to seven, was ideal summer. Hurrying across the river bridge, Lizette was only half conscious of the clean air and the quiet. She was thinking as she had been doing all night of Sister Simon and of Jinny. The police had not called, and their silence spoke loudly that no trace had been found of the missing girl. Her thoughts concerning Sister Simon were not so well defined. She should have understood the nun's adherence to duty, for very often she was overscrupulous herself. But when the rules hurt *you,* that's when they should be relaxed. Not for anyone else, only for you. And because the Sister hadn't made an exception for her, Lizette was bitterly resentful. That was most unfair. Still, when you remembered that the exception might have saved Dannie's life . . .

Lizette looked up abruptly from the pavement, for she was not going around that narrow, exasperating little race track again. Main Street was unnatural without its crowd of vacationers. The mind reader's tent on the portico of the Nickelodeon Palace was fastened shut. Down at the docks the excursion boats lay with their awnings furled and chairs tipped upside down on the decks. A solitary dog barked among the trailers, a few trucks roared by, pigeons walked cooing and nodding after yesterday's popcorn in the gutters. In the shooting gallery, wide open to the street, a colored boy was doing a lackadaisical job of sweeping. Farther along a girl with her head tied up in a bandana was giving a swish or two to the windows of the launderette.

"Oh, hi," the girl said as Lizette approached.

"Hi," Lizette replied, wondering at the quick friendliness. "You're up early."

"The guy I work for, he runs you day and night." The girl drew the squeegee down the window and wiped the blade. "Did your friend have a good time last night?"

"Wonderful," Lizette said without thinking.

"I was hopin' she would. She sure looked elegant."

Lizette stopped, her heart doing sudden flip-flops. "What friend?"

"Gosh, I dunno her name. The blondie. You an' her were both on duty in that do-it-yourself unit when I was in for X rays last spring. Always together, you two."

"And you saw her last night? *Here?*"

The girl nodded. "She said she was goin' out on a date."

"What on earth was she doing in the launderette?"

"She come for the suitcase. The woman sent her."

"The *woman* sent her?"

"Well, I dunno, I guess she said the woman couldn't come, I guess that was it. Anyways, she wanted the suitcase so I give it to her."

"What did it look like?"

"Kinda paper. Real light." The girl leaned on the handle of the squeegee. "Hey, was it hers all the time? Was she elopin' with the guy?"

"I really don't know."

"Listen, you all right? You look terrible."

"No, I—I'm just surprised. I never thought of her eloping." Lizette hardly knew what she was saying. She must get to a telephone, call Wakeley. "Did she say where she was going?"

"What's the good of runnin' away if you tell everybody?"

"That's right. And she was in a hurry, I suppose?"

"Oh, sure. Nervous, too. I sure hope the guy's good to her."

"He'd better be!"

The terrible conviction that the guy was not being good to Jinny started Lizette on a run up the hill toward Waddy's mortuary. The girl called after her, but she only waved her hand. She had to reach Ted before he could leave for his date with her. He would know what to do.

Her running steps carried her up the green matting and on to the welcome mat. Panting, she pressed the bell. Soft chimes sounded inside. She waited through an impatient minute. Then, since the door remained closed, she tried the knob.

Afterward she would remember that the latch was not quite caught. The door opened noiselessly. The hall was empty. Sunshine streamed through the windows of what was apparently a drawing room and touched the first of the nice gray steps leading upstairs.

"Ted?" Lizette inquired softly.

No answer. Judging from the very deep silence she was the only living soul in the entire building. The only *living* soul . . .

"Ted!" she called, but it was barely a whisper.

She could step back to the porch and keep pressing the bell until someone came. But ahead, tucked in behind the stair well, was a small doorway. The door stood open, showing light within the little room. Probably an office.

Lizette went forward, her steps dropping noiselessly on the gray carpet. She came into the little open door, and stopped.

Taking up most of the space was a casket, bronze finished, lined with pale pink. In the casket Dannie lay. Ted had described her well. You couldn't believe, looking at her, that she had died by violence.

Why, she's beautiful, Lizette thought, and moved a little farther into the room. Several chairs had been placed facing the casket. There was a red plush prie-dieu, and at the foot of the casket on a pedestal was a marvelous pink cyclamen in full bloom. Together, these things took up most of the space.

But not all of it. On the carpet between the chairs and the dark drapery of the casket truck lay a man, face down, his gray curls partly hidden by the velvet folds. He was very still. Beside him a red stain had spread in an ugly blot.

Somebody began to scream, long piercing screams that hurt Lizette's head. She didn't realize they were her own until Ted rushed in, said something, and caught her to him. She began to cry then, hysterically, and she clung to him until he picked her up and carried her out into the big room where the sunshine was.

"All right now, take it easy, honey, take it easy," he kept saying, but his voice shook.

He put her into a big chair and began to rub her hands.

"Liz, darling, maybe there's something I can do for him, maybe he isn't . . . Calm down, will you, honey, so I can go?"

"Go where?"

"Just to the phone. I've got to call a doctor. I'll be right here in the hall."

"Wakeley! Get Wakeley."

"O.K., I'll call 'em both."

Lizette felt Ted pat her hastily on the head and collapsed sobbing against the chair arm. Mr. Waddy was dead. Like Jim McArthur. And Elizabeth. And Dannie Grear.

And Jinny?

"Oh, no, no, no!" Lizette sobbed into the chair arm.

Out in the hall she could hear Ted talking frantically to Wakeley. Today, tomorrow, some day the same kind of call would be made concerning Jinny because the man with the gruff voice had lured her away. He had told her to pick up the suitcase at the launderette. It was a dangerous mission. And now Jinny was missing in the place of her dearest friend, Lizette.

"I believe," Sister Simon said, tapping the scrapbook in her lap, "I firmly believe that the whole thing dates back to here. Henry Waddy was the link, you see. His death proves it."

Lizette shook her head slowly. The nun had sent for her and Diane, and the three of them sat on the screened porch of the Octagon House. They were going to sift back through what they knew for facts that would fit together, Sister Simon had said, through what was in the scrapbook and what Lizette had seen of Dannie on the water front and all that Diane remembered of her aunt. Somewhere there must be an answer to this terrible puzzle. But the bees were making lazy attempts to draw honey from the blossoms of the moonseed vine and their humming was like a sedative to Lizette.

"How does Mr. Waddy's death prove anything, Sister?" she asked, and her voice sounded far away, as it did in dreams.

"Someone must have been desperately afraid of what he might tell."

"Something about Aunt Dannie?" Diane asked incredulously. "Sister, if you think . . . you just don't understand what she was like . . ."

"Nothing personal, dear. But I'm absolutely convinced that she and Henry Waddy were killed for the same reason, because of something they knew."

"But what could it be?"

Diane was like a peevish child, pale and on the verge of tears. We're all going to be like that, Lizette thought, if we don't stumble out of this quagmire pretty soon.

"They're all gone now," Sister Simon said, "all the men on the hunting trip, so we have to find another link if we can. Think hard, dear. Was there any friend, man or woman, about your aunt's age who might have known her through the past twenty years?"

"Nobody, Sister. Nobody except Mr. Barron."

"The lumberman? Vince Barron?" Lizette asked. "But he's . . . I mean . . ."

"He's a millionaire several times over. I know. And Aunt Dannie was poor as a church mouse. But he was her friend. He even came to see us quite regularly when I was small."

"But not lately?"

"How could I know that, Liz? I've been here at school."

"I wonder," the Sister said slowly. "I just wonder if he knows the same thing, whatever it might be, that Mr. Waddy knew, and Dannie."

Diane looked at her with wide eyes, started to speak, then suddenly jumped up and ran down the steps and away across the lawn. The two who remained on the porch watched her until she disappeared around a lilac bush.

"Sister," Lizette said after a moment, "Mr. Barron was a friend of Henry Waddy's. Ted mentioned him, what a strange sort of man he is. If he knows whatever this is, he could be the next victim."

"Yes. Or the murderer."

A bee worrying the last drop of nectar out of a moonseed blossom made a very loud buzzing. It seemed the most important thing in the world to Lizette that she wait until he had buzzed on to the next flower.

It took him a long time to finish.

"I'd like to go to see Mr. Barron," she said then. "I'd find out very casually where he was last night, because if he has an alibi so he couldn't possibly have had anything to do with Jinny's disappearance, or with Mr. Waddy's death, then he isn't the murderer. And he deserves a warning."

Sister Simon moved, easing herself in the chair. "He has an office, doesn't he, somewhere in town?"

"Straight over from the bank. You can see it, going to Waddy's."

"Well . . . then go in daylight, Lizette."

The girl smiled. "I'll be a student writing a term paper on the lumber industry, Sister. That ought to open him up. From what I've heard, it's been his whole life."

"Don't mention Dannie Grear. Or Virginia."

"I won't unless he does."

"Are you sure you want to do this, Lizette? You look so tired."

"I'll rest when I get back."

But there would be no rest for her until Jinny was found. Hurrying back to her room, changing her dress, giving her hair a dash with a comb, Lizette wondered how to begin her interview. A write-up for the school paper, perhaps that would be better. Still, how could she wind around to the vital question of where were you last night, Mr. Barron?

When she climbed the steps to the dismally bare house, Lizette was as fluttery as she had been on her first day in surgery. On the glass of the door in large gold letters was the name, "Barron Timberlands, Inc." Barron the millionaire, the little store clerk Dannie Grear, gentle Mr. Waddy, and young Jinny from the backwoods—how in the world could they all be linked together? And was the count three dead and one to go?

Lizette grasped the door latch and pushed. The hall was dim after the brilliant sunshine, but no amount of light could have made it cheerful. The walls were papered in brown oatmeal and in the corner was an ancient umbrella stand with a clouded mirror. A worn rubber runner led to a narrow stairs going up into more dimness. Nearest Lizette was a door with a beveled glass bearing the name, "V. W. Barron." There was darkness behind it. While she hesitated, wondering whether to knock, a door opened down the hall, seemed to be on the point of closing again, then swung barely wide enough to let a woman through. She was stocky and middle-aged, and she looked Lizette up and down, perhaps not with hostility but definitely taking her measure.

"Good afternoon," she said. She had a good voice and she was all competence, her hair cut like a man's, her blouse plain and very clean, and her shoes flat-heeled. Lizette felt frivolous in contrast. Mentally she stammered over the possible beginnings she had rehearsed on the way and found none of them adequate. Directness would be the best possible line with this person.

"I'd like to see Mr. Barron," she said. "If he isn't busy."

"Mr. Barron has not come in yet."

"Oh."

The only thing to do now was to leave. Or else state her business bluntly.

"I'm Lizette Carter, a student nurse at St. Matthew's. Diane McArthur is one of my friends." She paused, then since the woman showed no reaction she added, "Dannie Grear was Diane's aunt."

"I see."

It came casually enough, yet something changed in the woman's demeanor. She had not been smiling before, but now she looked as if she never had smiled in her life.

"And why did you wish to see Mr. Barron?"

Take the plunge, Lizette decided, get it over. "Diane said he was a friend of her aunt's, and I just thought . . . perhaps I should have come yesterday?"

"You'd have had to make it early. He's been gone since yesterday morning."

So Vince Barron was out of town when Jinny was lured away. He could have been the gruff voice on the telephone, but Tony would have known if it was a long-distance call. And if he had nothing to do with Jinny's disappearance, he wouldn't be involved in the death of Mr. Waddy, either.

"What is your business with Mr. Barron?"

"Sister Simon thinks—and so do I—that all this trouble about Dannie has come out of something that happened twenty years ago.

And since Mr. Barron was a friend of hers, he may know whatever it was she was killed for, and so he may be in danger, too!"

It was an impulsive confidence. The moment she had finished, Lizette wondered whether she had been wise. But if the disclosure was startling, the secretary gave no indication. With a quick nod, she led the way back to the open door, stood aside for the girl to enter, and then, although the silence seemed to imply that they were alone in the building, she closed the door.

"Sit down," she said.

The room had most likely been one of the double parlors of the old home for a wide archway had been filled in with compo-board, and steel filing cabinets were ranged against it. On top of the cabinets were piled folders and papers of all kinds. More folders were stacked on a big square table. The desk behind which the woman seated herself was littered; but it was an orderly litter, and it occurred to Lizette that this was the office of the executive rather than the other behind the darkened door.

"I'm Alice Armstrong," the woman stated. "I've been Mr. Barron's secretary for eighteen years. Now what's this about him being in danger?"

"We don't really know. The hunting party is the only . . ."

"What hunting party?"

"When Diane's father was killed. Jim McArthur. He and his brother Steve and Henry Waddy were deer hunting. It was an accident. Steve disappeared, afterward."

"And where does Dannie Grear come in?"

"She was a sister to Jim's wife, Elizabeth. Then when Elizabeth died in the fire only a short time later, Dannie took the baby, Diane, to raise her."

Lizette paused. Miss Armstrong was listening intently, her gaze on a glass bubble paperweight containing two cows in a barnyard.

"Dannie was a nun at the time of the fire," the girl continued. "She hadn't taken her final vows. She left in order to care for Diane."

"So that's why he gave them the house," Miss Armstrong said.

Lizette caught her breath. "The Octagon House? You mean Mr. Barron gave it to the Sisters when Dannie left?"

"When she entered. Twenty-two years ago." The secretary turned the paperweight upside down, then righted it, and watched the snow fall around the cows. "I found the record of it. I wondered why . . . he's not a specially charitable man . . . he wanted to think he provided a home for her, I suppose."

"But why?"

"You know the date today? August seventh. Every year on this day he'd go to visit her. Don't ask me why because I don't know . . . or do I?"

"You mean he was in love with her?"

"Why not?"

"From what I've heard of Mr. Barron, he wouldn't fall in love with anybody!"

"Nobody ever knows the why of loving someone, do they?"

Lizette fastened her gaze again on the cows. Was it possible that Miss Armstrong was in love with her boss? And Barron wouldn't even suspect it. He was too busy chasing after a woman who was so tangled up in something or other that she'd got herself murdered.

"He never mentioned Dannie Grear to me, naturally," the secretary added. "It's not a thing you'd discuss with somebody like him. Or me."

"Then how did you know about her?"

"A cousin of mine up in Beechwood Falls lived with Dannie for a while after Diane left to go to school. Nettie Julian. She's dead now." She picked up a pencil and drew a large X through the date on the calendar. "Who is this nun you mentioned?"

"Sister Simon. My supervisor."

"Is she doing some sleuthing on her own?"

"Not exactly. But Chief Wakeley doesn't feel that this business of the hunting accident has anything to do with Dannie and Mr. Waddy, and Sister Simon does. And since Mr. Barron was a friend of Dannie's . . ."

The secretary shoved away the calendar and rose. "I wouldn't worry about Mr. Barron. He can take care of himself. As for his friendship with Dannie Grear—well, he's paying her funeral expenses. Maybe if I stick with him long enough, he'll do the same for me, who knows?"

Lizette, letting herself out into the hot sunshine, thought hastily back over all the woman had told her. It wasn't evidence, exactly. The only real fact that emerged was the gift of the Octagon House to the Sisters, but Barron even in those days was a very rich man and the timing with Dannie's entrance into the convent might have been coincidence. According to Miss Armstrong, and Diane also, he had visited Dannie through the years. But it might not have been because he loved her. He could have been threatening her, too.

Down on the sidewalk, Lizette looked back up at the square, unlovely house. Barron was a good name for the man, that was what his life had been. And Miss Armstrong's must be barren, too. I wonder, Lizette thought, I wonder why I didn't mention Jinny to her? Quickly she turned away and hurried along the tree-shaded street.

Over on Main Street, Lizette turned left along the high walk which topped the retaining wall. People hung as usual against the railing, looking down on the park. She glanced toward the docks. The *Triton* was out. Ted would be declaiming the wonders of Stand Rock about now. On the portico of the Nickelodeon Palace the mind reader sat before his purple tent. He wore the garb of his profession, the white satin shirt and Paisley vest badly in need of cleaning, the orange turban dark with perspiration around the edges. The newspaper he held before him was a rather incongruous note. He should be gazing into a crystal ball. But he was not reading the newspaper, Lizette noted. He was looking past it, down at her.

She stopped. The man's eyes returned instantly to his paper. Merlin the mind reader had been present during that crucial time when Dannie had been so frightened down on the water front. And his client, Jinny, would certainly be known to him if he cared to remember her.

Rising, he stooped to pick up the stool on which he had been seated.

"Just a moment, please," Lizette said impulsively, and mounted the steps.

The mind reader paused, turning to her, his expression blank.

"I wonder if you'd remember the woman who was murdered? Dannie Grear? You were there that night, by the river."

He shook his head, the gold hoops dangling against his fat jowls. "I am seldom anywhere but here."

"Oh, but I saw you! You were on the stairs, and she was looking at the mud figures."

"I go many times to the park."

Lizette hesitated, wondering if she should remark the contradiction. "You must remember Dannie. She was so pathetic, lugging her suitcase. And frightened. Someone down there frightened her. I thought you might know who it was."

Merlin's eyes went to the stool he was folding. When an edge of canvas caught in the joint, he extracted it carefully.

"A mind reader does not glance over a crowd and read everyone's thoughts."

"But surely you remember her!"

"I see hundreds of people in a day."

Lizette was exasperated. He was not answering her questions at all, neither was he lying. She would try one more shot in the dark.

"Then you wouldn't remember my buddy, either. Jinny Johnson. She's come to you a couple of times this summer to have her palm read, but there's nothing remarkable about her. She's just—Jinny."

"Then why do you mention her?"

"Because she's missing."

Lizette thought later that she must have imagined the slight flare of alarm that crossed the man's face. He did not bother to reply. But it was with almost too much nonchalance that he proceeded into his tent. The first section was wide open, furnished with a dirty piece of carpet, a table holding a crystal ball, and two chairs. Inside, he raised another flap into an inner compartment, and Lizette had a glimpse of an unmade cot.

Slowly she went on down the long hill. The bridge had been built in the days of carriage traffic and the two lines of cars meeting one another nearly touched fenders. The sidewalk was too narrow for comfort. When the ambulance siren began to wail up on Main Street, Lizette hugged the rail. Even the ambulance could not pass swiftly here, and she had a good look into it as it went by. There was a sheeted figure on the stretcher and a white-coated attendant seated beside it. On the second seat was the woman Lizette had seen only minutes ago, Miss Alice Armstrong, who knew nothing of the whereabouts of her boss, which was strange, for the man on the stretcher could be none other than Vince Barron.

12

Sister Joe was not taking her customary pleasure in her little card game, and she was disappointed in herself. For years now, ever since she had educated Sister Jude to be her partner, she had looked forward to the recreation hour. Tonight, because the day had been so troubled, her anticipation had been even keener than usual. But something was wrong. She peered out over her spectacles at the assembled Sisters, thirty of them, all with lips moving in speech or laughter, all working at knitting or embroidery or jigsaw puzzles. The television was on, showing a pretty girl singing, but singing was just people opening their mouths when you couldn't hear. Sister Vitus was ripping her crocheting again, the same chalice design that Damian had been using for the altar cloth. . . .

Taking up the cards, Sister Joe began to shuffle them in long fans that appeared to rest in mid-air like a magician's trick. Frank had taught her to shuffle that way. It was he who had taught her to play cards back in the days when she had gone from one lumber camp to another collecting hospital insurance from the lumberjacks. With that money, St. Matthew's had made its beginning. Frank used to joke about it. Everything was funny to him. The sight of a nun dealing a poker hand was a huge joke. She never had played for money, of course, and never with anyone but Frank, her own brother. Those had been great days. Often, when the cook was sick or they were between cooks, she had turned in and fried the bacon. . . .

Sister Jude kicked her lightly under the table. Mother Richard had come in. Sister Joe lowered the cards to the conventional shuffle. Mother knew about the poker. She had participated once in a while before she had become superior, and she had been a reckless player. But now they all pretended she knew nothing about it. Not that there was a thing wrong with a game you played with buttons. Poker just sounded a little racy for a convent.

She dealt the cards expertly.

"Sweeten the pot, Sister."

She must have spoken too loudly because Sister Jude jumped and put her finger to her lips. The old nun's eyes went again around the circle. At times such as this she would have liked to hear, for Mother appeared to be telling something of high interest. Touching her thumb to her tongue, Sister Joe began to deal. Later, perhaps, someone would tell her the news. If not, she could offer the sacrifice of her curiosity for the poor souls.

"You open, Sister," she said.

The game began. But Sister Jude was so erratic in her playing it was difficult to tell what she meant, and finally she laid her cards face down on the table.

"Are you calling, Jude?" Sister Joe asked. "If you are, that's no way to go about it. Frank always said . . ."

"Sh!"

The old nun understood that well enough. She might as well gather up the buttons. Sister Jude's attention was gone from the game. Snapping the cover on the button box, she pushed back her chair and plodded out of the room and down the stairs. She was tired tonight. A half hour's reading in bed would send her off to sleep.

The lumberman had built his house well, but Sister Joe's tramp sent a shiver through half the cloister. The only light was a spare glimmer in the ceiling. All the doors were open upon oblongs of darkness. Except for one. In the third oblong from the end on the right there was a flash. Lightning? Sister Joe stopped. If she could feel the vibration of the thunder, then the storm was close and she would go back upstairs. Nothing happened. The light did not show again. Sister Edmond had sinus and was going to bed early, that was it. Everyone left her door open these hot nights. The old nun trudged forward. Perhaps Edmond would like some hot ginger tea.

SISTER SIMON'S MURDER CASE

The room, as she looked in, was dark hut against the grayness of the window she could see that the plain white bed was unoccupied. The curtains, clipped neatly back with clothespins, left the window available for any passing breeze. There were no screens on these windows because the wide porch was tightly screened. Sister Joe grunted. Lightning, it must have been.

And then, just as she was turning away, a black blot began rising against the lightness of the window, cautiously, slowly widening into shoulders and an arm braced against the window frame.

"Who's there?" Sister Joe boomed.

The figure swayed. There was something eerie in the way it remained poised half above the sill, featureless, incredibly quiet. Then, for no apparent reason, it began to sink away.

"Who is it?" she demanded again.

If there was a reply, she did not hear it. Never in all the years she had been in the convent had there been an intruder; but this person must be one. If he had legitimate business, why did he not come openly to the door and ring the bell?

For a long minute the old nun remained still, listening so intently that her fingers were pressed to numbness against the door jamb. Even the black blot of the head had disappeared now. There was nothing to indicate anything unusual had happened except the tingling sensation running along her spine.

Shutting the door with a slam she could hear herself, Sister Joe lumbered down the hall and out into the lobby, turned back to dip her finger in the holy-water cup, started up the stairs, and walked into her habit as she had not done since she was a novice. Jerking the habit out of the way, she ascended at a speed that brought her panting into the recreation room.

"Mother!" she boomed, and everyone jumped to face her. She still held her scapular clutched up in a bundle and she folded her arms across it. "Mother, there's a burglar in the cloister! In Sister Edmond's cell! He came through the window!"

She might have added something about calling the police but the Sisters, having waited mere seconds for Mother to lead the way, were already pouring past. When Sister Joe again reached the landing, the long stairs was a waterfall of waving veils being rapidly siphoned off into the cloister.

She came in with the last trickle. The door she had closed now stood open. Mother had turned on the light. Nobody was under the bed. The closet held nothing but Sister Edmond's other habit and her winter cloak and rubbers. The only proof that an intruder ever had been there was a dark smudge on the wall under the window.

"I don't wonder he's gone," Sister Joe observed. "He wouldn't stand around waiting to be caught."

No one answered her. Vaguely she could catch the word police. Mother was going to call them. It was the proper step. But they wouldn't find him. There had been so much trouble over Damian, perhaps this was part and parcel of it all.

Sister Joe went into her own cell and closed the door. Things she would just as soon remember were completely gone out of her head, but Damian's letter haunted her. She couldn't even forget where she had put it. Pushing aside the curtain of her closet, she looked up at the shelf. There it was, her new forgetting book, *Uranium Prospecting in Northern Minnesota*. She wouldn't take it down tonight. And possibly by morning she would have forgotten the letter.

Seating herself in her rocker, she took out her rosary.

Sister Simon came into the Octagon House just as Mother Richard hung up the telephone after calling the police. A prowler, the nuns babbled excitedly, had been in the cloister and goodness knew what might have happened if Sister Joe hadn't discovered him.

"There's even fingerprints on the wall!" young Sister Pius twittered. "Come and see!"

"We don't know why he'd want to get into the cloister," said Sister Jude. "We've never had a burglar before!"

"He could have mistaken it for the nurses' home," Sister Pius suggested, "only what would he be after there, either? He ought to know the girls don't have any money!"

"It wouldn't be money," Sister Simon murmured, already on her way out. The prowler could very well have mistaken the Octagon House for the nurses' home.

Out in the dark, the Sister began to run. Vince Barron had been admitted to the hospital this afternoon, unconscious from a bad concussion. The ambulance siren had barely sighed into nothing when Lizette, returned from her errand, had come hurrying up to pedes with a nervous account of a strange interview with a secretary who insisted Mr. Barron was out of town and yet a few minutes later was seen accompanying him in the ambulance, and of a second disturbing little conversation with Merlin the mind reader. Jinny was gone. And now Lizette?

Sister Simon was panting like a long-distance sprinter when she threw open the door to Lizette's room. Over by the window, in the dark, someone was seated. She snapped the light switch. In the sudden brightness Lizette blinked, then turned to bury her face in her arms on the sill.

"Sorry, dear," the Sister said, and flipped the switch again. "We'll have the lamp on instead. Why are you sitting here in the dark?"

"I'm thinking."

Turning on the small study lamp, Sister Simon glanced immediately at the window screen beyond Lizette. It was intact. He could have reached her so easily, sitting there. . . .

"What are you thinking about, Lizette?" the nun asked casually.

Lizette, still resting her head on her arms, faced the Sister. She was as pale as Diane had been in the afternoon, with the same drawn look, her dark eyes too big.

"I was thinking how unfair life is, Sister. Awful things happen to other people, but for me everything is perfect. I get along in school, I have a wonderful boyfriend, my folks are so good to me—but look at Jinny! She had a miserable life at home. Even if she graduates she'll be a terrible nurse, we all know that. The only bright spot was being Blueberry Queen. . . ."

She stopped, hiding her face again.

Sister Simon looked around the room. All of Jinny's clutter had been cleared away, her bed smoothly made, her stuffed rooster rakishly perched on the pillow. Deliberately the Sister sat down on that smooth bed and caught at the spread to wrinkle it a little.

"The only answer I can give you, Lizette, is that we aren't in a position to judge the fairness of life. There's an old story, you must have heard it, about a man who stood watching a nun scrubbing a floor, and he said, 'Sister, I wouldn't lead your kind of life for a million dollars.' And she smiled and said, 'Neither would I.' The purpose is what counts, you see. Jinny feels that she is really getting somewhere, she's not a bit sorry for herself. And there's a place for her in nursing. Couldn't you imagine what a comfort she would be to a bedridden old lady?"

Lizette straightened, smiling through tears. "What a dear thing to think of, Sister."

"Much more will be expected of you. So take your happiness and be thankful for it."

"Oh, I always am! Like yesterday morning. Ted and I had such a perfect time on our picnic up in the Gorge. A little boy came along with a rusty old gun over his shoulder and had breakfast with us. Ted told him the gun had undoubtedly belonged to Wyatt Earp, he even pretended he could see the initials on the stock, W E instead of W L. . . ." She paused, frowning. "That's been bothering me, Sister. Why should W L ring a bell?"

"It does with me, too. I seem to see it in print. What have I been reading lately? Sister Joe's old scrapbook?"

"That's it, Sister! Remember, right at the end of the clipping, it mentioned the other hunter who was missing, besides Steve McArthur? Willis Lawrence!"

"Where did the boy get the gun?"

"He said he found it in the river."

"Do you know his name?"

"No. Ted called him Jim Bowie. And the initials are changed now because Ted made the L into an E. For Wyatt Earp." Lizette rose, to lean on the end of the bed. "Sister, could this have any connection with the hunting accident?"

"I don't see how it could." But the nun spoke as if the breath had been knocked out of her. "No, of course not. Willis wasn't hunting with Henry Waddy's party. How could there be a connection?"

She was protesting too much, she well knew. But she couldn't look squarely at the terrifying possibility that had popped full fledged into her mind.

"You're thinking of something, Sister," Lizette accused her. "Something you're not going to tell me."

"Are you trying to be a mind reader, too, dear?" Sister Simon looked at her watch. "Nine o'clock. You can sleep for at least an hour and a half before you go on duty. And you should do it, Liz, you look tired."

"All right, Sister, I'll try."

The girl was puzzled and not quite pleased, the nun reflected as she hurried away. But far better to leave her that way than with nebulous imaginings. The only certain sure fact was that Willis had lost his gun.

The Sister, however, fled through the alley at such a pace that her stiff skirts made a clatter in the echoing old place. In the convent the Great Silence had begun and there was no sound except a few footsteps. There would be no more conversation until breakfast time. Sister Simon went straight to her cell and took the scrapbook from a drawer in her writing desk. Turning quickly to the page she had perused so often in the past hours, she ran her finger down to the bottom of the clipping. There it was, Willis Lawrence was missing. He had been on a deer hunting expedition with several people, among them his brother Bartholomew.

Returning to the hall, the Sister closed the cloister door tightly behind her. No one would hear her using the phone. There were several Lawrences listed in the telephone book, two of them Bartholomew, father and son because one of them was Junior. She dialed Senior.

Her heart thudded as she listened to the ringing, one, two, three—and the line opened.

"Hello," a woman's voice said.

"May I speak to Mr. Bartholomew Lawrence, please?"

"Just a moment."

Now what in the world would she say? She should have taken a few minutes to think this out carefully.

"Mr. Lawrence speaking," a man said into her ear.

"I'd like to get in touch with Willis Lawrence," Sister Simon told him. "I understand he's your brother."

There was a small hesitation. "Willis disappeared twenty years ago. We never knew what became of him. What did you want to get in touch with him for?"

Sister Simon would have given anything in the world if she could have dropped the telephone like the teen-agers who make bother calls and hang up as soon as you answer; because there was someone coming quietly through the long corridor from the front door, and the tread was unmistakably Mother Richard's.

"I believe something belonging to Willis has been found," Sister Simon said hurriedly. "I'll call you tomorrow morning. Good-by."

She did drop the receiver then. Poor Bartholomew, he would lie awake wondering who owned this voice out of the past; but she couldn't explain about a gun, not with Mother crossing herself at the cloister door, waiting for her. She should not have called Bartholomew in the first place; but Chief Wakeley would make light of this new clue, if such it could be called, and besides there was still her own lingering sense of guilt concerning Dannie's cry for help which she had not permitted to be answered. She couldn't dwell on her doubts, especially to a person who never had been mentally tousled herself. Mother would simply repeat her reassurances. Leave murder to the police. For yourself, sift the facts sensibly and you will see you did right, then forget it. With only a nod, so as not to break the Silence, Sister Simon followed Mother into the cloister.

In her own cell with the door closed, she could not shut off the terrible conclusion that was not merely a hunch any more. The facts were too indisputable. Willis Lawrence had not returned because he was dead. His gun had been found in the river. A skeleton, presumably that of Steve McArthur, was discovered in a ravine some years later, but the only identification was superficial, a watch with Steve's initials. The watch belonged to Steve. He had put it where it was discovered—on Willis Lawrence's wrist.

Slowly the nun walked over to the desk and gazed down at the clipping. Jim had died, Elizabeth had died—not by accident, either of them. Dannie had known that their deaths had not been accidental. Henry Waddy knew it. Vince Barron could be suspected of knowing and so an attempt had been made on his life. There was only one answer: Steve had come back. And the awful chain twenty years long would not be broken until he was found.

With the musket against his shoulder, Eddie skulked rapidly up the Witches' Gorge. He had to do his skulking rapidly because it would soon be dark and he was not supposed to be here at all. His mother had finally put her foot down. It was his own fault, in a way, because yesterday morning he had forgotten all about the time, with Ted carving the initial on the gun and telling stories about Wyatt Earp, and it was long past noon when Eddie got home. Mom had been worried sick. Anything could happen, she said, out in those hideous ravines. He could fall down a cliff and lie there with a broken leg until he died, she said, and all they'd ever find would be his bones. It was the end, she said, to the kid running wild. So now he would have to do his skulking when she didn't know about it, and this evening was his first chance. His mother and dad were gone somewhere, and Janet was on the front porch with her goony boyfriend and not caring a bit what her little brother did as long as he kept out of sight. And hearing. There was just about time for a quick trip through the Gorge.

It would be great, Eddie thought, if he could dally along until the last bunch of settlers came through the draw and say hello to Ted. Only he wasn't sure that Ted would be the guide, and he didn't dare stay away long enough to be missed. He'd better just bring down a few squirrels and head for home. Crouching on one knee, he sighted along the lofty top of the ravine. Nothing moved but a few ferns away up against the sky. His thumb rubbed softly at the initials on the stock of the gun. He'd thought so much about Wyatt Earp, after Ted's stories, that it almost seemed as if the weapon had really belonged to the famous frontiersman. It sure was a dandy shootin' iron.

Down the ravine behind him, Eddie heard a woman's high-pitched laugh. Settlers. Or Indians. He hadn't expected them in this neck of the woods. Hide, that's what Wyatt would do, until he'd see whether this was friend or enemy. Up ahead, just beyond the narrow turn they called Fat Man's Misery, was the old glacial cell he had explored the other day. Duck in there and he'd be safe. He could even pick off a few Indians as they filed by.

Laying the gun on the sidewalk, Eddie swung under the railing, took up the gun again, and on his knees backed into the circular cavity in the rock. It was a lot bigger than he'd thought before. There was a lip coming down and partly blocking the entrance; but right inside, the ceiling was nearly high enough so he could stand upright. Toward the back it curved down like an igloo, with a rounded wall. . . .

Eddie, pivoting on his knees, was suddenly motionless. He was not alone in the cell. A girl lay with her back against the wall, sound asleep. Out in the draw, the woman settler laughed again.

Lizette had turned off the light and lain down, but there was no way to turn off her thoughts. Staring up at the shadowy ceiling, she could see Sister Simon's pretty face, bewildered, even a little frightened. Exactly what the nun was thinking she could not quite deduce, for her head felt like a musty attic jammed full of the remains of things; but one fact she did know for sure: Sister's sudden brain wave had been inspired by the gun. The gun which had belonged to Willis Lawrence.

Lizette sat up, battered her pillow into another shape, and lay down again. She was not going to be shut out of making any discovery that could possibly help either to find Jinny or to throw light on the situation concerning Dannie and Henry Waddy. One obvious contribution would be to find the gun. She could do that very easily. At eleven she would go on duty, and Ted would have returned to the mortuary. She would call him and suggest another picnic up the Gorge in the morning. He'd agree, for he was more than ready to do anything she wished, these days. Jim Bowie had had such a good time yesterday morning with them that there was more than a possibility he would happen along again. And if he shouldn't come, Ted would think of a way to get in touch with him. Then they would borrow the gun. Sister Simon—or the police—could take it from there.

Sighing heavily, she closed her eyes.

Eddie watched the girl for a full minute. She was a real pretty girl. She had blond hair and it was fanned out over the dark rock, and her dress was about the color of Mom's lilacs last spring. Eddie didn't know whether he should wake her up or not. She certainly couldn't be very warm in this damp room. She'd catch her death of cold, lying there like that with no coat on.

"Hello," he said. The girl didn't move, so he said it louder. "Hello!" Still she didn't wake up. He inched over on his knees and touched her shoulder. It felt ice cold through the thin dress.

"Hey, listen, you're gonna get pneumonia," Eddie told her, and he gave her shoulder a small push against the wall. She rolled back a little but her arm, bent to lie along the rock, stayed in the same stiff position and on her dress, where her hand had been, there was a dark brown stain. Like the stain on the bandage when he'd cut his thumb so bad with the hatchet.

Eddie snatched back his hand. He had seen only one dead person—Grandpa, and he had looked like he was alive in his casket, only better. He suddenly was very sorry for this girl. Nobody would say like they did about Grandpa that it was a blessing she was gone, she had suffered so much. She was so pretty she ought to be alive. And somebody grown up had to come, not just a kid.

He scuffled over to the opening. The settlers were right at the curve. He could hear the guide explaining about the glacier, but it wasn't Ted's voice. While Eddie hesitated, other feet began to go by, girls' and men's and everything. And then a cautious thought struck him. He was not supposed to be here in the Witches' Gorge. Let him tell those people there was a dead girl in the cell and they'd never just say thanks, go on home now. They'd ask what's your name, how did you find her, where do you live, and his folks couldn't help hearing about it. Then he'd sure have some tall explaining to do. He could have trusted Ted. Ted would have worked out something to save his skin. As it was, he sure was in a pickle.

Shivering, his knees icy as the girl's shoulder on the cold rock, Eddie crouched in the dimness while the feet filed by. He didn't know what to do. It didn't seem right just to go off and leave the girl because nobody else would go diving into this place and she'd never be found. Nothing would hurt her, though, because animals didn't come down here from the forest above, there was nothing to eat for them, Ted had said so. Gol-*lee,* why hadn't he stayed home tonight and maybe crawled around under the porch and listened to Janet and the boyfriend if he'd wanted something to do? Only Mom had made him promise never to do that again after the time he'd choked with laughing and given himself away.

Eddie drew a long, trembling breath and hugged the gun. If he could figure out what Wyatt Earp would do in this case, maybe that would be the answer. Of course things were a lot simpler for Wyatt, not having folks to demand where in the world were you. Still, for other reasons he had to do things on the q.t., like when he was chasing outlaws and didn't want them to get wise to the fact that they were being trailed. If he'd discovered the girl while he was on a ride like that, and couldn't let anyone know he'd found her, he'd—well, wouldn't he lead somebody else to do the discovering all over again?

"You betcha!" Eddie whispered aloud. "You just betcha!"

The whole scheme fairly blasted out of his head. He had a beat up old crayon in his pocket. All he needed was a piece of paper, and he knew where to find one. The only chancy part was that he'd have to be out a little later than he'd planned, but Mom was going to mark up a hem for Aunt Margaret and that always led to more sewing talk, and Janet would be so glad he wasn't pestering that she'd never think of stirring him up by looking in his room. He'd be safe for quite a while yet.

The last of the feet went by and the voices drifted out of hearing, up the draw. The settlers wouldn't be coming back for a while, plenty long enough for what Eddie had to do. Scrambling out, he piled loose rocks in the open archway. The girl would be protected, and the rocks would be a landmark for Ted, doing the discovering. Then all he'd have to do would be to get the paper, write the note, a thought which sorta frightened him because he wasn't any good at spelling, and wait for the boat to depart from the landing at the foot of the Gorge. The waiting was so the wrong guy wouldn't get the note. It had to be Ted. And Ted, he knew from experience, would be the first guide up here tomorrow afternoon. He'd be sure to see the note, where Eddie would stick it.

He almost whistled as he ran down the sidewalk. Things were mighty easy when you worked them out like Wyatt Earp.

13

At one o' clock in the morning the water front was as quiet as it would ever be. The jukeboxes had stopped their blaring, the skates were all hung up in the roller rink and the rifles racked in the shooting gallery. Except for a big semitruck rolling down the hill to the bridge, Main Street was clear of traffic. The man trudged along the high sidewalk, his head down. Without the orange turban and in baggy tans, he was an inconspicuous figure. At the top of the boat company's fine stairs he glanced quickly up and down the street, then let himself down a careful step at a time to the river-side park. Cutting across the brown sod to the cluster of trailers, he went straight to a small, weatherbeaten one, knocked, and without waiting tried the door. It did not open. A fierce barking began inside, a voice swore, and the barking subsided to a growl.

The mind reader put his face close to the keyhole. "It's Smith. Let me in."

The voice swore again and muttered something about the middle of the night, but there was the creak of a bedspring and in a few moments the sound of a key turning in the lock. The man didn't wait for the door to open. Pushing hard, he slipped inside. The dog went into a fit of growling.

"Shut up, Barker!" Merlin snapped. "Lou, turn on a light before he takes a chunk out of me. Who does he think I am, a cop?

"You never know."

The light switch clicked. Even with her hair combed, Lou Tobias couldn't be called a good-looking woman. Routed out of bed, without the heavy make-up and in a crumpled housecoat, she was a hard-favored sight. Along her jaws was a stubble equal to Merlin's.

The mind reader tramped across to the davenport. Lou's trailer always looked as if she were having a rummage sale. Pushing aside some magazines and a bread wrapper, he sat down. He hated to say what he had to say, but after all it was what he had come for.

"I made a mistake tonight, Lou."

"What's different about that?"

He drew his sleeve across his forehead and looked at the dark streak. "I went out to the hospital."

"What for?"

"The girl. She's getting too close."

"And what were you going to do about it, Smith?"

"It was Pico's idea, not mine. Scare the daylights out of her, put her off snooping. But I . . ." He shrugged broadly. "Well, I picked the wrong place."

"How do you mean you picked the wrong place?"

Merlin's eyes went clear around the trailer, over the dingy bed, the sink filled with bottles, the cluttered table, and down to Lou's bare feet.

"I got into the convent and some old nosey caught me at it."

The dog had lain down and was licking a paw. Merlin watched him because he dared not look up at Lou. With a wide sweep of her arm she cleared a space on the table. A can of milk bounced to the floor and rolled, leaving a white path behind it. Barker stretched his neck to lick at the milk. Lou swung one leg up to half sit on the table.

"So you got into the convent," she said in a venomously soft tone. "You know what happens now? Now they'll put a cop there day and night. I told you we'd get around to her, but you can't wait! No, you gotta act, quick like an elephant, clumsy, stupid . . ."

Merlin spread his hands helplessly. "She was asking if I remembered the woman. Dannie Grear, Lou!"

"Well, what of it? You were there. So was I. So was Pico. So were a hundred other people. If you keep your head, we're all right."

"I had to do something!"

Lou, swearing quietly, dug a cigarette pack out of the mess on the table. "I run the shooting gallery open and above board, I make a production out of being respectable, I don't get in trouble with the cops, ever—and what happens? I'm in trouble up to my neck!"

"Not yet, Lou."

"What you mean, not yet?"

"Wakeley was here, he went away, didn't he?"

"He'll be back. He said we're all kind of a brotherhood, us carnies, we show up in the same places year after year, follow a route north in the summer, south in the winter. We'd stick together, he said."

Merlin gave a sour laugh. "How long would we stick together if we didn't have something on each other? Brotherhood, my eye!"

"Wakeley ain't a fool." Lou turned cold eyes on her visitor. "And mother's little helper, here, he comes along to make things double easy for the cop. You a mind reader? If you were worth your weight in garbage you'd still be a no-count bum!"

The dog leaped up, growling. There had been no knock but the doorknob turned. Almost with the turning the mud artist swung into the trailer. Lou showed no surprise. Barker went back to licking at the milk. The newcomer did not look as if he had been asleep. He glanced at Merlin.

"Oh, you," he said. "I saw the light. What's up?"

"More of same," Lou replied bitterly. "I'm sick of it."

"Too bad."

"It ain't grim enough we got cops diggin' around, this sharpie here, he's gotta crawl in the convent window!"

Pico threw back his head, roaring with laughter. "You're drinking the wrong brand again, Smith."

"What you laughing for?" Lou demanded.

Pico's face darkened. "I'll laugh whenever I feel like it, and don't you forget it," he said quietly. Going to the sink, he began to up-end bottles, tossing them in the direction of the trash box when he found them empty. Lou watched him in sullen silence. Merlin drew his tongue across his lips. It would have been so much better if he hadn't come here, he could see that now. He hated to be near Pico.

What if the fellow did hold the whip hand, he didn't have to be so brazen about it as he'd been lately.

"You and me, we're gonna have a talk pretty soon, Junior," Lou told Pico.

"What about?"

"Facts of life."

"Not interested."

"No?"

Lou jerked an empty sardine can toward her and ground out the cigarette. Going down on her knees, she shoved aside Merlin's feet, groped under the davenport, brought out a small, shabby suitcase and tossed it up on the pile of magazines. A sick trembling ran through Merlin. There was very little room for both him and the suitcase, and he drew away until he did not touch it. Lou sat back on her heels.

"Interested yet, Pico?"

He gave an insolent shrug. "That's your baby."

"What if I'm all through doing the dirty work?"

"Then I'd be ready to discuss the facts of life. Jailbreaks, for instance."

Lou's face turned beet red and she began to lumber to her feet, tripping on the housecoat. Merlin had been present during some of their brawls and he had no stomach for another. Squeezing past Lou, he brushed the sardine can off the table and stepped on Barker's paw; but he made it to the door and out. He'd certainly never talk to Pico like that, get him all riled up. Live and let live. Only things were certainly getting more complicated than they'd been in the beginning. . . .

Wiping his forehead, Merlin stood listening for the yelling to begin; but there were only a few gutturally vehement remarks and then silence. His nerves reached like antennae toward the trailer window. The sash was pushed out to let in air and there was a screen covered with a sagging curtain. He could see over the curtain if he could climb that high.

In the dark, being very quiet, he rummaged around until he found a washtub and a box. Turning the tub wrong side up, he set the box on top and mounted his perch. By stretching, he could see into the trailer.

The davenport was immediately under the window. Lou, facing Merlin, had opened the suitcase and was bent over it. Pico lounged against the sink, lazily lighting a cigarette, his beard like a shadow across his face. Merlin wanted to see what Lou was doing. He raised himself on tiptoe. Lou, bending over the suitcase, had let go of the housecoat and the front bagged open to the waist. The bare torso it disclosed was that of a man.

Merlin let himself down to the tub and then to the ground. He was always revolted somehow by any reminder that Lou merely pretended to be a woman. Good reason for a disguise, of course. Nobody would choose to go back to jail. But why not keep his male identity and go off to Siam or the North Pole?

Trudging away, Merlin tried to bring some sort of order out of his rattled thoughts. He was so keen at solving other people's problems, why not his own? He had tried, tonight. All he had accomplished was to arouse a conventful of women and make himself a laughingstock for Lou and Pico.

The river, at half past seven in the morning, was more quiet than it had been even in pioneer days. Then the still depths were rocky, murderous rapids where lumberjacks lost their lives breaking log jams and Indian canoes were caught in the eddies and whirled to pieces. Now in the great backwater above the dam there was only the tiny splash of oars as Ted rowed along. The swallows, although they appeared to be numbered in the thousands, made no slightest sound as they swooped low over the water after bugs or winged back to the cliffs honeycombed with their nests.

"You'd wonder how they all know which hole is theirs," Lizette said. "Do you suppose they ever get mixed up?"

"And feed the neighbors' wife and kiddies by mistake? I doubt it," Ted answered. "Instinct is a pretty trusty commodity."

"Instinct such as the birds have, maybe. Not ours."

"Like what?"

"Like self-preservation. That's what keeps our murderer going. He's killing now to protect himself."

"Could be. But you can't attribute killing to an instinct. That's using his intelligence, and he's gone berserk."

"Ted, if he's killed Jinny . . ."

"Let's not cross that bridge yet, honey."

Lizette trailed her fingers in the cool water. It was a shame to spoil the morning with talk of murder. But all night long she had run to listen every time Poppy answered the phone, hoping it was some word about Jinny, but none had come. She wasn't doing much, going after Jim Bowie and his gun, but it was better than nothing. Today would have to bring something in the way of a solution to Jinny's disappearance, it just wasn't possible to go on and on, waiting. Today, up in Marshlands, they would be having the Blueberry Festival. Without Jinny.

The little boat rounded a bluff and slid up beside the dock where the excursion boats stopped for the trip up the Witches' Gorge. Ted threw a rope around a post and tied it firmly. Then, with one foot in the boat and the other on the dock, he held out a hand to Lizette.

"Come on, lady. All ashore that's going ashore."

Lizette stepped out beside him. Above them, on top of the bluff, was the barny structure where the tourists bought coffee and postcards, its shutters closed at this early hour. A narrow path led past the flight of steps and immediately into the Gorge, the entrance used by all the guides. Starting along it, Lizette came to a sudden stop. In the middle of the path lay a small rock, and from under the rock protruded a folded piece of paper.

"What in the world . . ." she said, and stooped to push aside the stone. "Ted, it's a map. And it has your name on it!"

The lettering was done in crayon, "Ted," with a very crooked E.

"Some kid. Let's see, Liz."

The map was the printed sketch of the river and the tributary gorges which was given away free up above in the coffee shop. There was usually a box of the maps outside the door. A note was written in crayon on the back.

"Dont say nothing becas I am not spose to be here but I found a girl she is in the cave with the rocks pilled up good. You look and see. A frend."

Lizette read the note over Ted's elbow.

"Ted, what cave? *Is it Jinny?*"

His hand had fallen flat on the writing, crumpling it into a ball. "Liz, now let's not go off the deep end. This could be just a . . . a joke. You stay here and I'll . . . Liz, come back!"

But Lizette was already off at a staggering run up the narrow sidewalk leading into the Gorge. She could hear herself sobbing in the same way she had heard herself screaming when she found Henry Waddy, almost as if it were someone else making the noise. Slamming into the railing where it turned suddenly, she slid her palm along it and felt slivers piercing in. There were no rocks piled up here, no cave, nothing out of the ordinary except the chill dampness that always seemed odd on a summer day because it made you see your breath in steam. She could hear Ted behind her, begging her to stop. Once he caught hold of her but she pulled away. Squeezing through the Fat Man's Misery, she bumped her head on an outcropping and the sharp pain was like a stimulant to push her along. It couldn't be far now to the end of the ravine. If someone had played a cruel joke they would soon know. . . .

"Ted!" she screamed, "there it is! The rocks . . . the rocks . . ."

Lizette threw herself between the railing slats and began to tear at the stones, breaking her fingernails, bruising her hands. It was not a joke. The girl was in the cave, the girl who would have to be Jinny. . . .

"Darling, let me," Ted urged, trying to be calm; but he sent the rocks rolling. Daylight filtered past into the glacial cell. In the dimness, a little grayer than Lizette had seen it before, lay a fold of the orchid dress.

The small boat floated downstream so close to the riverbank that at times it struck a willow root and careened sideways. Merlin, trying to keep from being dumped by the swift current, swore softly to himself. He was no riverman. He should have stayed ashore, walked, hitchhiked, anything but this. Only he had to do something inconspicuous, and the boat had seemed like the ready solution. It was the same boat in which the girl and Ted had made their hasty return from some expedition up in the other direction. Merlin, prowling restlessly through the back quarters of the Nickelodeon Palace, had seen their almost frantic landing, Ted's fumbling with the painter, the girl's rush away from him toward the stairs. He didn't know, then, what it meant. Later, he did. Pushing out his lower lip he blew, trying to cool his face. It didn't help.

He peered ahead through the willows. Other than to put as much distance as possible between himself and Wakeley, he hadn't thought of any particular destination when he started out, but the ghost town would do as well as anything. It had to be along here somewhere. The journey already had felt like fifty miles, so it must be at least two. The current slammed the boat against a protruding stump, yanked it free, and shot it around the bend. There, straight ahead, were the remains of a rickety old dock.

Merlin dug the oars deep. The boat, for once, went where he intended and came up with a whack against the pilings. He climbed out thankfully.

He had the boat tied before he remembered that anyone coming down the river, hunting him, would surely see the craft. Turn it loose and let it drift away—but he might need it again. Pull it up into the willows, that would be safe. Getting the heavy boat into the underbrush was hard work for his soft muscles, and his tan shirt was dark down the back before the task was done to his liking. He had to sit down then on the dock, for his heart was thudding as if it would burst. He must decide, before it was too late to go back, whether absence was a good idea. The empty tent would naturally draw Wakeley's attention. But flight didn't have to be an indication of guilt. It could mean you merely wanted to get away and think things over, get the proper perspective. Well, get it quick.

Merlin wiped his face, stood up, and peeled off his shirt. Dipping it in the water, he wrung it out and put it on again. But there was no real defense against the muggy heat. The cool morning had become sultry by noon, and now in early afternoon the sky was overcast and yellow, seeming to cup the heat down against the earth. Puffing hugely, he trudged up through the wide-open space between the willows and came into the ghost town.

Empty houses showed windows empty of glass and doors hanging by one hinge. The place had never been very big. There was supposed to be a sawmill somewhere. Coming to the first house he sat down in the gaping doorway and stared at the ground in front of him.

They had found the girl. He had hoped it wouldn't be so soon. Exactly how the discovery had come about he didn't know, but the young snooper from the hospital and the guide had made it. That was one of the things he had heard Wakeley throwing at Lou, back there in the trailer. Lord, if he'd walked in on Lou as he had had every intention of doing, there would have been the two of them in jail now, not just Lou. Merlin began to shake again as he had when he cowered outside the trailer, listening. Lou had stayed too long in the housecoat, for Wakeley had torn off the disguise. You could tell, from the things he said. And then he searched the trailer, not very far, either, because he came on the suitcase right away. Merlin squirmed out of the wet shirt. It didn't feel good any more. He couldn't sit still. Lumbering to his feet, the shirt dragging from one hand, he started up the desolate, dusty expanse that used to be Main Street. Homely weeds sprangled where people had walked. Some of them must have had problems. But not like his. For the first time in years he wondered if the new life he had taken on shouldn't have been something safe. Like plumbing. Mind readers found out things. It was an occupational hazard, in a way, that people would sometimes think you'd found out far more than you had. They never stopped to realize that their behavior broadcast their state of mind to anyone who observed them keenly. Fear, for instance. Fear was unmistakably easy to read. . . .

In the middle of the street, among ragweed waist high, Merlin stopped and looked around. Where was he going? There was no refuge here. Nothing to eat, either. An ancient sign that said "Cafe" lay on the ground, face up to the sky like a dead man. He looked back to where the willows half hid the dock. No refuge anywhere. And no return. Would he starve to death in this God-forsaken place?

"Merlin the Magnificent," he said aloud.

A small garter snake slipped out of the ragweed, flashed its forked tongue at him, and glided on. In the whole wretched town, he and the snake appeared to be the only things alive.

As he stood there, a raindrop hit him on the head.

Sister Simon stood at the foot of Vince Barron's bed and watched the man's uneasy, jerking movements.

"He's been doing that for the last hour," the special nurse said. "I haven't telephoned Wakeley. He said to let him know the minute Mr. Barron came around, but there's no use yet."

"He hasn't spoken?"

"No, you know how they do, Sister, coming out of a concussion. You'd think they were wrestling the whole human race. Maybe he's fighting off his assailant. He could have passed out, fighting, and he's just carrying on from there."

"It's possible," said the nun. "Of course, for him there has been no interval of lying here in the hospital. They don't know how this happened, do they?"

"I guess not, Sister. The secretary said she didn't go into his office until after noon, and then she thought he had come in while she was out to lunch and gone to sleep. Something he never did before. He's hardly the type for afternoon naps."

"But she didn't see anything wrong with him?"

"No. And there's very little mark on his head. The blow must have been made with a flat weapon of some kind."

"If it came from behind, he wouldn't know who hit him."

"Not even what, Sister." The nurse straightened the already straight sheet. She was a stout white-haired woman, handsome in her white uniform. "Well, Wakeley's hoping for some scrap of a clue. This is really a crazy, mixed-up mess, isn't it, Sister? Finding that poor kid up the ravine, honestly, you wonder who's next."

Sister Simon left, walked down all the stairs and out across the alley to the nurses' home. The answer to the question of who's next was almost too obvious. Everyone who knew Steve from the old days had been put out of the way. The only remaining threat was the girl who had seen him on the water front. But she couldn't know him as Steve! If only there was some way to reassure him! He hadn't waited, before, to have his fears quieted. He had struck, brutally and finally. Three times. Four, counting Vince Barron. Would it be five before the total could be counted?

The Sister tapped on Lizette's door, heard a faint answer, and entered. The girl sat in the little rocker, a notebook open on her lap. Rain was pelting in the window, making inky puddles out of the writing on the open pages.

"You're getting all wet, dear," Sister Simon said, and went quickly to close the window.

Lizette touched her own arm, then looked at her fingers as if she were surprised to find them wet.

"It's not a very good day for the Blueberry Festival, is it, Sister?"

The nun had to swallow hard before she could reply. "Just a shower, I expect. Where can I find a towel?"

"Jinny has a clean one. On the back of the closet door."

They didn't talk while Sister Simon dried Lizette's arm and dabbed up the water on the floor. All the odds and ends of Jinny's life were still around, like the clean towel she hadn't had a chance to use. Her stuffed rooster was perched on the pillow, a brush with a few blond hairs on the dresser, in the wastebasket the face tissues she had probably used, her clothes still in the closet. But her folks were on their way to town and they would take the little physical things that remained of Jinny, and every trace of her would be blotted away like the puddle from the floor. But Jinny was only an element of a greater entity. Sorrow for her must not obliterate the real concern, which must be for the girl who sat like a rag doll in the rocker.

Sister Simon dropped the wet towel beside the door and returned to stand before Lizette. She didn't quite know how to begin because she had no real idea of what she wanted to say. A policeman had brought Lizette home this morning because Ted was needed to lead the rescue party up the Gorge, and Dr. Barney had given her a sedative. Even with that, she had not slept well, Sybil reported, and the grogginess still persisted. Mother Richard had done the only sensible thing in telephoning Lizette's parents. And yet, if they should take her home as they would undoubtedly want to do, wouldn't the killer follow? Three hundred miles was a short span for one who had brooded twenty years. Wakeley might refuse to let her go—but he was on the high road—where he might not see. . . .

Trembling, the nun sat down on Jinny's bed and clasped her hands tightly in her lap. Dear Lord, she prayed, don't let this poor child see how panicky and confused I am! Send us a solution . . . anything . . . anything to end this deathly suspense!

"Ted called up," she said. Her voice didn't sound too bad. "He asked for me when they told him you were asleep."

"Was I?"

"You had a nice long nap."

"Is he coming over?"

"After dinner this evening, yes. He said the boats won't be going out, not in the rain."

Ted had said a good deal more, too—that things were so disorganized at Waddy's it was like an anthill stirred up, everybody going off on tangents. The old gentleman had been the heartbeat of the place and without him there was chaos. But if there was anything Ted could do for Liz, he'd be right over. No, nothing, the Sister had said. And that was so terribly true. Nothing to do—except preserve her from the killer. Jinny had tried to do that very thing. I can't go chasing around the water front, Sister Simon pondered, a nun can't do things like that. I can't draw him out of his lair. . . . But Lizette could. Why not concoct some scheme using her as bait?

The idea was so repugnant that the Sister got up quickly and walked around the bed. Lizette was not watching. She was staring down at the ruined pages of her notebook, so drawn and limp that she seemed to be as drained of life as Jinny. That she was in danger now seemed as certain as the rain beating on the window. The killer was bound to strike at her, and there was no knowing where or when. *But if the time could he chosen for him. . . .*

"Lizette," the Sister said abruptly, "Lizette, would you do something to bring about a climax to this terrible situation? It may sound to you as if it would be dangerous, but actually you'd be safer than you are right now because the police would be protecting you. . . . Would you do it, Lizette?"

Lizette's dark eyes did widen with apprehension, but she said evenly enough, "Sister, I'd do anything—and I do mean anything—to get even for Jinny. What is it?"

Sister Simon found she had to sit down again, for her knees were giving way.

"Let me explain a little, Lizette. We know quite a few things about this man, whoever he is. He's connected with the water front, we know that. Dannie was frightened there, you talked to the mind reader and immediately a prowler crawls in the convent window, the laundromat girl told you that Jinny headed toward the water front with the suitcase."

"And she'd have had to be taken to the Gorge by boat. It's the only way you can get there from town." Lizette's face went even whiter. "Sister, do you think she was dead when he . . ."

"Dear, let's not do that, let's stick to what we know. Bartholomew Lawrence, for instance."

"Don't you mean Willis? And I didn't get the gun!"

"It doesn't matter. I called Bartholomew, the brother, this morning. He said Willis was a quiet boy, always satisfied with his job and his home and his girl. He was going to be married. There was no reason why he should disappear. So the only answer is that he was made to disappear."

"Somebody made him run away?"

"No. He was murdered. It's Willis' bones, not Steve's that were found in the ravine. Liz, Steve is still alive!"

The girl sat motionless for a long minute. Then she closed the notebook and laid it on the desk beside her.

"So he's the one Dannie saw that night."

"I'm sure of it, Liz."

"But why was she so scared to death?"

"Because she knew he was a killer."

"You mean of Jim McArthur?"

"Yes, the hunting accident that was not an accident at all. Somehow Elizabeth knew what had happened, and so Steve sneaked back and killed her, too. Perhaps he didn't think of Dannie's being a menace to him, not at that time. And Henry Waddy might have been inaccessible for some reason. Steve couldn't linger around town, waiting. Elizabeth was the only one who would have done anything to avenge Jim, anyway. He must have felt safe with her out of the way. He even dared come back here now, perhaps disguised in some manner."

"And then Dannie blundered onto him. But how, Sister?"

"I don't know. He didn't quite succeed with Vince Barron, but it's obvious he has killed everyone else who he thought could identify him."

"Jinny, too!"

"Everyone."

"Except me."

"Except you. . . ." Sister Simon took a deep and painful breath. "And you can be the one to—to bring him out into the open."

"What would I do, Sister?"

"Make him strike again. At you. And the police would catch him."

Sister Simon was amazed at herself, really. When she took the veil she had put off her identity as a policeman's daughter. Mother Richard would never approve. St. Augustine might get a kick out of it, but not Mother.

The girl stood up. "I'm ready, Sister. You want me to go down on the water front—is that it?"

"That's it, Lizette."

"Now?"

Sister Simon looked past her to the window. The rain would have driven away the crowd from the water front.

"No, no," she said quickly, "when the rain stops. Tomorrow morning. I'll call Chief Wakeley and explain all about it."

"He'll never agree, Sister."

"Oh, yes, he will!"

But the nun wondered, as she hurried out into the hall, whether Wakeley would be so easy to convince. For the present she need not concern herself with a decision. Perhaps, before she would find it necessary to make that decision, Wakeley's high road might have led him to the solution.

She opened the outside door and was hit by a splash of rain. Why walk down the long alley, unprotected, when she could just as well keep dry by going through the hospital? She darted across to the basement door and let herself in. Perhaps because the little dark door of the morgue was the dominant feature here, this corner of the hospital always reminded her forcibly of Dannie's murder. The Sister glanced at her watch. She had a few minutes before prayers, time enough to look in again on Vince Barron. Scarcely a half hour had passed since she had seen him, but he could have regained consciousness in the meantime. With these cases of concussion, you never knew. The elevator was down. She stepped in and pressed the second-floor button.

The door of Vince Barron's room was open a few inches, and Sister Simon tapped lightly, then put her head in. The white-haired nurse, standing at the foot of the bed, nodded.

"He woke up a few minutes ago, but he's still groggy."

"Has he said anything?"

"Nothing coherent. I gathered that somebody bopped him when he was putting his car away last night. He could have been knocked out for a minute and then came to enough to make it into the house. Funny thing how a blow on the head can work that way, sometimes. One patient I had—here he comes again, Sister."

The nurse moved close on the farther side of the bed. Vince was stirring restlessly and muttering. Sister Simon bent over him and took his limp hand in both of hers. She was almost certain he had mumbled the name of Steve.

"You're awake, Mr. Barron," she said quietly. "Open your eyes . . . come on . . . that's right. What about Steve? Was it he that hit you?"

He tried to shake his head, and winced with pain.

"Don't do that!" the nurse said. "Talking won't hurt you. But don't move your head."

"Did you see him?" Sister Simon persisted.

"No . . . no . . . nobody . . . but Steve . . . Steve's the killer."

"Why? Can you tell me why, Mr. Barron?"

"Always was a brat, never worked. Jim worked for what he had, but Steve wouldn't. Took everything away from Jim. Wanted Elizabeth, killed Jim to get her . . . but she wouldn't . . . wouldn't . . ."

The man's eyes closed. Sister Simon shook his hand gently.

"Why did he kill Dannie? Dannie, Mr. Barron?"

"She must have known him . . . and Henry . . . too. . . ."

"Is Steve in town?"

The small sound he made could have been "no," but it also could have been the sigh on which he slid back into unconsciousness.

Sister Simon straightened, frowning. It would be cruel, as well as impossible, to try to waken him.

"That's why I haven't called Wakeley yet," the nurse said. "By the time he'd get here our man would be gone again. By the way, Sister, who's this Steve character anyway?"

"If only I knew!" Sister Simon murmured, and she left quickly. Vince Barron's confirmation, hazy though it might be, was the first definite proof that her theory was right. Now she must decide whether to send Lizette off as bait and perhaps catch the murderer red-handed, or not to send her and leave him free to kill again. . . .

The nun, hurrying as always, traversed the old corridors to the alley, ducked out into the rain, and a moment later was running up the steps of the Octagon House. She had stopped to stamp off the bits of leaves which clung to her shoes when the door opened and Sister Joe came out. She had been crying. Carefully held against her she carried a letter in an envelope that had obviously been handled a good deal.

"Read it," she said, and thrust the letter at Sister Simon. "I couldn't forget it, although I tried. Read it, Sister, and tell me what I should have done."

Puzzled, Sister Simon looked down at the envelope. It was addressed to Sister Mary Joseph, St. Matthew's Hospital. And it had been postmarked a week earlier in Beechwood Falls.

14

Lizette changed her dress quickly, dug into her shoe bag for an old pair of sandals, and tied a kerchief over her head. She started to pull on her raincoat, then folded it instead and laid it over her arm. Opening her door, she looked both ways down the hall. No one was in sight. As quickly as Jinny had run away in the orchid dress, Lizette fled to the door and out. Under the portico she put on the raincoat. Then, forgetting to button it, she ran with the coat ballooning out behind.

It was easy running down the hill. Traffic was heavy on the bridge, but not with pedestrians, and she flew across and up the long slant of Main Street. The mind reader's tent was closed and deserted, the roller rink booming with young people in out of the rain. There was business too in the curio shops along the street. But not down in the river park. Lizette glanced over it as she hurried along the high sidewalk. At the top of the stairs where Dannie had paused in indecision, where Jinny had stood feeling so safe and courageous, Lizette also stopped. The rain beat upon her face and streamed down like tears. She hugged the coat around her. Over at the docks the *Triton* and the *Nautilus* were moored, stripped of their pennants and with the chairs turned upside down. The ticket booth was closed. No more desolate place existed on the face of the earth than this small, soaked area beside the river. Go back home, Lizette decided, bank down this terrific urge to do something instantly for Jinny. Tomorrow morning would be time enough—only Wakeley would never give in. That was why she had felt it so necessary to rush away immediately. Sister Simon could be right about who would be next—Lizette herself. If he could see her here, alone, whoever he was, surely he would realize what a perfect chance . . .

But there was no use lingering. The place was empty. She turned, hugging the coat, her foot on the step above, when she saw that she was not quite alone. Down by the wall, sheltered a little by the overhang of the sidewalk, the mud sculptor was at work. Completely absorbed in the mound of mud under his hands, he was paying no attention to her. She could even hear him whistling softly.

For a long minute she watched him. He had been one of those present when Dannie had become so frightened. And Jinny had found him fascinating. Slowly Lizette sidled down the stairs.

The sculptor evidently didn't know she was there until he stepped back to view his work. Then he gave her a mocking lift of the eyebrow and went on with the tune he was whistling. Lizette had not been able to see what he was doing, before. Now it was revealed, the lovely head of a girl. No body, just the head. The eyes were closed but she was laughing, and her hair was fanned out as if she had just tossed it gaily. Around the face, unbelievably delicate when you remembered it was all mud, was a wreath of flowers.

"That's beautiful!" Lizette exclaimed.

He paused as if he hadn't heard distinctly.

"Beautiful," she repeated.

He lifted a shoulder. "If you like mud."

Tilting his head, he studied the figure. For all the interest he took in Lizette, she might as well not have been there. He stood in the rain until his black shirt clung wet to his big shoulders. Then he returned to his work, down on one knee.

Oddly disappointed, Lizette turned to the stairs. But on the third one up, exactly where Dannie had paused, she stopped. Something stirred in the back of her mind—something she had seen. . . . Whirling, she stared at the man bent so devotedly over his modeling.

"Pico!" She said it rather loudly.

He took his time, but he sat back on his heel, finally looking at her.

Her breath was short, but she had to get it out.

"Pico, why are you modeling Jinny's head?"

Sister Simon stared down at the letter in her hand.

"You want me to read it?" she asked.

Sister Joe nodded so vigorously that a tear halfway down her cheek slipped sideways.

"Yes, dear. And don't spare me if you feel I did wrong in trying to forget it. There are so many sins of omission as well as commission, and I—well, read it, dear."

Sister Simon let herself down on the edge of a rocker. Opening the envelope, she took out the letter. It had been written in haste, half the t's not crossed and the dots nowhere near over the i's. Its message was urgent.

"Dear Mother Joseph, I may be in the Narrows by the time you receive this. I haven't quite decided what to do. But I was there three weeks ago, as you will remember, and I *saw Steve.*"

Those words were underlined. The pen, from there on, had trembled as it wrote.

"I believe I'll go back to the river park and have another look at him, and then if I'm sure, I'll go to the police. He murdered Elizabeth. That was why she brought Diane to me that morning of the fire, she was afraid for her. She didn't tell me, exactly. She said she had had a visitor the night before, and she was expecting him again, and she wanted the baby out of the way. I know now it must have been Steve. He may think Elizabeth told me all about it, and that I have told Diane, so the only way I can protect Diane is to see that he's charged with murder. He has changed his appearance a great deal, but I'm sure I'll know, this time. Love, and pray for me. Damian."

Sister Simon's hand fell to her lap. Here was the evidence to give to Wakeley, the meeting point of the high road and the low! Before her Sister Joe stood, weeping quietly, her hands gnarled together in anxiety.

"Did it matter terribly, dear? Me trying to forget?"

Sister Simon had to shake her head. How could she say that the chain might have been broken in time to save Mr. Waddy and Jinny?

"It didn't make one bit of difference," she said with all the confidence she could muster. "But it will help now. I'm going to telephone the policeman right away."

She smiled, taking the old nun by the arm to lead her inside, and Sister Joe's relief was pathetic. The central lobby was deserted. From up in the chapel came the needle-thin chanting of the Sisters at prayers. Old Sister Joe, unable to hear it, was not reminded of prayer time. She sat down on the stairs and mopped her wrinkled cheeks with her handkerchief.

Sister Simon dialed the number she had come to know by heart in the past few days. A young policeman answered and summoned Wakeley. She read him the letter.

"That's good, Sister," he said as she ended, but without the elation she had expected. "It ties up the loose bits. We've got the guy under lock and key. I gave you a ring a while ago but they couldn't locate you—yeah. All we need is his confession."

The nun was surprised at herself for feeling deflated. "What a relief!" Then with all the enthusiasm she could gather, she asked: "Who is it?"

"I don't suppose you know Lou, the woman from the shooting gallery? That's hardly your beat. Well, Lou is a man. He hasn't admitted a d—, a thing, but the fingerprints will sew it all up. We got his prints and a whole slew of others off bottles and stuff in the trailer, so as soon as we get the identification on them from Washington we'll round up his playmates, too. This was a toughie, Sister. It's a great feeling to have it licked. Tell Lizette she can sleep for a week now, nothing to worry about. She's safe."

"Indeed I'll tell her," Sister Simon promised. "Congratulations, Chief."

She laid down the telephone and nodded and smiled at Sister Joe. In a minute she would write it all out for her, every detail, and reassure her again. But right now she would call Lizette.

She dialed again. A girl answered. The Sister asked for Lizette.

"But if she's asleep, don't wake her," she added. "I have some very good news for her, but it can wait."

"Did they catch him, Sister?"

"Practically."

"Oh, boy, wait till I tell her!"

There was the clatter of the phone being laid down. The interval was rather long. As the minutes went by, Sister Simon grew impatient. Surely it wasn't too much to expect the girl—it had sounded like Tony—to come right back. She could imagine butterball Tony perched on Lizette's bed, chattering away. She was ready to hang up when a voice finally came,

"Sister? I'm sorry I took so long. I was hunting Liz, but she's not here."

"Not there? Tony, where did you look?"

"Well, in her room and the shower room, and Hazel is just in from the cafeteria and she wasn't over there. I can't imagine . . . just a minute, Sister." There was a murmur, then Tony again. "Sister, Jean says she saw her leave a while ago. She had a bandana and a raincoat. Maybe she went for a walk."

"Perhaps she did," the nun said. "Thank you, Tony."

She hung up. There was no reason why she should feel uneasy over Lizette going out alone for a walk. Uneasiness had become a habit in the past few days.

Sister Simon picked up the pencil. "Steve is in jail," she wrote on the pad, and handed it to Sister Joe. She must break her habit of uneasiness now. Lizette could go anywhere she liked in safety.

The old nun nodded. "That's the proper place for him, if he's going around killing people. But it's a shame he went so wrong because there was so much good in him. A perfect physical specimen, too, only a little hard of hearing. But he had real talent, Sister."

Sister Simon looked a question, and Sister Joe nodded again.

"Oh, real talent! You should have seen the pictures he was always drawing. And the little figures he used to make out of modeling clay or mud or anything." She smiled and added as if this were a confidential matter, "I always said he could have been a wonderful artist."

Pico watched the girl run up the stairs to Main Street. She hadn't waited for him to answer her question about someone named Jinny. He stood until she was gone, then turned slowly and looked down at the blanket where people threw their dimes, now a soggy heap in the rain; at the figure of the camp cook with its ears disintegrating in the wet, at the mother and baby, the dog and pups, finally at the lovely, laughing girl. The spade was thrown down beside that one. He stepped on the blade, jumping the handle up into his hand. Then, methodically but quickly, he dug into the face. He had gone

deep before the spade struck metal. He worked the object carefully out. It was a knife, short bladed and stocky. Picking up a dirty
rag, he wiped the knife, ran his thumb over the cutting edge, and
dropped it into his pocket. He left the spade where it had fallen,
hurdled his rope fence and leaped up the stairs two at a time. On
the street he stopped, then strolled toward the shooting gallery. Up
ahead, beyond the vacationers scattered outside the shops, he could
see the flying figure of the girl. She was heading straight for Waddy's.

Susan Chapin was having a dull afternoon. She expected quiet
days, working in a mortuary, but this one took the prize. Snodgrass
had looked in a while ago and said well, they certainly needed the
rain, and then gone mooching off somewhere, probably up to the
casket room to move things around again. Young Lombard had decided to clean the garage. Ted had taken the hearse down to the gas
station. Susan was used to being alone in the afternoons, but the
funereal stillness today was too profound a reminder that down in
the preparation room Mr. Waddy lay on one of his own slabs. She
jerked open the long drawer of her desk and glanced into the pocket
mirror she had set in there at the proper angle to give her a view of
her face. It wasn't ten minutes since she had done a complete job
of mascara, lipstick, and powder. She slammed shut the drawer and
reached out to turn on the radio.

The doorbell rang.

"Well, hallelujah," she said aloud, and tripped down the stairs
and across Mr. Waddy's fine gray carpet to the door. She was just
opening the door when the phone rang. It could go on for a ring or
two. . . .

"Good afternoon," she said with the detached friendliness Mr.
Waddy had taught her. Never let a person's appearance impress you,
lesson number one; we meet people in times of stress, you cannot
judge their status, either moral, physical, or financial, so treat them
all with consideration and politeness. It was a good thing Susan
remembered the lesson because the girl on the doorstep certainly
looked like a street waif blown in by the wind. Her bandana, dark
blue, was not meant for rain and it had run in streaks around her

collar. The coat itself dripped puddles. But with the right make-up she would have been pretty.

The phone rang for the third time.

"Will you please step in?" Susan invited. "I'll have to answer that, but I'll be with you in a minute."

The girl stammered something, but Susan didn't catch it. She had to get the call. Mr. Waddy was very strict about calls.

It was a man asking for Ted.

"He's not here right now. He took the hearse over for an oil change. If you'd like to leave a message. . . ."

There was a second's silence on the wire. "Never mind, I'll get him at the gas station. He'll have to go to Newport."

"On a call?"

"Yes," the voice said instantly.

'What name, please?"

"He's going to Newport," the man repeated roughly. Then the line went dead.

Susan hung up the telephone slowly. This was most irregular. Surely Mr. Waddy would never permit Ted to chase off with the hearse without knowing exactly the destination and the name of a responsible party. But Mr. Waddy was not here.

"I'd like to see Ted, please," the girl said from the doorway.

Susan jumped. She had forgotten about her.

"Oh, I'm sorry, but Ted is out."

"Out?"

She looked as if she might faint, and Susan went to her quickly. "Why don't you come in and wait for him?"

"When will he be back?"

"I couldn't say, now. This fellow that just called, he wants a pick-up in Newport. He's going to reach Ted at the gas station, so—"

"Nobody lives in Newport! That's a ghost town!"

"Well, even if nobody lives there, I guess somebody died there because this man said so and he sounded like he wasn't going to take no for an answer."

The girl went dead white and she seemed to speak with stiff lips. "A gruff voice, would you say?"

"Gruff is right. Muscles in it, if you know what I mean. You're Lizette, aren't you? Ted talks about you all the time."

"He sent Ted to Newport! Oh, he couldn't . . . no. . . ."

There was more to it but Susan didn't hear, because Lizette was gone, running down the steps and out along the rubber runner so fast she appeared to dodge between the raindrops.

"It's the big station right down on the corner!" Susan called after her. But the girl didn't stop or wave or anything. So Susan went back inside and closed the door.

She didn't feel right, not doing anything about the telephone message. Ted had been with Mr. Waddy longer than she herself, he'd have better judgment; and she might be able to reach him, yet. She took down the telephone book and was trying to remember the name of the gas station when the door chime again laid an urgent note on the silence.

A nun, just as wet as the girl, stood on the welcome mat. She had been running, or at least walking so fast the exertion had taken every speck of breath. She laid her hand on her chest and did nothing but breathe for a moment.

"Good afternoon, Sister," Susan said. "Won't you come in?"

"Lizette Carter—is she here?"

"No, she just left. Didn't you meet her on the hill, Sister?"

"I didn't meet anyone. Where was she going?"

"To the gas station." Susan's heart was doing uneasy leaps. There had been so much hanky-panky lately, and all revolving somehow around the hospital and the mortuary. "She's hunting Ted. He's down at—Harry's, that's it!—gassing up the hearse."

"I don't see how I could have missed her," the nun said, looking back down the street.

"Well, the way she chased off, she could have been to the moon by the time you came along," Susan said. "Ted had a call to go to Newport, and I guess she thought she'd catch him. If you want to wait a minute, Sister, I'll call Harry at the station."

"No, she could be there and gone while . . ."

Without finishing the sentence, the nun rushed off in the same way Lizette had gone.

"The big one on the corner, Sister!" Susan called.

The nun waved her hand. Again Susan closed the door. Just for her own satisfaction, she'd like to know what all the fuss was about. Leafing through the telephone book, she found Harry's number.

"Harry?" a man's voice answered her question. "No, Harry's doin' a battery. Whatcha want? Waddy's hearse? Just a minute, I'll look. I ain't Harry, but I'll look."

"O.K.," said Susan. "Even if you ain't Harry, you look."

After a moment the voice came again. "No hearse."

"Did a man leave a call for him?"

"Who for?"

"The driver of the hearse!"

"No. . . . Harry, any call for the hearse? . . . No call."

"Oh. Well, is a girl there?"

"What make?"

"Don't be funny!"

"I ain't. What make's she drivin'?"

"She's walking. In a raincoat."

"She ain't here neither. I'd of seen her."

"I bet you would," said Susan. "If the hearse comes, tell him to get in touch with me. Will you? Right away."

"I'll tell Harry, I ain't Harry."

"I know. Thanks anyway."

"Pleasure was all mine, ma'am."

Susan hung up. All she could do now was wait. Ted or Lizette or perhaps even the Sister would show up eventually, trailing one another. She might as well stroll to the kitchenette and see if there was any coffee.

Lizette, going past the filling station, did not even pause because all of the stalls were empty and the attendant stood under the awning chewing a wad of gum. Newport. Ted had been called to Newport, where nobody either lived or died, because he had been with her at the water front that night, he could have seen whoever it was that had frightened Jinny. Or Lizette herself might have told him. That was how the killer would work it out. So Ted too would have to be eliminated. But if he knew the plot, if he could be put on his guard before it would be too late . . . he was so strong, like a Roman gladiator, he could wrestle with an assailant . . . unless he was taken by surprise. . . .

Lizette was sobbing to herself when she reached the top of the long stairs. Peering over, she saw that Pico was gone. She wasn't afraid of him, exactly. He had remembered Jinny's face and modeled it without knowing who she was . . . or he had known . . . but what difference did it make? He wasn't here. Running down, she could see a couple of rowboats tied up, not the one they had used this morning, which was painted bright red, but two old green ones. Blinded by rain and tears, she stumbled down to the dock. One boat was half filled with water. She fumbled loose the painter of the other and jumped in.

The current carried her swiftly along without much help from the oars. It was a good thing. She couldn't think, much less fight a river. Reach Ted, warn him, get to him in time. . . . The rain felt refreshing on her face. But in spite of the laborious tussle she had with the boat, keeping it away from the willow roots, she was shivering when the dock came in sight. Someone was standing on the dock.

"Ted!" she screamed.

But almost with the cry, she knew it wasn't Ted. It was a short, dumpy figure . . . Merlin, the mind reader. She wasn't afraid of him. He would help her find Ted. Exerting all her strength, she pulled in quickly to the dock.

Sister Simon didn't even try to keep to a swift walk as she started down the hill toward the filling station. She ran. Her wet white skirts flapped noisily and her coif was beginning to wither around her face. People gaped at her, what few there were on the street, and several, she thought, would have asked what was the matter, Sister, if she hadn't chased on by. Cutting across the wide ramp at the station, she came to a panting stop before the attendant who stood under the awning chewing a cud of gum.

"Lizette," she choked out. "A girl! Has she been here?"

"In a raincoat?"

"Yes!"

"No, ma'am."

"Then how did you know she had a raincoat?"

"Somebody just called. Said so."

He had a long face like a horse. His jaw began to swing again.

"Was it a man?"

"Girl. Snippy."

Sister Simon made herself take a long, steadying breath. "What about the—the vehicle from Waddy's? Has it been here?"

"No, ma'am."

The nun caught hold of her wet veil which was flapping in the wind. Looking up and down the desolate street, she wondered almost despairingly what to do. Where was Lizette?

"She sure was skinnin' along," the fellow remarked.

"Who was?"

"That girl. In the raincoat."

"I thought you said she wasn't here!"

"Wasn't. She went by. Like she was shot out of a gun."

"Which direction?"

He jerked his head toward the river.

"You're sure about this?"

"Certain sure, ma'am. Ain't long, neither."

Sister Simon lifted her wet skirts slightly and stepped off the small landing. Evidently Lizette had gone to the mortuary to find Ted. Not finding him, she had decided to visit the water front. Alone. On an afternoon when no one would be around. . . .

"You from the hospital, Sister?"

"Yes."

"Harry's out for coffee. You wanta wait fi'teen minutes or so, I'll drive you back."

"Thank you, I can't wait. Thank you just the same."

She hurried away. She was getting wetter and wetter. Her veil slapped her back, her shoes made a squishing, a very continuous squishing because she went so fast. She certainly was doing all the things a nun ought never to do—being out in public alone, making herself conspicuous by talking to strangers—actually, in a way, chasing a murderer! Because murder could be the terrible climax to Lizette's escapade. I have to stop him, Sister Simon told herself, if only she would be in the park, not on her way to Newport. . . .

Looking down on the river park, the nun saw that it was totally, desolately empty. One rowboat, an old green one half filled with water, bobbed drearily at the end of the dock. Over close to the wall the mud figures were shiny wet in the rain. A newly dug hole was filling with water.

So Lizette had not come here. Ted could be in the same danger I'm in, how plainly she could hear the girl saying that, insisting on it. And she believed that Ted had gone to Newport. She would follow him.

Sister Simon leaned for a moment of weakness against the boat company's solid railing. Newport was two miles away. She was here. She had no money with her to hire a taxi, nothing but her rosary. She had to do something about Lizette. Call the police? Tell Wakeley he had the wrong man in jail, that Steve would have made a fine artist? But that would take time, for she would have to convince Wakeley first that there was very real danger. And in the meantime Lizette would be alone in Newport, the ghost town where nobody lived.

Groping for the crucifix of the big rosary that hung at her side, Sister Simon climbed the stairs and walked aimlessly to the curb. She had never felt more inadequate in all her life. There was no rule, no precedent to cover the situation of a soggy nun stranded on a street curb while, two miles away, a murderer made away with a victim she had delivered, although unwittingly, into his hands.

15

Lizette clambered up on the dock. Merlin did not heed her. He stood stiffly, not even turning his head. He wore no shirt, and his bare shoulders looked chilly after the heat.

"I'm so glad you're here!" she gasped. "I have to find Ted. . . ."

She stopped. The reason for Merlin's stiffness stood a few paces off, at the land end of the dock. Pico. With a gun.

Pico laughed.

"You don't expect to find Ted here, do you?"

"He had a call. . . ."

He laughed again. He was handsome in a brutal way, standing there with the rain beating on him.

"But you told the girl at Waddy's—was that because you knew I'd come here?"

"Exactly, my dear. Your devotion to your boyfriend touched me—don't move!"

The order was for Merlin, who had staggered slightly.

"I'm not quite ready to kill you yet, not either one of you. But I will be, soon."

"He means it," Merlin said, and licked his lips. "Don't move."

Lizette, holding herself immobile, saw the very inside of fear. It was a cave like the one Jinny had died in, built by the cruelly cold eyes of this man who called himself Pico.

"So you're Steve," she said. She was surprised that she could speak.

He seemed to be surprised, also, and his mocking smile held a hint of admiration.

"I'd like to keep you, my dear. I really would."

"Then why not do it?"

That didn't please him. "You don't need to think you can keep me talking until help arrives. There won't be any help, not until it's too late."

"He means it," Merlin said again.

"Keep still, you fat fool."

Lizette managed to meet the man's eyes levelly. She should be saying the Act of Contrition, preparing for the judgment that would soon be upon her; but all she could think of was the gun, so steady in Pico's big hands, and the river running quietly under the dock. From the highway over beyond the trees came the sound of traffic. But a scream would never penetrate so far.

"Everything I ever wanted, I never had," Pico said, watching her closely. "Jim had it. Everything. Even Elizabeth. I killed Jim to get Elizabeth."

"And then she wouldn't have you," Merlin said with soft derision. "So you killed her."

"Don't," Lizette begged, but it was no more than a whisper.

Pico's face darkened, swelling with rage. Leave him alone, the man's out of his mind, don't goad him into killing us, Lizette begged silently, every minute is a promise of delivery! But a change had come over the mind reader also. Cowed and fearful before, now he regarded Pico with contempt.

"A big man with a gun," he said, still softly, "a great big man. Powerful. Holding a gun on somebody is even better than your cheap blackmailing schemes."

Pico swore the vilest oaths Lizette ever had heard, but the stream did not deflect Merlin.

"Do you think we'd have had anything to do with you, Lou and me, if you didn't have something on us?"

"A jailbird and an old army deserter!"

Merlin shrugged. "We are what we are. You put us to good use, covering up for you. But we were not counting on covering up murder. Even if Wakeley hadn't pulled Lou in, the jig was up. I was going to the police."

"Public-spirited citizen!"

"Tonight, as soon as I could hitch a ride into town, I was going to the police."

"You've been spared the trouble, Smith."

"Of course," Merlin said. "Lou will take over." The gun wavered, but only a fraction of an inch. The mind reader continued evenly, "You don't imagine Lou will stay on the hook himself and not squeal on you? Why should he keep quiet? The ties of friendship? And how do you expect to make a getaway?"

"I got away once. I can do it again. I'll go back to South America." Then his hands tightened on the gun, and he raised it slowly.

Sister Simon had no time to begin the rosary. She hadn't been at the curb long enough to collect her thoughts even for the familiar rote when the truck pulled up before her. The gum chewer from the filling station leaned across the seat and threw open the door.

"Ride you to the hospital, Sister?"

She hesitated just a second. "I'd like a ride."

"Pile in."

She was in, and the door closed, and the truck moving before she added, "But not to the hospital."

"No? Well, just so's it ain't too far. Wife's waitin' for me to get home."

"To Newport. Please."

He was turning the narrow corner on to the bridge and he very nearly met a bus head on.

"Ain't nobody in Newport. I better drop you off at the . . . "

"Please take me to Newport! I don't want you to stay. Just get me there, quick!"

But he began to wag his head, thinking it over in time to his gum chewing. "Well, now, I wouldn't feel right about that. Ain't nobody there."

Oh, but there is, she wanted to cry out, there's a girl and a murderer. And I don't want you blundering along with me, alarming him so he'll stab her, or choke her, or something!

"I'm to meet someone there," she said. "It's perfectly all right."

He mulled this over thoroughly.

"She wants to go shoppin'," he said finally. "And to the doctor."

"Your wife?"

"Yuh. I'm s'pose to baby-sit the kids."

"Then you just drop me and go straight home. I'm absolutely able to take care of myself."

"Well . . . she's expectin'."

"Then you can't possibly disappoint her. It's very bad for women in that condition to be disappointed. And I'm sure she needs to see the doctor. So you go straight out this road, just follow the river. . . . How many children do you have?"

"This'll be five."

She asked him all the names and ages, who they looked like, everything she could think of. Any fewer children would not have served to get them to Newport. By the time they reached the ruined basement that was the only remaining emblem of the turn into the town, Sister Simon had the man's mind completely off the rather odd errand he was performing. With only a remark or two about hating to leave her, and how would she get home, he let her out of the truck. Then, making a turn that barely skirted the ditches, he drove back toward the Narrows.

Sister Simon struck at once into the woods. She was deep into the underbrush before she began to wonder in earnest whether this might not be a half-wit theory. Why hadn't she called Wakeley and at least tried to explain what she was about to do? Only he would have stopped her, of course, and done the investigating himself, taking his time . . . if he had believed in her idea at all. But there was nothing to do now but go on, plowing through grass waist high with burrs nipping at her ankles and a little wood's thing or two scuttling away as she approached.

And so she came out, before long, on the straggling, muddy expanse that had been Main Street. She stood still, listening. Rain hit dismally on ruined roofs. A big patch of ragweed in the middle of the place ducked its homely leaves under the onslaught of raindrops. Slowly she started forward. Would she have to look into every shell of a house that might shelter the killer and his victim, becoming a perfect target for him as she poked hither and yon? Because now she knew exactly how reckless she had been to come here alone. He could kill Lizette and her, dump them into some caved-in basement, and not even the father of the five children would ever be able to find them. Where would she begin?

And then, standing there so quiet in the patch of ragweed, she heard a man's voice. It was coming from the direction of the river. It sounded conversational, not in the least menacing. No girl's voice. Perhaps he had already—but then who would he be talking to?

As silently as the smallest thing in the woods, the Sister started toward the voice. The willows hid the speaker. She passed one after another of the ramshackle buildings and still the man was hidden. And then, suddenly, she saw him a short distance ahead, standing on the shore.

It was the black-haired artist. His back was to her. Facing her on the dock were Lizette and the mind reader from the Nickelodeon Palace.

Sister Simon paused. The gun was pointed directly at the two. If she were to alarm the fellow, if he were to feel any inkling of another person's presence, he would certainly shoot. So here she must remain, listening to this man's confession of murder, waiting for him to get around to shooting the two facing him, unable to do a thing to stop him. Jinny hadn't left the suitcase as she had been told, he was explaining. She had hung around, talked to him, and so he had had to take her for a boat ride. . . .

Revolted and sickened, Sister Simon made a movement and her toe hit a rusty tin can. The sound was tiny enough but she saw a faint reaction, quickly checked, by Lizette. If the girl had heard, so had the man. Stone still, the nun waited. Why didn't he whirl and shoot at her?

A perfect physical specimen but hard of hearing, that was what Sister Joe had said! Through a long frozen minute the Sister hardly drew a breath. The fellow didn't turn.

So he hadn't heard the slight noise. And if he actually couldn't hear well, then it might be possible to rescue the two out on the dock! How, she had no idea. She only knew that somehow she must try to overcome this man who stood with his insolent back toward her. And she must do it at once.

Praying in high gear, as she would tell Wakeley later, the nun walked slowly forward until she was only a few feet away from Pico.

Lizette and the mind reader were steadfastly keeping their eyes away from her; but the strain must be terrific, she must act quickly, rush him before he could turn. . . .

The skirt of her habit fluttering wildly, Sister Simon started at a dead run across the intervening space. Fortunately, Pico did not hear her; indeed he was unable to hear the swish of the river past the pilings or any other ordinary sounds. She rushed desperately toward him, both arms held straight out before her. The impact was stunning. The man, thrown violently off balance, flung out his hands futilely. On the slippery bank there was no foothold, and he plunged on down into the water. The gun flew into the air and landed at Sister Simon's feet.

"Sister!" Lizette screamed. "The gun!"

"I have it!"

The gun felt good in her hand. The weapon was well cared for, she saw at a glance, and fully loaded.

On the dock the mind reader stood watching with a somewhat whimsical smile as if he enjoyed the joke. Pico, swearing, regained his balance against the pilings and came wading in to shore, flushed with anger.

"Get up beside him," Sister Simon ordered, gesturing with the gun. "Step along!"

Pico, taking his time, gave her a derisive look. He would put up with this state of affairs just so long as it pleased him, his manner plainly said.

"Lizette, come here," the nun said.

As if she were in a daze, the girl obeyed.

"Are you all right, Liz?"

"Yes, 'Ster."

"They didn't harm you?"

"Oh, no!"

"Now you two," Sister Simon dipped the muzzle at the men, "walk backward to the far end of the dock."

Pico shrugged, but they both did as they were told. The Sister advanced until she stood on the last rim of shore.

"That's far enough. Now stay there. If you move, either one, I'll shoot the two of you."

"You will?" Pico jeered. "Well, well!"

Keep calm, the nun cautioned herself, don't let him rile you. Show him that you mean what you say.

"If you don't think I can use this weapon . . ." She shifted the muzzle toward an empty bottle floating toward the dock and fired. The bottle shattered and disappeared.

There was a startled silence. Sister Simon needed that small interval to recover her own senses. Slowly the men turned to her, respect in the careful way they moved as if they expected her to blast off again if they didn't please her. The mind reader was pale under his stubble.

"Lizette," the nun said briskly, "go out to the highway and flag down a car. Ask them to summon the police. Then come back here. Run along, fast."

The girl went without a word. Sister Simon was trembling inside, but the tremors were not disturbing the confidence in her aim. If the artist took a step toward her, made any movement whatsoever—and he was angry enough to do it—she would indeed shoot him without the slightest hesitation. The other man, too. But she was not afraid of him, somehow.

The trembling left her. The pounding of her pulse died away in her ears. Now the only sound was the soft lapping of the water around the old dock.

I'm dreaming, Lizette thought as she ran along the weedy old Main Street, I didn't leave Sister Simon down there with two desperate characters, I didn't face death a few minutes ago.

But her errand was very real in her mind. Get out to the highway, stop a car, ask them to call the police and Ted . . .

"Ted!" she cried.

Of course she was dreaming! He couldn't have come so soon! But there he was, leaping through the underbrush like a frantic Tarzan, saying her name as if he couldn't believe his eyes. He caught her in his arms, squeezing her so hard she couldn't breathe, holding her away to look at her and catching her tight again.

"Liz, Liz, you crazy kid! What the devil brought you out here?" But he gave her no time to answer. Answers were unimportant, anyway. The marvelous thing was that he was here, and that out on the highway a police siren wailed to a stop and it was easy to imagine Wakeley jumping out of the car and crashing like Ted through the undergrowth.

"How did you know where to come?" Lizette asked, clinging to Ted.

"Susan. She said you were following me to Newport. And something about a nun."

"Sister Simon. She's down on the dock."

"What's she doing there?"

Lizette took his hand, turned, and began to run although there was no real need for haste now, not with the police catching up and Ted sprinting along without asking questions.

They came around the last of the willows, and stopped. Even to Lizette, who had been a terrified part of it so short a time before, the scene was hardly to be believed. A white-garbed nun, very wet but seemingly very much at ease, stood holding a gun on two stalwart men who stood obediently at the very edge of the dock over the swift running river.

"Well, I'll be darned," Ted said softly.

Wakeley, pounding up, stopped beside the two.

"What would you give for a picture of that?" he asked.

"Not a penny," said Lizette. "I want to forget it."

Drawing his gun, Wakeley strode forward. Lizette, leaning against Ted, closed her eyes. For this was the end, there was no more to see. And she was suddenly very, very tired and too near to tears.

ABOUT THE AUTHOR

Margaret Ann Hubbard

MARGARET ANN HUBBARD

Margaret Ann Hubbard (1909-1992) was born in Souris, North Dakota. Her father, a widower with eight children, had moved to North Dakota to farm, where he met and married a young school teacher. They had two daughters, the youngest being Margaret Ann. After the family moved to Duluth, Minnesota, in 1924, Margaret Ann (who appears to have been born Margaret Lorraine, according to copyright records), graduated from high school and attended the Minnesota State Teachers College. She taught for two years, but decided elementary school teaching was not for her, and returned to school, attending the University of Minnesota to obtain an English degree. Jobs were scarce after graduation, and her widowed mother encouraged her to try writing. Margaret Ann began writing plays for the local children's theaters, and several were successfully published. She then wrote a number of books for children, both fiction and fictionalized biographies. Starting in 1950, Margaret Ann also began to write mysteries for adults (and adapting several of them as plays).

Her last published mystery, *Step Softly on My Grave* (1966), was reviewed in the *Chicago Tribune*: 'A Milwaukee publishing company is fortunate in having the talents of Miss Hubbard, who does not—as a press release stated—write in a "disarmingly serious style." Her story has biting domestic irony and nips of female cattiness which, in fairness, may have been missed by a male blurb writer. It *is* a disarming account of a spinster finding first love and neatly breaking not only her own shell, but a few family ties and the plans of an over-bearing sister-in-law. There's plenty of malice afoot in town, plus murder, ballet, and blackmail.' There may be a few unpublished mysteries in her papers, left to the University of Minnesota archives. Two manuscripts listed in that collection are intriguingly titled *Murder on Popple Run* and *Murder Walks in White*.

In 1955, Margaret Ann wed civic leader Joseph Priley, who became a St. Louis County commissioner. Together, they were responsible for constructing fountains and flower gardens at the Civic Center and heading city clean-up campaigns.

REFERENCES:

Cromie, Alice. 1967. 'Crime on My Hands.' *Chicago Tribune* (Jan. 8).

Ouse, David. 2012-2017. 'Margaret Ann Hubbard.' http://zenithcity.com/archive/people-biography/margaret-ann-hubbard/

COACHWHIP PUBLICATIONS

CoachwhipBooks.com

NARROW
GAUGE TO
MURDER

Carolyn Thomas

COACHWHIP PUBLICATIONS
CoachwhipBooks.com

THE
SARA ELIZABETH
MASON
MYSTERIES

MURDER RENTS A ROOM

THE CRIMSON FEATHER

COACHWHIP PUBLICATIONS
COACHWHIPBOOKS.COM

THE
SARA ELIZABETH
MASON
MYSTERIES

THE HOUSE THAT HATE BUILT

THE WHIP

COACHWHIP PUBLICATIONS
CoachwhipBooks.com

THE
RUMBLE
MURDERS

Henry Ware Eliot, Jr.

COACHWHIP PUBLICATIONS

COACHWHIPBOOKS.COM

KILL 'EM WITH KINDNESS

BY FRED DICKENSON

COACHWHIP PUBLICATIONS
CoachwhipBooks.com

A JUDGE MASSIE MYSTERY

THE CORPSE IS INDIGNANT

DOUGLAS STAPLETON
and HELEN A. CAREY

COACHWHIP PUBLICATIONS

CoachwhipBooks.com

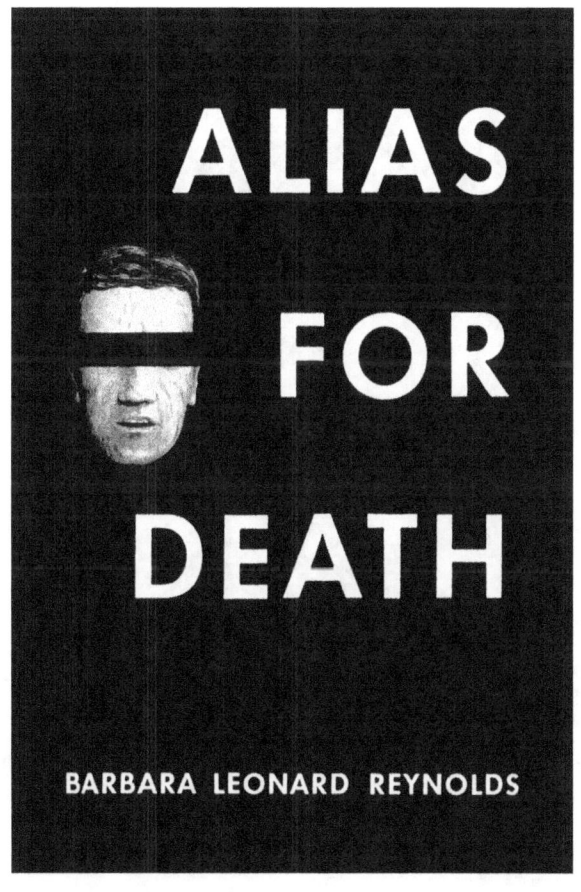

COACHWHIP PUBLICATIONS
CoachwhipBooks.com

The Serpentine Club Investigates
Murder in Washington, D.C.

THE CAPITAL
MURDER

JAMES Z. ALNER

COACHWHIP PUBLICATIONS
CoachwhipBooks.com

THE GOLF CLUB MURDER | OWEN FOX JEROME

www.ingramcontent.com/pod-product-compliance
Lightning Source LLC
Chambersburg PA
CBHW081131020726
47504CB00010B/2040